THE BOOK OF FATE

By Brad Meltzer

Novels

The Tenth Justice
Dead Even
The First Counsel
The Millionaires
The Zero Game
The Book of Fate
The Book of Lies
The Inner Circle

Nonfiction

Heroes for My Son

BRAD MELTZER

THE BOOK OF FATE

GRAND CENTRAL PUBLISHING

NEW YORK BOSTON

Grand Central Publishing
Hachette Book Group
237 Park Avenue
New York, NY 10017
www.HachetteBookGroup.com

Grand Central Publishing is a division of Hachette Book Group, Inc.
The Grand Central Publishing name and logo is a trademark of Hachette Book Group, Inc.

Printed in the United States of America

Originally published in hardcover by Hachette Book Group
First United States mass market edition: May 2007; Reissued: December 2010
First special one-time offer mass market edition: April 2009
First oversize mass market edition: October 2011
First special price mass market edition: September 2012

10 9 8 7 6 5 4 3 2 1
OPM

For Lila,
my girl,
who took my heart,
and with her sweet smile,
doubled its size

ACKNOWLEDGMENTS

It's been almost ten years since *The Tenth Justice* was published. I am thankful to everyone—especially you, our amazing readers—who offers the support that allows me to continue talking to my imaginary friends: First, always, my First Lady, Cori, for believing even before page one, and for somehow still loving me. Her brainpower, opinions, and editing are the true seeds in each book's bloom. Every day, I'm humbled by her. Every day, I wonder how I was so lucky to find her. Jonas and Lila, I find words for a living, yet there aren't words enough to define my love for you. You are my life's sweetest blessings and greatest joys. Jill Kneerim, wonderful agent, beautiful friend, whose guidance and insight have been there from the first photocopies; Elaine Rogers, forever the first; Ike Williams, Hope Denekamp, Cara Shiel, and all our friends at the Kneerim & Williams Agency.

For this book especially, I want to thank my parents: my father, whose experience became the launching pad for Wes, and my mother, for showing me the unquestioning support that went with it; my sister, Bari, whose strength I always draw upon; Dale Flam, for steering the rest of the ship into so many amazing new places; Bobby,

Matt, Ami, Adam, and Will, for their vital input and unwavering love; Noah Kuttler, who, after my wife, is the person I lean on most. His constant input and vital feedback are two of the key reasons this book is in your hands. I love him like family. Thank you, Calculator. Ethan Kline is just as valuable to this craft, and his insights into early drafts always shape the outcome; Steve "Scoop" Cohen, for giving me Dreidel and so much more; Edna Farley, Kim from L.A., and Dina Friedman, who do so much of the heavy lifting; Paul Brennan, Matt Oshinsky, Paulo Pacheco, Joel Rose, Chris Weiss, and Judd Winick, always my brothers, my Rogos, whose friendship inspires so much of my writing in ways they can never prove in a court of law.

Every novel is a lie that tries to sound like the truth. I owe the following people enormous thank-yous for giving me the truths that are weaved throughout this book. Without a doubt, I would've never been able to explore this world without the help of President George H. W. and Mrs. Barbara Bush and President Bill Clinton. The Bushes didn't need to open their world to me. Yet their generosity gave me so many of the details that made this book (which is all fiction!) come to life. I only hope they know how much I respect them. That same level of respect and thanks also goes to President Clinton, whose support I have treasured since my first novel. I don't care what side of the aisle you're on. Years later, it's still clear why we elected both of them. Staying with that theme, Jean Becker answered every one of my silly questions, but it's her friendship I cherish; Doug Band, Kris Engskov, Tom Frechette, and Andrew Friendly answered the rest of my inane queries, and in the process displayed why they were chosen to stand beside the most powerful men in the world; Thom Smith informed me on all things Palm Beach; Mary Louise Knowlton, Nancy Lisenby, Laura Cather Pears, Linda Casey Poepsel, and Michele Whalen are the best A-listers (and nicest people) in any presidency; Paul Bedard, Jessica Coen, Chuck Conconi, Joan Fleischman, Paula Froelich, Ann Gerhart, Ed Henry, Perez Hilton, Lorrie Lynch, John McCaslin, Roxanne Roberts, Liz Smith, Linton Weeks, and Ben Widdicombe taught me everything I know about gossip and are therefore all a part of Lisbeth's character. They are the best at what they do, and their kindness and class cannot be overstated. Mike Calinoff made me the second Jew in NASCAR and offered a wonderful friendship in the process; my friends Matthew Bogdanos, Eljay Bowron, Jo Ayn "Joey" Glanzer, Dave Leavy, Erik Oleson, Peter Oleson, Ken Robinson, Farris Rookstool, Adam Rosman, Alex Sinclair, and John Spinelli helped on all the law enforcement details—I hope they know how much I respect the work they do; Barry Kowitt brought Rogo's profession to life (www.ungerandkowitt.com); Mary Weiss gave me the 65 Roses Ball (www.cff.org); Dana Milbank helped with White House press; Shelly Jacobs answered more presidential library questions than she ever anticipated; Rags Morales, as always, drew his heart out; Dr. Lee Benjamin, Dr. Thomas Scalea, and Dr. Ronald K. Wright for their medical advice; Richard Ben Cramer's *What It Takes*, Max Skidmore's *After the White House*, and the works of Samantha Power were invaluable tools; Greg Apparcel, Steve Chaconas, Ron Edmonds, Sara Fritz, Mark Futch, Al Guthrie, Tim Krische, Jim Ponce, Walter Rodgers, Will Shortz, Laura Spencer, and Tiffini Theisen filled in all the rest of the details; my mentor and fellow schemer—and the true reason I am here—

Rob Weisbach, for being the first with faith all those years ago; and the rest of my family and friends, whose names once again inhabit these pages. I also want to thank Eli Segal, who gave me my very first shot. And my second shot. When I was a twenty-two-year-old kid, Eli treated me as an equal. It meant everything. I wouldn't be writing today without you, Eli.

Finally, I owe a huge thank-you to everyone at Warner Books: David Young, Larry Kirshbaum, Maureen Egen, Emi Battaglia, Tina Andreadis, Chris Barba, Martha Otis, Jen Romanello, Karen Torres, Becka Oliver, Evan Boorstyn, the nicest and hardest-working sales force in show business, and all the truly nice people who, through all these years, have become part of our family. Let me just say it as honestly as I can: They do the real work, and we'd be lost without them. I also want to stand on my desk and yell "O Captain! My Captain!" to my editor, Jamie Raab. I think the hardest part of being an editor is understanding your authors. Jamie has always understood me, watched out for me, taken care of me. No author is more blessed. So thank you, Jamie, for your encouragement, and most important, for your faith.

Whatever limits us, we call Fate.

Ralph Waldo Emerson

God does not roll dice.

Albert Einstein

1

Six minutes from now, one of us would be dead. That was our fate. None of us knew it was coming.

"*Ron, hold up!*" I called out, chasing after the middle-aged man in the navy-blue suit. As I ran, the smothering Florida heat glued my shirt to my chest.

Ignoring me, Ron Boyle darted up the tarmac, passing Air Force One on our right and the eighteen cars of the motorcade that idled in a single-file line on our left. As deputy chief of staff, he was always in a rush. That's what happens when you work for the most powerful man in the world. I don't say that lightly. Our boss was the Commander in Chief. The President of the United States. And when he wanted something, it was my job to get it. Right now President Leland "The Lion" Manning wanted Boyle to stay calm. Some tasks were beyond even me.

Picking up speed as he weaved through the crowd of staffers and press making their way to their assigned cars, Boyle blew past a shiny black Chevy Suburban packed with Secret Service agents and the ambulance that carried extra pints of the President's blood. Earlier today, Boyle was supposed to have a fifteen-minute sit-down with the

President on Air Force One. Because of my scheduling error, he was now down to a three-minute drive-by briefing sometime this afternoon. To say he was annoyed would be like calling the Great Depression *a bad day at the office.*

"Ron!" I said again, putting a hand on his shoulder and trying to apologize. "Just wait. I wanted to—"

He spun around wildly, slapping my hand out of the way. Thin and pointy-nosed with a thick mustache designed to offset both, Boyle had graying hair, olive skin, and striking brown eyes with a splash of light blue in each iris. As he leaned forward, his cat's eyes glared down at me. "Don't touch me again unless you're shaking my hand," he threatened as a flick of spit hit me in the cheek.

Gritting my teeth, I wiped it away with the back of my hand. Sure, the scheduling hiccup was my fault, but that's still no reason t—

"Now, what the hell's so damn important, Wes, or is this another vital reminder that when we're eating with the President, we need to give you our lunch orders at least an hour in advance?" he added, loud enough so a few Secret Service agents turned.

Any other twenty-three-year-old would've taken a verbal swing. I kept my cool. That's the job of the President's aide . . . a.k.a. the body person . . . a.k.a. the buttboy. Get the President what he wants; keep the machine humming.

"Lemme make it up to you," I said, mentally canceling my apology. If I wanted Boyle quiet—if we didn't want a scene for the press—I needed to up the ante. "What if I . . . what if I squeezed you into the President's limo right now?"

Boyle's posture lifted slightly as he started buttoning his suit jacket. "I thought you— No, that's good. Great.

Excellent." He even painted on a tiny smile. Crisis averted.

He thought all was forgiven. My memory's way longer than that. As Boyle triumphantly turned toward the limo, I jotted down another mental note. Cocky bastard. On the way home, he'd be riding in the back of the press van.

Politically, I wasn't just *good.* I was great. That's not ego; it's the truth. You don't apply for this job, you're invited to interview. Every young political gunner in the White House would've killed to clutch this close to the leader of the free world. From here, my predecessor had gone on to become the number two guy in the White House Press Office. *His* predecessor in the last White House took a job managing four thousand people at IBM. Seven months ago, despite my lack of connections, the President picked me. I beat out a senator's son and a pair of Rhodes scholars. I could certainly handle a tantrum-throwing senior staffer.

"Wes, let's go!" the Secret Service detail leader called out, waving us into the car as he slid into the front passenger seat, where he could see everything coming.

Trailing Boyle and holding my leather shoulder bag out in front of me, I jumped into the back of the armored limo, where the President was dressed casually in a black windbreaker and jeans. I assumed Boyle would immediately start talking his ear off, but as he passed in front of the President, he was strangely silent. Hunched over as he headed for the back left seat, Boyle's suit jacket sagged open, but he quickly pressed his hand over his own heart to keep it shut. I didn't realize until later what he was hiding. Or what I'd just done by inviting him inside.

Following behind him, I crouched toward one of the three fold-down seats that face the rear of the car. Mine was back-to-back with the driver and across from Boyle. For security reasons, the President always sat in the back right seat, with the First Lady sitting between him and Boyle.

The jump seat directly across from the President—the hot seat—was already taken by Mike Calinoff, retired professional race car driver, four-time Winston Cup winner, and special guest for today's event. No surprise. With only four months until the election, we were barely three points ahead in the polls. When the crowd was that fickle, only a fool entered the gladiator's ring without a hidden weapon.

"So she's fast, even with the bulletproofing?" the racing champ asked, admiring the midnight-blue interior of Cadillac One.

"Greased lightning," Manning answered as the First Lady rolled her eyes.

Finally joining in, Boyle scootched forward in his seat and flipped open a manila folder. "Mr. President, if we could—?"

"Sorry—that's all I can do, sir," Chief of Staff Warren Albright interrupted as he hopped inside. Handing a folded-up newspaper to the President, he took the middle seat directly across from the First Lady, and more important, diagonally across from Manning. Even in a six-person backseat, proximity mattered. Especially to Boyle, who was still turned toward the President, refusing to give up his opening.

The President seized the newspaper and scrutinized the crossword puzzle he and Albright shared every day. It had been their tradition since the first days of the campaign—and the reason why Albright was always in that coveted seat diagonally across from the President. Albright started each puzzle, got as far as he could, then passed it to the President to cross the finish line.

"Fifteen down's wrong," the President pointed out as I rested my bag on my lap. *"Stifle."*

Albright usually hated when Manning found a mistake. Today, as he noticed Boyle in the corner seat, he had something brand-new to be annoyed by.

Everything okay? I asked with a glance.

Before Albright could answer, the driver rammed the gas, and my body jerked forward.

Three and a half minutes from now, the first gunshot would be fired. Two of us would crumble to the floor, convulsing. One wouldn't get up.

"Sir, if I could bend your ear for a second?" Boyle interrupted, more insistently than before.

"Ron, can't you just enjoy the ride?" the First Lady teased, her short brown hair bobbing as we hit a divot in the road. Despite the sweet tone, I saw the glare in her leaf-green eyes. It was the same glare she used to give her students at Princeton. A former professor with a PhD in chemistry, Dr. First Lady was trained to be tough. And what Dr. First Lady wanted, Dr. First Lady fought for. And got.

"But, ma'am, it'll just take—"

Her brow furrowed so hard, her eyebrows kissed. "Ron. *Enjoy the ride.*"

That's where most people would've stopped. Boyle pushed even harder, trying to hand the file directly to Manning. He'd known the President since they were in their twenties, studying at Oxford. A professional banker, as well as a collector of antique magic tricks, he later managed all of the Mannings' money, a magic trick in itself. To this day, he was the only person on staff who was there when Manning married the First Lady. That alone gave him a free pass when the press discovered that Boyle's father was a petty con man who'd been convicted (twice) for insurance fraud. It was the same free pass he was using in the limo to test the First Lady's authority. But even the best free passes eventually expire.

Manning shook his head so subtly, only a trained eye could see it. First Lady, one; Boyle, nothing.

Closing the file folder, Boyle sank back and shot me the kind of look that would leave a bruise. Now it was my fault.

As we neared our destination, Manning stared silently through the light green tint of his bulletproof window. "Y'ever hear what Kennedy said three hours before he was shot?" he asked, putting on his best Massachusetts accent. "*You know, last night would've been a hell of a night to kill a President.*"

"*Lee!*" the First Lady scolded. "See what I deal with?" she added, fake laughing at Calinoff.

The President took her hand and squeezed it, glancing my way. "Wes, did you bring the present I got for Mr. Calinoff?" he asked.

I dug through my leather briefcase—the bag of tricks—never taking my eyes off Manning's face. He tossed a slight nod and scratched at his own wrist. *Don't give him the tie clip . . . go for the big stuff.*

I'd been his aide for over seven months. If I was doing my job right, we didn't have to talk to communicate. We were in a groove. I couldn't help but smile.

That was my last big, broad grin. In three minutes, the gunman's third bullet would rip through my cheek, destroying so many nerves, I'd never have full use of my mouth again.

That's the one, the President nodded at me.

From my overpacked bag, which held everything a President would ever need, I pulled out a set of official presidential cuff links, which I handed to Mr. Calinoff, who was loving every split second in his folded-down, completely uncomfortable hot seat.

"Those are real, y'know," the President told him. "Don't put 'em on eBay."

It was the same joke he used every time he gave a set away. We all still laughed. Even Boyle, who started scratching at his chest. There's no better place to be than in on an inside joke with the President of the United States. And on July 4th in Daytona, Florida, when you'd flown in to yell, "*Gentlemen, start your engines!*" at the legendary Pepsi 400 NASCAR race, there was no better backseat in the world.

Before Calinoff could offer a thank-you, the limo came to a stop. A red lightning bolt flashed by us on the left—two police motorcycles with their sirens blaring. They were leapfrogging from the back of the motorcade to the front. Just like a funeral procession.

"Don't tell me they closed down the road," the First Lady said. She hated it when they shut traffic for the motorcade. Those were the votes we'd never get back.

The car slowly chugged a few feet forward. "Sir, we're about to enter the track," the detail leader announced from the passenger seat. Outside, the concrete openness of the airport runway quickly gave way to rows and rows of high-end motor coaches.

"Wait . . . we're going out on the track?" Calinoff asked, suddenly excited. He shifted in his seat, trying to get a look outside.

The President grinned. "Did you think we'd just get a couple seats in front?"

The wheels bounced over a clanging metal plate that sounded like a loose manhole cover. Boyle scratched even more at his chest. A baritone rumble filled the air.

"That thunder?" Boyle asked, glancing up at the clear blue sky.

"No, not thunder," the President replied, putting his own fingertips against the bulletproof window as the stadium crowd of 200,000 surged to its feet with banners, flags, and arms waving. "Applause."

"*Ladies and gentlemen, the President of the United States!*" the announcer bellowed through the P.A. system.

A sharp right-hand turn tugged us all sideways as the limo turned onto the racetrack, the biggest, most perfectly paved highway I'd ever seen in my life.

"Nice roads you got here," the President said to Calinoff, leaning back in the plush leather seat that was tailor-made to his body.

All that was left was the big entrance. If we didn't nail that, the 200,000 ticket holders in the stadium, plus the ten million viewers watching from home, plus the seventy-five million fans who're committed to NASCAR, would all go tell their friends and neighbors and cousins and strangers in the supermarket that we went up for our baptism and sneezed in the holy water.

But that's why we brought the motorcade. We didn't *need* eighteen cars. The runway in the Daytona Airport was actually adjacent to the racetrack. There were no red lights to run. No traffic to hold back. But to everyone watching . . . Have you ever seen the President's motorcade on a racetrack? Instant American frenzy.

I didn't care how close we were in the polls. One lap around and we'd be picking out our seats for the inauguration.

Across from me, Boyle wasn't nearly as thrilled. With his arms crossed against his chest, he never stopped studying the President.

"Got the stars out too, eh?" Calinoff asked as we entered the final turn and he saw our welcoming committee, a small mob of NASCAR drivers all decked out in their multicolor, advertising-emblazoned jumpsuits. What his untrained eye didn't notice were the dozen or so "crew members" who were standing a bit more erect than the rest. Some had backpacks. Some carried leather satchels. All had sunglasses. And one was speaking into his own wrist. Secret Service.

Like any other first-timer in the limo, Calinoff was practically licking the glass. "Mr. Calinoff, you'll be getting out first," I told him as we pulled into the pit stalls. Outside, the drivers were already angling for presidential position. In sixty seconds, they'd be running for their lives.

Calinoff leaned toward my door on the driver's side, where all the NASCAR drivers were huddled.

I leaned forward to block him, motioning to the President's door on the other side. "*That* way," I said. The door right next to him.

"But the drivers are over *there*," Calinoff objected.

"Listen to the boy," the President chimed in, gesturing toward the door by Calinoff.

Years ago, when President Clinton came for a NASCAR race, members of the crowd booed. In 2004, when President Bush arrived with legendary driver Bill Elliott in his motorcade, Elliott stepped out first and the crowd erupted. Even Presidents can use an opening act.

With a click and a thunk, the detail leader pushed a small security button under the door handle which allowed him to open the armor-lined door from the outside. Within seconds, the door cracked open, twin switchblades of light and Florida heat sliced through the car, and Calinoff lowered one of his handmade cowboy boots onto the pavement.

"And please welcome four-time Winston Cup winner . . . Mike Caaaalinoff!" the announcer shouted through the stadium.

Cue crowd going wild.

"Never forget," the President whispered to his guest as Calinoff stepped outside to the 200,000 screaming fans. "*That's* who we're here to see."

"And now," the announcer continued, "our grand marshal for today's race—Florida's own . . . President Leeeee Maaaaanning!"

Just behind Calinoff, the President hopped out of the car, his right hand up in a wave, his left hand proudly patting the NASCAR logo on the chest of his windbreaker. He paused for a moment to wait for the First Lady. As always, you could read the lips on every fan in the grandstands. *There he is . . . There he is . . . There they are . . .* Then, as soon as the crowd had digested it, the flashbulbs hit. *Mr. President, over here! Mr. President . . . !* He'd barely moved three steps by the time Albright was behind him, followed by Boyle.

I stepped out last. The sunlight forced me to squint, but I still craned my neck to look up, mesmerized by the 200,000 fans who were now on their feet, pointing and waving at us from the grandstands. Two years out of college, and this was my life. Even rock stars don't have it this good.

Putting his arm out for a handshake, Calinoff was quickly enveloped by the waiting crowd of drivers, who smothered him with hugs and backslaps. At the front of the crowd was the NASCAR CEO and his surprisingly tall wife, here to welcome the First Lady.

Approaching the drivers, the President grinned. He was next. In three seconds, he'd be surrounded—the one black windbreaker in a Technicolor sea of Pepsi, M&M's, DeWalt, and Lone Star Steakhouse jumpsuits. As if he'd won the World Series, the Super Bowl, and the—

Pop, pop, pop.

That's all I heard. Three tiny pops. A firecracker. Or a car backfiring.

"Shots fired! Shots fired!" the detail leader yelled.

"*Get down! Get back!*"

I was still smiling as the first scream tore through the air. The crowd of drivers scattered—running, dropping, panicking in an instant blur of colors.

"*God gave power to the prophets . . .*" a man with black buzzed hair and a deep voice shouted from the center of the swirl. His tiny chocolate eyes seemed almost too close together, while his bulbous nose and arched thin eyebrows gave him a strange warmth that for some reason reminded me of Danny Kaye. Kneeling down on one knee and holding a gun with both hands, he was dressed as a driver in a black and bright yellow racing jumpsuit.

Like a bumblebee, I thought.

"*. . . but also to the horrors . . .*"

I just kept staring at him, frozen. Sound disappeared. Time slowed. And the world turned black-and-white, my own personal newsreel. It was like the first day I met the President. The handshake alone felt like an hour. Living between seconds, someone called it. Time standing still.

Still locked on the bumblebee, I couldn't tell if he was moving forward or if everyone around him was rushing back.

"*Man down!*" the detail leader shouted.

I followed the sound and the hand motions to a man in a navy suit, lying facedown on the ground. Oh, no. *Boyle.* His forehead was pressed against the pavement, his face screwed up in agony. He was holding his chest, and I could see blood starting to puddle out from below him.

"*Man down!*" the detail leader shouted again.

My eyes slid sideways, searching for the President. I found him just as a half dozen jumpsuited agents rushed at the small crowd that was already around him. The frantic agents were moving so fast, the people closest to Manning were pinned against him.

"Move him! *Now!*" an agent yelled.

Pressed backward against the President, the wife of the NASCAR CEO was screaming.

"You're crushing her!" Manning shouted, gripping her shoulder and trying to keep her on her feet. "Let her *go*!"

The Service didn't care. Swarming around the President, they rammed the crowd from the front and right side. That's when momentum got the best of them. Like a just-cut tree, the crush of people tumbled to the side, toward the ground. The President was still fighting to get the CEO's wife out. A bright light exploded. I remember the flashbulb going off.

"*. . . so people could test their faith . . .*" the gunman roared as a separate group of agents in jumpsuits got a grip on his neck . . . his arm . . . the back of his hair. In slow motion, the bumblebee's head snapped back, then his body, as two more pops ripped the air.

I felt a bee sting in my right cheek.

"*. . . and examine good from evil!*" the man screamed, arms spread out like Jesus as agents dragged him to the ground. All around them, other agents formed a tight circle, brandishing semiautomatic Uzis they had torn from their leather satchels and backpacks.

I slapped my own face, trying to kill whatever just bit me. A few feet ahead, the crowd surrounding the President collided with the asphalt. Two agents on the far side grabbed the First Lady, pulling her away. The rest never stopped shoving, ramming, stepping over people as they tried to get to Manning and shield him.

I looked as the puddle below Boyle grew even larger. His head was now resting in a milky white liquid. He'd thrown up.

From the back of the President's pile, our detail leader and another suit-and-tie agent gripped Manning's elbows, lifted him from the pile, and shoved him sideways, straight at me. The President's face was in pain. I looked for blood on his jacket but didn't see any.

Picking up speed, his agents were going for the limo. Two more agents were right behind them, gripping the First Lady under her armpits. I was the only thing in their way. I tried to sidestep but wasn't fast enough. At full speed, the detail leader's shoulder plowed into my own.

Falling backward, I crashed into the limo, my rear end hitting just above the right front tire. I still see it all in some out-of-body slow motion: me trying to keep my balance . . . slapping my hand against the car's hood . . . and the splat from my impact. Sound was so warped, I could hear the liquid squish. The world was still black-and-white. Everything except for my own red handprint.

Confused, I put my hand back to my cheek. It slid across my skin, which was slick and wet and raw with pain.

"Go, go, *go*!" someone screamed.

Tires spun. The car lurched. And the limo sped out

from under me. Like a soda can forgotten on the roof, I tumbled backward, crashing on my ass. A crunch of rocks bit into my rear. But all I could really feel was the tick-tock tick-tock pumping in my cheek.

I looked down at my palm, seeing that my chest and right shoulder were soaked. Not by water. Thicker . . . and darker . . . dark red. *Oh, God, is that my—?*

Another flashbulb went off. It wasn't just the red of my blood I was seeing. Now there was blue . . . on my tie . . . and yellow . . . yellow stripes on the road. Another flashbulb exploded as knives of color stabbed my eyes. Silver and brown and bright green race cars. Red, white, and blue flags abandoned in the grandstands. A screaming blond boy in the third row with an aqua and orange Miami Dolphins T-shirt. And red . . . the dark, thick red all over my hand, my arm, my chest.

I again touched my cheek. My fingertips scraped against something sharp. Like metal—or . . . is that bone? My stomach nose-dived, swirling with nausea. I touched my face again with a slight push. That thing wouldn't budge . . . *What's wrong with my fa—?*

Two more flashbulbs blinded me with white, and the world flew at me in fast-forward. Time caught up in a fingersnap, blurring at lightspeed.

"I'm not feeling a pulse!" a deep voice yelled in the distance. Directly ahead, two suit-and-tie Secret Service agents lifted Boyle onto a stretcher and into the ambulance from the motorcade. His right hand dangled downward, bleeding from his palm. I replayed the moments before the limo ride. He would've never been in there if I hadn't—

"He's cuffed! Get the hell off!" A few feet to the left, more agents screamed at the dogpile, peeling layers away to get at the gunman. I was on the ground with the rest of the grease stains, struggling to stand up, wondering why everything was so blurry.

Help . . . ! I called out, though nothing left my lips.

The grandstands tilted like a kaleidoscope. I fell backward, crashing into the pavement, lying there, my palm still pressed against the slippery metal in my cheek.

"Is anyone—?"

Sirens sounded, but they weren't getting louder. Softer. They quickly began to fade. Boyle's ambulance . . . *Leaving . . . They're leaving me . . .*

"Please . . . why isn't . . . ?"

One woman screamed in a perfect C minor. Her howl pierced through the crowd as I stared up at the clear Florida sky. *Fireworks . . . we were supposed to have fireworks. Albright's gonna be pissed . . .*

The sirens withered to a faint whistle. I tried to lift my head, but it didn't move. A final flashbulb hit, and the world went completely white.

"Wh-Why isn't anyone helping me?"

That day, because of me, Ron Boyle died.

Eight years later, he came back to life.

2

Eight years later
Kuala Lumpur, Malaysia

Some scars never heal.

"Ladies and gentlemen, the *ex*-President of the United States, Leland Manning," our host, the deputy prime minister of Malaysia announces. I cringe as I hear the words. Never call him *ex.* It's *former. Former* President.

The deputy prime minister repeats it again in Mandarin, Cantonese, and Malay. The only words I understand each time are: Leland Manning . . . Le*land* Manning . . . Leland *Manning.* From the way Manning tugs on his earlobe and pretends to glance backstage, it's clear that the only words he hears are *ex-President.*

"Here you go, sir," I say, handing him a letter-sized leather box that holds the pages of his speech. I've got a 101 fever and just stepped off an eleven-hour flight to Kuala Lumpur during which I didn't sleep a minute.

Thanks to the time difference, it feels like three in the morning. It doesn't slow Manning down. Presidents are built to run all night. Their aides, however, aren't. "Good luck," I add as I pull the burgundy curtain aside, and he bounds out from the right-hand side of the stage.

The crowd rises to a standing ovation, and Manning waves the speechbox in the air as if he's got the nuclear codes in there. We used to actually have them. A military aide would follow us everywhere, carrying the codes in a leather briefcase known as *the Football.*

These days, we don't have a mil aide . . . or the Football . . . or a motorcade . . . or a staff of thousands who will fly fax machines and armored limos around the world for us. These days, beyond a few Secret Service agents, I have the President, and the President has me.

Four months after the assassination attempt, President Manning lost his bid for reelection, and we all got tossed from the White House. The *leaving* was bad enough—they took everything from us . . . our jobs, our lives, our pride—but the *why* . . . the *why* is what haunts.

During the congressional investigations after the assassination attempt, Capitol Hill nitpickers were all too eager to point out every possible security flaw made on the racetrack trip, from the Secret Service agent in the local Orlando field office who had been stopped for a DUI two days before the President's visit . . . to the unexplainable holes that allowed the gunman to sneak through security . . . to the fact that the President's personal physician had accidentally ordered the wrong blood type for the ambulance on the day of the event. None of those mistakes mattered. But there was one that did.

After John Hinckley took a shot at President Reagan in 1981, Reagan's approval ratings shot up to 73 percent, the highest they reached during his eight years in office. After that day at the speedway, Manning's approval ratings kamikazed to a dismal 32 percent. The only thing to blame is the photo.

Pictures endure after every crisis. Even in the midst of the chaos, photographers manage to click their shutters and snap a shot. Some photos, like the one of Jackie Kennedy at the moment of JFK's shooting, show unapologetic terror. Others, like the one of Reagan, caught mid-blink during his shooting, show just how little time anyone has to react. It's the one thing politicians can't spin. They can manipulate their policies, their votes . . . even their personal backgrounds—but photographs . . . photographs rarely lie.

So when we heard about the photo in question—a crisp digital print of President Manning in mid-yell . . . standing behind the NASCAR CEO's wife . . . his hand on her shoulder as he was tugged backward by the Service . . . and best of all, trying to help push her out of the crushing crowd—we thought we'd have Reagan numbers. America's Lion in mid-roar.

Then we *saw* the photo. So did America. And they didn't see Manning pushing the CEO's wife *forward*, out of the way. They saw the President pulling her *back*, in front of him . . . cowering down behind his own personal shield. We trotted out the CEO's wife, who tried to explain that it wasn't how it looked. Too late. Five hundred front pages later, the Cowardly Lion was born.

"Roar," Manning whispers into the microphone with a wry smile as he grips the sides of the podium onstage.

When former President Eisenhower was lying on his deathbed, he looked at his son and one of his doctors and said, "Pull me up." They propped him up in bed. "Two big men," Ike groused. "Higher." They propped him even more. He knew what was coming. He died minutes later. All Presidents want to go out strong. Manning's no different.

He roars again, this time even softer. It took three years before he could make that joke. Today, it gets easy laughs and applause, which is why he opens every paid speech with it.

It's okay to make jokes now. The public even expects it—they can't get over it until you do. But as I learned during my first week on the job, just because the President is laughing doesn't mean he's laughing. Manning lost far more than the presidency that day at the speedway. He also lost one of his dearest friends. When the shots were fired, the President . . . myself . . . Albright and everyone else—we all went down. Boyle was the only one who never got back up.

I still see the milky pink puddle seeping out below him as he lay there facedown, his face pressed against the pavement. I hear the doors of his ambulance slam shut like a bank vault . . . the sirens fading into a muffled black hole . . . and the gasping, stuttering sobs of Boyle's daughter, struggling to get through the eulogy at her father's funeral. That was the one that cut deepest, and not just because her voice was shaking so much she could barely get the words out. His daughter, barely entering high school, had the same intonation as her dad. Boyle's whistling *s*'s and short Fl*o*rida *o*'s. When I closed my eyes, it sounded like Boyle's ghost speaking at his own memorial. Even the critics who once used his father's arrests to call him a *moral black eye on the administration* kept their mouths shut. Besides, the damage had already been done.

The funeral was televised, of course, which for once I appreciated, since the surgeries and the damage in my face meant I was watching it all from my hospital room. In a warped way, it was even worse than actually being there, especially as the President stood up to deliver the final eulogy.

Manning always memorized the opening lines of his speeches—better to look the audience in the eye. But that day at the funeral . . . That was different.

No one else even saw it. At the podium, the President had his chest out and his shoulders back in a conscious display of strength. He looked out at the reporters who lined the back walls of the crowded church. At the mourners. At his staff. And at Boyle's wife and now-bawling young daughter.

"C'mon, boss," I whispered from my hospital room.

The Cowardly Lion pictures were already published. We all knew it was the death of his presidency, but at that moment, it was just about the death of his friend.

Hold it together, I begged in my own silent prayer.

Manning pursed his lips. His velvet-gray eyes narrowed. I knew he'd memorized the opening line. He memorized every opening line.

You can do it . . . I added.

And that's when President Manning looked down. And read the first line of his speech.

There was no gasp from the audience. Not a single story was written about it. But I knew. And so did the staff, who I could see huddling imperceptibly closer whenever the cameras cut away to the crowd.

That same day, to add another knife in our necks, the man who killed Boyle—Nicholas "Nico" Hadrian—announced that although he had taken multiple shots at the President, he never intended to hit him, and that it was just a warning for what he called "the secret Masonic cult intent on seizing control of the White House in the name of Lucifer and his hordes in Hell." Needless to say, one insanity plea later, Nico was institutionalized at St. Elizabeths Hospital in Washington, D.C., where he remains to this day.

In the end, Boyle's death was the worst crisis we'd ever faced . . . a moment where something was finally bigger than the White House. The communal tragedy pulled everyone closer. And I watched it alone in a hospital room, through the one eye I could see out of.

"He's quite funny," says the Malaysian deputy prime minister, a man in his fifties with a slight acne problem. He sounds almost surprised as he joins me and Mitchel, one of our Secret Service agents, backstage. He eyes Mitchel, then cuts in front of me, turning back to study the profile of the President at the podium. After all this time as an aide, I don't take it personally.

"You've worked with him long?" the deputy prime minister asks, still blocking my view.

"Almost nine years," I whisper. It sounds like a long time to be just an assistant, but people don't understand. After what happened . . . after what I did . . . and what I *caused* . . . I don't care what my counselors said. If it weren't for me, Boyle would've never been in the limo that day. And if he hadn't been there . . . I clamp my eyes shut and refocus by visualizing the oval lake at my old summer camp. Just like my therapist taught me. It helps for a second, but as I learned in the hospital, it doesn't change the truth.

Eight years ago, when Boyle was yelling in my face, I *knew* the President would never be able to meet with him during a four-minute limo ride. But instead of taking the verbal lashing and simply rescheduling him, I avoided the whole headache and threw him the one bone I knew he'd go running for. I was so damn smug about it too. Dangling the President in front of him just to make my job easier. That decision took Boyle's life. And destroyed my own.

The only good news, as always, came from Manning. When most aides leave the job, they have half a dozen job offers. I had none. Until Manning was kind enough to invite me back on board. Like I said, people don't understand. Even out of the White House, this is still a once-in-a-lifetime opportunity.

"By the way, Wes," Mitchel interrupts, "you ever find out if they got the honey for the President's tea? You know he needs it for his throat."

"Already on it," I reply, wiping my forehead with the palm of my hand. Between the heat from the lights and my fever, I'm ready to pass out. Doesn't matter. The President needs me. "It should be waiting in the car when we're done." Double-checking, I pull my satellite phone from my pocket and dial the number for our Secret Service driver outside. "Stevie, it's Wes," I say as he picks up. "That honey get there yet?"

There's a short pause on the other line. "You're kidding, right?"

"Is it there or not?" I say, deadly serious.

"Yes, Wes—the all-important honey has arrived. I'm guarding it right now—I hear there's a gang of bumblebees in the neighborhood." He pauses, hoping I'll join him in the joke.

I stay silent.

"Anything else, Wes?" he asks dryly.

"No . . . that's all for now."

I can practically hear his eyes rolling as I hang up the phone. I'm not an imbecile. I know what they say about me. But they're not the ones who still see the puddle of blood under Boyle every time I hear an ambulance pass. Manning lost the presidency and his best friend. I lost something far more personal. It's no different than a trapeze artist who takes a bad fall during a triple backflip. Even when the bones are healed and everything's back in place . . . even when they put you back in the big top . . . you can swing as hard as you want, but it takes time before you'll ever fly as high again.

". . . though I still make 'em call me *Mr. President*," Manning jokes from onstage.

A swell of laughter gushes up from the audience, which is comprised of seven hundred of the top employees of the Tengkolok Insurance Corporation, the forty-third largest company in Malaysia. The good news is, they're paying $400,000 and private jet travel for the fifty-seven-minute speech . . . plus a short Q&A, of course. As a *Newsweek* reporter once told me, the post-presidency is like a prime-time hit in syndication: less visible, but far more profitable.

"They like him," the deputy prime minister tells me.

"He's had some practice in front of crowds," I reply.

He keeps his eyes locked on the President's silhouetted profile, refusing to acknowledge the joke. From this angle, the way Manning jabs a determined finger out toward the audience, he looks like he's back in fighting shape. The spotlight gives him an angelic glow . . . thinning out his extra fifteen pounds and softening every feature, from his sharp chin to his leathered skin. If I didn't know better, I'd think I was back in the White House, watching him through the tiny peephole in the side door of the Oval. Just like he watched over me in my hospital room.

I was there almost six months. For the first few, someone from the White House called every day. But when we lost the election, the staff disappeared, as did the phone calls. By then, Manning had every reason to do the same and forget about me. He knew what I'd done. He knew why Boyle was in the limo. Instead, he invited me back. As he taught me that day, loyalty mattered. It still does. Even after the White House. Even in Malaysia. Even at an insurance conference.

A yawn leaps upward in my throat. I grit my teeth and fight, trying to swallow it whole.

"Is boring for you?" the deputy prime minister asks, clearly annoyed.

"N-No . . . not at all," I apologize, knowing the first rule of diplomacy. "It's just . . . the time zone . . . we just flew in, so still adjusting . . ." Before I can finish, he turns my way.

"You should—"

Seeing my face, he cuts himself off. Not for long. Just enough to stare.

Instinctively, I try to smile. Some things you can't unlearn. The left half of my lip goes up, the right half stays flat, dead on my face.

Boyle went down that day at the racetrack. But he wasn't the only one hit.

"—should take melatonin," the deputy prime minister stammers, still staring at the faded slash marks on my cheek. The scars crisscross like interconnecting railroad tracks. When it first happened, they were dark purple. Now they're a shade redder than my pale chalky skin. You still can't miss them. "Melatonin," he repeats, now locking on my eyes. He feels stupid for gawking. But he can't help himself. He peeks again, then takes a second to glance down at my mouth, which sags slightly on my right side. Most people think I had a mini-stroke. Then they see the scars. "Very best for jet lag," he adds, again locking eyes.

The bullet that tore through my cheek was a Devastator—specially designed to fracture on impact and tumble into the skin instead of going straight through it. And that's exactly what happened when it ricocheted off the armored hood of the limo, shattering into pieces and plowing into my face. If it had been a direct hit, it might've been cleaner, the doctors agreed, but instead, it was like a dozen tiny missiles burrowing into my cheek. To maximize the pain, Nico even stole a trick from Mideast suicide bombers, who dip their bullets and bombs in rat poison, since it acts as a blood thinner and keeps you bleeding as long as possible. It worked. By the time the Service got to me, I was so bloody, they covered me, thinking I was dead.

The wound played punching bag with my facial nerve, which I quickly found out has three branches: the first gives nerve function to your forehead . . . the second controls your cheeks . . . and the third, where I got hit, takes care of your mouth and lower lip. That's why my mouth sags . . . and why my lips purse slightly off-center when I talk . . . and why my smile is as flat as the smile of a dental patient on Novocain. On top of that, I can't sip through straws, whistle, kiss (not that I have any takers), or bite my top lip, which requires more manipulation than I ever thought. All that, I can live with.

It's the staring that tears me apart.

"Melatonin, huh?" I ask, turning my head so he loses his view. It doesn't help. A face is what we hold in our memories. It's our identity. It shows us who we are. Worst of all, two-thirds of face-to-face communication comes from facial expressions. Lose those—which I have—and in the researchers' words, it's socially devastating. "I tried it years ago . . . maybe I'll give it another shot."

"I think you like it," the deputy prime minister says. "Help you feel good." He turns back to the lit silhouette of the President, but I already hear the shift in his voice. It's subtle but unmistakable. You don't need a translator to understand pity.

"I should . . . I'm gonna go check on that honey and tea," I say, stepping back from the deputy prime minister. He doesn't bother turning around.

Making my way through the backstage darkness of the Performing Arts Center, I sidestep between a papier-mâché palm tree and an enormous jagged rock made of plastic and foam—both pieces from the *Lion King* set which sits further behind the curtain.

". . . and countries look to the United States in ways that we still cannot underestimate . . ." Manning says as he finally segues into the more serious part of his speech.

". . . even now, when we're hated in so many corners of the world," I whisper to myself.

". . . even now, when we're hated in so many corners of the world . . ." the President goes on.

The line tells me he's got forty-one minutes to go in the fifty-seven-minute speech, including the moment thirty seconds from now when he'll clear his throat and take a three-beat pause to show he's extra-serious. Plenty of time for a quick break.

There's another Secret Service agent near the door at the back of the stage. Jay. He's got a pug nose, squatty build, and the most feminine hands I've ever seen.

Nodding hello, he reads the sheen of sweat on my face. "You okay there?" Like everyone, he gives my scars a quick glance.

"Just tired. These Asia flights take it outta me."

"We've all been up, Wes."

Typical Service. No sympathy. "Listen, Jay, I'm gonna go check on the President's honey, okay?"

Behind me, onstage, the President clears his throat. One . . . two . . . three . . .

The moment he starts speaking, I shove open the metal soundproof door and head down a long, fluorescent-lit, cement-block hallway that runs back past the dressing rooms. Jay's job is to fight every perceived and unperceived threat. With forty minutes left to go, the only thing I need to fight is my own exhaustion. Lucky me, I'm in the perfect place for a rumble.

On my right in the empty hallway, there's a room marked *Dressing Room 6.* I saw it when we came in. There's gotta be a couch, or at least a chair in there.

I grip the doorknob, but it doesn't turn. Same with dressing room 5 right across from it. *Crapola.* With so few agents, they must've locked them for security.

Zigzagging up the hallway, I bounce to dressing rooms 4 . . . 3 . . . 2. Locked, locked, and locked. The only thing left is the big number 1. The bad news is the sign taped to the door:

EMERGENCY USE ONLY

Emergency Use Only is our code for the President's private holding room. Most people think it's a place to relax. We use it to keep him away from the handshaking and photographing crowds, including the hosts, who're always worst of all. *Please, just one more picture, Mr.*

President. Plus the room's got a phone, fax, fruit, snacks, half a dozen bouquets of flowers (which we never ask for but they still send), seltzer water, Bailao tea, and . . . as they showed us during the walk-through . . . a connecting anteroom with a sofa and two ultra-cushy pillows.

I look at the other dressing rooms, then back to the closed metal door that leads to the stage. Jay's on the other side. Even if I ask, there's no way he'll unlock the other dressing rooms. I turn back to the *Emergency* sign on dressing room 1. My head's burning; my body's drenched. No one'll ever notice (thank you, soundproofing). Plus I've got over a half hour until the President's speech is— No. No, no, no. Forget it. This's the President's private space. I don't care if he won't notice. Or hear. It's just . . . going into his room like that . . . It's not right.

But as I turn to leave, I catch a flutter of light under the door. It goes dark, then white. Like a passing shadow. The problem is, the room's supposed to be empty. So who the hell would—?

Going straight for the doorknob, I give it a sharp twist. If this is that autograph nut from the parking lot . . . With a click, the door pops open.

As it swings wide, I'm hit with the smell of freshly cut flowers. Then I hear the cackling clang of metal against glass. Chasing the sound, I turn toward the small glass-top coffee table on the left side of the room. An older bald man in a suit but no tie rubs his shin from where he banged it. He's in mid-hop, but he doesn't stop moving. He's rushing right at me.

"Sorry . . . wrong room," he says with a slight hint of an accent I can't quite place. Not British, but somehow European. His head is down, and from the tilt of his shoulder, he's hoping to squeeze past me in the doorway. I step in front of him, cutting him off.

"Can I help y—?"

He slams into me at full speed, ramming my shoulder with his own. He's gotta be fifty years old. Stronger than he looks. Stumbling slightly back, I grab the doorjamb and try to stay in front of him. "You nuts?" I ask.

"Sorry . . . this was . . . I-I'm in the wrong place," he insists, keeping his head down and stepping back for another pass. The way he stutters and keeps shuffling in place, I start thinking he's got more problems than just being in the wrong room.

"This is a private room," I tell him. "Where'd you—?"

"The bathroom," he insists. "Looking for the bathroom."

It's a quick excuse, but not a good one. He was in here way too long. "Listen, I need to call the Secret Ser—"

Springing forward, he barrels at me without a word. I lean forward to brace myself. That's exactly what he's counting on.

I expect him to ram into me. Instead, he turns his foot sideways, pounds his heel down on the tips of my left toes, and grabs me by my wrist. I'm already falling forward. He tugs my wrist even harder, ducking down and letting momentum take care of the rest. Like a freshly spun top, I whip backward into the room, completely off balance. Behind me . . . the table . . .

The backs of my calves hit the metal edge, and gravity sends me plunging back toward the wide glass top. I paddle my arms forward to stop the fall. It doesn't help.

As my back hits the glass, I grit my teeth and brace for the worst. The glass crackles like the first few kernels of popcorn . . . then shatters like a thunderstorm of raining glass. The coffee table's smaller than a bathtub, and as I tumble in backward, my head hits the outer metal edge. A jolt of pain runs down my spine, but my eyes are still on the door. I crane my neck up for a better look. The stranger's already gone . . . and then . . . as I stare at the empty doorway . . . he sticks his head back in. Almost as if he's checking on me.

That's when our eyes lock. Contact.

Oh, God. My stomach sinks down to my kneecaps. Th-That's . . .

His face is different . . . his nose rounded . . . his cheeks more chiseled. I grew up in Miami. I know plastic surgery when I see it. But there's no mistaking those eyes—brown with a splash of light blue . . . He . . . he died eight years ago . . .

That was Boyle.

3

"Wait!"

He takes off in an eyeblink, darting to the left down the hallway—away from the doorway where Jay is. Boyl—whoever he is, he's smart.

I grab the edges of the coffee table and try to boost myself out. My hip and knees grind against the shards of glass as I twist into place. Stumbling to my feet, I rush forward, completely hunched over. I'm so off balance, I practically fall through the doorway, back into the hall, which is completely empty.

He barely had a five-second head start. It's more than enough.

Up ahead, the far end of the hallway bends around to the left. In the distance, a metal door slams shut. Damn. I run as fast as I can, gritting my teeth just to keep myself from hyperventilating. But I already know what's coming. Turning the corner, the hallway dead-ends at two more soundproof metal doors. The one on the right leads to an emergency set of stairs. The one straight ahead leads outside. If we were in the White House, we'd have two Secret Service guys standing guard. As a Former, we've barely got enough to cover the entrances that lead to the stage.

I shove open the door on my right. As it crashes into the wall, a low thud echoes up the concrete stairwell. I hold my breath and listen for footsteps . . . movement . . . anything. All I get is silence.

Spinning back, I slam into the metal bar of the remaining door, which whips open and flings me out into the sweet, steamy Malaysian air. The only light in the alley comes from the headlights of a black Chevy Suburban, a metal Cheshire cat with a glowing white stare. Behind the Suburban is a gaudy, white twelfth-grade-prom stretch limousine. Our ride back to the hotel.

"Everything okay?" an agent with cropped brown hair calls out as he steps around to the front of the Suburban.

"Yeah . . . of course," I say, swallowing hard and knowing better than to put him in panic. Jumping down the last three steps, my heart's racing so fast, I feel like it's about to kick through my chest. I continue to scan the alleyway. Nothing but empty dumpsters, a few police motorcycles, and the mini-motorcade.

The stairs . . .

I spin back to the doorway, but it's already too late. The door slams shut with a sonic boom, locking from the inside.

"Relax," the agent calls out. "I got the key right here."

He jogs up the stairs and flips through his key ring. "Manning still on time?" he asks.

"Yeah . . . he's perfect . . . right on time . . ."

The agent studies me carefully, fishing through his keys. "Sure you're okay, Wes?" he asks, pulling the door open as I run back inside. "You look like you've seen a ghost."

4

He's long gone.

A half hour later, after the final question in the President's Q&A ("*Do you miss the White House?*"), I'm sitting in the back of the prom limo, trying to read the President's mood.

"The crowd was good," Manning offers.

That means *they were flat.*

"I agree," I tell him.

That means *I understand.* Foreign speeches are always tough—the audience misses half the jokes, and Manning feels sorry for himself because the whole country no longer stops at his arrival.

In the front of the car, two of our Secret Service guys are dead silent, not even whispering into their radios. That means they're nervous. Back at the Arts Center, I reported the fact that I saw someone by the dressing rooms. When they asked for a description, I gave them everything I saw, though I left out his eye color and the fact it looked like Boyle. *Uh, yeah, it was our dead deputy chief of staff we buried eight years ago.* There's a fine line between being careful and looking like a whackjob.

As our car lurches to a stop in front of the Palace of the Golden Horses—Asia's most luxurious and overdecorated horse-themed hotel—three different valets open the limo's door. "Welcome back, Mr. President."

Well accustomed to dealing with VIPs, the Palace has eighteen elevators and seventeen different staircases to sneak inside. Last time we were here, we used at least half of them. Today, I asked the Service to take us straight through the front door.

"*There he is . . . There he is . . .* " simultaneous voices call out as we hit the lobby. A pack of American tourists are already pointing, searching for pens in their fanny packs. We've been spotted, which was the goal. Secret Service looks to me. I look to Manning. It's his call, though I already know the answer.

The President nods slightly, pretending he's doing a favor. But no matter how fast he buries it, I see the grin underneath. Anytime former Presidents travel abroad, the CIA arranges a quick briefing, which once again lets the Former feel like he's back in the thick of it. That's why all Formers love foreign trips. But when you're in a far-off land missing the adrenaline of attention, there's no better sugar rush than a quick fix of adoring fans.

Like the Red Sea before Moses, the agents step aside, leaving a clear path across the marble floor to the President. I pull a dozen glossy photos and a Sharpie marker from the bag of tricks and hand them to Manning. He needed this one. Welcome home, boss.

"Can you make it out to *Bobby-boy*? Just like that—*Bobby-boy*?" a man with oversize glasses asks.

"So where're you from?" Manning says, doing what he does best.

If I wanted to, I could stay at the President's side and

help the Service keep the line orderly. Instead, I step back, slip away from the crowd, and head for the front desk, just beneath the enormous golden dome with its hand-painted running horses.

It's been gnawing at me since the moment Boyle disappeared down that corridor. I'm not sure how he got backstage, but if he's trying to get near the President, there's only one other place to make the attempt.

"How can I help you today, sir?" a beautiful Asian woman asks in flawless English. To her credit, she glances at my scars but doesn't linger.

"I'm with President Manning," I tell her, hoping to grease the wheels.

"Of course, you are, Mr. Holloway."

I know we leave a hell of a calling card, but I'm still impressed.

"How can we help you?" she asks.

"Actually, I'm trying to track down one of the President's friends. He's supposed to be meeting us tonight, and I just wanted to see if he checked in yet . . . last name *Boyle.*"

Clicking at her keyboard, she doesn't even pause at his name. Fancy Malaysian hotels are good, but they're not that good.

"I'm sorry, sir, but we have no one under name *Boyle.*"

I'm not surprised. "How about *Eric Weiss*?" I ask. It was Boyle's fake name from our White House days when he didn't want reporters tracking us in hotels.

"Eric Weiss?" she repeats.

I nod. It's Houdini's real name—a dumb joke by Boyle, who collected old magician posters. But coming back from the dead? Even Eric Weiss couldn't pull off that trick.

"Sorry, no Eric Weiss," she says.

I glance over at the President. He's still got at least three more tourist autographs to get through.

"Actually, can you try one more: last name *Stewart*, first name *Carl.*"

"Carl Stewart," she repeats, tapping at her keyboard. It's a long shot, no doubt—the first and middle names of the President's father, and the hotel codename we used to use for the President when I first started in the White House . . . right before Boyle was—

"Carl Stewart," the front desk clerk says proudly. "I have him right here."

I feel the blood seep from my face. That codename was assigned to the President during our old trips as a way to hide what room he was in. No one knew that codename. Not even the First Lady. "You do?"

She squints at the screen. "But according to this, he checked out about an hour ago. I apologize, sir—looks like you just missed him."

"D'you have his address? Did he pay by credit card?" My questions tumble out before I can even catch myself. "I mean . . . we . . . were hoping to pay his bill for him," I add, finally slowing down. "Y'know . . . the . . . President's treat."

She stares straight at me. Now she thinks I'm nuts. Still, she checks her screen. "I apologize again, sir. It appears he paid by cash."

"What about his home address? I just want to make sure we have the right Carl Stewart." I add a laugh to put her at ease. That's when I realize Malaysians don't enjoy being laughed at.

"Sir, our guests' personal information . . ."

"It's not for me, it's for *him.*" I point back at the former

President of the United States and his three armed bodyguards. It's a hell of a trump card.

The clerk forces an uneasy smile. She looks over her shoulder. There's no one around but us. Reading from the screen, she says, "Mr. Stewart lives at . . . 3965 Via Las Brisas—Palm Beach, Florida."

My legs go numb. I grip the marble counter to keep from falling over. That's no codeword. That's President Manning's private home address. Only family has that. Or old friends.

"Sir, are you okay?" the desk clerk asks, reading my complexion.

"Yeah . . . just perfect," I say, forcing some peppy into my voice. It doesn't make me feel any better. My head's spinning so fast, I can barely stand up. Boyle . . . or whoever he was . . . he wasn't just in that dressing room . . . he was *here* last night. Waiting for us. For all I know, he would've been waiting for the President if I hadn't seen him first.

I replay the moments backstage at the speech. The metal clang as he banged into the coffee table. The panicked look on his face. Up till now, I assumed that when I saw him, he was in the process of breaking in. But now . . . him being here last night . . . and using that decade-old codename . . . Boyle's no idiot. With all the fake names to choose from, you don't use that name to hide. You use it so someone can find you. I twist the kaleidoscope and a new picture clicks into place. Sure, Boyle could've been breaking in. But he could've just as easily been invited. The problem is, considering that the only people on this trip are me and three Secret Service agents who never even worked in the White House, there's only one person left who would've recognized that old codename. One person who could've known Boyle was coming—and invited him inside.

I glance back at the President just as he finishes his final autograph. There's a wide smile across his face.

A knot of pain tugs the back of my neck. My hands start shaking at my sides. Why would . . . how could he do that? Ten feet away, he puts his arm around an Asian woman and poses for a photo, grinning even wider. As the flash explodes, the knot in my neck tightens like a noose. I clamp my eyes, straining to find the lake from summer camp . . . grasping for my focal point. But all I see is Boyle. His shaved head. The fake accent to throw me off. Even the sobs of his daughter, who I apologize to every time I see her grieving during the anniversaries of the event.

For eight years, his death has been the one wound that would never mend, festering over time with my own isolation. The guilt . . . everything I caused . . . Oh, Lord, if he's actually back . . .

I open my eyes and realize they're filled with tears. Quickly wiping them away, I can't even look at Manning.

Whatever Boyle was doing there, I need to figure out what the hell is going on. In the White House, we had access to the entire military. We don't have the military anymore. But that doesn't mean I don't have my own personal reserves.

I pull out my satellite phone and dial the number from memory. The sun should just be coming up in Washington.

Accustomed to emergencies, he picks up on the first ring. Caller ID tells him who it is.

"Let me guess, you're in trouble," Dreidel answers.

"This one's serious," I tell him.

"It involve your boss?"

"Doesn't everything?" Dreidel's my closest friend from the White House, and more important, knows Manning better than anyone. By his silence, it's clear he understands. "Now you got a second? I need some help."

"For you, my friend, anything . . ."

5

Paris, France

"With mayonnaise?" the thin woman with the red bifocals asked in a heavy French accent.

"Oui," Terrence O'Shea replied, nodding respectfully, but disappointed that she even asked. He thought his French was flawless—or as flawless as FBI training could make it—but the fact she asked the question in English and referred to the garlicky *aïoli* as "mayonnaise" . . . "Excusez-moi, madame," O'Shea added, "pourquoi m'avez vous demandé cela en anglais?" *Why did you ask me in English?*

The woman pursed her lips and smiled at his largely Swiss features. His thin blond hair, pink skin, and hazel eyes came from his mother's family in Denmark, but his fat, buckled nose was straight from his father's Scottish side—made only worse by a botched hostage rescue back from his days doing fieldwork. As the woman handed O'Shea the small container of french fries drenched with mayo, she explained, "Je parle très mal le danois." *My Danish is terrible.* Reading O'Shea's thin grin, she added, "Vous *venez* de Danemark, n'est-ce pas?" *You* are *from Denmark, yes?*

"Oui," O'Shea lied, taking a strange joy in the fact she didn't spot him as American. Then again, blending in was part of the job.

"J'ai l'oeiul pour les choses," the woman added.

"J'ai l'oeiul pour les choses," O'Shea repeated, dropping a few coins into the glass tip jar on the edge of the woman's sausage-and-french-fry pushcart. *Sometimes you just know.*

Heading further up Rue Vavin, O'Shea felt his cell phone vibrate in his pocket for the third time. He'd already convinced the pushcart woman that he wasn't American, and even though it didn't matter, he wasn't going to reveal himself by interrupting their conversation and picking up on the first ring.

"This is O'Shea," he finally answered.

"What're you doing in France?" the voice on the other line asked.

"Interpol conference. Some nonsense on trends in intelligence. Four whole days away from the pit."

"Plus all the mayo you can eat."

Just as he was about to bite his first mayo-dipped fry, O'Shea paused. Without another word, he pitched the basket of fries into a nearby trash can and crossed the street. As a Legat—a Legal Attaché—for the FBI, O'Shea had spent almost a decade working with law enforcement officials in seven foreign countries to help deter crime and terrorism that could harm the United States. In his line of work, the surest way to get yourself killed was being obvious and predictable. Priding himself on being neither, he buttoned his long black coat, which waved out behind him like a magician's cape.

"Tell me what's going on," O'Shea said.

"Guess who's back?"

"I have no idea."

"Guess . . ."

"I don't know . . . that girl from Cairo?"

"Let me give you a hint: He was killed at the Daytona Speedway eight years ago."

O'Shea stopped midstep in the middle of the street. Not in panic. Or surprise. He'd been at this too long to be fazed by bad intel. Better to confirm. "Where'd you get it?"

"Good source."

"How good?"

"Good enough."

"That's not—"

"As good as we're gonna get, okay?"

O'Shea knew that tone. "Where'd they spot him?"

"Malaysia. Kuala Lumpur."

"We have an office there . . ."

"He's already gone."

No surprise, O'Shea thought. Boyle was too smart to linger. "Any idea why he's out?"

"You tell me: It was the same night President Manning was there for a speech."

A red Fiat honked its horn, trying to blast O'Shea out of the way. Offering an apologetic wave, O'Shea continued toward the curb. "You think Manning knew he was coming?"

"I don't even wanna think about it. Y'know how many lives he's risking?"

"I told you when we first tried to bring him in—the

guy's poison. We should've never tried to flip him all those years ago." Watching the rush of Paris traffic, O'Shea let the silence sink in. Across the street, he watched the thin woman with the red bifocals dole out another basket of fries with *aïoli.* "Anyone else see him?" O'Shea finally asked.

"President's aide apparently got a look—y'know . . . that kid with the face . . ."

"He have any idea who he was looking at?"

"That's the question, isn't it?"

O'Shea stopped to think about it. "What about the thing in India next week?"

"India can wait."

"So you want me on a plane?"

"Say good-bye to Paris, sweetheart. Time to come home."

6

St. Elizabeths Mental Hospital
Washington, D.C.

"Make it quick, Nico—no futzing around," said the tall orderly with the sweet onion breath. He didn't shove Nico inside or stay with him while he undid his pants. That was only for the first few months after Nico's assassination attempt on the President—back when they were worried he'd kill himself. These days, Nico had earned the right to go to the bathroom alone. Just like he'd earned the right to use the telephone and to have the hospital stop censoring his mail. Each was its own victory, but as The Three had promised him, every victory brought its own cost.

For the telephone, the doctors asked him if he still had anger toward President Manning. For the mail, they asked him if he was still fixated on the crosses—the crucifix around his nurse's neck, the one the overweight lady wore in the law firm commercial on TV, and most important, the hidden ones only he knew were there: the ones created by windowpanes and telephone poles . . . in intersecting sidewalk cracks, and the T-shaped slats of park benches, and in perpendicular blades of grass, and—when they stopped letting him go outside because the images were too overwhelming—in crisscrossing shoelaces and phone cords and wires and discarded socks . . . in the seams of the shiny tile floor and the closed doors of the refrigerator . . . in horizontal shades and their vertical pull cords, in banisters and their railings . . . and of course, in the white spaces between the columns of the newspaper, in the blank spaces between the push buttons of the telephone, and even in cubes, especially when  is unfolded to its two-dimensional version

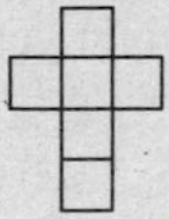

,

which then allowed him to include dice, luggage, short egg cartons, and of course, the Rubik's Cube that sat on the edge of Dr. Wilensky's desk, right beside his perfectly square Lucite pencil cup. Nico knew the truth—symbols were always signs.

No more drawing crosses, no more carving crosses, no more doodling crosses on the rubber trim of his sneakers when he thought no one was looking, his doctors had told him. If he wanted full mail privileges, they needed to see progress.

It still took him six years. But today, he had what he wanted. Just like The Three promised. That was one of the few truths besides God. The Three kept their promises . . .

even back when they first welcomed him in. He had nothing then. Not even his medals, which were lost—*stolen!*—in the shelter. The Three couldn't bring them back, but they brought him so much more. Showed him the door. Showed him what no one else saw. Where God was. And where the devil was hiding. And waiting. Almost two hundred years, he'd been there, tucked away in the one place the M Men hoped people would never look—right in front of their own faces. But The Three looked. They searched. And they found the devil's door. Just as the Book had said. That's when Nico played his part. Like a son serving his mother. Like a soldier serving his country. Like an angel serving God's will.

In return, Nico just had to wait. The Three had told him so on the day he pulled the trigger. Redemption was coming. Just wait. It'd been eight years. Nothing compared to eternal salvation.

Alone in the restroom, Nico closed the toilet seat and kneeled down to say a prayer. His lips mouthed the words. His head bobbed up and down slightly . . . sixteen times . . . always sixteen. And then he closed his left eye on the word *Amen.* With a tight squeeze of his fingertips, he plucked an eyelash from his closed eye. Then he plucked another. Still down on his knees, he took the two lashes and placed them on the cold white slab of the closed toilet seat. The surface had to be white—otherwise, he wouldn't see it.

Rubbing the nail of his right pointer finger against the grout in the floor, he filed his nail to a fierce, fine point. As he leaned in close like a child studying an ant, he used the sharpened edge of his nail to push the two eyelashes into place. What the doctors took away, he could always put back. As The Three said, it's all within him. And then, as Nico did every morning, he slowly, tenderly gave a millimeter's push and proved it. There. One eyelash perfectly intersecting with the other. A tiny cross.

A thin grin took Nico's lips. And he began to pray.

7

Palm Beach, Florida

"See that redheaded mummy in the Mercedes?" Rogo asks, motioning out the window at the shiny new car next to us. I glance over just in time to see the fifty-something redhead with the frozen face-lift and an equally stiff (and far more fashionable) straw hat that probably costs as much as my crappy little ten-year-old Toyota. "She'd rather die than call," he adds.

I don't respond. It doesn't slow him down. "But that guy driving that midlife crisis?" he adds, pointing at the balding man in the cherry-red Porsche that pulls out around us. "He'll call me right after he gets the ticket."

It's Rogo's favorite game: driving around, trying to figure out who'll be a potential client. As Palm Beach's least-known but most aggressive speeding ticket lawyer, Rogo is the man to call for any moving violation. As my roommate and closest friend since eighth grade, when he and his mom moved from Alabama to Miami, he's also the only person I know who loves his job even more than the President does.

"Oooh, and that girl right there?" he asks as he motions across two lanes of traffic to the sixteen-year-old with braces driving a brand-new Jeep Cherokee. "Pass the bread, 'cause that's my *butter*!" Rogo insists in a wet lick of a Southern accent. "New car and braces? Choo, choo—here comes the *gravy train*!"

He slaps me on the shoulder like we're watching a rodeo.

"Yee-hah," I whisper as the car climbs up the slight incline of Royal Park Bridge and across the Intracoastal Waterway. On both sides of us, the morning sun ricochets off glossy waves. The bridge connects the communities of working-class West Palm Beach with the millionaire haven known as Palm Beach. And as the car's tires rumble and we cross to the other side, the well-populated, fast-food-lined Okeechobee Boulevard gives way to the perfectly manicured, palm-tree-lined Royal Palm Way. It's like leaving a highway rest stop and entering Oz.

"Do you feel rich? 'Cause I feel *silver dollar*!" Rogo adds, soaking up the surroundings.

"Again, yee-hah."

"Don't get all sarcastic," Rogo warns. "If you're not nice, I'm not gonna let you drive me to work for the next week while my car's in the shop."

"You said it'd only be in the shop for a day."

"Ah, the negotiation continues!" Before I can argue, he does a double take on the braces girl, who's now right next to us. "Wait, I think she *was* a client!" he shouts, rolling down his window. "Wendy!" he yells, leaning over and honking my horn.

"Don't do that," I tell him, trying to push his hand

away. When we were fourteen, Rogo was short. These days, at twenty-nine, he's added bald and fat to his repertoire. And strong. I can't move him.

"Braces Girl!" he shouts, honking again. "Hey, Wendy, is that you!?"

She finally turns and rolls down her own window, struggling to keep her eyes on the road.

"Your name Wendy?" he yells.

"No," she calls back. "Maggie!"

Rogo seems almost hurt by his own misinformation. It never lasts long. He's got a smile like a butcher's dog. "Well, if you get a speeding ticket, go to downwithtickets.com!"

Rolling up his window, he scratches at his elbow, then readjusts his crotch, proud of himself. It's vintage Rogo—by the time he's done, I can't even remember what the argument's about. It's the same way he bulldozed into the legal profession. After two bad sets of LSAT scores, Rogo flew to Israel for his third attempt. Not even close to being Jewish, he'd heard that in Israel, they took a more relaxed approach to the concept of a *timed* exam. "What, an extra twenty minutes? Who's it gonna kill?" he asked for a full month, imitating his proctor in full Israeli accent. And with those twenty minutes, Rogo finally got a score that would get him into law school.

So as he found a home in speeding tickets and for the first time had some money in his pocket, the last thing he needed was a boring roommate who'd have trouble making the rent. Back then, my only job prospect was staying with the President, who'd moved to P.B. after the White House. *P.B.* being what the locals call Palm Beach, as in, "We'll be in P.B. all winter." I was living with my parents in Boca Raton; because of the low salary, I couldn't afford the tony neighborhood near the President's Palm Beach compound. With a roommate, though, I'd at least be able to live closer. It was right after the shooting. The scars were still purple on my face. Eighth grade goes a long way. Rogo didn't even hesitate.

"I still don't understand why you have to be in so early," Rogo adds in mid-yawn. "It's barely seven. You just got back from Malaysia last night."

"The President's—"

"—an early riser . . . the world's greatest guy . . . can heal the sick while cooking a six-course meal. Jesus and Emeril all in one body. I know how the cult works, Wes." He points out the window at a hidden cop car about two blocks up. "Careful, speed trap." Right back into it, he adds, "I'm just saying he should let you sleep in."

"I don't need to sleep in. I'm good. And FYI, it's not a cult."

"First of all, it *is* a cult. Second, don't say *FYI*. My mother says *FYI*. So does yours."

"That doesn't mean it's a cult," I push back.

"Really? So it's healthy that almost eight years after you left the White House, you're still running errands like some overhyped intern? What happened to grad school, or that event coordinator job, or even that threat of being a chef you made a few years back? Do you even enjoy work anymore, or d'you just stay there because it's safe and they protect you?"

"We do more good for the community than you'd ever know."

"Yeah, if you're chief of staff. You, on the other hand, spend half your day wondering whether he wants iceberg or romaine lettuce in his salad!"

I grip the steering wheel and stare straight ahead. He doesn't understand.

"Don't do that!" Rogo threatens. "Don't save your confidence for Manning. I just attacked you—you're supposed to fight back!"

There's a curdle in his voice that he usually saves just for traffic cops. He's getting riled, which isn't saying much for Rogo. In high school, he was the kid who threw his cards when he lost at Monopoly . . . and threw his tennis racket when he missed a shot. Back then, that temper got him in way too many fights, which was only made worse by the fact that he didn't have the physical size to back it up. He says he's 5'7". He's 5'6" if he's lucky.

"You know I'm right, Wes. Something internally bad happens when you give your entire existence to a single person. You feel me?"

He may be the smartest dumbest friend I have, but for once, he's reading me all wrong. My silence isn't from acquiescence. It's from my mental picture of Boyle, still staring at me with those brown and blue eyes. Maybe if I tell Rogo—

My phone vibrates in my pocket. This early in the morning, it's only bad news. I flip open the phone and check caller ID. I'm wrong. Here comes the cavalry.

"Wes here," I say as I answer.

"Got time to chat?" Dreidel asks on the other end.

I glance over at Rogo, who's back to hunting for potential clients. "Let me call you right back."

"Don't bother. How about meeting for breakfast?"

"You're in town?" I ask, confused.

"Just for a quick business meeting. I tried to tell you when you called from Malaysia. You were too busy panicking," he points out in his usual perfect calm. "So breakfast?"

"Gimme an hour. I got one thing to do at work."

"Perfect. I'm at the Four Seasons. Call me from the lobby. Room 415."

I shut the phone and for the first time enjoy the passing palm trees. Today's suddenly looking up.

8

Miami, Florida

O'Shea carried two passports. Both of them legal. Both with the same name and address. One was blue, like any other U.S. citizen's. The other was red . . . and far more powerful. For diplomats only. Fingering the embossed letters of the passports in his breast pocket, he could tell the red was on top. With a flick of his wrist, he could easily pull it out. And once the airport agents saw it, he'd no longer be stuck in the customs line that swerved through the back corridors of Miami International Airport. After the nine-and-a-half-hour flight from Paris to Florida, he'd walk right to the front. With a flick of his wrist, he'd be gone.

Of course, he'd also leave a trail of paperwork that tracked red passports everywhere. And as his FBI training taught him, all trails were eventually followed. Still, in most cases, that trail would be manageable. But in this one—between Boyle and The Three . . . and all they'd done—nothing was worth the risk. Not with so much at stake.

"Next!" a Latino customs clerk called out, waving O'Shea up to the small bulletproof booth.

O'Shea readjusted the U.S. Open baseball cap that he wore to blend in. His sandy-blond hair still peeked out, curling up under the edges. "How's everything going?" he asked, knowing the small talk would keep the clerk from making eye contact.

"Fine," the clerk responded, his head down.

Pulling out his blue passport, O'Shea handed it to the clerk.

For no reason, the clerk looked up. O'Shea had a smile waiting for him, just to keep things calm. As usual, the clerk immediately grinned back. "Coming back from work?" he asked.

"Lucky me, no. Vacation."

Nodding to himself, the clerk studied O'Shea's passport. Even tilted it slightly to inspect the new holograms that they recently added to crack down on forgeries.

O'Shea readjusted his U.S. Open cap. If he'd pulled the red passport, he wouldn't be waiting here.

"Have a great one," the clerk said, stamping O'Shea's passport and handing it back. "And welcome home."

"Thanks," O'Shea replied, tucking the passport back into his breast pocket. Right next to his FBI badge and ID.

Within a minute, O'Shea cut past the baggage carousels and headed for the signs marked *Nothing to Declare/Exit.* As his foot hit the sensor mat, two frosted-glass doors slid open, revealing a mob of family and friends pressed against short metal barriers, waiting for their loved ones despite the early hour. Two little girls jumped, then sagged, when they realized O'Shea wasn't their dad. He didn't notice. He was too busy dialing a number on his cell phone. It rang three times before his partner answered.

"Welcome, welcome," Micah said, finally picking up. From the soft humming in the background, it sounded like he was in a car.

"Tell me you're in Palm Beach," O'Shea replied.

"Got here last night. It's nice down here. Fancy. Y'know they got tiny water fountains on the sidewalks just for spoiled little dogs?"

"What about Wes?"

"Three cars in front of me," Micah said as the humming continued. "Him and his roommate just crossed the bridge a minute ago."

"I assume he hasn't seen you yet?"

"You said to wait."

"Exactly," O'Shea replied, stepping outside the airport and spotting his name on a handwritten sign. The private driver nodded hello and tried to grab O'Shea's small black piece of luggage. O'Shea waved him off and headed for the car, never taking the phone from his ear.

"He's dropping the roommate off right now," Micah added. "Looks like Wes is headed into work."

"Just stay with him," O'Shea replied. "I'll be there as quick as I can."

9

Washington, D.C.

The phone shrieked through the small office, but he didn't pick it up. Same on the second ring. He knew who it was—on this line, there was only one person it could be—but he still didn't move. Not until he knew for sure. Leaning both elbows on his desk, Roland Egen studied his phone's digital screen, waiting for caller ID to kick in. Black electronic letters popped into place: *Offices of Leland Manning.*

"You're early," The Roman said as he pressed the receiver to his ear. He had pale, rosy skin, bright blue eyes, and a shock of black hair. *Black Irish*, his fishing buddies called it. But never to his face.

"You said to make sure no one was here."

The Roman nodded to himself. Finally, someone who followed directions. "So the President's not in yet?"

"On his way. He sleeps late after overnight trips."

"And the First Lady?"

"I'm telling you, it's just me. Now can we hurry up? People'll be here any second."

Sitting at his desk and squinting out the window, The Roman watched as the light snow tumbled from the early morning sky. It may've been eighty degrees in Florida, but in D.C., winter was just unpacking its first punch. He didn't mind. When he was little, his grandmother had taught him to enjoy the quiet that came with the cold. Just as his grandfather had taught him to appreciate the calm that came to the waters of the Potomac. As any fisherman knew, winter chased away the jet skiers and pleasure boaters. And that was always the best time to put your line in the water. Especially when you had the right bait.

"What about Wes?" The Roman asked. "You get everything I sent?"

"Yeah . . . right here . . ."

He could hear the hesitation in his associate's voice. No one liked being the bad guy—especially in politics. "And you found something to put it in?" The Roman asked.

"We have a— That's why I came in early. We have this lapel pin—"

"You can get him to wear it . . ."

"I-I think so."

"It wasn't a question. Get him to wear it," The Roman shot back.

"You sure Wes'll even come in?" his associate asked. "Agents here said he was sick as a hound the entire flight back. Puked his lungs all over his pants."

Outside, a crack of blue light slit through the tired, gray sky. "I'm not surprised," The Roman said as the snow continued to fall. "If I were him right now, I'd be wrecking my pants too. Now about that pin . . ."

"Don't worry," his associate said. "Wes won't even look twice at it . . . especially when it's served by a friendly face."

10

Palm Beach, Florida

"Hold it!" I yell, darting around the corner of the lobby and heading for the elevator's closing doors. Inside the elevator, a blond woman looks away, pretending she didn't hear me. That's why I hate Palm Beach. As the doors are about to pucker in a tight kiss, I leap forward and squeeze through. Now stuck with me, the blonde turns to the floor selection panel and pretends she's searching for *Door Open.* I should call her on it and tell her off.

"Thanks," I say, bent over as I catch my breath.

"What floor?"

"Four."

"Oh, you're with—"

"Yeah," I say, finally looking up to see her.

She stares at my face, then quickly glances up at the electronic floor indicator. If she could run and scream "Monster!" she would. But like the best Palm Beach hostesses, she'll overlook anything if it means a good social climb. "Must be wild to work for him," she adds, my new best friend, even though she refuses to make eye contact. I'm used to it by now. I haven't had a date in two years. But every pretty girl wants to talk to the President.

"Wilder than you know," I say as the doors open on the fourth floor. Heading left toward a set of closed double doors, I sprint out as fast as I can. Not because of the blonde, but because I'm already—

"Late!" a scratchy voice scolds behind me. I spin back toward the open double doors of the Secret Service's suite, where a man with a neck as thick as my thigh sits behind a glass partition that looks like a bank teller's window.

"How late?" I call out, turning back toward the closed doors on the opposite side of the beige-carpeted hallway. Along with the Service's, they're the only doors on the whole floor—and unlike the law firm or the mortgage company just below, these doors aren't oak and stately. They're black and steel-lined. Bulletproof. Just like our windows.

"Late enough," he says as I pull my ID badge from my pocket. But just as I'm about to swipe it through the card reader, I hear a quiet thunk, and the closed doors unlock.

"Thanks, A.J.!" I call out, pulling the door open.

Inside, I check the left-hand wall for the Secret Service agent who usually stands guard. He's not there, which means the President's not in yet. Good. I check the reception desk. The receptionist is gone too. Bad.

Crap. That means they already . . .

Sprinting across the enormous presidential seal that's woven into the bright blue carpet, I cut to my left, where the hallway is lined with bad paintings and poor sculptures of the President. They've arrived every single day since we left office—all from strangers, fans, supporters. They draw, paint, pencil, sketch, bronze, and sculpt him in every possible permutation. The newest ones are a set of Florida toothpicks with his profile carved into each one, and a bright yellow ceramic sculpture of the sun, with his face in the middle. And that's not even including what the corporations send: every CD, every book, every DVD that's released, they all want the former President to have it, though all we do is ship it to his Presidential Library. Knocking over a beechwood walking cane with his childhood photos glued to it, I trip down the hall and head for the second-to-last office that's—

"Nice of you to join us," a raspy female voice announces as the entire room turns at my arrival. I do a quick head count just to see if I'm last—two, three, four, five . . .

"You're last," Claudia Pacheco, our chief of staff, confirms as she leans back in her seat behind her messy mahogany desk. Claudia's got brown, graying hair that's pulled back in an almost military-tight bun and smoker's lips that reveal exactly where the raspy voice comes from. "President with you?" she adds.

I shake my head, forgoing my one excuse for being late.

Out of the corner of my eye, I spot Bev and Oren smirking to themselves. Annoying and annoyinger. They both eye the small gold lapel pin that sits on the corner of Claudia's desk. Sculpted in the shape of the White House, the gold pin was no bigger than a hotel piece from Monopoly, but what made it memorable were the two gold poorly sculpted heads of the President and First Lady, pressed together and joined by one connecting ear, that dangled like charms just below it. The President bought it for Claudia years ago as a gag gift from a street vendor in China. Today, it's part of her leftover White House tradition: whoever's the last to arrive at the Monday morning staff meeting wears the pin for the next week. If you miss the meeting, you wear it for a month. But to my surprise, Claudia doesn't reach for it.

"What happened with the break-in backstage?" she asks in her barreling Massachusetts accent.

"Break-in?"

"In Malaysia . . . the guy in the President's holding room . . . the shattered glass table. My speaking Spanish here?"

In high school, Claudia was the girl who organized all the extracurricular events but never had any fun at them. It was the same when she ran Oval Office Operations, easily one of the most thankless jobs in the White House. She's not in it for the credit or the glory. She's here because she's dedicated. And she wants to make sure we are too.

"No . . . of course . . ." I stutter. "But it wasn't— That wasn't a break-in."

"That's not what the report said."

"They sent you a report?"

"They send us everything," Bev says from the two-person love seat perpendicular to Claudia's desk. She should know. As head of correspondence, she answers all the President's personal mail and even knows what inside jokes to put at the bottom of his friends' birthday cards. For a man with a good ten thousand "friends," it's tougher than it sounds, and the only reason Bev pulls it off is because she's been with the President since his first run for Congress almost twenty-five years ago.

"And they called it a *break-in*?" I ask.

Claudia holds up the report as Bev pulls the lapel pin from the corner of the desk. "Break. In," Claudia says, pointing to the words.

My eyes stay with the pin as Bev fidgets with it, running her thumb over the President's and First Lady's faces.

"Was there anything even worth stealing in the holding room?" Bev asks, brushing her dyed-black hair over her shoulder and revealing a V-neck sweater that shows off decade-old breast implants, which she got, along with the name *Busty Bev*, the year we won the White House. In high school, Bev was the girl voted Fabulous Face, and even now, at sixty-two, it's clear that appearances still matter.

"No one stole anyth— Trust me, it wasn't a break-in," I say, rolling my eyes to downplay. "The guy was drunk. He thought he was in the bathroom."

"And the broken glass table?" Claudia asks.

"We're lucky it was just broken. Imagine if he thought it was a urinal," Oren interrupts, already laughing at his own joke and scratching at his messy-prep eight a.m. shadow. At 6'1", Oren is the tallest, handsomest, toughest-looking gay man I've ever met in my life, and the only one close to my age in the office. From his seat across from Claudia's desk, it's clear he was the first one here. No surprise. If Bev was Fabulous Face, Oren was the smart kid who sent the dumb ones to buy beer. A born instigator, as well as our director of travel, he's also got the softest political touch in the entire office, which is why, with one simple joke, the room quickly forgets its obsession with the table.

I nod him a thank-you and—

"What about the table?" Bev asks, still fidgeting with the pin.

"That was me," I say way too defensively. "Read the report—I tripped into it as he was running out."

"Wes, relax," Claudia offers in her chief of staff monotone. "No one's accusing you of—"

"I'm just saying . . . if I thought it was serious, I'd still be hunting for the guy myself. Even the Service thought he was just a wanderer." On my left, Oren playfully taps his own lapel, hoping I don't notice. Motioning to Bev, he's trying to get her attention. He's only worn the pin once—on a day I told him, "Wait in your office, the President wants to see you." The President wasn't even in the building. It was an easy trick. This is just fourth-grade payback. He again motions to Bev. Lucky me, she doesn't notice.

"Listen, I'm sorry to do this, but are we done?" I ask, looking down at my watch and realizing I'm already late. "The President wants me to—"

"Go, go, go," Claudia says, closing her datebook. "Just do me a favor, Wes. When you're at tonight's cystic fibrosis event—I know you're always careful—but with the break-in . . ."

"It wasn't a break-in."

". . . just keep your eyes open a little bit wider, okay?"

"I always do," I say, dashing for the door and narrowly escaping the—

"What about the pin?" a rusty voice interrupts from his usual swivel chair in the back corner.

"Aaaaand you're screwed," Oren says.

"Red light, red light!" Claudia calls out. It's the same thing she yells at her kids. I stop right there. "Thanks, B.B.," she adds.

"Jes' doin' mah duty," B.B. says, the words tumbling out of the side of his mouth in a slow Southern crawl.

With a shock of messy white hair and a rumpled button-down shirt with the President's faded monogrammed initials on the cuffs, B.B. Shaye has been by the President's side even longer than the First Lady. Some say he's Manning's distant cousin . . . others say he's his senile old sergeant from Vietnam. Either way, he's been the President's shadow for almost forty years—and like any shadow, he'll creep you out if you stare at him too long. "Sorry, kiddo," he offers with a yellow-toothed grin as Bev hands me the gold White House with the dangling heads.

For authenticity, the sculptor used two flakes of green glitter for the First Lady's eye color. Since gray glitter is harder to come by, the President's eyes are blank.

"Just tell people they're your grandchildren," Oren says as I open the clasp and slide it into my lapel. Shoving too hard, I feel a sharp bite in my fingertip as the pin punctures my skin. A drop of blood bubbles upward. I've taken much worse.

"By the way, Wes," Claudia adds, "one of the curators from the library said he wants to talk to you about some exhibit he's working on, so be nice when he calls . . ."

"I'm on my cell if you need me!" I call out with a wave. Rushing to the door, I lick the drop of blood from my finger.

"Careful," B.B. calls out behind me. "It's the small cuts that'll kill ya."

He's right about that. Out in the hallway, I blow past an oversize oil painting of President Manning dressed as a circus ringmaster. Dreidel said he had info on Boyle. Time to finally find out what it is.

11

"Welcome back, Mr. Holloway," the valet at the Four Seasons says, knowing my name from countless visits with the President. Unlike most, he stays locked on my eyes. I nod him a thank-you just for that.

As I step inside the hotel, a blast of air-conditioning wraps me in its arms. Out of habit, I look over my shoulder for the President. He's not here. I'm on my own.

Cutting across the beige marble floor of the lobby, I feel my heart kicking inside my chest. It's not just Boyle. For better or worse, that's always been Dreidel's effect on me.

As Manning's original buttboy, Gavin "Dreidel" Jeffer isn't just my predecessor—he's also the one who put me on the President's radar and recommended mc for the job. When we met a decade ago, I was a nineteen-year-old volunteer in the Florida campaign officc, answering phones and putting out yard signs. Dreidel was twenty-two and Manning's right- and left-hand man. I actually told Dreidel it was an honor to meet him. And I meant it. By then, we'd all heard the story.

Back during primary season, Dreidel was just some

unaffiliated local kid setting up folding chairs during the first primary debate. Like any other roadie, when the show was over, he tried to get closer to the action by sneaking backstage. Where he found himself was the heart of the spin room, where the best liars in America were telling tall tales about why their candidate had just won. In a sloppy oxford shirt, he was the one silent kid in a room full of yammering adults. The CBS reporter spotted him instantly, shoving a microphone in his face. "What'd you think, son?" the reporter asked.

Dreidel stared blankly into the red light of the camera, his mouth dangling open. And without even thinking about it, he gave the God's honest response that would forever change his life: "When it was over, Manning's the only one who didn't ask his staff, *How'd I do?*"

That question became Manning's mantra for the next year and a half. Every news organization picked up the clip. Every major paper ran with the quote. They even passed out printed-up buttons saying *How'd I do?*

Three words. When Dreidel retold the story at his wedding a few years back, he said he didn't even realize what had happened until the reporter asked how to spell his name. It didn't matter. Three words, and Dreidel—the little Jewish spinner, as the White House press nicknamed him—was born. Within a week, Manning offered him a job as buttboy, and throughout the campaign, hundreds of young volunteers rolled their eyes. It's not that they were jealous, it's just . . . Maybe it's his smug smile, or the ease with which he stumbled into the job, but in the school yard, Dreidel was the kid who used to have the best birthday party, with the best presents, with the best favors for anyone lucky enough to be invited. For a few years, it puts him in the *in* crowd, but as cockiness sets in, he doesn't even realize he's on the outs.

Still, he's always been Manning's good luck charm. And today, hopefully mine.

"Good day, Mr. Holloway," the concierge calls out as I slide past him and head toward the elevators. It's the second person who knows my name, instantly reminding me of the need to be discreet. Of course, that's why I called Dreidel in the first place. The President would never admit it, but I know why he and the First Lady attended Dreidel's wedding and wrote his recommendation for Columbia Law School—and asked me to pick out a gift when Dreidel's daughter was born: rewards for years of good service. And in White House terms, *good service* means keeping your mouth shut.

As the elevator doors open on the fourth floor, I follow the directional arrows and start counting room numbers: 405 . . . 407 . . . 409 . . . From the distance between doors, I can tell these're all suites. Dreidel's moving up in the world.

The hallway dead-ends at room 415, a suite so big it's got a doorbell on it. There's no way I'm giving him the pleasure of ringing it.

"Room service," I announce, rapping my knuckles against the door.

No one answers.

"Dreidel, you in there?" I add.

Still no response.

"It's me, Wes!" I yell, finally giving up and ringing the doorbell. "Drcidel, are you—?"

There's a loud thunk as the lock flicks open. Then a jingling of metal. He's got the door chain on too.

"Hold on," he calls out. "I'm coming."

"What're you doing? Stealing the wood hangers?"

The door cracks open, but only a few inches. Behind it, Dreidel sticks his head out like an anxious housewife surprised by a salesman. His usually perfectly parted hair is slightly mussed, draping boyish bangs across his forehead. He pushes his circular wire-rim glasses up on his thin sculpted nose. From the little I can see, he's not wearing a shirt.

"No offense, but I'm not having sex with you," I say with a laugh.

"I said to call from downstairs," he shoots back.

"What're you getting so upset about? I figured you'd like showing off your big room and—"

"I'm serious, Wes. Why'd you come up here?" There's a new tone in his voice. Not just annoyance. Fear. "Did anyone follow you?" he adds, opening the door a bit more to check the hallway. He's got a towel around his waist.

"Dreidel, is everything—?"

"I said call from *downstairs*!" he insists.

I step back, completely confused.

"Honey," a female voice calls out from within the room, "is everything—" The woman stops midsentence. Dreidel turns, and I spot her over his shoulder, just turning the corner inside the room. She's dressed in one of the hotel's white overfluffed bathrobes—a thin African-American woman with gorgeous braids. I have no idea who she is, but the one thing I'm sure of is, she's not Dreidel's wife. Or his two-year-old daughter.

Dreidel's face falls as he reads my reaction. This is the part where he says it's not how it looks.

"Wes, it's not what you think."

I stare at the woman in the bathrobe. And Dreidel in his towel. "Maybe I should . . . I'll just go downstairs," I stutter.

"I'll meet you there in two minutes."

Stepping back, I study the woman, who's still frozen in place. Her eyes are wide, silently apologizing.

12

Where's he now?" O'Shea asked, pressing his palm against the window of the black sedan and feeling the warmth of the Florida sun. It was freezing in France. But somehow, even with the Palm Beach heat and the liquid-blue sky, he wasn't any warmer.

"He just took the elevator upstairs in the hotel," Micah replied.

"Elevator? You let him ride alone?"

"Better than me jumping in with him. Relax—there're only four floors. He's not getting far."

O'Shea rolled his tongue inside his cheek. "So what're you still doing in the lobby?"

"Waiting for one of the—"

Through the phone, O'Shea heard a slight ping followed by a low rumble. Micah's elevator had finally arrived. "I'll have him in—"

Micah's voice went silent. But from the background noise, O'Shea could tell Micah was still on the line.

"Micah, what happened?" he asked.

No response.

"Micah, you okay!?"

There was another low rumble. Elevator doors closing. Then a rough swishing. Like two windbreakers being rubbed together. Micah was moving. The swishing continued. At that pace, he was clearly not in the elevator, O'Shea thought. But if he wasn't in the elevator, that meant . . .

"Wes just stepped out, didn't he?" O'Shea asked as his sedan made a sharp left onto a well-manicured drive.

"Not bad, Watson," Micah whispered. "You should do this professionally."

"Anyone with him?"

"Nope. All alone," Micah said. "Something happened up there, though. Kid's got his tail between his legs. Like he got dumped."

"Is he leaving the hotel?"

"Nope again. Headed for the restaurant in back. I'm telling you, he really looks terrible . . . I mean, even more than those Frankenstein marks in his face."

"That's a shame," O'Shea said as his car curved into the horseshoe driveway of the main entrance. " 'Cause his day's about to get a whole lot worse." On his right, the car door sprang open and a valet with blond hair offered a slight tip of his hat.

"Welcome to the Four Seasons, sir. Are you checking in with us today?"

"No," O'Shea offered as he stepped out of the car. "Just grabbing a little something for breakfast."

13

Hunched forward in a big wicker armchair, I stir my coffee with a silver spoon and watch my reflection swirl into oblivion.

"Is it really that bad?" a voice teases behind me.

I turn just in time to see Dreidel enter the hotel's open-air restaurant. His black hair is gelled and parted. The boyish bangs are long gone. Combined with his monogrammed white shirt and antique wire-rim glasses, it's clear he's mastered the art of sending a message without saying a word. Right now he's selling confidence. Too bad I'm not buying.

Ignoring the foamy waves of the Atlantic Ocean on our left, he puts a hand on my shoulder and crosses around to the oversize wicker seat next to me. As he moves, his hand runs from my shoulder to the back of my neck, always holding tight enough to reassure.

"Don't use his moves on me," I warn.

"What're you—?"

"His *moves*," I repeat, pulling away so his hand's no longer on my neck.

"You think I'm—? You think I'd pull a Manning on you?"

Dreidel was with him for almost four years. I'm going on nine. I don't even bother to argue. I just stare back down at my overpriced, still-swirling coffee and let the silence sink in. This is why the in crowd turns on him.

"Wes, what you saw up there—"

"Listen, before you say it, can we just spare ourselves the awkwardness and move on? My bad . . . my fault . . . clearly none of my business."

He studies me carefully, picking apart every syllable and trying to figure out if I mean it. When you shadow a President, you become fluent in reading between the lines. I'm good. Dreidel's better.

"Just say it already, Wes."

I stare out across the open terrace and watch the waves kamikaze into the beach.

"I know you're thinking it," he adds.

Like I said, Dreidel's better. "Does Ellen know?" I finally ask, referring to his wife.

"She should. She's not stupid." His voice creaks like a renegade floorboard. "And when Ali was born . . . marriage is hard, Wes."

"So that girl up there . . ."

"Just someone I met at the bar. I flashed my room key. She thinks I'm rich because I can afford to stay here." He forces a grin and tosses his room key on the table. "I didn't realize you had so many money addicts in Palm Beach."

This time, I'm the one who's silent. A waiter approaches and fills Dreidel's cup with coffee.

"You guys talked about divorce?" I ask.

"Can't."

"Why not?"

"Why do you think?" he challenges.

I look over at the file folder that's lying between us on the table. The handwritten tab says *Fundraising.*

"I thought you said you were down here on business."

"And that's not business?" he asks.

A few months back, Dreidel called the President to tell him he was running for State Senate in the 19th District in his home state of Illinois. But when it comes to impending elections, "happily married father" polls far better than "recently divorced dad."

"See, and you thought you were the only one with problems," Dreidel adds. "Now assuming that was Boyle, you want to hear how he cheated death, or not?"

14

I sit up straight in my chair. "You actually found something?"

"No, I called you here to waste your time." With a deep sip of coffee, Dreidel's a different man. Like anyone in the White House, he's always better when he's in control. "So back to the beginning . . . the real beginning . . . On the day the two of you got shot at the speedway, you remember how long the drive was to get you to the hospital?"

A simple question, but I don't give him an answer.

"Just guess," he says.

I grit my teeth, surprised by how hard the memory hits. I can still see the ambulance doors closing on Boyle . . .

"Wes, I know you don't want to relive it, I just need—"

"I passed out," I blurt. "From what they said, the ambulance took about four minutes . . ."

"It was three minutes."

"Pretty fast."

"Actually, pretty slow considering Halifax Medical Center is only a mile and a half from the speedway. Now guess how long it took for the ambulance that drove there with Boyle, who was—no offense—a whole lot more important than you were to the administration, not to mention far more injured?"

I shake my head, refusing to play along.

"Twelve minutes," Dreidel blurts.

We sit in silence as I take it in.

"So?" I ask.

"C'mon, Wes. *Twelve minutes* for a speeding ambulance with a critically injured White House senior staff member to travel a mile and a half? The average person *walks* faster. My grandmother walks faster. And she's dead."

"Maybe they got stuck in the panicking riot outside."

"Funny, that's exactly what *they* said."

"They?"

From the briefcase that's leaning against the side of his chair, Dreidel pulls out a bound document about half as thick as a phone book. He drops it on the table with a thud that sends our spoons bouncing. I recognize the congressional logo immediately. *Investigation into the Assassination Attempt on President Leland F. Manning.* Congress's official investigation into Nico's attack. Dreidel leaves it on the table, waiting to see if I pick it up. He knows me better than I thought.

"You never read it, did you?" he asks.

I stare at the book, still refusing to touch it. "I flipped through it once . . . It's just . . . it's like reading your own obituary."

"More like Boyle's obituary. You lived, remember?"

I brush my hand against my face. My fingertips rise and fall in the craters of my scars. "What's your point?"

"Play the numbers, Wes. Two trains leave the station at almost the exact same time. Both race for the hospital. It's a matter of life and death. One takes three minutes. The other takes twelve. You don't see a problem there? And if that weren't enough, remember what the real security screwup was that Congress ripped our doctors apart for?"

"You mean bringing the President's wrong blood type?"

"See, that's where they always got it wrong. When Congress did their investigation, they tore out what little hair they had left in their heads because they found pints of O-negative blood along with the President's B-positive. Naturally, they assumed someone made a mistake and brought the wrong blood. But knowing who you saw at the speech that night—well, guess who else happened to be O-negative?"

"Boyle?"

"And that's how he pulled off his big magic trick."

"It wasn't a magic trick," I insist.

"No, you're right. But it *was* an illusion." Waving his left hand back and forth in front of me, he adds, "You're so busy watching the moving hand, you completely ignore the sly hand's misdirection." From his right hand, he drops a quarter on the table.

"Way to be melodramatic," I point out.

He shakes his head as if I'm missing the point. "Do you have any idea what you've stumbled onto? This thing was more fixed than a Harlem Globetrotters game. You, me, Congress, the whole world . . . we got—" He leans in close, lowering his voice. "We got *fooled*, Wes. They lied. I mean, if that was really Boyle—"

"It was him! I saw him!"

"I'm not saying you didn't. I just . . ." He looks around, his voice getting even quieter. "This isn't one of those petty news stories they save until the end of the broadcast."

He's right about that. "I don't understand, though—why would the President's ambulance be hauling around Boyle's blood?"

"I know. That's the question, isn't it?" Dreidel asks. "But when you pick it apart, only one explanation makes sense. They only carry around blood . . ."

". . . when they think someone's life is in danger." I pick up the quarter and tap it against the white tablecloth. "Oh, God. If they were expecting it . . . you think Boyle was wearing a vest?"

"Had to," Dreidel says. "He took two shots in the chest . . ."

"But all that blood—"

". . . and one shot that went through the back of his hand and straight into his neck. Read the report, Wes. Nico was an army-trained sniper who specialized in heart shots. Boyle went facedown the moment it happened. That shot to the neck . . . I'll bet that's what you saw pooling below him."

I close my eyes and hear myself offering to put Boyle in the limo. There's a jagged piece of metal in my cheek. The bumblebee's still screaming . . . "But if he was wearing a vest . . ." I look out toward the ocean. The waves are deafening. ". . . th-they knew. They had to've known . . ."

"Wes, will you stop—" Dreidel cuts himself off and lowers his voice. We don't need anyone staring. "They didn't know," he whispers. "They could've had an open threat on Boyle's life. He could've been wearing that vest for a month. In fact, according to the report, the President *wasn't* wearing *his* vest that day. Didja hear that?" He waits until I nod, just to make sure I'm focused. "If they'd known there was a gunman, Manning never would've been there, much less been allowed to go without that vest."

"Unless he *was* wearing one and that's just part of their story," I point out.

"Listen, I know you're close to this—"

"Close to it? It ruined my life! D'you understand that?" I finally explode. "This wasn't just some crappy afternoon. Little kids point at me and hide behind their moms! I can't fucking smile anymore! Do you have any idea what that's like?"

The restaurant goes silent. Every single person is looking at us. The preppy family with two twin girls. The sandy-haired man with the U.S. Open cap. Even our waiter, who quickly approaches, hoping to calm things down.

"Everything okay, sir?"

"Yeah . . . sorry . . . we're fine," I tell him as he fills our coffee cups that don't need refilling.

As the waiter leaves, Dreidel watches me closely, giving me a moment. It's how he taught me to deal with the President when he loses his cool. Put your head down and let the fire burn itself out.

"I'm okay," I tell him.

"I knew you would be," he says. "Just remember, I'm here to help."

I take a deep breath and bury it all away. "So assuming there was a threat on Boyle's life at the time, why not just take him to the hospital?"

"That's the nail I keep stepping on. They caught Nico . . . Boyle was injured, but obviously alive . . . why pretend you're dead and walk away from your life and your entire family? Maybe that's what they were talking about during those twelve minutes in the ambulance. Maybe that's when Boyle made his decision to hide."

I shake my head. "In twelve minutes? You can't just shuck your whole life in twelve minutes—especially when you're bleeding out of your neck. They had to've made plans before that."

"They?" Dreidel asks.

"C'mon, this isn't like hiding from your little brother in a pillow fort. To pull something this big off, you need the Service, plus the ambulance driver, plus the doctor who took care of his neck." I pause for a moment to make the point clear. "Plus someone to authorize it."

Dreidel lowers his chin, looking at me from just above the rounded rim of his glasses. He knows what I'm getting at. "You really think he'd—? You think he'd do that?"

It's the question I've been fighting with since the moment I saw Boyle's fake name back at that hotel. You don't use that name to hide. You use it so someone can find you. "I just . . . I don't see how the President *wouldn't* know. Back then, Manning couldn't pee in a bush unless someone checked it first. If Boyle was wearing a vest—which he clearly had to've been—there had to be a credible threat. And if there was a credible threat . . . and extra blood in the ambulance . . . and contingencies in place to make sure Boyle was safe . . . Manning had to've signed off on that."

"Unless Albright signed off for him," Dreidel counters, referring to our old chief of staff and the one other person in the limo with us that day at the speedway.

It's a fair point, but it doesn't bring us any closer to an answer. Albright died of testicular cancer three years ago. "Now you're blaming it all on a corpse?"

"Doesn't make it any less credible," Dreidel challenges. "Albright used to sign off on security details all the time."

"I don't know," I say, shaking my head. "Manning and Boyle had known each other since college. If Boyle was planning on disappearing, that's a hell of a prank to pull on a friend, much less the President of the United States."

"You joking? Boyle walked away from his family, his wife . . . even his own daughter. Look at the full picture, Wes: Nico the nutjob takes a potshot at the President. Instead, he hits Boyle square in the chest. But instead of going to the hospital to get patched up, Boyle takes that exact moment to fake his own death and disappear off the face of the earth. You do something like that, you've obviously got a damn good reason."

"Like father, like son?" I ask.

"Yeah, I thought about that. Problem is, Boyle's dad was just a petty scumbag. This is . . . this is big-league. With a capital *big*."

"Maybe Boyle hired Nico. Maybe the shooting was a giant smoke screen to give Boyle a way to get out."

"Way too *Mission: Impossible* sequels," Dreidel says. "If Nico misses, you're risking a head shot. More important, if the Service was helping, they're not putting the President, and his staff, and 200,000 spectators in danger while entrusting it all to some whacked looney tune. You've seen Nico in the interviews—he's Stephen King–movie crazy. If Boyle wanted to do this to himself, he'd fake a heart attack at home and be done with it."

"So you think when Nico fired those shots, Boyle and the Service just used the instant chaos to sneak him out of there?" I ask, trying hard to keep it to a whisper.

"I don't know what to think. All I know is, for Boyle to put on a bulletproof vest, he must've been expecting something. I mean, you don't bring an umbrella unless you think it's gonna rain, right?"

I nod, unable to argue. Still, it doesn't get us any closer to the *why*. Why was Nico taking shots at Boyle? Why was Manning's motorcade traveling around with Boyle's blood? And why would Boyle walk away from his life, his wife, and his teenage daughter? I mean, what could possibly tempt—or terrify—a man so much that he'd throw his entire life away?

"Maybe you should just ask," Dreidel blurts.

"Who, Manning? Oh, right—I'll just run up and say, 'By the way, sir, I just saw your dead buddy—yeah, the one whose assassination wrecked your entire presidency. Oh, and since he's alive, while I've been slaving for your ass every single day since I got out of the hospital, why'd you lie to me for over eight years about the single worst moment of my life?' Yeah, that'd be genius."

"What about the Service?"

"Same difference. Boyle could've never disappeared all those years ago if he didn't have their help. The last thing I need is to shout from the roof that I'm the one to blow it all open. Until I know what's going on, better to keep things quiet."

Dreidel leans back in his wicker chair. "When you saw Boyle backstage in that dressing room, you think he was trying to kill Manning?"

"Kill him?"

"Why else would he come out of hiding after almost eight years? Just to say hello?"

"I guess, but . . . to kill him? Isn't that—?"

"Kaiser Soze," Dreidel interrupts. "*Greatest trick the devil pulled off: convincing the world he didn't exist.*" He looks back up at me, and I swear there's almost a smile on his face. "Man, can you imagine? Being legally dead but still alive? Y'know how much freedom that gives you?"

I stare down at Dreidel's room key and try hard not to picture the fluffy white bathrobe that comes with it.

"Maybe that's what Boyle wanted all those years ago," he adds. "Just a way out."

I shake my head but still catch the deeper point. The only way to understand what's going on is to understand Boyle. "So where does that leave us?" I ask.

"*Us?* This ain't *my* disaster." He laughs as he says it, but he's definitely not joking. "C'mon, Wes, you know I'm just joking," he adds, knowing I get the point. Like any great political trickster, his first move is to remove his own fingerprints. It's why I called him in the first place. He spent almost four years by the President's side, but you'll never find him in the background of a single photograph. No one's better at being invisible, which is, right now, the number one thing I need if I plan on finding out the truth.

"Got any connections with law enforcement?" he adds, already two moves ahead. "If they can take a peek at Boyle's background—"

"I've got someone perfect for that," I tell him. But he's glancing over my shoulder, back toward the entrance to the restaurant. Following his stare, I turn around to find the black woman with the braids. She's traded the bathrobe for the other Palm Beach uniform: white slacks with a pale orange designer T-shirt. All set for a day on the town.

"Listen, I should run," Dreidel says, already out of his seat. "Just be smart about this."

"Smart?"

"Careful. Be careful. Because if Manning *is* in on this . . ." He takes another look around, then leans in close. "You thought America turned on him before? They'll crucify him, Wes. Seriously. Crucify."

I nod. Across the restaurant, his girlfriend shoots us a

look. "And while we're on the subject, Wes. I'm happy to keep your secret—just promise me you'll keep mine."

"O-Of course. I'd never say a word."

He turns to go, leaving me with the bill. "By the way, you interested in forking over five hundred bucks and coming to my fundraiser tonight?"

I shake my head in disbelief. "Dreidel, how much did your soul cost when you finally sold it?"

"You coming or not?"

"I would, but I've got a Manning event tonight."

Dreidel nods and doesn't linger. He knows who always comes first.

As he heads for the door, I decide not to turn and stare at the girl. Instead, I hold up my spoon and use the bottom of it as my own little fun-house mirror. Over my shoulder, I spot Dreidel just as he approaches her. He doesn't reach out to hold her hand until he thinks they're out of sight.

"Excuse me," someone says over my left shoulder. I turn, expecting to see the waiter. Instead, it's a blond guy in a black T-shirt. And a U.S. Open baseball hat.

"Wes Holloway?" he asks, opening his wallet to show me an FBI badge. "Terrence O'Shea. You have a few seconds to chat?"

15

St. Elizabeths Mental Hospital
Washington, D.C.

Breakfast bell's ringing, Nico. French toast or western omelet?" asked the petite black food service woman with the vinegar smell and the pink rhinestones set into her pink fingernails.

"What's for dinner?" Nico asked.

"You listening? We're on breakfast. French toast or western omelet?"

Putting on his shoes and kneeling just in front of his narrow bed, Nico looked up at the door and studied the rolling cart with the open tray slots. He'd long ago earned the right to eat with his fellow patients. But after what happened to his mother all those years ago, he'd rather have his meals delivered to his room. "French toast," Nico said. "Now what's for dinner?"

Throughout St. Elizabeths, they called Nico an NGI. He wasn't the only one. There were thirty-seven in total, all of them living in the John Howard Pavilion, a red brick, five-story building that was home to Nico and the other thirty-six patients *n*ot *g*uilty by reason of *i*nsanity.

Compared to the other wards, the NGI floors were always quieter than the rest. As Nico heard one doctor say, "When there're voices in your head, there's no need to talk to anyone else."

Still down on one knee, Nico yanked hard to fasten the Velcro on his sneakers (they took away the laces long ago) and carefully watched as the food service woman carried a pink plastic tray filled with French toast into his small ten-by-fifteen room, which was decorated with a wooden nightstand and a painted dresser that never had anything but a Bible and a set of vintage red glass rosary beads on it. The doctors offered to get Nico a sofa, even a coffee table. Anything to make it feel more like home. Nico refused, but never said why. He wanted it this way. So it looked like her room. His mom's room. In *her* hospital.

Nodding to himself, he could still picture the stale hospital room where his mother lay silent for almost three years. He was only ten when the Creutzfeldt-Jakob disease hit . . . when one faulty gene in her brain ignited the CJD protein that eventually kick-started her coma. When the diagnosis first came back, she didn't complain—not even when young Nico asked why God was taking her. She smiled, even then, and respectfully told him that's how it was written in the Book. The Book of Fate. Her head was shaking, but her voice was strong as she told him never to argue with it. The Book had to be respected. Had to be heeded. Let it guide you. But it wasn't just respect. She took strength from it. Security. No doubt, his mother knew. She wasn't afraid. How could anyone be afraid of God's will? But he still remembered his father standing behind him, squeezing his shoulders and forcing him to pray every day so Jesus would bring his mom back.

For the first few weeks, they prayed in the hospital chapel. After six months, they visited every day but Sunday, convinced that their Sunday prayers would be more effective if they came from church. It was three years later that Nico changed his prayers. He did it only once. During a frozen snow day in the fist of Wisconsin's winter. He didn't want to be in church that day, didn't want to be in his nice pants and church shirt. Especially with all the great snowball fights going on outside. So on that Sunday morning, as he lowered his head in church, instead of praying for Jesus to bring his mom back, he prayed for him to take her. The Book had to be wrong. That day, his mother died.

Staring at the plastic tray of French toast and still kneeling by his bed, Nico, for the third time, asked, "What's for dinner?"

"It's meat loaf, okay?" the delivery woman replied, rolling her eyes. "You happy now?"

"Of course, I'm happy," Nico said, flattening the Velcro with the heel of his hand and smiling to himself. Meat loaf. Just like his mom was supposed to have on *her* last night. On the day she died. The Three told him so. Just like they told him about the M Men . . . the Masons . . .

Nico's father had been a Freemason—proud of it too. To this day, Nico could smell the sweet cigar smoke that wafted in the door with his dad when he came back from Lodge meetings.

Nothing more than a social club, Nico had told them. All the Masons did was sell raffle tickets to raise money for the hospital. Like the Shriners.

The Three were patient, even then. They brought him the maps—taught him the history. How the Freemasons had grown worldwide hiding under the cover of charity. How they'd perfected their deceptions, telling people they were born out of the master stonemason guilds in the Middle Ages—a harmless organization where members could gather and share trade secrets, artisan-to-artisan. But The Three knew the truth: The Masons' craftwork had built some of the most holy and famous places in the world—from King Solomon's Temple to the Washington Monument—but the secrets the Masons protected were more than just inside tips for how to build archways and monuments. The night before Martin Luther King Jr. was killed, he was in a Mason Temple in Memphis. "I might not get there with you," King said that night to his followers. Like he knew that bullet was coming the next day. And the fact he was in a Masonic Temple . . . it was no coincidence. Fate. Always fate. At their highest levels, the Masons' ancient goal had never changed.

Even the church stood against the Masons at their founding, The Three explained.

It was a fair point, but Nico wasn't stupid. In the Middle Ages, there was much the church opposed.

The Three still didn't waver. Instead, they hit him with the hardest truth of all: what really happened to his mother the night she died.

16

But you can't tell anyone I told you," the woman whispered through the receiver.

Brushing a stray strand of red hair behind her ear, Lisbeth reached for the tiny tape recorder on her desk, double-checked it was plugged into the phone, and hit *Record.* "You have my word," Lisbeth promised. "Our secret."

As a reporter for the *Palm Beach Post*, Lisbeth was well aware that Florida law made it illegal to record private conversations unless the person recording first asked the other party. But as the gossip columnist for Below the Fold—the *Post*'s most popular section of the paper—Lisbeth also knew that the moment she asked permission, her source would freeze and fall silent. Plus she had to get the quote right. Plus she had to have proof for when the paper's lawyers gave her their usual libel thumbwrestle. It's the same reason why she had a mini-refrigerator stocked with wine and beer in the corner of her tiny beige cubicle, and a fresh bowl of peanuts on the corner of her desk. Whether it was her fellow reporters coming by to chat or a stranger calling on the phone, it was the sacred rule she learned when she took over the column six years ago: Always keep 'em talking.

"So about your story, Mrs. . . . ?"

"I'm just passing this along," the woman insisted. "Free of charge."

Making a note to herself, Lisbeth wrote the word *Pro?* in her spiral notepad. Most people fall for the name trap.

"Again, you didn't hear it from me . . ." the woman continued.

"I promise, Mrs. . . ."

". . . and I'm not falling for your little trick the second time either," the woman said.

Lisbeth crossed out the question mark, leaving only *Pro.*

Excited by the challenge, Lisbeth started spinning her phone cord like a mini–jump rope. As the cord picked up speed, the sheets of paper thumbtacked to the right-hand wall of her cubicle began to flutter. When Lisbeth was seventeen, her dad's clothing store had shut down, forcing her family into bankruptcy. But when her local newspaper in Battle Creek, Michigan, reported the story, the smart-ass reporter who wrote it up threw in the words *alleged poor sales*, implying a certain disingenuousness to her dad's account. In response, Lisbeth wrote an op-ed about it for her school newspaper. The local paper picked it up and ran it with an apology. Then the *Detroit News* picked it up from there. By the time it was done, she got seventy-two responses from readers all across Michigan. Those seventy-two letters were the ones that lined every inch of her cubicle walls, a daily reminder of the power of the pen—and a current reminder that the best stories are the ones you never see coming.

"Regardless," the woman said, "I just thought you'd

want to know that although it won't officially be announced until later this afternoon, Alexander John—eldest son of the Philadelphia Main Line Johns, of course—will be awarded a Gold Key in the National Scholastic Art Awards."

Lisbeth was writing the words *National Schola-* when she lifted her pen from the page. "How old is Alexander again?"

"Of course—seventeen—seventeen on September ninth."

"So . . . this is a high school award?"

"And national—not just statewide. Gold Key."

Lisbeth scratched at her freckled neck. She was slightly overweight, which she tried to offset with lime-green statement glasses that a rail-thin salesclerk promised would also shave some time off her thirty-one years. Lisbeth didn't believe the clerk. But she did buy the glasses. As she continued to scratch, a strand of red hair sagged from its ear perch and dangled in front of her face. "Ma'am, do you happen to be *related* to young Alexander?"

"What? Of course not," the woman insisted.

"You're sure?"

"Are you suggesting—? Young lady, this award is an honor that is—"

"Or are you in the employ of young Alexander's family?"

The woman paused. "Not full-time, of course, but—"

Lisbeth hit the *Stop* button on her tape recorder and chucked her pen against her desk. Only in Palm Beach would a mother hire a publicist for her eleventh grader's elbow macaroni art masterpiece. "It's a national award," Lisbeth muttered to herself, ripping the sheet of paper from her notepad. But as she crumpled it up, she still didn't hang up the phone. Sacred Rule #2: A crappy source today might be a great one tomorrow. Sacred Rule #3: See Sacred Rule #2.

"If I have space, I'll definitely try to get it in," Lisbeth added. "We're pretty full, though." It was an even bigger lie than the thinning and de-aging effects of her lime-green glasses. But as Lisbeth hung up the phone and tossed the crumpled paper into the trash, she couldn't help but notice the near-empty three-column grid on her computer screen.

Twenty inches. About eight hundred words. That's what it took every day to fill Below the Fold. Plus a photo, of course. So far, she had five inches on a local socialite's daughter marrying a professional pool player (B+, Lisbeth thought to herself), and four inches on a week-old cursing match between some teenager and the head of the DMV (C– at best). Eyeing the balled-up paper in the plastic garbage can, Lisbeth glanced back at her still mostly empty screen. No, she told herself. It was still too early in the day to be desperate. She hadn't even gotten the—

"Mail!" a voice called out as a hand reached over the top edge of the cubicle, wagging a short pile of envelopes in the air. Looking up, Lisbeth knew that if she reached for the stack, he'd just pull it away, so she waited for the hand . . . and its owner . . . to turn the corner. "Morning, Vincent," she said before he even appeared.

"Tell me you got something good today," Vincent said, his salt-and-pepper mustache squirming like a caterpillar on his lip. He tossed the pile of mail on Lisbeth's already oversubscribed desk. It wasn't until it fanned out accordion-style in front of her that Lisbeth saw the tear in each envelope.

"You opened my mail?" she asked.

"I'm your editor. That's my job."

"Your job is opening my mail?"

"No, my job is to make sure your column is the best it can be. And when it is, and when every person in this town is whispering to their neighbors about whatever scandal you so cleverly unearthed, we usually get about twenty to thirty letters a day, plus the usual press releases and invitations. Know what you got this morning? Six. And that's including the invites." Peering over her shoulder and reading from the mostly empty grid on Lisbeth's computer screen, Vincent added, "You spelled *DMV* wrong."

Lisbeth squinted toward the screen.

"Made you look," Vincent added, laughing his little huffing laugh. With his navy and red Polo-knockoff suspenders and matching bow tie, Vincent dressed like Palm Beach royalty on an editor's salary.

Annoyed, Lisbeth pulled his left suspender back like a bowstring and let it snap against his chest.

"Ow . . . that . . . that actually hurt," he whined, rubbing his chest. "I was making a point."

"Really? And what was that? That I should find more stories about handjobs in hot tubs?"

"Listen, missy, that was a fun story."

"*Fun?* I don't want fun. I want *good.*"

"Like what? Like your supposed top-secret source who whispered all those promises in your ear, then jumped off the face of the earth? What was her name again? Lily?"

"Iris." As Lisbeth said the word, she could feel the blood rush to her ears. Four months ago, a woman identifying herself only as Iris cold-called Lisbeth on the office's main line. From the shakiness in Iris's voice, Lisbeth could hear the tears. And from the hesitation . . . she knew what fear sounded like. For twenty minutes, Iris told her the story: about how, years ago, she used to do Thai massages at a local bathhouse . . . that it was there she first met the man she called Byron . . . and the thrill of secretly dating one of Palm Beach's most powerful men. But what got Lisbeth's attention was Iris's graphic detail of how, on a number of occasions, he lashed out physically, eventually breaking her collarbone and jaw. For Lisbeth, that was a story that mattered. And that was what the letters on her wall were there for. But when she asked for Byron's real name—and Iris's, for that matter—the line went dead.

"She was yanking your ya-ya," Vincent said.

"Maybe she was scared."

"Or maybe she just wanted some attention."

"Or maybe she's now married, and therefore terrified her husband will dump her the instant he finds out his lovely wife used to be a bathhouse girl. Think, Vincent. Sources only stay quiet when they have something to lose."

"Y'mean like their job? Or their career? Or their supposedly well read gossip column?"

Lisbeth stabbed him with a cold, piercing stare. Vincent stabbed her right back.

"Six," he said as he turned to leave. "Six letters in the stack."

"I don't care if it's one."

"Yes, you do. You're a great writer but a terrible liar, sweetie."

For once, Lisbeth stayed silent.

"By the way," Vincent added, "if a publicist calls for some art award for the John family . . . don't be such a snob. Think Page Six. Good bold names are good bold namcs."

"But if the story's crap—"

"I hate to break it to you, pumpkin," Vincent called out, already halfway down the hallway, "but there's no Pulitzer for gossip."

Alone in her cubicle, Lisbeth studied the empty grid on her screen, then looked down at the crumpled sheet of paper in her trash. She bent down below her desk to pull it from the garbage, and the phone rang above her. At the noise, she bolted upward, smashing the back of her head against the corner of her desk.

"Aaahh," she yelled, rubbing her head fiercely as she reached for the phone. "Below the Fold. This is Lisbeth."

"Hi, I . . . uh . . . I work over at the Four Seasons," a male voice began. "Is this the place you call for—?"

"Only if it's a good one," Lisbeth said, still rubbing, but all too aware what he was asking. It was the deal she made with all local hotel employees. A hundred bucks for any tip she used in the column.

"Well . . . uh . . . I was serving some of President Manning's old employees," he said. "And . . . I don't know if they count as celebrities, but if you're interested . . ."

"No, I'm definitely interested." She hit the *Record* button and scrambled for a pen. Even on her best days, there was no bigger bold name than *Manning.* "Those're exactly the type of people we love to write about."

17

"Maybe it'd be better if we stepped outside," O'Shea suggests, towering over me in the restaurant. He's got a buckled nose that makes it clear he's not afraid to take a punch. He tries to hide it with his sunglasses, but some things are hard to miss. The moment he flashed an FBI badge, people turned to stare.

"Yeah . . . that'd be great," I reply, calmly standing from my seat and following him through the open-air walkway that leads to the pool area outside. If I plan on keeping this quiet, the last thing I need is to be spotted with the FBI in a public place.

Surrounded by palm trees on all sides, the pool is a picture of privacy—this early in the morning, all the lounge chairs are empty—but for some reason, O'Shea doesn't slow down. It's not until we pass one of the many oversize potted plants that I see what he's looking at: two guys in a small wooden cabana folding towels, getting ready for the day. O'Shea keeps walking. Whatever he wants, he wants it in private.

"Listen, can you tell me where we're—?"

"How was your trip to Malaysia?" As he asks the question, I'm staring at the back of O'Shea's head. He doesn't even turn around to see my reaction.

"Um . . . it was fine."

"And the President had a good time?"

"I don't see why he wouldn't," I reply, annoyed.

"Anything else of note happen?" O'Shea asks, heading down a short path that's covered with water. A wave crashes in the distance, but it's not until a cascade of sand fills my loafers that I realize we're on the private beach behind the pool. Empty lounge chairs, empty lifeguard stands. The vacant beach goes on for miles.

As we pass a tiny hut that's used for snorkeling gear rentals, a man with finely combed brown hair steps out from behind it and pats me on the back. He's got a small nick that's missing from the top of his left ear.

"Say hi to my partner. Micah," O'Shea explains.

I turn back to the hotel, but thanks to the wall of palm trees, I can only make out a few terraces on the top floors of the building. Not a soul in sight. It's at that same moment I realize Micah has slowed his pace, so he's now slightly behind me.

"Maybe you should take a seat," O'Shea adds, motioning to one of the lounges.

"It'll only take a second," Micah adds behind me.

Spinning around, I start back toward the path. "I should really get—"

"We saw the report you filed with the Service, Wes. We know who you saw in Malaysia."

I stop right there, almost tripping in the sand. As I find my balance and turn to face them, O'Shea and Micah have the ocean at their backs. The waves pound ruthlessly. Subtlety isn't their strong point.

"What're you talking about?" I ask.

"The report," O'Shea says. "Fifty-something guy with Boyle's height, Boyle's weight, Boyle's shaved bald head, though for some reason you left out his eye color—and the fact you thought it was him."

"Listen, I don't know *what* I saw that night . . ."

"It's okay, Wes," Micah says with a singsong quality to his voice. "Boyle *was* in Malaysia. You're not crazy."

Most people would be relieved. But I've been around law enforcement long enough to know their tricks and treats. This one's called *tone matching.* Designed to subconsciously affect a target's mood, it's built on the fact that you tend to match the tone that's aimed at you. When someone yells, you yell back. Whisper, you whisper back. Usually, they use it to strengthen a witness who's depressed, or bring down a target who's cocky. Micah just sang to me, hoping I'd sing back. There's only one problem. FBI agents don't sing—and I don't either. If they're using mind games, there's something they're not saying.

"Boyle's really alive?" I ask, refusing to admit anything.

O'Shea studies me carefully. For the first time, he's staring at my scars. "I know this is personal for you—"

"That's *not* what this is about!" I shoot back.

"Wes, we're not here to attack," Micah says softly.

"And enough with the damn voice tricks! Just tell me what the hell is going on!"

The wind rockets across the shore, blowing Micah's tightly combed hair out of place. O'Shea shifts his weight, uncomfortable in the sand and well aware he picked the wrong button to press. It's not just their suits that make them stand out. The two agents exchange a glance. O'Shea offers a small nod.

"Boyle ever mention a group he called *The Three*?" Micah finally asks.

I shake my head no.

"What about *The Roman*?"

"Is that a group too?"

"It's a person," O'Shea says, watching my reaction.

"Am I supposed to know him?" I ask.

For the second time, the two agents share a glance. O'Shea squints against the morning sun as it burns through the clouds. "You have any idea how long we've been hunting Boyle?" O'Shea asks. "Y'think this all started with his miraculous 'death'? We were chasing him back in the White House, just waiting for him to screw up. And then when he did . . . poof . . . world's greatest get-out-of-jail-free card."

"So when he was shot . . ."

". . . we got snookered. Just like the rest of America. Even closed the case and filed the files. Three years later, he made his first mistake and got spotted in Spain by some local ex-pat who was just enough of a political junkie to recognize him. Lucky us, he calls it in, but before we could even do follow-up, the witness's car mysteriously blows up in front of his house. Pro job too—Semtex-H with a pressure-touch switch. Lucky us again, no one's hurt, but the message is sent. Witness decides he never saw anything."

"And you think Boyle knows Semtex-H? I mean . . . he's an accountant."

"Which means he knows how to pay people and manipulate and keep his fingerprints off everything no matter what he touches."

"But he . . ."

". . . makes his living preying on people. That's what he does, Wes. It's what he did in the White House . . . and with our agents . . . and especially with the Service."

Reading the confusion on my face, he adds, "C'mon, you must've figured this one out. The twelve minutes in the ambulance . . . the extra blood . . . Why do you think Manning and the Service helped him? Out of the kindness of their hearts? He's a termite, Wes—digging into the vulnerable, then exploiting their weaknesses. D'you understand what I'm saying? He thrives on weaknesses. All weaknesses."

The way he studies me . . . the way his glowing blue eyes lock onto mine . . . "Wait, are you saying *I*—?"

"We checked your file, Wes," O'Shea adds, pulling a folded sheet of paper from inside his jacket. "Seven months with a Dr. Collins White, who it says here is a *critical incident specialist.* Sounds pretty technical."

"Where'd you get that?" I ask.

"And the analysis: panic disorder and post-traumatic stress comorbidity . . ."

"That was eight years ago!" I tell them.

". . . triggering compulsive behavior involving light switches, locking and unlocking doors . . ."

"That's not even—"

". . . and a full-fledged obsession with the need for repetitive praying," O'Shea continues, unconcerned. "That true? What, was that your way of dealing with the shooting? Saying the same prayers over and over?" He flips over to the second page. "Not even religious, are you? That's a real Nico reaction."

To my own surprise, my eyes well up and my throat tightens. It's been a long time since anyone—

"I know it was hard for you, Wes," O'Shea adds. "Even harder than the way you stapled your fingers with Boyle. But if he has something over you, we can help you out of it."

Help me out of it? "You think I'd—?"

"Whatever he offered you, you'll only get burned."

"He didn't offer me *anything*," I insist.

"Is that why you were fighting?"

"Fighting? What're you—?"

"The broken coffee table? The shattered glass from where you hit it? We saw the report," Micah interrupts, his singsong voice long gone.

"I didn't know he was back there!"

"Really?" Micah asks, his voice picking up speed. "In the middle of a speech in a foreign country, you leave the President's side—where you were supposed to be . . ."

"I swear—"

". . . and disappear backstage to the one room where Boyle happens to be hiding—"

"I didn't know!" I yell.

"We have agents who were there!" Micah explodes. "They found the fake name Boyle used in the hotel! When they interviewed the desk clerks on duty that night, one of them picked out *your photo*, saying *you* were the one looking for *him*! Now do you wanna start over, or do you wanna bury yourself even deeper? Just tell us why Manning sent you instead of the Service to meet him."

It's the second time they've confirmed Manning and the Service being involved—and the first time I realize I'm not the one they're after. Big hunters want big game. And why take a cub when you can bag the Lion?

"We know Manning's been good to you—"

"You don't know anything about him."

"Actually, we do," O'Shea says. "Just like we know Boyle. Believe me, Wes, when they were in power, you didn't see half of what they—"

"I was with them every day!"

"You were with them for the last eight months, when all they cared about was reelection. You think that's reality? Just because you know what they like on their turkey sandwiches doesn't mean you know what they're capable of."

If I were Rogo, I'd rush forward and bury my fist in his jaw. Instead, I dig my foot in the sand. Anything to help me keep standing. From what they're saying, Manning definitely has some pretty dark dirt on his hands. Maybe they're just fishing. Maybe it's the truth. Either way, after everything Manning's done for me . . . after taking me back in and being by my side all these years . . . I'm not biting that hand until I know the facts myself.

"Ever see a three-car collision?" Micah asks. "Y'know which car suffers the most damage? The one in the middle." He pauses just long enough to let it all sink in. "Manning, you, Boyle. Which car d'you think *you* are?"

I grind my leg even deeper into the sand. "That's . . . that's not—"

"By the way, where'd you get the nice timepiece?" Micah interrupts, motioning to my vintage Franck Muller watch. "That's a ten-thousand-dollar bauble."

"What're you—? It was a gift from the president of Senegal," I explain. At home, I've got at least a half dozen more, including a platinum Vacheron Constantin given by the Saudi crown prince. When we were in office, they became gifts of the White House. Today, there're no rules on giving to former Presidents and his staff. But before I can tell him—

"Mr. Holloway," a voice calls out behind me.

I turn just in time to see my waiter from breakfast. He's up by the pool area, holding my credit card in his hand.

"Sorry . . . didn't want you to forget this," he calls out, now scrambling toward us on the beach.

O'Shea turns toward the ocean so the waiter can't hear. "Focus, Wes—are you really that blindly devoted? You know they lied to you. You keep covering for them and you're just gonna be someone who needs a lawyer."

"Here you go, sir," the waiter says.

"Thanks," I reply, forcing a half-smile.

O'Shea and Micah aren't nearly as kind. From the angry glares they drill my way, they still want more. The problem is, I don't have anything to give them. At least not yet. And until I do, I've got nothing to barter for protection.

"Wait up . . . I'll walk out with you," I say, pivoting in the sand and falling in line behind the waiter.

Years ago, I used to bite at a small callus on the side of my pointer finger. When I got to the White House, Dreidel made me stop, saying it looked bad in the background of the President's photos. For the first time in a decade, I start gnawing at it.

"See you soon," O'Shea calls out.

I don't bother to answer.

As we reach the pool area, there's a young family getting an early start on the day. Dad unpacks a newspaper, Mom unpacks a paperback, and their three-year-old boy with a bowl haircut is on his hands and knees, playing with two Matchbox cars, ramming them head-on, over and over, into each other.

I look over my shoulder and glance back at the beach. O'Shea and Micah are already gone.

They're right about one thing: I definitely need a lawyer. Fortunately, I know exactly where to find one.

18

Washington, D.C.

"*You know they lied to you. You keep covering for them and you're just gonna be someone who needs a lawyer.*"

"*Here you go, sir.*"

"*Thanks,*" Wes's voice said, coming through the small speaker on the edge of the short metal file cabinet. "*Wait up . . . I'll walk out with you.*"

Adjusting the volume, The Roman turned the knob slightly, his thick, steely hands almost too big for the job. When he was little, he only fit into his grandfather's gloves. But after years of tying lures onto fishing string, he'd mastered the art of a soft touch.

"*Have a wonderful day, Mr. Holloway,*" a voice squawked through the speaker.

Getting a small enough microphone was the easy part. So was getting a transmitter that ran on a satellite signal so it would broadcast halfway across the country. Protecting the

President was the Secret Service's specialty, but with jurisdiction over counterfeiting and financial crimes, their Intelligence Division had one of the most formidable surveillance operations in the world. Indeed, the only hard part was figuring out a place to hide it. And someone to put it there.

The phone rang on the corner of his desk, and The Roman glanced down at caller ID. Dark digital letters read *Offices of Leland Manning.* The Roman smiled to himself, brushing his black hair from his chalky skin. If only the bass were this predictable.

"Any problems?" The Roman asked as he picked up the phone.

"Not a one. I did it first thing this morning. Put it in that lapel pin just like you said."

"So I gathered from his last two hours of conversation."

Reaching down, The Roman tugged open the bottom drawer of the file cabinet, and his fingertips tap-danced to the last file in back. The only unmarked one in there.

"Wes say anything interesting yet?" his associate asked.

"He's getting there," The Roman replied, flipping open the file on his desk and revealing a small stack of black-and-white photos.

"What about you? If your investigation's so vital . . . I thought you were coming down here."

"I'll be there," The Roman said as he stared down at the pictures. Graying from age, all of them were from the day at the speedway. One of Nico with the Service tackling him to the ground, one of the President being shoved inside his limo, and of course, one of Boyle, in mid-clap moments before he was shot. The smile on Boyle's face looked unbreakable . . . his cheeks frozen, teeth gleaming. The Roman couldn't take his eyes off it. "I just have to take care of one thing first."

19

Palm Beach, Florida

"Where is he?" I ask, rushing through the welcome area of the small office with its dozens of potted plants and orchids.

"Inside," the receptionist says, "but you can't—"

She's already too late. I cut past her cheap Formica desk that looks suspiciously like the one I threw away a few weeks ago and head for the door covered with old Florida license plates. Beyond the plants, which were the standard thank-you gift from clients, the office had all the design sense of a fifteen-year-old boy. It didn't matter. Moving over the bridge a year ago, Rogo took this office so he'd have a proper Palm Beach address. When you're targeting the rich, and 95 percent of your business is done by mail, that's all you need.

"Wes, he's busy in there!" the receptionist calls out.

I twist the doorknob, shove open the door, and send it slamming into the wall. Standing at his desk, Rogo jumps at the sound. "Wes, that you?" His eyes are closed. As he tries to make his way toward me, he taps his blotter and pencil cup and keyboard like a blind man feeling his way.

"What happened to your eyes?" I ask.

"Eye doctor. Dilated," Rogo says, patting a picture frame of his childhood dog. The frame falls and he fumbles to pick it up. "Being blind sucks," he says.

"I need to talk to you."

"Meanwhile, ready for new levels of pathetic? When I was at the doctor, I *cheated* on my eye exam. Before he got in there, he left the eye chart up—y'know with the giant *E* and the little *N3QFD* at the bottom? I memorized it, then spit it right back at him. Suckaaaaaa!"

"Rogo . . ."

"I mean, that's even more sad-sack than—"

"Boyle's alive."

Rogo stops patting the picture frame and turns straight at me. "Wha wha?"

"I saw him. Boyle's alive," I repeat. I slowly slink toward one of the chairs across from his desk. Rogo turns his head, following me perfectly.

"You can see, can't you?" I ask.

"Yeah," he replies, still in shock.

"And is that my old desk out there in your reception area?"

"Yeah. I picked it up when you threw it away."

"Rogo, I left that desk for charity."

"And I thank you for that. Now would you like to tell me what the hell you're talking about with your dead former coworker?"

"I swear to you—I saw him . . . I spoke to him."

"Did he look—?"

"He got plastic surgery."

"Well, who wouldn't?"

"I'm serious. The shooting . . . that day at the speedway . . . it was . . . it wasn't how it looked."

It takes me almost a half hour to fill him in on the rest of the details, from backstage in Malaysia, to Dreidel's info about the O-negative blood, to the FBI cornering me on the beach and asking me about The Roman and The Three. Forever a lawyer, he never interrupts. Forever Rogo, his reaction is instantaneous.

"You told Dreidel before *me*?"

"Oh, please . . ."

"I was in the car with you this morning. What, you were so enraptured by classic hits from the eighties, nineties, and today that you forget to mention, 'Oh, by the way, that guy who died and cratered my life? Well, he must be on some all-bran diet, because he's actually *living*'?"

"Rogo . . ."

"Can I just say one more thing?"

"Is it about Dreidel?"

He crosses his arms against his chest. "No."

"Okay, then just—"

"You're in trouble, Wes."

I blink about four times trying to digest the words. Coming from Rogo, they hit even harder than the waves on the beach.

"I'm serious," Rogo continues. "They pinned you. Just by seeing Boyle, the FBI now thinks you're part of this. You don't help them and they stick you as an accessory to whatever Boyle and Manning were up to. You do help 'em and . . ."

". . . I kiss away whatever life I have left. What d'you think I'm doing here? I need help."

When I asked Dreidel, he hesitated, weighing the personal and political consequences. Rogo's always been built a little bit differently. "Just tell me who to punch."

For the first time in the last forty-eight hours, I actually half smile.

"What," he asks, "you think I'm letting you get beat up all by yourself?"

"I was thinking of going to Manning," I tell him.

"And I was thinking you should start worrying about yourself for once."

"Will you stop with that?"

"Then stop being the buttboy. Didn't you hear what the FBI said? The President was in on it, whatever the hell *it* is! I mean, how else do you explain Nico getting that close and sneaking a gun past all those Secret Service agents? Y'smell that? That's the whiff of an inside job."

"Maybe that's where The Roman and The Three come in."

"And those're the names the FBI mentioned?"

"That's why I want to go to Manning first. Maybe he'll—"

"Do you even hear yourself when you speak!? You go to Manning and you risk alerting the one person who has the best reason of all to put you in the guillotine. Now I'm sorry if that ruins the tiny safe haven you've built for yourself over the past eight years, but it's time to pay attention. The scars on your face, despite what you think, are *not penance.* You don't owe anybody anything."

"That's not the point."

"No, the point is: Leland Manning is a good man. Even a great man. But like any other man—especially one who runs for office—he will lie *straight to your face* when he needs to. Just do the math, Wes: How many U.S. Presidents you ever seen in jail? Now how many lower-level aides who swear they're innocent?"

For the first time, I don't answer.

"Exactly," Rogo continues. "Taking down a President is like demolishing a building—very little explosion and lots of gravity. Right now you're too damn close to getting sucked in the hole."

"That doesn't mean he's a monster."

"Please, you wouldn't even be here if you didn't think there were crawdads in your bed."

Sitting across from him, I keep my eyes on the carpet. During our final week in office, former Presidents Bush, Clinton, all of them called. But it was Bush Senior who gave Manning the best advice. He told him that "when you get off Air Force One, wave from the top of the steps . . . and when the lonely TV interviewer standing on the tarmac asks, 'How does it feel to be home?' you go, 'Great to be back!' And you look ahead and you try not to think what it used to be like just four or five hours before." When our plane touched down, Manning did just that. He told that lie with ease and a perfect grin.

Rogo watches me carefully as I bite at the callus on my hand.

"I know what he means to you, Wes."

"No. You don't." I shove my hand under my thigh. "Just tell me what you think I should do."

"You already know what I think," Rogo says with a grin. Even when he used to get his ass kicked, he's always loved a good fight. He pulls a notepad from his desk and starts hunting for a pen. "Y'know why I get a 96 percent dismissal rate on speeding tickets? Or 92 percent on illegal U-turns? Because I dig, dig, dig, and dig some more. Check the details, Wes: If the cop puts the wrong statute number on the ticket, dismiss. If he doesn't bring his ticket log, dismiss. Always comes down to the details—which is why I wanna know who the hell The Three and this guy The Roman are."

"You still have that buddy at the police station?"

"How else you think I get the list of speeding ticket violators two hours before anyone else? He'll run whoever we need."

"Dreidel said he'd look up some of the other stuff too. He's always good at—"

My phone vibrates in my pocket. Flipping it open, I spot a familiar number. Perfect timing.

"Any news?" I ask, picking up.

"Did you tip her?" Dreidel blurts, his voice racing.

"Excuse me?"

"The reporter—Lisbeth something—from the *Palm Beach Post* . . ." He takes a breath to stay calm. All it does is tell me something's wrong. "Did you call her this morning?"

"I don't know what you're—"

It's okay if you did . . . I'm not mad . . . I just need to know what you said."

It's the second time he's cut me off. And like any other young politician, the moment he says he's not mad is the exact same moment he'll rip your tongue out.

"Dreidel, I swear, I didn't—"

"Then how'd she know we were meeting!? She had that I drank coffee and ate some of your toast! Who'd you . . . ?" Catching himself, he again lowers his voice. "Just . . . who else did you tell?"

I look over at Rogo. "No one. No one that could've called her. I swear . . ."

"Okay, it's okay," he tells himself more than me. "I

just . . . I need you to kill the story, okay? She's calling you now for a quote. Can you do me that favor and kill it?" I've known Dreidel for almost a decade. Last time I heard him this panicked, he had the First Lady screaming at him. "Please, Wes."

"Fine . . . that's fine . . . but why're you so nervous about some dumb breakfast?"

"No, not a breakfast. A breakfast in Palm Beach. *Florida* . . . when my wife thought I was still checking out of my hotel from the meeting I had yesterday. In *Atlanta.*" He gives me a minute to connect the dots.

"Wait, so that woman . . . You didn't just meet her at a bar . . ."

"Jean. Her name's Jean. And yes, I left Atlanta and flew in early for her. I met her a few months ago. Okay? You happy? Now you got all the juice. All I'm asking is that you keep it away from this gossip woman, because if that story runs tomorrow and Ellen sees it—"

There's a click on my phone.

"That's her," Dreidel says. "All you have to do is bury it. Trade her something . . . give her ten minutes with Manning. Please, Wes—my family—just think of Ali," he adds, referring to his daughter. "And my State Senate race."

Before I can even react, there's another click. I hit the *Send* button on my phone and pick up the other line.

"Wes here," I answer.

"Mr. Holloway, Gerald Lang here," he says, his tone dry and professorial. "From the curator's office," he explains, referring to the Manning Presidential Library. "Claudia suggested I ring you and—"

"Now's not actually the best time."

"It'll only take a moment, sir. See, we're putting

together a new exhibit about presidential service, with a particular focus on the long history of the young men who have served as presidential aides. Sort of a . . . true retrospective, if you can imagine . . . everyone from Meriwether Lewis, who served under Thomas Jefferson, to Jack Valenti, who worked with LBJ, to eventually, hopefully, well . . . yourself."

"Wait . . . this exhibit's about . . . *me?*"

"Actually, more the others, of course. A true retrospective."

He's already backpedaling, which means he knows the rules. My job is to be the closest man to the President. Right beside him. But never in front of him. "I appreciate the offer, Mr. Lang . . ."

"Gerald."

"And I'd love to help, Gerald, but—"

"President Manning said it was okay," he adds, pulling the trump card. "Claudia too. A true retrospective. So when do you think we can sit down and—?"

"Later, okay? Just . . . call me later." Rushing off the phone, I click back to Dreidel.

"What'd she say? Does she know?" Dreidel asks, still panicking.

Before I can answer, my phone clicks again. Clearly, my curator friend didn't get the point. "Let me just get rid of this guy," I tell Dreidel, once again clicking over. "Gerald, I already told you—"

"Who's Gerald?" a female voice interrupts.

"E-Excuse me?"

"Hiya there, Wes, this is Lisbeth Dodson from the *Palm Beach Post.* How'd you like to have your name in bold?"

20

Washington, D.C.

The left front tire dove into the pothole at full speed, slicing through the puddle of melted snow and unleashing a jarring punch that shook the black SUV. With a twist of the steering wheel, the car jerked to the right. A second punch pummeled the car. The Roman cursed to himself. D.C. roads were bad enough. But southeast Washington was always the worst.

Flicking on his wipers, he brushed a light dust of snow from the windshield and made a sharp left onto Malcolm X Avenue. The burned-out cars, overpiled trash cans, and boarded-up buildings told him this wasn't a neighborhood to be lost in. Fortunately, he knew exactly where he was going.

Within a mile, the car bucked to a halt at the light where Malcolm X intersected with Martin Luther King Jr. Avenue. The Roman couldn't help but grin to himself. For eight years, he'd relied a great deal on peaceful coexistence. But now, with Boyle's reappearance . . . with Wes as a witness . . . even with O'Shea and Micah closing in . . . sometimes there was no choice left but the tough one.

It was no different eight years ago when they first approached Nico. Of course, not all three of them were there. For safety, only one went. Naturally, Nico was hesitant—even belligerent. No one likes seeing his family attacked. But that's when Nico was shown the proof: the records from his mother's stay in the hospital.

"What's this?" Nico had asked, scanning the sheet of paper filled with room numbers and delivery times. The single word *Dinner* was handwritten across the top.

"It's the hospital's meal delivery log," Number Three explained. "From the day your mother died."

Sure enough, Nico saw his mother's name. *Hadrian, Mary.* And her old room number. *Room 913.* And even what she ordered. *Meat loaf.* But what confused him was the handwritten notation in the column marked *Attempted Delivery.* On the sheet, every patient had a different delivery time: *6:03 p.m. . . . 6:09 p.m. . . . 6:12 p.m. . . .* Except for Nico's mom, where it simply said *patient deceased.*

Nico looked up, clearly confused. "I don't understand. This is from her final Sunday . . . from the day she died?"

"Not exactly," he told him. "Look at the date in the corner. September 16th, right?" As Nico nodded, he quickly explained, "September 16th was a Saturday, Nico. According to these records, your mom died on a Saturday."

"No," Nico insisted. "She died Sunday. Sunday, September 17th. I remember, I was— We were in church." Staring down at the meal delivery log, he added, "How could this happen?"

"No, Nico. The real question is, why would someone do that?"

Nico shook his head furiously. "No, there's no way. We

were in church. In the second row. I remember my father coming in and—"

Nico froze.

"That's the great thing about church, isn't it, Nico? When the whole town's packed into the pews and watching your concerned father praying with his two young kids . . . it really is the perfect alibi."

"Wait . . . you're saying my dad killed my—"

"What was it, three years since she'd lapsed into that coma? Three years with no mom. No one running the house. Every day—all those prayers and visits—her illness consuming your lives."

"He'd never do that! He loved her!"

"He loved you *more*, Nico. You'd already lost three years of your childhood. That's why he did it. For you. He did it *for you*."

"B-But the doctors . . . wouldn't the coroner . . . ?"

"Dr. Albie Morales—the neurologist who pronounced her dead—is the *worshipful master* in charge of your father's Masonic Lodge. Coroner Turner Sinclair—who filed the rest of the paperwork—is the deacon of that same Lodge. That's what Masons do, Nico. That's what they've done throughout histor—"

"You're lying!" Nico exploded, cupping his hands over his ears. "Please be lying!"

"He did it for you, Nico."

Nico was rocking fast—forward and back—as his tears rained down in thick drops to the sheet of paper that held his mother's final dinner order. "When she died . . . that was . . . she died for *my* sins! *Not his*!" he wailed like a ten-year-old boy, his entire belief system shattered. "She was supposed to die for *my sins*!"

And that's when The Three knew they had him.

Of course, that's also why they picked him in the first place. It wasn't difficult. With The Roman's access to military files, they focused on the records of Fort Benning and Fort Bragg, which housed two of the army's top sniper schools. Add the words *dishonorable discharge* and *psychological problems*, and the list narrowed quickly. Nico was actually third. But when they did some more digging—when they saw his religious devotion and found his father's group affiliation—Nico went right to the top of the list.

From there, all they had to do was find him. Since all transitional housing and homeless shelters receiving government funds must submit the names of those using the facility, that part was easy. Then they had to prove he could be controlled. That's why they took him back to his dad's mobile home. And gave him the gun. And told him that there was only one way to set his mother's spirit free.

During sniper training, Nico was taught to shoot between heartbeats to reduce barrel motion. Standing over his father, who was sobbing for mercy on the peeling linoleum floor, Nico pulled the trigger without hesitation.

And The Three realized they had their man.

All thanks to nothing more than a single sheet of paper with a fake hospital meal log.

As the traffic light blinked green, The Roman turned left and slammed the gas, sending his back wheels spinning and bits of slush spraying through the air. The car fishtailed on the never-plowed road, then quickly settled under The Roman's tight grip. He'd put in far too much time to lose control now.

In the distance, the old storefronts and buildings gave way to rusted black metal gates that fenced in the wide-open grounds and were supposed to make the neighborhood feel safer. But with twenty-two patients escaping in the last year, most neighbors understood that the gates weren't exactly living up to their expectations.

Ignoring the chapel and another towering brick building just beyond the gates, The Roman made a sharp right and stayed focused on the small guardhouse right inside the main entrance. It'd been almost eight years since the last time he was here. And as he rolled down his window and saw the peeling paint on the black and yellow gate arm, he realized nothing had changed, including the security procedures.

"Welcome to St. Elizabeths," a guard with winter-grizzled lips said. "Visitor or delivery?"

"Visitor," The Roman replied, flashing a Secret Service badge and never breaking eye contact. Like every agent before him, when Roland Egen first joined the Service, he didn't start in Protective Operations. With the Service's authority over financial crimes, he first spent five years investigating counterfeit rings and computer crime in the Houston field office. From there, he got his first protective assignment, assessing threats for the Intelligence Division, and from there—thanks to his flair for criminal investigations—he rose through the ranks in the Pretoria and Rome offices. It was raw determination that helped him claw his way up through the Secret Service hierarchy to his current position as deputy assistant director of Protective Operations. But it was in his after-hours work as *The Roman* where he reaped his best rewards. "I'm here for Nicholas Hadrian."

"Nico's in trouble, huh?" the guard asked. "Funny, he always says someone's coming. For once, he's actually right."

"Yeah," The Roman said, glancing up at the tiny cross on the roof of the old brick chapel in the distance. "Pretty damn hysterical."

21

Palm Beach, Florida

"Anyway, it's just a cute little squib with you and Dreidel eating at the Four Seasons," Lisbeth says as Rogo squeezes in next to me and puts his ear to the phone. "Sorta making the restaurant like a White House reunion in the sunny South. The President's boys and all that."

"Sounds fun," I tell her, hoping to keep her upbeat. "Though I'm not sure that's actually news."

"Amazing," she says sarcastically. "That's exactly what Dreidel said. You guys separated at birth, or does it just come naturally with the job?"

I've known Lisbeth since the day she took over the *Post*'s gossip column. We have a clear understanding. She calls and politely asks for a quote from the President. I politely tell her we're sorry, but we don't do those things anymore. It's a simple waltz. The problem is, if I don't play this carefully, I'll be giving her something to jitterbug to.

"C'mon, Lisbeth, no one even knows who me and Dreidel are."

"Yep, Dreidel tried that one too. Right before he asked if he could call me back, which I also know is a guaranteed sign I'll never hear from him again. I mean, considering he's got that little fundraiser tonight, you'd think he'd want his name in the local paper. Now do you just wanna give me a throwaway quote on how great it was for you and your friend to reminisce about your old White House days, or do you want me to start worrying that there's something wrong in Manningville?" She laughs as she says the words, but I've been around enough reporters to know that when it comes to filling their columns, nothing's funny.

Careful, Rogo writes on a scrap of paper. *Girl ain't stupid.*

I nod and turn back to the phone. "Listen, I'm happy to give you whatever quote you want, but honestly, we were only in the restaurant for a few minutes—"

"And that's officially the third time you've tried to downplay this otherwise yawn of a story. Know what they teach you in journalism school when someone tries to downplay, Wes?"

On the scrap of paper, Rogo adds an exclamation point next to *Girl ain't stupid.*

"Okay, fine. Wanna know the real story?" I ask.

"No, I'd much prefer the fake runaround."

"But this is off the record," I warn. She stays silent, hoping I'll keep talking. It's an old reporter's trick so she can say she never agreed. I fell for it my first week in the White House. That was the last time. "Lisbeth . . ."

"Fine . . . yes . . . off the record. Now what's the big hubbub?"

"Manning's birthday," I blurt. "His surprise sixty-fifth, to be exact. Dreidel and I were in charge of the surprise part until you called this morning. I told Manning I had some errands to run. Dreidel was in town and told him the same. If Manning reads in tomorrow's paper that we were together . . ." I pause for effect. It's a crap lie, but her silence tells me it's doing the trick. "You know we never ask for anything, Lisbeth, but if you could keep us out just this once . . ." I pause again for the big finale. "We'd owe you one."

I can practically hear her smile on the other line. In a city of social chits, it's the best one to bargain with: a favor owed by the former President of the United States.

"Gimme ten minutes face-to-face with Manning on the night of the surprise party," Lisbeth says.

"Five minutes is the most he'll sit for."

Rogo shakes his head. *Not enough*, he mouths silently.

"Deal," she says.

Rogo makes a double okay sign with his fingers. *Perfect*, he mouths.

"So my breakfast with Dreidel . . . ?" I ask.

"Breakfast? Come now, Wes—why would anyone care what two former staffers had on their morning toast? Consider it officially dead."

22

You know we never ask for anything, Lisbeth, but if you could keep us out just this once . . ."

As she listened to Wes's words, Lisbeth sat up in her seat and began to spin the phone cord, jump-rope-style. From the forced pause on the other line, Wes sounded like he was ready to trade. "We'd owe you one," he offered, right on cue. Lisbeth stopped the phone cord's spinning. Sacred Rule #4: Only the guilty trade. Sacred Rule #5: And the opportunists.

"Gimme ten minutes face-to-face with Manning on the night of the surprise party," she said, knowing that like any good publicist, he'd knock the time in half.

"Five minutes is the most he'll sit for."

"Deal," she said as she started rifling through the thick stack of invites on the far corner of her desk. Opening concert at the opera. The annual craft bazaar at the Sailfish Club. Baby naming at the Whedons. It had to be here somewhere . . .

"So my breakfast with Dreidel . . . ?" Wes asked.

Still flipping through the stack, Lisbeth was barely paying attention. "Breakfast? Come now, Wes—why would anyone care what two former staffers had on their morning toast? Consider it officially dead."

Manning's surprise party—and her promised five minutes—weren't for at least another month. But that didn't mean she had to stay away until then. Especially when there were so many other ways to get in close. Slamming down the phone, Lisbeth never took her eyes off the stack. Reception for the Leukemia Society, Historical Society, Knesset Society, Palm Beach Society, Renaissance Society, Alexis de Tocqueville Society . . . and then . . . there . . .

Lisbeth yanked the rectangular card from the middle of the stack. Like every other invite, the design was understated, the printing was meticulous, and the envelope had her name on it. But this one, with its cream-colored card stock and twirling black calligraphy, also had something more: *An Evening with President Leland F. Manning. Benefiting 65 Roses—the Cystic Fibrosis Foundation.* Tonight.

She didn't mind the fake stalling from Wes and Dreidel. Or the nonsense about Manning's so-called surprise party. But once Wes asked her to kill the piece . . . Sacred Rule #6: There were only two kinds of people in a gossip column—those who want to be in there, and those who don't. Wes just put himself on the *don't* side. And without a doubt, the *don'ts* were always far more interesting.

Picking up the phone, Lisbeth dialed the number on the invite.

"This is Claire Tanz," an older woman answered.

"Hi, Claire, this is Lisbeth Dodson from Below the Fold. I hope it's not too late to RSVP—"

"For tonight? No, no . . . oh, we read you every day,"

the woman said just a bit too excited. "Oooh, and I can call the President's staff and let them know you'll be there . . ."

"That's okay," Lisbeth said calmly. "I just got off the phone with them. They're already thrilled I'm coming."

23

T*hree and a half minutes*, Nico told himself as he watched the gray Acura cut through the snow and pass along the service road just outside his second-story shatterproof window. Pulling up the sleeve of his faded brown sweatshirt, he glanced down at the second hand on his watch, counting to himself. *One minute . . . two . . . three . . .* Nico closed his eyes and began to pray. His head bobbed sixteen times. *Three and a half . . .* Rocking slowly, he opened his eyes and turned to the door of his room. The door didn't open.

Perched atop the rusted radiator just inside his window, Nico continued to rock slowly, turning back to the falling snow and bowing the A-string of his well-worn maple violin. The violin had a tiny four-leaf clover inlay in the tailpiece, but Nico was far more interested in the way the fiddle's strings perfectly crossed the maple bridge as they ran up the fingerboard. When he first arrived at St. Elizabeths, he spent his first two weeks sitting in the exact same place, staring out the exact same window. Naturally, the doctors discouraged it—"*antisocial and escapist*," they declared.

It only got worse when they examined Nico's view: on his right, a burned-out brick building with an army crest on it ("*too symbolic of his military past*"); on his left, the edges of the Anacostia River ("*don't reward him with a quality view*"); and in the far distance, at the very edge of the property, half a dozen fenced-in fields with hundreds of crumbling headstones from the Civil War to World War I, when army and navy patients were still buried on the property ("*death should never be a focal point*"). Yet when Nico mentioned to a nurse that the dogwood tree just outside his window reminded him of his childhood home in Wisconsin, where his mother played cello and the wind sent the tree's branches swaying to the music, the doctors not only backed off, they got someone to donate the fiddle with the four-leaf clover inlay. "*Positive memories were to be encouraged.*" Nico knew it was a sign. Just as God had written in the Book. As God had sent them. The Fiddlers Three.

Eight years later, Nico still lived in the same room, surrounded by the same small bed, the same nightstand, and the same painted dresser that held his Bible and red glass rosary beads.

But what Nico always kept to himself was that while he did study the dogwood, and it did remind him of early days with his mom, he was far more focused on the well-worn service road that ran just in front of it, up from the main gate, across the property, and around to the parking lot that led to the entrance of the John Howard Pavilion. The tree was surely a sign—Christ's cross was built from a dogwood—but the road in front of it . . . the road was the path of Nico's salvation. He knew it in his heart. He knew it in his soul. He knew it the very first day he saw the road, littered with weeds and grass that cracked and clawed through its beaten, asphalt hide. Every year, the ground buckled slightly as the weeds shoved a bit further. Like a monster, Nico thought. A monster within. Just like the monsters who killed his mother.

He didn't want to pull the trigger. Not at first. Not even when The Three reminded him of his father's sin. But as he stared down at the proof—at the delivery log from the hospital . . .

"Ask your father," Number Three said. "He won't deny it."

Rocking to himself as he stared out the window of the hospital, Nico could still hear the words. Still smell his dad's sweet cigar smoke. Still feel the sharp Wisconsin wind cracking his lungs as he hopped up the metal front steps of his dad's mobile home. He hadn't seen his father in almost six years. Before the army . . . before the discharge . . . before the shelter. Nico didn't even know how to find him. But The Three did. The Three helped him. The Three, God bless them, were bringing Nico home. To punish the monster. And set things right.

"Dad, she was supposed to die for *my* sins!" he'd shouted, tugging the door open and rushing inside. Nico could still hear the words. Still smell the cigar smoke. Still feel the ball of his finger tightening on the trigger as his father begged, pleaded, sobbed—*Please, Nico, you're my— Let me get you help.* But the only thing Nico saw was his mother's photograph—her wedding photo!—perfectly preserved beneath the glass top of the coffee table. So young and beautiful . . . all dressed in white . . . like an angel. His angel. His angel who was taken. Taken by the monsters. By the Beasts.

"*Nico, on my life—on all that's holy—I'm innocent!*"

"Nobody's innocent, Dad."

The next thing Nico felt was his foot slipping across the peeling linoleum floor, which was soaked with . . . soaked with red. A dark red puddle. All that blood.

"Dad . . . ?" Nico whispered, flicks of blood freckled across his face.

His dad never answered.

"Don't doubt yourself, Nico," Number Three told him. "Check his ankle. You'll find their mark."

And as Nico moved in—ignoring the bullet hole in his father's hand (to make him feel Jesus's pain) and the other bullet hole in his heart—he lifted his father's leg and pulled down his sock. There it was. Just as Number Three had said. The hidden mark. Hidden from his son. Hidden from his wife. A tiny tattoo.

The compass and a square—the most sacred of all Masonic symbols. Tools of the trade for an architect . . . tools to build their doorway . . . plus a *G* for the Great Architect of the Universe.

"To show he's of them," Number Three explained.

Nico nodded, still reeling from the fact his father had kept it secret for so long. Yet now the monster was slain. But as Number Three pointed out, thanks to the Masons, there were more monsters fighting to get out. More Beasts. Still, by fighting now—by serving God—he could turn his mother's death into a blessing.

The Three called it *fatum.* Latin for *fate.* Nico's destiny.

Nico looked up as he heard the word. Fate. "Yes . . . that's what she— Like the Book."

Right there, Nico knew his mission—and why his mom was taken.

"Please . . . I need to— Let me help you slay the monsters," Nico volunteered.

Number Three watched him carefully. He could've dumped Nico right there. Could've left him . . . abandoned him . . . chosen to continue the fight by himself. Instead, he said the one thing only a true man of God could.

"Son, let us pray."

Number Three opened his arms, and Nico collapsed inside. He heard Number Three's sobs. Saw his tears. No longer just a stranger. Family. Like a father.

Fatum, Nico decided that day. His fate.

Over the next month, The Three revealed the full mission. Told him of the enemy and the strength on their side. From Voltaire to Napoleon to Winston Churchill, the Freemasons spent centuries cultivating the most powerful members of society. In the arts, they had Mozart, Beethoven, and Bach. In literature, Arthur Conan Doyle, Rudyard Kipling, and Oscar Wilde. In business, they grew with funding by Henry Ford, Frederick Maytag, and J. C. Penney.

In the United States, they built their power to new heights: From Benjamin Franklin to John Hancock, eight signers of the Declaration of Independence were Masons. Nine signers of the U.S. Constitution. Thirty-one generals in Washington's army. Five Supreme Court chief justices, from John Marshall to Earl Warren. Year by year, century by century, the Masons collected those with the greatest influence on society: Paul Revere, Benedict Arnold, Mark

Twain, John Wayne, Roy Rogers, Cecil B. DeMille, Douglas Fairbanks, Clark Gable, even Harry Houdini. Was it any coincidence that Douglas MacArthur became General of the Army? Or that Joseph Smith founded an entire religion? Or that J. Edgar Hoover was given the FBI? Or even that Buzz Aldrin was on that first rocket to the moon? All of those landmarks. All of them by Masons. And that didn't even consider the sixteen times they took the White House: Presidents George Washington, James Monroe, Teddy Roosevelt, FDR, Truman, LBJ, Gerald Ford . . . and most important, The Three explained, President Leland F. Manning and the monster known as Ron Boyle.

One month after the day they met, The Three revealed Boyle's sin. Just like they did with Nico's father.

Still rocking to himself and strumming on the A-string, Nico heard the throat-clearing grunt of tires scraping uphill against the ice. A black SUV rumbled into view, its windshield wipers swatting snow aside like a bothersome fly. Nico continued to strum, well aware that black SUVs usually meant the Service. But as the car cut in front of the dogwood, Nico saw that the passenger seat was empty. Service never came alone.

Three and a half minutes, Nico told himself as he studied the second hand on his watch. By now, he had it timed perfectly. Three and a half was the average. For his doctors, for his nurses, even for his sister before she stopped coming to visit. She'd always need an extra thirty seconds to steel herself, but even on the worst days—on that dark Sunday when he tried to hurt himself—three and a half minutes was more than enough.

Nico glanced down again at the second hand on his watch. *One minute . . . two . . . three . . .* He closed his eyes, bobbed his head, and prayed. *Three and a half.* Nico opened his eyes and turned to the door of his ten-by-fifteen room.

The doorknob twisted slightly, and the orderly with the bloodshot eyes appeared in the doorway.

"Nico, you decent? You got a visitor," the orderly called out.

Eight years watching. Eight years waiting. Eight years believing that the Book of Fate could never be denied. Nico could feel the tears flood his eyes as a man with pale Irish features and midnight-black hair entered the room.

"Nice to see you, Nico," The Roman said as he stepped inside. "Been far too long."

24

"Manning Presidential Library. How can I assist you?" the receptionist answers.

"I have some questions on presidential records," I say, checking for the second time that the door to my office is closed. Rogo said I could use his office to make the call, but between lunch and all our chatting, I've already been gone too long.

"Let me transfer you to the archivist of the day," the receptionist adds.

With a click, I'm on my way. And while I could just call the head of the entire library, like Rogo said, better to keep it low-key.

"Kara speaking. What can I help you with today?" a soft female voice asks.

"Hi, Kara. This is Wes over in the personal office. We're trying to get some of Ron Boyle's old files for a tribute book we're working on, so I was just wondering if you could help us pull some of those together?"

"I'm sorry, and your name again?"

"Wes Holloway. Don't worry . . . I'm on the staff list," I say with a laugh. She doesn't laugh back.

"I'm sorry, Wes, but before we release any documents, we need you to fill out a FOIA request stating who it's for—"

"President Manning. He requested them personally," I interrupt.

Every law has exceptions. Cops can run red lights. Doctors can illegally park during emergencies. And when your name is Leland Manning, you get any sheet of paper you want from the Leland Manning Presidential Library.

"J-Just tell us what you need. I'll start pulling it together," she offers.

"Fantastic," I say, flipping open the thick loose-leaf binder on my desk. The first page is labeled *Presidential Records and Historical Materials.* We call it the guide to the world's biggest diary.

For four years in the White House, every file, every e-mail, every Christmas card that was sent out was logged, copied, and saved. By the time we left Washington, it took five battle-sized military cargo planes to haul the forty million documents, 1.1 million photographs, twenty million printed e-mail messages, and forty thousand "artifacts," including four different Cowardly Lion telephones, two of which were handmade with the President's face on them. Still, the only way to find the needle is to jump into the haystack. And the only way to figure out what Boyle was up to is to pull open his desk drawers and see what's inside.

"Under White House Staff, let's start with all of Boyle's records as deputy chief," I say, flipping to the first few pages of the records guide, "and naturally, all of his own files, including correspondence to and from him." I flip to the next tab in the notebook. "And I'd also like to get his personnel records. Those would include any work complaints filed against him, correct?"

"It should," the archivist says, now suspicious.

"Don't worry," I laugh, hearing the change in her voice, "that's just to vet him so we know for sure where all the skeletons are."

"Yeah . . . of course . . . it's just—what do you need these for again?"

"A book the President's working on—about Boyle's years of service, from the White House to the shooting at the speedway—"

"If you want, we have the actual clip—y'know, with Boyle . . . and that young man who got hit in the face . . ."

When John Hinckley tried to kill Ronald Reagan, he hit the President, James Brady, Secret Service Agent Tim McCarthy, and police officer Thomas Delahanty. We all know James Brady. McCarthy and Delahanty became Trivial Pursuit answers. Just like me.

"So how fast do you think you can pull that together?" I ask.

She pants slightly into the phone. It's the closest thing she's got to a laugh. "Let me just . . . fourteen, fifteen, sixteen . . . you're probably looking at something like eighteen linear feet—or about . . . let's see . . . 36,000 pages."

"Thirty-six thousand pages," I repeat, my own voice sinking. The haystack just got eighteen feet taller.

"If you tell me a little bit more what you're looking for, I probably can help you narrow your search a little better . . ."

"Actually, there're a couple of things we were trying to get as soon as possible. The President said there were some other researchers on the book who were working with the library. Is there a way to tell us what files they pulled so we don't overlap?"

"Sure, but . . . when it comes to other people's requests, we're not supposed to—"

"Kara . . . it is Kara, right?" I ask, stealing one straight from Manning. "Kara, it's for the President . . ."

"I realize that, but the rules—"

"I appreciate the rules. I really do. But these are people working with the President. We're all on the same side, Kara," I add, trying not to beg. "And if I don't find this, then *I'm* the person who didn't get the President his list. Please tell me you know what that's like. I need this job, Kara—more than you'll ever realize."

There's a long pause on the other line, but like any librarian, Kara's a pragmatist. I hear her typing in the background. "What're their names?" she asks.

"Last name *Weiss*, first name *Eric*," I say, once again starting with Boyle's old Houdini codename.

There's a loud click as she hits the *Enter* key. I check my door for the third time. All clear.

"We've got two different Eric Weisses. One did some research the first year we were open. The other made a request about a year and a half ago, though it looks like it was a book report kid who wanted to know the President's favorite movie . . ."

"*All the President's Men*," we both say simultaneously.

She again laughs that panting laugh. "I don't think that's your researcher," she adds, finally warming up.

"What about the other Weiss?"

"As I said, he's from the first year we opened . . . mailing address in Valencia, Spain . . ."

"That's him!" I blurt, quickly catching myself.

"Certainly looks like it," Kara says. "He's got a few similar requests . . . some of Boyle's files . . . the President's schedule from the day of the shooting . . . The odd thing is, according to the notes here, he paid for copies—expensive too, almost six hundred dollars' worth—but when we sent them out, the package bounced back to us. According to the file, no one was listed at that address."

Like a photo in a darkroom, the edges of the picture slowly harden and flower into view. The FBI said Boyle was spotted in Spain. If that was his first request from the library, and then he ran, maybe he was worried people knew that his name was . . . "Try *Carl Stewart*," I say, switching to the codename Boyle used in the Malaysian hotel.

"Carl Stewart," Kara repeats, clicking away. "Yep—here we go . . ."

"You have him?"

"How could we not? Almost two hundred requests over the past three years. He's requested over 12,000 pages . . ."

"Yeah, no . . . he's thorough," I tell her, careful not to lose focus. "And just to be sure we have the right one, what's the last address you have for him?"

"In London . . . it's care of the post office at 92A Balham High Road. And the zip is SW12 9AF."

"That's the one," I say, scribbling it down, even though I know it's the British equivalent of a P.O. box. And just as untraceable.

Before I can say another word, the door to my office swings open. "He's in the closet," Claudia announces, referring to the President. I was afraid of this. *Closet* is her code for the bathroom—Manning's last stop before we head out to an event. If he's true to form—and he always is—that's my two-minute warning.

"So would you like me to just send you a list of what else he requested?" the librarian asks through the receiver.

"Wes, you hear what I said?" Claudia adds.

I hold a finger up to our chief of staff. "Yeah, if you can

send me the list, that'd be perfect," I tell the librarian. Claudia taps her watch, and I throw her a nod. "And if I can ask you one last favor—that last document he received—when was that sent?"

"Let's see . . . says here the fifteenth, so about ten days ago," the librarian replies.

I sit up straight, and the picture in the darkroom starts to take on brand-new details. Since the day the library opened, Boyle's been pulling documents and hunting through files. Ten days ago, he requested his final one—then suddenly came out of hiding. I don't know much, but it's pretty clear that finding that file is the only way out of the darkroom and into the light.

"Service are mobilizing," Claudia says, glancing up the hallway and watching the agents gather at the front door of the office.

I stand up and stretch the phone cord to the chair that holds my suit jacket. Sliding my arm in, I stay with the librarian. "How long would it take you to send me a copy of the last document he received?"

"Let's see, it went out last week, so it still might be in Shelly's . . . Hold on, let me check." There's a short pause on the line.

I look over at Claudia. We don't have many rules, but one of the vital ones is to never keep the President waiting. "Don't worry—I'm coming."

She looks over her shoulder and down the hallway. "I'm serious, Wes," she threatens. "Who you talking to anyway?"

"Library. Just trying to get the final list of the honchos who'll be there tonight."

In our office, when the President gets lonely for his old life, we'll catch him calling his Formers: former British prime minister, former Canadian prime minister, even the former French president. But the help I need is far closer than that.

"Got it right here. It's just a one-pager," the librarian interrupts. "What's your fax number?"

Relaying the number, I fight my other arm into my sleeve. The President's and First Lady's metal heads jingle on my lapel pin. "And you'll send it now?"

"Whenever you want . . . it's—"

"Now."

I hang up the phone, grab my bag of tricks, and dart for the door. "Just tell me when Manning's coming," I say to Claudia as I squeeze past her and duck into the copy room directly across from my office.

"Wes, this isn't funny," she says, clearly annoyed.

"It's coming through right now," I lie, standing in front of our secure fax machine. Every day at six a.m., Manning's NIDs—the National Intelligence Daily—arrive by secure fax in the exact same spot. Sent out by the CIA, the NIDs contain briefs on an array of sensitive intelligence topics and are the last umbilical cord all Formers have with the White House. Manning races for it like catnip. But for me, what's being transmitted right now is far more potent.

"Wes, go to the door. I'll take care of the fax."

"It'll just—"

"I said go to the door. Now."

I turn around to face Claudia just as the fax machine hiccups to life. Her smoker's lips purse, and she looks angry—angrier than anyone should be over a silly little fax.

"It's okay," I stutter. "I'll get it."

"Dammit, Wes—"

Before she can finish, my phone vibrates in my pocket. I pull it out as a simple distraction. "Just gimme one sec," I say to Claudia as I check caller ID. *Undisclosed caller.* There aren't many people who have this number.

"Wes here," I answer.

"Don't react. Just smile and act like it's an old friend," a grainy voice crackles through the receiver. I recognize him instantly.

Boyle.

25

"Nice room," The Roman said, eyeing the mostly bare, sun-faded walls of Nico's home for the past eight years. Above the nightstand was a free Washington Redskins calendar from the local grocery store. Above the bed was a small crucifix. On the ceiling, a spiderweb of cracked plaster rounded out the sum total of the decor. "Really nice," The Roman added, remembering how much Nico thrived on positive reinforcement.

"It is nice," Nico agreed, his eyes locked on the orderly as he left the room.

"And you've been well?" The Roman asked.

Keeping his arms wrapped around his violin and hugging it like a doll, Nico didn't answer. The way his ear was cocked, it was clear he was listening to the fading squeaks of the orderly's rubber soles against the linoleum.

"Nico—"

"Wait . . ." Nico interrupted, still listening.

The Roman stayed silent, unable to hear a thing. Of course, that was yet another reason why they'd picked Nico all those years ago. The average adult hears at a level of twenty-five decibels. According to his army reports, Nico was gifted with the ability to hear at ten decibels. His eyesight was even more uncanny, measured officially at 20/6.

Nico's army supervisors labeled it a gift. His doctors labeled it a burden, suggesting that overwhelming auditory and visual stimuli caused his desensitization with reality. And The Roman . . . The Roman *knew* it was an opportunity.

"Tell me when we're clear," The Roman whispered.

As the sound faded, Nico scratched his bulbous nose and studied The Roman carefully, his close chocolate eyes flicking back and forth, slowly picking apart his guest's hair, face, overcoat, shoes, even his leather briefcase. The Roman had forgotten how methodical he was.

"You forgot an umbrella," Nico blurted.

The Roman patted down the back of his slightly damp hair. "It's just a short walk from the parking lo—"

"You brought a gun," Nico said, staring at The Roman's ankle holster as it peeked out from his pant leg.

"It's not loaded," The Roman said, remembering that short answers were the best way to rein him in.

"That's not your name," Nico again interrupted. He pointed at the visitor ID sticker on The Roman's lapel. "I know that name."

The Roman didn't even bother looking down. He used his badge to get past the guards, but for the ID, of course the name was fake. Only a fool would put his real name on a list that regularly got sent to his supervisors at the Service. Still, with all Nico's years here, with all the drugs the doctors pumped into him, he was sharp. Sniper training didn't dull easily. "Names are fictions," The Roman said. "Especially the enemy's."

Still holding tight to his fiddle, Nico could barely contain himself. "You're of The Three." From the excitement in his voice, it wasn't a question.

"Let's not—"

"Are you One or Two? I only spoke to Three. He was my liaison—with me when my father—when he passed. He said the rest of you were too big, and that the President was one of—" Nico bit his lip, straining to restrain himself. "Praise all! Did you see the cross on the brick chapel?"

The Roman nodded, remembering what they told Nico all those years ago. That he should look for the signs. That physical structures have always been sources of inexplicable power. The Druids and Stonehenge . . . the Egyptian pyramids . . . even Solomon's First and Second Temples in Jerusalem. The Freemasons spent centuries studying them all—each one an architectural marvel that's served as a doorway to a greater miracle. Centuries later, that knowledge was passed to Freemason James Hoban, who designed the White House, and Freemason Gutzon Borglum, who did Mount Rushmore. But as they also explained to Nico, some doors weren't meant to be opened.

"Praise all!" Nico repeated. "He said when you came, redemption would—"

"Redemption will come," The Roman promised. "As the Book promises."

For the first time, Nico was silent. He lowered the fiddle to the ground and bowed his head.

"That's it, my son," The Roman said with a nod. "Of course, before redemption, let's start with a little . . ." He reached over to the dresser and picked up the red glass rosary beads. ". . . confession."

Dropping to his knees, Nico clasped his hands together and leaned on the side of his mattress like a child at bedtime.

The Roman wasn't surprised. He did the same thing when they found him in the shelter. And for almost two full days after he confronted his father. "There'll be time for prayer later, Nico. Right now I just need you to tell me the truth about something."

"I'm always truthful, sir."

"I know you are, Nico." The Roman sat on the opposite side of the bed and placed the rosary beads between them. The fading sun boomeranged through the prisms of red glass. Still on his knees, Nico studied it, mesmerized. From his briefcase, The Roman pulled out a black-and-white photo and tossed it between them on the bed. "Now, tell me everything you know about Wes Holloway."

26

Hey, how's everything?" I sing into my cell phone as Claudia stares me down from the doorway of the copy room.

"You know who this is?" Boyle asks on the other line. His tone is sharp, each syllable chiseling like an ice pick. He's impatient. And clearly riled.

"Of course. Good to hear your voice, Eric." I purposely use his old codename instead of *Carl Stewart.* He doesn't need to know I've figured that one out.

"You alone?" he asks as Claudia's lips purse even tighter and she lowers her chin with a burning glare.

"Sure, I've got Claudia right here—"

"Stay away from this, Wes. This isn't your fight. Y'hear me? It's not your fight."

The line goes dead. Boyle's gone.

He hung up.

"No, that's great," I say to the now-silent line. "See you soon." I'm not the world's greatest liar, but I'm still good enough to convince Claudia nothing's wrong.

"What's wrong?" she asks.

"That was . . . it was Manning. He said he'd be another few minutes . . ."

Her eyes narrow as she processes the news. Behind me, the fax machine grumbles to life. I jump at the sound, which hits me like a bullet.

"What?" she asks.

"No, it just . . . it startled me." For almost a year after the shooting, every car that backfired, every loud door that slammed . . . even action scenes in movies . . . the loud noises echoed from Nico's attack. The doctors said it would fade over time. And it did. Until now.

Knowing that look on my face, Claudia pauses and softens, but as always, reverts to her one priority. "You should still be out there," she says.

"I will . . . just let me get this. Y'know how he likes knowing names," I add, selling it as a benefit for Manning. That alone buys me a few more seconds.

By the time I spin back to the fax, the cover sheet is already through. So is half of the final page.

I grab the left-hand corner of the sheet as it churns out of the machine, then tilt my head, struggling to read it upside down. Top corner says *Washington Post.* From what I can tell, it's from the comics section of the paper. *Hagar the Horrible* . . . then *Beetle Bailey.* But as *Beetle Bailey* rolls out, there's something handwritten in the open space of the comic strip's second panel: boxy and clunky cursive lettering that looks like it was written on the dashboard of a moving car. It's almost unreadable to the untrained eye. Fortunately, my eyes've been trained for years. I'd know Manning's handwriting anywhere.

Gov. Roche . . . M. Heatson, I read to myself.

On the next line, it makes even less sense. *Host—Mary Angel.*

Roche is the former governor of New York, but Heatson or Mary Angel . . . nothing rings a bell.

As the rest of the fax shimmies from the machine, there's nothing but more comics. *Peanuts*, *Garfield*, and *Blondie.*

This was the final piece of Boyle's puzzle? I look back at the handwritten note. *Gov. Roche . . . M. Heatson . . . Mary Angel.* Doesn't even make sense. Three names with no information? I study it again, reading each letter. This is the last page Boyle found before coming out of hiding. Eight years dead, and *this* is what lured him back into his life? *Gov. Roche . . . M. Heatson . . . Host—Mary Angel.* Still means nothing.

"Wes, he's here," Claudia calls out, disappearing up the hallway.

"Coming," I say as the final lines of *Beetle Bailey* scroll out from the machine. As I spin around to take off, the cover sheet drops to the floor. Pausing to pick it up, I glance at the line that says *Number of Pages.* To my surprise, it says *3.*

The fax machine again hiccups, and a final sheet of paper crawls toward me. The librarian called it a one-pager. And it is one page . . . with two sides. Front and back.

I hunch down to the fax and try to read the document as each line of fresh ink is printed on the page. Like the comics page, it has the light gray tone of photocopied newsprint filled with more of the President's handwriting. But as I read it to myself, the picture in the darkroom feels overexposed, foggier than ever.

"Wes . . ." the President calls from the front door.

"On my way," I say, picking up my travel bag, ripping the sheet from the fax, and darting into the hallway. I give it one last glance before shoving it into my jacket pocket. It doesn't make sense. What the hell could Boyle possibly be doing with *this*?

27

"He's the one I shot, isn't he?" Nico whispered, staring down at the recent photo of Wes. "The innocent."

"In every war, there are innocents," The Roman said. "But what I need to know is—"

"He's older . . ."

"It's been years, Nico. Of course, he's older."

Nico pulled the picture close to him. "I broke him, didn't I? He's broken now."

"Excuse me?"

"In his eyes," Nico replied, focusing even tighter on the photo. "I've seen that look . . . in battle . . . kids in battle have that look."

"I'm sure they do," The Roman said, snatching the picture and fighting to keep Nico on track. "But I need you to tell me if—"

"We relieve them from duty when they have that look," Nico said, almost proudly. "They lose sight of the cause."

"Exactly. They lose sight of the cause. Let's focus on that." Tapping Wes's picture, The Roman added, "Remember what he said about you? At the hearing a few years back?"

Nico stayed silent.

"What'd he call you again? A savage?"

"A monster," Nico growled.

The Roman shook his head, well aware of Wes's description. But like any interrogation, the key was hiding the big questions. "And that's the last you heard from him?" The Roman asked.

"He blames me. Refuses to see what I saved us from."

The Roman watched Nico carefully, now convinced that Wes hadn't been in touch. Of course, that was only part of the reason for his visit. "Speaking of which, do you think about Boyle?"

Nico looked up, his eyes angry for barely a second, then calm. The hatred disappeared almost instantly. Thanks to the doctors, he'd finally learned to bury it. "Never," Nico said.

"Not at all?"

"Never," Nico repeated, his voice slow and measured. He'd spent eight years perfecting his answer.

"It's okay, Nico. You're safe now, so—"

"I don't think of him. I don't," he insisted, still on his knees and staring straight at the fiery red of the rosaries. "What happened to . . . him . . . he . . ." Swallowing hard, Nico reached for the beads, then stopped himself. "He put me in here. He . . ."

"You can say his name, Nico."

Nico shook his head, still eyeing the beads. "Names are fictions. He . . . Masks for the devil." Without warning, Nico's arm shot forward, snatching the rosary beads from the center of the bed. He pulled them to his chest, his thumb furiously climbing from bead to bead, counting to the rosary's small engraving of Mary.

"Nico, take it easy—"

"Only God is true."

"I understand, but—"

"God is true!" he exploded, climbing the beads quicker than ever. Turning away, Nico rocked back and forth . . . slowly, then faster. Gripping each bead, one by one. His shoulders sagged with each sway, and his body hunched lower and lower, practically curling into a ball at the side of the bed. He kept trying to speak, then abruptly cut himself off. The Roman had seen it before. The battle internal. Without warning, Nico looked back over his shoulder. The Roman didn't need 20/6 vision to spot the tears in his eyes.

"Are you here to redeem me?" Nico sobbed.

The Roman froze, assuming it was all about Boyle . . . and it was, but—

"Of course," The Roman said as he moved to the other side of the bed. Putting a hand on Nico's shoulder, he picked up the violin from the floor. He'd read enough of Nico's file to know it was still his best transitional item. "That's why I'm here," he promised as Nico embraced the neck of the violin.

"For redemption?" Nico asked for the second time.

"For salvation."

Nico eked out a smile, and the crimson beads sank to the floor. From the way Nico studied the violin with his half-closed eyes, The Roman knew he had a few minutes of calm. Better make it quick.

"In the name of The Three, I'm here for your cleansing . . . and to be sure that when it comes to Boyl— When it comes to the Beast, that his influence is no longer felt by your spirit."

"Who increases our faith . . . Who strengthens our hope . . . Who perfects our love," Nico began to pray.

"Then let us begin," The Roman said. "What is your last memory of him?"

"At the Revolt," Nico began. "His hand up in victory . . . preening for the masses with his white teeth glowing. Then the anger in his eyes when I pulled that trigger—he didn't know he'd been hit. He was angry . . . *enraged* as he gritted his teeth. That was his first reaction, even in death. Hatred and rage. Until he looked down and spotted his own blood."

"And you saw him fall?"

"Two shots in the heart, one in the hand as they tore me down. Sliced his neck too. I heard him screaming as they clawed at me. Screaming for his life. Begging . . . even amid the roar . . . for himself. *Me . . . someone help me* . . . And then the screams stopped. And he laughed. I hear things. I could hear it. Through his own blood. Boyle was laughing."

The Roman rolled his tongue against his teeth. No doubt, it was true. Laughing all the way to freedom. "What about since?" he asked, choosing each word carefully. Regardless of the risk, he needed to know if Boyle had been here. "Has he haunted you . . . recently?"

Nico stopped, looking up from the violin. "Haunted?"

"In . . . in your dreams."

"Never in my dreams. His threat was stopped when—"

"What about anywhere else, in visions or—?"

"Visions?"

"Not visions . . . y'know, like—"

"His power is that great?" Nico interrupted.

"No, but we—"

"To be able to do that . . . to call from beyond the ashes . . ."

"There's no such power," The Roman insisted, again reaching for Nico's shoulder.

Scootching back on his rear, Nico pulled away from The Roman's grasp. His back slammed into the radiator and his violin again dropped to the floor. "For the Beast to rise . . ."

"I never said that."

"You didn't deny it!" Nico said, his eyes zipping back and forth in full panic. Clenching his fists, he swung his hands wildly, like he couldn't control his movements. A thick vein popped from his neck. "But for him to be alive . . . the Great Tribulation lasts seven years—my time away—followed by resurrection of the dead . . ."

The Roman stepped back, frozen.

"You believe it too," Nico said.

"That's not true."

"I hear your voice. The quiver! I'm right, aren't I?"

"Nico—"

"He is! With resurrection . . . the Beast lives!"

"I never—"

"He lives! My God, my Lord, he *lives*!" Nico yelled, still on his knees as he turned toward the shatterproof window, screaming at the sky.

The Roman had been afraid it'd come to this. Reaching into his jacket pocket, he pulled out his cell phone, an old, thick model. With a shove of his thumb, he unlatched the back of the phone and unveiled a lead compartment holding a small syringe and a loose razor blade. His fake ID and Secret Service badge allowed him to bring in the gun that was tucked into his ankle holster, but syringes and razors? Not in a mental hospital.

"Nico, time to calm down," he said as he slid the syringe between his pointer and middle fingers. The fentanyl would easily knock him out, but it'd take the razor to make it look like a suicide.

"Y-You attack me?" Nico asked as he turned around and saw the needle. His eyes grew dark and his nostrils flared. "He sent you!" Nico shouted, pressed against the radiator and trapped in the corner. "You're of them!"

"Nico, I'm with you," The Roman soothed as he stepped closer. There was no pleasure in putting an animal down. "This is just to calm you down," he added, knowing he had no choice. Leaving a body would certainly bring questions, but it wouldn't be half as bad as letting Nico scream for the next month that The Three existed and that Boyle was still alive.

Nico's eyes narrowed, focusing on The Roman's gun in the ankle holster. As if he'd spotted an old friend.

"Don't think it, Nico. You can't—"

The door to the room whipped open, slamming into the wall. "What's all the hollering abou—? What the hell you think you're doing?!" a deep voice asked.

The Roman glanced back just in time to see two orderlies burst inside. That was all Nico needed.

Like an uncoiled snake, Nico sprang toward The Roman's legs. His right hand gripped The Roman's kneecap, twisting it like a bottle cap. His left hand went straight for the gun in the ankle holster.

"Gaaaah!" The Roman howled, crumbling backward toward the floor. Even before the impact, Nico was tearing the gun from its holster.

"Nico, don't—" the orderly with the hoop earring threatened.

It was already too late. Like a virtuoso painter reunited

with his long-lost brush, Nico grinned as the gun slid into his palm. Still on his knees, he bounced his hand slightly, letting the gun wobble in his grip. "Built-in silencer . . . neither muzzle nor butt heavy," he said to The Roman, who was still writhing on the floor. "Beautiful work," he added with a handsome squint as he smiled at the orderlies.

"Nico—!"

Four muffled shots hissed out. Both orderlies screamed. The first two shots pierced their hands. Just like he did with his father. And with Boyle. The stigmata. To show them Jesus's pain. Both slammed into the wall before they even realized the final two bullets were in their hearts.

Climbing to his feet, Nico didn't even watch as the orderlies wilted to the floor, their bodies leaving parallel red streaks down the white wall. Spinning around, he turned the gun toward The Roman, who was on his back, clutching something close to his chest. The shot would be quick and easy, but as Nico's finger hugged the trigger . . .

"Man of God!" The Roman shouted, holding up Nico's red glass rosary beads. They dangled down from his fist, swaying like a hypnotist's pocketwatch. "You know it, Nico. Whatever else you think . . . Never kill a man of God."

Nico paused, mesmerized by the rosary shimmering in the fading light. The beads continued to sway, matching pace with The Roman's quick breathing. A puddle of sweat gathered on The Roman's lip. Staring up from the floor, he could see straight into the barrel. Nico wouldn't make eye contact. Wouldn't even acknowledge he was there. Lost in the rosary beads, Nico searched for his answer, never moving the gun. His brow went from creased to calm to creased again, as if he were flipping a coin in his own head. And then the coin landed. Nico pulled the trigger.

The Roman shut his eyes as a single shot hissed out. The bullet pierced his empty left hand, straight through the center of his palm. Jesus's pain. Before he could even feel it, the blood puddled in his hand, rushing down his wrist toward his elbow.

"Where is he!?" Nico demanded.

"I-I'll kill you for that," The Roman growled.

"Another lie." Turning slightly to the right, Nico took aim at The Roman's other hand. "After everything you promised . . . to come to me now and protect him. What power does the Beast hold over you?"

"Nico, stop!"

Without hesitation, Nico pulled back the hammer of the gun. "Answer my question: Where is he?"

"I-I have no i—"

"Please move the rosary," Nico politely asked, motioning to the beads, which were down by The Roman's leg. As The Roman picked them up, Nico squeezed the trigger and a second silenced shot wisped through the air, burrowing through The Roman's foot. Both wounds burned like thick needles twisting through his skin. He gritted his teeth and held his breath, waiting for the initial sting to pass. All it did was get worse. "Nnnnuhhh!" he shouted.

"Where. Is. Boyle?" Nico demanded.

"If . . . if I knew, do you really think I'd come here?"

Nico stood silent for a moment, processing the thought. "But you've seen him?"

The Roman shook his head, still struggling against the pain. He could feel his foot swelling, filling his shoe.

"Has anyone else seen him?" Nico asked.

The Roman didn't answer. Nico watched him carefully, tilting his ear slightly toward him.

"Your breathing's starting to quicken. I hope you don't have a stroke," Nico said.

The Roman looked away from the bed. Nico looked right at it.

On the covers, just by the edge, was the black-and-white photograph of Wes. "Him?" Nico asked, reaching for the picture. "Is that—? That's why you asked me about him, yes? The one I broke . . . he's the one who saw the Beast."

"All he did was see hi—"

"But to communicate . . . to be in league with the Beast. Wes is corrupted now, isn't he? Polluted. That's why the ricochet—" Nico nodded quickly. "Of course! That's why God sent the bullet his way. No coincidences. Fate. God's will. To strike Wes down. And what God began . . ." Nico's eyes narrowed at the photo. "I will make him bleed again. I missed it before, but I see it now . . . in the Book. Bleeding Wes."

Looking up from the photo, Nico raised his gun and pointed it at The Roman's head. From the window over the radiator, the panes in the glass cast the thick shadow of a cross directly onto The Roman's face.

"God's mercy," Nico whispered, lowering his gun, turning his back to The Roman, and staring out the oversize shatterproof window. The gun's silencer was quiet, but security would be there soon. He didn't pause for a second. He'd had eight years to think about this moment. *Shatterproof.* Not bulletproof.

Two more shots snarled from the gun, piercing the bottom left and right corners of the glass, exploiting the foundation of the window.

Still on the floor, The Roman pulled off his tie to make a tourniquet for his foot. A tight fist eased the pain in his hand. The blood already filled his shoe, and his heartbeat felt like it was thumping up his arm and down his leg. A few feet away, he heard the thud of a bowling ball, then the crackling of glass. He looked up just in time to see Nico slamming his foot against the bullet hole on the bottom left of the window. True to its name, the glass wouldn't shatter, but it did give, popping like bubble wrap as the tiny shards fought to stay together in an almost bendable plastic sheet. Now he had an opening. Licking his lips, Nico put his foot against the glass and gripped the radiator for leverage. With another shove, a fist-sized hunk of the sea-green window broke off from the rest. He pushed again. And again. Almost there. There was a tiny tear and a kitten shriek as the window slowly peeled outward and upward like old wallpaper. Then a final thud and—Nothing.

The Roman looked up as a blast of cold air slapped him in the face.

Nico was already gone.

Crawling to the window, The Roman gripped the top of the radiator and pulled himself up. Two stories down, he spotted the small bluff of snow that had broken Nico's fall. Thinking about giving chase, he took another look at the height and felt the blood seeping through his own sock. *Not a chance*, he told himself. He could barely stand now.

Craning his neck out the window and following the footprints—out of the bluff, through the slush on the service road—he quickly spotted Nico: his sweatshirt creating a tiny brown spot plowing through the bright white layer of snow. Nico never looked back.

Within seconds, Nico's faded brown spot gained a speck of black as he raised the gun and pointed it downhill. From the angle of the window, The Roman couldn't see what Nico was aiming at. There was a guard at the gate, but that was over fifty yards a—

A whispered *psst* and a hiccup of smoke belched from the gun's barrel. Right there, Nico slowed his pace to a calm, almost relaxing walk. The Roman didn't need to see the body to know it was another direct hit.

Shoving the gun into the pouch of his sweatshirt, Nico looked like a man without a care in the world. Just strolling past the old army building, past the graveyards, past the leafless dogwood, and—as he faded from view—straight out the front gate.

Hobbling toward the door, The Roman grabbed the syringe and the razor blade from the floor.

"You guys okay?" a female voice asked through one of the orderlies' walkie-talkies.

The Roman leaned down and pulled it off the orderly's belt clip. "Just fine," he mumbled into the receiver.

Carrying it with him, he turned around and took a final survey of the room. It wasn't until that moment that he realized Nico had also taken the black-and-white photograph of Wes. Bleeding Wes.

28

Right this way," I say as I cup the elbow of the older woman with the beehive of blond hair and escort her and her husband toward President Manning and the First Lady, who're posed in front of a floral bouquet the size of a small car. Trapped in this small anteroom in the back of the Kravis Center for the Performing Arts, the President looks my way, never losing his grin. It's all the signal I need. He has no idea who they are.

I put it on a platter. "Mr. President, you remember the Talbots—"

"George . . . Leonor . . ." the First Lady jumps in, shaking hands and swapping air kisses. Thirty-four books, five unauthorized biographies, and two TV movies have argued she's the better politician in the family. All the proof is right here. "And how's Lauren?" she asks, pulling off their daughter's name as well. That's when I'm impressed. The Talbots aren't longtime donors. They're NBFs—new best friends, which is what we call the rich groupies who glommed onto the Mannings *after* they'd left the White House. Old friends liked the power; new friends like the fame.

"We just think you're the greatest," Mrs. Talbot gushes, her eyes solely on the First Lady. It's never bothered Manning. Dr. First Lady has always been a part of their political package—and thanks to her science background, the better at analyzing poll numbers, which is why some say she was even more crushed than the President when they handed over their keys to the White House. Still, as someone who was with the President that day as he flew home to Florida, and placed his final call on Air Force One, and lingered on the line just long enough to say his final good-bye to the phone operator, I can't help but disagree. Manning went from having a steward who used to wear a pager just to bring him coffee, to lugging his own suitcases back to his garage. You can't give away all that power without some pain.

"What'm I, chopped herring all of a sudden?" Manning asks.

"What do you mean, *all of a sudden*?" the First Lady replies as they all cocktail-party laugh. It's the kind of joke that'll be repeated for the rest of the social season, turning the Talbots into minor wine and cheese stars, and simultaneously ensuring that Palm Beach society keeps coming to these thousand-dollar-a-plate charity shindigs.

"On three," the photographer calls out as I squeeze the Talbots between the Mannings. "One . . . two . . ."

The flashbulb pops, and I race back to the receiving line to palm the next donor's elbow. Manning's look is exactly the same.

"Mr. President, you remember Liz Westbrook . . ."

In the White House, we called it the *push/pull.* I *pull* Mrs. Westbrook toward the President, which *pushes* the Talbots out of the way, forcing them to stop gawking and say their good-byes. True to form, it works perfectly—until someone pushes back.

"You're trying the push/pull with me? I *invented* it!" a familiar voice calls out as the flashbulb pops. By the time I spin back toward the line, Dreidel's already halfway to the President with a huge smile on his face.

Manning lights up like he's seeing his childhood pet. I know better than to get in the way of that. "My boy!" Manning says, embracing Dreidel. I still get a handshake. Dreidel gets a hug.

"We wanted it to be a surprise," I offer, shooting a look at Dreidel.

Behind him, the honcho line is no longer moving. Over the President's shoulder, the First Lady glares my way. I also know better than to get in the way of that.

"Sir . . . we should really . . ."

"I hope you're staying for the event," Manning interrupts as he backs up toward his wife.

"Of course, sir," Dreidel says.

"Mr. President, you remember the Lindzons," I say, pulling the next set of donors into place. Manning fake-smiles and shoots me a look. I promised him it was only fifty clicks tonight. He's clearly been counting. This is souvenir photo number 58. As I head back to the line, Dreidel's right there with me.

"How many clicks you over?" Dreidel asks.

"Eight," I whisper. "What happened to your fundraiser?"

"It was cocktails. We finished early, so I figured I'd come say hello. What happened with the gossip columnist?"

"All taken care of."

A flashbulb pops, and I grab the elbow of the next honcho, an overweight woman in a red pants suit. Falling back into old form, Dreidel puts a hand on the shoulder of her husband and motions him forward.

"Mr. President, you remember Stan Joseph," I announce as we drop him off for click number 59. Whispering to Dreidel, I add, "I also snagged Boyle's London address and his last request from the library."

Dreidel picks up speed as another flashbulb explodes. He's half a step ahead. He thinks I don't notice. "So what was on the final sheet?" he asks softly.

As I turn back to the honchos, there's only one person left in line. One click to go. But when I see who it is, my throat constricts.

"What?" Dreidel asks, reading my expression.

I stop right in front of our final honcho, a young redhead in a modest black suit. Dreidel goes to put a hand on her elbow to escort her forward. She brushes him off and puts a hand on his shoulder. "Just the people I'm looking for," she says proudly. "Lisbeth Dodson—*Palm Beach Post.* You must be Dreidel."

29

McLean, Virginia

Limping up the icy driveway and holding his fist against his chest, The Roman eyed the front windows of the classic stucco Colonial with the *For Sale* sign in the front yard. Although the lights were off, it didn't slow him down. After hiding his wound—by slipping his bloody foot into one of Nico's old shoes—he flashed his badge to push his way out of the hospital and quickly made the call. He knew Benjamin was home.

Sure enough, as he reached the side of the house, he grabbed the cold metal handrail and hobbled down a short cement staircase. At the bottom, he reached a door with a faint glow of light peeking out from under it. A small sign above the doorbell said *Appointments Only.* The Roman didn't have an appointment. He had something far more valuable.

"Les?" he called out, barely able to stand. Leaning against the doorjamb, he couldn't feel his left hand, which was still in the same blood-soaked glove that helped him hide it at the hospital. His foot had gone dead almost an hour ago.

"Coming," a muffled voice said from inside. As the pins and springs of the lock turned, the door opened, revealing a bushy-haired man with bifocals balanced on a plump nose. "Okay, what'd you do this ti—? Oh, jeez, is that blood?"

"I-I need—" Before he could finish, The Roman collapsed, falling forward through the doorway. As always, Dr. Les Benjamin caught him. That's what brothers-in-law were for.

30

"Mr. President, you remember Ms. Dodson . . . columnist for the *Palm Beach Post*," Wes said mid-handoff.

"Lisbeth," she insisted, extending a handshake and hoping to keep things light. She glanced back to Wes, who was already pale white.

"Lisbeth, I would've gotten your name," Manning promised. "Even if I don't know the donors, only a fool doesn't remember the press."

"I appreciate that, sir," Lisbeth said, believing his every word, even as she told herself not to. *Could I be more pathetic?* she asked herself, fighting off a strange desire to curtsy. Sacred Rule #7: Presidents lie best. "Nice to see you again, sir."

"Is that Lisbeth?" the First Lady asked, knowing the answer as she moved in for her own cheek-to-cheek hug. "Oh, you know I adore your column," she gushed. "Except that piece when you listed how much Lee was tipping local waitresses. That one almost had me take you off our invite list."

"You actually did take me off," Lisbeth pointed out.

"Only for two weeks. Life's too short to hold a grudge."

Appreciating the honesty, Lisbeth couldn't help but smile. "You're a smart woman, Dr. Manning."

"Dear, we're the ones who're supposed to be currying favor with you—though I will say you can do better than silly little squibs about what people are tipping, which, let's just admit, is below you." Slapping her husband on the arm, she added, "Lee, give the girl a nice quote about cystic fibrosis research so she can do her job."

"Actually," Lisbeth began, "I'm just here . . ."

"We should get you onstage, sir," Wes interrupted.

". . . to see your right-hand men," Lisbeth added, pointing at Dreidel and Wes. "I'm doing a piece on loyalty. Thought maybe I could grab their quotes and turn them into superstars."

"Good—you *should*," the President said, putting an arm around Dreidel. "This one's running for Senate. And if I still had the keys . . . he's Vice President caliber." The President paused, waiting for Lisbeth to write it down.

Pulling a notepad from her overstuffed black purse, Lisbeth took the cue and pretended to scribble. Over her shoulder, she could feel Wes seething.

"Don't worry," Lisbeth said to Manning. "I'll take it easy on them."

"Mr. President," a throaty female voice called out as they all turned to the middle-aged woman in the designer suit and matching designer hairdo. As honorary chairperson for the Cystic Fibrosis Foundation, Myrna Opal tapped her diamond Chopard watch, determined to keep the program running on time. "I think we're ready, sir."

The instant the President took his first step toward the stage door, Wes fell in line right beside him. "Wes, I'm fine."

"I know, but it's . . ."

". . . less than ten feet to the door. I'll make it. And Dreidel—I hope you're at my table later."

He says the words while looking at Wes. In the White House, they used to follow etiquette and make sure the President was always sitting next to whomever he needed to be near. For four years, he didn't pick his tablemates. These days, he no longer bothered with political favors. It was the only perk of losing the White House. The President could finally sit next to the people he liked.

"Just make sure you get these nice cystic fibrosis folks in tomorrow's column," the First Lady added, motioning to Lisbeth.

"Yes, ma'am," Lisbeth blurted, never taking her eyes off Wes. He'd been around the world's best politicians for almost a decade, but he still was a novice when it came to hiding his own emotions. Nose flaring . . . fists tight . . . whatever he was burying, it was eating him alive.

"This way, sir," one of two Secret Service agents said, motioning the President and First Lady toward the stage door. Like mice behind the piper, the cystic fibrosis chairperson, and P.R. person, and fundraising person, and photographer, and remaining honchos all fell in line behind them, an instant entourage that sucked every straggler from the room.

As the door slammed behind them, the quiet was overwhelming. To Lisbeth's surprise, Wes wasn't the only one to stay put. Dreidel was right next to him, a warm grin on his face.

"Come . . . sit," he offered, pointing to three empty seats at the cloth-covered round table that was used as a sign-in desk. Lisbeth obliged but wasn't fooled. Fear always brought out kindness. And if the hotshot state-senator-to-be was anxious, her B+ story just became an A–.

"So how'd the birthday party planning go?" she asked, pulling a seat up to the table.

"The what?" Dreidel asked.

"For Manning's birthday," Wes insisted. "Our meeting this morning . . ."

"Oh, it was great," Dreidel insisted, repatting the part in his hair and readjusting his wire-rim glasses. "I thought you meant my fundraiser."

"Figure out where you're gonna have it?" she added.

"Still deciding," Wes and Dreidel said simultaneously.

Lisbeth nodded. These guys were White House trained. They weren't falling for minor-league tricks. Better to go in soft. "C'mon, didn't you hear what the First Lady said?" she asked. "*Adores the column.* I'm not here to drink your blood."

"Then why'd you bring your cup?" Dreidel asked, pointing with his chin at her notepad.

"That's what's scaring you? What if I put it back in its holster?" she said, reaching under her seat and tucking the pad and pen back in her purse. Still bent over, she looked up, struggling to keep eye contact. "That better?" she asked.

"I was joking," Dreidel said, clearly playing nice. Without a doubt, it was his secret they were smuggling.

"Listen, fellas," Lisbeth begged. "Before you get all— Damn, sorry about this . . ." Reaching into the jacket pocket of her black suit, Lisbeth took out her cell phone and hit the *Receive* button. "Hey, Vincent . . . Yeah, I just . . . Oh, you're kidding. Hold on, gimme a sec," she said into the phone. Turning to Wes and Dreidel, she added, "Sorry, I gotta take this . . . it'll just be a minute." Before either of them could react, Lisbeth was out of her seat, speed-walking toward the main door. "Just watch my purse!" she called back to Dreidel and Wes, shoving her shoulder into the door and crossing into the ornate chandeliered lobby of the Kravis Center. With a tight grip on her phone, she pressed it to her ear. But the only things she heard were the voices of the two young men she'd just left inside.

"You told her we were *party planning*?" Dreidel hissed.

"What'd you want me to say?" Wes shot back. "That I was trying to save what was left of your marriage?"

Sacred Rule #8: If you really want to know what people think about you, leave the room and listen to what they say. Lisbeth learned this one the hard way on the Palm Beach party circuit, when a local socialite paid a parking valet $1,500 to eavesdrop on Lisbeth's conversation with a confidential source. A week later, Lisbeth saved the $1,500 and simply signed up for two separate cell phones. Today, cell phone A was in her purse, back with Wes and Dreidel. Cell phone B was pressed to her ear. When she put her notepad away, all it took was the press of a button for A to speed-dial B. One faked important call later, Sacred Rule #8 proved why it would forever be in the top ten.

"But if she finds out about Boyle . . ." Wes said on the other line.

"Easy, poppa—she's not finding out about Boyle," Dreidel shot back. "Though speaking of which, tell me what you found . . ."

Alone in the lobby, Lisbeth stopped short, almost falling out of her scuffed high heels. *Boyle?* She looked around, but no one was there. They were all inside, lost in the hum of *An Evening with President Leland F. Manning*. Lisbeth could hear his voice rumbling off the main stage. A rush of excitement flushed her freckled cheeks. Finally . . . after all these years . . . an honest-to-God A+.

31

"Ahhh!" The Roman roared as Benjamin used sterilized scissors to cut the dead gray skin from the edges of the wound in his palm. "That *hurts*!"

"Good—that's a sign of no nerve damage," Benjamin said dryly in the small basement office his ex-wife used to use for her electrolysis practice. The Roman sat on a modern leather sofa; Benjamin swiveled slightly on a stainless-steel rolling chair. "Hold still," he added. Pressing his thumb in The Roman's palm and his fingers on the back of The Roman's hand, Benjamin squeezed tightly on the wound. This time, The Roman was ready. He didn't scream at all.

"No bony tenderness or instability . . . though I still think you should have it X-rayed to be sure."

"I'm fine."

"Yeah, I could tell that by the way you passed out in the doorway. Just a picture of health." Unbending a paperclip, Benjamin twisted the metal until the two tips of the clip were almost touching, barely half a centimeter apart. "Do me a favor and close your eyes." As the Roman obliged, Benjamin lightly pressed the tips of the paperclip against the side of The Roman's thumb. "How many points do you feel?"

"Two," The Roman said.

"Good." Finger by finger, Benjamin repeated the question, then wrapped The Roman's hand in fresh gauze. Eventually working down to The Roman's bloodied foot, he tweezed pieces of sock and shards of shoelace from the wound and applied the same paperclip test to each toe. "How many now?"

"One."

"Good. Y'know, it's a miracle you didn't fracture any tarsal bones."

"Yeah, God's on my side," The Roman said, wiggling his fingers and tapping the gauze bandage on his palm. The blood was gone, but the pain was still there. Nico would pay for that one.

"Just keep it clean and elevated," Benjamin said as he eventually wrapped The Roman's foot.

"So I'm okay to fly?"

"Fly? No . . . forget it. This is rest time. Understand? Take it easy for a few days."

The Roman stayed silent, leaning down and carefully sliding his foot into the shoes Benjamin had brought from upstairs.

"Did you hear what I said?" Benjamin asked. "This isn't the time to run around."

"Just do me a favor and call in those prescriptions," The Roman said, fighting the urge to limp as he headed for the door. "I'll call you later." Without looking back, he stepped outside and pulled his cell phone from his pocket.

Ten digits later, a female voice answered, "Travel Office, how can I assist you?"

"I'm trying to make a reservation," The Roman said, walking out into the darkness as a gust of Virginia chill tried to blow him sideways. "I need the next flight you have for Palm Beach."

32

"This?" Dreidel asks as he stares down at the unfolded fax. "This's the last thing Boyle got from the library?"

"According to the archivist."

"It doesn't even make sense," Dreidel moans. "I mean, a personnel file, I could understand . . . even an old targeting memo for some attack that went wrong . . . but a *crossword puzzle*?"

"That's what she sent: one sheet with some names on a stupid *Beetle Bailey* cartoon—and on the opposite side, a faded, mostly finished . . ."

". . . crossword puzzle," Dreidel repeats. He studies the crossword's handwritten answers. "It's definitely Manning's writing."

"And Albright's," I say, referring to our former chief of staff. "Remember? Albright started the puzzles . . ."

". . . and Manning finished them." Turning back to the crossword, he points to a jumble of doodles and random letters on the right side of the puzzle. *AMB* . . . *JABR* . . . *FRF* . . . *JAR* . . . "What're these?"

"No idea. I checked the initials, but they're no one he knows. To be honest, it looks like gibberish."

Dreidel nods, checking for himself. "My mother does the same thing when she's working a puzzle. I think it's just work space—testing letters . . . trying different permutations." Focusing back on the puzzle itself, he reads each answer one by one. "What about the actual boxes? Anything interesting?"

"Just obscure words with lots of vowels. *Damp . . . aral . . . peewee*," I read across the top, leaning over his shoulder.

"So the answers are right?"

"I've had a total of twelve seconds to look at it, much less solve it."

"Definitely looks right," Dreidel says, studying the finished puzzle. "Though maybe this's what the FBI guy meant by *The Three*," he adds. "Maybe it's a number in the crossword."

I shake my head. "He said it was a group."

"It could still be in the crossword."

Eyeing the only "three" in the puzzle, I point to the four-letter answer for 3 down. *"Merc,"* I say, reading from the puzzle.

"Short for *mercenary*," Dreidel says, now excited. "A mercenary who knew to leave Boyle alive."

"Now you're reaching."

"How can you say that? Maybe that's exactly what we're missing . . ."

"What, some hidden code that says, *At the end of the first term, fake Boyle's death and let him come back years later in Malaysia*? C'mon, be real. There's no secret message hidden in a *Washington Post* crossword puzzle."

"So where does that leave us?" Dreidel asks.

"Stuck," a female voice announces from the corner.

Spinning around, I almost swallow my tongue. Lisbeth enters quieter than a cat, her eyes searching the room to make sure we're alone. The girl's not dumb. She knows what happens if this gets out.

"This is a private conversation," Dreidel insists.

"I can help you," she offers. In her hand is a cell phone. I glance down at her purse and spot another. Son of a—

"Did you record us!? Is that why you left?" Dreidel explodes, already in lawyer mode as he hops out of his seat. "It's illegal in Florida without consent!"

"I didn't record you . . ."

"Then you can't prove anything—without a record, it's all just—"

"*It could still be in the crossword . . . Merc . . . short for mercenary . . .*" she begins, staring down at her left palm. Her voice never speeds up, always a perfect, unsettling calm. "*A mercenary who knew to leave Boyle alive . . .*" She turns her palm counterclockwise as she reads. "*Now you're reaching.* I can keep going if you want. I haven't even gotten to my wrist yet."

"You tricked us," I say, frozen at the table.

She stops at the accusation. "No, that's not— I was just trying to see why you were lying to me."

"So you do that by lying to *us*?"

"That wasn't what I—" She cuts herself off and looks down, weighing the moment. This is harder than she thought. "Listen, I'm . . . I'm sorry, okay? But I'm serious . . . I can work with you on this."

"Work with us? No, no no!" Dreidel shouts.

"You don't understand . . ."

"Actually, I'm pretty damn fluent at this stuff—and the

last thing I need right now is more time with you, listening to your bullshit! I have a *no comment* on all this, and anything you print, I'll not only deny, but I'll sue your ass back to whatever crappy high school newspaper taught you that damn phone trick in the first place!"

"Yeah, I'm sure a public lawsuit will really help your state election campaign," Lisbeth says calmly.

"Don't you dare bring that into— *Dammit!*" Dreidel screams, spinning around and slamming both fists against the welcoming table.

Still standing in the doorway, Lisbeth should be wearing a smile so wide, there'd be canary feathers dangling from her lips. Instead, she rubs the back of her neck as her front teeth click anxiously. I wore that same look when I walked in on one of the many fights between the President and First Lady. It's like walking in on someone having sex. An initial thrill, followed instantly by the hollow dread that in a world of infinite possibilities, physical and temporal happenstance have conspired to place you at the regrettable, unreturnable moment that currently passes for your life.

Lisbeth takes a step back, bumping into the door. Then she takes a step forward. "I really can help you," she says.

"Whattya mean?" I ask, standing up.

"Wes, don't," Dreidel moans. "This is stupid. We already—"

"I can get you information," Lisbeth continues. "The newspaper . . . our contacts—"

"Contacts?" Dreidel asks. "We have the President's Rolodex."

"But you can't call them," Lisbeth shoots back. "And neither can Wes—not without tipping someone off."

"That's not true," Dreidel argues.

"Really? So no one'll raise an eyebrow when Manning's two former aides start dissecting his old assassination attempt? No one'll tattle to the President when you start sniffing around Boyle's old life?"

We're both speechless. Dreidel stops pacing. I brush some imaginary dirt from the table. If the President found out . . .

Lisbeth watches us carefully. Her freckles shift as her eyes narrow. She reads social cues for a living. "You don't even trust Manning, do you?" she asks.

"You can't print that," Dreidel threatens.

Lisbeth's mouth falls open, shocked by the answer. "You're serious . . ."

It takes me a second to process what just happened. I look to Lisbeth, then back to Dreidel. I don't believe it. She was bluffing.

"Don't you dare print it," Dreidel adds. "We didn't say that."

"I know . . . I'm not printing it . . . I just—you guys really punched the hornet's nest on this, didn't you?"

Dreidel's done answering questions. He storms at her, jabbing a finger at her face. "You have no proof of anything! And the fact that—"

"Can you really help us?" I call out from the table.

Turning to me, she doesn't hesitate. "Absolutely."

"Wes, don't be stupid . . ."

"How?" I ask her.

Dreidel turns my way. "Wait . . . you're actually *listening* to her?"

"By being the one person no one can ever trace back to you," Lisbeth explains, stepping around Dreidel and heading toward me. "You make a phone call, people'll know something's up. Same with Dreidel. But if I make it, I'm just a crackpot reporter sniffing for story and hoping to be the next Woodward and Bernstein."

"So why help us?" I ask.

"To be the next Woodward and Bernstein." Through her designer eyeglasses, she studies me with dark green eyes—and never once glances down at my cheek. "I want the story," she adds. "When it's all over . . . when all the secrets are out, and the book deals are falling into place, I just want to be the one to write it up."

"And if we tell you to go screw yourself?"

"I break it now, and the news vans start lining up outside your apartment, feeding your lives to the cable news grinder. Lying to all of America . . . a giant cover-up . . . They'll eat you like Cheerios. And even if you get the truth out there, your lives'll be like picked-over bones."

"So that's it?" Dreidel asks, rushing back and tapping his knuckle on the table. "You threaten us, and we're supposed to just comply? How do we know you won't break it tomorrow morning just to get the quick kill?"

"Because only a moron goes for the quick kill," Lisbeth says as she sits on the edge of the table. "You know how it works: I run this tomorrow and I'll get a nice pat on the head that'll last a total of twenty-four hours, at which point the *Times* and the *Washington Post* will grab my football, fly a dozen reporters down here, and dance it all the way to the end zone. At least my way, you're in control. You get your answers; I get my story. If you're innocent, you've got nothing to fear."

I look up from my seat. At the edge of the table, Lisbeth's right leg swings slightly. She knows she's got a point.

"And we can trust you on that?" I ask. "You'll stay quiet until it's over?"

Her leg stops swinging. "Wes, the only reason you know Woodward and Bernstein is because they had the ending . . . not just the first hit. Only a fool wouldn't stick with you till we get all the answers."

I've been burned by reporters. I don't like reporters. And I certainly don't like Lisbeth. But as I glance over at Dreidel, who's finally fallen silent, it's clear we're out of options. If we don't work with her, she'll take this whole shitstorm public and unleash it in a way that we'll never be able to take back. If we *do* work with her, at least we buy some time to figure out what's really going on. I give another look to Dreidel. From the way he pinches the bridge of his nose, we've already stepped on the land mine. The only question now is, how long until we hear the big—?

"Nobody move!" a deep voice yells as the door whips into the wall and half a dozen suit-and-tie Secret Service agents flood the room, guns drawn.

"Let's go!" a beefy agent with a thin yellow tie says as he grabs Dreidel by the shoulder and shoves him toward the door. "Out. Now!"

"Get off me!"

"You too!" another says to Lisbeth as she follows right behind. "Go!"

The rest of the agents swarm inside, but to my surprise, run right past me, fanning out in onion-peel formation as they circle through the room. This isn't an attack; it's a sweep.

The only thing that's odd is none of these guys look familiar. I know everyone on our detail. Maybe we got a bomb threat and they called in local—

"Both of you, *move*!" the yellow-tie agent barks at Dreidel and Lisbeth. I assume he doesn't see me—Lisbeth's still in front of me near the table, but as I shoot out of my seat and follow them toward the door, I feel a sharp tug on the back of my jacket.

"Hey, what're you—?"

"You're with me," Yellow Tie insists, yanking me backward as my tie digs into my neck. With a hard shove to the left, he sends me stumbling toward the far corner of the room. We're moving so fast, I can barely keep my balance.

"Wes!" Lisbeth calls out.

"He's fine," an agent with bad acne insists, grabbing her elbow and tugging her to the door. He says something else to her, but I can't hear it.

Looking back to me over her shoulder, Lisbeth is still off balance as she staggers toward the doorway's white rectangle of light. With one last wrench, she disappears. When the first agent grabbed her, she was pissed. But now . . . the last look I see before the door slams behind her . . . the way her eyes go wide . . . whatever the agent said to her, she's terrified.

"Let go—I'm a friendly!" I insist, fighting to get to my ID.

Yellow Tie doesn't care. "Keep moving!" he tells me, practically holding me up by my collar. The last time the Service moved this fast was when Boyle was— No. I stop myself, refusing to replay it. Don't panic. Get the facts.

"Is Manning okay?" I ask.

"Just move!" he insists as we rush toward the corner of the room, where I spot a carpeted, almost hidden door.

"C'mon!" Yellow Tie says, undoing a latch and ramming me into the door to shove it open. Unlike the door that Lisbeth and Dreidel went through, this one doesn't dump us in the lobby. The ceiling rises up, and the concrete hallway is gray and narrow. Loose wires, grimy fire extinguishers, and some random white pipes are the only things on the walls. Maintenance corridor from the ammonia smell of it.

I try to break free, but we're moving too fast. "If you don't tell me where the hell we're going, I'll personally make sure you're—"

"Here," Yellow Tie says, stopping at the first door on my right. A red and white sign reads *Storage Only.* He reaches the door with his free hand, revealing a room that's bigger than my office. With one final shove, he lets go of my collar and flings me inside like the evening's trash.

My shoes slide against the floor as I fight for balance, but it's not until I spot two other sets of black shiny shoes that I realize I'm not alone.

"All yours," Yellow Tie calls out as I hear the door slam behind me.

My skidding stops as my funny bone bangs into a metal utility rack. A hiccup of sawdust belches into the air.

"Busy day, huh?" the man in the U.S. Open hat says, arms folded across his chest. His partner scratches at the nick of skin missing from his ear. O'Shea and Micah. The FBI agents from this morning.

"What the hell's going on?" I demand.

"Nico Hadrian escaped from St. Elizabeths about an hour and a half ago. What we wanna know is, why was your name in the hospital's log as his last visitor?"

33

Richmond, Virginia

It was easy for Nico to get the jeans and the blue button-down shirt from the dryer in the Laundromat. Same with the Baltimore Orioles baseball cap he took from a dumpster. But once he made his way into Carmel's Irish Pub, it took a full nine minutes before an older black man, nursing whiskey and a runny nose, hobbled over to the restroom and left his faded army jacket sagging like a corpse on the seat of his bar-stool. Approaching the stool, Nico was calm. The Lord would always provide.

It was the same thought swirling through his head right now as he stood on the gravelly shoulder of I-95 and an eighteen-wheel truck ferociously blew by, kicking up a trail of tiny pebbles and chocolate-brown slush. Shielding his eyes, Nico squinted through the instant hurricane as the pull of wind sent him reeling to the right. One hand was pressed down on his head to keep his Orioles hat from blowing away, while the other gripped his cardboard sign that flapped like a kite in the truck's backdraft. As the truck disappeared and the wind died, the sign went limp, brushing against Nico's right leg. Calmly as ever, Nico raised his hand and put out his thumb.

He was already in Richmond, well out of the thirty-mile radius that the FBI and D.C. Police were currently combing near St. Elizabeths. The first driver took him up South Capitol Street. The second helped him navigate I-295. And the third took him down I-95, all the way to Richmond.

Without question, Nico knew he couldn't afford to be standing out in the open for long. With the nightly news approaching, his picture would be everywhere. Still, there wasn't much he could do. From a statistical standpoint, the odds of a fourth driver picking him up in the next few minutes were already low. Anyone else would be panicking. Not Nico. As with anything in life, statistics meant nothing if you believed in fate.

Spotting the pair of owl-eyed headlights in the distance, he calmly stepped toward the road and once again held up his handmade sign with the big block letters: *Fellow Christian Looking for a Ride.*

A piercing screech knifed through the night as the driver of a beat-up flatbed hit his brakes, and all ten wheels clenched and skidded along the ice on the shoulder of the road. Even now, as the semi rumbled to a stop fifty yards to his right, Nico relished the belches, shrieks, and hisses of the outside world. He'd been locked away too long.

Tucking his sign under his armpit, he strolled to the side of the main cab just as the door to the passenger side flew open, and a faint light within the cab poured outward. "God bless you for stopping," Nico called out. In his pocket, he fingered the trigger of his gun. Just in case.

"Where you need to get at?" a man with a blond mustache and beard asked.

"Florida," Nico replied, mentally replaying Revelation 13:1. *And I stood upon the sand of the sea, and saw a beast.* It was all coming together. Heed the Book. Finish God's will. Finish Wes, and in his blood, he'd find the Beast. "Palm Beach, to be exact."

"Sick of the cold, eh? Tallahassee good enough?"

Nico didn't say a word as he stared up at the olive wood rosary and silver cross that dangled from the man's rearview. "That'd be perfect," Nico said. Reaching for the grab handle, he tugged himself up into the main cab.

With a lurch and a few more belches from the transmission, the oversize flatbed grumbled back onto I-95.

"So you got family down in Florida?" the driver asked, shifting into gear.

"Naw . . ." Nico said, his eyes still on the wooden cross as it swayed like a child's swing. "Just going to see an old friend."

34

"What're you talking about?" I ask anxiously.

"Your name, Wes. It was on the—"

"When'd he break out?"

"That's the point. We think he had—"

"A-Are you looking for him? Is he gone, or— Are you sure he's gone?" A needle of bile stabs my stomach, making me want to bend over in pain. It took me seven months of therapy before I could hear Nico's name and not feel puddles of sweat fill my palms and soak my feet. It was another year and a half before I could sleep through the night without him jarring me awake as he lurked in the periphery of my dreams. Nico Hadrian didn't take my life. But he took the life I was living. And now . . . with this . . . with him out . . . he could easily take the rest. "Doesn't he have guards?" I ask. "How could they . . . how could this happen?"

O'Shea lets the questions bounce off his chest, never losing sight of his own investigation. "Your name, Wes. It was on the hospital sign-in sheet," he insists. "According to their records, you were there."

"Where? Washington? You saw me here on the beach this morning!"

"I saw you leave the Four Seasons at almost nine-thirty. According to the receptionist in your office, you didn't return to work until after three. That's a long time to be gone."

"I was with my fr—my lawyer all morning. He'll tell you. Call him right now: Andrew Rogozinski."

Micah laughs softly. "And I assume the fact he's also your high school pal and current roommate means he'd never lie to protect you? You were gone for almost six hours, Wes. That's more than enough time to—"

"To what? To jump on my private jet, fly two and a half hours to Washington, go free Nico—who, oh yeah, once tried to *kill me*—and then fly back to work, hoping no one noticed I was gone? Yeah, that sounds like a genius plan. Go see the one guy I still have nightmares about, be dumb enough to use my real name on the sign-in sheet, and let him loose so he can hunt me down."

"Who says he's hunting you?" O'Shea challenges.

"What're you talking about?"

"Enough with the idiot act, Wes. You know Nico's just a bullet. Even back then, someone else pulled the trigger."

"Someone else? What does that—?"

"You speak to Boyle today?" O'Shea interrupts.

I try to bite my top lip, momentarily forgetting the nerve damage that makes it impossible.

"We're not here to hurt you, Wes. Just be honest with us: Are you chasing him or helping him?" Micah adds. He grabs a nearby mop, tossing its handle from one hand to the other, then back again, like the tick-tock of a metronome.

"You know I didn't free Nico," I tell them.

"That wasn't the question."

"And I haven't spoken to Boyle," I shoot back.

"You're sure about that?" O'Shea asks.

"I just told you—"

"Did you speak to him or not? I'm asking you as an officer in an ongoing investigation."

Micah's mop ticks back and forth. They're acting like they know the answer, but if they did, I'd be in handcuffs right now instead of trapped in a supply closet. I look them dead in the eyes. "No."

O'Shea shakes his head. "At noon today, an unidentified male came into St. Elizabeths requesting a private visit with Nico by identifying himself as a member of the Secret Service, complete with a badge and picture ID, both of which you have access to. Now, I'm willing to accept that only a moron would use his own name, and I'm also willing to keep your name from the press—for no other reason than out of respect for your boss—but in a situation you claim to know nothing about, it's sorta fascinating that yours is the only name that keeps popping up outta the daisy patch."

"What's your point?"

"My point is, when you're in Malaysia, Boyle's there . . . when your name's on a sign-in sheet in Washington, Nico escapes. This isn't exactly Morse code. You tracking the trend?"

"I didn't go to Washington!"

"And you didn't see a dead man in Malaysia. And you didn't get sent backstage by the President, who wanted you to pick up the message from Boyle, right? Or was that just something we invented to make ourselves feel better—y'know, kinda like your old door-locking and light-switch-on-and-off obsessions? Or better yet, the repetitive praying that—"

"Just because I saw a counselor—"

"*Counselor?* It was a shrink."

"He was a critical incident specialist . . ."

"I looked it up, Wes. He was a clinical psychologist who had you medicated for the better part of a year. Alprazolam for the anxiety disorders, coupled with some heavy-duty olanzapine for all the compulsions. That's an antipsychotic. Plus his notes, which said that in a strange way, he thought you actually relished your scars—that you saw the pain as atonement for putting Boyle in that limo. Doesn't say much about the shape you were in."

"The guy blew my friggin' face off!"

"Which is why you've got the best motive and the worst alibis—especially in Malaysia. Do me a favor—for the next few days, unless you're traveling with the President, stay put for a bit. At least until we figure out what's going on."

"What, so now I'm under house arrest? You can't do that."

"Wes, I've got a homicidal paranoid schizophrenic on the loose, who, two hours from now, will feel a brand-new tingling on the right side of his brain as the drugs that help manage his psychosis slowly wear off. He already shot two orderlies and a security guard—all three in their hearts and, like Boyle, with stigmata through their hands—and that's when he was *on* medication. So not only can I do whatever the hell I want, I'm telling you right now, if you try to take another little jaunt out of town, and I find out you have *any* involvement with this case—trying to contact Boyle, or Nico, or even the guy who was selling popcorn in the stands at the speedway that day—I will slap you with obstruction of justice charges and rip you apart faster than that nutbag ever did."

"That is, unless you want to tell us what message

Boyle was bringing the President in Malaysia," Micah offers, the mop-handle metronome smacking into his left palm. "C'mon, Wes—they were clearly trying to meet that night—and trying to maintain all the dirt they thought they'd covered up. You're with him every day now. All we want to know is when they're meeting again."

Like before—like any FBI agents trying to make a name for themselves—all they really want is Manning, who no doubt had a major hand in helping Boyle hide and lie to the entire country. I rat on him, and they'll happily let me out of the mousetrap. The problem is, I don't even know what I'm ratting about. And even when I try scraping deeper . . . Back at the beach, they mentioned Boyle's ability to work people's weaknesses. Fine, so what were Manning's weaknesses? Something from their past? Or maybe that's where The Roman and The Three came in. Whatever the reason, I'm not finding it out unless I buy some time.

"Let me just . . . let me think about it for a bit, okay?" I ask.

O'Shea nods, knowing he's made his point.

I turn to leave the closet but stop short at the door. "What about Nico? Any idea where he's heading?" I add, feeling my fingers start to shake. I shove them into my pants pockets before anyone notices.

O'Shea studies me carefully. This is the easiest moment for him to be a prick. He readjusts his U.S. Open baseball cap. "D.C. Police found his clothes in a Laundromat about a mile away from St. Elizabeths. According to his doctors, Nico hasn't talked about Manning in years, but the Service is still adding double duty just to be safe."

I nod but still don't take my hands out of my pockets. "Thanks."

Micah's about to give me some good cop, but O'Shea puts a hand on his chest, cutting him off. "You're not alone, Wes," O'Shea adds. "Not unless you want to be."

It's a perfect offer presented in the kindest way. But that doesn't make it any less of a tactic. Tattling to the FBI . . . taking on Manning . . . all start a domino game that eventually sends me falling. From here on in, the only safe way out of this mess is finding the truth and wrapping myself in it. That's the only bulletproof vest that works.

In my pocket, my phone begins to vibrate. I pull it out and spot Lisbeth's name on the caller ID. Good-bye rock, hello hard place. "It's my mother," I tell O'Shea. "I should go. She probably heard about Nico on the news."

"Be careful what you say," Micah calls out.

No doubt about that. Still, it's a simple choice. Going with the FBI means they'll ram me at Manning. But before I put the knife in Caesar's back, I need to make sure I have the right target. At least with Lisbeth, I'll buy that time to figure out what's really going on.

"Think about it, Wes. You're not alone," O'Shea calls back as I duck out of the closet. Back in the hallway, I wait until the third ring just to make sure I'm out of earshot.

"Wes here," I answer.

"Where are you?" Lisbeth asks. "You okay? Did they tell you Nico—?"

"Just listen," I interrupt. "What you said earlier about finding stuff out for us . . . were you serious?"

There's a slight pause on the other line. "More serious than a Pulitzer."

"You sure? I mean, if you put yourself in this— You sure you're ready to put yourself in this?"

Now the silence lasts even longer. This isn't some

fifty-word favor about the First Lady's new dress. However they did this—Boyle, Manning, the Secret Service—you don't pull this off without help from people at the highest levels of government and law enforcement. That's the fight she's picking. Even worse, when the word gets out, they'll be using all that power to make us look like lunatics who saw a ghost. And the worm in the apple is, with Boyle alive, Nico has the best reason of all to come back here and finish his original job.

At the end of the hallway, I ram my hip into the metal latch of the door, which opens to the empty lobby of the theater. A rumble of laughter echoes from the auditorium. The Secret Service may've swarmed the back rooms, but from the sound of it, the President's still killing onstage. On my right, a woman with white hair sells a four-dollar bottle of water to a man in a pin-striped suit. A set of two other Secret Service agents rushes through the lobby on a standard sweep. But what catches my eye is the slightly overweight redhead standing outside the theater, just beyond the tall plate-glass doors. Her back's to me, and as she paces slightly in the cottony moonlight and presses her phone to her ear, Lisbeth has no idea I'm there.

"This is why I became a reporter, Wes," she says through the phone, her voice strong as ever. "I've waited my whole life for this."

"And that's a nice speech," I tell her, still watching from behind. "But you do know who you're messing with, right?"

She stops pacing and takes a seat on the edge of one of the half dozen concrete planters that serve as a barrier against any sort of vehicular attack on the Kravis Center. When Manning moved to town, they went up all over. But as Lisbeth scootches back, her body practically sags into it. She can barely keep her head up as her chin sinks down, kissing her neck. Her right hand still holds the phone, but her left slithers like a snake around her own waist, cradling herself. The concrete planters are built to withstand an impact from an almost five-thousand-pound pickup truck traveling over forty-five miles per hour. But that doesn't mean they offer any protection against the sickening recognition of your own self-doubt.

Lisbeth said she'd been waiting her whole life for this. I believe her. But as she looks out at the crush of Secret Service black sedans, their flashing red lights spraying crimson shadow puppets across the facade of the building, it's clear she's wondering if she has what it takes to make it happen. She sinks slightly as her arms cradle her waist even tighter. There's nothing more depressing than when aspirations get guillotined by limitations.

Standing alone in the lobby, I don't say a word. Eight years ago, Nico Hadrian served me my own limits on a public platter. So as I watch Lisbeth sink lower, I know exactly how she—

"I'm in," she blurts.

"Lisbeth—"

"I'll do it . . . I'm in. Count me in," she demands, her shoulders bolting upright. Hopping off the planter, she looks around. "Where are you anyw—?" She cuts herself off as our eyes lock through the glass.

My instinct is to turn away. She comes marching toward me, already excited. Her red hair fans out behind her. "Don't say no, Wes. I can help you. I really can."

I don't even bother to argue.

35

St. Pauls, North Carolina

Nico told himself not to ask about the maps. Don't ask for them, don't talk about them, don't bring them up. But as he sat Indian-style in the cab of the flatbed truck . . . as the olive wood rosary beads swayed from the rearview mirror . . . he couldn't help but notice the frayed edge of paper peeking out from the closed glove compartment. Like the crosses he saw in every passing telephone pole and lamppost that lined the darkness of the highway, some things were better left unsaid.

Focusing his attention through the front windshield, he watched as the highway's bright yellow dividing lines were sucked one by one beneath the truck's tires.

"You don't have any maps, do you?" Nico asked.

In the driver's seat next to him, Edmund Waylon, a rail-thin man hunched like a parenthesis, gripped the wide steering wheel with his palms facing upward. "Check the glove box," Edmund said as he licked the salt of his sour cream and onion potato chips from the tips of his blond mustache.

Ignoring the scratch of Edmund's fingernails against the black rubber steering wheel, Nico popped open the glove box. Inside was a pack of tissues, four uncapped pens, a mini-flashlight, and—tucked between a thick manual for the truck and an uneven stack of napkins from fast-food restaurants—a dog-eared map.

Twisting it around as it tumbled open like a damaged accordion, Nico saw the word *Michigan* printed in the legend box. "Any others?" he asked, clearly disappointed.

"Might be some more in the doghouse," Edmund said, pointing to the plastic console between his seat and Nico's. "So you were saying about your momma . . . she passed when you were little?"

"When I was ten." Studying the truck's swaying rosary to bury the image, Nico leaned left in his seat and ran his hand down past the cup holders, to the mesh netting attached to the back of the console. Feeling the tickle of paper, he pulled at least a dozen different maps from the netting.

"Man, losing your momma at ten . . . that'll mess you up good. What about your daddy?" Edmund asked. "He passed too?"

"Everyone but my sister," Nico replied, flipping through the stack of maps. North Carolina, Massachusetts, Maine . . . It'd been almost twelve hours since he last had his medication. He never felt better in his life.

"Can't even imagine it," Edmund said, eyes still on the road. "My daddy's a sombitch—used to smack all of us . . . my sisters too . . . fist closed, knuckles right across the nose—but the day we have to put him in the ground . . . when a man loses his daddy, it cracks him in two."

Nico didn't bother to answer. Georgia, Louisiana, Tennessee, Indiana . . .

"Whatcha looking for anyway?" Edmund asked with a quick lick of his mustache.

Don't tell him Washington, Nico insisted.

"Washington," Nico said, shuffling the maps into a clean pile.

"Which—state or D.C.?"

Tell him state. *If he hears otherwise . . . if he sees the proof of the Masons' sin . . . and their nest . . . The last hour approaches. The Beast is already loosed—communicating, corrupting Wes.*

"State," Nico said as he reached around the console, tucking the maps back into the mesh netting. "Washington State."

"Yeah, now you're outta my range. I'm all Northeast corridor and east of Mississippi." Covering his mustache with his palm and hooking his nose in the groove between his thumb and pointer finger, Edmund slid his hand down, unsuccessfully trying to contain a long-overdue yawn. "Sorry," he apologized, violently shaking his head to stay awake.

Nico glanced at the football-shaped digital clock glued to the dashboard. It was almost two in the morning.

"Listen, if you still need one of them maps," Edmund said, "right as we pass I-20 in Florence, there's one of those Circle 'n Stations with the big magazine sections—they got maps, travel guides, I swear I might've even seen an atlas or two. If you want, we can make it our next stop."

Nico asked the voices what they thought. They couldn't be more excited.

"Edmund, you're a fine Christian," Nico said, staring out at a passing telephone pole. "Your rewards will be bountiful in the end."

36

As I pull into the parking lot at the back of my apartment building, I feel my phone vibrate and look down at caller ID. Crap. *New York Times.*

Surprised it took them this long, I push the *Send* button and brace myself. "Wes here."

"Hey, Wes—Caleb Cohen. From the *Times*," he announces with the forced familiarity of every reporter. Caleb used to cover Manning during White House days, meaning he called every day. But these days, we're in the former-President rotation, which is barely a notch above second cousin once removed. Until right now.

"You have a statement on the escape yet?" Caleb asks.

"You know we never comment on Nico," I tell him, following years of protocol. Last thing we need is to let some runaway quote rile up the mad dog.

"No, I don't mean from Manning," Caleb interrupts. "I mean from you. You're the one with the scars. Aren't you worried he's out there, ready to hit you with something harder than a ricochet?"

He says it to get a rise, hoping I'll blurt a quick

response. That worked once, with *Newsweek*, right after the accident. I'm not twenty-three anymore.

"Nice talking to you, Caleb. And if you want to talk again, don't print a *no comment* from us either. Just say we couldn't be reached."

I slam the phone shut, but as Caleb disappears, I'm swallowed by the haunting silence of the open-air parking lot, which is tucked just behind my apartment building. It's almost midnight on a Thursday. At least fifty cars surround me, but no one's in sight. Squeezing between two matching Hondas, I push the *Door Lock* button on my key ring just to hear the noise. It fades far too fast, leaving me alone with the reality of Caleb's question: If Nico's out there, what's preventing him from coming back to finish the job?

Glancing around the empty parking lot, I don't have an answer. But as I study the tall, slender shadows between the twelve-foot shrubs that surround the lot, I suddenly can't shake that awkward, stomach-piercing anxiety that I'm no longer alone. Ignoring the skeleton arms of overgrown branches, I scan the darkness between the tall shrubs, holding my breath to listen even closer. My only reward is the droning buzz of crickets who fight for dominance against the hum of the lot's overhead lampposts. Catching my breath, I take a few steps.

That's when I hear the tiny metal jingling. Like coins rattling in a pocket. Or someone hitting a chain-link fence. I turn around slightly, scanning between the branches and spotting the fence that surrounds the parking lot and runs behind the hedges.

Time to get inside. Spinning back toward the building, I speed-walk toward the yellow-striped awning that juts out over the back entrance. On my far left, the crickets fall silent. There's a rustling by the group of hedges that blocks the view to the pool area. Just the wind, I tell myself as I pick up my pace and move even faster toward the awning, which seems almost submerged in darkness.

Behind me, the rustling from the hedges gets louder. *Please, God, just let me—*

My phone vibrates in my hand as caller ID shows me a 334 prefix. *Washington Post.* Last year, Manning, like LBJ before him, had a secret actuarial done to see how long he'd live. The way things are going, I can't help but wonder the same about myself. And while I'm tempted to pick it up just to have some sort of audio witness, the last thing I need right now is another reminder that Nico's out there, waiting.

Shifting from speed walk to jog, I fumble through my shoulder bag and search for my house keys. I glance over my shoulder as the leaves continue to shake. Forget it. I go to full-fledged sprint. Under the awning, my feet slide against the blacktop. I ram the key into the lock and twist to the right. The metal door clicks open, and I slip inside, colliding with the shopping cart that people use to move their groceries. My knee slams into the corner of the cart, and I shove it out of the way, hobbling up the narrow beige hallway and into one of the lobby's waiting elevators.

Crashing against the brown Formica walls of the elevator, I jab the button for the fifth floor and smash the *Door Close* button like a punching bag. The elevator door's still open. In the hallway, a broken fluorescent light sizzles at half-power, adding a yellow, mucusy pallor to the floor and walls. I close my eyes for some quick calm, but as I open them, the world goes black-and-white, my own personal newsreel. In the distance, a woman screams in C minor as Boyle's ambulance doors bite shut. *No, that's not* . . . I blink again and I'm back. *There's no one screaming.* As the door eventually rumbles shut, I touch my ear as my hand shakes uncontrollably. *C'mon, Wes . . . hold it together . . .*

Pressing my back into the corner to keep myself upright, I grit my teeth to slow my breathing. The elevator rises with a lurch, and I focus on the indicator lights. Second floor . . . third floor . . .

By the time I step out on the fifth floor, beads of sweat ski down across my rib cage. Leaving nothing to chance, I check the left side of the hallway before darting out and heading right.

I run for apartment 527, ram my key in the lock, and twist the knob as fast as I can. Inside, I flick on every light I can find . . . the entryway . . . the living room . . . the lamp on the end table . . . I even double back to do the hall closet. No . . . better to leave it off. I flick it on, then off. On, then off. On, then off. *Stop* . . . Stepping backward and crashing into the wall, I shut my eyes, lower my head, and whisper to myself. "Thank you, God, for keeping my family safe . . ." *Stop* . . . "For keeping me safe, and the President safe . . ." *Find a focal point*, I tell myself, hearing the counselor's voice in my head. ". . . for me and . . ." *Find a focal point.*

Pounding myself in the ear, I stumble around, almost tripping over the ottoman from my parents' old leather sectional sofa in the living room. *Find her.* Sprinting up the hallway that leads to the back half of the apartment, I run past the flea market picnic bench we put in our dining room, past Rogo's room with the stack of unread newspapers outside the door, past the hallway's life-size cutout of President Manning with a hand-drawn word balloon on his head that says *I don't remember how to drive, but I lovey that downwithtickets.com!* and eventually make a sharp right into my bedroom.

Tripping over a pile of dress shirts on the floor, I race for the square metal birdcage that sits atop my dresser. As the door slams into the wall, Lolo pulls back, wildly flapping her beige wings and bobbing her yellow head from side to side. Watching her reaction, I catch myself and quickly find my calm. Lolo does the same, lowering her wings and grinding her beak. Her head sways slowly as I catch my breath. Just seeing her, just the sight . . .

"Hi, Melissa—whattya doin'?" my cinnamon cockatiel asks. She's got a bright orange circle on each cheek and a pointy yellow crest on her head that curves forward like a feathery tidal wave. "Melissa, whattya doin'?"

The joke's too old to make me laugh—Lolo's been calling me by her old owner's name for almost seven years—but the counselor was right. Focal points are good. Though familiar voices are even better.

"Crap away," I tell Lolo, who for some reason was trained to poop on command.

True to form, three tiny runny droppings splatter through the bottom of the cage onto the waiting newsprint, which I quickly replace, along with fresh food and water.

The bird was my dad's idea. It was six months after the accident, when light switches and repetitive prayers were starting to overwhelm me. He'd heard the story from one of his students about a rape victim whose parents bought her a dog so she wouldn't feel alone when she came home every night. I rolled my eyes. And not just because I'm allergic to dogs.

Still, people never understand. It was never just the bird. It was the need. The need to be needed.

With a quick flick of the lock, I open the cage and offer my left pointer finger as a perch. Lolo hops on immediately, riding it up to her usual spot on my right shoulder. I turn my face toward her, and she tries to bite at my cheek, which means she wants to be scratched. I crouch down to my tan-carpeted floor and cross my legs into Indian position as the stress of the day starts to wash away. Lolo nuzzles in close, her feathers tenderly tickling the grooves of my face. For all their vaunted eyesight, birds don't see scars.

Her talons loosen their grip on my shoulder, and she lowers her crest, slicking it back Elvis-style. Within a minute, she's already calmed down, and on most nights, that'd be enough to get me to do the same. But not tonight.

In my pocket, my cell phone vibrates. As I check caller ID, I also see that I got two new messages just during the ride in the elevator. Scrolling down, I see all the old numbers. Current call is *L.A. Times.* Messages are CNN and Fox News. My answering machine at home is no better. Nineteen new messages. Family, friends, and the few reporters smart enough to track my home address. They all want the same thing. A piece of the action . . . piece of the story . . . piece of me.

The front door to the apartment swings open down the hall. "Wes, you still up?" Rogo calls out. His voice grows louder as he turns the corner. "Your light's on, so if you're touching yourself, now's the time to stop!"

Lolo's talons dig deep into my shoulder. I know exactly how she feels. The last thing I need is another person reminding me about Nico and Manning and Boyle and every other time bomb ticking in my life. *How you doing? How you feeling? How you holding up?* Enough with the damn—

My bedroom door opens slowly. Rogo's been around long enough to know if he kicks it in, it'll send Lolo flapping.

I look up from the carpet, just waiting for the onslaught of questions.

Rogo scratches at his bald head and leans his meatball physique against the door frame. "So . . . uh, I rented *Purple Rain*," he says, pulling the movie from the red knapsack he calls his briefcase. "Figured we could . . . I don't know . . . order some pizza, maybe just hang—and then, of course, spend some time rewinding the part where Apollonia jumps naked into the river."

I sit there for a moment, digesting the offer.

"Hi, Melissa—whattya doin'?" Lolo squawks.

"Shut up, bird. I ain't talking to you," Rogo threatens.

A tiny smile lifts my left cheek. "Apollonia gets naked? You sure?" I ask.

"Wes, when I was sixteen, I wanted my first car to be a purple motorcycle. Now, who's ready for some bad pizza and Prince doing that pouty thing with his lips? C'mon, Melissa, time to party like it's 1999!"

He runs back up the hallway before I can even say thank you.

37

Florence, South Carolina

Nico knew they'd have them.

"Maps?" Nico asked, stepping into the gas station minimart and holding up the map of Michigan he took from Edmund's truck.

"Back left," a ponytailed attendant with peach-fuzz sideburns said without looking up from the small TV he was watching behind the counter.

Before Nico could even take a step, a loud chime rang from where he crossed into the electric eye of the automated doorbell. Wincing at the sound, he still wasn't used to being out in public. But the way his heart was jackhammering with excitement, it didn't slow him down.

Counting three surveillance cameras—one by the attendant, two in the aisles—Nico hit the brakes and eased his pace to a walk as he headed for the spinner rack of maps in the back. It was no different from his old assignments: No need to rush. Don't look around. Disappear in the mundane.

He read most of the maps from halfway down the aisle. California, Colorado, Connecticut, Delaware . . .

It was a good sign. But not half as good as stepping in and seeing that the central spine of the spinner rack was made up of dozens of intersecting metal crosses. Exhaling with relief, Nico practically laughed out loud. Of course his map would be here. Just like with Wes. As in the Book, God's will was always clear.

Tucking his Michigan map under his armpit, he gave the spinner rack a confident whirl, going straight to the end. Sure enough. Second from the top. Right between Washington State and West Virginia. Washington, D.C.

Lightning bolts of adrenaline surged up Nico's legs. He covered his mouth as his eyes flooded with tears of joy. Even though he never doubted . . . to finally see it after being denied for so long. *The nest . . . the devil's nest . . . the M Men buried it so long ago. And now the proof was back.* "Thank you, Father," Nico whispered.

Without even hesitating, he pulled the D.C. map from its metal tower, replacing it with the Michigan map he'd brought from the truck. Fair trade.

Wiping his eyes with the heel of his palm, he took a moment to catch his breath. Slowly heading back for the door, he tipped his baseball cap at the attendant. "Thanks for the help."

As the ding-dong of the automated chime sounded, the attendant nodded without even looking up.

Outside, a deep gulp of the crisp South Carolina air chilled Nico's lungs, but it didn't come close to cooling the rising thrill bubbling inside his chest. Seeing Edmund pumping gas at the back of the flatbed, Nico darted for the front. As he ducked into the narrow gap between the front grille of Edmund's truck and the back bumper of the truck in front of them, Nico blinked a fresh set of tears from his eyes. For eight years at St. Elizabeths, it was the one thing he never spoke of. The one truth they'd never understand. Sure, they figured out the crosses through observation, and the whispering to himself that he used to do in the early years. But this . . . like Number Three taught . . . Some secrets weren't meant to be shared. And when it came to the nest . . .

Open it! he insisted, nodding to himself.

Like a child sneaking a cookie from the jar, Nico kept his shoulders pitched as he studied the front page of the map. Closing his eyes, he took one last scan of the area: the metal clicking of the truck's idle engines . . . the garden hose hiss from the pumps . . . even the chalky scratch of claws against concrete as a raccoon prowled toward the dumpster around back.

"Thank you, Father," Nico whispered, keeping his eyes shut as he tugged the map open and let it unfold in front of him. His head bobbed up and down sixteen times as he mouthed his final prayer. *Amen.*

His eyes sprang open, staring straight at the familiar blue and black grid of the D.C. streets. Orienting himself on the wide-open patches of the Tidal Basin and National Mall, he quickly found the marker for the Washington Monument. From there, he traced a path up to Dupont Circle, where—

"D.C?" Edmund asked, resting a hand on Nico's shoulder and peeking over at the map. "I thought you wanted Washington *State*?"

Refusing to turn around, Nico stood up straight as his legs, arms, and whole body stiffened. If it weren't for his sniper training, his hands would've been shaking. Still, he felt the bad vein between his eyebrows. The vein that swelled, pregnant and full, when they took away his violin . . . when his father told him his mother was gone . . . when The Three told him the truth.

Just to keep himself steady, he clenched his toes into tiny fists that gripped the earth right through his shoes. The vein still throbbed. Pulsating even faster. Picking up speed. *Father, please don't let it burst* . . . And then . . . as Nico clamped his lips shut and held his breath and focused everything he had on the web of veins swelling against his sinuses, it all went away.

Turning just his head, Nico slowly peered over his own shoulder at Edmund.

"Whoa . . . y'okay?" Edmund asked, stepping back slightly and pointing at Nico's face. "Your nose . . . it's bleedin' like a bitch, bro."

"I know," Nico said, dropping the map as he reached out and palmed Edmund's shoulder. "Blood of our savior."

38

Reagan National Airport
Washington, D.C.

"And you're all set, Mr. Benoit," the airline attendant said at the boarding gate.

"Great," The Roman replied, careful to keep his head tilted down to the left. He didn't have to hide. Or use the fake name. Indeed, the one benefit of Nico's escape was that it gave The Roman the perfect excuse to justify his trip down South. As deputy assistant director, that was his job. Still, he kept his head down. He knew where the cameras were hidden. No need to tell anyone he was coming.

After heading toward the plate-glass window behind the check-in desk and sitting at the far end of a long row of seats, The Roman dialed a number on his phone, ignored the chitchatting of his fellow passengers, and focused on the black, predawn sky.

"D-Do you have any idea what time it is?" a groggy voice begged, picking up the other line.

"Almost six," The Roman replied, staring outside. It was still too early to see slivers of orange cracking through the horizon as prologue to the sun's arrival. But that didn't mean he had to sit in the dark.

"Did you get the new schedule yet?" The Roman asked.

"I told you last night, with Nico running around, Manning's entire day is in flux . . . you of all people should know that."

Staring at his own reflection in the glass, The Roman nodded. Behind him, an armed agent in a *Security* windbreaker weaved through the food court, scanning the crowd. Back by the metal detectors when he first came in, he'd counted three more agents doing the same—and that didn't include the dozen or so who operated in plainclothes to stay out of sight. The FBI wanted Nico back—and in their minds, the best way to get him was to cover every airport, train station, and travel hub. It was a good plan, following years of typical FBI procedure. But Nico was far from typical. And at this point, in all likelihood, far from here.

"What about Wes? When does he get his copy of the schedule?" The Roman asked.

"It's not like the White House anymore. No matter how close he is to Manning, he gets it same as the rest of us—first thing in the morning."

"Well, when he does get it—"

"You'll have it," his associate said. "Though I still don't understand why. You already have the microphone f—"

"Send it!" The Roman roared. On his right, a few passengers turned to stare. Refusing to lose it, he shut the phone and calmly slipped it back into the pocket of his overcoat. It wasn't until he unclenched his fist that he saw a tiny dot of blood seeping through the gauze.

39

"A reporter?" Rogo asks in full Southern twang as we weave through morning traffic on Okeechobee Boulevard. "You're sitting on the biggest political scandal since Boss Tweed started Teapot Dome, and you threw it in the lap of a reporter?"

"First, Boss Tweed had nothing to do with Teapot Dome. They were fifty years apart," I tell him. "Second, what happened to all that *Purple Rain* calmness from last night?"

"I was trying to make you feel better! But this . . . You threw it in the lap of a reporter?"

"We didn't have a choice, Rogo. She heard us talking." Just below the glove compartment, his feet barely touch the Yosemite Sam floor mat with the words *Back Off!* in giant white letters. He bought the mat for me for my birthday a few years back as some sort of personal lesson. From the look on his face, he still thinks I need to learn it. "If she wanted, she could've run the story today," I add.

"And this is she? Below the Fold?" he asks, flipping open the newspaper and turning to Lisbeth's column in the Accent section. The headline reads *Still the One—Dr.*

First Lady Outshines All. It opens with a fawning item about Mrs. Manning's chartreuse Narciso Rodriguez suit as well as her gold eagle pin, which Lisbeth calls "Americana elegance." To her credit, she doesn't even go for the snarky mention of Nico's escape.

"See, she's making nice," I point out.

"That's just so you don't notice that she's maneuvering you in front of the bull's-eye. Think for a sec."

"Believe me, I know what Lisbeth wants."

"Yet you're ignoring the fact she'll eventually stop writing about the First Lady's suit and instead be using *your* name to cut to the head of the class. Screw the gossip column, Wes—she'll have the whole front page to herself."

"She can have it right now! Don't you understand? She heard it all last night: Boyle being alive, us not trusting Manning . . . but like me, she knows that if she goes public now, it'll bring a tidal wave of feces crashing down on all of us."

"Actually, it'll just be crashing down on Manning and Boyle. Y'know, the people who, well, *actually caused this*!"

"Are you even listening, Rogo? Whatever happened that day, it was pulled off by some of the most powerful people around, including—according to these FBI guys—the former President of the United States, who's also been like a father to me for nearly a decade . . ."

"Here we go—always afraid to hurt Daddy."

"I'm not afraid to hurt anyone—especially whoever the hell did this to me," I say, pointing to my cheek. "But your solution? You want me—before I even know what's going on—to shout everything from the rooftops and go stick a fistful of dynamite into the dam."

"That's not what I said."

"It *is* what you said. But if I unleash this, Rogo—if I go public—I can't take it back. And you know that the moment I open my mouth, these people—people who were powerful and connected enough to convince millions that their illusion was real—are going to aim all their resources and energy at making me look like the crackpot who swears he saw a dead man. So if the water's gonna be raging, and I'm wrecking every professional relationship in my entire life, I want to be absolutely sure before I blow it all up."

"No doubt," Rogo says calmly. "Which is why if you go with the FBI—"

"I what? Save myself? I have nothing to offer the FBI. They already know Boyle's alive. They only want me so they can get Manning and light the dynamite themselves. At least my way, I'm the one holding the fuse, and we'll get some information, which is more than we got from your so-called law enforcement buddies."

"They're trying their best. They're just . . ."

". . . traffic cops. I understand. And I appreciate you trying. But between The Roman and The Three, we need some actual answers."

"That doesn't mean you have to sacrifice yourself. Lisbeth's still gonna burn you in the end."

Holding tight to the wheel, I pump the gas and speed through a yellow light. The car dips and bounces as we climb up Royal Park Bridge.

"Sixty-nine bucks for the ticket and three points on your license," Rogo warns as the yellow light turns red just above us. "Though I guess that's nothing compared to wrecking your life with an overanxious reporter."

"Rogo, y'know why no one knew who Deep Throat was all those years? Because he controlled the story."

"And that's your grand plan? Be Deep Throat?"

"No, the grand plan is to get all the facts, put my hands around Boyle's throat, and find out why the hell all this actually happened!" I don't motion to my face, but Rogo knows what I'm talking about. It's the one thing he won't argue.

Rogo goes back to reading Lisbeth's column, which ends with a quick mention of Dreidel stopping by. *Old Friends Still Visit*, according to the subhead. It's Lisbeth's way of reminding us that she could've easily gone with the mention of Dreidel's and my breakfast.

"Dreidel was there last night?" Rogo asks. "I thought he had a fundraiser."

"He did. Then he came over to see Manning."

Rogo scratches at his bald head, first on the side, then back behind his ear. I know that scratch. He's silent as the car reaches the peak of the bridge. Three, two, one . . .

"You don't think that's odd?" he asks.

"What, that Dreidel likes to suck up to Manning?"

"No, that on the day after you spot Boyle, Dreidel happens to be in Palm Beach, and happens to get you in trouble with the press, and just *happens* to be raising money in Florida for a congressional race that only matters to people in *Illinois*. That doesn't smell a little stinky feet to you?"

I shake my head as we leave the metal droning of the bridge and glide onto the perfectly paved Royal Palm Way. On both sides of the street, tucked between the towering, immaculate palm trees, are the private banks and investment firms that juggle some of the biggest accounts in the city. "You know how fundraising works," I tell Rogo. "Palm Beach was, is, and will always be the capital of Manningland. If Dreidel wants to cash in on his old connections, here's where he has to come to kiss the rings."

Rogo scratches again at his head. He's tempted to argue, but after seeing the shape I was in last night, he knows he can only push so far. Lost in the silence, he taps a knuckle against the passenger window to the tune of "Hail to the Chief." The only other sound in the car comes from the jingling of the two dangling presidential faces on the lapel pin that's attached to my navy suit jacket.

"Here's hoping you're right," Rogo offers as he stares down at Yosemite Sam. "Because, no offense, pal—but the last thing you need right now is another enemy."

40

What'd she write?" Micah asked, gripping the steering wheel and trying to read the newspaper in O'Shea's lap. Four cars ahead of them, Wes's Toyota chugged back and forth through traffic.

"Some fluffy mention about the First Lady's suit," O'Shea said from the passenger seat, still scanning Lisbeth's column. "Though she did manage to work in a Dreidel mention."

"You think Wes told her what's going on?"

"No idea—though you saw the body language last night. All the hesitations . . . just barely looking her in the eyes. If he hasn't said anything, he's thinking about it." Pointing ahead to the Toyota, O'Shea added, "Not so close—pull back a hair."

"But for him to go to the press," Micah began, hitting the brakes and dropping back a few cars. "He's safer with us."

"Not in his eyes. Don't forget, the kid's been wrecked by the best, and he's somehow still standing. Deep down, he knows how the world works. Until he gets a better bargaining chip, in his mind, he's not safe with anyone."

"See, that's why we should just offer him straight clemency. *Okay, Wes, next time you hear from Boyle, tell him Manning wants to meet with him and give him a time and place. Then call us and we'll take care of the rest.* I know you've got big eyes, O'Shea, but unless we finally put hands on Boyle—"

"I appreciate the concern, Micah—but trust me, we stick with Wes and we'll get our Boyle."

"Not if Wes thinks we're gonna bite back. I'm telling you, forget the vague promises—put a deal on the table."

"No need," O'Shea said, knowing that Micah always went for the easy way out. "Wes knows what we want. And after everything Boyle's so-called death put him through, he wants him more than any of us."

"Not more than me," Micah insisted. "After what him and Manning pulled—"

"Get up there! He's running the red light!"

Micah punched the gas, but it was already too late. With a screech, the car in front of them came to an abrupt halt, forcing them to do the same. In the distance, Wes's Toyota climbed up the bridge and out of sight.

"I told you to—"

"Relax," Micah said. "He's just going to work. Losing him for two minutes isn't gonna kill anyone."

41

Woodbine, Georgia

". . . but that's the problem with hiding a treasure," Nico said as the early morning sun punched through the damp Georgia clouds. "You don't pick the right spot, some stranger's gonna come along and dig it up."

But to say they hid it in a map . . .

"Dammit, Edmund, it's no different than hiding it in a crossword or a—" Cutting himself off, Nico gripped the steering wheel and turned toward his friend in the passenger seat. It was harder than he thought. Trusting people never came easy. But Nico understood the power of the Lord. The power that delivered Edmund to his side. From the rearview mirror, the wooden rosary swayed in a tight circle, like a marble in its last seconds before circling down an open drain. Edmund was sent for a reason. And Nico knew never to ignore the signs. Even if it meant exposing his own weaknesses. "I'm not crazy," Nico said, his voice soft and tender.

I never thought you were. By the way, you sure you're okay driving?

"I'm fine. But just know, if you wanna help, you need to understand that this battle didn't start eight years ago. It started in '91."

1991?

"*1791*," Nico said, watching Edmund's reaction. "The year they drew the battle lines . . . by drawing the city lines," he explained, jabbing a finger against the map that was spread out across the wide dashboard between them.

City lines to what? Washington, D.C.?

"That's what they were designing—the layout for our nation's capital. President George Washington himself picked out a U.S. army major for the job: French-born architect Pierre Charles L'Enfant. And when you look at his early plans . . . it laid the groundwork for everything here today," Nico said, pointing Edmund back toward the map.

So when this French guy designed the city—

"No!" Nico insisted. "Unlock yourself from history's lies. L'Enfant is the one most often credited with the plans, but after being hired by President Washington, a known Freemason, there was one other man who helped sketch the details of the city. *That's* the man who marked the entryway. And used the skills of the Masons to build the devil's door."

Is it someone I know, or some other French guy?

"Unlock yourself, Edmund. Ever hear of Thomas Jefferson?"

42

"ID, please," the burly African-American security guard insists as I step through the glass doors and into the gray marble lobby of our building. Most mornings I pass with nothing more than a wave to Norma, the overweight Hispanic woman who's worked the morning shift for the past three years. Today, Norma's gone. A quick glance at the new guard's hand shows me the beige sleeve-microphone concealed in his fist. The patch on his shoulder reads *Flamingo Security Corp.* But I know Secret Service when I see it.

With Nico loose, no one's taking any chances.

It's no different when I step out of the elevator on the fourth floor. In addition to the regular suit-and-tie agent who stands guard by the flags in our welcoming area, there's an agent outside our bulletproof doors, and a third just outside the President's personal office at the end of the hallway. Still, none of it surprises me half as much as the familiar voice I hear a few doors down as I cut into my own office.

"You're sure it's okay?" the voice asks from our chief of staff's office.

"Absolutely," Claudia promises as they step into the hall. "In fact, if you didn't call—oh, I would've *killed* you. And so would *he*," she says, referring to the President.

She stops short right in front of my door. "Wes, guess who's going to be working out of our office for the next week?" she asks, stepping inside and waving like a magician's assistant toward the door.

"H-Hey, pal," Dreidel says as he enters my office, a thick file folder pressed against his hip.

I clap my hands, pretending to be amused. *What're you doing?* I ask with a glance.

"My firm asked if I could—"

"They didn't *ask*," Claudia jumps in, already seizing control. "They had a last-minute rescheduling on a deposition, and since he was down here, they *told* him to stay. But we can't let him scrounge in some hotel executive center, right? Not when we've got all this office space here."

"It's just for a week," Dreidel says, already reading my reaction.

"Wes, you okay?" Claudia asks. "I figured with all this Nico mess, it'd be nice to have someone familiar to—" She cuts herself off, realizing what she's missed. "Nico. Oh, how could I be so *stupid*? Wes, I'm so sorry . . . I didn't even think that you and Nico—" She steps back, tapping the tight bun in her hair as if she wants to bury herself under it. From there, the pity comes quickly. "How're you holding up? If you need to go home—"

"I'm fine," I insist.

"After all these years, it's just . . . I don't even think of you as—" She doesn't say the word, but I still hear it. *Disabled. Scarred.*

"A *victim*," Dreidel clarifies as Claudia offers a thankful nod.

"Exactly. A victim," she repeats, finding her footing. "That's all I meant. Just that you . . . you're not a victim, Wes. Not now, not ever," she insists as if that makes it so. Like any career politician, she doesn't let the apology linger. "Meanwhile, Dreidel, let me show you the volunteer room in back—it's got a computer, a phone—you'll be set for the week. Wes, just so you know, I talked to the Service this morning, and they said they're not expecting any incidents, so unless we hear otherwise, schedule stays pretty much the same."

"Pretty much?"

"They're keeping him home most of the day—y'know, just to be safe," she says, hoping to soothe. The problem is, the last time Manning altered his schedule was when they thought he had rectal cancer a few years back. Life-or-death. "So forget the PSA taping," she quickly adds, heading for the door. "Though he'll still need you for the Madame Tussaud thing at the house tonight."

Before I can say a word, my phone rings on my desk.

"If it's press . . ." Claudia says.

I shoot her a look.

"Sorry," she offers. "I just, if you saw how many calls I got last night . . ."

"Believe me, I've been saying no all morning," I tell her as she waves and leaves. I let the phone ring, waiting for Dreidel to trail behind her. He stays put.

"Claudia, I'll be there in a sec," he calls out, standing next to me at my desk.

I stare at him in disbelief. "What the hell're you doing here?" I whisper.

He looks back with the same disbelief. "You kidding? I'm helping you."

The phone rings again, and I glance down at caller ID,

which is angled so Dreidel can't read it from his side of the desk. *Presidential Library.*

"Could be the archivist," Dreidel says, leaning forward for a quick glance. "Maybe she got Boyle's papers ready."

The phone rings again.

"What, now you don't want the papers?" he adds.

I roll my eyes but can't ignore the logic. Grabbing the receiver, I answer, "Wes here."

Dreidel makes a beeline for the door, peeking out into the hallway to make sure we're alone.

"Heya there, Wes," a soft voice says through the phone. "Gerald Lang . . . from the curator's office? Wondering if you had a moment to talk about that presidential aide exhibit?"

As Dreidel cranes his neck into the hall, a sudden, fake smile lights up his face. Someone's there.

"Heeey!" he announces, motioning them into my office.

"Dreidel, *don't*!" I hiss, covering the phone. I don't need the circus to—

"Dreidel?" Lang asks on the line, clearly overhearing. "I was just trying to reach him. He was Manning's aide in the White House, no?"

In front of me, Bev and Oren embrace Dreidel in a Mary Tyler Moore group hug. Bev squeezes him so tightly, her fake boobs practically crush the personalized Manning letter she's holding. The prodigal son's returned. But as I watch them celebrate, a hollow pain crawls through my stomach. Not out of jealousy. Or envy. I don't need them to ask me about Nico or how I'm holding up. I don't need more pity. But I do need to know why Dreidel, still in mid-hug, keeps glancing over his shoulder, studying me on the phone. His eyes are tired, the dark moons below them betraying his lack of sleep last night. Whatever kept him up, kept him up late.

"Wes, you there?" Lang asks on the other line.

"Yeah, no—I'm here," I reply, crossing around to the seat side of the desk. "Let me just . . . can I think about it for a bit? With all this Nico mess, we're just running a little crazy."

Hanging up the phone, I look back at my friend. My friend who got me my job. And taught me everything I know. And visited me when . . . when only my parents and Rogo visited. I don't care what Rogo says. If Dreidel's here, it's for a good reason.

With a back pat for Oren and a cheek kiss for Bev, Dreidel sends them on their way and bounces back into my office. Curling one leg under my tush, I take a seat behind my desk and study the smile on his face. No doubt about it. He's here to help.

"So *no* on the archivist, huh?" he asks. "What about Lisbeth? What time we seeing her?" When I don't answer immediately, he adds, "Last night . . . I was there, Wes. You said you were meeting this morning."

"We are, but—"

"Then let's not be stupid." He heads for the door and slams it shut for privacy. "Instead of rushing in like imbeciles, let's make sure we're ready for once." Reading my reaction, he adds, "What? You do want me to come, right?"

"No . . . of course," I stutter, sinking slightly in my seat. "Why wouldn't I want that?"

43

Kingsland, Georgia

T*HE Thomas Jefferson?*

"A trinity—can't you see it?" Nico asked, both hands on the six o'clock position of the steering wheel. Motioning Edmund to the map on the dashboard between them, he added, "Washington, Jefferson, L'Enfant. The original Three."

The original three what?

"The Three, Edmund. From the earliest days, there have always been The Three. The Three who were born to destroy—and today, The Three who're here to save."

So The Three are chasing The Three—sorta like a circle . . .

"Exactly! Exactly a circle," Nico said, already excited as he reached up to the sun visor above his seat and pulled out a pen. "That's how they picked the symbol!" Holding the steering wheel and leaning over toward the dashboard, Nico sketched furiously on the corner of the map.

A circle with a star?

"Five-pointed star, also known as a pentagram—the most widely used religious symbol in history—vital to every culture, from the Mayans to the Egyptians to the Chinese."

And Washington and Jefferson somehow unearthed this?

"No, no, no—pay attention—Washington was a Freemason . . . Jefferson was rumored to be one too. D'you really think they didn't know what they were doing? This wasn't something they unearthed. This was something they were *taught.* Five points on the star, right? In ancient Greece, five was the number of man. And the number of elements: fire, water, air, earth, and psyche. Even the church used to embrace the pentagram—just look at it—the five wounds of Jesus," Nico said, giving a quick glance to the wood rosary on the rearview. "But when the symbol is inverted—turned upside down— it becomes the opposite of that. A sign embraced by witches, by the occult, and by . . .

. . . the Freemasons.

"You see it, don't you? I knew you would, Edmund! They've been invoking the symbol for centuries—placing it on their buildings . . . above their archways . . . even *here,*" Nico said, jabbing down at the map, his pointer finger stabbing the most well known block of Pennsylvania Avenue.

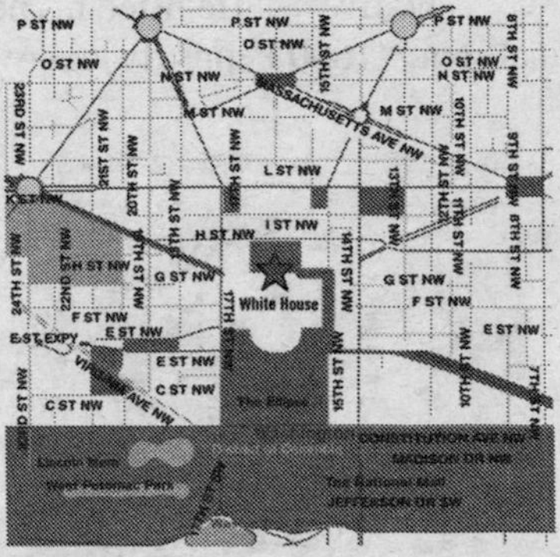

The White House?

"They tried it for centuries all over the world. Fortresses in Spain, castles in Ireland, even in the old stone churches in Chicago. But for the doorway to open, they needed more than just the right symbols and incantations . . .

. . . they needed power.

"Supreme power. That was the lesson of the pyramids and Solomon's Temples—centers of power—to this day, the Freemasons still call Solomon their first grand master! That's why they collected all of history's leaders! The access to power! I knew you'd see it! Praise be all!" Just watching Edmund's reaction, Nico could barely contain himself. "I knew you'd see!"

But . . . how could no one in the White House notice there was a door with a pentagram on it?

"*Door?* Doors can be removed and replaced, Edmund. Even the White House has been burned and renovated. No, for this, the Masons marked something far more permanent . . ." Nico again turned to the map. "Follow the landmarks," he explained, already circling each point on the map. "One—Dupont Circle . . . two—Logan Circle . . . three—Washington Circle . . . four—Mount

Vernon Square . . . and five—" He lifted his pen and jabbed down at the final spot: "1600 Pennsylvania Avenue."

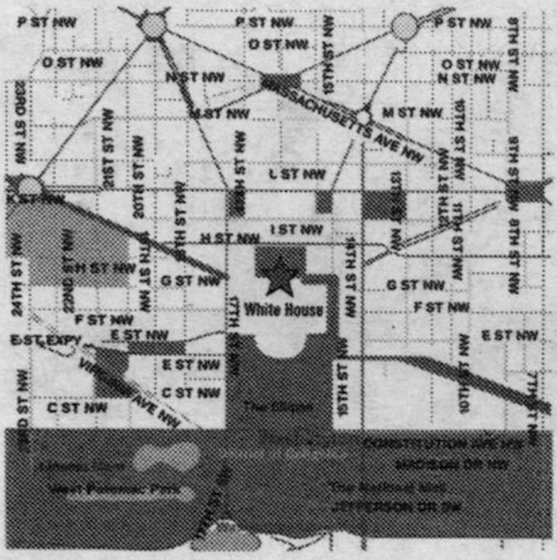

"The building *is* the door. Right in front of us for over two hundred years," he added as he connected the dots. Just as The Three had done for him.

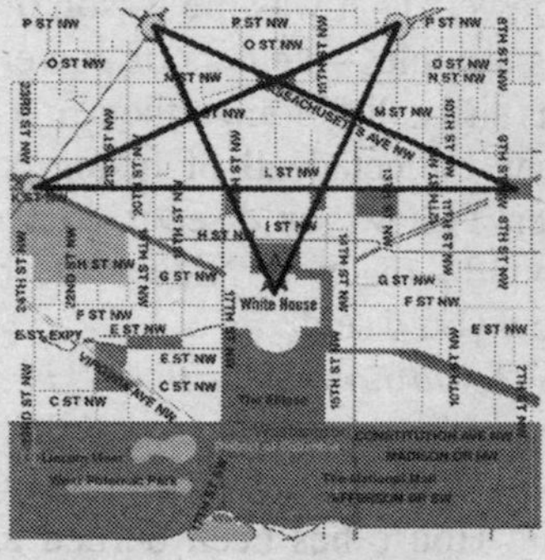

Oh, God.

"God had nothing to do with it, Edmund. Monsters," Nico insisted. "That's who we're fighting. To mark the territory, Jefferson even branded it with their own emblem."

On the edge of the map, Nico again started to draw. To his own surprise, his eyes welled up with each scratch of his pen. It was the one symbol he'd never forget.

Nico, you okay there?

Nico nodded, grinding his teeth and refusing to look back down at the symbol—the compass and the square. *Remember the lessons. No tears. Just victory.* Locked on the road, he gave the coordinates he'd learned all those years ago. "Start at the Capitol and run your finger down Pennsylvania Avenue, all the way to the White House," Nico explained, feeling the pressure building in his skull. *Fight it. Fight the monster back.* "Now do the same from the Capitol down Maryland Avenue—follow it all the way to the Jefferson Memorial—his own shrine! Now go to Union Station and draw a line down Louisiana Avenue, then on the south side of the Capitol, draw another down Washington Avenue. The lines will connect in front of the Capitol . . ."

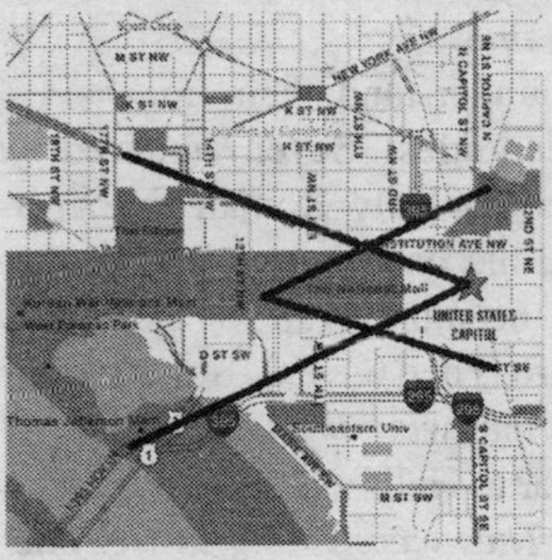

This time, Edmund was silent.

"The compass and the square. The most sacred Masonic symbol . . ."

. . . pointing right to the doorway of the White House . . . all that power in one place. Why would—? What're they doing, trying to take over the world?

"No," Nico said coldly. "They're trying to *destroy* it." Already forgetting the pain in his skull, he added, "Welcome, Edmund—welcome to the truth."

I . . . I can't believe this.

"Those were my words . . . my thoughts too."

But to get this done with no one knowing . . .

"They did it in plain view! On October 13, 1792, Maryland's Masonic Lodge number 9 laid the cornerstone of the White House in a ceremony filled with Freemason rituals. Look it up—it's true! The inscription on the brass plate of that cornerstone says it was laid on the twelfth, but every reputable history book in existence says it was laid on the *thirteenth*!"

Thirteen. The number of the Beast.

"Thirteen blocks north from the White House is where they built the House of the Temple, national headquarters of the Freemasons!"

Thirteen again!

"Now you understand their treachery. They've been waiting for centuries! Seven hundred years ago, we thought it was the Holy Roman Emperor—the one the church labeled the first enemy. But the Masons knew to wait. Wait for the signs. Wait for the true world power to emerge. Prepare. Then the end-times would come!"

So the door they were trying to open . . .

". . . the door to Hell."

Of course! They were trying to free the Creatures . . .

begin the motions! Nico, do you have any idea what you're on to? Scripture predicts it! It begins when the Two Beasts arrive . . .

". . . they come through hosts! First, a disciple—a man of sin . . ."

That's Boyle, right? The man of sin!

"Then the Leader—a man of power . . ."

Manning!

"Through him the Dark One—the true Beast—will arise, creating the most powerful kingdom of all!"

So the Beast they were trying to free . . .

"The Antichrist, Edmund. They want the Antichrist! If it weren't for The Three, he would've come! Tell me you see that! Without The Three, Manning's reelection was imminent! Supreme power in Manning! A man of sin in Boyle! Together, the keys to open the door!"

The original Three dedicated to birthing him—the final Three dedicated to destroying him! Alpha and Omega! Their destiny fulfilled!

"Yes, yes . . . destiny—their fate—just as in scripture! '*Dear children . . . the antichrist is coming. He is now already in the world!*' " Nico screamed as spit flew from his mouth and sprayed the inside windshield.

So the reason you shot Boyle instead of Manning . . .

"In a coliseum of his admirers? Surrounded by his supplicants? *Manning's influence was at its peak!* What if that were the catalyst for his awakening? No—like The Three said . . . better to go with Boyle, who was—was—was— *Don't you see?*" he yelled, pounding the steering wheel. "Without Boyle, there'd be only *one* Beast! *One key instead of two! With only one, the door couldn't open!*" He kept looking to Edmund, then back to the road. His breathing was galloping, his whole body shaking.

Being silent for so long . . . to finally let it out . . . he could barely catch his breath.

"Th-Th-The man of sin—like my father—has always been the sign! Have you not . . . have you not heard of Boyle's sin?" Nico shouted, gasping between breaths as a sudden flush of tears blurred the road in front of him. He hunched forward, gripping the wheel as a dry heave clenched his stomach. "What he did to his own—? And then to my—?" He jabbed a finger at his eyes, digging away the tears. They rolled down his face, dangling like raindrops from his jaw. *Don't fight it,* he told himself. *Be thankful to get it out . . . Heed the Book . . . Thank you, Mother . . . Thank you . . .*

"D-D'ya understand?" he pleaded with Edmund, his voice cracking with the Wisconsin accent he'd buried years ago. "People know nothing, Edmund. Teacher and student. Master and supplicant. Manning and Boyle," he repeated, sinking forward on the steering wheel. "Like father and son. That's why I was chosen. Why my mother was taken. To test me . . . to stop my father . . . to close the devil's door. To keep the door shut and the Great Darkness from coming."

In the passenger seat next to him, Edmund didn't say a word.

"P-Please, Edmund . . . please tell me you understand . . ."

Once again, Edmund was silent. As silent as he'd been for the past five hours when they pulled out of the gas station in South Carolina.

With his seat belt in a diagonal bear hug across his chest, Edmund slumped slightly to the right, his shoulder pressed against the passenger door. His arms dangled at his side, his left wrist bent in his lap.

As the flatbed truck rumbled onto the overpass that ran across St. Marys River, a bump of uneven concrete sent Edmund's head sagging to the right, his forehead thumping lightly into the glass of the passenger window. With each new seam in the asphalt, the flatbed hiccupped. With each hiccup, Edmund's head thumped over and over against the glass.

"I knew you would, Edmund," Nico said excitedly. "Thank you. Thank you for believing . . ."

Thump . . . thump . . . thump. Like a hammer to a stubborn nail, Edmund's head banged the glass. The baritone drumbeat was ruthlessly unavoidable. Nico didn't notice. Just like he didn't notice the slurpy sound of Edmund's bloody fingers sticking and unsticking from the truck's vinyl seats. Or the dried waterfall of blood that'd poured down Edmund's chest from where Nico slit his throat with his car keys.

"I know, but I'm just glad you understand," Nico said, catching his breath and wiping the last of the tears from his eyes. With one final thump, the truck cleared the St. Marys River overpass and officially crossed the state line of Georgia. On the right, they blew past a faded orange and green highway sign. *Welcome to Florida—The Sunshine State.*

44

An hour and a half later, I pull up to the curb in front of First of America Bank, which houses Rogo's offices on the second floor. As my car bucks to a stop, Rogo trudges slowly out the building's front door, heading for the front passenger door. He's still pissed I'm meeting with Lisbeth. But not half as pissed as seeing Dreidel sitting in his seat.

"How's the world of traffic tickets?" Dreidel calls out as he rolls down the window.

"Same as Chicago politics," Rogo replies, shooting me a look as he opens the door for the backseat. "Completely corrupt."

It was no better the first time they met, years ago. Both lawyers, both opinionated, both too stubborn to see anything but the other's flaws.

For the rest of the ride, Rogo sulks in the back as we blow by the past-their-prime mom-and-pop shops that line South Dixie Highway. Every once in a while, he peers out the back to make sure we're not being followed. I use my side mirror for the same.

"There . . ." Dreidel points as if I haven't been here a

dozen times. Hitting the brakes, I make a sharp right into the front lot of our destination: the wide, off-white office building that takes up most of the block. Just in front of the building is a small plaza with a statue of a turtle dressed in a black suit and sunglasses, comically playing an electric keyboard. It's supposed to be funny. None of us laugh.

"Park underneath," Rogo says, pointing to the two-story concrete parking garage that connects to the building. "The fewer people who see us, the better." He glares at me in the rearview. It doesn't take a genius to get the point. It's bad enough I brought us here. It's even worse that I brought Dreidel.

Still, Dreidel doesn't seem to notice Rogo's tantrum. Staring out the window, he's far too focused on the huge brown sign that's partially blocked by the building's faux-cement pillars: *Palm Beach Post.*

"You sure this is smart?" Dreidel asks as the sun disappears, and we wind our way up to the second level of the already dark garage.

"You got a better place?" I challenge.

And that's the point. No matter where we go, it's a cakewalk for anyone to listen in. But here, in the heart of it . . . I don't care how powerful they are—Manning, the FBI, even the Service—none of them can afford to fistfight with the press.

"What's the backup plan for when she screws us?" Rogo asks as we head through the front door of the building and across the lobby's salmon and black marble floor. It's his last-ditch effort to turn us around. Dreidel nods to show he agrees, but he still doesn't slow down. Like me, he's got a personal stake. And based on what I saw in his hotel room, he doesn't want to give Lisbeth another excuse to put his name in bold.

"Cell phones and pagers," a tan guard with silver hair announces as we approach the metal detector and X-ray. I put my shoulder bag on the belt, along with my phone. But as I step through the X-ray, a loud beep echoes through the tall marble canyon.

Feeling myself up, I check for a pen or a—

"Your pin," the guard blurts, pointing to my lapel.

Rolling my eyes and stepping back through the X-ray, I fight my way out of my suit jacket and lay it across the conveyor.

"You should just throw the pin away," Dreidel says, following right behind me. "Those creepy shrunken heads bobbling like that—"

"Hey, fellas," the security guard interrupts, his head cocked sideways as he studies the video monitor for the X-ray. He taps the screen and makes a face. "Think you might wanna take a glance at this . . ."

45

"Ladies and gentlemen, welcome to Palm Beach International Airport," the flight attendant announced through the plane's intercom. "Please remain seated with your seat belts fastened until the aircraft comes to a complete stop and the captain turns off the seat belt sign."

Flicking the metal clasp, The Roman undid his seat belt, reached under the seat in front of him, and pulled out a thick aluminum photographer's briefcase with the Secret Service logo on it. He flexed his thumbs, triggering the clasps that opened the case. From inside, tucked into a gray foam protective shell, he pulled out a small receiver that reminded him of the old transistor radios his grandfather used to collect. Unwrapping a black wire from around the receiver, he inserted the earpiece in his right ear and flicked the *On* switch on the side of the receiver.

"*. . . pin away,*" Dreidel said, his voice far more muffled than before. "*Those creepy shrunken heads bobbling like that—*"

Checking the reception on the square electronic screen, The Roman saw four out of five digital bars. It was no different than a cell phone with a souped-up military battery.

"Hey, fellas," a new voice interrupted. *"Think you might wanna take a glance at this . . . "*

The Roman put a finger in his free ear and turned a dial to raise the volume. All he got was silence.

Up above, a loud chime sounded in the plane as a metal symphony of unfastened seat belts filled the cabin. Sitting perfectly still, The Roman turned up the volume even higher. Still nothing. For a moment, there was some mumbling, but nothing audible.

"What floor?" Rogo asked, coming through loud and clear.

"Second," Wes replied.

"Just do me a favor," Rogo added. *"When dealing with Lisbeth, let's try to be smart about this, okay?"*

Closing his suitcase and following his fellow passengers into the aisle, The Roman nodded to himself. Them being smart was exactly what he planned.

46

Gotta give the boy credit," Micah offered, circling through the parking lot as Wes, Rogo, and Dreidel disappeared inside the *Palm Beach Post* building.

"Who, Wes?" O'Shea asked, watching from the passenger seat of their government-rented Chevy. "Why, because he's running for help?"

"See, that's where you're underestimating. I don't think he's running. Once he steps inside that building, he's zipping himself in a force field he knows we won't pierce."

"Either that or he's running out of options."

"Maybe," Micah said, holding the steering wheel and facing his longtime partner. "But when I was trailing him yesterday morning, every single person he ran into was staring at his face. The valet, the doorman, the guests he passed in the lobby . . . if he can handle that on a daily basis, he can take more punches than you think."

"And that's supposed to impress me?"

"I'm just saying, the immovable object is just as deadly as our unstoppable force."

"Yeah, but the unstoppable force is still the one people're afraid of. And until we catch Boyle's ass, that's the one I'd rather be."

". . . because it's served us so well thus far," Micah said.

"You're missing the point. Even if Boyle knows we're searching . . ."

". . . which he does. He's known for years."

"But what he *doesn't* know is that Wes has suddenly become the best carrot on our stick. Turn—in there," O'Shea added, pointing to the entrance to the two-story parking garage.

Rounding the turn and weaving up to the second level, it didn't take long for them to pull up to Wes's rusted black Toyota. As soon as he saw it, Micah hit the brakes.

"Just pull in back there," O'Shea said, motioning to an open parking spot diagonally across from the Toyota.

Tapping the gas, Micah eased into the spot. Through the back window, the view of Wes's car was perfect.

"We got the carrot," O'Shea said. "When you hold tight to that, the horse'll always follow."

47

Crowding around the small TV monitor of the X-ray, we all stand frozen as the guard points to the screen. The rectangular outline of my lapel pin glows dark gray. Just below it, the two sculpted heads dangle like matching gray tears. But what's far more interesting are the tiny metal pieces—they almost look like shards of shattered glass—glowing bright white at the center of the rectangle.

We're all squinting, struggling to make them out, until the guard hits a button on his keyboard and pulls in on the picture. On-screen, the pieces—a coiled antenna, a miniature microchip, and an even smaller hearing-aid battery—bloom into view.

As always, Rogo's mouth opens first. "Sonofa—"

I pinch his elbow and shoot him a look.

"That's just . . . that's my voice recorder—all digital—y'know, to save good ideas," I whisper, trying to sound like I have a sore throat. "Cool, huh?"

"They make 'em even tinier than those little cassettes," Rogo adds, quickly catching on.

"Here, try it," I bluff to the guard as the conveyor

returns my jacket. Folding it over my arm and shoving it toward him, I hold out the lapel to give him a closer look. He waves me off, satisfied by the offer.

Quickly heading for the elevators, we paint on fake smiles as if everything's perfect. The way Dreidel's eyes are dancing back and forth, he's in full panic. I don't blame him. Whoever's listening knows about what he was doing in that hotel room. But now's not the time. I glance back at the guard, who's still watching us, then down at the metal White House, which is presumably still broadcasting.

Just wait, I say to Dreidel with nothing but an open palm aimed in his direction. His eyes dance even faster. As we step into the waiting elevator, he bites at his manicured thumbnail, unable to contain himself. But just as he's about to whisper a response, Rogo grabs him by the biceps.

"What floor?" Rogo asks, leaning in and motioning upward with his chin. In the corner of the elevator, a security camera stares down at us.

"Second," I reply as casually as possible.

"Just do me a favor," Rogo adds. "When dealing with Lisbeth, let's try to be smart about this, okay?"

No one says another word until the door pings open on the second floor. I make two quick lefts, following the gray carpet down the main hallway. Along the left wall are the closed glass doors and private offices of the paper's top editors. We go straight for the cubicles in back.

"This is stupid," Dreidel whispers as my hand covers the lapel pin. "We should get out of here. Just dump the jacket and abort."

For once, Rogo agrees. "Take it as a sign, Wes. For all we know, she's only gonna make it worse."

"You don't know that," I whisper.

"Hey," Lisbeth calls out, popping her head over the cubicle just as we approach. She reads our reactions instantly. "What's wr—?"

I put a finger to my lips and cut her off. Holding up my jacket, I point to the lapel pin and mouth the word *bug.* "Thanks again for having us over," I add as she pantomimes and points to her own ear.

They can hear us? she asks.

I nod and drape the jacket across the back of her chair.

"Sorry about the air-conditioning," she adds, already one step ahead of us as she grabs a thick file folder from her desk. "If you want, just leave your jackets here . . ." Before we can react, she's out of the cubicle and darting up the hallway, her red hair bouncing and her arms swaying at her sides. The way the sleeves of her crisp white shirt are rolled up to her elbows, I can see the pale freckles that dot most of her forearm. Trailing behind her, Rogo sees them too, but he doesn't say a word. He either hates her or loves her. As always with him, it's hard to tell which.

"I'm Rogo," he says, extending a hand and racing to catch up to her.

"In here," she says, ignoring him and pulling open the door to a sunny conference room with three glass walls, each of them with open vertical blinds. Lisbeth circles the room and, one by one, tugs on the pull cords, snapping the blinds shut. She does the same with the blinds on the plate-glass window that looks out over the front parking lot. Within three seconds, sunlight's replaced by the quiet drone of fluorescents.

"You sure no one can hear us?"

"Editorial board meets here every morning to decide

whose lives they're ripping apart each day. Rumor is, they sweep it for bugs at least once a week."

Unlike Dreidel or Rogo, or even myself, Lisbeth's not the least bit thrown or intimidated. We've been out of fighting shape since the day we left the White House. She picks public battles every day. And she's clearly good at it.

"So who gave you the pin?" Lisbeth asks as we take seats around the large oval conference table.

"Claudia," I stutter, referring to our chief of staff as I accidentally back my chair into the black Formica credenza that runs against the back wall. "It goes to whoever's late . . ."

"You think she's the one that put the mike in there?" Dreidel asks.

"I-I have no idea," I say, replaying yesterday's meeting in my head. Oren . . . Bev . . . even B.B. "It could've been anyone. All they needed was access to it."

"Who was wearing it last?" Lisbeth asks.

"I don't know . . . Bev maybe? Oren never wears it. Maybe B.B.? But by the end of the week, people sometimes just leave it on their desk. I mean, I wouldn't have noticed if someone went into my office and pulled it off my jacket . . ."

"But to squeeze a wireless mike into something so small," Dreidel says. "Doesn't that seem a little high-tech for—no offense, Wes—but for the scrubs on the White House B-team?"

"What's your point?" I ask, ignoring the snobbery.

"Maybe they had help," Dreidel says.

"From who? The Service?"

"Or the FBI," Rogo suggests.

"Or from someone who's good at collecting secrets,"

Lisbeth adds, a bit too enthusiastically. The way her fingertips flick at the edge of her file folder, she's clearly got something to say.

"You got someone who fits the bill?" Dreidel asks skeptically.

"You tell me," she says, flipping open her file folder. "Who wants to hear the real story behind The Roman?"

48

Mostly, it was like the hum of an escalator or the churn of an airport conveyor belt. Soothing at first, then maddening in repetition.

For The Roman, it'd been almost half an hour since he'd heard Wes's scratchy voice echo through the wiretap. If he was lucky, it wouldn't be much longer. But as he picked up his rental car, fought through the airport traffic, and eventually made his way down Southern Boulevard, the wiretap hummed with nothing but emptiness. Every once in a while, as two people passed by Lisbeth's cubicle, he'd pick up the distant buzz of a conversation. Then back to the hum.

Gripping the steering wheel as his white rental car scaled up the Southern Boulevard Bridge, he tried to calm himself with the aquamarine views of the Intracoastal Waterway. As usual, it did the trick, reminding him of the last time he was here: during Manning's final year, casting in Lake Okeechobee, and reeling in nothing smaller than nine-pounders. No question, the bass were bigger in Florida—back in D.C., a six-pounder was considered huge—but that didn't make them any easier to catch. Not unless you were willing to have some patience.

With a glance at his silver briefcase that sat wide-open on the passenger seat, The Roman double-checked the wiretap's signal strength and readjusted his earpiece. After a sharp left on Ocean Boulevard, it wasn't long before he saw the top of the squat, glass office building peeking above the green leaves of the banyan trees that were relocated there to shield it from public view. As he turned left into the main driveway, he knew they'd have security. What he didn't know was that they'd also have two police cars, two unmarked Chevys, and an ambulance right outside the building's entrance. They were definitely starting to panic.

The Roman banked into a nearby parking spot, shut his briefcase, and pulled the earpiece from his ear. Wes was smarter than they'd bargained for. He wouldn't be hearing Wes's voice anytime soon. But that was why he made the trip in the first place. Having patience was fine for catching fish. But the way things were going, some problems required an approach that was more hands-on.

From the bottom of the briefcase, The Roman pulled his 9mm SIG revolver, cocked it once, then slid it into the leather holster inside his black suit jacket. Slamming his car door with a thunderclap, he marched straight for the front entrance of the building.

"Sir, I'll need to see some ID," an officer in a sheriff's uniform called out with a hint of North Florida twang.

The Roman stopped, arcing his head sideways. Touching the tip of his tongue to the dip in his top lip, he reached into his jacket . . .

"Hands where I can—!"

"Easy there," The Roman replied as he pulled out a black eelskin wallet. "We're all on the same side." Flipping open the wallet, he revealed a photo ID and a gold badge with a familiar five-pronged star. "Deputy Assistant Director Egen," The Roman said. "Secret Service."

"Damn, man, why didn't you just say so?" the sheriff asked with a laugh as he refastened the strap for his gun. "I almost put a few in ya."

"No need for that," The Roman said, studying his own wavy reflection as he approached the front glass doors. "Especially on such a beautiful day."

Inside, he approached the sign-in desk and eyed the sculpted bronze bust in the corner of the lobby. He didn't need to read the engraved plaque below it to identify the rest.

Welcome to the offices of Leland F. Manning. Former President of the United States.

49

The Roman's a hero," Lisbeth begins, reading from the narrow reporter's pad that she pulls out of her folder. "Or a self-serving narc, depending on your political affiliation."

"Republican vs. Democrat?" Dreidel asks.

"Worse," Lisbeth clarifies. "Reasonable people vs. ruthless lunatics."

"I don't understand," I tell her.

"The Roman's a C.I.—confidential informant. Last year, the CIA paid him $70,000 for a tip about the whereabouts of two Iranian men trying to build a chemical bomb in Weybridge, just outside of London. Two years ago, they paid him $120,000 to help them track an al-Zarqawi group supposedly smuggling VX gas through Syria. But the real heyday was almost a decade ago, when they paid him regularly—$150,000 a pop—for tips about nearly every terrorist activity hatching inside Sudan. Those were his specialties. Arms sales . . . terrorist whereabouts . . . weapons collection. He knew what the real U.S. currency was."

"I'm not sure I follow," Rogo says.

"Money, soldiers, weapons . . . all the old measuring

sticks for winning a war are gone," Lisbeth adds. "In today's world, the most important thing the military needs—and rarely has—is good, solid, reliable intel. Information is king. And it's the one thing The Roman somehow always had the inside track on."

"Says *who*?" Dreidel asks skeptically. After all his time in the Oval, he knows that a story's only as good as the research behind it.

"One of our old reporters who used to cover the CIA for the *L.A. Times*," Lisbeth shoots back. "Or is that not a prestigious enough paper for you?"

"Wait, so The Roman's on *our* side?" I ask.

Lisbeth shakes her head. "Informants don't take sides—they just dance for the highest bidder."

"So he's a good informant?" I ask.

"*Good* would be the guy who ratted out those Asian terrorists who were targeting Philadelphia a few years back. The Roman's great."

"How great?" Rogo asks.

Lisbeth flips to a new sheet of her notepad. "Great enough to ask for a six-million-dollar payout for a single tip. Though apparently, he didn't get it. CIA eventually said no."

"That's a lot of money," Rogo says, leaning in and reading off her notepad.

"And that's the point," Lisbeth agrees. "The average payout for an informant is small: $10,000 or so. Maybe they'll give you $25,000 to $50,000 if you're really helpful . . . then up to $500,000 if you're giving them specific info about an actual terrorist cell. But six million? Let's put it this way: You better be close enough to know bin Laden's taste in toothpaste. So for The Roman to even demand that kind of cash . . ."

"He must've been sitting on an elephant-sized secret," I say, completing the thought.

"Maybe he tipped them about Boyle being shot," Rogo adds.

"Or whatever it was that led up to it," Lisbeth says. "Apparently, the request was about a year before the shooting."

"But you said the CIA didn't pay it," Dreidel counters.

"They wanted to. But they apparently couldn't clear it with the higher-ups," Lisbeth explains.

"Higher-ups?" I ask. "How higher up?"

Dreidel knows where I'm going. "What, you think Manning denied The Roman's pot of gold?"

"I have no idea," I tell him.

"But it makes sense," Rogo interrupts. "'Cause if someone got in the way of *me* getting a six-million-dollar payday, I'd be grabbing my daddy's shotgun to take a few potshots."

Lisbeth stares him down. "You go to those action movies on opening night, don't you?"

"Can we please stay on track?" I beg, then ask her, "Did your reporter friend say anything else about what the six-million-dollar tip was about?"

"No one knows. He was actually more fascinated with how The Roman kept pulling rabbits out of his hat year after year. Apparently, he'd just appear out of nowhere, drop a bombshell about a terrorist cell in Sudan or a group of captured hostages, then disappear until the next emergency."

"Like Superman," Rogo says.

"Yeah, except Superman doesn't charge you a few hundred grand before he saves your life. Make no mistake, The Roman's heartless. If the CIA didn't meet his price, he was just as happy to walk away and let a hostage get his head sawed off. That's why he got the big cash. He didn't care. And apparently still doesn't."

"Is he still based in Sudan?" I ask.

"No one knows. Some say he might be in the States. Others wonder if he's getting fed directly from inside."

"Y'mean like he's got someone in the CIA?" Rogo asks.

"Or FBI. Or NSA. Or even the Service. They all gather intelligence."

"It happens all the time," Dreidel agrees. "Some midlevel agent gets tired of his midlevel salary and one day decides that instead of typing up a report about Criminal X, he'll pass it along to a so-called informant, who then sells it right back and splits the reward with him."

"Or he makes up a fake identity—maybe calls himself something ridiculous like *The Roman*—and then just sells it back to himself. Now he's getting a huge payday for what he'd otherwise do in the course of his job," I say.

"Either way, The Roman's supposedly dug in so deep, his handlers had to design this whole ridiculous communication system just to get in touch with him. Y'know, like reading every fifth letter in some classified ad . . ."

"Or mixing up the letters in a crossword," Dreidel mutters, suddenly sitting up straight. Turning to me, he adds, "Let me see the puzzle . . ."

From my pants pocket, I pull out the fax of the crossword and flatten it with my palm on the conference table. Dreidel and I lean in from one side. Rogo and Lisbeth lean in from the other. Although they both heard the story last night, this is the first time Rogo and Lisbeth have seen it.

Studying the puzzle, they focus on the filled-in boxes, but don't see anything beyond a bunch of crossword answers and some random doodling in the margins.

"What about those names on the other sheet?" Lisbeth asks, pulling out the page below the crossword and revealing the first page of the fax, with the *Beetle Bailey* and *Blondie* comic strips. Just above Beetle Bailey's head, in the President's handwriting, are the words *Gov. Roche . . . M. Heatson . . . Host—Mary Angel.*

"I looked those up last night," I say. "The puzzle's dated February 25, right at the beginning of the administration. That night, Governor Tom Roche introduced the President at a literacy event in New York. In his opening remarks, Manning thanked the main organizer, Michael Heatson, and his host for the event, a woman named Mary Angel."

"So those names were just a crib sheet?" Lisbeth asks.

"He does it all the time," Dreidel says.

"*All* the time," I agree. "I'll hand him a speech, and as he's up on the dais, he'll jot some quick notes to himself adding a few more people to thank—some big donor he sees in the front row . . . an old friend whose name he just remembered . . . This one just happens to be on the back of a crossword."

"I'm just amazed they save his old puzzles," Lisbeth says.

"That's the thing. They don't," I tell her. "And believe me, we used to save *everything*: scribbled notes on a Post-it . . . an added line for a speech that he jotted on a cocktail napkin. All of that's work product. Crosswords aren't, which is why they're one of the few things we were allowed to throw away."

"So why'd this one get saved?" Lisbeth asks.

"Because *this* is part of a speech," Dreidel replies, slapping his hand against Beetle Bailey's face. *Gov. Roche . . . M. Heatson . . . Host—Mary Angel.* "Once he wrote those, it was like locking the whole damn document in amber. We had to save it."

"So for eight years, Boyle's out there, requesting thousands of documents, looking for whatever he's looking for," Lisbeth says. "And one week ago, he got these pages and suddenly comes out of hiding." She sits up straight, sliding her leg under her rear end. I can hear the speed in her voice. She knows it's in here.

"Lemme see the puzzle again," she says.

Like before, all four of us crowd around it, picking it apart.

"Who's the other handwriting besides Manning's?" Lisbeth asks, pointing to the meticulous, squat scribbles.

"Albright's, our old chief of staff," Dreidel answers.

"He died a few years ago, right?"

"Yeah—though so did Boyle," I say, leaning forward so hard, the conference table digs into my stomach.

Lisbeth's still scanning the puzzle. "From what I can tell, all the answers seem right."

"What about this stuff over here?" Rogo asks, tapping at the doodles and random lettering on the right side of the puzzle.

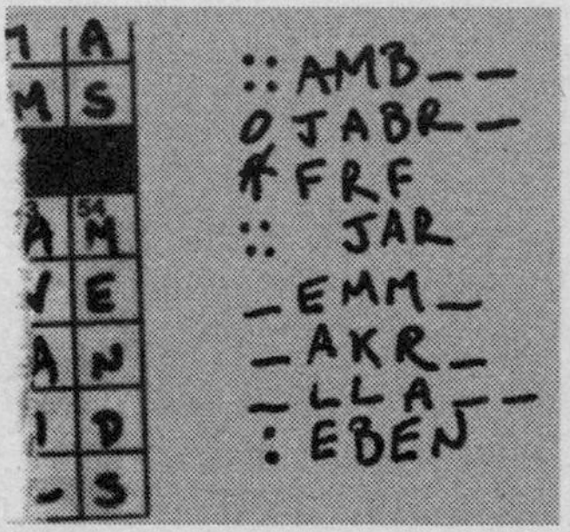

"The first word's *amble* . . . see 7 across?" I ask. "The spaces are for the *L* and the *E.* Dreidel said his mom does the same thing when she does puzzles."

"Sorta scribbles out different permutations to see what fits," Dreidel explains.

"My dad used to do the same," Lisbeth agrees.

Rogo nods to himself but won't take his eyes off it.

"Maybe the answer's in the crossword clues," Lisbeth suggests.

"What, like The Roman had an in with the puzzle-maker?" Dreidel asks, shaking his head.

"And that's more insane than it being hidden in the answers?"

"What was the name of that guy from the White House with the chipmunk cheeks?" Rogo interrupts, his eyes still on the puzzle.

"Rosenman," Dreidel and I say simultaneously.

"And your old national security guy?" Rogo asks.

"Carl Moss," Dreidel and I say again in perfect sync.

I stay with Rogo. Whenever he's this quiet, the pot's about to boil. "You see something?" I ask.

Looking up slightly, Rogo smiles his wide butcher's dog smile.

"What? Say it already," Dreidel demands.

Rogo grips the edge of the crossword and flicks it like a Frisbee across the table. "From the looks of it, the names of all your staffers are hidden right there."

50

In the lobby, The Roman didn't hesitate to sign in. Even made small talk about crummy assignments with the agent behind the desk. At the elevators, he rang the call button without worrying about his fingerprints. Same when the elevator doors opened and he hit the button for the fourth floor.

It was exactly why they got organized. The key to any war was information. And as they learned with the crossword puzzle all those years ago, the best information always came from having someone on the inside.

A loud ping flicked the air as the elevator doors slid open.

"ID, please," a suit-and-tie agent announced before The Roman could even step out into the beige-carpeted hallway.

"Egen," The Roman replied, once again flashing his ID and badge.

"Yes . . . of course . . . sorry, sir," the agent said, stepping back as he read the title on The Roman's ID.

With a wave, The Roman motioned for him to calm down.

"So if you don't mind me asking, what's the mood at headquarters?" the agent asked.

"Take a guess."

"Director's pretty pissed, huh?"

"He's just mad he'll be spending the next six months on the damage control circuit. Ain't nothing worse than a daily diet of cable talk shows and congressional hearings explaining why Nico Hadrian wandered out of his hospital room."

"Those congressmen sure like having their faces on TV, don't they?"

"Doesn't everyone?" The Roman asked, eyeing the surveillance camera and heading toward the black bulletproof doors of the President's office.

"Pop the locks, Paulie," the suit-and-tie agent called out to another agent sitting just inside the Secret Service offices on the right-hand side of the hallway.

On the left, there was a muted thunk as the magnetic lock unlatched. "Thank you, son," The Roman said. He tugged the door open without ever looking back.

"Hell-o," a Hispanic receptionist with a high-pitched voice sang as the heavy door slammed behind The Roman. "How can I help you today?"

Crossing the presidential seal in the carpet, The Roman scanned the left-hand wall for the agent who usually stood guard by the American flag. The agent wasn't there, which meant neither was the President. The only other good news was the yellow Post-it note on the side of the receptionist's computer monitor. In swirling, cursive writing were the words *Dreidel—Ext. 6/Back office.*

"Dreidel's not in, is he?" The Roman asked.

"No, he's out with Wes," the receptionist replied. "And you are . . . ?"

The Roman again flashed his ID and badge. "Actually, I'm here to see Ms. Lapin . . ."

"Sure . . . of course," the receptionist said, pointing to The Roman's left. "You want me to call her or—"

"No need," The Roman insisted, calmly marching down the hallway. "She's already expecting me."

On the right-hand side of the hall, The Roman breezed past nearly a dozen glass frames filled with ribboned Medals of Honor from every major country. Poland's Great Cross of the Order, Qatar's Collar of Independence, even the U.K.'s Order of the Bath. The Roman didn't even glance at them, already focused on the open door on his left.

Across the hallway, he peeked into the office with the *Chief of Staff* nameplate attached to it. The lights were off, the desk empty. Claudia was already at lunch. Good. The fewer people around, the better.

Cutting left, he stepped into the well-lit office that smelled like fresh popcorn and stale vanilla mint candle. From his angle looking down at her desk, he had a perfect view of the tight red V-neck sweater that fought against her decade-old breast implants.

Before she could even react, The Roman gripped the spine of the door, slowly closing it behind himself.

"Nice to see you, Bev," he said as it slapped shut. "Florida looks good on you."

51

Right here," Rogo says, pointing to the column of scribbles on the right side of the puzzle. "In the work space . . ."

I recheck the vertical column of doodles and

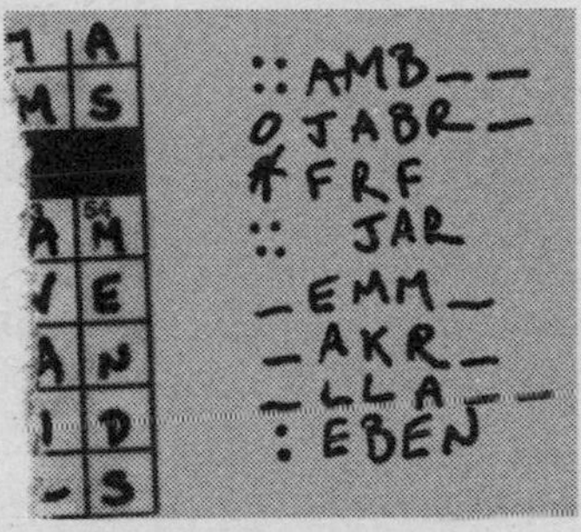

"AMB? JABR? FRF?" Dreidel asks. "Those aren't any initials I know."

"Don't go left to right. Go up and down . . ." With his pen, Rogo makes a circle from top to bottom.

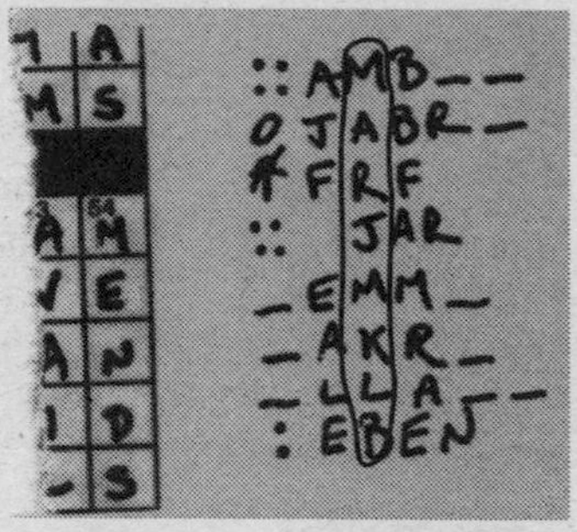

"M, A, R, J, M, K, L, B," Rogo says, starting me off. "Fill it in: Manning, Albright, Rosenman . . ."

"Jeffer," I add.

"Who's Jeffer?" Lisbeth interrupts.

"Me," Dreidel says.

"Moss, Kutz, Lemonick," I add, hitting the rest. "And B . . ."

"For Boyle," Rogo says proudly. "Eight people, all with major Oval Office access."

Lisbeth nods, still studying the crossword. "But why would the President keep a list with his top staffers' names on it?"

We all look to Dreidel. "I've never seen it in my life," he says with a laugh. But from the shake in his voice, it's the one time he's not thrilled to be included on an exclusive list.

Already impatient, Rogo hops from his seat, walking toward the head of the table. "Manning wrote down eight people's names, then camouflaged it with doodles so no one would notice they were there. Not to play Nancy Drew, but what do they all have in common?"

Lisbeth slides the crossword back to the middle of the

conference table. I look down at the list of names. Lemonick was White House counsel, Rosenman was press secretary, Carl Moss was national security adviser. Combined with Manning, Albright, and Boyle, they were the biggest names we had—the knights of our own round table. "It's clearly a power list."

"Except for Dreidel," Rogo points out. "No offense," he adds, turning Dreidel's way.

"Were you all working on something at that time?" Lisbeth asks. "When was it again, February during the first year?"

"We weren't even there a month," Dreidel points out. But as he sees the seniority of the people on the list, I can already hear the change in his voice. "Maybe it's who he wanted at the morning sessions—for the PDB." Reading the confusion of Lisbeth's and Rogo's faces, he explains, "Every morning at six a.m., an armed courier comes from CIA headquarters to the White House with a legal briefcase handcuffed to his wrist. Inside is the President's Daily Brief—the summary report of the most highly classified news that's happening around the world. Troop movements in North Korea . . . spy networks in Albania . . . whatever the President needs to know, he gets at his first meeting of the day, along with a few select others."

"Yeah, but everyone knew who was invited to those meetings," I point out.

"They knew *eventually*," Dreidel says. "But during those first weeks, you think Rosenman and Lemonick didn't try to elbow their way inside?"

"I don't know," Lisbeth says, staring at the list with a small crease between her eyebrows. "If you're just cutting names, why be so secretive?"

"People're only secretive when there's a reason," Dreidel says. "And it seems pretty clear they didn't want anyone else seeing what they were writing."

"Okay, fine—so what're the things you could write about your top dozen or so staffers that you wouldn't want anyone else to see?" Lisbeth asks. "You don't like the person . . . you don't want them there . . . you're afraid of them . . ."

"There you go—blackmail's juicy," Rogo says. "Maybe one of them had a secret . . ."

"Or *knew* a secret," Dreidel says.

"You mean about the President?" I ask.

"About anyone," Lisbeth agrees.

"I don't know," I say. "The level of people you're talking about . . . that's the group you're not supposed to worry about keeping their mouths shut."

"Unless one of them gets you worried that they *can't* keep their mouth shut," Dreidel blurts.

"You mean like a *trust* list?" Lisbeth asks.

"I guess . . . sure," Dreidel replies. "That's what *I'd* want to know if I had a new staff." For the first time, he's stopped biting his manicured hand.

"I'm not sure I follow," I say.

"Think about what was actually going on those first few weeks we were in the White House. That bus bomb in France and all the internal arguing over whether Manning's response took it seriously enough. Then we had all those slap-fights about redecorating the Oval . . ."

"Those I remember," Lisbeth says. "There was that piece in *Newsweek* about the red-striped carpet . . . what'd they say the First Lady called it again?"

"Fruit-stripe gum," Dreidel says dryly. "The bombing and the bad carpet—those were nonsense stories about internal arguments. *Uh-oh, captain can't steer his new ship* . . . But the only reason those things got out was because some loudmouthed staffer decided to take it out."

Lisbeth nods, knowing this one all too well. "So what Manning was really worried about back then . . ."

". . . was finding out who was leaking all our internal baggage," Dreidel says. "When you have that many new staffers flushed with that much new power, there's always someone who wants to rush off and brag to their friends. Or the press. Or their friends who happen to be press. And until you can plug the leaks, those stories take away from your entire agenda."

"Okay," I say. "Which means when this list was made, Manning was hunting for staffers who were leaking to the press?"

"Not just staffers," Dreidel adds. "Those stories were from conversations happening at *senior staff* levels. That's why Manning was so nuts back then. It's one thing when some intern leaks that the President's wearing unmatched socks. It's another to open up the *Washington Post* and read a verbatim blow-by-blow on the front page from a meeting with your five most trustworthy lieutenants."

"If that's the case, then why include himself on the list?" Rogo asks as we all glance back at the crossword.

"Maybe it's a list of who was at a particular meeting—Manning, Albright, Boyle, etc.—then they were just trying to narrow who let a particular piece of info out," I say.

"That would explain why *I'm* there," Dreidel adds. "Though maybe it wasn't just leaking to the press."

"Who else is there?" Lisbeth asks.

"Think back to what you said about The Roman and the six-million-dollar prize they wouldn't approve. Those top informant payments are in the PDB too."

I nod, remembering the old meetings. "It's not a bad call. Whoever was leaking the info could've leaked it to The Roman, telling him who was responsible for denying his payout."

"And you think that's why Boyle got shot?" Lisbeth asks. "Because Boyle was the one who said no to The Roman's payday?"

"I'd believe that," Rogo says. "Six million bucks is a lot of money."

"No question," Dreidel says. "But it seems pretty clear that if you want to know who on the list couldn't be trusted, it's the guy who, until recently, we thought was dead. Y'know, the one the FBI is chasing . . . rhymes with *Doyle* . . ."

"That's why I had the Presidential Library pull Boyle's files," I say. "They've got everything: his schedules, what issues he was working on, even his official personnel file with his FBI background check. We'll have every single sheet of paper that was ever in Boyle's desk, or written about him."

"That's fine—so two of us can go to the library," Lisbeth says. "But it still doesn't tell us why a secret list Manning made during the first year of the administration has anything to do with Boyle being shot three years later."

"Maybe Boyle was mad at the President for not trusting him," Rogo says.

"No," Dreidel says. "According to Wes's FBI guys, whatever Boyle and Manning were up to, they were in it together."

"Which has to be true," I point out. "The ambulance . . . having the blood type ready . . . how else could Boyle possibly pull that off without help from Manning and the Service?"

"So what're you saying? That they didn't trust someone *else* on the list?" Lisbeth asks, her eyes already on Dreidel.

I shake my head. "All I'm saying is President Manning and Albright spent one of their very first days in office building a hidden list with the names of eight people that shared daily access to some of the best-kept secrets in the entire world. More important, by keeping that list on a crossword puzzle, they figured out a way to create the impossible: a presidential document—potentially containing Manning's innermost thoughts—that wouldn't be inspected, cataloged, studied, or seen by anyone else around him."

"Unless, of course, you absentmindedly jot a few notes to yourself on the back," Rogo says.

"The point is, the list still needs narrowing," I say. "And as far as I can tell, besides the President, the only people on here who were at the speedway that day were Boyle and Albright—and Albright's dead."

"You sure those were the only two?" Lisbeth asks.

"Whattya mean?"

"Have you ever looked at any of the archival footage from that day? Maybe take a peek to see if everything you think you remember matches up with reality?"

I shake my head. A week after the shooting, when I was still in the hospital, I caught a clip of the footage while flipping through channels. It took three nurses to calm me down that night. "I haven't seen the footage for a bit," I tell her.

"Yeah, I figured this isn't exactly your favorite home movie. But if you really want to know what happened, you have to start at the scene of the crime." Before I can react, she reaches into her file folder and pulls out a black videocassette. "Lucky for you, I've got connections at the local TV stations."

As she pops out of her seat and heads for the black Formica credenza with the VCR/TV combo, my throat tightens and my hands flood with sweat.

I can already tell this is a bad idea.

52

What about Claudia?" The Roman asked calmly, strolling over to Bev's window and staring down at the agents, sheriff, and ambulance crew crowded into the rotary at the front of the building.

"You told me not to—that it was an internal investigation," Bev said as she watched The Roman from her desk and anxiously picked at an open bag of microwave popcorn.

"And Oren?"

"I just told you—"

"Tell me again!" The Roman insisted, turning from the window, his pale skin and black hair practically glowing in the noon sunlight.

Bev stayed silent, her hand frozen in the popcorn.

The Roman knew he'd scared her, but he wasn't about to apologize. Not until he had what he wanted.

"You said not to tell anyone—I didn't tell anyone," Bev finally offered. "Not B.B., not the President . . . no one." Fidgeting with the tips of her dyed-black hair, she added, "Though I still don't get how any of this helps Wes."

The Roman turned back to the window, taking a moment to choose his words. Bev had known Wes since his first days in the White House. Like any protective parent, she wasn't turning on her kid unless it was for his own good. "What helps Wes is finding out just who he ran into that night in Malaysia," The Roman explained. "If what he said in the report is right—that it was just some drunk looking for the bathroom—then there's nothing to worry about."

"But to have me put a microphone in his pin . . . to hide it from everyone on staff . . . Why can't you just tell me who you think approached him?"

"Bev, I told you from the start, this is part of a long-term inquiry that we believe—and hope—Wes accidentally stumbled onto. Trust me, we want to protect him as much as you do, which is why—"

"Does it have to do with Nico? Is that why he escaped?"

"This has nothing to do with Nico," The Roman insisted.

"I just thought . . . with your hand . . ." she said, motioning to the white gauze wrapped around his palm.

The Roman knew that was the risk coming to the office. But with the wiretap silent, and Boyle still unaccounted for . . . some things had to be done face-to-face.

Sitting on the edge of Bev's desk, The Roman cupped her hand between his palms. "Bev, I know you don't know me. And I know it's odd to suddenly get a call from an agent about an investigation you know nothing about, but I swear to you, this has nothing to do with Nico. Understand? *Nothing.* Everything I've asked of you . . . it's only in the interests of national security and for Wes's benefit," he added, his pale blue eyes locked on hers.

"Now I appreciate how you look out for him . . . we all know the pity you took . . ."

"It's not pity. He's a sweet kid . . ."

". . . who should've left this job years ago, but didn't because he's terrified of stepping out of the thoughtful but crippling security blanket you've all tucked him into. Think about it, Bev. If you really care that much about him, *this* is the moment he needs you. So, is there anyone else out there we might've overlooked? Old White House contacts? Current in-house contacts? Anyone you can think of that he might turn to if he's in trouble?"

Rolling backward on the wheels of her desk chair, Bev was silent at the onslaught of questions. For a moment, her eyes stayed with The Roman's pale blues. But the more he pushed, the more she glanced around. At her keyboard. At her leather blotter. Even at the blurry 5×9 perched under her computer monitor, from her office birthday party a few years back. In the photo, the entire staff was in mid-laugh as the President blew out the candles on Bev's birthday cake. It was the kind of photo that never existed in the White House, but decorated nearly every office here: slightly off-center, slightly funny, and slightly out of focus. Not a professional photo taken by a White House photographer. A family photo—taken by one of their own.

"Sorry," Bev said, pulling her hand away and glancing down at The Roman's gauze pad. "There's no one else I can think of."

53

"—ies and gentlemen, the President of the United States!" the announcer bellows through the P.A. system as the tape begins to roll, and the shiny black Cadillac One lumbers out onto the racetrack.

From the wide angle—showing half the motorcade in profile—I'm guessing it's from a camera up in the stadium's press box.

"There's the ambulance with Boyle's blood," Dreidel points out, running around the conference table so he can get closer to the TV. He stops right next to Lisbeth, who's just to the left of the screen. On my far right, Rogo's back at the head of the oval table. But instead of moving toward the screen, he circles back. Toward me.

He doesn't have to say a word. He juts his chin slightly to the left and lowers his eyebrows. *You okay?*

Tightening my jaw, I nod confidently. Rogo's been my friend since before I could drive. He knows the truth.

"Lisbeth," he calls out. "Maybe we should . . ."

"Leave it—I'm fine," I insist.

As the limo leaves the final turn and heads toward the finish line, the camera pulls out to reveal the entire motorcade, which is now headed straight at us. I used to call it a funeral procession. I had no idea.

On-screen, the camera slowly pulls in on Cadillac One. I swear, I can smell the leather seats of the car, the oily whiff of Manning's daily shoeshine, and the sweet tinge of gasoline from pit road.

"Okay, here we go," Lisbeth says.

The video jump-cuts to a brand-new camera angle from the infield of the track—we're now at eye level. On the passenger side, the Secret Service detail leader gets out of the limo and races to open the back door. Two other agents swoop into place, blocking any clear shot from the crowd. My feet ball up as my toes try to dig through the soles of my shoes. I know what's coming. But just as the door opens, the picture freezes and pauses.

"Slow motion?" Dreidel asks.

"It's the only way to get a good look at who's in the background," Lisbeth explains, gripping the edge of the top left corner of the TV. Dreidel crosses over and does the same on the right corner. Both lean in. They don't want to miss a thing.

On the other side of the conference table, I twist in my seat. In slow motion, two more Secret Service agents slowly creep into the background near the open door that faces the crowd.

"And these are all guys you know?" Lisbeth asks, making a big circle around the five suit-and-tie agents on-screen.

"Geoff, Judd, Greg, Allan, and . . ." Dreidel pauses on the last one.

"Eddie," I call out, never taking my eyes off the screen.

"It'll be done in a sec," Dreidel promises as if that's supposed to make me feel better. He turns back toward the TV just in time to see five fingertips peek out like tiny pink worms above the roofline of the limo. My toes dig even deeper, practically burrowing through my shoes. I close my eyes for a second and swear I can smell popcorn and stale beer.

"Here he comes," Dreidel whispers as Manning slowly leaves the limo, one hand already up in a frozen, celebratory wave. Behind him, with her own hand raised, the First Lady does the same.

"Now watch the President here," Lisbeth says as each frame clicks by, and he slowly turns toward the camera for the first time.

On-screen, Manning's grin is so wide, his top gums are showing. Same with the First Lady, who holds his hand. They're definitely enjoying the crowd.

"Doesn't exactly look like a man who knows shots are about to be fired, does he?" Lisbeth asks as Manning continues to wave, his black windbreaker bubbling up like a helium balloon.

"I'm telling you, he didn't know it was coming," Dreidel agrees. "I mean, I don't care what they were prepared for, or how much of Boyle's blood they had in the ambulance, there's no way Manning, the Service, or anyone else is going to risk a head shot."

"You're still assuming they were aiming for Manning," Lisbeth says as Albright appears on-screen, rising at a turtle's pace from the limo. "I think Nico hit exactly who he wanted to hit. Just look at his escape from the hospital last night. Both orderlies shot through the heart and the palm of their right hand. Sound like anyone you know?"

On TV, at the center of a bushy mess of gray hair, a tiny bald spot rises above the limo's roofline like the morning sun. Here comes Boyle.

"Now *he's* the one who's anxious," Lisbeth says, tapping his face on the monitor.

"He was always miserable, though. Even on day one," Dreidel replies.

I swallow hard as Boyle's profile glows on-screen. The olive skin's the same, but his thin, pointy nose is far sharper than the stubby nose job I saw him with two days ago. His jowls are longer now too. Even plastic surgery can't stop the aging process.

"See, he's not even looking around," Dreidel adds as Boyle follows behind the President. "They've both got no idea what's coming."

"There you are," Dreidel says, tapping the far right-hand corner of the screen, where you can barely see me in profile. As I leave the limo, the camera pans left—away from me—as it tries to stay with the President. But since I'm only a few steps behind, there's a tiny shot of me gawking in the background.

"Man, you were a *baby*," Lisbeth says.

The video flickers, and my head turns like a creaky robot toward the camera. It's the first time we all get a clear look. In my right hand, my middle and ring fingers quickly knead at the heel of my palm. My eyes well up just seeing it. My face . . . God, it's been so long—but there it is . . . the real me.

On-screen, President Manning's hand rises to meet the NASCAR CEO and his now-famous wife. The First Lady adjusts her sapphire necklace, her lips spread in an eternal *hello*. Albright sticks his hands in his pockets. Boyle straightens his tie. And I chase behind them all, frozen midstep with my bag of tricks dangling from my shoulder and a sharp, cocky squint in my eyes.

I know what happens next.

Pop, pop, pop.

On TV, the camera angle jerks upward in a blur, panning past the fans in the stands as the cameraman ducks at the shots. The screen is quickly filled with the blue sky. But to me, it's already fading to black and white. A boy in a Dolphins T-shirt screams for his mom. Boyle falls to the ground, facedown in his own vomit. And a bee sting rips through my cheek. My head whips back at just the thought of it.

The camera jerks again, sliding back down to earth, past the blur of fans running and shouting and stampeding from the stands. On the left side of the screen, Cadillac One rumbles and takes off. The President and First Lady are already inside. Already safe.

As the car leaves, the camera whizzes back and forth, searching the aftermath and sifting through the ballet of slow-motion chaos: Secret Service agents with their mouths frozen open in mid-yell . . . bystanders darting in every direction . . . and on the top right of the screen, just as the limo pulls away, a pale, skinny kid crashing to the ground, twisting in pain like a worm along the concrete, his hand gripping his face.

The tears tumble down my cheeks. My fingers press so tight into the heel of my palm, I feel my own pulse. I tell myself to look away . . . to get up and turn on the lights . . . but I can't move.

On-screen, two suit-and-tie agents carry Boyle off the battlefield and to the ambulance. Since their backs are to us, it's impossible to make them out. But in the swirl of dust behind the limo, I'm still lying on my back, pressing my face so hard, I look like I'm pinning the back of my head to the asphalt. And while it's all in full color on TV, I still see it in black and white. A flashbulb goes supernova.

My fingertips scratch against the sharpened metal in my face. Boyle's ambulance doors slam shut.

"Wes, you with us?" Rogo whispers.

Why won't they stop slamming shut—?

"Wes . . ." Rogo continues to whisper. He says it again, and I realize it's not a whisper. His voice is loud. Like he's yelling.

Something clenches my right shoulder, shaking.

"Wes!" Rogo shouts as I blink back to reality and find his meaty paw holding my shirt.

"No, no . . . yeah . . . I'm fine," I insist, pulling my shoulder free of his grip. It's not until I look around the conference room that I realize the videotape is no longer running. In the corner, Lisbeth flicks on the lights, looking back to see what's going on.

"He's fine," Rogo insists, trying to block her view. "He's just . . . just give him a second, okay?"

Heading back from the light switch, Lisbeth still continues to stare, but if she sees what's going on, she's kind enough to keep it to herself.

"So that basically accomplished a big fat nothing, huh?" Dreidel asks, still clearly annoyed we're even here. "I mean, except for giving Wes a few brand-new nightmares to deal with."

"That's not true," Lisbeth says, heading back to the opposite side of the table. Instead of sitting next to Dreidel, she decides to stand. "We got to see the agents that carried Boyle off."

"Which means nothing since we can't see their faces—not to mention the fact that since the Service clearly helped, I personally don't think it's safe asking any of their agents for help."

"We would've gotten more if the camera weren't

swirling like my mom taking home movies," Lisbeth points out.

"Yeah, that cameraman was a real jerk-off for ducking down and trying to protect his life like that," Dreidel shoots back.

"Dreidel," I interrupt.

"Don't *Dreidel* me, Wes."

"How 'bout if *I* Dreidel you?" Rogo threatens.

"How 'bout you sit back down and let the boy fight his own fight for once?" Dreidel pushes back. "Wes, no offense, but this was stupid. Except for getting inside juice for when Drudge-ette here writes her best-selling tell-all, there's not a single good reason to come here. She could've just sent us the info we needed."

"I was trying to help," Lisbeth insists.

"This was helping? We've got a thousand unanswered questions, half a dozen absurd theories, and you wanna spend the day watching the one video that Congress, the public, and every conspiracy junkie in the world has combed through and *still* didn't find anything suspicious? It didn't even give us a good shot of Nico to see if there's anything else we might've been missing."

I shake my head. "That's not—"

"He's right," Lisbeth admits from just behind Dreidel, who has to spin around to see her. She's got her back to us as she stands in front of the big plate-glass window. "We *didn't* get any good shots." Turning back to us with that same crooked little smile from when she was picking fights with us last night, she adds, "Fortunately, I know exactly how to change that."

54

Y'know there *is* a back entrance," Micah pointed out, tucked into a *Compacts Only* parking spot and checking his rearview mirror for the third time in the last minute. Diagonally behind them in the parking garage, Wes's empty Toyota hadn't moved. "I can take a quick look and—"

"No need," O'Shea said from the passenger seat, his elbow perched on the edge of the car's open window as he worked the morning's crossword. "This is Florida—he's not going anywhere without his car."

"Unless he takes someone else's. Remember that woman in Syria?"

"Syria was different. We needed her to run."

"Why? So you had a good excuse to bring her in?"

"She would've killed you, Micah. You know that."

"I was luring her in."

"That's your interpretation," O'Shea shot back. "But if you try anything as hotheaded as Syria, I promise you right now, *I'll* be the one putting the gun to *your* head." Refusing to look up from the crossword, O'Shea pointed over his own shoulder with the back of his pen. "See that junk shop Subaru diagonally down at the bottom there . . . with the Grateful Dead stickers? We saw it last night. That's Lisbeth's. The one up here is Wes's. Rogo's is still in the shop. No one's going anywhere."

Unconvinced, Micah checked his rearview for the fourth time, then glanced over at O'Shea's elbow resting in the open window. "You should close that up," he said, motioning to the window. "In case he comes . . ."

"Micah, it's seventy-two degrees here. In December. You know how cold it was in France? Let me enjoy the damn warmth."

"But Wes could—"

"It's under control."

"Yeah, just like this," Micah said, jabbing a finger at the photo of Nico on the front page of the newspaper that wilted across the armrest between them.

"What, you still think that was The Roman?" O'Shea asked.

"How could it not be? Boyle gets spotted . . . Nico gets out . . . hell of a coincidence, don't you think?"

O'Shea nodded, finally looking up from the crossword. "But if he used Wes's name to get in . . ."

"I'm just glad you got it purged from the official report. If that went out, the whole world would've swarmed Wes's front steps, and we'd've lost our best—"

"*Tsssttt!*" O'Shea hissed, cutting Micah off. Behind them, a familiar voice echoed off the walls of the garage.

"—e should still call the office," Wes said as Dreidel followed him up the concrete incline.

"Why, just to panic them?" Dreidel asked.

Studying their respective side mirrors, O'Shea and Micah watched the scene unfold diagonally behind them. From their spot in the garage, they had a perfect view of the passenger side of Wes's Toyota. And it didn't take anything more than that to notice Rogo was missing.

"Where's the fat kid?" Micah whispered.

"Hitting on the girl?" O'Shea guessed.

Just as Wes stepped around to the driver's-side door and opened the locks, his car keys slipped from his hand. Spinning to catch them, he twisted toward Micah and O'Shea, who didn't flinch. From their angle in the garage, they were near impossible to spot.

There was a loud clink as the keys hit the pavement. For a fraction of a second, O'Shea saw Wes's glance turn toward him. O'Shea still didn't move. No way was Wes that good.

"What's wrong?" Dreidel called out to his friend.

O'Shea stared in his passenger-side mirror and stood his ground. Next to him, watching his own rearview, Micah did the same. They'd been at this too long to panic.

"You hear something?" Wes asked.

"Don't get paranoid," Dreidel warned.

In the edge of his mirror, O'Shea could see the outline of the back of Wes's head as he turned to his Toyota, picked his keys up off the ground, and slid into the car.

"No, you're right," Wes replied.

Within seconds, the Toyota's engine grumbled to life and its wheels screeched against the concrete.

Following years of training, Micah waited before going for the ignition. At least until they heard the metallic thunk of Wes's Toyota cresting over the speed bump just outside the garage.

By the time Micah and O'Shea reached the speed bump, Wes's Toyota was pulling into traffic, making a sharp left back onto South Dixie.

"Any idea where he's headed?"

"I'm guessing his office . . ."

"Guess again," O'Shea said as the Toyota made another sharp left at the first traffic light—in the opposite direction of Manning's office.

Carefully staying at least three cars back, Micah pulled his own quick left just as the Toyota blew past a sign for I-95. "He's driving fast."

"Maybe headed for the highway," O'Shea guessed as the Toyota took off, shrinking in the distance. Calm as ever, Micah stayed tucked behind two minivans and a white Honda, never losing focus on the two heads in the front seat of Wes's car.

Sure enough, a minute later, the Toyota veered left, following signs for I-95 South and hugging to the curve of the on-ramp at Belvedere Road. But as they merged onto the highway, Micah and O'Shea were surprised to see that Wes wasn't picking up speed. He was slowing down.

"He's at fifty-five exactly," Micah said, checking the speedometer. "Think he's trying to flush us out?"

Pointing to the nearest exit sign, O'Shea said, "Maybe he's just headed home."

"Strike one," Micah said as the Toyota merged into the middle lane of the highway. "Okeechobee's the other way."

"What about the airport?"

"Strike two," Micah said as Wes's car chugged past the runways at Southern Boulevard. "Wanna go for a third?"

Falling silent, O'Shea reached outside his window and readjusted his side mirror.

"You got something?"

"Unclear," O'Shea replied, studying the cars behind him. "Just don't let him get too far."

Tucked behind a car carrier filled with SUVs, O'Shea

and Micah spent the next twenty minutes trailing Wes's Toyota as it continued south on 95, past Lake Worth, and Lantana, and Boynton Beach, and Delray . . . cruising past each city, but never going more than sixty miles an hour, never weaving through traffic, never leaving the middle lane. Through the unwashed back window, with cars zipping past them on both sides, Wes and Dreidel sat perfectly still, never panicking or checking over their shoulders. It was almost as if they weren't in a rush. Or didn't have a place to—

"Pull up," O'Shea blurted.

"What're you—?"

"Let's go—get up there," he insisted, patting the dashboard and pointing through the windshield. "*Now.*"

Micah punched the gas, and O'Shea's head snapped back, his sandy-blond hair bumping for a half second against the headrest. As their car slid out from behind the car carrier, it didn't take Micah long to weave across traffic and pull right behind Wes.

For the first time since he got on the highway, Wes merged into the far left lane, speeding up just enough to keep pace with a convertible Mercedes on their right.

With another punch of the gas, Micah tugged the wheel to the left, plowing the car into the poorly paved emergency lane on the inside shoulder of the road. Pebbles, trash, and shards of shattered glass spun under the tires, swirling in the car's wake. Careful to keep the driver's side from scraping against the concrete divider, Micah had no trouble catching up to Wes's Toyota, which was still barely doing sixty.

As they pulled neck and neck, Wes's window slowly rolled down.

"Careful driving in that lane—it's *illegal*!" Rogo

shouted from the driver's seat, tapping his thumbs against the steering wheel as the two cars whipped down the highway. The only other occupant was Dreidel, who refused to make eye contact.

"Son of a—"

Ramming the brakes at a sign marked *Emergency Vehicles Only*, Micah cranked the steering wheel toward the open patch of grass on his left, skidding into a U-turn and heading back the way they came.

At this rate, Wes already had at least an hour head start.

55

Flat on my back underneath a silver Audi, I press my chin to my chest and stare out between the back tires and sagging muffler into the silence of the *Palm Beach Post*'s parking garage. It's been nearly fifteen minutes since Rogo and Dreidel pulled out in my Toyota. And nearly fourteen minutes since O'Shea and Micah's blue Chevy slinked down the incline of the garage and trailed Rogo out to the street.

Based on the mic in my lapel pin, we knew we were dealing with pros. Dreidel said it was the FBI. We needed to see if he was right.

When Dreidel and I first came down to my car, I pulled out my keys and popped the locks. But it wasn't until I gripped the door handle that I spotted his shadow underneath. Below the car, Rogo stuck his head out like a mechanic and pumped his eyebrows.

"You owe me a new suit," he'd whispered from a puddle of grease.

All he needed was ten minutes of lead time to crawl on his stomach underneath the cars.

"You're lucky I fit," he'd said.

Looking up at the grease- and dirt-caked axle directly above me, he was right about that. Just like he was right that if we pulled it off fast enough, no one would notice.

I had to step back to give him some room, but from there, Rogo was a pro. I pulled open the car door just as he rolled out from underneath. Dropping my keys covered most of the sound. Even I started to get excited. Climbing to his knees, Rogo held up his fingers to count. *One . . . two . . .*

In one quick motion, I ducked down to pick up my keys just as Rogo popped up in my place and slid into my car.

"No, you're right," I'd called out from the ground to complete the illusion. With a quick roll, I went under the car next to mine, which is where I've been ever since. Houdini would've been proud.

Staring out between the back tires, I turn on my side, and my elbow slides through the grease. By now, Rogo should have O'Shea and Micah halfway to Boca Raton. Still, I'm not sure what's worse. The fact that they were watching, or the fact we got rid of them. With Nico still out there . . . At least with the FBI around, I was safe.

As I'm about to roll out, there's a faint creak on my left. Hushed . . . like corduroy rubbing together. Craning my neck and peering out from under the car, I search the pocked concrete floor of the garage. The sound's long gone. But something else takes its place.

I know it from years of people's stares. It's even worse in public places—at a movie or in the supermarket—when they're trying to pretend they don't care. There's no scientific term to explain it. But I feel it every day. At this point, I've probably honed it. That haunting tug at the back of your skull . . . the nearly telepathic scream that demands you turn around. That indescribable feeling when you know you're being watched.

A single set of footsteps echoes through the garage, followed by the mild roar of another engine.

Right on time.

Tires churn and brakes squeal as the car flies in reverse up the ramp, backing halfway into my Toyota's now-empty parking spot. Rolling out from my hiding place, I'm face-to-face with a full row of Grateful Dead bumper stickers, which lurch to a stop barely an inch from my forehead.

"Hey, magic man—David Copperfield called . . . wants to know if you can still sub for him next Thursday?" Lisbeth says, leaning out the driver's-side window.

Most people would laugh, which is the only reason I force a grin. She doesn't buy it for a second. Fake smiles are a gossip columnist's bread and butter. Climbing to my feet, I brush the dirt from my clothes.

"If it makes you feel better, Wes, all the hiding and rolling under cars? That was the scary part."

She waits for some plucky response like I'm some lantern-jawed action-movie hero. "That's not even true," I tell her.

Shaking her head, she studies me carefully. "Is it actually against the law to try and cheer you up?"

Again, she waits for a smile. Again, I don't give it.

"Just get in the car, Wes. The only way we're pulling this off is if we move fast."

She's right about that. Hopping in the passenger seat, I slam the door as Lisbeth tosses me a silver cell phone with a little ladybug sticker on it.

"I traded with a friend who writes for the gardening section," she explains. "Now we're untraceable."

Refusing to celebrate, I flip open the phone and punch in the number.

"It's a beautiful day in President Manning's office. How can I help you?" the receptionist answers.

"Jana, it's Wes. Can you put me through to Oren?"

"Hiya, Wes. Of course—transferring you to Oren right now." There's a soft click, two chirps, and then . . .

"This is Oren," my officemate answers.

"How we looking?"

"They're getting it set up right now," he replies. He's even faster than I thought. "All you have to do is go pick it up."

I nod to Lisbeth. She rams the gas. And away we go.

56

Got everything you need?" the secretary asked The Roman as he left Bev's office and trudged across the presidential seal carpet in the main reception area.

"Apparently so," The Roman replied, hiding his bandaged hand from view. "Though I—"

The receptionist's phone rang on her desk. "Oop—excuse me," she said, putting on her headset. "It's a beautiful day in President Manning's office. How can I help you?"

The Roman headed for the door.

The receptionist waved good-bye, never taking her attention away from the caller on her headset. "Hiya, Wes. Of course—transferring you to Oren right now . . ."

The Roman stopped midstep, the toe of his left foot digging into the head of the eagle on the presidential seal. A thin grin returned to his face as he pivoted around.

Tapping a few buttons on her phone, the receptionist sent the call on its way and looked up at her guest. "I'm sorry . . . you were saying?"

"Just that I need some directions," The Roman replied,

pointing left, then right. "Which way is Oren's office again?"

"Second on your right. See it?" the receptionist called out.

The Roman nodded. "You're an angel."

He paused outside the office and waited for the click of Oren hanging up his phone. With a sharp rap of knuckles against the door, he stepped inside and flashed his badge. "Oren, right? Agent Roland Egen. United States Secret Service."

"Everything okay?" Oren asked, already halfway out of his chair.

The Roman shrugged. "You have a few minutes to chat?"

57

Standing outside the Mediterranean cypress plank doors set into an arched coral stone entryway, I ring the pearl doorbell and offer a smile for the security camera that stares down at us.

"Who's calling?" a delicate female voice asks through the intercom, even though she just buzzed us in three minutes ago when we first pulled up to the twenty-foot-tall hedges and wrought-iron gate that protect the estate.

"Mrs. Sant, it's Wes Holloway," I say into the intercom. "From President Manning's office."

With a click, the front door opens by remote control. Ten feet away, a young woman with perfectly arched eyebrows, sheer lip gloss, and flowing blond hair straight out of a shampoo commercial strolls toward us through the anteroom. She's wearing a peach cashmere sweater with a low enough V-neck to reveal why she's a trophy wife. And like the best trophies in town, she has breasts that are perfect and real, just like the diamond bracelet that engulfs most of her wrist.

Anxious to be out of sight, I go to step inside. Lisbeth tugs on the back of my button-down, keeping me in place.

Protocol says I'm supposed to wait to be invited in. And with money this big, protocol rules.

"So nice to see you again," Mrs. Sant says in an Australian accent, even though we've never met. Like most Palm Beach wives, she knows better than to take a chance.

Finally reaching the doorway, she studies my face, then glances over my shoulder at Lisbeth's beat-up car. Again, perfect Palm Beach. Judgment first, niceties later.

"I take it the President's not with you," she adds, still staring at our car. It's not until she's done with me that she even notices Lisbeth.

"No, he's actually meeting us in—"

"Ms. Dodson?" she asks excitedly, grabbing Lisbeth's hand as if she were proposing marriage. "I met you that night at the Alsops—oh, I'm sorry," she adds, patting her own chest. "Cammie Sant—my husband's Victor," she explains as if that's all the introduction she needs. "Oh, what a treat! I read you every day! Come in, come in . . ."

I don't know why I'm surprised. When you cover society, part of the job is having society suck up. But instead of reveling in the moment, Lisbeth shrinks from it, consciously slowing down so she's a full step behind me as we enter the anteroom.

"Oh, and that mention you did of Rose DuVall . . . *good* for you. We all knew it was her husband who dragged the kids to court."

Next to me, Lisbeth looks away, fighting to avoid eye contact. At first, I thought it was modesty. But the way her face falls . . . the way she anxiously scratches at the freckles on her neck . . . I know shame when I see it. Especially when it comes from not meeting your own personal expectations.

"Oh, and please ignore the mess," Cammie adds, leading us through the sumptuous Mediterranean-style living room and pointing to the white billowy painter's cloths that're draped over every piece of artwork on the walls. "The jury's coming tomorrow."

Two years ago, the previous owners of Cammie's spectacular fourteen-bedroom, twenty-thousand-square-foot home were brutally gunned down by their only son. With the parents dead, the house was sold to Cammie and her husband, an heir to the Tylenol fortune, who, according to the stories, were so desperate to make a splash in the P.B. social scene, they swooped in and bought it for twenty-seven million even before they wiped the chalk marks off the wide, cypress plank floors.

"The sheets were Victor's idea," Cammie explains. "You know, with the jury set to walk through the old crime scene, we just thought . . . when it comes to the collection . . . we don't need everyone knowing how many Francis Bacons we have." She raises her eyebrows at us.

I nod, staring at the stark white sheets. Traveling with the President, I've been to plenty of billionaires' homes with a Rembrandt or Monet or Warhol on the wall. Some'll even have two or three. But here . . . as we pass from the living room, through the library, through the blood-red billiard room in back, I count at least thirty covered pictures.

"Of course. Of course, you'd want to be discreet," Lisbeth says, finally looking up.

Stopping short at the double French doors that lead out back, Cammie spins around at the word *discreet.* A lesser clubwoman would take it as a threat. It's not. And Cammie's not *lesser* at anything. Tugging on the bottom of her peach sweater, she smooths it over her flat stomach and smiles to herself. It's every hostess's dream: being owed a favor by the local gossip queen.

"Listen, I have some errands to run—what a pleasure meeting you," Cammie adds, happily excusing herself. "Tommaso's out back. He'll take perfect care of you."

With a flick of the antique brass doorknob, the French doors swing open, leading us out across a stone path that takes us past the saltwater pool, through an expansive formal garden, and into a fruit orchard filled with the sweet smells of grapefruits, tangerines, and Persian limes.

"Am I shallow for hating her perfect, yoga-trainered ass?" Lisbeth asks as we pass one of the lime trees. "Or should I just be content in despising her for the mere fact that I now owe her one?"

"If you wanna get technical, we actually owe her *two*," I say, pointing to our destination.

Beyond the orchard, beyond the stone amphitheater, even beyond the football-field-sized patch of meticulously mowed grass that runs down toward the water, sits a pristine, 160-foot, three-deck, black-and-cream-colored mega-yacht that towers over every other boat floating behind it on the calm currents of Lake Worth. *The Pequod*, it says in fine gold script along the transom at the stern. It's not until we're right alongside it that I even appreciate how big the yacht is—from front to back, it's gotta be three eighteen-wheelers parked end-to-end.

"You sure it's fast enough?" Lisbeth asks, craning her neck back and shielding her eyes from the sun.

She's not talking about the boat. As fast as we need to move, we don't have time for a pleasure cruise. Nor can we afford to risk heading to the local airport and getting tracked by our IDs and airline tickets. I take two steps back to get a clearer view of our target. It sits on the rear sundeck with its three still blades arched slightly downward.

A car would take over four hours. A seaplane would take an hour and forty minutes. But a French-built, twin-engine helicopter with no boarding, taxi, or wait time since it's parked on a yacht? We'll be there in an hour, easy. Plenty of time to get what we need and be back at Manning's house tonight.

"She's gorgeous, no?" a man calls out in a heavy Spanish accent. Sticking his head over the railing, Tommaso stares down at us from the edge of the deck. "The President is joining us, yes?"

"No," I say, still craning my neck up. "He's meeting us there."

Tommaso shrugs it off without a care. In a pilot's navy blazer and a blue-and-white-striped shirt, he's dressed as staff, which means he's used to spoiled honchos changing their minds at the last minute. "Come, let us go," he adds, motioning palms-up to a metal staircase that leads up to the main deck. Within seconds, we're aboard.

That's why I called Oren in the first place. When we went to Saudi Arabia, Oren found a sheik who was happy to loan the President his jet. When we flew to North Carolina for vacation, he found an heir of the Kentucky Fried Chicken family to do the same. It's not snobbery. It's Oren's job. As director of travel, he's there to collect the name of every person who says the phrase that's uttered most often to every former U.S. President: *Let me know if you ever need anything.*

On most trips, the President just needs privacy. Today, I need the same.

Naturally, Oren was hesitant. But when I told him that I was having trouble breathing . . . that Nico's escape . . .

just seeing his face on the news . . . and the pains in my chest . . . *Please, Oren, you know I never ask. I just need to get away . . . as fast as possible . . .*

Forget the presidency—the most powerful cards to play are pity and guilt. One phone call later, recent donors and NBFs Victor and Cammie Sant were honored, just honored, to offer up their personal helicopter for the President and his staff. No questions asked, no flight plan to file, no possible way to be traced.

"Welcome to the *Pequod*," Tommaso says as we reach the top of the metal stairs and climb on board the yacht. Across the sundeck-turned-landing-pad, he twists a latch and opens the door to the matching black and cream helicopter. "Ready to ride the white whale?"

"Palm Beach Tower, thees copter two-seven-niner-five-Juliett lifting off," Tommaso says into his radio.

"Seven-niner-five," a radio voice calmly crackles back. "Depart at your own risk."

Lisbeth looks to me as she hears the words through the intercom, then raps her knuckles against the Plexiglas divider that separates our cabin—with its four leather club chairs—from the two seats up by the pilot. *"At our own risk?"* she calls to Tommaso, flipping a switch on the intercom.

"Is fine, miss. Regulation," he explains as he pushes a button to start the first engine.

Behind us, just above our heads on the back of the helicopter, an exhaust pipe clears its throat, hacking itself awake. I jump at the sound, which rings louder than a gunshot.

A few seconds later, Tommaso hits another button, starting engine two. A second exhaust pipe explodes with a sputter. I jump again, searching over my shoulder, even though I know no one's there. My eyes blink over and over and over.

"Take a breath," Lisbeth says, reaching over from her seat and grabbing my wrist. The whole helicopter starts vibrating as the blades begin to spin. *Vrrrrrrrr . . . rrr . . . rrr . . .* like a race car whipping around the track.

"Just pretend it's Marine One," she adds, referring to the helicopter I used to ride at the White House.

I turn to the wide window on my right and hold my breath. It doesn't help. A tidal wave of nausea pirouettes through my stomach.

Vrrrrrr . . . rrr . . . rrr . . . the blades pick up speed. Leaning closer to the window, I press my forehead against the glass. The blades whip so fast, they disappear above us.

"Wes, I swear to you, there's no one out there. We're in good shape."

She thinks I'm staring at the lush grounds that lead back to the Sants' Mediterranean mansion. Or that I'm scanning every tree, shrub, and Greek Revival statue looking to see if we were followed. But as the helicopter pitches forward and lifts off the landing pad, the only thing I see in the window is my own reflection.

"And you wanted to sit inside all day," Lisbeth reminds me, hoping to reassure as we climb straight up into the blue sky and the Sants' yacht shrinks below us. "Bye-bye, rich people with perfect lives who make me feel inadequate and fat—we're off to endanger ourselves!"

Staying silent, I keep my forehead pressed to the window. At the sandy tip of the Palm Beach inlet, where Lake Worth flows into the Atlantic Ocean, the glowing blue-green water expands to the horizon, its colors more mesmerizing than a peacock's tail. It barely registers.

"C'mon, Wes—you've earned a smile," Lisbeth adds, her voice still racing. "We've got a lead on The Roman, some hints into the crossword, Rogo and Dreidel are on their way to dig up the scoop on Boyle, and we, in a mad stroke of your own genius, are now flying on a three-million-dollar whirlybird to the one person who was in the absolute best position to show us what happened that day. I'm not saying you should order the confetti and schedule the victory parade, but you definitely can't just sit there and sulk."

With my head still pressed against the glass, I shut my eyes and replay the video. She'll never understand.

"Listen, I know it was hard watching that tape . . ."

I press even harder.

". . . and just to see yourself without the scars . . ." Unlike most, she doesn't shrink from the issue. I can feel her looking—not staring—right at me. The helicopter banks into position, heading south down the golden coastline, then quickly cutting right and heading inland, southwest over the carpeted green waves of the country club golf course. At five hundred feet, we're about as high as a plane coming in for a landing. Golf carts scurry like tiny white ants across the grass, while the course's sand traps dot the landscape like dozens of round beige kiddie pools. Within minutes, the beachfront homes and breathtaking yachts of Palm Beach give way to the mossy, mosquito-filled brown marshes of the Everglades. It changes so damn quickly.

"I'm just saying," she adds, "whatever you've been through . . . it's still the same you."

Staring out the window, I watch as the tall strands of sawgrass peek out and sway in the Everglades' shallow brown waters. "It's not about my face," I blurt.

Ignoring my reflection and pulling back slightly, I use the polish of the window to stare over my shoulder. Behind me, Lisbeth doesn't move, still watching me carefully, with no hesitation as she studies my face.

"You saw the tape," I add. "The way I stepped out of that limo . . . waving to the crowd . . . the swaggering sway in my shoulders . . ."

"You're better off. You looked like Dreidel."

"See, but that's the point. When I see that tape . . . when I see the old me . . . I don't just miss my face. What I miss—what I *mourn*—is my old life. *That's* what they took from me, Lisbeth. You can see it on the tape: A twenty-three-year-old cocky kid strutting like only a twenty-three-year-old cocky kid can. Back then, when I imagined my future, from the White House to—I was rocketing so high, I couldn't even pick the next coordinate. The whole damn world was possible. I mean, that's the promise, right? I run and run and run this race—and then, in one stupid day, with one stupid ricochet . . ." My chin starts to quiver, but after all these years, I know exactly how to grit my teeth to bury it. ". . . I find out I'm never getting any further th-th-than . . . than halfway there." The quivering's gone. It's not much of a victory. "That's my life. Halfway there."

In the reflection of the window, Lisbeth tucks a red curl behind her ear. "You got further than halfway, Wes."

"Why, because I fetch the President's Diet Coke and know which of his friends he hates? Rogo said it for years, but I wouldn't listen. It was supposed to be a stepping-stone. Somehow it became a destination. Can you possibly fathom how pathetic you have to be to let that happen?"

"Probably as pathetic as settling for a local gossip job,

even though the real dream was to challenge the world with risky, investigative news items."

For the first time since we've taken off, I turn away from the window and stare at Lisbeth. "That's different," I tell her.

"It's *not*," she shoots back. "You saw my office—all those letters on the walls of my cubicle . . ."

"The ones to your dad."

"Not *to* him. *About* him. Those letters are proof, Wes. They're proof that you can use this job to change someone's life for the better. They're proof that there's a power in reporting. And what do I do with that power? I spend every day trying to find twenty inches' worth of local divorces, country club backstabbing, and all-around nail-biters, like who got stuck at the crappy table at Morton's? When I took this job, I promised myself it was for a year or two, until I could properly feed my cats. That was seven years ago, Wes," she says, more serious than ever. "And y'know what the worst part is?"

"That you gave up your dream?"

She shakes her head. "That I can leave at any time."

As I study her, she scratches at the freckles on her cheek.

"It's still different," I insist, turning back to the window. "My goal is to walk down the street and not be noticeable. You're at least the same person you always were."

She shifts in her seat as the leather crunches below her. "My dad used to say that God puts cracks in everything. That's how the light gets in."

"Yeah, well, your dad stole that from an old Leonard Cohen song."

"Doesn't make it any less true."

Through the window, I stare down at the river of grass, its muted green and brown strands braided across the water like a head of wet hair. About a hundred feet down, a small flock of white birds glides through the sky.

"Those herons?" Lisbeth asks, staring out her own window.

"Egrets," I reply. "Beaks are blacker and pointier."

Staring downward, I think of my own bird, Lolo, and how much she'd enjoy the view. Then I remind myself that she can't fly. Not while her wings are clipped.

For the second time, I turn away from the window and look over my shoulder at Lisbeth. She's got caramel freckles along her neck. "You really that miserable with your job?" I ask her.

"Last month, I didn't go to my ten-year high school reunion because the little bio of me in the program listed me as 'gossip queen.' I know it's so seventh grade, but I just . . . I couldn't show my face there."

"Imagine that," I tease, turning my head so she gets a good look at my scars.

"Oh, jeez, Wes, you know I didn't—"

"I know," I tell her, flashing the best full smile I can offer. As always, the right half of my mouth doesn't move. But for once, as the left half rises toward the roof of the helicopter, it actually seems like enough.

58

What about phone records?" O'Shea asked, sitting in the passenger seat as Micah steered through the lunch-hour traffic that clogged I-95.

"Goose egg," Paul Kessimian replied through O'Shea's phone in a fat Chicago sausage accent. As a student of applied mathematics and a dropout from the U.S. Naval Academy, Paul wasn't a scholar. As a senior associate in the FBI's Investigative Technology Division, he was a genius. And rarely wrong. "Kid hasn't made a cell call since late last night."

"Credit cards?"

"I ran it all—cards, ATM withdrawals, airline reservations, even his Blockbuster card. Whoever he is, this Wes's no schmuck. Kid's quieter than a caterpillar."

"Then track the phone itself," O'Shea said into his cell as their Chevy came to a short stop just shy of a black pickup. Tapping the dashboard with his fist, he pointed to the far left shoulder of the road, pantomiming for Micah to keep moving. "He should be pinging off some nearby cell tower as we speak."

"Really? I'd totally forgotten how GPS and, indeed, my entire job worked," Paul said.

O'Shea didn't laugh. "Don't fuck with me on this, Paul."

"Hey, hey . . . easy with the mouth. You didn't say it was that important."

"It's that important. Now is he pinging or not?"

"He *should* be," Paul began as O'Shea heard the clicking of computer keys through the phone. "But if his phone's issued by Manning's office—which according to this it is—they cloak all their GPS so our former Presidents can get some privacy."

"So you can't track it?"

"Of course, we can track it. You really think we let these guys run around without protection? The annoying part is, I'm not getting anything traceable."

"Why? He's got his phone off?"

"Even if it's off, GPS should still be transmitting," Paul explained as Micah cut back into traffic, finding an opening in the center lane. "Which means he's in the air, underground, or otherwise out of range."

"He's in the air," O'Shea said to Micah, pointing to the exit ramp for Palm Beach Airport. "Get off here!"

Without even hesitating, Micah swerved the blue Chevy across two lanes of traffic, ramming toward the exit. Angry car horns faded behind them. "Maybe Wes is using someone else's phone," Micah said, his eyes locked on the road. "Ask him to trace Dreidel's calls."

"Paul, do me a favor and run those other three names—the two guys and the girl," O'Shea said as they curved along the off-ramp. "Call you back in a minute."

"What're you doing?" Micah asked as O'Shea ended the call. "We need that info *now*."

"Which is why I'm getting it," O'Shea said, his thumb pounding at a brand-new phone number. "If Wes isn't using credit cards or his own ID, he's not getting on a plane without some heavyweight help."

"It's a beautiful day in President Manning's office," the receptionist said through the phone. "How can I help you?"

"Hi there, this is Agent O'Shea calling from the FBI. We're doing some work on the current Nico investigation. Can I speak to the person in charge of the President's transportation? We need to make sure he's aware of all the recent precautions we and the Service have put in place."

"Of course," the receptionist replied. "Let me transfer you to Oren."

There was a quick click followed by two sharp chirps.

"This is Oren."

"Oren, Agent O'Shea calling from—"

"Wow, I'm getting popular—two in one day," Oren interrupted.

"Pardon?"

"You're calling from the Service, right? Just spoke to your buddy—left here a minute ago."

"Absolutely," O'Shea said without even a stutter. "So you already spoke to Agent . . ."

"Egen . . . Roland Egen? I say that right?"

"He's the one," O'Shea replied, squeezing his phone in his fist. "Pale skin and black hair, right?"

Micah turned at the description, his jaw almost hitting the steering wheel. "Wait, is he—?"

O'Shea put up his hand, cutting Micah off. "So you gave him the quick update on Wes?"

"Of course. Though all I had was his flight to Key West," Oren explained. "We really appreciate you looking out for him, though. I mean, he's always been a little more, y'know, *jumpy* since the accident, but with Nico suddenly on the loose, I could hear it in his voice—he sounded pretty torn apart."

"Who could blame him?" O'Shea asked, anxious to get off. "Oren, you've been a lifesaver. Thanks for all the help."

As O'Shea shut his phone, Micah could read the look on his partner's face.

"Motherf—"

"Please tell me The Roman was just standing in his office," Micah demanded.

"Enough," O'Shea said. "Either we just hit the lottery or we jumped face-first on an even bigger land mine."

Nodding in agreement, Micah punched the gas and pointed with his eyebrows at a billboard offering daily charter flights to Key West. O'Shea was already dialing.

"Hi, I'd like to rent one of your seaplanes," he said into the phone. "Think you can have it ready in the next five minutes?"

59

"You sure he didn't call?" Dreidel asked from the passenger seat as the car idled in the stranglehold of traffic that regularly gripped Miami's US-1. "Do me a favor and just check your phone."

Tapping his thumbs against the steering wheel, Rogo didn't bother checking his phone. "He didn't call."

"But if something happened . . . if he didn't get to Key West—"

"Wes is smart—he knows they'll trace it if we call. If there was a problem, we'd know."

"Unless there was a problem and we *didn't* know," Dreidel insisted. "Dammit, why didn't we get his info: the name of the helicopter guy . . . where they're flying from . . . we don't even have the address he's at in Key—" Before Dreidel could finish, his own phone vibrated in his pocket. Ripping it out, he anxiously flipped the phone open, checking caller ID. Rogo glanced across the seat just in time to see the 202 prefix. Washington, D.C.

"Hello?" Dreidel answered. His jaw quickly slid off-center. "Listen, I'm in the middle of something. Can we talk about it later? . . . Yeah, I will . . . *I will* . . . Bye."

Turning to Rogo as he closed the phone, Dreidel added, "My wife."

"With a Washington phone number?" Rogo asked, his thumbs no longer tapping. "I thought you lived in Chicago."

"My old cell. We kept the number from D.C.," Dreidel explained.

Speeding up, then slowing back to a full halt, the car stood motionless in traffic. Rogo didn't say a word.

"What, you think I'm lying?" Dreidel blurted.

"I didn't say anything. Enough with the witch trials."

Shifting in his seat, Dreidel looked over his own shoulder and checked the lane next to them. "You're clear on the right."

Clenching the steering wheel, Rogo didn't make a move.

"Rogo, you hear what I—?"

"Traffic's bad enough. Don't tell me how to drive."

In the middle lane, the car inched past the cause of the slowdown: a tow truck with yellow sirens loading up a tan Cadillac on the left side of the road.

"I'm not an imbecile, Rogo. I know what you think of me."

"Dreidel . . ."

"I see it in your face . . . and how, when we split up, how quick you were to keep me from going with Wes. Don't tell me I'm wrong. Instead, let me paint this picture as best I can: I'd never do anything to hurt him. *Never.*"

"I'm sure you wouldn't," Rogo said.

"I'm not saying I'm the best husband, okay? But I'm still a damn good friend. Don't forget, I'm the one who got Wes the job in the first place."

"That fact hasn't been lost on me."

"Oh, so now that's my fault too?" Dreidel asked. "This

was my master plot to somehow put him in my old job so a once-in-a-lifetime ricochet could hit him in the face?"

"That's not what I said."

"Then be clear for once instead of your lovable facade that treats Wes like some fragile, overprotected china doll. I know why you do it, Rogo—I know plenty of underachievers who love to be needed."

"Just like I know plenty of overachievers who love abandoning people the instant they don't need those people anymore. Enough rewriting history. I was there with him the week they took the bandages off . . . and when that *Times* reporter used the front page to describe his face as *ruined* . . . and when Wes finally decided to look at himself only to say he wished he was the dead one instead of Boyle. But that's the thing, Dreidel—for eight years, Wes *has* been the dead one. You and the rest of your White House crew may have gone on to your own TV shows and newspaper columns, but Wes was the one who never got to move on to his new life. Now that that chance is here, I'm not letting anyone rip it away from him."

"That's a wonderful speech, Rogo, but do me a favor: If you don't trust me, have the balls to say it and just let me out right here."

"If I didn't trust you, Dreidel, I would've left you in Palm Beach."

"That's not even true," Dreidel challenged. "You brought me here because you wanted to see Boyle's files, and you know I'm the only one who can get you in."

With a flick of his blinker, Rogo turned into the far right lane. Looking over at the passenger seat, he was silent.

Dreidel nodded to himself, biting at the skin on the inside of his bottom lip. "Fuck you too, Rogo."

Tapping his thumbs on the steering wheel, Rogo made a sharp right on Stanford Drive and headed toward a guard gate and lawn that served as the main entrance to the campus. On their right, a forest-green and gold metal sign bolted into a concrete wall read:

WELCOME TO THE UNIVERSITY OF MIAMI
HOME OF THE LELAND F. MANNING
PRESIDENTIAL LIBRARY

Neither said another word to each other until they were inside.

60

Jacksonville, Florida

Nico, maybe we should stop.

"There's no need."

But if you don't rest—

"I've been resting for eight years, Edmund. This is the calling," Nico said, sitting so far forward in the driver's seat, his chest nuzzled the steering wheel of the giant flatbed. Just behind him in his seat was the balled-up army jacket he'd stolen from the Irish Pub. With Florida's noon sun burning overhead, winter seemed long gone. He didn't need the jacket. Or Edmund's blood, which soaked the front of it.

You're telling me you're not tired?

Nico glanced over at Edmund's lifeless body drooping in the seat next to him. His friend knew him all too well.

You've been driving nearly ten hours, Nico. It's okay to take a break—in fact, it's necessary, son. Especially if we plan on staying out of sight.

Nico knew what he was getting at. "So you still think—?"

Nico, I don't care how cautious a driver you are—you take a forty-ton flatbed through the dainty streets of downtown Palm Beach, someone's gonna bat an eye.

Staring at the wooden rosary beads swaying from the rearview, Nico knew Edmund was right. They'd been lucky so far, but if a cop pulled them over . . . if they were taken into custody . . . No, after all this, the cause was too great. And when they were this close . . . to Wes . . . to Boyle . . . to completing God's will and delivering the redemption for his mother . . . No, this was no time for risk.

"Tell me what you think is best," he said, looking to Edmund.

Hard as it is to say, we need to dump the truck and get something that's a bit less noticeable in traffic.

"That's fine, but how do we do that?"

How do we do anything, Nico? As the truck hit a divot in the road, Edmund's head jerked up and back, crashing into the headrest and revealing the bubbling black and red gash across his neck. *You look outside your window and search for the opportunity.*

Following Edmund's gaze through the front windshield, Nico searched the blacktop of highway, eventually spotting what his friend was staring at in the distance. The moment he saw it, a broad smile lifted his cheeks.

"You think we should—?"

Of course, we should, Nico. Heed the Book. Why else would God put them there?

Nodding to himself, Nico hit the brakes, and the truck rumbled and shuddered, eventually screeching to a stop right behind a maroon Pontiac on the shoulder of the highway. On the passenger side of the car, a woman with cropped black hair watched as her tank-topped boyfriend fought to change the flat tire on their car.

"You guys need some help?" Nico asked as he hopped out of the cab.

"You from Triple A?" the woman asked.

"No. It just looked like you needed an assist, so we thought we'd pitch in."

"I actually think I'm done," the boyfriend said, tightening the last lug nut.

"Wow, a real Good Samaritan," the woman teased.

"Funny," Nico replied, stepping into the woman's personal space. "Though I much prefer the term *guardian angel.*"

The woman stepped back. But not nearly fast enough.

61

Key West, Florida

Here you go," the cabdriver says as his bright pink Key West cab jerks to a stop. He's got thick white sunblock caked all over his nose, and a ratty *Shrek* beach blanket with the words *Can I Get a Whoop Whoop* draped over the back of his seat. "Three twenty-seven William Street."

"You kidding? We barely went three blocks," Lisbeth barks from our seats in the back. "Why didn't you just tell us we could walk?"

"You got in the cab," the driver says, not the least bit riled as he turns up the dial on the *Paul & Young Ron* radio show. Standard Key West—everything's sunny. "That'll be two bucks," he adds, poking a button on the meter.

"I shouldn't pay you a single—"

"Thanks for the ride," I interrupt, tossing three bucks into the front seat. When our helicopter touched down on another private yacht in Key West's Historic Seaport, we decided that the rest of the trip should be low-key and untraceable. The driver studies my face in his rearview mirror, and I realize we're already well off course. Fortunately, we've still got a few tricks left.

Kicking the door open and hopping outside, we watch as the cab disappears up the lush but narrow residential street. We're standing in front of a modest two-story conch cottage at 327 William, but as the cab turns the corner at the end of the block, we cross the street and trace the house numbers to our actual destination: the pale peach cottage with the white shutters and gingerbread trim at 324.

Grabbing the wooden railing that leans slightly when you put weight on it, Lisbeth bounds up the weather-beaten front porch like she's racing home for lemonade. But before she reaches the front door, her phone rings. Or rather, her colleague's phone rings, since they switched back at the paper. "Lemme just check this," Lisbeth says as she pulls the phone from her purse. She told her friend to only call if it was life-or-death. I look over her shoulder as we both check caller ID. The number is Lisbeth's work line. Here comes death.

"Eve?" Lisbeth answers.

"Oh, thank God," her colleague from the gardening section says, loud enough that it's easy to hear. "Hold on, I'm patching her in right now."

"Huh—patching *who* in?"

"Your phone call. I know you said not to pick up, but when I saw who it was . . . I mean, how'm I gonna say no to Lenore Manning?"

"Wait . . . *what?* The First Lady?"

"She asked for you—says she wants to talk to you about your column this morning."

I nod, telling her it's okay, and with a click, Eve announces, "Dr. Manning, you're on with Lisbeth."

"Hi, there," the First Lady opens, always first out of the gate.

"H-Hi, Dr. Manning."

"Oh, dear—you sound busy," the First Lady says, reading it perfectly as always. "Listen, I don't mean to waste your time—I just wanted to thank you for the generous mention for cystic fibrosis. You're a darling for that."

Lisbeth is speechless as she hears the words. But for Lenore Manning, it's standard fare. She used to do the same thing in the White House—anytime a mention ran, good or bad, she'd call or send a thank-you note to the reporter. It's not out of kindness. It's a trick used by nearly every President. Once a reporter knows there's a person on the other end, it's twice as hard for them to tear you down.

"No, happy to help," Lisbeth says, meaning every word.

"Ask her if Manning went into the office," I whisper in Lisbeth's ear.

"Ma'am, can I also—?"

"Let me let you run," the First Lady says, sidestepping with such grace, Lisbeth barely realizes she hasn't even gotten the question out. With a click, Dr. Manning is gone.

Lisbeth turns my way and shuts her phone. "Wow, she doesn't miss an opportunity, huh?"

"She's just happy you called her an icon."

"She actually cares abou—?"

"Let me tell you something: On days like today, when the wires are filled with Nico's escape, and old clips are running from the Manning administration, she misses it more than anyone."

Lisbeth races back across the sun-faded porch, where a

hand-painted wooden crab on the front door pinches a sign that says *Crabby on more than just Mondays.* She tugs on the screen door and reaches for the doorbell.

"It's open!" a throaty, cigarette-stained voice calls from inside, awakening a flush of old memories.

I reach over Lisbeth's shoulder and give the door a shove. Inside, the bitter acidic smell of chemicals drills through my sinuses.

"Sorry, been airing out the darkroom," a short, overweight man with a spotty gray beard and a matching head of brushed-back thinning gray hair announces. Wiping his hands with a baby wipe, he rolls up the sleeves of his creased shirt and steps a bit too close to Lisbeth. That's the problem with White House photographers—always overstepping their limits.

"You're not Wes," he says to Lisbeth with no hint of irony.

"You must be Kenny," she says, shaking his hand and taking half a step back. "Lisbeth. From the President's library."

He doesn't even notice. He's far too focused on me as I step inside. Never taking his eyes off his subject.

"The Boy King," he says, whipping out my old nickname.

"Popeye the Photographer Man," I say, whipping his right back. He taps his pointer finger against the crow's-feet of his left eye. After years of looking through a lens with his right eye, Kenny's left is always closed a hair more.

"C'mere, Bluto, gimme a kiss," he teases, embracing me with the kind of hug you get from an old camp friend—a deep-tissue squeeze that brings with it a flush of memories. "You look fantastic," he says, believing every word.

During trips on Air Force One, Kenny ran the press pool's poker game in back. As I step inside, he's already searching for my tells.

"Still can't leave it behind, can you?" he asks, tracing my glance to the *New York Times* on his painted Arts and Crafts–style kitchen table. On the front page, there's a huge picture of current President Ted Hartson standing at a podium, his hands resting just below the microphone.

"Who took that? Kahan?" I ask.

"Arms resting flat . . . no motion . . . no reaction shot . . . of course, it's Kahan. President might as well be a corpse."

In the world of podiums and White House photographers, the only real action shot comes when the President moves. A hand gesture. Raised eyebrows. That's when the firing squad of cameras pulls its triggers. Miss that and you miss the shot.

Kenny rarely missed the shot. Especially when it mattered. But after thirty-five years of running city to city and country to country, it became clear that even if it's not a young man's game, it's not an old one's either. Kenny never took it personally. Even the best horses get put out to pasture.

"So how're the twilight years?" I joke, even though he's barely pushing sixty.

Cocking his Popeye eye, he motions us into his living room, which is clearly more of a welcome area for his studio. Centered around a pine cocktail table surrounded by four Mission-style armchairs, the room is covered almost to the ceiling with dozens of black-and-white photographs, all displayed in sleek white matting and museum-quality black frames. As I step toward them, I'm surprised to see that while most of the photos are in the candid journalistic style that White House photographers are famous for, the shots themselves are of young brides throwing bouquets, and well-clad grooms being fed mouthfuls of cake.

"You're doing *weddings*?" I ask.

"Six Presidents, forty-two kings, countless ambassadors . . . and Miriam Mendelsohn's bridal party, complete with a reunion shot of her Pi Phi pledge class," Kenny says, all excitement and no shame.

"You're serious?"

"Don't laugh, Wes—I work two days a month, then get to go sailing all week. All I gotta do is make 'em look like the Kennedys."

"They're really beautiful," Lisbeth says, examining the photos.

"They should be," Kenny says, straightening one of the frames. "I pour my heart into them. I mean, life doesn't just peak in the White House, right?"

I nod instinctively. So does Lisbeth, who reaches out and straightens another frame. Just over her shoulder, on a nearby end table, I spot one of Kenny's most famous photos of Manning: a crisp black-and-white shot of the President in the White House kitchen, fixing his tie in the reflection of a shining silver water pitcher just before his first state dinner. Turning back to the wall of brides, I find a blond beauty queen looking over her own shoulder and admiring her French braid in the mirror. The new shot's just as good. Maybe even better.

"So how's the Kingfish?" Kenny adds, referring to Manning. "Still mad at me for taking the shot?"

"He's not mad at you, Popeye."

"Really? You tell him you were coming here?"

"You crazy?" I ask. "You have any idea how mad he is at you?"

Kenny laughs, well aware of his social standing in the Manning house. "Some laws are immutable," he says, pulling a thick three-ring binder off the end table with Manning's picture. "White used cars sell best . . . strip clubs only shut down if there's a fire . . . and President Leland Manning will never forgive the man who gave him *this* . . ." Flipping open the three-ring binder, Kenny reveals a plastic-encased, pristine copy of the most famous presidential photo since Truman held up the *Dewey Defeats Truman* headline: the black-and-white Cowardly Lion shot—Manning in mid-scream at the shooting, tugged down in the pile as the CEO's wife became his human shield.

"God, I remember seeing this on the front page the next day," Lisbeth says, sitting in one of the armchairs as he lowers the binder onto her lap. "This's . . . it's history . . ."

"What paper?" Kenny asks.

"*Palm Beach Post,*" Lisbeth replies, looking up.

"Yep, that was me. Another few thousand dollars I'll never see."

Reading the incomprehension on Lisbeth's face, I explain, "Since Kenny was working for the AP at the time, they made all the money from the reprint sales."

"Hundreds of newspapers and forty-nine magazine covers—all for bubkes," Kenny says. "Meanwhile, that college kid NASCAR hired to take some shots for their Web site? He was freelance, lucky schmuck. Made $800,000—*eight hundred thousand*—and he *missed the shot*!"

"Yeah, but who's the one who got the Pulitzer for the full sequence?" I point out.

"Pulitzer? That was a pity vote," Kenny interrupts. "I

didn't squeeze the shutter in a hail of gunfire. I panicked at the noise and accidentally hit the button. Manning's only in three of the frames." Turning back to Lisbeth, he adds, "It happened so fast, if you looked away and then looked back, you missed it."

"Doesn't look like you missed anything," Lisbeth says as she turns past the first page of the book and stares down at the double-page spread of contact sheets filled with sixty or so tiny black-and-white shots, each one barely bigger than a postage stamp.

"If you keep flipping, there should be six more—eight rolls total, including reaction shots," Kenny says. "I've got most of them blown to 8×10, but you said the library was looking for some new angles, so . . ." From his pocket, he pulls out a photographer's loupe—a small, round magnifier to see the details of the photos—and hands it to Lisbeth.

For a half second, she forgets that she introduced herself as library staff. "No . . . no, that's great," she says. "With the ten-year anniversary of the shooting coming up, we just want an exhibit that does more than reprint the same old stuff."

"Sure, that makes perfect sense," Kenny says dryly, his Popeye eye narrowing as he calmly stares me down. "With two years to go, it's much smarter for you to come all the way to Key West than to have me make a few copies and mail them to you at the library."

Lisbeth freezes. So do I. The Popeye eye is barely a sliver.

"No bullshit, Wes. This for you or for *him*?" Kenny asks. He says *him* in that tone that people reserve for God. The same tone we all used during our days in the White House.

"Me," I say, feeling my throat go dry.

He doesn't respond.

"I swear, Kenny. On my mom."

Still nothing.

"Kenny, please—"

"Listen, that's my phone," Kenny interrupts, even though the house is dead silent. "Lemme go grab this call. I'll be upstairs if you need me. Understand?"

I nod, holding my breath. Kenny pats me on my scars like a godfather, then disappears up the staircase, never looking back. It's not until I hear his upstairs bedroom door close that I finally exhale.

Lisbeth pops open the notebook's binder rings with a metallic thunk. "You take the loupe—I'll take the 8×10s," she says, unlatching the first eight sheets and sliding them my way.

Kneeling over the cocktail table, I put the loupe over the first photo and lean in like a jeweler studying a diamond.

The first shot is a close-up on the limo just as we pulled into the pits of the racetrack. Unlike the video at Lisbeth's office, the background here is crisp and clear. But the camera's so close up on the car, all I see are the backs of a few NASCAR drivers' heads and the first row of people sitting in the stands.

One picture down . . . 287 to go . . .

62

"We're looking for Kara Lipof," Rogo said, stepping into the messy room that was as wide and long as two side-by-side bowling lanes.

"Two to the right," a male archivist with a phone number written on his hand said as he pointed his thumb two desks away.

Housing all eight archivists in a shared space with nothing but a metal bookshelf to separate each desk from the one next to it, the room was littered with paper on every desk, shelf, chair, computer monitor, mini-fridge, and window ledge. Fortunately for Rogo, the paper didn't cover the plastic nameplate on the front of Kara's desk.

"Kara?" Rogo asked warmly, always preferring to charm.

From behind her desk, a woman in her early thirties with auburn hair and a trendy floral-print blouse looked up from her computer screen. "Can I help you?"

"I hope so," Rogo replied, adding a smile. "I'm Wes Holloway—from the personal office. I spoke to you yesterday about Ron Boyle's files." Before she could register any difference in Wes's and Rogo's voices, Rogo added the one thing guaranteed to get her attention. "The President wanted to know if you'd pulled them together yet."

"Yes . . . of course," Kara said, fidgeting with the piles on her desk. "It's just . . . I'm sorry, I didn't realize you were coming to pick them up."

"You said there were 36,000 pages to copy," Rogo added, keeping the smile as he repeated the details Wes gave him. "We figured if we came down here and flipped through them first, we'd save you on the Kinko's bills."

Kara laughed. So did Dreidel, just for effect.

"You have no idea how much you're saving my life right now," Rogo added. "Thanks to you, I'll actually live to my twenty-third birthday. Okay . . . twenty-fifth. Twenty-ninth, tops."

"Don't go turning me into a saint just yet," Kara said, pulling out a thin manila folder. "Faxing you a crossword was one thing—but if you want access to Boyle's full file, I need an official FOIA request, plus authorization that—"

"See, that's the tickle," Dreidel interrupted, putting a hand on Rogo's shoulder and trying to get him to step aside. Rogo didn't budge. "If the President makes an official request, people take notice. They start thinking something's happened. That there must be news with Boyle's case. Next thing we know, Boyle's family wants to know what the government's hiding. We say *nothing*, they say *everything*, and that's how conspiracies are born. So how about saving all of us the migraines and instead treating this as an *unofficial* request? As for authorization, I'm happy to sign for it."

"I'm sorry . . . do I know—?"

"Gavin Jeffer," Dreidel replied before she could even finish the question. "Y'know . . . from *here* . . ."

Pointing a finger down toward her desk, Dreidel stabbed a piece of library letterhead just next to where his name appeared along the left margin.

To this day, it was Dreidel's greatest get. In order to build the Manning Library, a separate foundation was set up with a board of directors that included the President's closest friends, biggest donors, and most loyal staff. The select group included Manning's daughters, his former secretary of state, the former CEO of General Motors, and—to almost everyone's surprise—Dreidel. It took surgically precise phone calls and begging in all the right places, but those were always Dreidel's specialties.

"So the files?" he said to the archivist.

Kara looked to Rogo, then back to Dreidel. The way she flicked her thumb against the edge of the manila folder, she was clearly still on the bubble.

"Kara, if you want, call the President's office," Dreidel added. "You know Claudia's number."

"That's not what I—"

"It's not like we're talking about NSC staff," Dreidel said, continuing to pound away as he referred to the National Security Council. "Boyle's domestic."

"And dead," Rogo said, bouncing on his feet to keep the mood upbeat. "C'mon, what's the worst that happens? He suddenly comes back to life?"

For the second time, Kara laughed. For the second time, Dreidel pretended to.

"And you'll sign off on it?" she asked Dreidel.

"Gimme the form and I'm your man. And if it makes you feel better, I'll have President Manning write you a thank-you note personally."

Shaking her head, she stood from her desk. "This better not get me fi—"

Rogo's phone rang in his pocket. "Sorry," he said, fishing it from his pants and flipping it open. Caller ID said *PB Sher. Off.* Palm Beach Sheriff's Office.

"I'll catch up in a second," he said to Dreidel and Kara as they headed for the door. Turning to the phone, he answered, "This is Rogo."

"Hey, fatty, we missed you in court today," a man teased with a high voice and unforgivable New York accent. Rogo knew it instantly. Deputy Terry Mechaber. Palm Beach County's number one writer of illegal U-turn tickets . . . and Rogo's oldest friend in law enforcement.

"Yeah, receptionist was sick, so I had to stay back and kiss my own butt this morning," Rogo replied.

"That's funny, because I just spoke to your receptionist. Sounded like her lips were just fine—especially when she said you'd been gone since this morning."

For a moment, Rogo was quiet. "Listen, Terry—"

"I don't wanna know, I don't wanna hear, I don't wanna read about it in tomorrow's paper," Terry said. "And based on this fight you're picking, I don't even wanna see the bad TV movie with the scene of me passing this along to you."

"Wh-What're you—?"

"The Three . . . y'know, the guys you asked me to run through the databases here . . ."

"Wait, you found something?"

"Yeah, here in the Florida DMV, we have records of all the international bad guys. No, I passed it to my partner's sister's brother-in-law, who's been spending the last few years doing some high-tech computer job I still don't understand for DOD."

"Dee-oh-dee?"

"Department of Defense," Terry replied, his voice slow

and serious. "And when he ran *The Three* through there, well, remember the time when that eighteen-wheeler hauling all that rebar triple-flipped on I-95, sending metal javelins through the air and impaling nearly everyone in the ten nearest cars behind it?"

"Yeah . . ."

"It's worse than that."

63

"Welcome to Key West," the pilot called out, brushing his wispy blond hair back on his head.

Following him out of the seaplane door and down the scaffolding to the white pontoon floats that gave the orange and red plane its buoyancy, O'Shea and Micah barely waited for the plane to be tied to the dock.

"How long you gonna be?" the pilot asked.

"Not long," O'Shea said, careful to time his jump just right. Waiting for the seaport's light waves to sink, then swell, he hopped from the edge of the pontoon float and landed square on the dock. "Just make sure—"

"Don't stress so much," the pilot called back. "I know every dockmaster working this place. Soon as I tie us up, I'll take care of it—no one'll ever know we were here."

"We should call Wes's office again," Micah said, only a few steps behind. "Maybe he checked in."

"He didn't check in."

Tracing the maze of wooden planks past dozens of sailboats and charter boats that swayed against the docks, O'Shea didn't stop until he reached the end of William Street. As Micah skidded to a stop next to him, the sound of acoustic folk rock drifted in from the bar on their far right. O'Shea narrowed his eyes, searching through the crowds of tourists clogging the shops along the docks. From the side streets, a steady stream of cars and cabs circled the block, replenishing the tourist supply.

"What're you—?"

"All the cabs are pink," O'Shea blurted. *"Taxi!"*

On their right, a bright pink cab shrieked and stopped. Opening the back door, O'Shea slid inside. "You have radios in these cars?"

The skinny African-American cabbie glanced over his shoulder at O'Shea's dark blue suit, then over at Micah, whose tie dangled downward as he leaned in through the open door. "Let me guess—lost your wallet in a pink cab."

"Actually, I lost my friend." O'Shea laughed, playing nice. "He's pretty unforgettable, though—huge mess of scars on the side of his face. Plus the redhead he's running around with. So whattya say," he added, lowering a twenty-dollar bill onto the armrest of the front seat. "Think you can help me track him down?"

The cabbie grinned. "Damn, man, why didn't you just say so in the first place?"

One quick description later, a slow, easy voice squawked through the radio's receiver. "Yeah, I seen 'em, Rogers. Kid with the scars . . . Dropped 'em twenty minutes ago. Three twenty-seven William Street."

"That far from here?" O'Shea asked as the cabbie looked at him in the rearview.

"You can walk if you want."

Micah hopped inside, tugging the door shut.

"We'll drive," O'Shea said as he tossed another twenty onto the armrest. "Fast as you can."

"Like your life depended on it," Micah added.

64

With my knees digging into the carpet, my chest pinned against the coffee table, and the weight of my face pressed against the photographer's loupe, I study a black-and-white profile shot of the President and First Lady as they leave Cadillac One, their chins up toward the astonished crowd. Like the best White House photos, the moment is flush with the pomp of the presidency mixed with the humanity of the players involved.

Manning has his hand on the small of his wife's back, gently edging her out of the limo and into his world. As she leaves the car, one foot already on the pavement of the racetrack, she's in mid-blink, frozen awkwardly between the private quiet of the limo and the public roar of the crowd. For support, the First Lady holds the hand that the President's extended to her. But even in that moment—her holding him, his fingertips on the curve of her back—whatever tenderness exists between husband and wife is swallowed by the fact that instead of looking at each other, both smile up to the fans in the stands.

"These are unreal," Lisbeth says, flipping through the notebook of 8×10s in her lap.

I glance over to see what she's looking at. She's about ten seconds ahead of my sequence, moments after the last shot was fired and Manning was pulled down by the swarm of drivers, guests, and Secret Service agents. In her photo, people in the stands scream and scurry in every direction, their hair spiked as they run.

In mine, they're enraptured and calm, completely immobile on the edge of their seats. In Lisbeth's, I hear the screams. In mine, I hear the thrill of their first true look at the President and his wife. *There he is . . . There he is . . . There they are . . .*

Ten seconds apart. Ten seconds to change everyth—

No. It didn't change everything. It changed me.

An electronic ring interrupts the thought as I quickly trace the noise to the cell phone we borrowed from Lisbeth's coworker at the paper. Pulling it from my inside jacket pocket, I see *Pres. Manning Library* on caller ID. At least he's smart enough not to call from his—

"They're all in it together," he insists before I can even say hello. "That's how they pulled it off."

"What're you—?"

"It's just like we said, Wes—you can't do this without help."

"Slow down . . . who're you talking about?"

"The Three—that's what Boyle called them. But they're not what you—"

"Who'd you get this from? Dreidel or someone else?"

"My—"

"Does Dreidel even know?"

"Will you shut the hell up and let me tell you!?" Rogo shouts through the phone. I turn to see if Lisbeth hears, but she's too lost in the 8×10s.

Catching his breath in the silence, Rogo starts at a

whisper. Wherever he is, he's definitely not alone. "They started as a myth, Wes. Like some old law enforcement ghost story. You've heard it for years: politicians bitching and moaning that all our law enforcement groups don't work well together—that the FBI won't share information with the CIA, who won't share with the Secret Service. The result leaves half the agencies complaining that they're in the dark. But there are some who argue—not publicly, of course—that the lack of coordination isn't such a bad thing. The more adversarial they are, the more each agency is a check on the other. If the CIA does something corrupt, the FBI is there to call them on it. But if they all got together and ganged up against us . . . well, y'know what kinda power's in those numbers?"

"Wait, so now you're trying to tell me that someone's convinced *thousands* of our country's top, most trusted agents to suddenly switch sides?"

"Not thousands," Rogo says, his voice still a whisper. "Just three."

Climbing from my knees, I sit back on the couch. Next to me, Lisbeth's carefully studying one of the photos.

"Hey . . . uh . . . Wes," she says, pointing to a photo.

I give her the *one minute* sign with my pointer finger and stay focused on the phone.

"Three members," Rogo adds. "One from the FBI, one from the CIA, one from the Secret Service. Alone, they can only do limited damage. Together, fully aware of all the tricks, including how to sidestep three of our most powerful agencies? They can pull down the whole damn sky."

"Wes, I think you should look at this," Lisbeth says.

Once again, I put up the *one minute* sign.

"Apparently, it was the great urban myth of law

enforcement—until eight years ago, when the first internal investigation was opened," Rogo says. "My guy said there's some sky-level memo from Boyle to the President, warning him to look into it."

"So Manning and Boyle were chasing The Three?"

"Or The Three were chasing them—for all we know, they were fighting over the same corrupt pie," Rogo replies.

"And you think three guys could really keep their jobs and stay hidden that long?"

"You kidding? Robert Hanssen spent twenty years selling secrets from within the FBI before anyone took notice. The Three are pros within their agencies. And the way they're backing each other up, they're doing triple damage. Oh, and just to crap on your day a little more: The last—and only—known sighting for one of these guys was that beautiful little terrorist hot spot known as Sudan."

"Sudan? As in, the one country The Roman specializes in?"

"Wes, I'm serious," Lisbeth says, popping open the rings of the notebook.

"Just one sec," I tell her. "No jokes, Rogo," I say into the phone. "You think The Roman gets info from The Three?"

"Or *gives* info *to* The Three. Hell, for all we know, The Roman's *part of* The Three, though I guess it could be anyone in the Service."

Next to me, Lisbeth pulls the photo from the notebook, then holds it almost to her nose to check it up close.

"You mean that he's CIA or FBI?" I ask Rogo.

"No, he's Secret Service," Rogo says a bit too confidently. I know that tone.

"Rogo, don't play games. Say what you're saying."

"Wes, just take a second to look at this," Lisbeth says, now annoyed I'm ignoring her.

"It was actually Dreidel's brainstorm," Rogo says. "Once he heard *FBI*, he asked my guy if he could look up your favorite investigators, Agents O'Shea and Micah. According to his records, O'Shea started with the Bureau in July of 1986. Same exact year as Micah."

"So what's the problem?"

"Wes . . ." Lisbeth pleads.

"The problem," Rogo says, refusing to slow down, "is that Micah doesn't work for the Bureau. As near as we can tell, he works as a case officer. For the CIA."

"Just look!" Lisbeth adds, shoving the photo into my lap.

My lungs crater, like someone's shot an arrow into my chest. It only gets worse as I look down at the photograph. In my lap is a black-and-white reaction shot taken a few minutes after the shooting. Unlike the others, this one faces the infield of the raceway, where NASCAR drivers, mechanics, and their staff embrace, hug, sob, and retell the story that just unfolded in front of them. Most look shell-shocked. A few look angry. And one—all alone in the far right corner of the photo, glancing over his shoulder as he walks away—looks oddly curious.

At first, he blends right in because of his racing jumpsuit. But there's no mistaking the finely combed hair and the small nick missing from the top of his ear. Eight years ago, I was shot in the face, Boyle was supposedly killed, and the Manning presidency was decimated. Micah was there to witness it all.

"That's him, right?" Lisbeth asks. "That's Micah . . ."

The Secret Service is in charge of presidential protection. The FBI handled the investigation of Nico. "What the hell was the CIA doing there that day?" I blurt.

"CIA?" Lisbeth asks.

"Wes, don't answer her!" Rogo calls out through the phone.

"What're you talking about?"

"Think for a second," he tells me. "You've always been alone when O'Shea and Micah corner you, right? So if Lisbeth never met Micah before, how the hell can she pick him out of a photograph?"

I look over at Lisbeth, who's still next to me on the couch. "What's wrong?" she asks, reaching for the picture. She pulls it out of my hands before I can react.

"Lemme call you right back," I say to Rogo as I hang up the phone.

65

Sorry I couldn't be more help," an elderly black woman with a beaded bracelet said as she walked O'Shea to the door of her modest conch cottage at 327 William Street. "Though I do hope you find him."

"I'm sure we will," O'Shea replied, stepping back outside and tucking his badge back into his jacket pocket. "Thanks for letting us look around, though."

A few steps behind him, Micah held his phone to his ear, trying hard not to look frustrated. He didn't say a word until the woman shut the door behind them.

"Told you the kid's sharp," The Roman said through Micah's phone.

"That's real helpful," Micah shot back. "Almost as helpful as showing up in Florida and heading into Manning's office without telling anyone."

"You know the rules," The Roman said calmly. "No contact unless—"

"You telling me this isn't a fucking emergency?" Micah exploded. "We got Wes sniffing everywhere, no bead on Boyle, and you're waltzing into the one place that has the very best chance of asking what the hell're you doing here in the first place? When'd you plan on filling us in—before or after they start staring at you and report you back to headquarters?"

Just as he did before, The Roman stayed calm. "I *did* call you, Micah. That's why we're talking. And if it makes you feel better, no one's reporting me anywhere. I'm here because it's my job, which is more than I can say about you and the half dozen people you've held yourself out to as an FBI agent. The Agency teach you to be that dumb, or were you just panicking that O'Shea would turn on you if you didn't stay close to him?"

"I told headquarters my father was sick. O'Shea said he had his niece's graduation. You think we didn't clear ourselves for being back here?"

"And that makes you think you can hold hands in public like that? Using your real names, no less? O'Shea I understand—just in case Wes calls the Bureau to check him out. But *you*!? Have you forgotten how we got this far in the first place?"

"Actually, I haven't forgotten any of it," Micah shot back. "Which is why, when I first started smelling the flames from the *Towering Inferno*, I called O'Shea instead of you. So don't *you* forget, pinhead—in the FBI, O'Shea's a Legal Attaché, meaning he coordinates resources for foreign investigations. That means he's authorized—hell, he's *encouraged*—to pair up with Agency folks like me. That's his job! So no offense, but as long as it's my ass on the clothesline, I plan on being front and center for saving it!"

For a moment, The Roman was silent. "No contact," he finally said. "*Ever.*"

Micah turned to O'Shea, who mouthed the words *Hang up*. After almost ten years together, they both knew it wasn't worth the argument. When The Roman wanted something, he always went after it himself. It was the same for all of them. Personal drive was what brought them together all those years ago at War College. It was no coincidence that each was invited to attend one of the army's prestigious leadership conferences, where top military officials and representatives from the State Department, CIA, FBI, DIA, Customs, and Secret Service spend two weeks studying national defense and military interactions. It was there that they were lectured on military tactics. There that they learned strategic leadership. And there that each realized how much they'd given to their government—and how little the government had given back. That's where The Three was born.

No doubt, personal drive made them successful over time. It helped them maneuver through the system, maintaining their jobs to this day without any of their colleagues being the wiser. Yet personal drive, they also knew, would someday be their undoing. Boyle called them The Three, but even on their best days, they were always looking out for number one.

"Just find Wes—he's still the only one Boyle's contacted, which means Boyle'll reach out again," The Roman added. "And even with the fake address Wes gave, you should still be able t—"

With a click, Micah hung up the phone. "Guy's unreal," he bitched to O'Shea. "First, he snakes in without telling us, now he wants to play quarterback."

"He's just nervous," O'Shea said. "And personally, I don't blame him."

"But to let Nico out—"

"By accident . . ."

"You believe him on that?"

"Micah, Roman's a scumbag, but he's not a moron. He knows Nico can *Hindenburg* at any moment, which is why he needed to see if Boyle had been in touch. But let me tell you right now, if we don't find Wes—and Boyle—quickly, I'm done. No joke. It's enough."

"Can you please stop with the ultimatums?"

"It's not an ultimatum," O'Shea insisted. "Just being here—snooping this close and giving this kid every reason to look us up—you have any idea what we're risking?"

"We're being smart."

"No, being smart is walking away now, and being thankful we made some cash and lasted this long."

"Not when there's so much more cash to be made. The Roman said next month in India, there's a—"

"Of course, it's India. And eight months ago, it was Argentina, and eight years ago, it was Daytona. It's enough, Micah. Yes, we added some feathers to the nest egg, but the giant pot of gold? It's never coming."

"You're wrong."

"I'm right."

"You're *wrong*!" Micah insisted, his finely combed hair flying out of place.

O'Shea stopped at the curb, knowing better than to keep arguing. It didn't matter anyway—he'd made his decision the moment he got the call yesterday: If they could wrap this up quickly, fantastic. If not, well, that's why he saved his money and bought that bungalow in Rio. Eyeing Micah, he knew that if it all cratered and it came down to finger-pointing, he had no problem breaking a few fingers.

"Everything okay?" Micah asked.

O'Shea nodded from the curb, both of them studying each house on the lush, narrow street. O'Shea checked windows and doors, searching for shadows and suddenly closed curtains. Micah checked front porches and pathways, searching for footprints in the light layer of sand that regularly blew across the Key West sidewalks. Neither found a thing. Until . . .

"There," O'Shea said, marching diagonally across the street and heading straight for the peach cottage with the white shutters and gingerbread trim.

"Where?" Micah asked, still searching for himself.

"The car."

A few steps behind O'Shea, Micah studied the old red Mustang parked in the driveway at 324 William Street. Florida license plate. Registration stickers up to date. Nothing out of the ordinary. Except for the ratty, weatherworn Washington Redskins bumper sticker on the back left bumper.

"Go Skins," Micah whispered, barely able to contain his grin. Picking up speed, he followed his partner up the steps to the front door with the hand-painted wooden crab sign hanging on it.

"One sec," Micah added as he reached into his suit jacket and flicked off the safety on his gun. Signaling to O'Shea with a nod, he took a half-step back, just in case they'd have to knock down the door.

With a jab of his finger, O'Shea rang the doorbell and checked on his own gun. "Coming," a voice called from inside.

Micah checked the street behind them. No one in sight.

The doorknob twisted with a creak, and the door flew open.

"Hey there," O'Shea announced, purposely not pulling his FBI badge. "We're friends of Wes Holloway and just wanted to check in and make sure he's okay."

"Oh, he's great," Kenny said, purposely blocking the doorway, even though the only thing to see was his empty kitchen and living room. "But I'm sorry to say he's long gone."

Craning his neck to look over Kenny's shoulder, Micah ignored the kitchen and living room and instead focused on the far back wall of the house, where a painted screen door led out to the backyard.

"Yeah, we thought that might be the case," O'Shea said. "But even so, you mind if we come inside and just ask a few questions?"

66

"So you've been down to the stacks before?" Kara asked as the elevator doors slid open, revealing a concrete hallway with narrow windows on either side and all the charm of a prison.

"Absolutely," Rogo replied, keeping his voice peppy and his head down as they passed the first of two security cameras attached to the wall. Two steps in front of him, next to Kara, Dreidel fidgeted with his tie and did the same.

When a President builds his library, it's his chance to rewrite history. In LBJ's library, there's an exhaustive exhibit on why the U.S. *had* to go to Vietnam. In Manning's, the only mention of the Cowardly Lion was down in the stacks.

"We really appreciate you pulling everything so fast," Dreidel said.

"That's our job," Kara replied as they approached a steel-reinforced door that was nearly as thick as a bank vault. "I just hope you guys aren't claustrophobic . . ."

"No—in fact, we hate the sunlight," Rogo said. "Darn vitamin D *pisses* me off!"

Glancing over her shoulder, Kara offered another panting laugh. This time, Dreidel didn't join in. "Just point us to the files and we'll be gone before you know it," he said.

Kara punched in a five-digit code just above the doorknob. "You asked for it," she said as the thick metal door swung open, and the sweet smell of an old bookstore wafted through the air. In front of them, in a room as big as a basketball court, was row after row of gray metal storage shelves. But instead of being filled with books, they were stacked with thousands of square and rectangular acid-free storage boxes. On their far right, well past the shelves, a metal cage ran from floor to ceiling, separating them from another set of about ten metal shelves: secure storage for national security files. Just in front of the cage, a lanky Hispanic man with reading glasses sat in front of one of two computer terminals.

"If you have any problems, ask Freddy," Kara explained, motioning to one of the library's four research room attendants.

Freddy waved to Rogo and Dreidel. Rogo and Dreidel waved back. But the way Kara eyed Freddy, and Freddy eyed Dreidel . . . Even Rogo took the hint. Kara may've been nice enough to let them in the stacks, but there's no way she was dumb enough to leave them unsupervised in the heart of the archives.

"So our stuff . . ." Dreidel asked.

". . . is right here," Kara said, pointing to the end of one of the metal stacks, where a small worktable was buried under at least forty boxes. "These small ones have already been processed through FOIA," she explained, waving her open palm at the dozen or so narrow, vertical boxes that looked like they each held a phone book. "And these FRCs . . . these're the ones from closed storage," she added, pointing to the thirty or so square boxes that were each about the size of a milk crate.

"And this is everything Boyle had?" Rogo asked.

"If you went back in time and pulled open his desk drawers in the White House, here's what you would've found—his files, his memos, his printed-out e-mails—plus you asked for his personnel file and those 12,000 pages that were requested by your other researcher . . ."

"Carl Stewart," Rogo said, remembering Wes's instructions as Kara handed him the list of every file Boyle requested under his fake name.

"You already have the crossword, right?" Kara asked.

"Right here," Rogo said, patting the breast pocket of his shirt.

"Kara, we can't thank you enough," Dreidel added, anxious to send her on her way.

Taking the cue, Kara headed for the door. Never forgetting her role as protector of the archives, though, she called out, "Freddy, thanks for supervising."

As Kara turned the corner and disappeared, Dreidel shot a smile at the attendant, then quickly turned back to Rogo. "How 'bout you take Boyle's desk drawers, and I'll start hunting through the list of his requests."

"I got a better idea," Rogo challenged. "You take the drawers, and *I'll* go through the requests."

For a moment, Dreidel was silent. "Fine," he said, flipping open the nearest box. Behind him, Rogo did the same.

As Rogo pulled out the first file, he licked his fingers and turned to the first page. "Okay, Boyle, you sneaky son of a bitch—time to see what you were searching for."

67

Melbourne, Florida

"No, not her," Nico said, glancing out the front windshield of his maroon Pontiac Grand Prix as a petite Peruvian woman sipped her coffee and headed toward her own car.

Why? What's wrong with her?

Nico looked shaken. "She looks like my nurse. Pick someone else."

What about him?

Nico didn't even turn toward Edmund's selection. From their corner spot in the Waffle House parking lot, he was still watching the woman who looked so amazingly like his night nurse. It'd been nearly a full day since he thought about the hospital. The doctors were wrong. So were the lawyers. All wrong. Out on his own—even without his meds—he felt just fine. Better even. More clear. Crackling crystal clear.

Nico, focus. What about him?

Following Edmund's glance, Nico studied the bearded man with teeny eyes and obvious hair plugs.

"I can't. No. I can't. He was in my dream last night."

Fine, then her—the mom with the two boys . . .

"The short child has to pee—look how he grabs himself. She won't stop. I think the older boy wants M&M's. You can read his lips. *M . . . and . . . M's . . .*"

Nico, don't get loopy on me.

Sitting up straight, he pushed Edmund's imagined hand from his shoulder. "I'm not—I'm good. I just need to—" Cutting himself off, he locked on a plump, middle-aged waitress with beautiful brown eyes coming out of the restaurant for a cigarette break. On the strap of her purse was an *Ask Me About Avon* button.

"There. Her. She knows rejection," Nico announced, diving for the door handle and leaping out of the Pontiac. "Hurry!" he called to Edmund as he crossed the parking lot and approached the waitress.

"Can I borrow your phone?" Nico asked, slowing down just as he reached the woman. "It's an emergency. My—I have to call my mother."

Seeing Nico's handsome squint, the waitress didn't even hesitate. "Of course," she replied, her chubby hand lowering like a skill-crane into her fake-leather purse.

Tell her you won't be long.

"I won't be long," Nico said.

"Take as much time as you want, hon—I get a thousand minutes every month, God praise my divorce lawyer."

Flipping the phone open, Nico turned his back to the waitress and dialed a simple three-digit number. There was a chime on the other line.

"Welcome to local 411. What city and state?" a female operator asked.

"Wes Holloway," Nico said as he lowered his voice.

"*City* and *state*," the operator repeated, clearly annoyed.

"Palm Beach. Florida."

There was a short pause. "Sir? I've got a Wes Holloway in *West* Palm Beach. Please hold for the—"

"Not the number," Nico said. "The address."

Once again, there was a short pause. "Eight three eight five Okeechobee Boulevard, apartment 527. And you sure you don't want the phone number—y'know, just in case?"

"No number," Nico said, giving a quick thumbs-up to Edmund. "No, no. No. This is a surprise."

68

"What, now you don't believe me?" Lisbeth calls out.

"Just c'mon . . . let's go," I say, cutting between two tourists and running past the ice cream store on our way to the docks. She wasn't happy when I asked her how she knew what Micah looked like, but it's tough to argue with her answer.

"Wes, when we were at the newspaper, they drove right past me in the garage," she insists. "I was hiding right by the entrance—your idea, remember?—waiting for them to leave so I could pick you up. Any of this sounding familiar?"

If I were Rogo, I'd ask her how she knew which was Micah and which was O'Shea.

"I believe you," I tell her as I leap down two short steps and my feet slap against the wood of the docks. Over the past two days, I could've easily described Micah and O'Shea. More important, with everything we've been through, everything she's seen . . . After eight years of dealing with political schemers, I'm fluent in bullshit. Far as I can tell, Lisbeth doesn't speak a word of it.

"Wes, if I wanted to burn you—"

"I know—I just had to ask, okay?"

"But if you—"

"Lisbeth, I swear—we're fine," I call out, weaving through the maze of docks, back toward the yacht that holds our helicopter. "I swear to you. If we weren't, you wouldn't be holding the picture."

As she runs behind me, the photo we swiped from Kenny flaps in the wind. It's the only proof we have that Micah was there that day—and the main reason we darted out Kenny's back door. For the past two days, O'Shea and Micah have played relatively nice in the vain hope that I'd help them get Boyle and Manning. But if they find out we know the truth . . . that one of them is actually CIA . . . that he was there at the racetrack and potentially part of The Three . . . I glance over my shoulder at Lisbeth, who's glancing over her shoulder at the mostly empty docks. Whoever they were shooting at that day, Micah and O'Shea weren't afraid to send bullets at the most powerful men in the world. I don't even want to think how fast they'd make us disappear.

"You think they're close?" Lisbeth asks, her voice shaking.

Right now it's the only question that matters. To answer it, I slam the brakes, stopping short right in front of a small wooden hut no bigger than a phone booth. "Keep going," I say to Lisbeth, waving her along. "Tell Tommaso to get our ride ready. We need to leave now!"

She slows down, already worried I'm ditching her. "Then why're you—?"

"Just looking for our *friends*," I insist, shooting her a look as a man in a blue button-down and a wide-brimmed straw hat steps out of the hut. As dockmaster, he assigns all the boats to their different slips. Which means he sees every person coming and going. Lisbeth takes the hint and keeps running.

"Signing in or heading out?" the man asks, angling his hat back to reveal a mess of muddy tobacco chew in his mouth.

"Actually, was wondering if you happened to see some buddies of mine—probably just came in on a seaplane or helicopter from Palm Beach."

"Sorry, we don't log departure cities," he says quickly.

"What about in the last hour? Anybody new fly in?"

"Naw, we been pretty quiet all morning."

"You're sure?"

The dockmaster studies me, checking out my shirt, my slacks, even my shoes. He grins slightly and two dimples dot his cheeks.

"Positive, Dapper Dan. Nobody's flown in 'cept the billionaires in back," he says, motioning to our black and cream helicopter at the far end of the docks.

Nodding a thank-you, I dart back toward the yacht and breathe the smallest sigh of relief. At least for now, no one knows we're here—and as long as we have that . . . as long as they don't know what we found . . . we've finally got the advantage.

"Tommaso, you ready?" I call out to the back deck of the yacht.

"Waiting for you, sir," he calls back with a thumbs-up sign.

"Where's Lisbeth?"

He points to the glass cabin right next to him. Lisbeth's inside with her back to the glass. I don't blame her. Better to be out of sight than be spotted.

Scrambling up the metal steps two at a time, I leap for the door on the main deck and shove it open. "Good news," I say. "I think we're sa—"

Lisbeth spins around, her hands fighting to stuff what looks like a small cell phone into her purse.

"This for you or for him?" Kenny's voice echoes from the device.

"*Me. I swear—*" my own voice says. She hits a button and the playback stops with the loud pop of a . . . *tape recorder.*

My mouth gapes open, and my chest caves in.

Lisbeth looks at me, her wide eyes already shoveling up the apology.

"Wes, before you say anything," she pleads, stuffing the recorder into her bag.

"You were recording us?"

"It's not how y—"

"How long were you doing it?"

"It's not for attribution—just to keep my notes strai—"

"That's not the question."

"Listen, Wes—you . . . you knew I'd be writing the story. That was our deal."

"How *long?*"

"You told me it was our deal."

"Dammit, Lisbeth! *How fucking long?*"

She watches me carefully, then turns away to avoid the conflict. With her back to me, she stares out at the drumming waves of the Gulf of Mexico. "Since you walked in this morning," she eventually whispers.

"Including the helicopter ride here?"

She freezes, finally realizing what I'm getting at. Every reporter has a line they promise themselves they'll never cross. From the look on her face as she turns back to me, Lisbeth just skipped, hurdled, and jumped over it. "I never would've used that stuff, Wes."

My legs buckle, barely able to hold my weight.

"You know that's true, right?" she asks, reaching out for my shoulder.

As I pull away, an adrenaline surge crackles under my skin. I grit my teeth so tightly, I swear I have feeling in my lip again instead of just phantom pain. "Gimme the recorder," I growl.

She doesn't move.

"*Gimme the damn recorder!*"

Fumbling as she pulls it from her purse, she offers a look that says, *You don't have to do this.* But I'm done believing. I snatch the recorder from her hand and stride back to the deck.

"Wes, I know you don't believe this, but I never meant to hur—"

"Don't say it!" I snap, whipping back to face her and jamming a finger at her face. "You knew what you were doing! You *knew* it!"

Shoving my way outside and plowing toward the stern of the yacht, I cross over to the far railing, chuck the tape recorder into the water, and pivot back toward the helicopter.

"Everything okay?" Tommaso asks as he holds the helicopter door open and ushers us inside.

"Perfect," I snap. "Just get us the hell out of here."

69

Sitting cross-legged on the linoleum floor and surrounded by piles of stacked-up acid-free archival boxes, Rogo flipped through his fourth file folder in the past fifteen minutes. "What's *I&W*?"

"I&W for what?" Dreidel asked, hunched forward on a wooden chair and reading through one of Boyle's files.

"Doesn't say. Just *I&W* with lots of dates next to—wait, here's one: *I&W for Berlin.*"

"*Indicators and Warnings.* Or as General Bakos used to put it: all the trash talk and warning signs that our intelligence picks up about specific threats," Dreidel explained. "Why? Is that what—?" He looked over at the attendant and kept his voice to a whisper. "Is that what Boyle was requesting? All the different I&Ws?"

"Is that bad?"

"Not bad—just—indicators and warnings are the kinds of things you usually find in the PDB."

"President's Daily Brief. That's the report you were talking about before, with the CIA guy and the handcuffed briefcase?"

"And the place where The Roman's payouts were

decided," Dreidel added. "Don't forget, a year before the shooting, The Roman was denied a major sum of money for some hot tip in Sudan, which also, since they clearly were never stupid enough to be seen in the same place together, tells us which one of them used Sudan as their last—and only—known location."

"I'm not sure I follow."

"The Three—The Roman, Micah, O'Shea—are from the Service, the CIA, and FBI. When they link brains, think of all the information they have access to."

"I understand how they work . . . but to do all that—to set it all up—no offense, but . . . just for a six-million-dollar payout?"

"What makes you think they were only doing it once? For all we know, if the payment went through, they would've come back every few months—and if they upped each payment, six million becomes ten million becomes an easy seventy to eighty million dollars by the time they're done. Not a bad annual salary for preying on America's fears."

"So you think they—?"

"Don't just focus on the *they*—think of who else had access to that same info. I mean, nothing happens in a vacuum. To even ask for that first six-million-dollar payment, they clearly had to've known something big was about to happen. But what if they weren't the only ones?"

"So you think someone else knew?" Rogo asked.

"All this time, we've been assuming that The Three and Boyle were enemies. But what if they were *competitors*? What if that's why The Three's multimillion-dollar payday got turned down—because the White House already had a similar tip—a similar indicator and warning—from someone else?"

"I got ya—so while The Three or The Roman or whatever they call themselves kept bringing the White House their best hot tips, Boyle—or someone else in that meeting—was trying to prove he was a bigshot by leaking those very same tips to the press."

"And in the process, making The Roman's so-called scoops look like day-old newspapers."

"Which takes us back to the crossword—if it really was a trust list—if Manning and his chief of staff used the puzzle to try and figure out who was leaking to the press, maybe that's who Boyle was looking for," Rogo said. "The only thing I don't get is, why would Manning and his chief pass notes in secret code when they could just wait a few hours and discuss the matter in private?"

"Private? In a building where they once had secret tapes recording all conversations in the Oval?"

"Is that true? They still do those recordings?"

"Don't you see? That's the point, Rogo. In that world, everybody's listening. So if you plan on saying something bad about one of your top lieutenants, you better be sure not to say it out loud."

"Even so, how's that get us any closer to figuring out who Manning was singling out in the puzzle?"

"You tell me. What's it say in the files?" Dreidel asked. "Any other names mentioned in there?"

Rogo glanced around at the thirty-eight boxes and 21,500 sheets of paper, hundreds of schedules, and thousands of briefings they still had to go through. "You really think we can get through all this before the library closes?"

"Have a little faith," Dreidel said, fingering through a set of files. His eyes lit up and a sly grin spread across his face. "For all we know, the smoking gun is right in front of us."

"What? You got something?"

"Only Boyle's personnel file," Dreidel said as he plucked the inch-thick file from its box. "Which means we're about to find out what the President *really* thought of his old buddy Ron Boyle."

70

"Listen, I'm kinda busy," Kenny said as he closed the door on O'Shea and Micah. "Maybe you can come back another—"

O'Shea jammed his foot in the doorway, forcing it open. From his pocket, he pulled his FBI badge and slid it through the opening toward Kenny's nose. "*Now* is actually a better time for us," O'Shea insisted. He wasn't surprised by Kenny's reaction. After family, old friends were the hardest to crack.

Kenny's Popeye eye glared at Micah, then back to O'Shea's badge. "Wes is a good kid," he insisted.

"No one said he wasn't," O'Shea replied as he and Micah stepped inside. O'Shea quickly scanned the kitchen. It didn't matter that Wes was gone. What mattered was what he saw while he was here.

"So you from Key West?" Micah asked as he made eye contact with his partner. Micah stayed in the kitchen. O'Shea took the living room.

"No one's from Key West," Kenny shot back, already riled.

"Then where do you know Wes from?" O'Shea asked

as he approached the wall of black-and-white wedding photos.

"D'you mind telling me what this is about?" Kenny asked.

"These are beautiful," O'Shea replied, stepping toward a shot of a short-haired bride playfully biting the ear of her groom. "You take these?"

"I did, but—"

"Did you work at the White House with Wes?" Micah interrupted, keeping him off balance.

"Kinda," Kenny replied. "I was there as a—"

"Photographer," O'Shea blurted as he scooped up the framed photo of President Manning checking his reflection in the White House water pitcher. "I remember this one. You're a hotshot, aren't you, Mr.—I'm sorry, I forgot your name."

"I never gave it to you," Kenny said.

"Well, why don't we fix that?" O'Shea demanded, laying the silver frame flat down on its back. "I'm Agent O'Shea and you're . . ."

"Kenny. Kenny Quinn."

"Wait . . . Kenny Quinn?" Micah asked. "How do I know that name?"

"You don't," Kenny said. "Not unless you're a photo editor or working the White House press pool."

"Actually, I spent some time in D.C.," Micah said, leaving the kitchen and heading toward Kenny in the living room.

Just behind Kenny, O'Shea eyed the closed three-ring binder on the cocktail table.

"You're the guy who won the award, didn't you?" Micah asked, working hard to hold Kenny's attention.

"The Pulitzer," Kenny replied dryly.

"So you were there that day?" Micah asked.

"At the racetrack? There were plenty of us there."

"But you're the one who took the photo, right? The Cowardly Lion photo?"

"I'm sorry," Kenny said, turning back toward O'Shea, "but until you tell me what you're looking for, I don't think I shou—"

A hushed hiss carved through the air, and a dark red bullet hole singed Kenny's skin as it pierced his forehead. As Kenny crumpled lifelessly to the floor, Micah stared at O'Shea, who had his gun in one hand and the open three-ring binder in the other.

"You *nuts*!?" Micah exploded.

"They IDed you, Micah."

"What're you talking about? There's no way!"

"Really? Then what the hell is *this*?" O'Shea shouted, tapping his gun against an empty Mylar protective sleeve in the binder.

"There could've been anything in—"

"Not the sleeve—*underneath*!" O'Shea said as he flipped aside the empty sheet to reveal a clear view of the photo on the next page. "You're telling me that's not you?" he asked, pointing to the enormous crowd shot where, when you looked closely enough, Micah was tucked away, glancing to the side.

"It's . . . it's not possible—we bought every photo out there . . . went through every tape . . ."

"Well obviously, there were a few more Kenny decided to keep in his collection! Don't you get it, Micah? Wes knows! He's got the thread of the sweater—and when he starts pulling, *you're* gonna be the first one they look at!"

"Big deal, so they ask me a few questions. You know

I'll never say anything. But *this* . . . y'know what kinda avalanche you just started?"

"Don't worry," O'Shea said calmly. "If I set the bodies right, it'll just look like a botched robbery."

"Bodies?" Micah asked, confused. "What're you talking about? You've got more than one?"

O'Shea raised his gun and pointed it straight at his partner's chest.

Following years of training, Micah spun to his right, then leaped like a cheetah at O'Shea. The way Micah's pointer and middle fingers were curled—like claws—it was clear he was aiming for O'Shea's eyes.

O'Shea was impressed. No doubt, Micah was fast. But no one was that fast.

As O'Shea tugged the trigger, his fair blond hair glowed in the afternoon Key West sun. "Sorry, Micah."

There was a soft *ssstt.* Then a grunt.

And The Three became The Two.

71

"Don't tell me you lost him. Don't say those words."

"I didn't *lose* him," Lisbeth told her editor, clutching her cell phone as she walked in through the front door of the building. "I let him go."

"Did I tell you not to tell me that? Do I speak and you not hear?" Vincent asked. "What's Sacred Rule #1?"

"Always keep 'em talking."

"Fine, then Sacred Rule #26½: Don't let Wes out of your damn sight!"

"You weren't there, Vincent—you didn't see how upset he was. For fifty minutes—the entire flight back—the only thing he said to me was—" Lisbeth went silent.

"Lisbeth, you there?" Vincent asked. "I can't hear you."

"*Exactly!*" she replied, waving to security and heading for the elevators. "Fifty minutes of dead silence! The guy wouldn't look at me, wouldn't talk to me, wouldn't even curse me out. And believe me, I gave him every opportunity. He just stared out the window, pretending I wasn't there. And when he dropped me off, he wouldn't even say good-bye."

"Okay, so you hurt his feelings."

"See, but that's the thing—I didn't just hurt his feelings. He's been at this too long to feel burned by a reporter, but the pain on his face . . . I hurt *him.*"

"Spare me the sentimental, Lisbeth—you were doing your job. Oh, wait, you actually weren't. If you were, the moment he dropped you off, you would've turned around and followed him."

"In what? He has my car."

"He *stole* your car?"

Lisbeth paused. "No."

Vincent paused even longer. "Oh, jeez—you *gave* it to him? You gave him your car?" Vincent shouted. "Sacred Rule #27: Don't go soft! Rule 28: Don't fall in love with a dreamer. And 29: Don't let sad disfigured boys pluck your heartstrings and send you sailing on a guilt trip just because they're sad and disfigured!"

"You don't even know him."

"Just because someone's in a wheelchair doesn't mean they won't roll over your toes. You know what this story means, Lisbeth—especially for you."

"And you."

"And *you*," he said as Lisbeth stepped into the waiting elevator and hit the button for the second floor. "You know the job: You have to piss on people to be read. So please make my month and at least tell me you were smart enough to get it on tape."

As the doors slid shut and the elevator started to rise, Lisbeth leaned against the brass railing, her head tilting back against the Formica wall. Letting the day's events wash over her, she lifted her head and lightly tapped it back against the wall. *Tap, tap, tap.* Over and over against the wall.

"C'mon, you *did* get it on tape, right?" Vincent asked.

Opening her purse, Lisbeth pulled out the miniature cassette tape that held the last part of their conversations. Sure, she'd handed Wes the recorder, but it didn't take much for her to palm the cassette while he was ranting. Of course, now—no, not just now. Even as she was doing it—so damn instinctively—another part of her brain was watching in disbelief. Every reporter needs instinct. But not when it overwhelms ideals.

"Last time, Lisbeth—yes tape or no tape?"

The elevator pinged on the second floor, and Lisbeth stared at her open palm, rubbing her thumb against the tiny cassette. "Sorry, Vincent," she said, tucking it back in her purse. "I tried to stop him, but Wes tossed it overboard."

"Overboard. Really?"

"Really."

As she left the elevator and followed the hallway around to the left, there was a long pause on the line. Even longer than the one before.

"Where are you right now?" Vincent asked coldly.

"Right behind you," Lisbeth said into her phone.

Through an open door up the gray-carpeted hallway, Vincent stopped pacing in his office and spun around to face her. Still holding the phone to his ear, he licked his salt-and-pepper mustache. "It's four o'clock. I need tomorrow's column. Now."

"You'll have it, but . . . the way things were left with Wes, I still think we should take another day before we push a story that's—"

"Do what you want, Lisbeth. You always do anyway."

With a swing of his arm, Vincent slammed his door shut, unleashing a thunderclap that echoed in front of her and through her cell phone. As her fellow employees turned to stare, Lisbeth trudged to her cubicle just across the hall. Collapsing in her seat, she flicked on her computer, where a nearly empty three-column grid filled the screen. On the corner of her desk, a crumpled sheet of paper held all the vital info about young Alexander John's recent victory in the ultra-competitive world of high school art. This late in the day, there was no escaping the inevitable.

Flattening the crumpled paper with the heel of her hand, she reread the details and instinctively punched in the code for her voice mail.

"You have seven new messages," the robotic female voice announced through her speakerphone. The first five were from local maître d's hoping to get some free press for their restaurants by ratting out who was eating lunch with whom. The sixth was a follow-up call on Alexander John's art award. And the last . . .

"Hi . . . er . . . this message is for Lisbeth," a soft female voice began. "My name's . . ."

The woman paused, causing Lisbeth to sit up straight. The best tips always came from people who didn't want to identify themselves.

"My name's . . . Violet," she finally said.

Fake name, Lisbeth decided. *Even better.*

"I just . . . I was reading your column today, and when I saw *his* name, my stomach just . . . it's not right, okay? I know he's powerful . . ."

Lisbeth mentally ran through every mention in today's column. *The First Lady . . . Manning . . . does she mean Manning?*

". . . it's just not right, okay? Not after what he did." She's careful how she puts the knife in. She knows to punch, but not too hard. "Anyway, if you can give me a call . . ."

Furiously scribbling the number, Lisbeth flipped open her cell phone and immediately started dialing. Her ears flushed red as it rang.

C'mon . . . pick up, pick up, pick up, pick—

"Hello?" a woman answered.

"Hi, this is Lisbeth Dodson from Below the Fold—I'm looking for Violet."

There was a second or two of dead silence. Lisbeth just waited. New sources always needed an extra moment to decide.

"Hiya, honey—hold on one second," the woman said. In the background, Lisbeth heard a bell chime and the sudden wisp of wind buzzing the phone. Whatever store Violet was in, she just left for privacy. Which meant she was willing to talk.

"This isn't . . . you're not recording this, right?" Violet finally asked.

Lisbeth glanced at the digital recorder that always sat on her desk. But she didn't reach for it. "No recordings."

"And you won't give my name out? Because if my husband . . ."

"We're off the record. No one'll ever know who you are. I promise you that."

Once again, the line was drowned in silence. Lisbeth knew better than to push.

"I just want you to know, I'm no snitch," Violet said, her voice cracking. Based on Violet's inflection and speed, Lisbeth wrote *mid-30s?* in her notepad. "Understand, okay? I don't want this. He just . . . seeing his name in print again . . . and so happy . . . people don't realize—there's a whole 'nother side of him . . . and what he did that night . . ."

"What night?" Lisbeth asked. "What was the date?"

"I don't think he's a bad person—I really don't—but when he gets angry . . . he just . . . he gets angry with the best of 'em. And when he's *real* angry . . . You know how men get, right?"

"Of course," Lisbeth agreed. "Now, why don't you just tell me what happened that night."

72

I don't wanna talk about it," I insist.

"She was recording the whole time?" Rogo asks, still in shock as his voice crackles through the cell phone.

"Rogo, can we please not—?"

"Maybe it's not how it looked. I mean, she gave you her car *and* her phone, right? Maybe you misread it."

"I heard my voice on the tape! How else could that possibly be read!?" I shout, squeezing my fist around the steering wheel and jamming even harder on the gas. As I blow past the thick twisting banyan trees that shield both sides of County Road from the sun, I hear the shift in Rogo's voice. At first, he was surprised. Now he's just hurt, with a dab of confused. When it comes to judging someone's character, he's usually a master.

"I told you she'd burn us—didn't I call it?" Dreidel hisses in the background. His voice is barely a whisper, which means someone's there with them.

"Did she say why?" Rogo adds. "I mean, I know Lisbeth's a reporter, but—"

"Enough already, okay? How many times do I need to say it? I don't wanna talk about it!"

"Where are you now anyway?" Rogo asks.

"No offense, but I shouldn't say. Y'know, just in case someone's listening."

"Wes, you're full of manure—where the hell are you?" Rogo insists.

"On US-1."

"You're lying—that was too fast."

"I'm *not* lying."

"Too fast again. C'mon, Pinocchio—I know the little stutter and stammer when you're fibbing. Just tell me where you are."

"You have to understand, Rogo, he—"

"He? *He?* The royal *He,*" he moaned, more angry than ever. "Son of Betsy Ross, Wes! You're going to see Manning?"

"He's expecting me. Schedule says I have to be there at four."

"Schedule? The man's been lying to you for eight years about the single greatest tragedy in your life. Doesn't that—?" He lowers his voice, forcing himself to calm down. "Doesn't that let you say F-you to the schedule for once?"

"He's going to Manning?" Dreidel asks in the background.

"Rogo, you don't understand—"

"I *do* understand. Lisbeth made you sad . . . The Three got you scared . . . and as always, you're running for your favorite presidential pacifier."

"Actually, I'm trying to do the one thing we should've done the first moment I saw Boyle alive: go to the source and find out what the hell actually happened that day."

Rogo's silent, which tells me he's seething. "Wes, let me ask you something," he finally says. "That first night you saw Boyle, why didn't you go to Manning and tell him the truth? Because you were in shock? Because it seemed that Boyle was somehow invited to that hotel by his old best friend? Or because deep in the pit of your chest, no matter how much you've rationalized it over the years, you know that before he's a father, a mentor, or even a husband, Leland F. Manning is a politician—one of the world's greatest politicians—and for that alone, he's fully capable of lying to your face for eight years without you ever knowing it."

"But that's what you're missing, Rogo—what if he didn't lie? What if he's just as clueless as we are? I mean, if O'Shea and Micah and whoever this Roman guy is—if they're the ones who sent Nico to shoot Boyle—maybe Manning and Boyle aren't the villains in all this."

"What, so now they're victims?"

"Why not?"

"Please, he's the—" Catching himself and knowing I won't listen if he yells, Rogo adds, "If Boyle and Manning were complete angels—if they had nothing to hide and were only doing good—why didn't they just take Boyle to the hospital and let the authorities investigate? C'mon, Wes, these two guys lied to the entire world—and the only reason people lie is because they have something to hide. Now, I'm not saying I have all the pieces, but just by the lie alone, there's no way Manning and Boyle are just helpless victims."

"That still doesn't mean they're the enemy."

"And you really believe that?"

"What I *believe* is that Ron Boyle's alive. That The Three, with all their connections, helped Nico sneak into the racetrack that day. That O'Shea, Micah, and this Roman, as members of The Three, clearly have some grudge against Boyle. And for that reason, they're now doing anything in their power to find out where he is. As for how Manning fits into this, I've got no idea."

"Then why race to him like a battered wife back to her abuser?"

"What're my other choices, Rogo? Go to the FBI, where O'Shea works? Or the Service, where The Roman is? Or better yet, I can go to the local authorities and tell them I saw dead man walking. Ten minutes after that happens, you think O'Shea and his little posse won't show up with their federal badges, take me into private custody, and put a bullet in the back of my head claiming I was trying to escape?"

"That's not even—"

"It *is* true and you *know* it's true, Rogo! These guys went after one of the most powerful men in the White House at a stadium filled with 200,000 people. You think they won't slice my neck open on some deserted road in Palm Beach?"

"Tell him not to mention my name to Manning," Dreidel calls out in the background.

"Dreidel wants you to—"

"I heard him," I interrupt, twisting the steering wheel into a sharp left on Via Las Brisas. As I curve around a well-manicured divider, the street narrows, and the privacy hedges rise, stretching as tall as twenty feet and blocking my view of all thc multimillion-dollar homes hidden behind them. "Rogo, I know you don't agree, but for the past two days, the only reason I stayed away from Manning is because O'Shea and Micah convinced me to. D'you understand? The man's been by my side for eight years, and the only reason I doubted him is because they—*two strangers with badges*—told me to. No offense, but after all our time together, Manning deserves better than that."

"That's fine, Wes, but let's be clear about one thing: Manning hasn't been *by your side* for eight years. You've been by his."

I shake my head and pull up to the last house on my right. For security reasons, they don't allow parking in the driveway, so I head for the shoulder of the grassy divider and park directly behind a navy-blue rental car that's already there. His guests are early—which means, as I hop out and rush across the street, I'm officially late.

Even before I stop at the ten-foot-high, double-planked wooden fence, the intercom that's hidden in the shrubs crackles. "Can I help you?" a deep voice asks.

"Hey there, Ray," I call out to the agent on duty. "It's Wes."

"You don't have to do this," Rogo pleads through my phone.

He's never been more wrong. This is exactly what I need to do. Not for Manning. For me. I need to know.

A metallic thunk unlocks the wooden gate, which slowly yawns open.

"Wes, at least just wait until we get through Boyle's personnel file," Rogo begs.

"You've been searching for four hours already—it's enough. I'll call you when I'm done."

"Don't be so stubborn."

"Good-bye, Rogo," I say, hanging up the phone. It's so easy for someone outside the ring to tell a fighter how to fight his fight. But this is *my* fight. I just never realized it.

As I walk up the driveway, there's no house number on

the front door, and no mailbox to identify the occupants. But the four suit-and-tie Secret Service agents standing outside the garage are quite a giveaway. With Nico on the loose, they kept Manning at home. Fortunately, as I lift my chin and stare up at the pale blue British Colonial, I know where the former President lives.

73

"And how'd you meet him again?" Lisbeth asked, holding her cell phone with one hand and taking notes with the other.

"Mutual friend," Violet replied, her voice already shaking. "It was years ago. At that point on the job, it was personal introductions only."

"Introductions?"

"You have to understand, with a man like him, you don't just walk up and swing your tail. In this town—with all the money . . . with everything these guys have to lose—the only thing they care about is discretion, okay? That's why they sent him to me."

"Of course," Lisbeth said as she scribbled the word *Hooker* in her notepad. "So you were . . ."

"I was twenty, is what I was," Violet said with a verbal shove. She didn't like being judged. "But lucky me, I could keep a secret. That's why I got the work. And with him . . . our first two appointments, I didn't even say his name. That alone guaranteed he'd invite me back. Gladiators need to conquer, right?" she asked, her laughter soft and hollow.

Lisbeth didn't laugh back. There was no pleasure in someone else's pain.

"I know what you're thinking," Violet added, "but it was nice in the beginning. He was, honestly . . . he was tender—always asking if I was okay . . . he knew my mother was sick, so he'd ask about her. I know, I know—he's a politician, but I was twenty and he was . . ." Her voice trailed off.

Lisbeth didn't say anything. But as the silence wore on . . . "Violet, are you—?"

"It sounds so damn stupid, but I was just thrilled he liked me," she blurted, clearly trying to stifle a sob. From the sound of it, the flush of emotion surprised even her. "I'm sorry—let me just . . . I'm sorry . . ."

"You have no reason to be sorry."

"I know—I just . . . it mattered that he liked me . . . that he kept coming back," she explained, sniffling it all back in. "I wouldn't see him for a while, then the phone would ring, and I'd be jumping up and down, like I'd been asked to the prom. And that's how it was until . . . until he left one night and I didn't hear from him for almost three months. I was . . . to be honest, at first, I was worried. Maybe I did something wrong. Or he was mad. And then, when I heard he was in town, I did the one thing I never should've done—the dumbest thing I could possibly do, against every rule," Violet explained, her voice barely a whisper. "I called him."

Right then Lisbeth stopped writing.

"He was at my place in ten minutes," Violet said, another sob clogging her throat. "Wh-When I opened the door, he stepped inside without a word . . . made sure he was out of view . . . and then he just—I swear to you, he never did it before . . ."

"Violet, it's okay to—"

"I didn't even see the first punch coming," she said as the tears flooded forward. "He just kept screaming at me, 'How dare you! How *dare* you!' I tried fighting back—I did . . . I'm . . . I've never been weak—but he grabbed the back of my hair and he . . . he sent me straight for . . . there was a mirror above my dresser."

Staring at her own rounded reflection in her computer screen, Lisbeth didn't move.

"I could see him behind me in the mirror . . . just as I hit it . . . I could see him behind me . . . his face . . . the red in his eyes. It was like he pulled off a mask and let out . . . like he freed something underneath," Violet cried. "And—and—and when he was gone . . . when the door slammed and the blood was pouring from my nose, I still—I know it's—can you believe I still missed him?" she asked, weeping uncontrollably. "I-I mean, could I possibly be more pathetic than that?"

Lisbeth shook her head to herself, trying hard to stay focused. "Violet, I know this is hard for you—I know what it takes to tell the story—but I just need— Before we do anything, I need to ask: Do you have any way of proving this . . . anything at all . . . videotapes, physical proof . . . ?"

"You don't believe me," she insisted.

"No, no, no . . . it's just, look who you're fighting with here. Without a way of verifying—"

"I have proof," Violet said, clearly annoyed as she caught her breath. "I've got it right here. If you don't believe me, come get it."

"I will, I'll come right now. Lemme just . . . hold on one second . . ." Pressing her cell phone to her chest and hopping out of her seat, Lisbeth grabbed the uncrumpled art award notes, darted out of her cubicle, and ducked into a blond reporter's cubicle directly across the hall. "Eve, can I borrow your car?" Lisbeth asked.

"First my phone—which I still haven't gotten back—now my car—"

"Eve!"

Eve studied her friend, reading her expression. "This's the one, isn't it?"

"Column's on my computer. Here's the last item," Lisbeth said, tossing her the art award notes. "Can you—?"

"On it," Eve said as Lisbeth said thank you, took off up the hallway, and pressed her cell to her ear. "Violet, I'm on my way," she said, doing her best to keep her talking. Sacred Rule #9: Never let go of the big fish. "So . . . how long were you two actually together?"

"A year and two months," Violet replied, still sounding angry. "Right before the shooting."

Lisbeth stopped running. "Wait, this was when he was still in the White House?"

"Of course. Every President goes home for vacation. Besides, he couldn't pull this off in Washington. But down here . . . I'd get the phone call and he could—"

"Violet, no bullshitting anymore—you're trying to tell me that despite all the security—despite dozens of Secret Service agents—you were sleeping with and got beat up by the President of the United States *while he was still in office*?"

"President?" Violet asked. "You think I was sleeping with Manning? No, no, no . . . the other mention—about running for Senate . . ."

"You mean—"

"The little animal who mauled me. I was talking about Dreidel."

74

"Think he'll go through with it?" Dreidel asked, readjusting his wire-rim glasses as he read from Boyle's personnel file.

"Who, Wes? Hard to say," Rogo replied, still sitting on the floor and flipping through the documents in Boyle's requests. "He was talking a tough game, but you know how he gets with Manning."

"You've obviously never been on the receiving end of Manning." Looking down at the file, Dreidel added, "Y'know Boyle spoke Hebrew and Arabic?"

"Says who?"

"Says here: Hebrew, Arabic, and American Sign Language. Apparently, his sister was deaf. That's why they moved to Jersey—had one of the early schools for the hearing impaired. God, I remember filling this out," he added, reading from Boyle's National Security Questionnaire. "According to this, he won a Westinghouse prize when he was in high school—plus a Marshall Scholarship at Oxford. Guy was scary smart, especially when it came t— Hold on," Dreidel said. "*Have you been over 180 days delinquent on any debts? Yes. If yes, explain below . . .*"

Flipping to the next page, Dreidel read the single-spaced page that was stapled to the application. "*. . . to a total debt of $230,000 . . .*"

"Two hundred and thirty *thousand*? What'd he buy? Italy?"

"I don't think he bought anything," Dreidel said. "From what it says here, it was his *father's* debt. Apparently, Boyle volunteered to take it over so his dad wouldn't have to declare bankruptcy."

"Boy loves his daddy."

"Actually, hates his daddy. But loves his mom," Dreidel said, reading even further. "If Dad declared bankruptcy and the creditors swooped in, Mom would've been kicked out of the family restaurant that she'd worked in and run since Boyle was a kid."

"Nice work by Dad—put the family business at risk, boot your wife out on the street, and stick your kid with all the leftover debt."

"Wait, that's the good part," Dreidel said, turning to the last few pages of the application. Here: *Is there anything in your personal life that could be used by someone to embarrass the President or the White House? Please provide full details.*" Flipping the page and revealing another single-spaced typed document, Dreidel shook his head, remembering the stories that Boyle had disclosed early in the campaign. Even at the beginning, Manning stood by his friend. "Most of this we know: Dad was first arrested before Boyle was born. Then arrested again when Boyle was six, then again when he was thirteen—the last time for assault and battery on the owner of a Chinese laundry in Staten Island. Then he actually wound up staying out of trouble until just after Boyle left for college. That's when the FBI picked him up for selling fake insurance policies in a New Brunswick nursing home. The list keeps going . . . importing stolen scooters, check kiting for a few thousand bucks, but somehow, barely serving any time."

"It's a Freudian field day, isn't it? Dad breaking all the rules with the con man shtick, while Boyle throws himself into the preciseness of accounting. What was that *Time* story when Dad got arrested for shoplifting? Black eye . . ."

". . . on the *White* House. Yeah, clever. That's almost as good as that political cartoon where they had him robbing Toys for Tots."

"I still can't—" Rogo cut himself off, shaking his head. "All this time, we're hunting for Boyle like he's the great white evil, but when you hear all the details: miserable childhood, deaf sister, working-class Italian mom . . . and yet he still manages to claw his way out and make his way to the White House . . ."

"Oh, please, Rogo—don't tell me you're feeling bad for him."

". . . and then his dad lies, cheats, steals, and on top of it all, leaves Boyle holding the bill. I mean, just think about it—how does a father do that to his own son?"

"Same way Boyle did it to his own wife and daughter when he disappeared from their lives and turned them into mourners. People are scumbags, Rogo—especially when they're desperate."

"Yeah, but that's the thing. If Boyle were really that bad, why'd they even let him work in the White House? Isn't that the purpose of all these forms—to screen people like him out?"

"In theory, that's the goal, but it's not like it was some uncovered secret. Everyone knew his dad was trash. He used to talk about it—use it for sympathy in the press. It only became a problem when we won. But when your best friend is President of the United States, oh, what a surprise, the FBI can be convinced to make exceptions. In fact, let me show you how they . . . here . . ." Dreidel said, once again thumbing through the folder. "Okay, *here*," he added, unclipping a sheet of stationery-sized paper as Rogo took a seat on the edge of the desk and started flipping through the rest of the file.

"Boyle had codeword clearance. Before they dole that out, they need to know what side you're on. FBI . . . Secret Service . . . they all take a look. Then Manning gets to see the results . . ." On the small sheet of paper was a list of typed letters lined up in a single column, each one with a check mark next to it:

BKD ✓
MH ✓
WEX ✓
ED ✓
REF ✓
<u>AC</u>
PRL ✓
FB ✓
PUB ✓

"Is that the same as *this*?" Rogo asked as he turned a page in the file and revealed a near-identical sheet.

"Exactly—that's the same report."

"So why's Boyle have two?"

"One's from when he started, the other's probably

from when they renewed his clearance. It's the same. *BKD* is background—your general background check. *MH* is your military history. *WEX* is work experience . . ."

"So this is all the dirt on Boyle?" Rogo asked, staring down at the sparsely covered page.

"No, *this* is the dirt—everything below *here*," Dreidel said, pointing to the underlined letters *AC* halfway down the page.

"AC?"

"Areas of concern."

"And all these letters below it: *PRL . . . FB . . . PUB . . .*"

"*PRL* is Boyle's personal history, which I'll wager refers to all the crap with his father. *FB* is his financial background; thanks again, Dad. And *PUB* . . ." Dreidel paused a moment, reading from his sheet as Rogo followed on his own copy. "*PUB* is the public perception issues if Boyle's background gets out, which in this case, it already was."

"What about *PI*?" Rogo asked.

"Whattya mean?"

"PI," Rogo repeated, turning his sheet toward Dreidel. "Isn't your last one *PI*?"

Dreidel looked at his own sheet, which ended with *PUB*, then turned toward Rogo's, squinting to read the letters with the handwritten message next to them:

PI—*note May* 27

Dreidel's face went white.

"What?" Rogo asked. "What's it mean?"

"What's the date on yours say?"

Reading from the top corner of the sheet, Rogo could

barely get the words out. "June 16th," he said. "Right before the shooting."

"Mine's January 6th—days before we moved into the White House."

"I don't understand, though. What's *PI*?"

"Paternity issues," Dreidel said. "According to this, just before he was shot, Boyle had a kid no one knew about."

75

What'd you *do*?" The Roman asked, his voice squawking through the scrambled satellite phone.

"It's fine. Problem solved," O'Shea replied, keeping the phone close and staring out the small oval window of the chartered seaplane.

"What does that mean? Let me speak to Micah!"

"Yeah, well . . . that's a little harder than it used to be," O'Shea said as the plane dropped down, approaching the aquamarine waves of Lake Worth. From the current height—barely a few hundred feet above the water—the backyards of the Palm Beach mansions whizzed by in a blur.

"O'Shea, don't tell me— What'd you do to him?"

"Don't lecture me, okay? I didn't have a choice."

"You *killed* him?"

O'Shea stared out the window as the plane sank down to just a few feet above the waves. "Be smart. He's covert in Directorate of Operations. He shouldn't be working on U.S. soil. And for some reason, he's caught standing on the track at the speedway? Once Wes IDed him, they would've brought him right in."

"That doesn't mean he'd talk!"

"You think so? You think if they offered him a deal and said they'd go easy on him, every one of Micah's fingers wouldn't've pointed our way?"

"He's still CIA!" The Roman shouted through the phone. "You have any idea what kinda fire that starts? You just lit the damn volcano!"

"You think I enjoyed it? I've known Micah since War College. He was at my niece's communion."

"Well, I guess there goes his invite for her sweet sixteen!"

With a final jolt, the plane dropped down for its landing. The instant the floats hit the water, the plane bounced and wobbled, slowing down until it was cruising with the current.

"Enough," O'Shea warned as the floating plane chugged toward the floating dock of the Rybovich Spencer boatyard. "It was hard enough as it is."

"Really? Then maybe you should've thought twice before you decided to put a bullet in him! You know how hard it's gonna be to find another person inside the Agency?"

"*You're* lecturing *me* about forethought? Have you forgotten why we're even stamping around in all this manure? It's the same jackass thing you did with our so-called six-million-dollar payment for *Blackbird.* You rush in, stick your finger in all the electrical sockets, then get mad at me when I have to deal with the cleanup."

"Don't even— *Blackbird* was a mutual decision!" The Roman exploded. "We voted on that!"

"No, *you* voted. You're the one who put the number that high. Then when they decided they weren't paying it, you came crying that we needed an assist from the inside."

"Okay, so now you didn't want that six mil?"

"What I didn't want was to have to ask for that kinda cash *twice.* We spent nearly a decade building up your damn Roman identity—all those tips we snatched and passed your way so it looked like you had some big, great informant out there—hell, they still think The Roman's a real person who feeds the government info—all for the goal of going in for that one huge multimillion-dollar hit. One time! One ask! That's all it was supposed to be—until you got the dollar signs in your eyes and thought we could do it on a regular basis."

"We *could've* done it on a regular basis—fifty, sixty, seventy million, easy. You *know* you agreed."

"Then you should've listened to us and never approached Boyle first," O'Shea said, his voice calmer than ever. "And unlike last time, I'm done letting a loose end come back to bite us in the ass. As long as Wes is out there with that photo, we've both got targets on our chests."

"What, so now you're putting Wes on your hit list as well? I thought you agreed he was just bait."

Without a word, O'Shea watched as the seaplane angled past half a dozen pristine yachts and nosed up to the floating dock.

"Check out that sailboat in front of us," the pilot announced as he pulled off his headphones and entered the back of the plane. "That's Jimmy Buffett's day sailer. You see the name of it? *Chill.*"

O'Shea nodded as the pilot opened the hatch, stepped outside, and tossed the grab line to the dock.

"O'Shea, before you get stupid, think about next month," The Roman said through the phone. "If this thing comes through in India . . ."

"Are you even listening? There is no next month! There's no India! Or Prague! Or Liberia! Or Lusaka! We brought our resources together—we created the perfect virtual informant—and we made some cash. But now I'm done, pal. D'you understand? The pot of gold—the seventy million—it's bullshit. I'm over."

"But if you—"

"I don't care," O'Shea said, heading for the door and stepping out to the edge of the plane's floats. A short hop took him onto the dock, where he waved a thank-you to the pilot and followed the path toward the buildings of the boatyard.

"O'Shea, don't be such a mule," The Roman continued. "If you touch Wes now—"

"Are you listening? I. Don't. Care. I don't care that he's bait. I don't care that he's our best bet for getting Boyle. I don't even care that Nico might get to him first. That kid knows my name, he knows what I look like, and worst of all—"

There was a soft beep on O'Shea's phone. He stopped midstep, halfway up the dock. Caller ID said *Unavailable.* On this line, there was only one person that could be.

"O'Shea, listen to me," The Roman threatened.

"Sorry, signal's bad here. I'll call you later." With a click, he switched over to the other line. "This is O'Shea."

"And this is your conscience—stop having sex with men at truck stops. Go to a bar—it's easier," Paul Kessiminan said, laughing, in his fat Chicago accent.

O'Shea didn't even bother responding to the joke. Tech guys—especially those in the Bureau's Investigative Technology Division—always thought they were funnier than they were. "Please tell me you got a hit on Wes's phone," O'Shea said.

"Nope. But after taking your advice and watching his friends, I did get a hit on the fat kid's."

"Rogo's?"

"For the past few hours, it's quiet as death. Then ping, incoming call from a number registered to an Eve Goldstein."

"Who's Eve Goldstein?"

"Which is why I looked her up. Y'know how many Eve Goldsteins there are in Palm Beach County? Seven. One owns a Judaica store, one's a school principal, two retirees—"

"Paulie!"

". . . and one who writes the gardening section for the *Palm Beach Post*."

"They switched phones."

"Ooooh, you're good. You should get a job with the FBI."

"So Wes is still with Lisbeth?"

"I don't think so. I just called the newsroom. She's apparently on another line. I think she gave Wes her friend's phone and ditched his on the plane or something. Telling you—boy's smart," Paul said. "Lucky for you, I'm smarter."

"But you traced the new phone to his current location?"

"It's an old model, so there's no GPS. But I *can* get you to the closest cell tower. Cell site 626A. On County Road, just a few blocks south of Via Las Brisas."

At the center of the long dock, O'Shea froze. "Las Brisas? You think he went to—?"

"Only one way to find out, Tonto. Be careful, though. With Nico out there, headquarters just opened their own investigation."

Nodding to himself, O'Shea reached into his inside jacket pocket and pulled out a black ostrich-skin wallet and matching CIA badge. As he flipped it open, he took one last look at the picture in Micah's driver's license. From the messy brown hairstyle and the crooked bottom teeth, the photo had to be almost a decade old. Before the teeth were fixed. Before the hair got meticulously slicked back. Before they were making real money.

O'Shea didn't like lifting his old friend's wallet, but he knew it'd buy him at least a day in IDing the body. Though right now, as he readjusted his shoulder holster and rechecked his gun, all he needed was an hour or so to wrap things up and leave this life behind.

They'd created an alter ego for Egen as The Roman. Certainly, O'Shea could create something new for himself.

"How fast you think you can get there?" Paul asked through the phone.

Grinning to himself, O'Shea tossed Micah's IDs from the dock into the water. They floated for half a second, then sank out of sight. "At this rate? I'll be in and out lickety-split."

76

"Try calling him again," Dreidel said as he spun the acid-free archival box around and checked the dates on its typed spine: *Boyle, Ron—Domestic Policy Council—October 15–December 31.*

"Just did," Rogo said, working his way through his own stack and checking the last few boxes in the pile. "You know how Wes gets on the job—he won't pick up if he's with Manning."

"You should still try him agai—"

"And tell him what? That it looks like Boyle had a kid? That there's some note referencing May 27th? Until we get some details, it doesn't even help us."

"It helps us to keep Wes informed—especially where he is right now. He should know that Manning knew."

"And you're sure about that?" Rogo asked. "Manning knew about Boyle's kid?"

"It's his best friend—and it's in the file," Dreidel said. His voice cracked slightly as he looked up from the last few boxes. "Manning definitely knew."

Rogo watched Dreidel carefully, sensing the change in his tone. "You're doubting him, aren't you, Dreidel? For the first time, you're realizing there might be a crack in the Manning mask."

"Let's just keep looking, okay?" Dreidel asked as he tilted the final two milk-crate-sized boxes and scanned the dates. One was labeled *Memoranda—January 1–March 31.* The other was *Congressional AIDS Hearing—June 17–June 19.* "Damn," he whispered, shoving them aside.

"Nothing here either," Rogo said, closing the last box and climbing up from his knees. "Okay, so grand total—how many boxes do we have that include the May 27 date?"

"Just these," Dreidel said, pointing to the four archival boxes that they'd set up on the worktable. "Plus you pulled the schedule, right?"

"Not that it helps," Rogo replied as he waved Manning's official schedule from May 27. "According to this, the President was with his wife and daughter at their cabin in North Carolina. At noon, he went biking. Then lunch and some fishing on the lake. Nothing but relaxing the whole day."

"Who was staffing him?" Dreidel asked, well aware that the President never traveled without at least some work.

"Albright . . ."

"No surprise—he took his chief of staff everywhere."

". . . and Lemonick."

"Odd, but not out of the ordinary."

"And then those same names you said were from the Travel Office—Westman, McCarthy, Lindelof—"

"But not Boyle?"

"Not according to this," Rogo said, flipping through the rest of the schedule.

"Okay, so on May 27th, barely two months before the shooting, Manning was in North Carolina and Boyle was presumably in D.C. So the real question is, what was Boyle doing while the cat was away?"

"And you think the answer's in one of these?" Rogo asked, circling the tops of the four boxes with his hand.

"Those're the ones that have date ranges that include May 27th," Dreidel said. "I'm telling you," he added as he flipped off the top of the first box, "I've got a good feeling. The answer's in here."

"There's no *way* it's in here!" Rogo moaned forty-five minutes later.

"Maybe we should go through them again."

"We already went through them twice. I picked through every sheet of paper, every file, every stupid little Post-it note. Look at these paper cuts!" he said, extending his pointer and middle fingers in a peace sign.

"Voice down!" Dreidel hissed, motioning to the attendant by the computers.

Rogo glanced over at Freddy, who offered a warm smile and a wave. Turning back to Dreidel, he added, "Okay, so now what?"

"Not much choice," Dreidel said as he scanned the remaining thirty-eight boxes that were stacked like tiny pyramids across the floor. "Maybe they filed it out of order. Flip through each box—pull out anything that has the date May 27th on it."

"That's over 20,000 pages."

"And the sooner we start, the sooner we'll know the full story," Dreidel said, tugging a brand-new box up to the worktable.

"I don't know," Rogo said as he gripped the handholds of a beaten old box and heaved it up toward the desk. As it landed back-to-back with Dreidel's box, a puff of dust swirled like a sandstorm. "Part of me worries we're sifting through the wrong haystack."

77

Port St. Lucie, Florida

Edmund had been dead for nearly twelve hours. During hour one, as Nico strapped him into the passenger seat of the truck, thick frothy blood bubbles multiplied at the wound in Edmund's neck. Nico barely noticed, too excited about telling his friend about Thomas Jefferson and the original Three.

By hour four, Edmund's body had stiffened. His arms stopped flopping. His head, bent awkwardly back and to the right, no longer bobbed with each bump. Instead of a rag doll, Edmund was a frozen mannequin. Rigor mortis had settled in. Nico still didn't notice.

By hour ten, the cab of the truck began to take its own beating. On the seats . . . the floor mat . . . across the vinyl interior of the passenger-side door, the blood began to decompose, turning each stain a darker, richer red, tiny speckles of liquid rubies.

But even when they left all that behind—when they

abandoned the truck and used Edmund's wool blanket to switch to the clean maroon Pontiac—there was no escaping the smell. And it wasn't from the body. That would take days to decompose, even in the Florida heat. The true foul horror came from what was inside, as Edmund's lack of muscle control caused everything from feces to flatulence to leak out, soaking his clothes, his pants, all the way through to the once-parchment-colored cloth seat and the dusty blanket that covered Edmund from the neck down.

In the driver's seat next to him, Nico couldn't have been happier. Up ahead, despite rush hour, traffic looked clear. On his right, out west, the sun was a perfect orange circle as it began its slow bow from the sky. And most important, as they blew past another green highway sign, they were even closer than Nico expected.

PALM BEACH 48 MILES

Less than an hour and we're there.

Barely able to contain himself, Nico smiled and took a deep breath of the car's outhouse reek.

He didn't smell a thing. He couldn't. Not when life was this sweet.

Quickly picking up speed, Nico reached for the wipers as a late-day sun-shower sent a few speckles against the Pontiac's front windshield. But before he could flick the wipers on, he thought twice and left them off. The rain was light. Just a drizzle. Enough to cleanse.

Maybe you should—

"Yeah, I was just thinking the same thing," Nico said, nodding to himself. With the push of a button on the dash, he opened the sunroof of the car, held his stolen Orioles baseball cap, and tilted his head back to stare up at the gray sky.

"Hold the wheel," he told Edmund as he clamped his eyes shut.

At eighty miles an hour, Nico let go of the steering wheel. The Pontiac veered slightly to the right, cutting off a woman in a silver Honda.

Saying a prayer to himself, Nico kept his head back. The wind from outside lashed against the brim, blowing his baseball cap from his head. Needles of rain tap-danced against his forehead and face. The baptism had begun. Wes's home address was clutched in his hand. Salvation—for Nico and his mom—was less than an hour away.

78

Lisbeth thought the neighborhood would be a dump. But as she drove west on Palm Beach Lakes Boulevard and followed Violet's directions—past the Home Depot and Best Buy and Olive Garden, then a right on Village Boulevard—it was clear she didn't need to lock the car doors. Indeed, as she pulled up to the guard gate for *Misty Lake—A Townhome Community*, the only thing she had to do was lower her window.

"Hi, I'm visiting unit 326," Lisbeth explained to the guard, remembering Violet's instructions to not use her name. Of course, it was silly. Lisbeth already had her address—who cared about her name?

"ID, please," the guard said.

As she handed over her driver's license, Lisbeth added, "I'm sorry, I think it's unit 326—I'm looking for . . ."

"The Schopfs—Debbie and Josh," the guard replied, handing her a guest parking pass for the dashboard.

Lisbeth nodded. "That's them." Waiting until the security gate closed behind her to scribble the name *Debbie Schopf* in her notepad, she followed the signs and never-ending speed bumps past row after row of identical pink townhomes, eventually pulling into the guest spot just outside the narrow two-story house with blinking holiday lights dangling from above the door and an inflatable snowman in the thriving green garden. Christmas in Florida at unit 326.

Heading up the front path, Lisbeth tucked her notepad into her purse and out of sight. Violet was already nervous on the phone. No reason to add to—

"Lisbeth?" a female voice called out as the door of the townhouse swung open.

Lisbeth looked up at eye level, which put her directly at Violet's dark brown neck. It wasn't until she craned her neck up that Lisbeth saw the full picture of the stunning 5'10" African-American woman standing in the doorway. Wearing faded jeans and a white V-neck T-shirt, Violet almost seemed to be trying to dress like a mom. But even standard suburban uniforms couldn't mask the beauty underneath.

"You . . . uh . . . you wanna come in?" Violet asked, her voice shaky as she lowered her head and looked away.

Lisbeth assumed she was being shy. Probably embarrassed. But as she got closer—walking past Violet and entering the house—she got her first good look at Violet's left eyebrow, which appeared to be cut in two by a tiny white scar that sliced through her dark, otherwise perfect skin.

"That from— He do that?" Lisbeth asked, even though she knew the answer.

Violet looked up, her shoulders arching like a cornered cat—then just as quickly, her posture leveled as she regained her calm. For Lisbeth, it was like glancing too late at a just-missed lightning bolt. Two seconds ago, rage detonated in Violet's eyes, then disappeared in an eyeblink. Still, like the lost lightning bolt, the afterimage was too strong. Lisbeth couldn't miss it. And in that moment, she saw the brash, confident, and swaggering self-assured woman that the young twenty-six-year-old Violet used to be. And who she'd never be again.

"I don't want my picture in the paper. Or my name," Violet whispered, tugging her bangs over the fleshy white scar.

"I'd never do that," Lisbeth promised, already kicking herself for pushing too fast. From the plastic pink tea set scattered along the floor and the baby doll stroller in the entryway, Violet had a great deal to lose. No way Lisbeth was getting the story without a softer touch.

"Adorable," Lisbeth said, heading up the main hallway and admiring a framed family photo of a little white girl running through a sprinkler, her mouth open with her tongue licking the water.

Violet barely responded.

Lisbeth turned. Every parent likes to talk about their kids.

Halfway up the main hallway, Lisbeth scanned the rest of the family photos along the wall. The girl in the sprinkler. Pictured again with a redheaded woman at the beach. And again with the redhead at a pumpkin patch.

As Lisbeth scanned all the photos, she noticed that every shot had white people in it. Indeed, not one—not a single one—had anyone who was black.

Lisbeth underestimated her. Violet—or whatever her name was—wasn't some dumb novice.

"This isn't your house, is it?" Lisbeth asked.

Violet stopped in the small, cluttered kitchen. A child-size plastic Cinderella table sat next to a full-size faux-wood one. Half a dozen photos cluttered the refrigerator door. Again, everyone was white.

"And your name's not Debbie Schopf, is it?" Lisbeth added.

"Leave Debbie out of this—"

"Violet, if she's your friend . . ."

"She's just doing me a favor."

"Violet . . ."

"Please don't drag her in— Oh, God," Violet said, shielding her eyes with her hand. It was the first time Lisbeth got a look at the thin gold wedding band on Violet's ring finger. The one detail Lisbeth believed.

"Listen," Lisbeth said, touching Violet's shoulder. "You listening? I'm not here to catch you or trap you or drag your friends in. I swear. I just need to know if what you said about Dreidel—"

"I didn't make it up."

"No one thinks you did."

"You just said my name wouldn't be used. You told me that."

"And I stand by it, Violet," Lisbeth said, knowing the fake name put her at ease. "No one knows I'm here. Not my editor, not my colleagues, nobody. But let's remember: You invited me here for a reason. What Dreidel did to you . . . when he raised his hand—"

"He didn't raise his hand! He put his fist in my face, then gashed me with the mirror!" Violet erupted, her fear quickly smothered by rage. "That bastard hurt me so bad I had to tell my mother I was in a car accident! She believed it too—after I kicked my headlight in to prove it! But when I saw him in the paper . . . If he thinks I'm just gonna keep it all quiet while he holds himself out there as State Senator Boy Scout . . . Oh, no, no, *no*!"

"I hear you, Violet—I do. But you need to understand, I can't do anything, I can't even help you, until I verify it. Now you said you had proof. Are they photos or—?"

"Photos? Even when he's dumb, Dreidel's not that stupid." Leaving the kitchen, Violet headed into the family room, where beige vertical blinds kept the last bits of sun from peeking through the sliding glass doors. Taking a moment to calm down, she put her five fingertips against the center of her chest.

"Y'okay?" Lisbeth asked.

"Yeah, just—just hating the past a little, know what I mean?"

"You kidding? I even hate the present."

It was an easy joke, but exactly what Violet needed to catch her breath. "When we first—y'know, when we started," she said, kneeling down and fishing under the L-shaped flower-print sofa, "I wasn't even allowed to ask him about work. But these White House boys . . . they're no different than the money boys in Palm Beach or Miami or anywhere . . . all egomaniacs love to talk about themselves," she added as she tugged a small pile of paperwork from under the sofa. Bound by a thick rubber band, it looked like a stack of catalogs and mail. As Violet whipped off the rubber band, the pile fanned out across the cream-colored Formica coffee table.

"President Manning's Remarks for APEC Summit. Signed program from the Moroccan king's funeral . . ." Skimming through the pile, Violet rattled them off one by one. "Look at this—personal business card of the owner of the Miami Dolphins with his direct dial and cell numbers handwritten on the back, along with a note that says *Mr. President, Let's play golf.* Asshole."

"I don't understand. Dreidel left this stuff here?"

"Left it? He gave it to me. *Proudly* gave it to me. I don't know, it was his pathetic way of proving he was actually by the President's side. Every time he visited, I'd get another piece from the presidential junk drawer: Manning's handwritten lunch orders, scorecards from when he played bridge, military coins, crossword puzzles, luggage tags—"

"What'd you say?"

"Luggage tags?"

"Crossword puzzles," Lisbeth repeated as she sat next to Violet on the couch and leaned toward the pile on the coffee table.

"Oh, I definitely got one," Violet replied, digging through the stack. "Manning was a nut at those. Dreidel said he could do a full puzzle while chatting on the phone with— Ah, here we go," she added, pulling an old folded-up newspaper from the stack.

When Violet handed it over, Lisbeth's arms, legs, and whole body went cold as she finally got a look at the puzzle . . . and the President's handwritten answers . . . and the jumble of initials scribbled in the left-hand margin.

Her hands were shaking. She read it, then reread it to be sure. *I don't believe it. How could we be so—?*

"What?" Violet asked, clearly confused. "What's wrong?"

"Nothing . . . just— I can reach you at this number, yes?" As Violet nodded, Lisbeth copied the phone number that was handwritten on the base of the phone. Standing from her seat, she continued to clutch the crossword in her hand. "Listen, can I make a copy of this? I'll bring it right back as soon as I'm done."

"Sure, but—I don't get it. What'd you find, Dreidel's handwriting?"

"No," Lisbeth said, sprinting for the door, flipping open her cell phone, and already dialing Wes's number. "Something far better than that."

79

Silent for almost twenty-five minutes, Rogo was hunched over the archival box in his lap as his fingertips walked through each page of the open file. "Who d'ya think the mom is?" he finally asked as the sun faded through the nearby window.

"Of Boyle's kid?" Dreidel replied, picking through his own box. "I've got no idea."

"You think it was someone big?"

"Define *big*."

"I don't know—he could've been sleeping with anyone: a senior staffer . . . some intern . . . the First Lady—"

"First Lady? You joking? You think we wouldn't notice if Mrs. Manning—*while in the White House*—started vomiting, gaining weight, and suddenly seeing a doctor—not to mention if she showed up one day with a kid that looked like Boyle?"

"Maybe she didn't have the kid. It could've been—"

"'Paternity issue' means the kid was born," Dreidel insisted, crossing to the other side of the table and picking up a new box. "It would've said *ABT* if they thought there was an abortion. And even if that weren't the case—the

First Lady? Please . . . when it came time to leave the White House, she was more upset than the President himself. No way she'd put any of that at risk for some dumb fling with Boyle."

"I'm just saying, it could've been anyone," Rogo said, nearly halfway through the file box as he reached a thick brown accordion folder that held two framed photos. Pulling out the silver frame in front, he squinted down at the family shot of Boyle with his wife and daughter.

Posed in front of a waterfall, Boyle and his wife playfully hugged their sixteen-year-old daughter, Lydia, who, at the center of the photograph, was in mid-scream/mid-laugh as the ice-cold waterfall soaked her back. Laughing right along with her, Boyle had his mouth wide open, and despite his thick mustache, it was clear that Lydia had her father's smile. A huge, toothy grin. Rogo couldn't take his eyes off it. Just one big happy—

"It's just a photo," Dreidel interrupted.

"Wha?" Rogo asked, looking over his shoulder.

Behind him, Dreidel stared down at the framed shot of the Boyles at the waterfall. "That's it—just a photo," he warned. "Believe me, even though they're smiling, doesn't mean they're happy."

Rogo looked down at the photo, then back to Dreidel, whose lips were pressed together. Rogo knew that look. He saw it every day on his speeding ticket clients. We all know our own sins.

"So the mom from Boyle's paternity problem . . ." Rogo began.

". . . could be anyone," Dreidel agreed, happy to be back on track. "Though knowing Boyle, I bet it's someone we've never even heard of."

"What makes you say that?" Rogo asked.

"I don't know—it's just . . . when we were in the White House, that's the way Boyle was. As Manning's oldest friend, he was never really part of the staff. He was more—he was *here*," Dreidel said, holding his left hand palm-down at eye level. "And he thought the rest of us were *here*," he added, slapping his right palm against the worktable.

"That's the benefit of being First Friend."

"But that's the thing—I know he kinda got sainthood when he was shot, but from where I was standing on the inside, Boyle spent plenty of days in the doghouse."

"Maybe that's when Manning found out about the kid."

For the second time, Dreidel was silent.

Rogo didn't say a word. Unloading the second picture from his own box, he propped open the back leg of the black matte picture frame and stood it up on the worktable. Inside was a close-up photo of Boyle and his wife, the apples of their cheeks pressed together as they smiled for the camera. From the bushiness of his mustache and the thickness of his hairline, the photo was an old one. Two people in love.

"What else you got in there besides photos?" Dreidel asked, turning the box slightly and reading the word *Misc.* on the main label.

"Mostly desk stuff," Rogo said as he emptied the box, pulling out a hardcover book about the history of genocide, a softcover about the legacy of the Irish, and a rubber-banded preview copy of a highly critical book called *The Manning Myth.*

"I remember when that came out," Dreidel said. "Pompous ass never even called us to fact-check."

"I just can't believe they keep all this crap," Rogo said

as he pulled out a decade-old parking pass for the Kennedy Center.

"To you, it's crap—to the library, it's history."

"Let me tell you something—even to the library, this crap is crap," Rogo said, unloading a small stack of taxi receipts, a scrap of paper with handwritten directions to the Arena Stage, a blank RSVP card to someone's wedding, a finger-paint drawing with the words *Uncle Ron* neatly printed on top, and a small spiral notebook with the Washington Redskins football logo on the front.

"Whoa, whoa, whoa—what're you doing?" Dreidel interrupted.

"What, *this*?" Rogo asked, pointing to the finger-paint drawing.

"That," Dreidel insisted as he grabbed the spiral notebook with the football logo.

"I don't get it—whattya need a football schedule for?"

"This isn't a schedule." Opening the book, Dreidel turned it toward Rogo, revealing a daily calendar for the first week of January. "It's Boyle's datebook."

Rogo's eyebrows rose as he palmed the top of his buzzed head. "So we can see all his meetings . . ."

"Exactly," Dreidel said, already skimming through it. "Meetings, dinners, everything—and most particularly what he was up to on the night of May 27th."

80

"Mr. President?" I call out as I open the front door.

No one answers.

"Sir, it's Wes—are you there?" I ask again, even though I know the answer. If he weren't here, the Secret Service wouldn't be outside. But after all our years together, I'm always careful to know my place. It's one thing to walk into his office. It's quite another to step into his home.

"Back here," a man's voice calls out, ricocheting down the long center hallway that leads to the living room. I pause a moment, unable to place the voice—polished, with a hint of British accent—but quickly step inside and shut the door. It was hard enough making the decision to come here. Even if he's got guests, I'm not turning back now.

Still trying to identify the voice, I head for the hallway and steal a glance at the poster-sized, framed black-and-white photograph that sits above the antique credenza and the vase of fresh flowers on my right. The photo is Manning's favorite: a panoramic view of his desk in the Oval Office, taken by a photographer who literally put the camera in the President's chair and hit the shutter.

The result is an exact re-creation of Manning's old view from behind the most powerful desk in the world: the family photos of his wife, the pen left for him by the previous President, a personal note written by his son, a small gold plaque with the John Lennon quote "A working class hero is something to be," and a shot of Manning sitting with his mom on the day he arrived at the White House—his first official meeting in the Oval. On the left of the desk, Manning's phone looms as large as a shoebox, the camera so close you can read the five typed names on his speed dial: *Lenore* (his wife), *Arlen* (the V.P.), *Carl* (national security adviser), *Warren* (chief of staff), and *Wes*. Me.

With the push of a button, we'd all come running. Eight years later, I haven't changed. Until now.

Plowing through the hallway, I head into the formal living room, where, at the center of the Tibetan rug, Manning is standing on a small stool while a fair-skinned man with messy blond hair that barely covers his large forehead flits around him like a tailor working on his suit.

"Please, Mr. President, I just need you still," he pleads in what I now realize is a genteel South African accent.

Just behind Big Forehead, a twenty-something female photographer with short spiky hair lowers her chin and a flashbulb explodes.

It's not until I see that Forehead is holding measuring calipers—which look like a ruler with an adjustable wrench on the end of it—that I even realize what's going on. The photographer snaps another picture of Manning. On the sofa, a square box that can easily be mistaken for a Chinese checkers set holds a dozen rows of glass eyeballs, each one a different shade of Manning gray. Manning himself stands perfectly still and the calipers *klik-klik* around his wrist, a digital readout giving Forehead another measurement. Madame Tussauds Wax Museum prides itself on accuracy. Even for celebrities no longer in the public eye.

"Whattya think—they're darker now, right?" a petite African-American woman says as she holds out two gunmetal-gray eyeballs that stare directly at me. The odd part is, even held out in the air, they look eerily like Manning's. "These were from our original White House figure—hand-done, of course—but I feel like he's gone deeper gray in the past few years."

"Yeah . . . sure," I stutter, already looking at my watch. "Listen, do you know how long this is going t—?"

"Relax, Wes," Manning interrupts with the last kind of laugh I want to hear. The only time he's this excited is during the annual meeting where the board of his library gets together. With his old staff reunited, he once again feels like he's holding the power. It lasts four hours at most. Then he goes back to being yet another former President whose two-car motorcade still has to stop at the red lights. Today, the Tussauds folks bring with them the attention of the glory days. Manning's not letting it go. "The schedule's clear," he tells me. "Where else you got to be?"

"Nowhere, sir. But now that—with Nico out there—"

"Now you sound like Claudia." But as he turns and takes his first actual look at me, he cuts himself off. I may know how to read him perfectly, but he knows how to read me even better—especially when it comes to Nico. "Wes," he says, not even needing words.

I'm fine, I reply with nothing more than a nod. He knows it's a lie, but he also knows why. If I'm having this discussion, it's not going to be in front of an audience.

Determined to get things moving, I head for Forehead, who seems to be the one in charge.

"Declan Reese—from Madame Tussauds. Thanks for having us back," Forehead says, saluting me with the calipers and extending a handshake. "We try to never call on our portraits twice, but the popularity of President Manning's figure—"

"They just think I'm getting old and want to make sure they get my wattle right," Manning says, playfully swatting his own jowls.

All the Tussauds people laugh. Especially because it's true.

"No problem," I say, never forgetting the job. "Just remember—"

"Thirty minutes," Declan promises as another flashbulb explodes. "Don't worry—I did Rudy Giuliani in twenty-seven minutes, and we still got his cracked lips and the bright redness of his knuckles."

As the eyeball woman readies a bite plate for a tooth impression, Declan pulls me aside and cups my elbow. "We were also wondering if we could possibly get a new piece of clothing. Something to reflect the more casual post-presidency," he whispers just loud enough so Manning can hear. "Bush's and Clinton's offices sent us some golf shirts."

"Sorry . . . we don't really do that kind of—"

"What'd Bush and Clinton send? Golf shirts?" Manning calls out, never wanting to be left out. Every day, we turn down dozens of endorsements, from *Got Milk?* ads, to presidential chess sets, to autograph deals, to a ten-million-dollar role for a two-day cameo in a movie. But when his fellow Formers are involved, Manning can't help himself. "Wes, do me a favor and go grab them one of my blue blazers. We give 'em a golf shirt, they'll dress us like the Three Stooges."

As the room again laughs, I sneak a look at Declan, who knows exactly what he's doing. He got Woody Allen's prescription glasses—he can swindle the clothes off a former President.

"Thank you, good sir," Declan adds in his spit-shined accent as I head back through the hallway and toward the stairs. Usually, I'd fight—but the sooner they're out of here, the sooner I can find out what's going on with Boyle.

Focusing on just that, I clutch the banister, already role-playing the moment in my head. When it comes to giving Manning bad news, the best way is to just put it out there. *Sir, I think I saw Boyle the other night in Malaysia.* I know Manning's tells—how he grins when he's mad or raises his chin when he's feigning surprise. Just seeing his reaction'll give me all I need to know.

At the top of the stairs, my phone vibrates in my pocket. Caller ID says it's Lisbeth. I shut the phone, refusing to answer. My bullshit quota for the day is filled. The last thing I need is another fake apology.

More annoyed than ever, I quickly plow down the second-floor hallway that's lined with two American flags: one that flew over the White House on Manning's first day in office, the other that flew the day he left. By the time I approach the bedroom on my left, I'm already rethinking my Manning strategy. Maybe I shouldn't just blurt it. He's always better with a soft touch. *Sir, I know this'll sound odd . . . Sir, I'm not sure how to say this . . . Sir, am I really as big a puss as I think I am?* Knowing the answer, I shove open the bedroom door and—

"Daaah . . . !" the First Lady yelps, jumping back in

her seat at the antique writing desk in the corner of the room. She spins to face me so fast, her reading glasses fly from her face, and even though she's fully dressed in a light blue blouse and white slacks, I cover my eyes, immediately backtracking.

"Forgive me, ma'am. Didn't realize you were—"

"I-It's okay," she says, her right hand patting the air to reassure me. I'm waiting for her to rip me apart. Instead, she's caught so off guard, it doesn't come. Her face is flushed as her eyes blink over and over, searching for calm. "Just . . . you just surprised me is all."

Still mid-apology, I reach down for her glasses and stumble forward to hand them back. It's not until I'm right in front of her that I see her left hand tucking something under the cushion of her seat.

"Thank you, Wes," she says, reaching for the glasses without looking up.

Spinning back on my heel, I make a beeline for the door—but not before taking one last glance over my shoulder. Dr. Lenore Manning has been through two presidential elections, three battles for governor, two natural childbirths, and four years of never-ending attacks against her, her husband, her children, her family, and nearly every close friend, including a *Vanity Fair* cover story with the homeliest picture ever taken of her, over the headline *The Doctor First Lady Is* In: *Why Pretty Is Out—and Brains Are All the Rage.* At this point, even the worst attacks roll off her. So when I see her glance back at me—when our eyes lock and I spot the bloodshot redness that she quickly tries to hide with a smile and another thank-you . . . Right there, my legs lock. She can blink all she wants. I know tears when I see them.

As I stumble back to the door, the awkwardness is

overwhelming. *Go . . . move . . . disappear.* This isn't where I'm supposed to be. Without even thinking, I rush into the hallway and head back toward the stairs. Anything to get out of there. My brain's racing full speed, still struggling to process. *It's not even . . . In all my years with them . . . What's so god-awful, it could possibly make her cry?* Searching for the answer, I stop at the top of the stairs and glance back over my shoulder. On my right is the flag from the day we left the White Hou— No. We didn't *leave* the White House. We were thrown out. Thrown out for Manning's reaction that day at the speedway. Thrown out after Boyle was shot. Thrown out after Boyle *died* in that ambulance.

I watched the funeral on TV from my hospital bed. Naturally, they kept cutting away to the President's and First Lady's reactions. Hidden by her wide-brimmed black hat, she kept her head steady, trying to hold it in—but as Boyle's daughter started to speak . . . The camera caught it for half a second, never even realizing what was happening. The First Lady wiped her nose, then sat up straighter than ever. With that, it was done. It was still the only time I'd seen the First Lady cry.

Until just now.

Still looking over my shoulder, I stare up the hallway at the open door of the bedroom. No doubt, I should go downstairs. This isn't my business. There are infinite reasons she could be crying. But right now, two days after seeing Boyle's brown and light blue eyes . . . a day after Nico escaping from St. Elizabeths . . . plus whatever the First Lady was hiding under her seat . . . I hate myself for even thinking it. They should fire me for even thinking it. But with everything that's swirling, to just walk away now—to give up, to pretend it's not there, to walk downstairs without finding out why one of the most powerful women in the world is suddenly devastated . . . No. I can't. I need to know.

Pivoting back toward the bedroom, I take a silent step across the handwoven gold carpet that runs up the hall. I hear a soft sniffle from her direction. Not crying. A strong, final sniff that buries everything back down. Clenching my fists and holding my breath, I take two more tiptoed steps. For eight years, I've fought to protect their privacy. Now I'm the one invading it. But if there's something she knows . . . something about what happened . . . I keep my pace, almost at the door. But instead of heading to the bedroom on my left, I crane my neck, check to make sure the First Lady can't see me, and duck into the open door of the bathroom that's diagonally across the hall on my right.

With the sun fading outside, the bathroom's dark. As I duck behind the door, my heart's pounding so fast, I feel it in the sides of my temples. To be safe, I shut the door halfway and peek out from the thin vertical gap between the door spine and the frame. Across the hall, in her bedroom, the First Lady's back is to me as she sits at her writer's desk. From the angle I'm at, I only see the right half of her body—like she's split vertically in two—but it's the only half I need, especially as she reaches under her seat cushion and pulls out whatever it was she hid.

Pressing my nose into the opening, I squint hard trying to see what it is. A photograph? A memo? I don't have a chance. Her back blocks everything. But as she holds the item, lowering her head to examine it, there's no mistaking the sudden droop in her posture. Her shoulders sag. Her right arm begins to tremble. She reaches up, as if she's pinching the bridge of her nose—but as another sniffle cuts through the air, followed by an almost inaudible whimper—I realize she's not pinching her nose. She's wiping her eyes. And once again cryi—

Just as quickly, her posture stiffens and shoulders rise. Like before, she buries the moment, a final sniffle patting the last bits of dirt on the grave of whatever previous emotion she momentarily let through. Even in solitude, even as her arm continues to tremble, the President's wife refuses to suffer weakness.

Moving like she's in a rush, she promptly folds up the memo or photo or whatever it is, and stuffs it between the back pages of what looks like a paperback on her desk. I almost forgot. Manning isn't the only one the Madame Tussauds folks are here to see. With a final deep breath, the First Lady smooths out her skirt, dabs her eyes, and lifts her chin. Public mask back in place.

As she turns to leave the bedroom, she stares across the hallway, at the dark space where I am, pausing for half a second. I shrink back from the sliver of doorway, and she keeps moving, looking away just as quickly. No, no way. She didn't see a thing. Hidden by the darkness, I watch as she plows toward me, cutting to my left as she reaches the hallway. Within seconds, her footsteps sound against the wooden stairs, fading with each step. I don't even take a breath until I hear her footsteps disappear into the carpet at the bottom. Even then, I still count to ten, just to be safe. A swell of nausea already has me reeling. What the hell am I doing?

Trying to shake it, I flush the toilet, run the faucet, and step out of the bathroom as if everything's normal. A quick scan of the hallway tells me no one's there. "Dr. Manning?" I say softly. No answer. I'm all alone.

Through the open door of the Mannings' bedroom, the

antique writer's desk is less than ten feet away. In all our years together, I've never once betrayed their trust. I tell myself that again as I stare at the book on her desk. It's just sitting there. With the answer inside.

If I were Rogo, I'd do it. If I were Dreidel, I'd do it. If I were Lisbeth, I'd have done it two minutes ago. But I'm me. And therein lies the *real* problem. I know myself. I know my limitations. And I know if I go in there, it's an action I can never take back. The old me would've never even considered it. But I don't think I'm that man anymore.

Tightening my fists, I take four steps into the bedroom and up to the desk. The black book is thick with gold embossing on the cover. *Holy Bible.* I don't know why I'm surprised.

As I pick up the Bible and thumb through it from back to front, the folded-up sheet practically leaps out. I unfold it so fast, it almost rips. I thought it was a photograph or some kind of official memo. It's not. It's a letter. Handwritten on plain, unmarked stationery. The handwriting is unfamiliar but precise—perfect tiny block letters undistinguished by any style or idiosyncrasy. Like it was written by someone who's spent years perfecting ways to go unnoticed.

To be sure, I flip the sheet over to the signature on the back. Like the rest, the letters are simple, almost commonplace. The tip of the *R* drags longer than the rest. *Ron.* Ron Boyle.

Dear Lenore, I read as I flip it back, my brain hurtling so fast, all I can do is skim. *Please forgive me . . . never meant to mislead you . . . I just thought, for everyone's good . . . for all my sins . . . to finally protect those I hurt . . . My punishment, Lenore. My atonement. Please understand, they said it could be anyone—that it could've been you . . . And after there was no payment for Blackbird, when I found what he . . .*

He? Who's he*?* I wonder, still skimming. *And Blackbird? Is that what they called the six-million-dollar—?*

"Hey!" a female voice calls out behind me.

My lungs collapse and my body freezes. I'm already off balance as I spin back to face her.

The First Lady stands in the doorway, her leaf-green eyes on fire. "What the hell do you think you're doing?"

81

You gotta be kidding me."

"It's bad?" Rogo asked, leaning in and reading over Dreidel's shoulder.

On the worktable in front of them, Boyle's datebook was opened to the week of May 22. In the square labeled *Monday, May 23* was the handwritten note *Manning in NY.* On Wednesday the twenty-fifth was the note *Elliot in the Morning interview.* And on Thursday the twenty-sixth was the note *Senator Okum fundraiser—Wash. Hilton—7 p.m.* But what caught Rogo's eye was the box for May 27, which was blacked out with a thick marker:

[redacted]

"They crossed it out?" Rogo asked.

"That's the library's job—read through all the files and figure out what can be released to the public."

"I understand *how.* I just mean . . . Hold on—" he said, cutting himself off and reaching down to touch the right-hand page of the calendar. Even before he rubbed it with his fingers, Rogo could see it was made from a thinner and brighter paper stock than the off-white sheets that filled the rest of the datebook. "This isn't even the original, is it?"

"Photocopy—that's how redactions are done," Dreidel explained. "They can't ruin the original, so they make a second copy, black that out, and staple it back in the original's place."

"Okay, fine—so how do we get the original?"

"Actually, they usually— Here, lemme see," Dreidel said, reaching for the datebook and flipping back to the front inside cover. Sure enough, folded up and stapled to the first page was another photocopied sheet of paper. As Dreidel unfolded it, Rogo read the words *Withdrawal Sheet* across the top.

"Anytime they redact something, they have to document it," Dreidel said as they both read from the sheet.

DOCUMENT TYPE	SUBJECT/TITLE	DATE	RESTRICTION
1. calendar	Boyle schedule 1p., partial	5/27	B6
1. calendar	Boyle schedule 1p., partial	6/3	B6

"What's B6?" Rogo asked.

Squinting to read the tiny font, Dreidel skimmed through the list of restrictions at the bottom of the withdrawal sheet.

"B1 is when it's classified . . . B2 is when an agency forbids it . . ."

"And B6?"

"Release would constitute a clearly unwarranted invasion of personal privacy," Dreidel read from the sheet.

"So this is some secret from Manning's personal life?"

"Or his own," Dreidel clarified. "The meetings and the schedules may be work product of the White House, but if

Boyle writes something . . . I don't know, like his ATM PIN code or his Social Security number . . . that clearly has nothing to do with the presidency and therefore gets the black pen as well."

Rogo flipped the book back to the May 27 redaction.

[redacted]

"Looks like a few more letters than a PIN code."

"Or a Social Security number," Dreidel agreed.

"Maybe we can go back to the archivist, and you can pull rank on her again until she shows us the original."

"You kidding? After everything we've said, she's already suspicious enough."

"Can we find it ourselves? Is it in there?" Rogo asked, pointing to the metal cage in the far corner of the room where at least another ten sets of shelves were piled to the ceiling with archival boxes.

"Right—we'll just randomly search through an additional five million documents—right after we sidestep the guy who's watching us, and figure out how to break open the bombproof lock that guards all the other national security files. Look at that thing—it's like the *Die Hard* vault."

Rogo turned around to check the cage. Even from across the room, the thickness of the battered steel lock was unmistakable. "So that's it? We just give up?"

Lowering his chin and shooting Rogo a look, Dreidel grabbed the datebook and stuffed it underneath the worktable. "Do I look like Wes to you?" he asked as he stared over Rogo's shoulder.

Following Dreidel's gaze, Rogo again turned around as he traced it to Freddy the attendant, who was still clicking away at the bank of computers.

"Guys, you ready to wrap up?" Freddy asked. "It's almost five o'clock."

"Ten more minutes—tops," Dreidel promised. Outside, through the tall plate-glass windows that overlooked the shiny bronze statue of Manning, the December sun sank early in the sky. No doubt, it was getting late. Hunching down in his seat and blocking himself from Freddy's view, he whispered to Rogo, "Move an inch to your left."

"What're you—?"

"Nothing," Dreidel said calmly, his hands still out of sight as he held the datebook under the worktable. "And I'm certainly not defacing government property by tearing out a sheet of paper from this historically treasured calendar." As a small smirk spread up Dreidel's cheeks, Rogo heard a quiet *kk, kk, kk* below the table—like the last few pimples of bubble-wrap popping . . . or a page being tugged from the teeth of a half dozen staples.

With a final tear, Dreidel freed the last piece, then folded up the May 27 calendar page and tucked it into his jacket pocket. "I'm telling you, it's not here!" he called out, raising his voice as he brought the datebook back up to the worktable. "Hey, Freddy, can you take a look at this? I think there's a page missing from one of the files."

Hopping out of his seat, Dreidel held the datebook out to Freddy and pointed to the withdrawal sheet. "See, it says here that there's a redaction on the entry for May 27th, but when you flip here," he explained, turning back to the May calendar pages, "it just picks up with the beginning of June."

Freddy flipped back to the withdrawal page, then back to June. "Yeah . . . no . . . the page is definitely missing. Can this hold till tomorrow? We're about to close and—"

"Trust me, we're on deadline too," Dreidel said, glancing at his watch. "Listen, can you do us a favor and just pull the original? If we don't bring this to Manning tonight, he'll have our testicles. Really. He'll reach down and take them away."

"Listen, I'd love to help you guys, but if it's redacted—"

"Freddy, when I left Palm Beach this morning, the President said he wanted a full copy of this datebook for the memorial piece he's doing for Boyle's family," Dreidel pleaded. "Now we're talking about a nearly ten-year-old file for a man who's been dead for that entire time. If there's something embarrassing in that entry—if it says, *I hate the President* or *I'm a terrorist spy* or anything that truly affects national security—don't show it to us. But if it's just some dumb little detail nobody cares about like his sister's birthday, you'd really be saving us."

Scratching his finger in the dimple of his chin, Freddy glanced down at the datebook, then up at Dreidel and Rogo.

"Just take a peek," Rogo begged. "If it's anything embarrassing, put it back on the shelf."

Standing there, Freddy pointed them back to their file-covered worktable. "Just give me the folder numbers on the box. I'll see what I can do . . ."

"Freddy," Rogo began, his voice racing down the runway, "when I get married, brother, you're my bridesmaid!"

"Folder OA16209," Dreidel called out from the front of the archival box.

Fifteen minutes later, in the far corner of the room, the metal door to the cage opened, and Freddy walked out with a single sheet of paper in his hand.

"Here you go," Freddy said as he handed it to Dreidel. "Though I think you would've been better off getting his sister's birthday."

82

"I-I-I was just—"

"Rummaging through my desk!" the First Lady explodes. "That I can see for myself! You—you—after all our time together—to violate that trust!"

"Ma'am, please don't—"

"Don't bullshit me, Wes! I know what I saw. I see it right now! But this isn't your *business*!" she growls, ripping Boyle's letter from my hand.

I step back, my body shaking. Forget firing me; for a moment, I'm actually terrified she might hit me. But as she blurts the last part—*This isn't your business!*—something swells and erupts in my stomach. Blood flushes my cheeks, and I can't help but shake my head. "That's not true," I whisper, my eyes locked on her.

Right there, she pounces. "Ex*cuse* me?"

I stay silent, still amazed the words came from my lips.

"*What'd* you just say?" she challenges.

"It's—that's not true," I repeat, searching her face. "I was at the speedway too—it *is* my business."

Her eyes narrow. I stare out the window over her shoulder. Like all the windows in this house, it's bulletproof and doesn't open. But right now she looks like she's ready to toss me through one. Waving the Boyle letter, she asks, "Who put you up to this?"

"What?"

"Was it a reporter? Did they pay you to write this?"

"Ma'am, you really think I'd—?"

"Or is it just some sick practical joke to test my reaction? I've got a great idea," she says in mock impersonation. "Let's revisit the worst moment in Dr. Manning's life, then see if we can rip apart her reality until she finally snaps."

"Ma'am, this isn't a joke—"

"Or better yet, let's have her husband's aide sneak into her bedroom . . ."

"Ma'am . . ."

". . . take it from her desk . . ."

"Dr. Manning, I saw him."

". . . and that way, she'll start panicking, wondering if it was even real to begin with."

"I saw Boyle. In Malaysia. He's alive."

She freezes, the tips of her fingers touching her lips. Her head shakes slowly. Then faster. *No—no. Oh, no, no.*

"It was him, ma'am. I saw him."

Her head continues to shake as her fingers move from her lips, to her chin, to her own shoulder. Curling forward and gripping her shoulder, she practically shrinks into a ball. "How could he—? How could they both—? Oh, God . . ." She looks back up at me, and her eyes well with tears so fast, there's no time to blink them away. Earlier, I thought they were tears of guilt—that she might be hiding something. But to see her now—the frightened anguish that contorts her face, the shock that keeps her head shaking in denial—these tears are born in pain.

"Dr. Manning, I'm sure this . . . I know it seems impossible—"

"That's not—God!—it's not like I'm naive," she insists. "I'm *not* naive. I mean, I-I-I knew he'd keep things from me—not to deceive—that's just what he has to do. That's the job of being President."

As she stumbles through the words, I realize she's no longer talking about Boyle. She's talking about her husband.

"There are secrets he *has* to keep, Wes. Troop positions . . . surveillance capabilities . . . those are the secrets we *need*," she says. "But something like this . . . good Lord, I was at Ron's funeral. I read a psalm!"

"Ma'am, what're you—?"

"I went to his house and cried with his wife and daughter! I was on my knees praying for his peaceful rest!" she shouts, her sadness shifting to rage. "And now to find out it was all a sham . . . some weak-minded escape for his own cowardice . . ." The tears again flood forward and she sways off balance. "Oh, Lord, if what Ron says . . . if it's true . . ." Stumbling toward me, she grabs the corner of the low Empire dresser on my left, barely able to stay on her feet.

"Ma'am!"

She holds up a hand to keep me back. Her eyes flit around the room. At first, I assume she's mid-panic-attack. But the way she keeps looking . . . from the side table on the left of the bed, to Manning's side table on the right, to the writer's desk, back to the Empire dresser . . . each is covered with picture frames—all shapes and sizes—all with photos of Manning. "H-How could he . . . how could they do that?" she asks, looking at me for the answer.

All I can offer is a shell-shocked stare. I can't feel my arms. Everything's numb. Is she saying that Manning knew abou—?

"Did Boyle say anything when you saw him? Did he offer any explanation?"

"I just . . . I walked in on him," I explain, barely hearing my own words. "He took off before I even realized what was happening."

The First Lady's hand starts shaking again. She's like me in Malaysia. Thanks to the letter, she's finally hearing that her dead friend is actually alive. And from what Boyle wrote, for some reason he blames himself, saying he did it to protect his family. Overwhelmed by the moment, Dr. Manning takes a seat on the hand-painted American flag chest at the foot of the bed and stares down at Boyle's handwritten letter. "I just can't—"

"He called me yesterday and told me to stay away," I add for no good reason. "That it wasn't my fight." I feel a flush of rage. "But it *is* my fight."

She looks at me absently as if she'd forgotten I was there. Her jaw tightens, and she presses her hand against her lap until it stops shaking. It's bad enough she's so emotionally distraught. It's even worse that it's happening in front of me. Within an eyeblink, her chin and posture stiffen, and her political instincts, honed by years of keeping private matters private, kick in. "He's right," she blurts.

"What're you talking about?"

"Listen to Boyle," she says. Then, as an afterthought, "Please."

"But, ma'am—"

"Forget you ever saw him, forget he ever called you." As her voice cracks, I realize I was wrong. This isn't about her being emotionally exposed. It's about her being protective. And not just of her husband. Of me too. "Wes, if you walk away now, at least they won't know that you—"

"They already know. They know I saw him . . ."

"*They?* Who's *they*?" she asks, cocking an anxious eyebrow.

"The Three," I insist.

She looks up as I say the words, and I spot the recognition in her eyes. They were messing with her friend too—of course, she knows the details. But that doesn't mean she wants to drag me into the rest of it.

"I know who they are," I tell her.

"I don't think you do, Wes."

"How can you—?" I cut myself off as adrenaline buries the nauseous undertow I'm feeling. I've let her protect me for eight years. It's enough. "I know The Three were fighting with the President and Boyle. I know *Blackbird*, whatever it was, was worth a quick six-million-dollar payout for The Roman, who apparently was one of the government's top informants. I know that the payout was rejected by the President in one of the national security briefings. And I know that losing that kind of cash—and whatever else they would've made after it—had to've enraged them. The only thing I can't figure out is, where'd Boyle fit in, and what'd he do that had The Three angry enough to pull the trigger?"

I expect her to be relieved to have someone with her, but she looks more frightened than ever, which quickly reminds me that this letter is as much of a shock to her as spotting Boyle was to me. And even with me digging up her worst family secrets, regardless of what Boyle or her husband did, she doesn't want to see me hurt by it.

"How did you learn about The Three?" she asks.

I hesitate at first. "Friend of a friend who works for DOD."

"And who told you they were fighting with the President?"

"That part I guessed on."

Panicking, she studies me, weighing the permutations. She knows I'm not her enemy. But that doesn't mean she's letting me be her friend. Still, I'm definitely close. Too close to just send me on my way.

"I can help you," I tell her.

She shakes her head, unconvinced.

"Ma'am, they know I saw Boyle. If you're trying to keep me safe, it's already too late. Just tell me what Boyle did and—"

"It's not what Boyle *did*," she whispers. "It's what he *didn't* do." She catches herself, already regretting it.

"Didn't do to *who*? To the President?"

"*No!*" But that's all she tosses my way. Looking down, she curls back into a ball.

"Then to who? To you? To Albright? Just tell me who it was."

She's dead silent.

"Dr. Manning, please, you've known me eight years. Have I ever done anything that would hurt you?"

She continues to stare down, and I can't say I blame her. She's the former First Lady of the United States. She's not sharing her fears with some young aide. I don't care. I need to know.

"So that's it? I'm supposed to just walk away?"

Still no answer. No doubt, she's hoping I'll be my usual self and shrink from the conflict. Two days ago, I would've. Not today.

"That's fine," I tell her as I head for the door. "You have every right to keep it to yourself, but you need to understand this: When I leave here, I'm not giving up. That bullet hit *my* face. And until I find out what really happened that day, I'm going to keep searching, keep digging, keep asking questions of every single person that was—"

"Don't you see? It was an offer."

I turn, but I'm not surprised. Whatever Boyle did, if she tells me the truth, at least she has a chance of containing it. And for someone who already has third-degree burns from the glare of the public spotlight, containment is all.

"An offer for what?" I ask, well aware of the box she lives in. If there's something she needs to keep hidden, she can't risk letting me walk out of here armed with embarrassing questions.

But she's still hesitating.

"I'm sorry you don't trust me," I say, heading for the door.

"You said it yourself, Wes. As an informant, The Roman started bringing in tips."

"But The Roman was actually a Secret Service agent, right?"

"That's what they think *now*. But no one knew that back then. In those days, the agencies were just happy to get The Roman's tips. Especially after Iraq, a correct, well-corroborated tip about a hidden training camp in Sudan? You saw how the war on terror works—indicators and warnings are all we have. Amazingly for The Roman, if he brought an assassination tip to the Secret Service, when the Service would go verify it with other agencies, the FBI would confirm it, as would the CIA. If he brought a tip to the FBI, it'd get authenticated by the

CIA and the Service—and that verification is exactly what he needed for them to pay him as a source."

"So under the guise of The Roman, The Three would bring the tips into their separate agencies, then just corroborate them amongst themselves . . ."

". . . making it look like everyone—FBI, CIA, and the Service—were all in agreement. Sad to say, it happens all the time—last year in the State Department, someone made up a tip. The difference is, in most cases, they get caught because it doesn't match what the other agencies are saying. But here . . . well, if they hadn't gotten so greedy, it might've been a simple way to supplement their midlevel government salaries."

"But they got greedy?"

"Everyone's greedy," the First Lady says as years of buried anger rise again to the surface. "They knew the system. They knew that small tips about some hidden training camp would only net them fifty thousand or so. And they also knew that the only way to get the big money they were after was to lie low and save their energy for those onetime shock-and-awe tips: The Golden Gate Bridge is being targeted . . . that shoe warehouse in Pakistan is really a chemical factory. Once everyone's convinced that The Roman's last nine tips were right, they'll pay anything for the jumbo-sized tenth—even if it never happens. And when the FBI and CIA and Service all corroborate it and agree the threat is real? That's how the informant who brought it in gets his multimillion-dollar payday."

"So what was their problem?" I ask, trying to sound strong. Adrenaline only lasts so long. With each new detail of our old lives, the nauseous undertow floods back.

"The problem was, FBI and CIA case officers can only

approve payouts of $200,000. To get into the multimillion range that would put The Three in retirement, the payday had to be approved by the White House."

"And that's what *Blackbird* was, right? They were starting to cash out with their first big tip, but it got shot down by the President."

She nods, and eyes me, impressed. "That's when they realized they needed someone on the inside. Boyle was warned about it back then—that they might try approaching him, especially because of his background . . ."

"Wait, whoa, whoa—so The Three—"

"Stop calling them that. Don't you see? None of this happened because of The Three. It happened because they got smart and reached out for a new member. The Three was done. This is about The Four."

83

"You sure that's right?" Rogo asked, reading from the original May 27 entry in Boyle's datebook. He held it up to the redacted photocopy just to make sure it was a perfect fit. Underneath the

[redacted]

were the handwritten words

Dr. Eng 2678 Griffin Rd. Ft. L.

"That's the big secret they were hiding from the masses?" Rogo added. "That Boyle had a doctor's appointment?"

"It *is* personal information," Freddy pointed out, slowly approaching them as Rogo tucked the original into a nearby file.

"Makes complete sense," Dreidel agreed. "In every White House, half the staff lines up to see a shrink."

Standing at the edge of one of the long research stacks, Rogo turned to his friend, who was sitting on the corner of a nearby desk. "Who says he's a shrink?" Rogo challenged.

"Wha?"

"Dr. Eng. What makes you think he's a shrink?"

"I don't know, I just assumed he—"

"Listen, guys, I'd love to spend the rest of the night debating the merits of Eng's particular practice," Freddy interrupted, "but this is still a government building, and like any government building, when the little hand reaches the five—"

"Can you just run one more quick search?" Rogo asked, pointing to the library computers.

"I'm trying to be helpful. Really. But c'mon—the library's closed."

"Just one more search."

"It's already—"

"Just put in the words *Dr. Eng*," Rogo pleaded. "Please—it'll take less than thirty seconds. It's just typing two words—*Dr.* and *Eng*—into the bat-computer. You do that and we'll be gone so fast, you'll be home in time for the early early news."

Freddy stared at Rogo. "One last search and that's it."

A few keystrokes later, as Freddy hunched over the keyboard, the answer popped on-screen.

No other records found.

"And you—?"

"I checked everything: the WHORM file, staff and office collections, e-mail, even the few odd bits of microfiche from the old national security stuff," Freddy said, well past annoyed. "The library's now officially closed," he added, standing from his seat and pointing to the door. "So unless you'd like to be introduced to our well-trained security staff, I suggest you have a nice day."

Walking swiftly through the brick and concrete courtyard in front of the library, Rogo was a full five feet in front of

Dreidel as they headed toward the car. "A business. Yes, in Fort Lauderdale," Rogo said into his cell phone. "I'm looking for the number of a Dr. Eng. E-N-G."

"I have a Dr. *Brian* Eng on Griffin Road," the operator said.

"Two six seven eight, exactly," Rogo said, reading the address off the sheet of paper they had copied it to. "And does it say what kind of doctor he is?"

"I'm sorry, sir—we don't list occupations. Please hold for that number."

Within seconds, a mechanized female voice announced, "At the customer's request, the number is nonpublished and is not listed in our records."

"Are you friggin'— What kinda doctor keeps an unlisted phone number?" As he turned back to Dreidel, he added, "Anything on the Web?"

Staring down at the tiny screen on his phone, Dreidel fidgeted with the buttons like a grandparent with a remote control. "I know I'm set up for Internet access—I just can't figure out how to—"

"Then whattya been doing for the past five minutes? Give it here," Rogo snapped, snatching the phone from his hand. With a few clicks and shifts, Rogo entered the name *Dr. Brian Eng* and hit *Enter.* For almost a full two minutes, he scrolled and clicked but didn't say a word.

"Anything?" Dreidel asked as they weaved around cars in the parking lot.

"Unreal," Rogo moaned, still clicking buttons on the phone. "Not only is his number unlisted—the guy's somehow managed to stay out of every major search engine. Google . . . Yahoo! . . . you name it—put in *Dr. Brian Eng* and nothing comes up—it's ridiculous! If I put in the words *Jewish Smurfs*, I get a page full of hits, but

Dr. Brian Eng gives me goose egg?" Approaching the driver's side of the Toyota, Rogo slapped the phone shut and tossed it across the roof of the car to Dreidel. "Which leads us right back to, what kinda doctor keeps himself so hidden, he's almost impossible to find?"

"I don't know . . . a mob doctor?" Dreidel guessed.

"Or an abortion doctor," Rogo countered.

"What about a plastic surgeon—y'know, for the really rich who don't want people to know?"

"Actually, that's not a bad call. Wes said it looked like Boyle changed some of his features. Maybe the May 27th appointment was his first office consult."

Sliding into the passenger seat, Dreidel glanced down at his watch. Outside, it was already starting to get dark. "We can swing by when they open tomorrow morning."

"You kidding?" Rogo said as he started the car. "We should go right now."

"He's probably closed."

"Still, if the building's open, I bet the directory in the lobby'll at least tell us what kind of practice he has."

"But to trek all the way to Fort Lauderdale . . ."

Halfway out of the parking spot, Rogo jammed the brakes and shifted the car back into *park.* Turning to his right, he glared at Dreidel, who was still staring out the front windshield.

"What?" Dreidel asked.

"Why don't you want me driving to this doctor right now?"

"What're you talking about? I'm just trying to save us time."

Rogo lowered his chin. "Good," he said, jerking the car back into gear. "Next stop, Dr. Brian Eng."

84

"Wait, you're telling me Boyle—"

"They invited him in," the First Lady explains, her voice shaking with each word. "Why be three horsemen when you can be more effective as four?"

"And Boyle said yes?"

"We didn't know . . ." She pauses, wondering whether to tell me the rest. But she knows I'll run out and ask the questions myself if she doesn't. "We didn't think so," she says.

"I don't understand," I say, my chest in knots.

"You think they gave Ron a choice? The Three had access to the same FBI files we did. They knew his weakness—the child he thought none of us knew about . . ."

"Child? He had a—?"

"I told Lee that would come back to rip us. I *told* him," she insists, more angry than ever. "I said it on the campaign—you could tell even back then. When you have a scab like that, someone's bound to come pick at it."

I nod, knowing better than to slow her down. "But for Boyle to actually join them—"

"That's not what I said. I said they *approached* him. But The Three didn't understand—with Ron . . . even with his child . . . with all the self-destructive messes he'd made . . . he'd never turn on us. Never. No matter the cost," she says, looking up. I get the point. She expects the same from me.

"Dr. Manning, I'm sorry—but the way you said it . . . You knew all this back then?"

"Wes, you were there with us. You know what was at stake. With someone like Ron . . . that kind of pressure point to exploit . . . you really think the FBI doesn't keep an extra eye on him?"

She stabs me with a look that almost knocks me to the ground. "Hold on . . . you're saying the FBI was watching Boyle? While we were in office?"

"They were trying to keep him safe, Wes. And even then, Lee fought them watching on every front—called Barry and Carl personally," she says, referring to our old FBI director and national security adviser. "Two days later, they found the deposit. Eleven thousand dollars in a bank account with Ron's daughter's name on it. Can you imagine? Using his *daughter's* name! They said that was probably The Three's opening offer. Take the money they slipped into his account, or they'd wreck his life and tell his wife about the child he was hiding on the side."

As she says the words, I'm the one who needs to lean on the dresser to stand. "But in . . . in the briefing book . . . I never saw anything about that."

"Every file wasn't for you, Wes."

"Still, if The Three were that close, couldn't you call—?"

"You think we weren't pulling up the floorboards? At

that point, we didn't even have a name for who we were chasing. We knew they had someone from FBI because they'd clearly accessed Ron's files. Then when they transferred the money into Ron's bank account—Secret Service does financial crime—they said the way the money was sent, they were using techniques from inside. And blackmail? That's CIA bread and butter. We alerted every agency with an acronym and started telling them to look within!"

"I know . . . I just—" I catch myself, always careful to know my place. "Maybe I'm missing something, ma'am, but if you knew Boyle was being pressured into joining The Three, why didn't you just warn *him*—or at least tell him that you knew he was being blackmailed?"

Looking down at the handwritten letter, Lenore Manning doesn't say a word.

"What?" I ask. "He *was* being blackmailed, right?"

She sits on the hand-painted chest, still silent.

"Is there something I'm not—?"

"We needed to see what he would do," she finally says, her voice softer than ever.

A sharp chill seizes my spine. "You were testing him."

"You have to understand, when The Roman got that close—to penetrate our circle like that—it wasn't about Boyle anymore—we were trying to catch The Three." Her voice trembles—she's been holding this in for so long—she's practically pleading for forgiveness. "It was the FBI's request. If the myth was real, if a group of dirty agents were truly in contact, this was their chance to catch them all."

I nod like it makes sense. Ron Boyle was their oldest and dearest friend, but when The Three forced his head toward the mousetrap, the Mannings—the President and

First Lady of the United States—still waited to see if he'd take the cheese.

"I know what you're thinking, Wes, but I swear to you, I was trying to protect Ron. I told them that: Give him time to resign. Make sure to look out for—" She swallows hard, shaking her head over and over and over. I've seen the First Lady angry, upset, sad, offended, enraged, distressed, anxious, worried, and even—when she came out of hip replacement surgery a few years back—in pain. But I've never seen her like this. Not even when we left the White House. Catching herself, she presses her chin against her chest to stop her head from shaking. The way she turns away from me, she hopes I don't notice. But as always, in this job, I see it all. "They were supposed to look out for him," she whispers, lost in her own broken promise. "They . . . they swore he'd be safe."

"And Boyle never told you The Three approached him?"

"I was waiting for it . . . praying for him to take us aside. Every day, we'd get a report on whether he'd accepted their offer. *No response*, they kept saying. I knew Ron was fighting it. I knew it," she insists as she hugs her own shoulder, curling even tighter. "But they told us to keep waiting . . . just to be sure. And then when he was shot . . ." She stares down at the floor as a surprise sob and a decade of guilt seize her throat. "I thought we'd buried him."

As I stare across at the handwritten letter in her lap, the mental puzzle pieces slide into place. "So all this time, the real reason Boyle was shot wasn't because he crossed The Three, it was because he refused to *join* them?"

She looks back, cocking her head. Her voice is still

barely a whisper. "You don't even know who you're fighting, do you?"

"What're you—?"

"Have you even read this?" she asks, slapping the letter against my chest. "On the day he was shot, Ron hadn't given The Three a decision yet!" There's a shift in her tone. Her eyes widen. Her mouth hangs open. At first, I think she's angry, but she's not. She's afraid.

"Dr. Manning, are you okay?"

"Wes, you should go. This isn't . . . I can't—"

"You can't what? I don't underst—"

"Please, Wes, just go!" she pleads, but I'm already staring back at the letter. My brain's racing so fast, I can't read it. But what she said—on the day of the shooting, if Boyle hadn't given The Three a decision yet . . . for all they knew, he still could've gone to join them.

My forehead crinkles, struggling to process. But if that was the case . . . "Then why kill him?" I ask.

"Wes, before you jump to conclusions—"

"Unless they knew Ron was having second thoughts . . ."

"Did you hear what I said? You can't—"

". . . or maybe they thought they'd revealed too much . . . or . . . or they realized he was under surveillance . . ."

"Wes, why aren't you listening to me!?" she shouts, trying to pull the letter from my hands.

"Or maybe they found someone better to fill the fourth spot," I blurt, tugging the letter back.

The First Lady lets go, and the page hits my chest with a thunderclap. My whole body feels a thousand pounds heavier, weighed down by the kind of numbing, all-consuming dread that comes with bad news at a doctor's office. "Is that what happened?" I demand.

Her answer comes far too slowly. "No."

My mouth goes dry. My tongue feels like a wad of damp newspaper.

"That's not . . . Ron didn't . . ." the First Lady says. "Maybe Ron's wrong . . ."

"Boyle was deputy chief of staff. There aren't that many people who're better at getting the—"

"You don't understand. He's a good man . . . he must've been tricked," she continues, practically rambling.

"Ma'am . . ."

"He never would've done it on purpose . . ."

"Ma'am, please—"

". . . even if they promised four more years—"

"Can you please calm down!" I insist. "Who could they possibly get that's bigger than Boyle?"

Still hunched forward on the trunk at the foot of her bed, the First Lady lifts her chin, staring straight at me. Like the President, like everyone in our office, she doesn't look at my scars. She hasn't for years. Until right now.

The question echoes over and over through my brain. They were looking for a fourth. Who would be the biggest fourth of all?

I glance down at the letter that's still in my hands. On the bottom of the page, the meticulous handwritten note reads:

But I never thought they'd be able to get him.

Blood drains from my face. That's what she realized. That's why she asked me to leave. She'd never turn on—

"*Him?*" I ask. "You can't mean—?"

"Wes, everything okay up there?" President Lee Manning shouts from the base of the stairs. "We're still waiting for that sport coat!"

I turn to the First Lady. The President's footsteps hammer up the stairway.

85

The First Lady starts to say something, but it's like she's talking underwater. Teetering backward, I crash into the desk with all the Manning photos, which wobble and shake. Like me. To do that to me— The room whirls, and my life swirls into the kaleidoscope. All these years . . . to lie to my— God, how could he—? There's no time for an answer. From the footsteps outside the bedroom, it's clear the President is almost at the top of the stairs. If he sees me with her—

"Wes?" he calls out.

"Coming, sir!" I yell as I rush to his closet, tug a navy sport coat off its hanger, and shoot one last look at the First Lady, who's still frozen on the hand-painted trunk. Her eyebrows lift, her cheeks seem almost hollow. She doesn't say a word, but the cry for help is deafening.

"He'd never—he wouldn't do that—not on purpose," she whispers as I drop Boyle's note back in her lap. Nodding repeatedly, she's already convincing herself. "In fact, maybe . . . maybe he was tricked. Maybe he got approached by The Roman and he didn't realize who he was talking to. He would look like a real agent, right? So—

so—so maybe they got worried that Ron was taking so long, and they tried a more manipulative route that went straight to the top branch of the tree. And then . . . he could've thought he was actually *helping* the Service. Maybe—maybe he didn't even realize what he'd done."

I nod. Maybe she's right. Maybe it wasn't intentional. Maybe it was Manning's greatest, most horrible mistake that he prayed would somehow go away. The problem is, I can still picture the President on his last walk across the South Lawn, clutching the First Lady's hand and refusing to look back as they headed for Marine One. Back then, the leaks from our own staff said she was more devastated than he was. But I was there. I saw how tightly he was squeezing her fingers.

The President's footsteps are nearly at the top of the stairs.

I wobble toward the door, burst into the hallway, and make a sharp right, almost ramming into the President's chest.

"H-Here you go, sir," I say as I skid to a halt, my arm outstretched with his navy blazer.

He takes another step toward me. I stand my ground, making sure he doesn't go any farther.

For a moment, Manning's eyes narrow, his famous grays flattening into matching icy slivers. But just as quickly, a broad, warm smile lifts his cheeks and reveals a hint of yellow on his teeth. "By the way, have you seen the wigs yet?" he asks, referring to the Madame Tussauds folks downstairs. "They brought the one from when we left office. I'm telling you, Wes, it's grayer than I am now. I think I'm getting younger."

I force a laugh and head for the stairs before he gets a good look at me.

"What's wrong?" he asks, barely a step behind.

"No . . . nothing," I say, motioning with the navy sport coat and feeling a flush of hot blood rushing through my neck. "I just wanted to be sure I didn't give away one of your good jackets."

"I appreciate your looking out for the wax me," he teases, putting a hand on my shoulder. That's the move. Hand on shoulder for instant intimacy and guaranteed trust. I've seen him use it on prime ministers, senators, congressmen, even on his own son. Now he's using it on me.

Halfway down the stairs, I pick up my pace. He stays right with me. Even if working with The Roman was his mistake, to lie to my face every single— Is that why he kept me here? Penance for his own guilt?

In my pocket, my phone starts vibrating. I pull it out and check the phone's tiny screen. Text message:

wes, it's lisbeth. pick up.
i solved puzzle.

A second later, the phone vibrates in my hand. "Excuse me one second, sir," I say to the President. "It's Claudia, who— Hello?" I say, answering the phone.

"You need to get out of there," Lisbeth says.

"Hey, Claudia. I did? Okay, hold on one sec." Nearing the bottom step, I keep Lisbeth on hold and turn back to Manning, feeling like my body's on fire. "She says I left my house keys in her office. I'm sorry, sir, but if it's okay, I may just run back there and—"

"Relax, Wes, I'm a big boy," he says with a laugh, his shoulder grasp turning into a quick, forceful back pat that almost knocks me off the bottom step. "Go do what you have to. I've handled one or two problems bigger than this."

Handing him his sport coat, I laugh right back and head for the front door. I can feel the President's eyes burning into the back of my head.

"By the way, Wes, do me a favor and let the Service know where you're going too," he says loud enough so the agents outside can hear. "Just in case they need to get in touch."

"Of course, sir," I say as I jog down the front steps.

"You alone yet?" Lisbeth asks through the phone.

The moment the door slams behind me, the two suit-and-tie agents who're standing outside the garage look up.

"Everything okay?" the shorter agent, Stevie, asks.

"Don't look suspicious," Lisbeth says through the phone. "Tell him you forgot your keys."

"Yeah, no . . . I forgot my keys," I say, speed-walking to the tall wooden privacy gate at the end of the driveway and pretending that everything I've built my life on isn't now coming apart. My breathing starts to gallop. I've known Stevie for almost three years. He doesn't care whether I check in or not. But as I reach the gate and wait for it to slide open, to my surprise, it doesn't move.

"So where you headed to, Wes?" Stevie calls out.

"Wes, listen to me," Lisbeth pleads. "Thanks to your low-life friend Dreidel, I found another puzzle. Are you listening?"

I turn back to the two men, who're still standing in front of the closed garage and the matching Chevy Suburbans parked a few feet away. Stevie's hand disappears into his pants pocket. It's not until that moment that I realize that on the night I first saw Boyle, Stevie was driving the lead car in Malaysia. "Wes," he says coldly. "I asked you a—"

"Just back to the office," I blurt. Spinning clumsily to the gate, I stare at the double-plank wooden slats that keep people from looking in. I grip the phone to stop my hand from shaking. The sun's about to set in the purple-orange sky. Behind me, there's a metallic click. My heart leaps.

"See you soon," Stevie calls out. There's a loud *rrrrrr* as the wooden gate rolls to the right, sliding open just enough for me to squeeze through.

"I'm out," I whisper to Lisbeth.

"Fine—then pay attention. Do you have the old puzzle on you?"

Staggering across the street to the car, I don't answer. All I see is Manning's grin and his yellow Chiclet teeth—

"Wes! Did you hear what I said!?" she shouts. "Take out the original one!"

Nodding even though she can't see me, I reach into my pocket and hastily unfold the original crossword.

"See the handwritten initials down the center?" she asks. "M, A, R, J . . ."

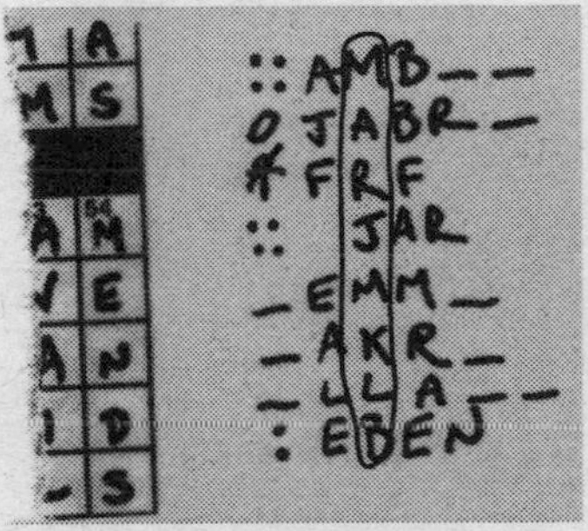

"Manning, Albright, Rosenman, Jeffer . . . what about them?"

"He's got the same list on the new puzzle. Same initials down the middle. Same order. Same everything."

"Okay, so? Now there're two lists of top senior staff," I say, stopping just outside the car. I have to lean against the door to keep standing.

"No. Pay attention, Wes. Same *everything*. Including those scribbles down the side."

"What're you talking about?"

"On the left—before each set of initials: the four dots in a square, the little oval, the cross with a slash through it . . ."

I look at each one: , , . "The chicken scratch?"

"That's the thing, Wes," she says, deadly serious. "I don't think it's chicken scratch. Unless he's got some majorly smart chickens."

86

But those doodles," I say as I study Manning's scribbles on the side of the crossword.

"Are you listening?" Lisbeth shouts through the phone. "That's what they wanted it to look like—random doodles and extra letters that make the hidden initials disappear. But if you look at this new crossword, the exact same scribbled images are in the *exact same order.* There's nothing random about it, Wes! The four dots . . . the small oval—Manning was using them as some sort of message."

"Why would—?"

"You said it yourself: Every politician needs allies—and every President needs to figure out who he can trust. Maybe this is how Manning ranked those closest to him. Y'know, like a report card."

Nodding at the logic, I glance again at the list, mentally adding the real names.

 Manning

 Albright

 Rosenman

∷ Dreidel
—— Moss
—— Kutz
—— Lemonick
: Boyle

"And no offense," Lisbeth adds, "but your boy Dreidel? He's a piece of shit. Real shit, Wes—as in beating-up-prostitutes-and-ramming-their-faces-into-mirrors kind of shit."

As she relays Violet's story, I can still picture the woman in the bathrobe peeking out from Dreidel's hotel room. Still, to go from that to smashing faces . . . "You sure you can trust this Violet woman?" I ask.

"Look at the list," Lisbeth says. "That *is* Manning's handwriting, right?" When I don't answer, she adds, "Wes, c'mon! Is that Manning's handwriting or not?"

"It's his," I say as my breathing again quickens.

"Exactly. So if he's the one filling in this report card, then the grade he gives himself—those four dots—you think in his own personal ranking, he's giving himself an A or a big, steaming F?"

"An A?" I say tentatively, staring at the ∷.

"Absolutely an A. He's the cipher. In fact, I'll wager those four dots are a sparkling A+. Now look who else was lucky enough to get the exact same ranking."

I look down at the list. It's the first time I realize Manning and Dreidel are both ranked with four dots.

"Red rover, red rover, we call Dreidel right over," Lisbeth says through the phone.

"Lisbeth, that doesn't prove anything. So what if he trusted Dreidel more than any of the others?"

"Unless he trusted Dreidel to do what none of the others would."

"Wait, so now Dreidel's a legbreaker?"

"You were there, Wes. You're telling me the President never had any personal issues that needed dealing with?"

"Of course, but those usually went to—" I cut myself off.

"What? Those were the problems that went to Boyle?"

"Yeah, they . . . they were supposed to. But what if that's the point? What if they *used* to go to Boyle . . ."

". . . and suddenly they stopped?"

"And suddenly they started going to Dreidel," I say with a nod. "No one would even know the President made the switch unless . . ."

". . . unless they happened to find their ranking on the list," Lisbeth agrees, her voice now racing. "So when Boyle found this, when he saw that Dreidel and Manning were ranked together . . ."

". . . he could see the real ranking of the totem pole."

An hour ago, I would've told Lisbeth she's crazy—that there's no way the President and Dreidel were scheming together. But now . . . I replay the last ten minutes in my head. What the First Lady said . . . what Boyle accused the President of . . . and what Lisbeth's already confirming . . . if even half of it's true . . . I inhale a warm burst of muggy air, then grit my teeth to slow my breathing. But it won't slow down. My chest rises and falls. My neck, my face—I'm soaked.

Up the block, on the corner of County Road, there's a white car with its blinker on, waiting to turn toward me.

"Get the hell out of there," Lisbeth says.

"I'm leaving right now."

Ripping the door open, I hop into the car and frantically claw through my pocket for my keys. I came here to confess . . . to get help from the biggest and the best. But now—with the President as The Fourth, and Dreidel feeding us directly to the Lion . . . I ram the key at the ignition, but the way my hand's shaking, the key bounces off the steering column. I try again. *Dammit, why won't it—?* I take another stab, and the tip of the key scratches across the metal column, pinching my fingertip. The pain's sharp, like being jabbed with a needle. But as my eyes swell with tears, I know it's not from the pain. Or at least not this pain.

A sob rises like a bubble in my throat. I again clench my teeth, but it won't go down. *No, don't do this . . . not now,* I beg as I press my forehead as hard as I can against the steering wheel. But as I picture the President—all these years—I didn't just learn his shoe size and pillow preference. I know what he thinks: who annoys him, who he trusts, who he hates, even who he thinks is still using him. I know his goals, and what he's afraid of, and what he dreams about, and what he hopes . . . what I hoped . . . The bubble in my throat bursts and my body begins to shake with silent, heaving sobs. After eight years . . . every single day . . . *Oh, God—how could I not know this man?*

"Wes, you there?" Lisbeth asks through the phone.

Still breathing heavily and fighting for calm, I swallow hard, sit up straight, and finally shove the key into the ignition. "One sec," I whisper into the phone. Punching the gas, I feel the wheels gnaw through the grassy divider, eventually catching and whipping me forward. As I wipe the last tears from my eyes, I notice a Chinese restaurant menu tucked underneath my windshield wiper. Steering with one hand and lowering the window with the other, I flick on the wipers, reach outside, and nab the menu just as the wiper blade slings it across the glass. But as I toss the menu into the passenger seat, I spot familiar handwriting running across the back page of the menu, just below the coupons. I jam my foot against the brake, and the car skids to a halt a full twenty feet shy of the stop sign at the end of the block.

"You okay?" Lisbeth asks.

"Hold on . . ."

I dive for the menu. The handwriting's unmistakable. Perfect tiny block letters.

Wes, turn around. Make sure you're alone.
(Sorry for the melodrama)

Whipping around in my seat, I check through the back window and sniff away the rest of the tears. The gate to the Mannings' house is shut. The sidewalks are empty. And the grassy divider that splits the narrow street holds only the quiet navy-blue rental car of the Madame Tussauds folks.

"Did you find something?" Lisbeth asks.

Struggling to read the rest of the note, I can barely keep my hands from shaking.

You need to know what else he did. 7 p.m. at—

My eyes go wide when I see the location. Like before, it's signed with a simple flourish. The tip of the *R* drags longer than the rest. *Ron.*

There's a flush of sweet-sour wetness across the left half of my tongue. I touch my lip and spot the bright red liquid on my fingertips. Blood. I was biting my lip so hard, I didn't even feel myself break the skin.

"What is it, Wes? What's there?" Lisbeth asks, now frantic.

I'm about to tell her, but I catch myself, remembering what she's done.

"Wes, what's wrong?"

"I'm fine," I say as I reread the note. "Just nervous."

There's a pause on the line. She's been lied to by the best. I'm not even in the top ten. "Okay, what're you not saying?" she asks.

"Nothing, I just—"

"Wes, if this is about the tape, I'm sorry. And if I could take it back—"

"Can we not talk about this?"

"I'm just trying to apologize. The last thing I wanted was to hurt you."

"You didn't hurt me, Lisbeth. You just treated me like a story."

For the second time, she's silent. It's cutting her deeper than I thought. "Wes, you're right: This *is* a story. It's a big story. But there's one thing I need you to understand: That doesn't mean it's *only* a story to me."

"And that's it?" I ask. "You make the pretty speech, the musical score swells, and now I'm supposed to trust you again?"

"Of course not—if I were you, I wouldn't trust *anyone.* But that doesn't mean you don't need help. Or friends. And just FYI, if I were trying to burn you, when I got the new crossword . . . when I got the Violet and Dreidel story . . . I would've called my editor instead of you."

I think on that for a moment. Just like I think about our first ride in the helicopter.

"And remember that trade where you promised that you'd give me the story?" she asks. "Forget it. I'm off. I don't even want it anymore."

"You're serious about that?"

"Wes, for the past ten minutes, my notepad has been in my purse."

I believe Lisbeth. I think she's telling the truth. And I'm convinced she's trying to do the right thing. But after today . . . after Manning . . . after Dreidel . . . after damn near everyone . . . the only person I can really put my faith in is myself.

"What about your visit to the Mannings?" she adds. "They say anything I can help you with?"

I stare down at Boyle's handwritten note and the signature with his long-tipped *R.*

"No—just the usual," I reply, rereading the message for myself.

You need to know what else he did. 7 p.m.

87

What about your visit to the Mannings?" Lisbeth said into her phone as she walked briskly through the rain just outside the townhouse where she met Violet. "They say anything I can help you with?"

Wes paused barely half a second. For Lisbeth, it was more than enough. If he wanted to lie, he would've already made up some story. A pause like this . . . whatever he's debating, it's tearing at him. And to her own surprise, the more she saw what he'd been through—and was still going through—the more it tore at her as well. Sacred Rule #10, she told herself: Get attached to the story, not the people in it.

"No—just the usual," Wes finally offered. He added a quick good-bye to sidestep the awkwardness. It didn't.

Lisbeth couldn't blame him. By bringing that tape recorder, she'd shaken his trust. Yet as she slid behind the steering wheel of her car and started dialing a new number, it was clear she wasn't going to just sit still and let him hold her at a distance.

"*Palm Beach Post*," a female voice answered on the other line. "This is Eve."

"Eve, it's Lisbeth. Are you—?"

"Don't worry, the column's all done."

"Forget the column."

"Even got the dumb art award in."

"*Eve!*"

There was a pause on the other line. "Please tell me you didn't wreck my car."

"Can you please listen?" Lisbeth pleaded as she stared down at the crossword puzzle Violet had given her and spread it across the steering wheel. "Remember that old guy from comics—y'know, with the creepy glasses and the moon-chin—"

"Kassal? The guy who designed our crossword puzzles?"

"Yeah, that's the—wait, whattya mean *designed*? Don't tell me he's dead."

"Lisbeth, this newspaper's so cheap, they shrunk the font size on our headlines to save money on ink. You really think they'd pay an extra employee, extra benefits, extra health insurance, when they can get a syndicated daily crossword for thirty bucks?" Eve pointed out. "They fired him two years ago. But lucky you, I happen to be staring at an employee directory from *three* years ago."

"You really haven't cleaned your desk in that long?"

"You want the number or not?"

Ten digits later, Lisbeth watched a light rain skate down her windshield. Her foot anxiously tapped the floor mat as she waited for someone to pick up. "Be home, be home, be home . . ."

"Hiya," an older man with a horse voice and a creaky Midwest accent answered.

"Hi, I'm looking for Mr. Kassal," Lisbeth explained.

"Martin to you. And you are . . ."

"Lisbeth Dodson—we used to work together at the *Palm Beach Post*—and I promise you, sir, this'll be the strangest question you get all d—"

"Up the pace, sweetie. I got pancakes cooking for dinner, and it'll kill me to see 'em burn."

"Yeah, well, a good friend of mine has a problem . . ." Lisbeth took a full breath, reaching for her pen, then stopping herself. "How good are you at solving puzzles?"

88

With the sunroof open and the light rain still drizzling inside, Nico veered off the highway, cutting in front of a white Lexus and following the exit ramp to Okeechobee Boulevard.

"Edmund, what's the address again?" Nico asked, readjusting the blanket on Edmund's chest as they approached the red light at the end of the ramp.

8385 Okeechobee Boulevard.

Nodding to himself, Nico leaned forward in his seat, craning his neck past the steering wheel to get a better look at the street that ran perpendicular in front of them. On his right, the light traffic coasted past gas stations and a lawn-mower repair shop. On his left, the open blue water of Clear Lake ran in front of the Performing Arts Center, while a green highway sign pointed toward the beautiful high-rises in the distance. In the photo Nico stole, Wes was broken, shattered, corrupted by Boyle's touch. Nothing beautiful about him.

Tugging the wheel to the right, Nico cut off the same white Lexus, who bitched with his horn for a good five seconds. Not hearing it, Nico pumped the gas and dove into traffic.

"Can you read that one?" Nico asked as he pointed to the address on a nearby car dealership. A droplet of rain whizzed through the sunroof and flicked Edmund on the cheek.

2701.

"What about *that* one?" Nico asked, pointing to a cash-advance store half a block ahead.

That one's, lemme see . . . 2727.

Nico beamed with a beady twinkle in his eyes and hit the gas even harder.

Breathtaking work, Nico. Lord's definitely on your side with this one.

Thinking the exact same thing, Nico reached for the wooden rosary beads that swayed from the Pontiac's rearview. "Do you mind, Edmund?"

I'd be honored. You've earned them, my son.

My son. Nico sat bolt upright at the words. Surely, Edmund knew what they meant . . . and once Nico heard them, he could smell the black licorice and hickory whiff of his dad's old hand-rolled cigars. Back when . . . back before Mom got sick. When they'd go to church. When things were good. Barely able to hide his grin, Nico nodded over and over as he slipped the rosary beads around his neck and glanced back at the passenger seat.

What? What's wrong, Nico?

"Nothing . . . I just . . ." He nodded again and took another deep breath of black licorice. "I'm happy," he said. "And in a few more minutes, Mom—like Dad—is finally gonna get her justice."

89

Five minutes ago, I started telling Rogo the story about The Four, and the note from Boyle, and what Lisbeth said about Dreidel. Under normal circumstances, Rogo would've been screaming for a fistfight and stacking up the I-told-you-sos. But like any good actor, he's well aware of his audience.

"What's he saying?" Dreidel asks in the background.

"Tell him the Mannings gave me tomorrow off," I shoot back through the phone, my newfound anger barely covering my still-smoldering anxieties.

"The Mannings gave him tomorrow off—just to calm down from all the Nico mess," Rogo says like an old pro. Back to me, he adds, "You have any idea why he did it?"

"Who? Manning? I have no idea—the First Lady said maybe they suckered him. All I know is when The Three recruited Boyle, they were blackmailing him with this supposed kid. But to get something on a sitting President of the United States . . ."

". . . we're talking one hell of a secret," he agrees. "Wes, you're gonna need to be careful."

"Careful of what?" Dreidel interrupts, clearly frustrated. "What's he saying?"

"Rogo," I warn, "don't give him—"

"Just relax, okay? We're talking about O'Shea and Micah," Rogo says, clearly in control. When Dreidel doesn't respond, I wonder if I'm being too harsh. Even if what Lisbeth said is true—about Manning and Dreidel being ranked the same . . .

"Ask Wes if he wants to meet up," Dreidel calls out in the background. "Just so we can compare our notes in one place."

"Actually, that's a great idea," Rogo says. For Dreidel, Rogo's tone is completely enthusiastic. For me, his undertone is just as clear: He'd gnaw his own thumbs off before letting that meeting ever happen.

As Rogo continues to hold him at bay, I make a sharp right out of the rush-hour traffic on Okeechobee Boulevard and cut through the wide-open space of the Publix supermarket parking lot. It's not my usual path, but as I check the rearview, the vast emptiness of the lot is the best way to see I'm still alone.

"So when should we meet?" Rogo asks, still trying to keep Dreidel happy.

"I assume you're joking, right?" I ask, looping back through the parking lot and following the narrow two-lane street to the familiar building at the end of the block.

"Ya-huh . . . of course."

"Fine, then just keep him away," I say. "Away from me and away from Boyle."

"Dammit, Rogo, you missed the turn!" Dreidel shouts in the background. "The on-ramp's back that way!"

Without a word, I know Rogo understands. By the time

they get to Dr. Eng's office, then back to Palm Beach, Dreidel's officially one less crisis I have to deal with.

"Okay, eight o'clock tonight at Dreidel's hotel—you got it, Wes," Rogo says. "Ya-huh, yeah . . . of course," he adds, even though I'm silent. Through the phone, he takes a deep breath. His voice slows down. "Just make sure you're safe, okay?" I know that tone. The last time I heard it, he was standing by my hospital bed. "I'm serious, Wes. Be safe."

"I will," I tell him as a sharp right takes me up the paved brick driveway that's shaped like a horseshoe in front of my apartment building. Driving past the main entrance, I pull around to the open-air parking lot in back. "Though I gotta be honest, Rogo—I figured you'd be happy I was finally fighting back."

"Yeah, well . . . next time try swimming a few laps before you decide to cross the English Channel."

"I gave my life to him, Rogo. I need to get it back."

"You're telling *me*? Wes, I fight with everyone. I *love* fighting with everyone—I fight with the snot bagboy who tries to cheap me out by giving me plastic instead of paper. But let me tell you something: You don't fight with people like this. You get your proof, you lock it up somewhere safe, and then you run to the press . . . to the authorities . . . to whoever's in the best position to keep them from knocking your teeth out through your colon. And believe me, when they find you, they're gonna hit back."

"You still talking about Micah and O'Shea?" Dreidel interrupts in the background.

"Who else would we talk about?" Rogo shoots back.

"Rogo," I interrupt, "I *know* how they hit. They're not getting another crack."

"Good—that's what I wanna hear. Okay, so if you can't go home, where you gonna hide out for the next few hours: that crappy hotel my mom stayed at, or maybe somewhere more out in the open, y'know, like the lobby of the Breakers or something?"

I'm silent for a moment, coasting toward my parking spot in back. "Whattya mean?"

"Look at the time, Wes—you've still got two hours to kill—so assuming you don't wanna be at home . . ."

I'm silent again.

I swear I can hear Rogo shaking his head. "You're home right now, aren't you?"

"Not exactly," I say as the car bounces over a speed bump.

"*Not exactly?* What's *not exactly*?"

"It's . . . it means I'm . . . it means I'm kinda in the parking lot."

"Aw, jeez! Wes, why would you—? Get out of there!"

"You don't think our security in front can—?"

"That's not security. It's a doorman with a sewn-on badge!"

"I'm talking about the cameras, Rogo. That's what they're afraid of—being seen! And no offense, but until you just blurted it to Dreidel, I probably would've been fine."

"Just go. Now!"

"Y'think?" I ask, pulling into an open spot for a quick three-point turn.

"Just turn the car around and get your ass outta there before—!"

As I throw the car into reverse, there's a knock against the driver's-side window. Turning to my left, I spot the tip of a gun tapping against the glass.

O'Shea points his pistol right at me and raises his pointer finger to his lips.

"Tell them you're fine," O'Shea says, his voice muffled through the window.

I stare at the gun. "L-Listen, Rogo—I'm fine," I say into the phone.

Rogo says something, but I can't hear him.

"Tell them you'll call back when you find someplace safe," O'Shea adds.

For a moment, I hesitate. O'Shea tightens his finger against the trigger.

"Rogo, I'll call you back when I find someplace safe."

I shut the phone. O'Shea rips open my car door.

"Nice to see you again," he says. "How was Key West?"

90

"Let's go, Wes. *Out,*" O'Shea says, gripping the shoulder of my shirt and dragging me from the Subaru. As I stumble across the asphalt of the parking lot, I realize the car's still running. He doesn't care. He doesn't think this'll take long.

"Keep going . . . toward the fence," he adds, barely a step behind. His gun is no longer out in the open. But through the outline in his jacket pocket, it's still clearly pointed at me.

We head toward the back corner of the parking lot, where there's an opening in the tall shrubs that leads to a shaded dog run that runs parallel to the lot. The dog run is narrow and not too long. But tucked behind the shrubs, it'll keep us out of sight.

"So Key West," O'Shea says, still right behind me. "Your buddy Kenny says hi."

I glance over my shoulder just as we reach the two lampposts that flank the entrance to the dog run. O'Shea offers a smug grin, but the way his sandy-blond hair is matted to his head, he's had a tougher day than he's saying. The drizzle of rain looks like beads of sweat across his pug nose.

"I don't know what you're talking about," I say, turning back to face him.

He doesn't even bother calling me on it. "Where's the photo you took, Wes?"

"I told you, I don't—"

In a blur, his fist cocks me in the face, jamming into my left eye and sending me crashing to the muddy path. As I skid backward on my butt through the damp grass, my whole eye socket's throbbing, like a just-rung bell.

"I know you have the photo. Hand it over, and you're free to go."

"It-it's in the glove compartment," I say, pointing to the car with one hand and holding my eye with the other.

He glances back at the Subaru just as two more cars glide into the parking lot. Their headlights are on, slicing through the early darkness and turning the light drizzle into tiny fireworks that flicker in the distance. Fellow tenants coming home from their day's work. Planting his foot on my shoulder, O'Shea studies the entire scene like he's reading someone's palm.

Without a word, he reaches down, grips the front of my shirt, and pulls me to my feet. Even before I get my balance, he whips me around, and I crash chest-first into the nearest tree. My cheek scrapes against the bark, momentarily forcing me to forget the pain in my eye.

Behind me, O'Shea kicks my legs apart and starts frisking through my pockets, tossing the contents to the ground: wallet, house keys, the folded-up sheet of paper with Manning's daily schedule on it.

"What're you doing?" I ask as he pats my chest and works his way down my legs. "I told you it's in the glove compar—"

There's a soft crackle as his fingers pat my ankle.

I look down at him. He looks up at me.

I try to fight free of his grip, but he's too strong. Choking my ankle, he hikes up my pant leg, revealing the glossy black-and-white photo that's curled around my shin, the top half of it sticking out of my sock.

Enraged, O'Shea rips it free and shoves me aside. His anger swells as he stares down at the speedway photo of Micah, crumpling the corner of it in his hand—but just as quickly, he finds his calm and catches his breath. Relieved that he's not in it, he locks back on me. The fact I'm still alive means the photo isn't the only thing he's here for.

"Where's Lisbeth?" he asks.

"We had a disagreement."

"But she still let you use her car? Sounds like she's being plenty helpful."

"If you want to know if she's writing a story—"

"I want to know where she is, Wes. Now. And don't say *I don't know.*"

"But I don—"

"*Don't say I don't know!*" he shouts, pulling his gun and pointing it directly at my face. Lowering his voice, he adds, "I know you were speaking to her about the crossword. Now—"

There's a crack of broken sticks and a jingle that sounds like Christmas bells. Behind O'Shea, through the opening that leads to the parking lot, a short woman in a pin-striped business suit shakes a metal dog leash as she leads her fluffy beach-colored cocker spaniel through the entrance of the dog run.

Before the woman even realizes what's happening, O'Shea crosses his arms, hiding his gun under his armpit.

"Sorry," the woman says, laughing nervously as she ducks down and cuts between us. "Didn't mean to interrupt."

"No problem at all," O'Shea replies, turning just enough that she never gets a clear look at his face. "We're just waiting for our dogs to come back—they love running down to the end."

The woman nods, glancing back just long enough to see that neither of us is carrying a leash. Quickly turning away and pretending not to notice, she follows her dog's lead as she's tugged to a small patch of grass about ten feet away.

I'm tempted to run. She's a perfect distraction—and a witness. But as O'Shea lowers his chin and his hazel eyes disappear in the darkness of his brow, I hear the message loud and clear. If I make a move, he'll kill her too.

"Good girl, Murphy—there you go," the woman says, tugging the dog back between us and reentering the parking lot. For a full minute, we watch her from behind as she crosses the lot and heads for the back door of the building. The woman looks at her dog, at her watch, for her keys—but to her credit, she never looks back. With a faint crack, the metal door to the building slams, and the woman disappears. O'Shea's arms unfold, and his gun goes right back to my face.

"Sorry, Wes," O'Shea says as he pulls back the hammer of his gun. "This is gonna sting."

"Wait . . . what're you doing?" I ask, stumbling backward into a nearby tree.

The light rain taps against his face, but he barely notices. His fair skin shines with a yellow glow in the darkness.

"O'Shea, if you do this . . . the investigation they'll open: You'll never be able to cover it up."

O'Shea grins as his finger tightens on the trigger. "Funny. That's what they said to us last ti—"

Pop, pop, pop.

The sound hiccups through the air. My body goes cold. Not from pain. From the sound. *Pop, pop, pop*—an echo from the past—firing now.

Across from me, O'Shea, a look of angry surprise frozen on his face, shudders and shifts, crashing backward into the lamppost. He slaps his shoulder like he's slapping a bug bite. His knees start to buckle. His head dips slightly to the side. Still, it's not until I spot the blood coming from his shoulder that I even realize he's been shot. His blood looks black in the dim light as it runs down his suit.

"Nuuh!" O'Shea grunts as his head slams back into the lamppost. His gun drops to the muddy ground. The way he's teetering and leaning on the lightpost, he's about to follow. Behind me, there's another crunch of broken sticks. Before I even register the sound, a tall blurred shadow in a black windbreaker races past me, right for O'Shea.

"Move, Wes! *Move!*" the shadow shouts, ramming his forearm into my back and shoving me out of the way. But as I slip on the grass and fight for my own balance, there's no mistaking that voice. The voice from Malaysia . . . from the warning on my phone . . .

Boyle.

91

"Wes, get the hell out of here! Now!" Boyle hisses, his gun pointed at O'Shea. A wisp of smoke twirls from the barrel.

Sliding to the ground with his back against the lamppost, O'Shea crumples to his knees. Fighting to stand up, he doesn't get anywhere. He's already in shock. Taking no chances, Boyle rushes in and jams the barrel of his gun against O'Shea's head. "Where's Micah?" he demands.

Down on his knees, O'Shea grits his teeth in obvious pain. "You finally found his name, huh? I told him this wou—"

"I'm asking you one more time," Boyle threatens. Moving the gun from O'Shea's head, he jabs the barrel into the wound in O'Shea's shoulder. O'Shea tries to scream, but Boyle puts his hand over O'Shea's mouth. "*Last time, O'Shea! Where's he hiding?*" Pulling back the hammer, he digs his gun into O'Shea's wound.

O'Shea's body shakes as he tries to speak. Boyle lets go of his mouth. "H-He's dead," O'Shea growls, more pissed than ever.

"Who did it? You or The Roman?"

When O'Shea hesitates, Boyle twists the gun even deeper. "M-M-Me . . ." O'Shea grunts, his eyes wild like an animal's. "Just like I'll do with y—"

Boyle doesn't give him the chance, pulling the trigger and shooting him through the same wound. There's a muffled pop and a splat as a hunk of flesh explodes out the back of his shoulder. The pain's so intense, O'Shea doesn't even have time to scream. His eyes roll back. His arms go slack.

Crumpling like a sack of pennies, O'Shea rag-dolls forward. The instant he hits the dirt, Boyle's all over him, pulling O'Shea's hands behind his back and snapping his wrists into plastic flex cuffs that Boyle's pulled from his pocket.

"Wh-What're you doing here?" I ask, barely catching my breath.

With a loud *zzzip*, the cuffs clench, locking O'Shea's wrists behind his back. If Boyle wanted him dead, he'd fire another shot. But the way he's wrapping him up, he clearly wants something else. What's more amazing is the way Boyle moves—patting down O'Shea's body, working so fast . . . the way his triceps tense underneath his windbreaker . . . he's been training for this.

"Wes, I told you to leave!" Boyle shouts, finally turning my way.

It's the first time I get a good look at his eyes. Even in the dim light, they glow like a cat's. Brown with a splash of blue.

In the distance, a car door slams with a metal *chunk*. Boyle jerks to the left, following the sound. The tall shrubs block his view, but the way he freezes, leaning in to listen . . . like he knows someone's coming.

"We gotta go!" he insists, suddenly frantic as he pulls O'Shea's gun from the mud and pockets it.

"How'd you know I'd be here?"

Refusing to answer, he furiously rolls the unconscious O'Shea like a log, flipping him on his back. "Help me get him up!" Boyle demands.

Without even thinking, I move in, grabbing O'Shea under his left armpit. Boyle grabs the right.

"Were you following me?" I add as we lug O'Shea to his feet.

Boyle ignores the question, cutting in front of O'Shea and dropping to one knee. As O'Shea topples forward, Boyle hoists his shoulder under O'Shea's midsection, boosting him up like he's lugging an old rolled-up carpet.

"I asked you a—"

"I heard you, Wes. Get out of my way." He tries to step around me. I sidestep, staying in front of him.

"You *were* following me? Is that to track them down or—?"

"Are you paying attention, Wes? Nico can be here any minute!"

I stumble at the words. My mouth goes dry, and I swear, every sweat gland in my body opens.

"Now get the hell out of here before you get both of us killed!" Shaking his head, Boyle rushes around me with O'Shea on his shoulder. I spin back and watch as he plows down to the end of the dog run.

"Where're you taking him?"

"Don't be stupid!" he calls out, shooting me one last look and making sure I get the point. "There'll be time for chatting later."

In the distance, as he turns away from me, Boyle's black windbreaker camouflages everything but his bald head. Draped over his shoulder, it's the same for O'Shea, whose pale neck shines as his head dangles toward the ground. Boyle yells something else, but I can't hear it. At the clip they're going down the tree-lined path, they quickly fade in the darkness. The sun's already set. And I'm once again standing in silence. In shock. All alone.

Behind me, a car door slams in the parking lot. On my left, a cricket's chirp scratches the night air. The drizzle continues and another twig cracks. Then another. It's more than enough.

Spinning back toward the parking lot, I run as fast as I can. Another car door slams. This one's quiet—like it's on the very far end of the lot. No time to take chances. Scooping up my wallet, house keys, and the photo, I dart between the lampposts, back to the parking lot. As I cut between two cars, no one's there.

After stuffing my wallet back into my pocket—and the photo back inside the ankle of my sock—I run through the lot, searching row by row and scanning the hood of each car. Along every metal roof, the overhead lamps cast a circular reflection that ripples with each raindrop. Still no one in sight. It doesn't make me feel any safer. If Boyle's been following me the whole time, then anyone cou— No, don't even think about it.

Shifting into a full sprint, I plow toward Lisbeth's car, rip open the door, and practically dive into the driver's seat. The car's still running. My phone's still sitting on the armrest.

Flipping open my cell, I frantically punch in Rogo's number and throw the car in reverse. But as I listen to it ring, all I can think about is who Rogo's traveling with . . . and how many questions Dreidel was asking . . . and how—somehow—O'Shea knew I was talking to Lisbeth. Rogo and I were convinced that Dreidel couldn't hear anything from our last conversation, but if we were wrong . . .

Jamming my thumb against the *End* button, I hang up, replaying Boyle's words in my head. *There'll be time for chatting later.* I look down at the digital clock on the dash. An hour and forty-five minutes, to be precise.

As my thumb pounds out a brand-new number and my foot pounds the gas, I tell myself it's the only way. And it is. However Boyle pulled it off, even if he was using me as bait for The Three, by nabbing O'Shea and finding out Micah's dead, he finally gave us a chance. So instead of just showing up at seven tonight—instead of just rushing in blind—I need to make the most of it. Even if it means taking some risks.

As I finish dialing the last digit, all I have to do is hit *Send.* Still, I stop myself. Not because I don't trust her. But because I *do.* Rogo would tell me I shouldn't. But he didn't hear her apology. He didn't hear the pain in her voice. She knew she'd hurt me. And that hurt her.

I hit *Send*, praying I won't regret it. I listen as the phone rings. And rings again. She's got caller ID. She knows who it is.

The phone rings for a third time as I zip through the parking lot toward the front of the building. I don't blame her for not picking up. If I'm calling, it only means trou—

"Wes?" Lisbeth finally answers, her voice softer than I expected. "That you?"

"Yeah."

It's not tough to read my tone. "Everything okay?" she asks.

"I-I don't think so," I say, gripping the steering wheel. She doesn't even hesitate.

"How can I help?" she asks.

92

Driving up the curving brick driveway in front of Wes's building, Nico rechecked Edmund's wool blanket and nudged the brakes, reminding himself to take it slow. From the army to the speedway to this, his first goal was never to get noticed. Still, just being this close . . . Nico took his foot off the brake and gave a tap to the gas. The wooden rosary beads seemed to burn against his chest.

Almost there, son. Don't get riled.

Nico nodded, throwing a wave to one of the tenants running out the front door for a jog. As the Pontiac followed the road to the parking lot in back, its headlights stabbed through the dusk like twin glowing lances.

Know where you're going?

"Five twenty-seven," Nico replied, pointing with his chin at the black apartment numbers painted on the concrete stops at the front of each parking spot.

Within a minute, he'd weaved up and down the first two aisles.

525 . . . 526 . . . and . . .

Nico hit the brakes, bucking the car to a halt. 527. Wes's apartment number. But the parking spot was empty.

He could still be upstairs.

Nico shook his head. "He's not upstairs."

Then we should go up there and wait for him.

"I don't think that's a good idea," Nico said, still studying the lot. Refusing to give up, he took another pass down the next aisle. His eyes narrowed, and he lowered the windows for a better look. To his ears, the rain on the nearby cars sounded like a ten-year-old letting loose on a drum set.

Weaving up and down each aisle, the Pontiac eventually looped back around to the far side of the lot where they first came in.

D'you even know what kind of car he drives?

Slowing down, Nico shook his head and opened the driver's-side door. "I'm not looking for his car."

What're you—?

The Pontiac was barely in park as Nico hopped outside, crossed in front of his own headlights, and squatted down toward the ground. On the asphalt, a matching set of curved tire marks formed identical, partially overlapping Vs just outside a parking spot. Like someone left in a hurry.

Standing up straight, Nico looked over his shoulder, rescanning the full length of the lot. Lamppost by lamppost, aisle by aisle, he took in every piece, including the twenty-foot shrubs that completely circled the whole— No. Not the whole lot. Cocking his head, Nico blinked twice to make sure he was seeing it right.

It was easy to overlook—tucked back between the cars and filled with even more shrubbery, the narrow opening in the shrubs practically disappeared in its own natural camouflage. Fortunately for Nico, he had plenty of training with camouflage.

Nico, you got something?

Nico pulled his gun from his pants, tapping the barrel against the rosary beads on his chest. But as he strode toward the cutaway and into the dog run, all he found were muddy footprints scattered like buckshot, and patches of matted-down grass. At first glance, it looked like there could've been a struggle, but with the rain . . . the muddy runoff from the lot . . . it could've just as easily been nothing.

Undeterred, Nico searched the branches (so many crosses), the bushes, the trunks of each tree. God brought him here. The Lord would provide. He squatted down on his knees, peering under shrubs, swishing his free hand through shallow puddles. There were dog prints and footprints under a few overhanging branches, but most of the ground was already too muddy to read.

Crawling through the flooded grass, Nico felt the mud seeping through the knees of his jeans. His heart plummeted. He didn't understand. God was . . . God was supposed to provide. But as Nico frantically searched . . . as he continued to crawl like a dog, pawing through the mud—the proof . . . where Wes went . . . all of it was gone.

"Please—please stop raining," Nico pleaded to the now-dark sky.

The drizzle continued, falling like a mist from above.

"Please . . . *stop raining!*" Nico exploded, throwing a fistful of mud and wet grass in the air.

The drizzle continued.

Down on all fours, Nico lowered his head, watching the rosary beads swaying from his neck. How could . . . ? Why would God bring him this far? As the rain ran down his face, Nico climbed to his feet and walked deliberately between the lampposts, back to the parking lot.

His head was still down as he approached the Pontiac. He clutched the rosary, trying to say a prayer, but nothing came out. He tried closing his eyes, but all he could picture was the mess of mud and grass and sticks that covered all tracks. His fist tightened around the rosary, pulling tighter, ever tighter. God promised. He . . . He swore to me—*swore!*—that the devil's door would remain shut—that avenging my mother's death would bring redemption. And now to just abandon me like—

With a sharp crack, the rosary necklace snapped, spilling dozens of wooden beads like marbles down on the asphalt of the parking lot.

"No . . . God—I'm sorry—I'm so sorry!" Nico begged hysterically, scrambling to pick them all up as they bounced, rolled, and scattered in every direction. Diving sideways as he scooped them against his chest, Nico lurched for a stray wooden bead like a five-year-old trying to catch a cricket. But it wasn't until he skidded down on his already-wet knees . . . until the bead hopped, hopped, hopped, and rolled beneath the Pontiac . . . that Nico saw the mushy wet pamphlet stuck to the ground. Just in front of the right front tire.

From the look of it—the top half perfectly flat, the bottom half swollen and soggy from the rain—the pamphlet had already been run over. But even in the moonlight, even with the top half of it flaking away and pancaked from tire treads, Nico could still read the big red-lettered restaurant name at the top of the Chinese menu. And more important, the handwritten note at the bottom.

You need to know what else he did. 7 p.m. at Woodlawn. —Ron

Ron.

Nico read the name again. And again. The Beast.

Ron.

The letters blurred in front of him. Gently peeling the menu from the asphalt, he could barely stop his hands from trembling . . . trembling just like his mom's head. Half the menu ripped away as he tugged. He didn't care. Clutching the soggy remains to his chest, Nico looked up at the sky and kissed the fistful of loose rosary beads in his other hand.

"I understand, God. Wes and Boyle—the traitors—together. One final test . . . one last chapter," Nico whispered to the sky. He began to pray. "I won't fail you, Mom."

93

The scratched metal door to the old apartment yawned open, and the stale smell of pipe tobacco swirled across Lisbeth's face.

"The reporter, right?" asked a stubby, sixty-year-old man with brown-tinted glasses, a short-sleeve white button-down, and a pointy, crescent-moon chin. He looked no different than the last time she saw him—except for his forehead, where a jagged oval hunk of skin the size of a campaign button had been sliced from the top of his receding white hairline down to his eyebrows, leaving a lump of fresh pink skin in its place.

"Squamous cell skin cancer," he blurted. "Not pretty, I know, but—aheh—at least it didn't reach my skull," he added with an awkward shrug and laugh.

Eve had warned her about this. Like the comic strip folks and the obituary guys downstairs, every crossword designer could use a few lessons in social graces.

As Lisbeth stepped inside, Martin Kassal followed a bit too closely, trying to hide a small limp while trailing her into the living room, where packed bookshelves clogged every wall. Even the tops of the bookcases were stacked to the ceiling with newspapers, magazines, dictionaries, thesauruses, and full sets of the 1959 and 1972 *Encyclopedia Britannica.* Just past the living room, a small sitting area held a white Formica desk that was yellowed from the sun, a two-person beige love seat buried under newspaper clippings, and a freestanding chalkboard that was framed with at least fifty diamond-shaped, suction-cup Baby on Board signs: *Student Driver on Board*, *Twins on Board*, *Marlins Fan on Board*, *Gun Owner on Board*, *Mother-in-Law in Trunk*, *Michigan Dad on Board*, *Nobody on Board*, a bright pink *Princess on Board*, and of course, a black and white *Crossword Lover on Board*, where the *o*'s in *Crossword* and *Lover* intersected.

"June 1992," Kassal beamed, his moon-chin rising. "We did a scavenger hunt for the weekend section. Impossible stuff: an old pull tab from a soda can, a baseball card with a player not wearing a baseball cap, and *these*," he said, pointing to the Baby on Board collection. "Anything but *BABY on Board.*"

Nodding politely, Lisbeth looked past the suction-cup signs and focused on the actual blackboard, which held an oversize hand-drawn grid. The top half of the grid was filled with words and darkened boxes; the bottom half was almost completely blank.

"You still design them by hand?" she asked.

"Instead of what, some computer program that'll do all the work for me? No offense, but—aheh—I'm obsolete enough as it is. Last thing I need to do is wave the white flag and bury myself, if that makes sense."

"Perfect sense," Lisbeth agreed, staring down at the two crossword puzzles in her hand.

"So those the puzzles you were talking about?" Kassal asked, raising his nose and peering through the reading half of his tinted bifocals. As Lisbeth handed him the crosswords, he scanned the top one for a moment. "Fifty-six across should be *taser*, not *tasks*."

"It's not the puzzle that's the problem," Lisbeth pointed out. "It's the symbols on the side."

Following Lisbeth's finger to the side of the puzzle, Kassal studied each symbol: the handwritten , , , and .

"Sure it's not just doodling?"

"We thought the same—until we found *this*," she explains, flipping to the crossword Violet gave her.

"Aheh," Kassal said with his wimpish little laugh. "Clever buggers. Their own little message."

"See, but that's the thing. I don't think they made it up themselves . . ."

Already lost in the game, Kassal whispered to himself. "If the four dots represent the letter *D* as the fourth letter, and the two dots stand for *B* . . . No, no—it's not a cryptogram—not enough symbols for letters. Not an anagram either." Looking over the tops of his glasses at Lisbeth, he added, "They could be weather symbols . . . maybe Navajo signs. Who'd you say drew this again?"

"Just a friend."

"But is it a clever friend, a dumb friend, a—?"

"Clever. Really clever. Head-of-the-class clever."

"And what do you need it for again?"

"Just . . . y'know . . . just for fun."

Kassal stared at her, picking her apart like she was the crossword. "This isn't going to get me in trouble, is it?"

"Sir, the guys in comics—they said you were the best at deciphering these kinds of things."

"Now you're trying to flatter me, dearie."

"No, that's not—"

"It's okay. These days, I don't get flattered too often by pretty young redheads. I miss it." Hobbling over to the yellowed Formica desk, Kassal pulled out a legal pad and copied the symbols one by one.

"So you'll help?" Lisbeth asked.

"Less talking—more working," he said, once again engrossed in the puzzle.

Lisbeth moved behind him, barely able to hide her excitement.

"Let's start with the four-dot sign you have here," he said, pointing to the ∷. "If you draw a vertical line down the middle of it, like this:

". . . and a horizontal line like this:

". . . the symbol is the same on both sides of the line, which means this sign is multi-axis symmetric."

"And that matters *why*?" Lisbeth asked.

"Ever try to look up a symbol in a dictionary? *Four-dots-in-a-square* isn't filed under *F.* But the same way every puzzle has a solution, every symbol has its own classification, which breaks down into four distinct subgroups: First, whether it's symmetrical or not. Second, whether it's *closed* like a triangle or *open* like your four dots here. Third, are its lines straight or curved? And fourth, does the symbol have lines that cross, which opens up a whole new religious can of tuna."

"And when you answer those questions?"

"When you answer those," Kassal said, limping to his

bookcases and pulling thick, phone-book-sized texts from his shelves, "then you go to the references." With a thud, he dumped the pile of books on his desk. *Elsevier's Dictionary of Symbols and Imagery, Encyclopedia of Traditional Symbols, Franken's Guide to Religious Images, The Visual Almanac of Occult Signs, Passer's Handbook of Native American Symbols . . .*

"This is gonna take some time, isn't it?" Lisbeth asked, flipping open one of the books to a section titled *Multi-Axis, Closed, Soft Elements, Crossing Lines.* The open pages contained four encyclopedia entries for ∞ (including its denotations in mathematics, genealogy, and botany) and six listings for ⚭, ◎, and various other overlapping circles.

"Of course, it'll take time," Kassal replied, already cataloging the other symbols from the crossword. "Why? You got someplace t—"

Lisbeth's cell phone erupted with a high-pitched ring. Flipping it open, she was about to pick up, then caught herself when she saw caller ID.

"Bad news?" Kassal asked, reading her reaction.

"No, just—not at all," she insisted as the phone rang again.

"You say so," Kassal replied with a shrug. "Though in my experience, looks like that are reserved for two people: bosses and boyfriends."

"Yeah, well . . . this one's a whole different problem." But as the phone rang for the third time, Lisbeth couldn't ignore the fact that even though her notepad was sticking out of her purse, she wasn't reaching for it. Of course, that didn't mean it was easy for her. But after nearly a decade of trying to turn four-inch stories into front-page headlines, well . . . some things were more important than the front page. Finally picking up, she asked, "Wes? That you?"

"Yeah," he replied, sounding even worse than when they watched the video of the shooting.

"Everything okay?"

"I-I don't think so."

Hearing the pain in Wes's voice, Lisbeth turned back to Kassal.

"Go," the old man told her, readjusting his bifocals. "I'll call you as soon as I find something."

"Are you—?"

"Go," he insisted, trying to sound annoyed. "Young redheads are just a distraction anyway."

Nodding a thank-you and scribbling her number on a Post-it for him, Lisbeth ran for the door. Turning back to her cell, she asked Wes, "How can I help?"

On the other end, Wes finally exhaled. Lisbeth couldn't tell if it was relief or excitement.

"That depends," he replied. "How fast can you get to Woodlawn?"

"Woodlawn Cemetery? Why there?"

"That's where Boyle asked to meet. Seven p.m. At his grave."

94

Fighting traffic for nearly an hour, Rogo veered to the right, zipping off the highway at the exit for Griffin Road in Fort Lauderdale.

"Y'know, for a guy who deals with traffic tickets every single day," Dreidel said, gripping the inside door handle for support, "you think you'd appreciate safe driving a bit more."

"If I get a ticket, I'll get us off," Rogo said coldly, jabbing the gas and going even faster down the dark off-ramp. Wes had enough of a head start. Priority now was finding why Boyle was seeing Dr. Eng—in Florida—the week before the shooting.

"There's no way he'll even be there," Dreidel said, looking down at his watch. "I mean, name one doctor who works past five o'clock," he added with a nervous laugh.

"Stop talking, okay? We're almost there."

With a sharp left that took them under the overpass of I-95, the blue Toyota headed west on Griffin, past a string of check-cashing stores, two thrift shops, and an adult video store called AAA to XXX.

"Great neighborhood," Rogo pointed out as they

passed the bright neon purple and green sign for the Fantasy Lounge.

"It's not that ba—"

Directly above them, a thunderous rumble ripped through the sky as a red and white 747 whizzed overhead, coming in for a landing at Fort Lauderdale Airport, which, judging from the height of the plane, was barely a mile behind them.

"Maybe Dr. Eng just likes cheap rents," Dreidel said as Rogo reread the address from the entry in Boyle's old calendar.

"If we're lucky, you'll be able to ask him personally," Rogo said, pointing out the front windshield. Directly ahead, just past a funeral home, bright lights lit up a narrow office park and its modern four-story white building with frosted-glass doors and windows. Along the upper half of the building, a thin yellow horizontal stripe ran just below the roofline.

2678 Griffin Road.

95

During the first year, Ron Boyle was scared. Shuttling from country to country . . . the nose contouring and cheek implants . . . even the accent modification that never really worked. The men in Dr. Eng's office said it'd keep him safe, make his trail impossible to follow. But that didn't stop him from bolting upright in his bed every time he heard a car door slam outside his motel or villa or pensione. The worst was when a spray of firecrackers exploded outside a nearby cathedral—a wedding tradition in Valencia, Spain. Naturally, Boyle knew it wouldn't be easy—hiding away, leaving friends, family . . . especially family—but he knew what was at stake. And in the end, when he finally came back, it'd all be worth it. From there, the rationalizations were easy. Unlike his father, he was tackling his problems head-on. And as he closed his eyes at night, he knew no one could blame him for that.

By year two, as he adjusted to life in Spain, isolation hit far harder than his accountant brain had calculated. Unlike his old friend Manning, when Boyle left the White House, he never suffered from spotlight starvation. But the loneliness . . . not so much for his wife (his marriage was finished years ago), but on his daughter's sixteenth birthday, as he pictured her gushing, no-more-braces smile in her brand-new driver's license photo—those were the days of regret. Days that Leland Manning would answer for.

In year three, he'd grown accustomed to all the tricks Dr. Eng's office taught him: walking down the street with his head down, double-checking doors after he entered a building, even being careful not to leave big tips so he wouldn't be remembered by waiters or staff. So accustomed, in fact, that he made his first mistake: making small talk with a local ex-pat as they both sipped *horchatas* in a local bodega. Boyle knew the instant the man took a double take that he was an Agency man. Panicking, but smart enough to stay and finish the drink, Boyle went straight home, frantically packed two suitcases, and left Valencia that evening.

In December of that same year, the *New Yorker* commissioned a feature article about Univar "Blackbird" computers showing up in the governments of Iran, Syria, Burma, and Sudan. As terrorist nations unable to import from the United States, the countries bought their computers from a shady supplier in the Middle East. But what the countries didn't know was that Univar was a front company for the National Security Agency and that six months after the computers were in the terrorist countries' possession, they slowly broke down while simultaneously forwarding their entire hard drives straight to the NSA—hence the *Blackbird* codename—as the info flew the coop.

But as the research for the *New Yorker* article pointed out, during the Manning administration, one Blackbird computer from Sudan didn't forward its hard drive to the NSA. And when the others did, the remaining Blackbird was removed from the country, eventually making its way to the black market. The informant who held it wanted a six-million-dollar ransom from the United States for its return. But Manning's staff, worried it was a scam, refused to pay. Two weeks before the *New Yorker* story was to be handed in, Patrick Gould, the author of the article, died from a sudden ruptured brain aneurysm. The autopsy ruled out foul play.

By year four, Boyle was well hidden in a small town outside London, in a flat tucked just above a local wedding cake bakery. And while the smell of fresh hazelnut and vanilla greeted him every morning, frustration and regret slowly buried Boyle's fear. It was only compounded when the Manning Presidential Library was two months behind its scheduled opening, making his search for papers, documents, and proof that much harder to come by. Still, that didn't mean there was nothing for him to dig through. Books, magazines, and newspaper profiles had been written about Nico, and the end of Manning's presidency, and the attack. With each one, as Boyle relived the sixty-three seconds of the speedway shooting, the fear returned, churning through his chest and the scarred palm of his hand. Not just because of the ferocity of the attack, or even the almost military efficiency of it, but because of the gall: at the speedway, on live television, in front of millions of people. If The Three wanted Boyle dead, they could've waited outside his Virginia home and slit his throat or forced a "brain aneurysm." To take him down at the speedway, to do it in front of all those witnesses . . . risks that big were only worth taking if there was some kind of added benefit.

Year four was also when Boyle started writing his letters. To his daughter. His friends. Even to his old enemies, including the few who missed his funeral. Asking questions, telling stories, anything to feel that connection to his real life, his former life. He got the idea from a biography of President Harry Truman, who used to write scathing letters to his detractors. Like Truman, Boyle wrote hundreds of them. Like Truman, he didn't mail them.

In year five, Boyle's wife remarried. His daughter started college at Columbia on a scholarship named after her dead father. Neither broke Boyle's heart. But they certainly jabbed a spike in his spirit. Soon after, as he'd been doing since year one, Boyle found himself in an Internet café, checking airfares back to the States. A few times, he'd even made a reservation. He'd long ago worked out how he'd get in touch, how he'd contact his daughter, how he'd sneak away—even from those he knew were always watching. That's when the consequences would slap him awake. The Three . . . The Four . . . whatever they called themselves, had already—Boyle couldn't even think about it. He wasn't risking it again. Instead, as the Manning Presidential Library threw its doors open, Boyle threw himself into the paperwork of his own past, mailing off his requests and searching and scavenging for anything to prove what his gut had been telling him for years.

By year six, he was ankle-deep in photocopies and old White House files. Dr. Eng's people offered to help, but Boyle was six years past naive. In the world of Eng, the only priority was Eng, which was why, when Manning had him introduced to Dr. Eng's group all those years ago, Boyle told them about The Three, and their offer to make him The Fourth, and the threats that went along with it. But what he never mentioned—not to anyone—was what The Three had already stolen. And what Boyle was determined to get back.

He'd finally gotten his chance eleven days ago, on a muddy, rainy afternoon in the final month of year seven. Huddled under the awning as he stepped out of the post office on Balham High Road, Boyle flipped through the newly processed releases from Manning's personal handwriting file. Among the highlights were a note to the governor of Kentucky, some handwritten notes for a speech in Ohio, and a torn scrap from the *Washington Post* comics section that had a few scribbled names on one side . . . and a mostly completed crossword puzzle on the other.

At first, Boyle almost tossed it aside. Then he remembered that day at the racetrack, in the back of the limo, Manning and his chief of staff were working a crossword. In fact, now that he thought about it, they were *always* working a crossword. Staring down at the puzzle, Boyle felt like there were thin metal straps constricting his rib cage. His teeth picked at his bottom lip as he studied the two distinct handwritings. Manning's and Albright's. But when he saw the random doodles along the side of the puzzle, he held his breath, almost biting through his own skin. In the work space . . . the initials . . . were those—? Boyle checked and rechecked again, circling them with a pen.

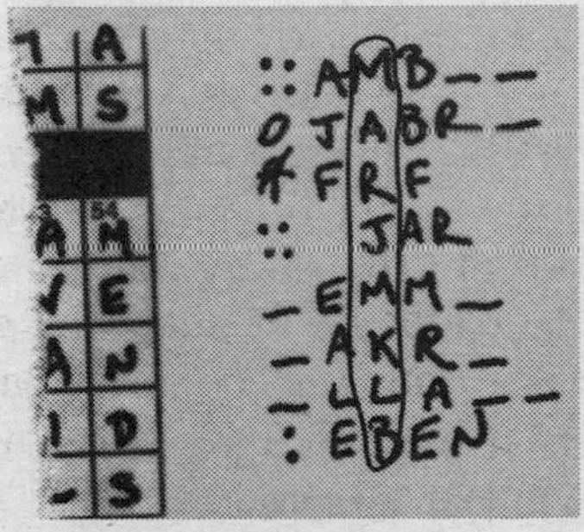

Those weren't just senior staff. With Dreidel and Moss and Kutz—those were the people getting the President's Daily Briefing, the one document The Three asked him for access to.

It took three days to crack the rest: two with a symbols expert at Oxford University, half a day with an art history professor, then a fifteen-minute consultation with their Modern History Research Unit, most specifically, Professor Jacqui Moriceau, whose specialty was the Federalist period, specifically Thomas Jefferson.

She recognized it instantly. The four dots . . . the slashed cross . . . even the short horizontal dashes. There they were. Exactly as Thomas Jefferson had intended.

As Professor Moriceau relayed the rest, Boyle waited for his eyes to flood, for his chin to rise with the relief of a seemingly lifelong mission complete. But as he held the crossword in his open palm . . . as he slowly realized what Leland Manning was really up to . . . his arms, his legs, his fingertips, even his toes went brittle and numb, as if his whole body were a hollowed-out eggshell. God, how could he be so blind—so trusting—for so long? Now he had to see Manning. Had to ask him to his face. Sure, he'd unlocked the puzzle, but it wasn't a victory. After eight years, dozens of missed birthdays, seven missed Christmases, six countries, two surgeries, a prom, a high school graduation, and a college acceptance, there would never be victory.

But that didn't mean there couldn't be revenge.

Fifteen minutes south of Palm Beach, Ron Boyle pulled to the side of the highway and steered the beat-up white van to the far corner of a dead-empty emergency rest stop. Without even thinking about it, he angled just behind a crush of ratty, overgrown shrubs. After eight years, he had a PhD in disappearing.

Behind him, sprawled along the van's unlined metal floor, O'Shea shuddered and moaned, finally waking up. Boyle wasn't worried. Or scared. Or even excited. In fact, it'd been weeks since he felt much of anything beyond the ache of his own regrets.

On the floor, with his arms still tied behind his back, O'Shea scootched on his knees, his chin, his elbows, slowly and sluggishly fighting to sit up. With each movement, his shoulder twitched and jumped. His hair was a sopping mess of rain and sweat. His once-white shirt was damp with dark red blood. Eventually writhing his way to a kneeling position, he was trying to look strong, but Boyle could see in the grayish coloring of his face that the pain was taking its toll. O'Shea blinked twice to get his bearings.

That's when O'Shea heard the metallic click.

Crouching in the back of the van, Boyle leaned forward, pressed his pistol deep into O'Shea's temple, and said the words that had been haunting him for the better part of a decade:

"Where the fuck's my son?"

96

Can I help you?" a deep voice crackled from the intercom as the man pulled his car up to the closed wooden security gate.

Refusing to answer, the driver pulled his ID from his jacket pocket and shoved it toward the hidden camera stuffed into the tall shrubs.

The intercom went silent. Moments later, a metallic click released the magnetic lock, and the security gate swung open.

Slowly easing his foot against the gas, the man inched the car up the private brick driveway, where three suit-and-tie Secret Service agents turned and stared. When they didn't approach his car, he knew they were getting the news of his arrival in their earpieces. And by the looks on their faces, they were unnerved by it. No one likes when the boss comes to check on things. But with Nico on the loose, they weren't the least bit surprised.

With a tug to the left, he steered his car between the matching black Chevy Suburbans, then readjusted his leather shoulder holster and made sure the strap that held his gun in place was unsnapped. This wasn't like his trip to the office. With the principals here, he needed to be ready. And if the reports were true—that a neighbor had already found Kenny's and Micah's bodies and that fingerprints were already making the rounds—well, this was now about much more than seventy million dollars in payouts and four more years in office.

It was so much easier back when they started. After War College, they spent the first six months doing nothing but running simulations and war-gaming. No need to rush. Better to make it a science. Take no chances, make no contact, and make sure nothing's traced back. Of course, the key to that was creating The Roman, right down to the stolen thumb they snatched from a Tanzania morgue to use with the fingerprint cards required for every informant payout. From there, people would just be chasing a ghost. Once The Roman was "real," the true work began.

It was Micah who struck gold first. As a CIA case officer stationed in Khartoum, he received a tip about someone in the Sudanese security agency trying to sell eleven pristine U.S. visas—all of them sterile and untraceable—to al-Zaydi, a known terrorist organization. According to Micah's source, al-Zaydi was paying with its usual mode of untraceable African diamonds—$500,000 worth, which would be delivered in Taormina, Sicily, on October 15.

That morning, to communicate with his fellow members, Micah left piecemeal coded messages in the agreed-upon online chat rooms. Then he wrote up his full official report, which detailed only *one* of the facts—that the Sudanese security agency was rumored to be selling eleven visas. He intentionally left out the rest. That afternoon, O'Shea—in his position as an FBI Legat in Brussels assigned to working with foreign law enforcement officials—took full advantage of the info Micah had sent about the diamonds. Now knowing what to look for, and reaching out to overseas security agencies, he combed through foreign customs reports, eventually finding a suspected al-Zaydi member traveling through Italy—legally—with nearly $500,000 of diamond jewelry. That night, Secret Service Agent Roland Egen—as the resident agent in charge of the Service's office in Pretoria, South Africa—put the cherry on top. Calling up his supervisor in the Rome office, he said, "I've got a source bragging about black market U.S. visas for sale—and that he'll give us the time and place for the drop."

"What kinda payoff does he want?" the supervisor had asked.

"Fifty thousand dollars."

There was a short pause. "Who's the source?"

"He calls himself The Roman," Egen said with a grin.

Within minutes, the Service started vetting the tip. Throughout the community, they called it backstopping—checking with other agencies to corroborate the source. After Iraq, it was a necessity. And after the information-sharing from 9/11, the info came quick. Thanks to O'Shea, the FBI showed a similar report. Thanks to Micah, so did the CIA. All three pieces corroborating the same picture.

"Pay it," Egen's supervisor said.

Twenty-four hours later, Micah, O'Shea, and The Roman—by simply corroborating one another—split their first $50,000 payout. Not a bad day's work.

Years ago, it was easier. But that was before they invited others to join in the game.

"Welcome, sir," a brown-haired agent called out as the

man left the car and marched toward the pale blue Colonial with the American flag above the door.

Halfway there, a fourth suit-and-tie agent approached from the front steps.

Well aware of the protocol, the man again handed over his ID, waiting for it to be looked at.

"Sorry, sir . . . I didn't . . . You're here to see the President?" the agent asked, anxiously handing the ID back.

"Yeah," The Roman replied as he stepped inside the President's home. "Something like that."

97

"Wanna try that one again?" Boyle growled in the back of the van as he dug the barrel of his gun into O'Shea's temple.

"You can demand all you want, it's the truth," O'Shea said, spitting up blood and contorted by the lightning bolt of pain coursing through his shoulder. As he kneeled in the van, his voice was purposely soft. Boyle shook his head, knowing it was just a trick to bring his own volume down. O'Shea still pushed on. "I know this is emotional for you, Boyle, but you need t—"

"Where the hell's my son!?" Boyle exploded, shoving the gun so hard against O'Shea's head, it sent O'Shea backward like a turtle on his shell. But even as he worked his way back to his knees, O'Shea didn't thrash, panic, or fight. Boyle couldn't tell if it was exhaustion or strategy. The only thing he knew was that, like a wounded leopard still locked on its prey, O'Shea never took his eyes off Boyle's gun.

Eight years ago, Boyle's hands would've been shaking. Today, he was perfectly still. "Tell me where he is, O'Shea."

"Why, so you can wait outside his school—what is he, nine, ten years old now?—so you can wait outside his fourth-grade class and tell him you want visitation rights? You think your girlfriend Tawana—"

"Her name's Tiana."

"Call her what you want, she told us the story, Boyle—how you flirted during the campaign, how she followed you to D.C.—"

"I never asked her to do that."

"—but you didn't have any problem hiding her from your wife and daughter for almost four years. And then when she got pregnant—darn!—better do something about that."

"I never asked her to get an abortion."

"Oh, I'm sorry—I didn't realize you were a saint." In the distance, a pack of cars whipped past them on the highway. O'Shea curled downward and lowered his head for a moment, yielding to the pain. "C'mon, Boyle," he stuttered as he looked back up, "you hid the kid from the entire world—insisted that they never approach you in public—and *now* you suddenly wanna take him to the father-son White House picnic?"

"He's still my son."

"Then you should've taken care of him."

"I did take care of him!"

"No, *we* took care of him," O'Shea insisted. "What you did was send fifty bucks a week, hoping it would buy food, diapers, and her silence. We're the ones who gave her—and him—a true future."

Boyle shook his head, already agitated. "Is that how The Roman sold it to you? That you were giving them a future?"

"She needed cash; we offered it."

"Or, more accurately: You paid her to hide, then refused to tell me where they were unless I agreed to be your fourth turncoat," Boyle said, his voice now booming. "So don't make it look like you were *doing her any favors*!"

Pressing his chin down against his shoulder, O'Shea looked up from the floor, his hazel eyes glowing in the darkness of the van. A slow grin rose like a sunrise on his face. "Boy, we really picked the right push button, didn't we? To be honest, when The Roman said you cared for her, I thought he was full of crap."

Boyle aimed the gun at O'Shea's face. "Where are they? I'm not asking you agai—"

Leaning back on his knees, O'Shea erupted with a deep rumbling laugh that catapulted from his throat and echoed through the van. "C'mon, you really think we kept track after all this time? That somehow we kept them as pen pals?"

As the words left O'Shea's lips, Boyle could feel each syllable clawing straight through his belly, shredding every organ inside his chest. "Wh-What're you talking about?"

"We killed you, jackass. Or at least that's what we thought. For all I cared, from that moment on, Tiana and her little bastard could've moved right back to that dump where we found them in D.C."

Hunched over, Boyle took a half-step back. His hand started to shake.

"Wait . . . oh, you . . . wait," O'Shea said, already chuckling. "You're telling me that in all the time you spent trying to track us down, that . . . that you never once considered the possibility that we wouldn't know where they are?"

For the second time, O'Shea leaned back for a loud bellowing laugh. Then, without warning, he sprang forward, like a frog, with a ramming headbutt that plowed into Boyle's chin before he even saw it coming. On impact, Boyle's head whipped back, sending him crashing into the bucket seats.

"You feel that?!" O'Shea screamed, his eyes wide with rage. "This time I'll kill you myself!"

Boyle shook his head no. Slow at first. Then faster. O'Shea charged forward like a truck. Boyle was already in mid-swing, lashing out with his right hand. And the gun he was still holding in it.

In a blur, the butt of the pistol slammed O'Shea like a ten-pound weight to the head. Colliding with the corner of his brow, it sent him tumbling sideways toward the wall behind the passenger seat. With his hands still tied behind his back, he didn't have a chance. Already off balance, he turned just enough to hit the metal wall shoulder-first.

"That's for my son," Boyle snarled, buzzing with adrenaline.

O'Shea sank to the floor of the van. Boyle didn't let up, rushing in and pressing the barrel of his gun against O'Shea's forehead. "And this one's for my daughter, you thieving piece of shit!"

Boyle cocked the gun's pin and started squeezing the trigger.

O'Shea erupted with another haunting laugh. "Do it," he demanded, his voice breathless and raw as he lay there, sprawled on his back. His chest rose and fell rapidly as his body twisted on the floor. Between the bullet wounds from the dog run and his current impact, the pain was overwhelming. "With these metal walls . . . go ahead . . . I-I'd love to see you risk the ricochet."

Boyle glanced around at the walls of the van. "It won't ricochet," he insisted.

"You sure about that?" O'Shea gasped, fighting for air and kicking his heel against the metal floor. There was a loud deep thud. "Sounds . . . sounds pretty damn solid to me."

Boyle didn't respond. His hand twitched slightly as he tightened his grip on the trigger.

"That's . . . it's a frightening thought, isn't it?" O'Shea asked. "Here you are all ready to wreck the few remaining shards of your life by becoming a killer, and . . . and now you have to worry if you'll shoot yourself in the process."

Boyle knew he was lying. He had to be.

"C'mon, Boyle—here's your chance to blow my head off. Take your shot!" Defiantly, O'Shea leaned forward, pressing his forehead even harder against the gun.

Boyle's finger rattled against the trigger as a dribble of blood ran from his nose to his top lip. This was it. The moment he'd begged for . . . prayed for . . . the revenge that had fueled him all these years. The problem was, O'Shea was still right about one thing: Whatever else they'd taken from him, whatever cold shell of himself they turned him into, he'd never be a killer. Though that didn't mean he couldn't have his vengeance.

Shifting his arm to the right, Boyle pointed the barrel at O'Shea's still-seeping shoulder wound and pulled the trigger. A single bullet tore through O'Shea's shoulder, taking another chunk of meat with it. To maximize the pain, Boyle kept the gun at an angle, hoping to hit some bone as well. From O'Shea's scream—which faded into a silent breathless gasp as his eyes rolled back and he finally lost consciousness—it was more than enough to do the trick.

Kicking O'Shea onto his side, Boyle knelt down to the splatter of blood on the floor. Underneath the mess, through the metal floor of the van, was a small jagged bullet hole. Sticking a finger in and feeling the musty air outside, Boyle shook his head. Of course, it wouldn't ricochet. Only the President's limo is bulletproof.

Wasting no time, Boyle ducked into the front of the van and wriggled into the driver's seat. Far to his left, another swarm of cars buzzed by on the highway. As he looked down, the digital clock on the dashboard said it was 6:57 p.m. Perfect, he thought as he punched the gas, spun the wheels, and sent bits of gravel chainsawing through the air. One more stop and it'd all be done.

98

Haven't these people ever heard of a parking lot?" Rogo asked as he drove past the landscaping by the frosted-glass entrance and veered around to the back of the white office building.

"There," Dreidel pointed out as they turned the corner. Around back, a wide lot was dotted with eight or ten cars.

"That's a good sign, right? People still working?"

"Unless it's just janitorial staff," Dreidel said, eyeing the building through the passenger window.

"How many janitors you know drive brand-new Mustangs?" Rogo asked, parking next to a shiny black convertible Ford Mustang. "The only thing I can't figure out is why they have all that space in the front of the building and instead put the parking lot around back?"

"Maybe it's a zoning issue."

"Yeah, maybe," Rogo said.

"What, you still think it's some kinda mob doctor?"

"All I know is, they're about a block away from the Bada-Bing and the porn shop, there's a funeral home next door, and that Mustang has a personalized license plate that says *Fredo*."

Dreidel glanced down at the license plate, which read *MY STANG.* "Will you please stop? It's a doctor's office, Rogo. You can tell it from here."

"Well, color me a stickler, but I'd still prefer to see it for myself," Rogo added, flicking the car door open, hopping out into the drizzling rain, and running for the back door of the building. Halfway there, he looked straight up as a soft high-pitched whistle exploded into a deafening, rumbling earthquake. Another 747 coming in for a landing. Behind him, he noticed that Dreidel was at least ten steps behind.

Rogo finally reached two sliding frosted-glass doors that were almost identical to the entrance in front. Stepping onto the pressure mat, he waited for the doors to slide open. They didn't move.

"Anybody home?" Rogo announced, knocking on the frosted glass, then pressing his face against it, trying to peer inside. Diagonally up on his right, a pinprick of red light revealed a shiny black security camera that was as thin as a calculator with a tiny round lens no bigger than a dime. Rogo turned away, too smart to stare. No way was a doctor's office spending money on high-end tech like that.

"Don't look up," Rogo whispered as Dreidel stepped next to him.

"You sure no one's—?"

Rogo raised a knuckle to knock again, but before he could tap the glass, the doors slid open, revealing an annoyed security guard with stringy brown hair and a close-cropped mustache.

"Can I help you?" he asked, looking at Dreidel, then Rogo, then back at Dreidel.

"Yeah, we're looking for Dr. Eng," Rogo said, trying to step inside. The guard stepped in front of him, cutting him off, but Rogo kept going, his short meatball build ducking quickly under the guard's arm and into the salmon-colored marble lobby.

"Sorry . . . it's just . . . it's raining," Rogo said, pointing outside and flicking excess water from his hands.

The guard didn't say a word, still staring at Dreidel. Rogo noticed that the guard was armed with a 9mm pistol in his belt.

"Anyway," Dreidel interrupted, "we're here to see Dr. Eng."

"Sorry, he left already," the guard shot back.

"That's fine—if we could just see his office assistant."

"Dr. Eng is gone. His office is closed for the day."

Up the hallway, Rogo spotted a tenant directory on the wall next to the elevators. "Listen, if we came at a bad time, I apologize, but can I just ask one favor?" Rogo pleaded. "I've been driving for over an hour in tear-your-hair-out traffic. We'll get out of your way—we'll call Dr. Eng tomorrow—but first, can I *please* just use your bathroom? We're talking real emergency here."

The guard stared at him, unmoving.

"Please," Rogo pleaded, doing an anxious shuffle with his feet. "If I wait any longer—"

"Men's room is past the elevators on the left-hand side," the guard said, pointing up the hall.

"My bladder thanks you," Rogo said, taking off.

Dreidel took a step to follow behind him. The guard shot him a look, and Dreidel stopped.

"We'll . . . I'll just wait here," Dreidel decided.

"Great idea," the guard said.

Without looking back, Rogo cruised up the hallway, which, like the outside of the building, was worn and weary: cracked marble along the floor, cheap art deco light fixtures overhead, and eighties-era aqua and seafoam modern art paintings on the wall. Brushing past it all, Rogo focused on the office directory next to the elevators.

"Did I pass it yet?" he called back to the guard as he stopped in front of the directory's gold metal frame. Skimming the alphabetical list, he saw:

Eng, Dr. Brian——Suite 127

But to Rogo's surprise, it didn't list the type of practice or even a business name. Same with every other doctor in the directory. Six in total, but not a single one included their practice.

"Next door down," the security guard called back. "On the left."

Waving his thanks, Rogo ducked into the small restroom, which greeted him with the sharp reek of bleach. Knowing he had to take some time before rushing out, he walked to the sink, hit the lever on the dispenser for a few paper towels, and wiped the rest of the rain from his face. He looked in the mirror to make sure he got it all. That's when he noticed the oak door behind him, just over his shoulder.

Turning back, he studied it carefully. To anyone else, it was nothing more than a storage closet. And to him, on any other day, it would be too. But tonight . . . with everything going on . . . Rogo glanced to his left. There was already a narrow door with the word *Storage* stenciled on it.

Stepping toward the oak door, Rogo gave the doorknob a twist. Locked.

Quick as he could, he glanced around the restroom—the stalls, the urinals, the garbage can in the corner—searching for—*there.*

Next to the sink, Rogo rushed for the paper towel dispenser, slamming the lever as hard as he could. A single paper towel stuck its tongue out. Perfect, Rogo decided, pulling the plastic case off the dispenser and leaving just the lever and the exposed paper towels. He hit the gray plastic lever again, but this time, didn't let go of it, gripping as tight as he could with his fingertips, leaning in with his chest, and putting his full weight against it.

Within seconds, he could hear the damage. There was a loud plastic pop as the dispenser started to crack. Rogo held on, standing on his tiptoes and lifting one foot off the ground to increase the weight. Another pop pierced the air. Almost there. Rogo didn't let up, gritting his teeth and breathing hard through his nose. Don't let go . . . not until . . . With a final short hop, he picked his other foot off the ground. That was it. Plastic shattered with a crack as the boomerang-shaped metal lever snapped free through the bottom of the dispenser. Rogo crashed to the tile floor, and a grin took his face.

As he climbed to his feet, he examined the metal lever, turning the boomerang sideways. Definitely thin enough. Lunging for the oak door, but trying to keep quiet, he slid the boomerang-shaped sliver of metal into the narrow gap between the angled latch and the door's threshold. His forehead and nose were pressed against the door seam as he peered downward and pulled the boomerang toward his belly. Like a child fishing for coins through a sewer grate, he wiggled his hand, trying to jigger the lever against the door's latch. Slowly, the latch started to giv—

Click.

With a frantic tug, he pulled the oak door open. Rogo craned his neck to look inside. "Hello?" he whispered.

Inside, it was dark, but as the light from the bathroom

flooded forward, it was clear this wasn't a little storage closet. The room was deep, almost as big as his and Wes's living room. And as Rogo stepped forward—as he saw what was inside—his eyes widened. It didn't make sense. Why would they—?

"What the hell you think you're doing?" a deep voice asked from the bathroom door.

Rogo spun around just in time to see the security guard coming at him.

99

I know where Boyle's grave is. I've been there before.

The first time was after my sixth and final surgery—the one where they tried to dig the last bits of metal shrapnel from my cheek. Fifteen minutes into it, the doctor decided the pieces were too deep—and far too small, like steel grains of sand—so better to leave them where they are. "Lay it to rest," Dr. Levy told me.

Taking his advice, I left the hospital and had my mom drive me here, to Woodlawn Cemetery. Seven months after Boyle was buried on national television, I approached his grave with my right hand stuffed deep in my pants pocket, clutching my newest prescription and silently, repetitively apologizing for putting him in the limo that day. I could hear my mother sobbing behind me, mourning me like I wasn't even there. It was one of the toughest visits of my life. To my own surprise, this one's tougher.

"Stop thinking about it," Lisbeth whispers, plowing through the unmowed, shin-high grass that wraps like tiny bullwhips around our ankles. As we approach the chain-link fence behind the back of the cemetery, I try to hold the umbrella over both of us, but she's already two steps ahead, not even noticing the light rain. I don't blame her for being excited. Even if she's not writing the story, the reporter in her can't wait to get the truth. "Y'hear what I said, Wes?"

When I don't answer, she stops and spins back to face me. She's about to say something; most likely, *Calm down . . . take it easy.*

"I know it's hard for you," she offers. "I'm sorry."

I nod and thank her with a glimpse of eye contact. "To be honest, I didn't think it'd—I thought I'd be more eager."

"It's okay to be scared, Wes."

"It's not scared—believe me, I *want* Boyle's answers—but just being here . . . where they buried—where they buried whatever they buried. It's like a—it's not the best place for me."

I look up, and she steps toward me, back under the umbrella. "I'm still glad you let me come."

I smile.

"C'mon, I got a good vibe," she says, tugging my shoulder as she sprints back out from under the umbrella. Gripping the top of the four-foot-tall chain-link fence, she stabs her toe into one of the openings.

"Don't bother," I reply, motioning to a mound of dirt that's piled so high it buries the fence and leads right inside. Despite the pep talk, I still hesitate. That's extra dirt from the graves. Lisbeth has no such problem. Ignoring the rain, which is still a light drizzle, she's up the small mound and over the fence in an instant.

"Careful," I call out. "If there's an alarm—"

"It's a cemetery, Wes. I don't think they're worried about people stealing."

"What about grave rob—?" But as I follow her over the dirt mound, we're met with nothing but the soft buzz of crickets and the thick black shadows of two-hundred-year-old banyan trees, whose branches and tendrils stretch out like spiderwebs in every direction. Diagonally to our left, the eighteen acres of Woodlawn Cemetery expand in a perfect rectangle that measures over seventeen football fields. The cemetery eventually dead-ends, with no apparent irony, at the back of the Jaguar dealership, which probably wasn't the intention in the late 1800s when city founder Henry Flagler plowed over seventeen acres of pineapple groves to build West Palm Beach's oldest and most lavish cemetery.

I take off for the main stone-paved path. Grabbing the umbrella, Lisbeth pulls me back and leads us to our left, behind a tall meatball-shaped shrub just inside the back fence. As we get closer, I spot another huge meatball next to it, then another, then another . . . at least a hundred in total, ten feet tall . . . the row of them lining the entire back length of the graveyard. Her instinct's perfect. By staying back here, we're off the main path, meaning we're out of sight, meaning no one can see us coming. With what we've got planned, we're not taking chances.

As we duck behind the first meatball shrub, we quickly see it's not a meatball at all. Hollowed out from the back and shaped like a *U*, the shrub hides a collection of empty Gatorade bottles and soda cans scattered along the ground. The shrub next to it contains a folded-up piece of Astroturf that they use to cover open graves.

"Wes, these are perfect for—"

"No question," I say, finally getting caught up in her excitement. Still, that doesn't mean I'm putting her at risk. Checking to make sure we're alone, I turn left, toward the center of the lot, where a glowing white flagpole is lit up by floodlights and serves as the graveyard's only light source. But from where we are, surrounded by trees in the corner of the far end zone, all its pale glow does is cast angled shadows between the branches and across the path.

"You're slowing down," she says, grabbing the umbrella and tugging me forward.

"Lisbeth, maybe you should—"

"I'm not going anywhere," she insists, doubling our pace and glancing to the right, where a skinny bone-white military headstone has a crest that reads:

CPL
TRP E
13 REGT CAV
SP AM WAR
1879–1959

"He's buried near people from the Spanish-American War?" she whispers. "You sure he's not in the new section?"

We'd seen it when we first drove up. On our far left, past the floodlit flagpole, past the thousands of silhouetted crosses, crooked headstones, and family crypts, was a wide-open field dotted with flat ceremonial markers. Like most Florida cemeteries, Woodlawn learned the hard way what happens when a hurricane hits a graveyard. Nowadays, the newly dead get only flat markers set flush into the earth. Unless, of course, you know someone big enough to tug some strings.

"Trust me, he's not in the new section," I say. The further we go down the path, the more clearly we hear a new sound in the air. A hushed murmur, or a whisper. Dozens of whispers—coming and going—as if they're all around us.

"No one's here," Lisbeth insists. But on our left, behind a 1926 headstone with a marble set of rosary beads dangling from the front, there's a loud scrape like someone skidding to a stop. I spin to see who's there. The headstones surround us. The rain continues to dribble down our backs and soak our shoulders, its mossy smell overwhelming the stench of wet dirt. Behind us, the rumble of thunder starts to—no, not thunder.

"Is that . . . ?"

The rumbling gets louder, followed by the deep belch of an air horn. I wheel back toward the meatball shrubs just as the *ding-ding-ding* of the crossing gate pierces the air. Like a glowing bullet through the darkness, a freight train bursts into view, slicing from right to left, parallel with the low fence that runs along the back of the graveyard.

"We should keep going!" Lisbeth yells in my ear, leading us deeper down the path. The train continues to rumble behind us, taking all sound with it, including the rustling and scraping that would let us know someone's coming.

What about in there? Lisbeth pantomimes as we pass an aboveground crypt with stained-glass double doors. The crypt is one of the largest here—nearly as big as a dumpster.

"Forget it," I say, yanking her by the elbow and taking the lead. She doesn't realize how close we are to our goal. Three graves down from the crypt, the path dead-ends at the trunk of the enormous banyan tree, which, during the day, shields every nearby grave from the battering sun. That alone makes this one of the most select areas in the entire cemetery. President Manning made the call himself and personally secured the double plot of land that now holds the imported Italian black marble headstone with the slightly curved top and the stark white carved letters that read:

RONALD BOYLE

TREASURED HUSBAND, FATHER, SON

WHOSE MAGIC WILL ALWAYS BE WITH US

"This is him?" Lisbeth asks, spotting the name and almost crashing into me from behind.

It was Manning's last gift to his friend—a final resting place that kept Boyle out of the land of flat markers, and instead put him next to a general from World War II, and across from one of Palm Beach's most respected judges from the 1920s. It was vintage Palm Beach. Even in death, honchos still want the best seat in the house.

Behind us, the train fades and the sound of crickets returns, engulfing us on all sides. I just stand there, staring at Boyle's grave in the dim light.

"Y'okay?" Lisbeth asks.

She thinks I'm afraid. But now that we're here . . . now that I know there isn't a body underneath this stone . . . and most important, that I never put him there . . . My fists tighten as I reread the epitaph. Like everything in their lives, it's polished and pretty—and a festering tumor of lies. For eight years, Manning—my boss, my mentor—for eight years, he knew I was eating shit, but he never once took it off my plate. He just served it. Day after day. With a perfect presidential grin.

My fists clench. Then I feel Lisbeth's hand on the small of my back. She doesn't say a word. She doesn't need to.

I take one last look around the empty cemetery. For eight years, I've been afraid. That's what death does when it haunts you. But right now, as I stand here in the soft rain and bleeding darkness, I'm ready to meet my ghost. And so is Lisbeth.

We take our separate places, just like we discussed. Lisbeth looks down at her watch. All we have to do is wait.

100

"Outta there! Now!" the guard yelled as he gripped the back of Rogo's shirt.

"Get off me!" Rogo shouted back, tugging free and running deeper into the poorly lit room. Two steps later, motion sensors kicked in, flooding the room with the buzz of fluorescent light. On Rogo's left was a single bed with a beat-up oak headboard, immaculately folded white sheets, and a Bible sitting on a fuzzy, olive-green wool blanket. Rounding out the cheap motel decor was a mismatched white Formica side table and a faux-wood dresser that held a pile of old magazines and a ten-year-old twelve-inch TV. To the right, oak double doors opened into what looked like a conference room, complete with a long mahogany table and half a dozen modern black leather chairs. None of it made sense. Why's a public bathroom connect to a separate bedr—?

From behind, Rogo felt a sharp tug on his shirt. He again tried to pull away, but this time, the guard was ready, yanking him backward toward the bathroom.

"Y'know how much trouble you just got me into?!" the guard shouted.

"I was just—the door was open—"

"Bull . . . *shit*," the guard insisted, whipping Rogo around and sending him smashing face-first into the room's half-closed door, which slammed into the tile wall as he shoved Rogo into the bathroom.

"Are you nuts?!" Rogo screamed, twisting to break free. The guard held tight, marching him back through the men's room and toward the door to the hallway. A full head taller than Rogo, he gripped Rogo's wrists and held them behind his back.

"I'm a lawyer, you stupid monkey. By the time I'm done suing, I'm gonna own this place and turn it into an Arby's!"

As Rogo stumbled from the bathroom into the salmon marble hall, the guard shoved him to the right, back toward the lobby's white frosted-glass doors.

"Dreidel, tell him who you are!" Rogo called out, his voice echoing up the hall.

"W-What'd you do?" Dreidel asked, already stepping backward, away from the check-in desk.

"Don't move!" the guard warned Dreidel.

Panicking, Dreidel spun around and took off for the sliding doors.

"No . . . *don't!*" the guard shouted.

Too late.

Before Dreidel even registered the words, his foot hit the sensor mat. But it wasn't until the doors started to slide open that Rogo noticed shadows on the other side of the frosted glass.

With a hushed swoosh, the doors yawned open, revealing a thin bald man with chiseled cheeks and a crusted-up bloody nose. Slumped over his shoulder was a fit blond man whose head was drooped down, unconscious. His shirt was soaked with what looked like blood.

"Guess who I found?" Boyle announced as he stepped inside. "All that's left is—" Spotting Dreidel, he froze. Without even thinking, he let go of O'Shea, who clattered to the ground, splayed out across the sensor mat.

"Boyle," Dreidel blurted.

"*Boyle?*" Rogo asked.

"Don't move!" the guard yelled at Boyle, pulling his gun and shoving Rogo aside.

"Put your gun away," Boyle ordered.

"I said *don't move*!" the guard repeated. Turning to his radio, he shouted, "Fellas, *I need some help down here*!"

Regaining his balance, Rogo couldn't take his eyes off Boyle. It was just like Wes said. The pointy features . . . the gaunt cheeks . . . but still so much the same.

"R-Ron, are you okay?" Dreidel asked, still in shock.

Before Boyle could answer, his brown and blue eyes locked with Rogo's. "You're Wes's roommate, aren't you?"

Rogo nodded, his head bobbing slowly. "Why?"

"Is Wes here too?" Boyle asked, his eyes swiftly scanning the lobby.

Confused and completely overwhelmed, Rogo followed Boyle's glance, searching the lobby, the elevators, the check-in desk, almost half expecting Wes to jump out. "I-I thought he was meeting *you*."

"Meeting *him*?" Dreidel asked.

"Meeting *me*?" Boyle replied.

"Yeah, no—*you*," Rogo shot back. "That note you sent . . . for Wes to meet you . . . seven p.m. Y'know, at the graveyard."

Staring at Rogo, Boyle shook his head, clearly clueless. "I don't know what you're talking about, son. Why would I invite Wes to meet me at a graveyard?"

101

It took him six seconds to flick the four pins and pop the rusted old padlock, and that was with an umbrella in his hand. He knew there was no alarm—that was why he'd come by earlier. Indeed, as the lock sprang open, he quietly tugged the rusted metal chain and unthreaded it from the iron front gates of the cemetery without even looking to see if anyone was coming. With a final push, he shoved the gates open just enough for the two of them to squeeze inside.

"This is where you—? Who would possibly meet you here?"

"Just trust me," the man said, tipping his umbrella back and glancing up at the ornate stone archway that framed the gates. Sandblasted into the stone, in classic block letters, was the one epitaph that had been on the cemetery's entrance since it was built two hundred years ago: *That which is so universal as death must be a blessing.* "Wait here," he said.

"Why? Where're you going?" his partner asked, shielded under a separate umbrella and carefully hanging back. "You're not leaving me in a graveyard."

"What I'm leaving you is *out of sight,*" the man insisted, knowing that Wes had to be here already. "If you want me to clean up this mess—which I assume you do—I suggest you stay here until I tell you it's clear." Leaving his partner behind, he eyed the floodlit flagpole that bathed the main entrance in light, then quickly cut left and plowed across a plot of graves. Ignoring the stone pathways, he strode toward the south end of the cemetery, using the trees for cover.

Behind him, he could hear his partner following, holding back far enough to stay hidden. But still following. Good. That's what he needed.

Heading toward Wes, he stopped behind a cracked limestone column on the corner of a crypt with a pointed cathedral roof. To his right, across from the crypt, a small gray 1928 headstone for someone named *J. G. Anwar* was engraved with a Masonic  and a five-pointed star. Hidden in the darkness, he couldn't help but grin at the irony. How perfect.

Still ignoring his partner creeping twenty feet behind him, he peered around the crypt as the tines of his umbrella scratched against the mushy wet moss that was slowly working its way up the limestone column. Diagonally across the graveyard, at the base of an oversize banyan tree, Wes's single thin shadow paced back and forth, hunched under his own crooked umbrella.

"That him?" his partner whispered, quickly catching up and staying hidden by the crypt.

"I told you t—"

But before he could get the words out, the shadow by the grave pivoted toward him, and he could immediately tell who it was. The ankles were the giveaway.

The man's fist tightened on his umbrella handle. His eyes narrowed, and as he leaned forward, the umbrella tines scratched deeper against the mossy crypt. With a burst, he raced forward. *That stupid motherf—*

"Wait . . . where're you—?"

"*Stay here!*" he seethed at his partner, this time meaning it. All this time . . . All he needed was for Wes to be alone. Half running, he cut diagonally across a row of graves. He knew full well they'd hear him coming.

Sure enough, the shadow turned his way, lifting its umbrella and revealing a glint of auburn hair.

"Boyle, that you?" Lisbeth called out. Getting no answer, she cocked her head, squinting into the darkness. "Boyle . . . ?"

Barely ten feet away, the man reached into his pocket and used his good hand—his left hand—to grab his gun.

"Boyle, just relax," Lisbeth said, backing up as the man approached, his face still hidden by his umbrella. For a split second, he ducked under a wayward branch that caught the umbrella and pulled it aside. The instant Lisbeth saw his jet-black hair, she knew she was in trouble. According to Wes, Boyle was bald. "Listen, whoever you are, I'm just here to—"

Ramming through a row of bushes and bursting from the darkness, he pulled his gun, pointed it at Lisbeth's chest, and stepped in so close, he forced her back against a tall clay-colored headstone with a carved Celtic cross on top.

"I don't care why the hell you're here," The Roman exploded, knocking her umbrella from her hand. As he moved closer, his skin glowed as gray as the headstones. "But if you don't tell me where Wes is, I swear to my God, you'll be begging me to blow your face off."

Frozen in shock, Lisbeth glanced over The Roman's shoulder and spotted his associate stepping between the bushes.

The reporter's mouth sagged open as the final member of The Four came forward.

102

Martin Kassal could read when he was three years old. He could write when he was four. And by five, he would sit next to his father at the breakfast table, eating his raisins and French toast while reading the headlines in the newspaper. But it wasn't until he was seven that he finished his first crossword puzzle. Designing it, that is.

Sixty-one years later, Kassal tapped at his moon-chin, skimming his way through a small beaten paperback called *Myths and Symbols in Indian Art and Civilization.* Even with his tinted reading glasses, he still needed to lean close to see, and as he pulled back slightly to flip to a new page, he was so engrossed in the symbols of the sacred rivers, he didn't even register his phone until the third ring.

"Is this Ptomaine1?" a female voice asked with an accusatory tone.

"I'm sorry—who's this?" Kassal asked.

"*Tattarrattat* is my screen name. Also known as Mary Beth Guard to my friends," she added with a huffy laugh at her use of the longest palindrome in the Oxford Dictionary, second edition. "I saw your posting on the message boards . . . about the glyphs you were trying to identify . . . the four dots and the cross with the slash . . ."

"Of course. No, of course. And thank you for getting back so quickly."

"Hey, you posted your phone number. I figured it was an emergency. By the way, I like your screen name. Ptomaine. From NPR, right? *Famous historic American. Put his first name inside his last name to get a word.* Ptomaine. Tom Paine. Cute," the woman said, almost as if she were looking for a date.

"Yeah, well . . . aheh," Kassal said, wiping his forehead. "So about those symbols . . ."

"The glyphs—sure—I knew them immediately. I mean, I stare at them every day."

"I'm not sure I follow."

"I work at Monticello. Y'know, Virginia? Home of our wisest and greatest President, Thomas Jefferson—and I don't just say that as an employee."

"These were symbols used by Jefferson?"

"Actually, by Meriwether Lewis."

"Of Lewis and Clark?"

"Oooh, you know your history, Ptomaine," she said sarcastically. "Of course. But what people don't realize is that the main reason Meriwether Lewis was picked to explore the Louisiana Purchase—in fact, maybe the *only* reason he was trusted with the task—was because a few years earlier, he did such an incredible job as Jefferson's personal secretary."

"Huh," Kassal said, already scribbling a note to use the info in an upcoming puzzle. "I didn't realize Lewis was Jefferson's aide."

"Very first aide to any President. Right after Jefferson

was elected in 1801, one of his first jobs as President was decreasing the number of officers in the army. The Revolutionary War was long over, the conflict with France was winding down, and they were trying to shrink the ranks."

"So the political consequences . . ."

"Very good. Were staggering," Mary Beth explained. "You have the political bug too, eh? Have you ever been to Monticello? I'd be happy to show you around."

That was always the problem with the message boards. The odds were good, but the goods were odd. "I'm sorry, I'm just in a bit of a rush—"

"Okay, I get it—you're married. My apologies. I'm just not good at reading these things—"

"Yes, so, aheh—you were saying about Jefferson . . . that the political consequences of firing officers . . ."

"Of course, of course. The politics were tricky to say the least, so to avoid putting his foot in it, Jefferson asked Lewis to secretly rank the loyalty of each army officer. That way, they'd know who to fire and who to keep on board."

"So those symbols," Kassal said, looking down at the , , , and , "those were . . ."

". . . Lewis and Jefferson's coded rating system to make sure none of the officers would ever find out what Jefferson's opinion of them actually was: whether they were trustworthy, apathetic, or a political enemy. So when the War Department supplied Jefferson with the list of all the brigadier generals and lieutenants, Lewis took his secret symbols and put . . ."

". . . a handwritten mark next to each name," Kassal said, studying the exact same symbols two hundred years later on the crossword. "To everyone else, it looked like the random blots of a fountain pen . . ."

". . . right again . . . but to Jefferson, it was a guide to which of his officers were honest Abes. In fact, if you ever do come h— We actually have the original list on display, plus the key that Jefferson used to decipher the codes. It's beautiful to see up close—all the flourishes in the old script."

"Certainly sounds *tempting*," Kassal said, making the kind of face that usually goes with biting a lemon. "But . . . Mary Beth, is it?"

"Mary Beth," she said proudly.

"If I could ask you one last favor, Mary Beth: Now that I have the signs—the four dots and the cross with the slash through it—can you just read me the cipher so I know what each of these stands for?"

103

You're telling me you didn't send him a note?" Rogo asked Boyle as he readjusted his shirt from where the guard had pulled it.

"Note? Why would I send him a note?" Boyle asked, sounding annoyed as his eyes flicked between Rogo and the guard.

"I said don't move!" the guard shouted, his gun pointed at Boyle.

"You yell at me again, you're gonna be picking that gun outta your teeth," Boyle growled back. "Now I want my contact man, or at the very least, a supervisor, and I mean *now.*"

"What the hell's going on?" Dreidel asked, his hands raised in the air, even though the gun wasn't anywhere near him. "You said we were meeting at my hotel. Since when is Wes meeting at a graveyard?"

"Dreidel, this isn't about you," Rogo insisted. Turning to the guard, he added, "Listen, I know you don't know me, but my friend's life is in—"

"So is yours," the guard said as he pointed his gun back at Rogo. Turning his attention to his walkie-talkie, he pushed a button and added, "Rags, we got a problem—I need you to find Loeb."

"So wait . . . when Wes called . . . you *both* lied to me?" Dreidel asked, still putting the pieces together. "Now you have Wes not trusting me too?"

"Don't you dare play victim," Rogo warned. "Lisbeth spoke to your old girlfriend—the one with the crossword puzzle—"

Boyle turned at the words. "You found the puzzle?"

"Boyle, keep your mouth shut!" the guard warned.

"How'd she find Violet?" Dreidel asked, his face paste white as he slowly lowered his hands.

Rogo shook his head at Dreidel but knew enough to stay with the guard, who knew enough to stay with Boyle. Rogo shifted his weight anxiously, barely able to stand still. Every second they wasted here meant that Wes— He cut himself off. *Don't think about it.*

"When'd you find the puzzle?" Boyle added, still trying to get Rogo's attention.

Rogo glanced his way, smelling the opening. Until he could get to Wes, he might as well get some answers. "Does that mean you're gonna tell me what's in it?" Rogo asked.

Boyle ignored the question like he didn't even hear it.

"No—don't do that," Rogo warned. "Don't just— If you can help Wes—if you know what's in the puzzle—"

"I don't know *anything*."

"That's not true. You went to Malaysia for a reason."

"Loeb, you there?" the guard said into his radio.

"C'mon, Boyle—I heard Wes talk about you. We know you tried to do the right thing."

Boyle watched the guard, who shook his head.

"Please," Rogo pleaded. "Wes is out there thinking he's meeting you."

Boyle still didn't react.

"Someone lured him out there," Rogo added. "If you know something and you keep it to yourself, you're just letting him take your place."

Still nothing.

"Forget it," Dreidel said. "He's not—"

"Where'd he find it?" Boyle blurted.

"Find what?" Rogo asked.

"The note. You said Wes found a note. For the graveyard."

"Boyle . . ." the guard warned.

"On his car," Rogo sputtered. "Outside Manning's house."

"Since when?" Dreidel asked. "You never said that. They never said that," he added to Boyle.

Boyle shook his head. "And Wes just assumed it was—? I thought you said you unlocked the crossword."

"We unlocked the names—all the initials," Rogo said. "Manning, Albright, Rosenman, Dreidel . . ."

"These . . . with Jefferson's old cryptogram," Boyle said as he pulled a worn, folded-up sheet from his pocket. Furiously unfolding it, he revealed the crossword and its hidden code, plus his own handwritten notes drawn in.

"That's the one," Rogo said. "But aside from telling us that the President trusted Dreidel, we couldn't—"

"Whoa, whoa, time out," Boyle interrupted. "What're you talking about?"

"Boyle, you know the rules on clearance!" the guard shouted.

"Will you stop worrying about clearance?" Boyle barked back. "Tell Loeb he can blame it on me." Turning back to Rogo, he added, "And what made you think Dreidel was trustworthy?"

"You're saying I'm not?" Dreidel challenged.

"The four dots," Rogo explained as he pointed at the ⁘. "Since the President and Dreidel are both ranked with four dots, we figured that was the inner circle of who he trusted."

Boyle went quiet again.

"That's *not* the inner circle?" Rogo asked.

"*This* is the inner circle," Boyle said, pointing to the O next to Manning's chief of staff, the man he used to do the puzzles with.

"So what're the four dots?" Rogo asked, still lost.

"Boyle, that's enough," the guard warned.

"This has nothing to do with clearance!" Boyle challenged.

"Those four dots are good," Dreidel insisted. "Manning trusted me with everything!"

"Just tell me what the four dots were," Rogo demanded in a low voice.

Boyle glared at Dreidel, then back to Rogo. "The four dots were Jefferson's shorthand for soldiers without any political creed—the opportunists who would give up anything for their own advancement. For us, it was meant to describe who Manning and Albright thought were leaking to the press. But when The Three found a copy and deciphered it, that's how they knew who to pick for their fourth."

"I'm not The Fourth!" Dreidel insisted.

"I never said you were," Boyle agreed.

Rogo glanced down at Manning's old crossword, studying the two names with the four dots.

∷ Manning

∷ Dreidel

None of it made sense. Wes swore that the handwriting—that all the rankings—were Manning's. But if that's true . . . "Why would the President give himself such a low ranking?"

"That's the point. He wouldn't," Boyle said.

"But on the crossword . . . you said the four dots—"

Boyle raked his bottom teeth across his top lip. "Rogo, forget your biases. The Three wanted someone close to every major decision, and most important, someone who could *affect* those decisions—that's why they first picked me instead of Dreidel."

"Boyle, that's *enough*! *I'm serious!*" the guard shouted. But Boyle didn't care. After eight years, there was nothing more they could take from him.

"You see it now, don't you?" Boyle asked as Rogo stared down at the page. "You've got the right name. Even the right reasoning—never underestimate what they'd do for four more years. But you got the wrong Manning."

Confused, Rogo shook his head, still locked on the puzzle. "What other Manning is th—?"

A burst of bitter cold seized Rogo's body, as if he'd been encased in ice.

Oh, shit.

104

I know her shadow anywhere. I know it better than my own. I've watched it nearly every day for almost a decade. That's my job: trailing three feet behind her, close enough to be there the moment she realizes she needs something, but far enough that I'm never in the photo. Back during White House days, even when she was swarmed by entourages of dignitaries and foreign press and our press and staff and crowds and Secret Service, I could still stand at the back of the horde, peer through the sea of legs, and find her silhouette at the center—and not just because she was the only one in high heels.

It's no different tonight. Indeed, as I squat down in the shadowy graveyard and hide behind one of the meatball shrubs, as I clamp my eyes into paper-thin slits and try to squint through the braided crisscrossing branches and the nearly fifty yards of headstone-lined darkness, I stare down the crooked stone path and instantly recognize the thick calves, sharp shoulders, and pointed silhouette of Dr. Lenore Manning.

An aching pain swells like a balloon inside my rib

cage. No . . . she—she'd never— I shake my head, and my ribs feel like they're about to splinter. How can—? Why would she do that?

At the end of the path, stopping at the tree, she tips her umbrella slightly, and in the light from the distant flagpole, I see anger and annoyance—and even fear—in her face. I can still picture her leaving the White House—the President squeezing her fingertips as they walked to Marine One. She said it herself: When it came to staying in power, they would've done almost anything.

She barks something at the man next to her, but I'm too far away to hear it. She's not happy to be here. Whatever she did, she's clearly regretting it. I pull back, blinking violently. But Boyle . . . If the First Lady's here, and the man next to her, with the bandages on his right hand (is that a gun?), if that's The Roman . . . A rush of blood throbs up from my chest, all the way to my face. I hold my cheek, which burns against my hand, just like when I was shot.

Closing my eyes, I see it all, another black-and-white newsreel. Back at the Mannings' house, she knew I was watching—when she was crying, showing me the letter from Boyle—and then the note on my car. That's why the handwriting matched. She . . . and The Roman . . . oh, God.

I stare back down the path at Lisbeth, who's in just as much shock as I am. It was her idea that we switch places before Boyle showed up: I'd be the lure to bring him in; she'd be the friendly reporter who'd give him more incentive to stay. But Boyle's not coming. He never was.

The Roman steps toward Lisbeth, who straightens up, trying to look strong. But the way she watches his gun . . .

and backs up, colliding with the tall clay-colored headstone . . . she knows she's in trouble. We all are. Unless I can get some—

Spinning back toward the fence just behind me in the graveyard, I pull my phone from my pocket and sprint as fast as I can. But before I press a single digit, I slam face-first into the chest of a tall, slim man facing the distant light. He has thin expressionless lips, buzzed black hair, and tiny chocolate eyes that seem almost too close togeth— My cheek burns like it's on fire. I know him immediately. From every one of my nightmares.

Nico snatches my phone from my hand, chucks it to the ground, and buries it in the mud with his heel. Reaching out and seizing me by the ear, he puts the barrel of his gun against my cheek, right against the scars he created all those years ago.

"You've been corrupted by the Beast, Wesley," he says calmly, almost kindly. "Now tell me where Ron Boyle is, or you will again face God's wrath."

105

You didn't know she was The Fourth?" Boyle asked.

"I said *that's enough*!" the guard shouted, gripping his gun with two hands. He had a build—and a face—like a rhino, but as he stepped closer, Rogo saw the guard's feet shuffle with hesitation. Eight years ago, Ron Boyle was an accountant. Today, he was clearly something more.

"Who'd you think it was? The President?" Boyle added.

"He really ranked me that low?" Dreidel asked.

"Why'd you think you were fired?" Boyle asked.

"I wasn't fired. I got promoted."

"Sure you were."

"I'm counting to three!" the guard warned Boyle.

"Listen, please," Rogo begged, turning to the guard. "You need to call the police . . . my friend's about to be killed!"

"You hear me, Boyle?" the guard said.

"Didn't you realize who you were up against?" Boyle shouted at Rogo. "You should've called the cops days ago."

"We did! We thought we did!" Rogo replied. "Micah and O'Shea said they were—"

One . . . !" the guard shouted.

"Or at least called in some favors," Boyle added, turning to Dreidel.

Turning away, Dreidel was silent.

Rogo raised an eyebrow.

"Two . . . !" the guard continued.

Boyle watched them both carefully, then rolled his tongue, more annoyed than ever. He'd worked in the White House for nearly four years. He'd seen that look before.

"You did, didn't you?" Boyle challenged.

"And you did anything different?" Dreidel shot back. "Spare me the judgment."

"Wait . . . *what?*" Rogo asked. "You went for help without telling us?"

Before Dreidel could answer, the guard pulled back the hammer on his gun.

Still locked on Dreidel, Boyle ignored the threat. "Who'd you run to first? NSA? FBI? Or'd you go to Bendis at—?"

"The Marshals," Dreidel blurted. "I went to the Marshals Service."

Hearing the words, the guard turned toward Dreidel. And took his eyes off Boyle.

That was the end.

Leaping forward, Boyle slammed the guard from behind, wrapping his left arm around the guard's neck and gripping his stringy brown hair with his right.

"Are you—? Get the hell off!" the guard screamed. He reached back to grab Boyle—which was exactly what Boyle was hoping for.

Seizing the momentum, Boyle threw himself backward, taking the guard with him as they plunged toward the floor. It wasn't until they were in mid-fall that the guard realized what he was in for.

"Boyle, don't—!"

Pivoting at the last second, Boyle spun to the left, twisting around so that instead of falling backward, the guard was falling forward. Straight toward the salmon-colored marble floor. At the last second, with a sharp tug of brown hair to steer the ship, Boyle turned the guard's head to the side, so his right ear was facing down.

"Get off me, you lunati—!"

Like a cupped hand slapping water, the guard's ear smacked the ground with a loud hollow pop, followed half a second later by a louder pop as his gun backfired from the impact. Boyle, Rogo, and Dreidel all jumped back as the bullet zinged from his gun, piercing the base of the welcome desk and lodging in the marble wall. Before they'd even realized what happened, the guard's head slumped unconscious against the floor, blood trickling out from his burst eardrum.

"What're you, *on drugs*!?" Dreidel demanded as Boyle climbed to his feet.

Without answering, Boyle motioned to the door. "We should go. He's got backup coming."

Still in shock, Rogo just stood there, his eyes hopping from Boyle and Dreidel to the limp figures of O'Shea and the guard. "I don't . . . I'm not—"

"Dreidel, you don't live down here, do you?" Boyle asked.

"No, but I can—"

"I need you to show me the fastest route to the cemetery," Boyle said as he turned to Rogo.

Rogo nodded, first slowly, then faster, his eyes eventually settling on Dreidel, who quickly approached to make peace.

"Rogo, before you say anything . . ."

"You made a deal, didn't you?" Rogo challenged.

"Just listen—"

"What'd the Marshals offer you?"

"Rogo . . ."

"What'd they offer you, you cancerous little parasite!?" Rogo shouted.

Dreidel shook his head as his jaw shifted off-center. "Full immunity."

"I *knew* it!" Rogo said.

"But it's not—"

"And what was the trade? That you'd spy on us—help them catch The Three—as a way to prove your own innocence?"

"I *am* innocent!" Dreidel snapped.

"So is Wes! So am *I*! But you don't see us running to the authorities, making private deals, and then tattling on our friends *without telling them*!"

"Rogo—both of you—we need to go," Boyle insisted.

Enraged but well aware of Wes's current situation, Rogo spun back to the main entrance, followed Boyle through the sliding doors, and burst into the parking lot with Dreidel right behind him.

As flicks of rain bombarded from above, Dreidel quickly caught up so they were running side by side, heading for Boyle's van. "I didn't tattle on you," Dreidel said.

"So you never told them what we were up to?" Rogo shot back.

"I didn't have a choice, Rogo. Once Wes came to my

hotel room that first day . . . I needed the help. They said if I kept my eyes on you and Wes—kept them informed on where you were—they'd do their best to keep us protected as well as keeping our names out of the papers."

"And that's not spying on your friends?"

"Listen, don't be mad at me for being the only one smart enough to realize that in an emergency, you're supposed to break the glass and call for help. C'mon, Rogo, think for a second. I can't afford—" As they approached the white van, he explained, "I'm running for State Senate."

Rushing around to the passenger side of the van, Rogo felt his fingers tighten into a fist. He almost bit through his own lip as he fought to contain his rage. "Let's go—open the door," he called out to Boyle.

"I swear, Rogo, I wasn't trying to hurt you," Dreidel insisted.

As the locks popped, Rogo ripped open the passenger door, reached inside, and hooked his arm around to pound down the lock on the van's sliding door.

"What're you doing?" Dreidel asked. "Unlock it!"

Rogo didn't say a word as he leaped into the front passenger seat, which was covered with thick piles of cluttered files, photocopies, old newspapers, and a brand-new digital camera. Leaning in Rogo's door, Dreidel stuck his arm behind the passenger seat and tried to open the lock himself. Without even hesitating, Rogo tugged the door shut. Dreidel tried to pull away. He wasn't fast enough. The sixty-pound door chomped down, sinking its metal teeth into his manicured fingertips.

"*Gahhhhh!* Open it! *Open it, motherf—!*"

"Ooh, sorry," Rogo offered as he nudged the door open, and Dreidel tucked his hand under his own armpit. "I swear, Dreidel, I wasn't trying to hurt you either."

Staring downward from his seat in the van, Rogo shot him the kind of glare that comes with an ice pick. "Don't pretend you're Wes's friend, dickface."

With a hiccup, the van roared to life, and Rogo slammed the door shut. Dreidel just stood there, pelted by the rain.

"C'mon, we going or not?" Rogo shouted at Boyle.

"Don't bark orders at me," Boyle countered. "I didn't shoot your friend in the face."

"But if you—"

"I didn't shoot him, Rogo. They shot *me*. And if I really wanted to see Wes hurt, I wouldn't be running to save him right now," Boyle said as he shifted the car into reverse and jammed his foot on the gas.

Staring dead ahead as they squealed out of the spot and away from Dreidel, Rogo rolled his jaw, forever looking for the fight. For once, he couldn't find it. "Just tell me one thing," he finally said as he motioned back toward the modern building with the thermal security cameras. "What the hell is that place, and why'd they have a bed and conference table connected to the bathroom?"

"Didn't you hear who Dreidel made his deal with?" Tapping the glass of his own window, Boyle motioned to the four-story building that was perfectly located two miles from the airport. "Dr. Eng's just the name that lets them hide in plain sight. Forget what it says on the front door. That's a WITSEC safehouse."

"Wit sack?"

"WITSEC. As in *Witness Security*."

"You mean like the Witness Protection Program?"

"Exactly like the Witness Protection Program—which, along with judicial protection, is run solely under the jurisdiction of . . ."

". . . the Marshals Service," Rogo said, shaking his head and finally realizing why Dreidel hadn't wanted to come.

"Starting to stink now, isn't it?" Boyle asked. "But that's how they work. They've got fake offices in every city in America. The only difference here is, it's Witness Protection 2.0. Instead of just putting you in hiding, they make everyone think you're dea—"

Overhead, a 747 shredded the night sky, buzzing down toward the airport and drowning out Boyle.

Rogo stared at the frosted-glass building as the adrenaline from fighting with Dreidel drained away and the dread of his new reality seeped into his system. "So when the guard called on his radio, he . . ."

". . . wasn't just calling his buddies," Boyle agreed as they tore past the front of the building. "He was calling the United States Marshals Service. And unless we get out of here, we're gonna get a personal introduction."

106

Lisbeth's elbow scraped against the jagged granite as she backed into the clay-colored headstone with the Celtic cross on top.

"Tell me where Wes is hiding," The Roman demanded, his gun so close to her head, she saw her own distorted reflection in the tip of the barrel.

When she didn't answer, he asked again, but Lisbeth barely heard the words. All her attention was still focused just over The Roman's shoulder, where the First Lady read Lisbeth's shock for herself.

Soaked by the falling rain, Lisbeth tried to back up even further, but the headstone held her in place.

"Wes?" the First Lady hissed like an angry cat at The Roman. "You brought me to see Wes?"

"I told you to stay back, ma'am," The Roman said, never taking his glance or his gun off Lisbeth.

"And I told you to never contact me again—but that didn't stop you from showing up at my house—entering *my home*! Do you have any idea what kind of risk that—?" She cut herself off as the consequences sank in. "Good God! He's—Wes is here right now?" She anxiously looked up the stone path, scanning nearby headstones. "You brought him here t— Is that why you had me give him that note?"

The Roman stared at Lisbeth, then glared back at the First Lady. "Don't play for the reporter, Lenore."

"*Playing?* That's not— *Why didn't you tell me!?*" the First Lady exploded, her umbrella jerking wildly with each syllable.

The Roman laughed softly, his sandpaper voice grating. "No different than a decade ago, is it? You're telling me you really wanted to know?"

The First Lady went silent as the rain tapped on her umbrella. Across from her, Lisbeth stood unprotected, the drizzle slowly soaking her red hair, which flattened and dangled across her face like wet yarn.

"Please tell me they blackmailed you," Lisbeth pleaded, her voice cracking and her eyebrows knotting.

The First Lady ignored the question, still searching the lot for Wes. Just in front of her, The Roman flashed the smallest of grins.

"And that's it? You just did it?" Lisbeth asked.

"I didn't do anything," Dr. Manning insisted.

"But you knew. He just said it: Even if you ignored it, you—"

"I didn't know anything!" she screamed.

"That's because you didn't want to!" Lisbeth shot back.

The First Lady did her best to stay calm.

"They came to me through the Service, saying they could help on security issues—that our senior staff was holding us back by not paying for *Blackbird* and other good tips. Back then, I . . . we needed to show we were strong. *I thought I was helping!*"

"And so you just did whatever they said?"

"Are you listening? They were from the Service! *From our side!*" she insisted, her voice booming. "I figured they knew best—d'you understand? I never thought they'd— *I was helping!*"

"Until what? Until Boyle suddenly turned up dead and you realized you'd been had?" Lisbeth asked. No question, that could certainly be the case. But it didn't explain why the First Lady had continued to stay silent in the days that followed—or how, when she was first approached by The Roman—when the White House was swarming with an internal investigation of Boyle and the group they started calling The Three—how she could've been so naive and not even questioned what The Roman was selling. It's not like national security was her pet issue. In fact, that close to reelection—especially when they were down in the polls—the only issue *any* First Lady should've been focused on was bringing home a second ter—

"You wanted to win," Lisbeth blurted.

"Roman, I'm leaving now," the First Lady said, turning away, her pinkie flicking the strap of her umbrella handle.

"That's why you never reported him, isn't it? Maybe you wanted to believe it; maybe you just turned the blind eye. But as long as he could help you on security issues—if he could give you the bump in the polls, just this one time—"

"Did you hear me?" she shouted at The Roman, almost crying.

"They learned their lesson with Boyle, didn't they? They approached you with a softer touch. Then suddenly, Boyle got shot . . ."

"Roman, tell her I didn't know! I never knew you'd do that!"

"And now they had it all," Lisbeth added. "A sitting President behind in the polls . . . the guaranteed bump from some hired whackjob's assassination attempt. If it all went right and the President hadn't been pulled back by the crowd, The Three would say good-bye to Boyle, while putting you, their unknowing new member with far more inside influence than Boyle, in the perfect spot to pass along your *helpful* new recommendations to your husba—"

The Roman's good hand jabbed forward in a blur, pounding the butt of his gun into Lisbeth's face. Blood burst from her top lip, and her head whipped back, cracking against the headstone. Gasping, she swallowed something tiny and jagged. A lick with her tongue quickly told her it was the tooth next to her left front. *"Hkkkkk!"* As it scraped down her throat, she hunched forward like she was about to throw up, then dry-heaved twice as a mouthful of blood drooled down to her shoes and the soaking grass.

Two miles away, the faint wail of an approaching train moaned.

Staring at the ground as a dry heave flushed all the blood to her face, Lisbeth didn't even hear the whistle. Indeed, as the rain dripped like a leaky faucet from her hair, her chin, her nose, the only thing Lisbeth registered was the squish of The Roman's shoes as he stepped forward.

"She's gonna need an ambulance, Wes," he called out calmly into the darkness. Reaching down to the back of Lisbeth's head, he grabbed a fistful of her soaking hair, holding her so she was bowed down in front of him.

"Get the hell off me!" Lisbeth shouted.

"Keep hiding, Wes!" The Roman announced, clenching her hair even tighter and taking a half-step back. Almost like he was winding up.

The last thing Lisbeth saw was the flecks of mud on the tips of The Roman's black calfskin shoes. And the ball of his knee as he rammed it toward her face.

107

He smells like hospital antiseptic and hamburger meat gone bad. But as Nico digs the barrel of his gun into my scars, it's not the smell that churns my stomach. I swallow so hard, it feels like there's a brick in my throat.

"How could you help him? How *could* you?" he demands. "Do you even know what you've unleashed?" His eyes jackrabbit side to side to side to side. He's been off his medication for two days.

"Answer me!" he seethes, forcing me back with a shove of his gun. He doesn't even blink as the rain hits his face.

Stumbling off balance, I crash backward into the shrub. A wayward branch stabs me in the spine, but I barely feel it. Just seeing Nico, hearing him—I'm back at the speedway. The crowd roaring. Manning smiling. A hundred thousand fans stand up, pointing and waving. At us. At me. And the bumblebee. *Pop, pop, pop.* The ambulance doors close on Boyle.

"—ven listening to me?" Nico demands as I blink back to reality. His gun grinds against my cheek, but I still don't feel it. I don't feel anything. I haven't for years.

"Where's Boyle?" he says.

"I don't kn—"

His left hand springs out like a cobra, sinking its fangs into the center of my shirt and tugging me toward him. He pivots to his left, tripping me, and I fall back again, down into a puddle, sending water everywhere. Nico's right on me, straddling my chest, pinning my biceps with his knees, and never moving his gun from my scarred cheek.

"I found your letter," Nico growls as the Chinese menu peeks out from the inside pocket of his army jacket. *"Where's Boyle!?"*

I want to tell him it's fake . . . that The Roman . . . and the First Lady . . . that I don't want to die. But after eight years of imagining this moment, imagining every minute of finally confronting Nico—what I'd say, where I'd stand, how I'd cross my arms against my chest, even what I'd do if he tried to lash out and throw a punch . . . how I'd duck down at the last instant, how I'd be ready this time, and he'd miss me, and then, before he ever saw it coming, how I'd spin back and clench his throat in my hands, squeezing so hard, hearing him gasp, and still clutching tighter, my fingers digging into his windpipe as we tumbled to the ground and he gasped for mercy—the only words that leave my lips are the ones that have been there since the day he shredded my face. The one question that the doctors, the shrinks, the President, my family, my friends, my parents, and I have never been able to answer:

"Nico," I blurt. "Why did you do this to me?"

He cocks his head as if he understands perfectly. Then his brow contracts. He hasn't heard a word I've said.

"I know you've been in contact with him," he says. "That's why God steered the bullet your way. The ricochet. That's why you got broken."

"That's not true!" I shout as a brand-new rage swells within me.

"It is true! The Book of Fate is written! Everything for a reason!" he insists in a puff of hot breath that smells like beef jerky. "You sided with the Beast! That bullet in your face—your fate is written—that's God's will!"

"Nico, they lied!"

"Did you not speak to him? *Did you!?* See . . . it's true!" he shouts, reading my expression and digging the gun into my cheek. "God gave you your chance at redemption, and you spit at it! That's why He brought me here—to finish His job! To see your blood!" he insists, his finger tightening around the trigger. I try to fight, but he's too strong. All I see is the outline of Nico above me, the light behind him, his head shielding me from the rain, the rosary around his neck swaying like a hypnotist's pocket watch. He pulls the hammer back on his gun. "This is meant to hurt, Wesley." He tugs me toward him.

I clamp my eyes shut at the sudden beam of light, but all I hear is—

"Oh, Lord! Y-You have it," Nico whispers as his hand starts to tremble. I see his eyes glitter in the dark.

"What're you—? *What?*" I ask, confused.

"I couldn't see in the photo . . . but this close," he stutters, staring at my face. "It's so clear," he insists. "Your scars! The way they intersect . . . jagged in your flesh . . . one cutting through the other. The papers said it was like railroad tracks, but it's really a perfect—a perfect—a perfect—a perfect . . . *cross*," he blurts. "Of course! Mother of God, how could I not—? You weren't meant to die on that day, Wesley—you were meant to be born on it!" Craning his head back and staring up at the sky, he adds, "You transformed him, didn't You? By my actions . . . through Your will. That was his role—*the crossbearer*," he insists, his head still up as he mumbles a brief prayer.

In the sudden silence, I faintly hear the First Lady's voice in the distance. Lisbeth shouts something back. They're too far for me to make it out, but with his heightened hearing, Nico should—

His eyes pop wide as if he's heard his own name. Slowly, he lowers his chin, following the—

"That's not true," he whispers, holding his stomach like someone put a corkscrew in his gut. I can't hear what Lisbeth's saying, but as I look up at Nico, it's not hard to translate. "No . . . The Three never—"

Nico's knees still pin my arms, but his weight—all the pressure—is gone, and his body starts shuddering with his own personal earthquake. Behind us and miles to the left, a train engine's faint howl pierces the air.

Nico's chin quivers; his eyes swell with tears. Reaching up to the sides of his head, he clutches the tops of his ears, tilts his head down, and pulls tight, as if he's trying to rip them from his skull. "Please, God," he begs. "Tell me they're lying . . ."

"She's gonna need an ambulance, Wes," The Roman bellows in the distance.

Lisbeth.

Jerking wildly, I struggle to sit up. Nico doesn't bother to fight. Sliding from my chest, he crumbles like a rag doll onto the wet grass and curls in full fetal position. Sixty to zero in less than ten seconds.

"Don't say that, God," he sobs and pleads, his hands tugging at his ears. "Please . . . don't . . . don't turn Your back on me! Help me heed the Book! *Please!*"

"Keep hiding, Wes!" The Roman shouts, even louder than before.

Scrambling to my feet, I peer through the shrub's branches, down the stone-paved, tree-lined path, straining to see shapes in the faint light. Down at the end, at the base of the ancient banyan tree, I can just make out two figures as The Roman rams his knee into Lisbeth's face and she lurches backward. Just behind them, the First Lady has her back turned. Seeing her, I should be boiling, raging. But as I study the back of her crooked neck . . . all I feel now is a bitter empty chill. I need to get to Lis—

"I know you're there!" The Roman taunts. For the first time, it pisses me off.

Lisbeth's still—

"She's hurting, Wes!" The Roman adds. *"Ask her!"*

I tense to run, but there's a tug on my slacks. And a familiar click.

Behind me, Nico rises from the mud—climbing to one knee, then the other—his tall frame unfolding like an Erector set. His short black hair is soaked and matted against his head, while his gun is pointed at my chest.

"Nico, let go of me."

"You're my crossbearer, Wesley," he says as he wipes tears from his eyes. "God selected you. For me."

"She's bleeding pretty bad, Wes!" The Roman shouts.

Lisbeth yells something too, but I'm so focused on Nico, I can't hear it.

"Nico, listen to me—I know you heard them . . ."

"The crossbearer carries the weight!" Smiling sweetly,

he points his gun at his own head. "Will you catch my body when I fall?"

"Nico, don't—"

"Will you catch me when I fall, fall, fall from grace . . . the crossbearer to bear witness . . . ?" He lowers his gun, then raises it up again, pressing it against his temple. I hear Lisbeth moaning.

"God sent you to save her too, didn't He?" He stares at me, transfixed, the gun still at his head. "Save me as well, my angel."

Behind us, the train whistle howls, so close it's almost deafening. Nico presses his lips together, trying to look like he's not cringing. But I can see his jaw tightening. For me, it's noisy. For him, it's overwhelming. Wild-eyed, he points the gun back at me to keep me from running.

I don't care. "I'm innocent," I tell him as I step toward him. He knows it's a warning.

"Nobody's innocent, Dad."

Dad?

"Lord have mercy on my son," he continues, his gun moving from my chest, to my head, back to my chest. He's crying again. He's in agony. "You understand, Dad, right?" he begs. "I had to do it. They told me . . . *Mom said to follow the Book!* Please tell me you understand!"

"Y-Yes," I say as I put a hand on his shoulder. "Of course, I understand. Son."

Nico laughs out loud, the tears still streaming down his cheeks. "Thank you," he says, barely able to contain himself as he clutches his rosary. "I knew . . . I knew you'd be my angel."

Turning left, I glance through an opening in the shrub. The Roman's aiming his gun down at Lisbeth.

"Nico, *move*!" I say as I shove my way past him. All I need to do is—

Blam!

I jump back as The Roman's gun explodes. Down the path, a tiny supernova of light breaks the darkness like a burst firefly, then disappears.

I run as fast as I can.

Lisbeth's already screaming.

108

You don't believe me, do you?" Boyle asked Rogo as the white van skidded out of the parking lot and swerved onto Griffin Road.

"Does it matter what I think?" Rogo replied, gripping the console between their bucket seats and staring out the front window. "C'mon, make this light."

The van blew through the 25th Avenue intersection as Rogo checked his side mirror to see if anyone was following. So far, all clear.

"You still need to hear it, Rogo. If something happens t— Someone needs to know what they did."

"And you couldn't just write a letter to the editor like everyone else?" When Boyle didn't respond, Rogo shook his head and again glanced in the side mirror. The Marshals' white building was barely a dot in the horizon. "So all this time, you were in Witness Protection?"

"I told you, version 2.0. *Witness Fortification*," Boyle clarified. "Not that they'd ever acknowledge its existence. But once I told Manning what was happening—usually, it takes the President one phone call to make something happen. It took Manning three separate calls to get me inside."

"And they do this a lot? I mean, c'mon, making families think their loved ones are dead?"

"How do you think the government prosecutes their terrorism cases against these suicidal maniacs? You think some of those witnesses would've talked if the Justice Department couldn't absolutely guarantee their safety? There are animals in the world, Rogo. If The Three, The Four, whatever they call themselves—if they thought I was alive and hiding, they'd slit my wife and kids' throats, then go out for a beer."

"But to lie to people like that . . ."

"I didn't choose this life. The Three chose me. And once that happened, once they tossed me aside for the First Lady, this was the only way to keep my wife safe, and my kid—both kids—alive."

"You still could've—"

"Could've what? Taken the family into hiding with me? Put everyone at risk and hoped for the best? The only absolutely unassailable hiding spot is the one where no one knows you're hiding. Besides, The Three have single-handedly compromised our top law enforcement agencies, picked apart our databases for their private use, and collected thousands of dollars in Title 50 money for confidential tips about terror attacks—all without us ever knowing who the hell they were."

"Until two days ago when they panicked and went after Wes."

"They didn't panic," Boyle said as he slowly pressed the brakes. Two blocks in front of them, the three lanes of Griffin Road narrowed into one. Something was definitely blocking the road. "Is that construction?" Boyle asked, craning his neck and squinting through the dark.

"I think it's an accident."

"You sure?"

"Isn't that an ambulance?

Boyle nodded as the cars came into view—an ambulance, a tow truck, and a silver car turned sideways from the collision. Boyle glanced to his left, already eyeing the side streets.

"Something wrong?" Rogo asked.

"Just being cautious." Refusing to lose his thought, he added, "Anyhow, The Three didn't panic. They got greedy and fat—thanks mostly to The Roman."

"So what the First Lady told Wes was true," Rogo said. "That they started with all these small tips—VX gas in Syria, training camps in Sudan—and then used that to build credibility until they could find the monster threats and ask for the multimillion-dollar let's-all-retire paydays."

"No, no, no. Don't you see?" Boyle asked, quickly pulling out of the single-file line of traffic and rechecking what was causing the accident. But all was normal. Ambulance. Tow truck. Wrecked silver car. Flipping open the console between them, Boyle checked on a small box the size of a videotape, then closed it just as fast. He tried to hide it with his elbow, but Rogo saw the word *Hornady* in bright red letters on the box's side. Growing up in Alabama, he knew the logo from his dad's hunting trips. Hornady bullets. "Once they established The Roman as a solid informant, they didn't even need the big threat. Why do you think people are so worried about agencies working together? The Roman would bring his info into the Service, then Micah and O'Shea would serve it again from their outposts in the FBI and CIA. Now, each one's confirmed the other. That's how informants get verified: You check it with someone else. And once all three agencies agree, well, fiction becomes fact. It's like that bombing threat on the New York City subways a few years back—not a single grain of truth behind it, but the informant still got paid. Meanwhile, is this the only way to get to I-95?"

Rogo nodded and cocked an eyebrow. "I don't get it—they made it all up?"

"Not in the beginning. But once they built that reputation for The Roman, they could sprinkle bad tips in with the good and earn a little more cash. And with the big stuff—you think six-million-dollar tips just jump in your lap?"

"But to make something that big up—"

"It's like making the Statue of Liberty disappear—it's the kind of magic trick you pull off once, then disappear until the dust settles. So when their first attempt . . ."

"Blackbird."

". . . when *Blackbird* was set up, they had it perfect: hold a fake NSA computer hostage and reel in the cash. It was big enough to get serious money, but unlike promising that a building was about to blow up, there was no penalty or suspicion if the White House decided not to pay. Then when *Blackbird* failed and we *didn't* pay, they were smart enough to realize they needed an inside track at the White House just to make sure the next request went through."

"That's when they approached and threatened you."

"When they approached and threatened me, *and* when they tried the softer sell on someone with even more power than that."

"But to assume that you or the First Lady would go for it—much less be able to pull six-million-dollar strings over and over . . ."

"Y'ever been fishing, Rogo? Sometimes, you're better off throwing in a few lines with different bait and seeing who nibbles. That's the only reason they approached both of us. And though she'll forever deny it—in fact, she probably doesn't even think she did anything wrong anymore—but the First Lady's the one who swam toward the hook," Boyle explained. "And as for making their *next* six million happen, or the ten million after that, look at any White House in history. The most powerful people in the room aren't the ones with the big titles. They're the ones with the President's ear. I've had that ear since I was twenty-three years old. The only one who's had it longer is the person he's married to. Whatever they came in next with—if *she* had a hand in it and thought it'd help them on security issues—believe me, it'd have gotten through."

"I don't get it, though. Once *Blackbird* got nuked, didn't they at least need *some* kinda results before they could make another big request like that?"

"Whattya think I was?" Boyle asked.

Rogo turned to his left but didn't say a word.

"Rogo, for the snake-oil scam to succeed, people only need to see the cure work once. That's what The Three gave them—courtesy of two bullets in my chest."

Sitting up in his seat, Rogo continued to study Boyle, who was staring at the open back doors of the ambulance that was less than a car's length away.

"Twenty minutes before the shooting, the Secret Service Web site was sent a tip about a man named Nico Hadrian who was planning to assassinate President Manning when he stepped out of his limo at Daytona International Speedway. It was signed *The Roman*. From that moment on, anything he would've given them—especially when it was corroborated by the FBI and CIA—well, you know the paranoid world we live in. Forget drugs and arms sales. Information is the opiate of the military masses. And terrorist information about attacks on our own soil? That's how you print your own money," Boyle said. "Even better, by taking their stealthier approach with the First Lady, they wouldn't've even had to split the cash four ways."

As they pulled past the ambulance, they both looked to their left and peered into its open back doors. But before they could even see that there wasn't a victim, a gurney, or a single medical supply inside, there was a metal thud against the back door. Then one from above. On both sides of the van, a half dozen plainclothes U.S. marshals swarmed from the tow truck and silver car, fanning out and pointing their guns against the side windows and front windshield. Outside Boyle's door, a marshal with bushy caterpillar eyebrows tapped the barrel of his gun against the glass.

"Nice to see you again, Boyle. Now get the fuck out of that van."

109

She's hurting, Wes!" The Roman called out to the empty darkness as the rain ticked against his umbrella. "Ask her!"

"H-He's not stupid," Lisbeth whispered, down on her rear in the wet grass. With her back against the Celtic headstone for support, she pressed both hands against her eye, where The Roman had rammed his knee into her face. She could already feel it swelling shut.

Back by the tree, the First Lady stared coldly at The Roman. "Why did you bring me here?" she demanded.

"Lenore, this isn't—"

"You said it was an emergency, but to bring me to Wes!"

"Lenore!"

The First Lady studied The Roman, her expression unchanging. "You were planning to shoot me, weren't you?" she asked.

Lisbeth looked up at the question.

Turning to his right, The Roman squinted up the crooked stone path and, as his Service training kicked in, visually divided the graveyard into smaller, more manageable sections. A grid search, they called it. "Be smart, Lenore. If I wanted to kill you, I would've shot you in the car."

"Unless he wanted to make it look like—*puhhh,*" Lisbeth said, violently spitting flecks of saliva at the ground as the train whistle screamed of its impending arrival, ". . . like Wes killed you, and he killed Wes. Th-Then he's the hero and there's no one left to point fingers."

Shaking his head, The Roman stayed glued to the meatball shrubs. "*She's bleeding pretty bad, Wes!*"

The First Lady turned toward Boyle's grave, then back to The Roman, her pinkie flicking harder than ever at the strap of her umbrella as she said in a poisonous, low voice, "She's right, isn't she?"

"She's just trying to rile you, Lenore."

"No, she's— *You swore no one would ever be hurt!*" the First Lady exploded. She spun back toward the front entrance of the cemetery.

There was a metallic click.

"Lenore," The Roman warned as he raised his gun, "if you take one more step, I think we're going to have a serious problem."

She froze.

Turning back toward Lisbeth, The Roman took a deep breath through his nose. It was supposed to be cleaner than this. But if Wes insisted on hiding . . . Carefully aiming his gun, he announced to Lisbeth, "I need you to put your hand up, please."

"What're you talking about?" she asked, still sitting on the ground.

"*Put your damn hand out,*" The Roman growled. "Palm facing me," he added, holding up his bandaged right palm to Lisbeth.

Even under the shadows of the umbrella, it was impossible to miss the tight white bandage with the perfectly round, blood-red circle at the center of it. Lisbeth knew what he was planning. Once her body was found with stigmata—like a signature—all the blame would shift to—

Lisbeth stopped seeing the rain. Her whole body started to shake.

"Put your hand up, Lisbeth—or I swear to God I'll put it in your brain."

Curling both arms toward her chest, she looked over at the First Lady, who again started to walk away.

"Lenore," The Roman warned without turning. The First Lady stopped.

Lisbeth felt the wet ground soaking her rear end. Her hands still hadn't moved.

"Fine," The Roman said, aiming at Lisbeth's head as he cocked the hammer. "Have it in your brai—"

Lisbeth raised her left hand in the air. The Roman squeezed the trigger. And the gun roared with a thunderclap that left a ringing silence in its wake.

A spurt of blood erupted from the back of Lisbeth's hand, just below her knuckles. Before she even felt the pain and screamed, blood was running down her wrist. Already in shock, she kept staring at the dime-sized burned circle in her palm as if it weren't her own. When she tried making a fist, the pain set in. Her hand went blurry, like it was fading away. She was about to pass out.

Without a word, The Roman aimed his gun at Lisbeth's now-bobbing head.

"Don't!" a familiar voice yelled from the back of the cemetery.

The Roman and the First Lady turned to the right, tracing the voice up the tree-lined path.

"Don't touch her!" Wes shouted, his body a thin silhouette as he rushed out from the shrub. "I'm right here."

Just like The Roman wanted.

110

Aided by the glow from the floodlit flagpole in the distance, I study the outline of The Roman from the top of the stone path. He stares right back at me, his gun still pointed at Lisbeth.

"That's the right choice, Wes," he calls out from the base of the tree. His voice is warm, like we're at a dinner party.

"Lisbeth, can you hear me?" I shout.

She's fifty yards away and still on the ground. Among the shadows and the overhang of the banyan tree, she's nothing but a small black blob between two graves.

"She's fine," The Roman insists. "Though if you don't come help her, I think she might pass out."

He's trying to get me closer, and with Lisbeth bleeding on the ground, I don't have a choice.

"I need to check she's okay first," I say as I head toward the path. He knows I'm trying to stall. "Step back and I'll come forward."

"Go fuck yourself, Wes." Turning back to Lisbeth, he raises his gun.

"No! Wait—I'm coming!" Rushing down the stone path, I put my hands in the air to let him know I'm done.

He lowers his gun slightly, but his finger doesn't leave the trigger.

If I were smart, I'd continue to watch him, but as I stumble down the path between the rows of headstones, I turn toward the First Lady. Her wide eyes are pleading, her whole body is in a begging position. This time, her tears aren't fake. But unlike before, she's looking in the wrong place for help.

"Don't take it so personally," The Roman tells me, following my gaze.

Moving toward Lisbeth, watching my footing, I keep looking at the silhouette of Lenore Manning. For eight years, she's known I blamed myself for putting Boyle in that limo. For eight years, she's looked into what's left of my face and pretended I was part of her family. On my birthday three years ago, when they were teasing me that I should go on more dates, she even kissed me on my cheek—*directly on the scars*—just to prove I shouldn't be so self-conscious. I couldn't feel her lips because they were touching my dead spot. But I felt it all. Leaving the office, I cried the whole way home, amazed at what a beautiful and thoughtful gesture it was.

Right now, walking past a shadowed stone crypt with red and blue stained-glass doors, I again well up with tears. Not from sadness. Or fear. My eyes squint, squeezing each drop to my cheeks. These tears sting from rage.

Down on my left, Lenore Manning's lips pucker like she's starting to whistle. She's about to say my name.

I glare back, telling her not to bother.

Even in this dim cemetery, she's fluent in reading her staff. And that's all I've ever been. Not family. Not friend. Not even a wounded puppy that you take in to clear your conscience from the other crap you do in your life. Hard as it is to admit, I've never been anything more than staff.

I'm tempted to yell, curse, scream at what she did to me. But there's no need. The closer I get, the more clearly she can see it for herself. It's carved deep into my face.

For a second, her eyebrows tilt. Then she takes a tiny step back and lowers her umbrella so I can't see her face. I'll take it as a victory. Lenore Manning has faced just about everything. But at this moment, she can't face me.

Shaking my head, I turn back to The Roman, who's now forty feet away.

"Keep coming," he says.

I stop. Diagonally to my right, between two stubby headstones, Lisbeth is down on her knees, cradling her bloody hand toward her chest. In the eerie bluish light, I can see that her hair is soaked, her left eye puffy and already swollen. I'm nearly there.

"I'm sorry," she stutters as if it's her fault.

"I said *keep coming*," The Roman insists.

"Don't!" Lisbeth interrupts. "He's gonna kill you."

The Roman doesn't argue.

"Promise me you'll let her leave," I say.

"Of course," he sings.

"Wes!" Lisbeth says, her breathing growing heavy. It's all she can do to stay conscious.

There are no sirens in the distance, no one riding to the rescue. From here on in, the only way Lisbeth's getting out of here is if I step forward and try to make the trade.

The train gets louder in the distancc. There's a whisper over my shoulder. I turn back to follow the sound, but the only thing there is my own reflection in the red and blue stained-glass doors of the crypt. Inside, behind the glass, I swear something moves.

"You're hearing ghosts now?" The Roman teases.

As the whispers get louder, I continue toward him on the path. I've got barely twenty feet to go. The rain lightens overhead as I reach the cover of the tree. Its tendrils dangle from above like a puppeteer's fingers. I'm so close, I can see Lisbeth's body shaking . . . and the First Lady's pinkie flicking her umbrella strap . . . and the hammer on The Roman's gun as he cocks it back with his thumb.

"Perfect," he says with a wry grin. Before I can even react, he turns to the side and raises his gun. Directly at Lisbeth's heart.

111

"N*o—don't!*" I shout, already running.

There's a high-pitched hiss. But not from his gun. From behind me.

Before I even realize what's happening, a burst of blood spurts from The Roman's right hand, through the back of his palm, just below his knuckles. He's been shot. At the impact, The Roman's own gun goes off.

Out of the corner of my eye, I see Lisbeth slapping her shoulder like she's swatting a mosquito. I can make out something dark—blood—leaking out between her fingers, like water seeping from a cracked well. She pulls her hand away from her shoulder and holds it up in front of her face. When she sees the blood, her face goes white, and her eyes roll back in her head. She's already unconscious.

"Shit, shit, *shit*!" The Roman yells, bent over, jerking wildly and holding his shattered right hand to his chest. On his right, the First Lady takes off, running back toward the main entrance and disappearing into the darkness. The Roman's in too much pain to stop her. On the back of his hand, the hole's no bigger than a penny. But the signature with the stigmata is unmistakable.

"You lied to me! He's an angel!" Nico howls from the back of the graveyard, up by the shrubs. He plows toward us through the darkness, his gun straight out, ready for the kill shot. He's in silhouette. I can't see his face. But his arm is steady as ever.

"Y-You're going to Hell," The Roman whispers as he anxiously throws his own personal Hail Mary. "Like Judas, Nico. You're Judas now."

The way Nico flinches, it's clear he hears it. It still doesn't slow him down. "God's laws last longer than those who break them!" he insists as he gathers his strength. "*Your fate is rewritten!*" Up the path, he grips his rosary with one hand and aims the gun with the other.

"Nico, think of your mother!" The Roman begs.

Nico nods as the tears again stream down his face. "I am," he growls, but as he takes aim, there's a loud whoosh from behind the back fence of the cemetery. Up on the train tracks, a silver passenger train bursts into view, moving so fast it almost appears from nowhere. The clanking is deafening. My ears pop from the sudden vacuum in the air. For Nico, it's fifty times worse.

He still fights it, gritting his teeth as he squeezes the trigger. But the noise is already too much. His arm jerks for half a second, the shot hisses from his gun, and as the bullet zings past The Roman's shoulder and shatters a hunk of bark from the nearby tree, Nico Hadrian actually misses.

A dark grin returns to The Roman's face as the train continues to whip by. Barely able to hold his gun with his right hand, he tosses aside the umbrella and switches the gun to his bandaged left. The way his right fist is shaking, he's clearly in pain. He doesn't care. His shoulders straighten. His knees steady. As he raises his gun and takes aim, I'm already running at him. So is Nico, who's at least thirty feet behind me.

The Roman has time for just one shot. There's no question who's more dangerous.

Bam!

As the shot explodes from The Roman's gun, it's drowned out by the still-passing train. Behind me, just over my right shoulder, there's a deep guttural grunt as Nico takes it in the chest. He still keeps running toward us. He doesn't get far. Within two steps, his legs lock and his too-close-together eyes widen into full circles. Tumbling forward and off balance, his body hurtles face-first toward the ground. In mid-fall, the rosary flies from his hand. He's not getting up.

As Nico crashes, The Roman turns his gun toward me. I'm already moving too fast. Lost in momentum, I collide with The Roman like he's a tackling dummy, my arms wrapping around his shoulders as I ram him at full speed. The impact sends him staggering backward to his left. To my own surprise, it feels like there's a metal plate against his chest. He learned it from Boyle. Bulletproof vest. The good news is, he's already weakened from being shot in the hand. We trip over his umbrella in the dirt. I hold tight to his chest, riding him like a lumberjack on a falling tree.

As we crash to the ground, his gun flies from his hand across the wet grass. His back slams into a zigzagging tree root bursting up from the earth, while his head smacks backward into a jagged rock. The vest helps with his back, but his face clenches in pain as the rock jabs his skull.

Scrambling up and digging my knee into his stomach, I grab the collar of The Roman's shirt with my left hand, pull him toward me, and punch as hard as I can with my right, ramming my fist just above his eye. His head whips into the jagged rock again, and a small cut opens above his left eye. He grits his teeth at the pain, his eyes squeezing shut to protect his sockets. Flushed with adrenaline, I hit him again, and the cut reddens and widens.

The real damage, though, comes from the rock under The Roman's head. With each of my punches, there's a sickening dull *gkkkk* as it drills through his black hair, into the back of his head. Still reeling from being shot, he thrashes his bandaged left hand toward his head, trying to protect himself from the rock.

Refusing to let up, I punch him again. And again. This one's for all the surgeries. And for having to learn to chew on the left side of my cheek. And for not being able to lick stuff off my lips . . .

Below me, The Roman shoves his bandaged hand between his head and the rock. It's not until that moment, with my arm cocked in the air, that I realize he's not protecting his head from the rock. He's pulling it from the dirt.

Oh, crap.

I punch down as hard as I can. The Roman swings his left arm like a baseball bat. He's got the jagged gray rock clutched in his fist. I'm fast. He's faster.

The sharp edge of the rock drills into my jaw like a razor on the tip of a missile, sending me falling to the right and crashing on my shoulder in the soaking grass on the edge of the path. Tasting victory, The Roman's almost up. Climbing to my feet, I scramble as fast as I can, clambering to get out of there before he can—

He jabs me with the rock, his own personal pile driver. It's a solid shot too—just above my neck at the base of my skull. I feel every ounce of it. As I stumble forward, unable to slow down, my vision goes blurry, then blinks back. No, don't pass out . . .

I crash down on my knees and palms as tiny rocks from the stone path gnaw into my hands. The Roman is right behind me. He breathes heavily through his nose. His feet pound at the path, kicking a spray of pebbles at my back. "You're—!" He grips the back of my shirt. I try to run, but he's pulling too hard. *"You're fuckin' dead!"* he roars, whipping me around like an Olympic hammer throw and flinging me backward toward the polished stone crypt with the X-shaped wrought-iron bars that protect the red and blue stained-glass doors. If I hit the bars at this speed . . .

There's a sickening crunch as my spine smacks against it. A half dozen panels shatter and pop like Christmas lights, one right where my head hits the glass. There's something warm and wet on the back of my neck. If I can feel it, I'm bleeding bad.

As he tugs me forward, my neck goes limp and my head tips back. The rain comes down in slow motion, millions of silver frozen pine needles. My vision goes blurry again. The sky fades to bl—

"Nnnnnnnn," I hear myself say, fighting awake as he drags me away from the crypt. Still gripping my shirt, he looks around for a moment. Lisbeth's unconscious. The First Lady's gone. Nico's down. Whatever The Roman had planned, he needs to improvise now. His eyes scan the— That's when he sees it.

He yanks hard, and I stumble forward, barely able to stay on my feet. Tucking my head under his arm, The Roman spins around, grips me in a headlock, and leads me across the stone path like a dog being tugged from the dining room. The way his sausage wrist wraps around my throat, it's nearly impossible to breathe. I try to dig in my heels, but my fight's long gone. Still, it's not until we cross the stone path that I finally spot our destination. Diagonally behind two matching husband-and-wife gray headstones sits a small patch of grass that shines a bit greener than the rest of the surrounding mossy plots. At the bottom edge of the patch, a small piece of the grass puckers. Like a carpet. Oh, God. That's Astroturf. He's dragging me toward— That's a freshly dug grave.

112

Tugged toward the open hole, I frantically backpedal, almost vomiting up my Adam's apple. The Roman squeezes the headlock tighter, lugging me toward the hole.

"Get off me!" I scream, clawing at his arm and trying to free my neck. He doesn't budge, pulling the leash even harder. As my feet slide from the path, through the damp grass, and toward the husband-and-wife graves, my arms and legs flail wildly—at the ground, in the air—searching for something to latch onto. At the foot of the matching rectangular headstones, I grab a branch from a nearby bush. I try holding on, but we're moving so fast, the sharp woody stems stab into my palm. The pain's too intense. With a final grunt, The Roman yanks me free, dragging me forward.

The freshly dug grave is dead ahead, but as we squeeze between the matching graves, I lunge to my left and clench one of the headstones. My fingers creep like tarantulas across the front, digging into the engraved letter *D* in the word *HUSBAND*.

Enraged, The Roman tightens his vise grip around my

throat. I feel my face swell with blood. I still don't let go. He tugs harder, and my fingers start to slide. From the angle he's pulling, the sharp granite corner of the rectangular headstone scratches the underside of my forearm. The Roman yanks so hard, I feel like my head's about to come loose from my neck. My shoulder's burning. My fingertips start to slide. The granite's already slick with rain.

Stretching out his leg to the foot of the grave behind us, The Roman kicks off the Astroturf covering. I look up just long enough to see the seven-foot hole . . . the crumbling dirt walls . . .

I dig my fingers in, but the engraving's only so deep.

The Roman's right hand is soaked in blood, useless from being shot. No doubt, he's in pain. But he knows what's at stake. Leaning forward and closing the vise, he puts his full weight into it. My feet slowly slide across the grass. I try to take a breath, but it doesn't come—he's holding too tight. My arm is numb. My fingers start shaking, skidding from their perch. Darkness again presses in from the sides. *Please, God, take care of my mom and d—*

Blam! Blam!

Small stones spray across my face. The Roman's grip loosens. And I fall to the wet grass, coughing and hacking as oxygen reenters my lungs.

Above me, the top edge of the husband's grave is shattered from one of the bullets. I stare at The Roman, who spins to face me. His blue eyes flit anxiously. There's a brand-new hole in his shirt, at the center of his chest. But no blood. He staggers backward, but not for long.

On my left, just a few feet away, Lisbeth is on her feet and breathing heavily, her own hand bleeding as she grips The Roman's gun. As she lowers it, she thinks she's won.

"Lisbeth . . ." I cough, fighting to get the words out. *"His vest!"*

Lisbeth's eyebrows leap up.

Snarling like a cheetah, The Roman lunges toward her.

Panicking, Lisbeth raises the gun and clenches the trigger. Two shots go off. They both plow into The Roman's chest. He's moving so fast, they barely slow him down. Inches away, he grabs for the gun. Lisbeth pulls the trigger one final time, and as the pistol explodes, a single bullet rips through the side of The Roman's neck. He's so lost in rage, I don't think he feels it. Lisbeth steps backward, barely able to get a scream out. He's all over her within seconds.

Ripping the gun from her hands, The Roman tackles her head-on. As they fall onto the stone path, Lisbeth's head slams back into the concrete. Her body goes limp. Taking no chances, The Roman pins his forearm against her throat. Her legs aren't thrashing. Her arms sag at her sides.

Shaking off my own beating, I hop to my feet and run my hands through the grass, my fingers brailling against the scattered shards of broken granite. On any given day, I'd have no chance against a six-foot, 220-pound, Secret Service–trained steel wall of a man. But right now The Roman's got a fresh wound in his neck and another in his hand. And I've got a sharp hunk of granite headstone clenched in my fist. As I run toward him, he's still bent over Lisbeth. I don't know if I can take him. But I do know I'll leave one hell of a dent.

Cocking the jagged shard back, I grit my teeth and swing at the back of The Roman's head with everything I have left. The shard is shaped like a brick cracked in half, with a tiny point in the corner. It strikes right behind his ear. His scream alone is worth it—a throaty whimpering grunt even he can't contain.

To his credit, as he slaps his hand against the side of his head, he doesn't fall over. Instead, he catches his balance, turns back to face me, and lumbers to his feet. Before he can completely turn around, I take another full swing, cracking the granite block across his face. He stumbles back, falling on his ass. I still don't let up. Stealing from his own playbook, I grip the front of his shirt, pull him toward me, and aim for the cut above his eye. Then I wind up and hit him again. The blood comes quickly.

A strand of drool falls like a silk thread from my bottom lip. He's the reason my mouth won't close, I tell myself as I swing again, driving the edge of the granite into his wound and watching the blood cover the side of his face. Like me. Like mine.

His eyes roll back in his head. I hit him again, determined to widen the wound. My drool sags lower, and I pummel him harder than ever. I want him to know. I want him to stare at it. Each granite blow takes another hunk of skin. I want him to live with it. I want him to turn away from his *own reflection in storefront windows*! I want him t—

I stop right there, my arm in midair, my chest rising and falling as I catch my breath. Lowering my fist, I wipe the saliva from my lip and once again feel the polite rain as it drips from the tip of my nose and chin.

I wouldn't wish it on anyone.

And with that, I let go of The Roman's shirt. He collapses across my shoes.

The granite block falls from my hand, clunking against the concrete. I spin back to Lisbeth, who's still lying on the ground behind me. Her arm is twisted awkwardly above her head. Dropping to my knees, I check her chest. It's not moving.

"Lisbeth, are you—? *Can you hear me?*" I shout, sliding on my knees next to her.

No response.

Oh, God. No. No, no, no . . .

I grab her arm and feel for a pulse. There's nothing there. Wasting no time, I tilt her head back, open her mouth, and—

"Hggggh!"

I jump back at the sound as she violently coughs. Her right hand instinctively covers her mouth. But her left—with the wound—stays stranded awkwardly above her head.

She spits and dry-heaves as the blood rushes back to her face.

"Y-You okay?" I ask.

She coughs hard. Good enough. Glancing sideways without moving her neck, she spots The Roman's body just a few feet away. "But we need—we hafta—"

"Just relax," I tell her.

She shakes her head, more insistent than ever. "But wh—what abou—?"

"Slow down. We got him, okay?"

"Not him, Wes—*her*." My throat locks as the light rain pats my shoulders. "Where's the First Lady?"

113

Striding up the block, her umbrella still over her head, the First Lady glanced over her shoulder. Behind her, from the cemetery, two more gunshots exploded. Her ankle twisted at the sound. She didn't slow down. Hobbling for a moment, she quickly found her balance and continued to march forward, still trembling.

She knew it would end like this. Even when things were quiet, even when she first realized whom she'd inadvertently aligned with, she knew it would never go away. There was no escaping this mistake.

Another two shots rang out, then a final one that echoed from behind the tall trees. She flinched hard at each blast. Was that The Roman or—? She didn't want Wes to die. Along with Boyle, Wes's being shot at the speedway was the thing she'd never been able to shake, even after all these years. That's why she always tried to be supportive . . . why she'd never objected when her husband brought him back on board. But now that Wes knew the truth . . . She shook her head. No. She was tricked. She was. And only trying to help.

With a sharp right, The First Lady turned the corner, her

heels clicking against the pavement as she entered the small parking lot that ran along the south side of the cemetery. At this hour, it was empty—except for the shiny black Chevy Suburban that The Roman had brought her over in.

Racing for the driver's door, she ripped it open and climbed inside, already rehearsing her side of the story. With Nico there . . . with the hole in Lisbeth's hand . . . that part was easy. America loves to blame the psycho. And even if Wes managed to survive . . .

Playing out the permutations, she reached up to adjust the rearview mirror. There was a sharp hiss from behind. A dime-sized black circle burst through the back of the First Lady's hand as the rearview mirror shattered. At first, she didn't even feel it. In the few remaining shards of glass, she could see a familiar figure in the backseat, his fingers creeping along his rosary.

"I saw you when you drove in," Nico said, his voice calm.

"Oh, God . . . my hand," she cried, seeing it and clutching her shaking palm as the fiery pain shot up to her elbow.

"You're taller than I thought. You were sitting during the competency hearings."

"Please," she begged, the tears already welling in her eyes as her hand went numb. "Please don't kill me."

Nico didn't move, his right hand holding his gun in his lap. "It surprised me to see you with Number One. What did they call him? The Roman? He hurt me too."

In the cracked mirror, the First Lady saw Nico look down at the top of his rib cage, where he'd been shot.

"Yes . . . yes, of course," the First Lady insisted. "The Roman hurt both of us, Nico. He threatened me—made me come with him or he'd—"

"God hurt me also," Nico interrupted. His left hand gripped the rosary, his thumb slowly climbing from wooden bead to wooden bead, counting its way to the engraving of Mary. "God took my mother from me."

"Nico, you . . ." Her voice cracked. "God . . . please, Nico . . . we've all lost—"

"But it was The Three who took my father," he added as he lifted the gun and pressed it to the back of the First Lady's head. "That was my error. Not fate. Not the Masons. The Three took him. When I joined them . . . what I did in their name . . . don't you see? Misreading the Book. That's why God had to send me the angel."

Shivering uncontrollably, the First Lady raised her hands in the air and struggled to glance over her shoulder. If she could turn around . . . get him to look at her face . . . to see her as a human being . . . "Please don't . . . please don't do this!" she begged, facing Nico and fighting back tears. It'd been nearly a decade since she'd felt the onslaught of a deep cry. Not since the day they left the White House, when they returned home to Florida, held a small press conference on their lawn and realized, after everyone was gone, that there was no one but themselves to clean up the reporters' discarded coffee cups that were scattered across their front yard. "I can't die like this," she sobbed.

Unmoved, Nico held his gun in place, pointing it at her head. "But it wasn't just The Three, was it? I heard the reporter, Dr. Manning. I know. The Four. That's what she said, right? One, Two, Three, you're Four."

"Nico, that's not true."

"I heard it. You're Four."

"No . . . why would I—?"

"One, Two, Three, you're Four," he insisted, his fingers moving across four beads of the rosary.

"Please, Nico, just listen . . ."

"One, Two, Three, you're Four." His fingers continued to calmly count, bead by bead. He was over halfway through. Just sixteen beads to go. "One, Two, Three, you're Four. One, Two, Three, you're Four."

"Why aren't you listening!?" the First Lady sobbed. "If you—I can—I can get you help . . ."

"One, Two, Three, you're Four."

". . . I can . . . I'll even . . ." Her voice picked up speed. "I can tell you how your mother died."

Nico stopped. His head cocked sideways, but his expression was calm as ever. "You lie."

His finger slithered around the trigger, and he squeezed it. Easily.

There was a sharp hiss, and a *pfffft* that sounded like a cantaloupe exploding. The inside front windshield was sprayed with blood.

The First Lady slumped sideways, and what was left of her head hit the steering wheel.

Barely noticing, Nico pointed the gun at his own temple. "Your fate is mine, Dr. Manning. I'm coming to get you in Hell."

Without closing his eyes, he pulled the trigger.

Click.

He pulled again.

Click.

Empty . . . it's empty, he realized, staring down at the gun. A slight, nervous laugh hiccupped from his throat. He looked up at the roof of the car, then back down at the gun, which quickly became blurred by a swell of tears.

Of course. It was a test. To test his faith. God's sign.

"One, Two, Three, you're Four," he whispered, his thumb climbing up the last wooden beads and resting on the engraving of Mary. Flushed with a smile even he couldn't contain, Nico looked back up at the roof, brought the rosary up to his lips, and kissed it. "Thank You . . . thank You, my Lord."

The test, at long last, was complete. The Book could finally be closed.

114

Ten minutes after seven the following morning, under an overcast sky, I'm sitting alone in the backseat of a black Chevy Suburban that's filled with enough new-car smell to tell me this isn't from our usual fleet. Usually, that's cause for excitement. Not after last night.

In the front seats, both agents sit uncomfortably silent the entire ride. Sure, they toss me some small talk—*Your head okay? How're you feeling?*—but I've been around the Service long enough to know when they're under orders to keep their mouths shut.

As we make the left onto Las Brisas, I spot the news vans and the reporters doing stand-ups. They gently push forward against the yellow tape as they see us coming, but the half dozen agents out front easily keep them at bay. On my left, as the car pulls up to the manicured shrubs out front, and the tall white wooden gate swings open, an Asian female reporter narrates—. . . *once again: former First Lady Lenore Manning* . . .—but gracefully steps back to give us room.

For the reporters and press, all they know is she's dead

and that Nico killed her. If they knew her hand in it . . . or what she did . . . an army of agents wouldn't be able to hold them back. The Service, pretending to be clueless, said that since Nico was still out there, they thought it'd be safer to chauffeur me inside. It's a pretty good lie. And when the agents knocked on my door this morning, I almost believed it.

As the gate slowly closes behind us, I know better than to turn around and give them a shot of my face for the morning news—especially with the cuts on my nose and the dark purple swelling in my eye. Instead, I study the Chicago-brick driveway that leads up to the familiar pale blue house. Flanking both sides of the Suburban, six agents I've never seen before watch the gate shut, making sure no one sneaks in. Then, as I open my door and step outside, they all watch me. To their credit, they turn away quickly, like they don't know what's going on. But when it comes to spotting lingering glances, I'm a black belt. As I head for the front door, every one of them takes another look.

"Wes, right?" an African-American agent with a bald head asks as he opens the front door and welcomes me inside. On most days, agents aren't stationed in the house. Today is different. "He's waiting for you in the library, so if you'll just follow—"

"I know where it is," I say, moving forward to cut around him.

He takes a step to the side, blocking my way. "I'm sure you do," he says, throwing on a fake grin. Like the agents out front, he's in standard suit and tie, but the microphone on his lapel . . . I almost miss it at first. It's tinier than a small silver bead. They don't give that kind of tech to guys on former-President duty. Whoever he is, he's not from the Orlando field office. He's from D.C. "If you'll follow me . . ."

He pivots around, leading me down the center hallway, into the formal living room, and past the gold velvet sofa that yesterday held Madame Tussauds' set of Leland Manning eyeballs.

"Here you go," the agent adds, stopping at the double set of French doors on the far left side of the room. "I'll be right here," he says, motioning back to the main hallway. It's not meant as a comfort.

Watching him leave, I bite the dead skin on the inside of my cheek and reach for the American eagle brass doorknob. But just as I palm the eagle, the doorknob turns by itself, and the door opens. I was so busy watching the agent, I didn't see him. Our eyes lock instantly. This time, though, as I spot the brown with the splash of light blue, my stomach doesn't plummet. And he doesn't run.

Standing in the doorway and scratching his fingers against the tiny stubble on his head, Boyle forces an unconvincing smile. From what Rogo told me late last night, I should've known he'd be here. Silly me, though, I actually thought I'd be first. Then again, that's always been my problem when it comes to the President.

Stepping forward and closing the door behind him, Boyle blocks me even worse than the Service. "Listen, Wes, do you . . . uh . . . do you have a sec?"

The President's expecting me in the library. But for the first time since I've been in Leland Manning's personal orbit, well, for once . . . he can wait. "Sure," I say.

Boyle nods me a thank-you and scratches from his head down to his cheek. This is hard for him. "You should put a warm compress on it," he finally says. Reading my confusion, he adds, "For your eye. Everyone thinks cold is better, but the next day, warm helps more."

I shrug, unconcerned with my appearance.

"By the way, how's your friend?" Boyle asks.

"My friend?"

"The reporter. I heard she got shot."

"Lisbeth? Yeah, she got shot," I say, staring at Boyle's sharpened features. "The one in her hand was the worst."

Boyle nods, glancing down at the old stigmata scar at the center of his own palm. He doesn't linger on it, though.

"Wes, I—I'm sorry I had to keep you in the dark like that. In Malaysia, when I was trying to get to Manning . . . All these years, I thought he might've screwed me—that maybe *he* was The Fourth—so to find the crossword . . . to see it was her—and then when I saw you, I just—I panicked. And when O'Shea and Micah started trailing you . . ."

He waits for me to complete the thought—to yell at him for using me as bait these past few days. To blame him for the lies, for the deception . . . for every ounce of guilt he dumped on my shoulders for eight years. But as I stare across at him . . . as I see the deep circles under his eyes and the pained vertical line etched between his brows . . . Last night, Ron Boyle won. He got everyone—The Roman . . . Micah and O'Shea . . . even the First Lady—everyone he'd hunted for so long. But it's painful to see him now, anxiously licking his lips. There's no joy in his features, no victory on his face. Eight years after his ordeal began, all that's left is an aged man with crummy nose and chin jobs, a haunted vacancy in his eyes, and an unstoppable need to keep checking every nearby door and window, which he does for the third time since we started talking.

Suffering is bad. Suffering alone is far worse.

My jaw clenches as I try to find the words. "Listen, Ron . . ."

"Wes, don't pity me."

"I'm not—"

"You *are*," he insists. "I'm standing right in front of you, and you're still mourning me like I'm gone. I can see it in your face."

He's talking about the swell of tears in my eyes. But he's reading it wrong. I shake my head and try to tell him why, but the words feel like they're stapled in my throat.

He says something else to make me feel better, but I don't hear it. All I hear are the words that're trapped within me. The words I've practiced in my sleep at night—every night—and in my mirror every morning, knowing full well they'd never get to leave my lips. Until this moment.

I swallow hard and again hear the crowd at the speedway that day. Everyone happy, everyone waving, until *pop, pop, pop,* there it is, the scream in C minor as the ambulance doors close. I swallow hard again and slowly, finally, the screams begin to fade as the first few syllables leave my lips.

"Ron," I begin, already panting hard. "I—I . . ."

"Wes, you don't have to—"

I shake my head and cut him off. He's wrong. I do. And after nearly a decade, as the tears stream down my face, I finally get my chance. "Ron, I . . . I'm sorry for putting you in the limo that day," I tell him. "I know it's stupid—I just—I need you to know I'm sorry, okay? I'm sorry, Ron," I plead as my voice cracks and the tears drip from my chin. "I'm so sorry I put you in there."

Across from me, Boyle doesn't respond. His shoulders

rise, and for a moment, he looks like the old Boyle who screamed in my face that burning July day. As I wipe my cheeks, he continues staring at me, keeping it all to himself. I can't read him. Especially when he doesn't want to be read. But even the best facades crack in time.

He rubs his nose and tries to hide it, but I still spot the quivering of his chin and the heartbroken arch of his eyebrows.

"Wes," he eventually offers, "no matter what car you put me in, that bullet was always going to hit my chest."

I look up, still fighting to catch my breath. Over the years, my mom, Rogo, my shrinks, Manning, even the lead investigator from the Service, told me the exact same thing. But Ron Boyle was the one I needed to hear it from.

Within seconds, a tentative smile spreads across my face. I spot my own reflection in the glass panels of the French doors. The smile itself is crooked, broken, and only lifts one of my cheeks. But for the first time in a long time, that's plenty.

That is, until I spot the flash of movement and the familiar posture on the other side of the glass. With a twist, the brass eagle doorknob once again turns, and the door opens inward, behind Boyle's back. Boyle turns, and I look up. Towering above us, President Manning sticks his head out and nods at me with an awkward hello. His mane of gray hair is matted just enough that I can tell it's unwashed; the whites of his eyes are crackling with red. His wife died last night. He hasn't slept ten minutes.

"I should go," Boyle offers. From what I heard last night, he's blaming his death and reappearance on Nico and The Three. Not The Four. For that alone, Manning'll make him a hero. I'm not sure I blame him. But as Manning knows, I deal with things differently than Boyle.

Before I can say a word, Boyle walks past me, offers a quick shoulder pat, and casually leaves the room, like he's going to lunch. The problem is, I'm the one about to be eaten.

On most days, Manning would simply head back into the library and expect me to follow. Today, he opens the door wider and motions me inside. "There you are, Wes," the President says. "I was starting to worry you weren't coming."

115

"I appreciate your getting here so early, Wes."

"Believe me, I wanted to come last night."

Nodding soberly and ushering me to the seat in front of his desk, Manning turns his back to me and scans the framed photos and leather-bound books that line the built-in maple shelves that surround us on all sides. There are pictures of him with the pope, with both Presidents Bush, with Clinton, Carter, and even with an eight-year-old boy from Eritrea, who weighed barely twenty pounds when Manning met him during one of our first trips abroad. Unlike his office, where we cover the walls, here at home he displays only the pictures he loves best—his own personal greatest hits—but it's not until I sit down in the antique Queen Anne chair that I realize that the only photo on his desk is one of him and his wife.

"Sir, I'm sorry about—"

"The funeral's Wednesday," he says, still scanning his shelves as if some brilliant answer were there among the peace prizes, bricks from the Hanoi Hilton, and imprints of the Wailing Wall. Across from him, I also stare—at the bronze casting of Abraham Lincoln's fist that sits on the edge of the desk.

"We'd like you to be a pallbearer, Wes."

He still doesn't face me. The snag in his voice tells me how hard this is. The way his hand's shaking as he shoves it in his pocket shows me the same. As President, Leland Manning buried three hundred and two American soldiers, nine heads of state, two senators, and a pope. None of it prepared him for burying his wife.

"A pallbearer?" I ask.

"It was her request," he says, trying to pull it together. "From her checklist."

When a President and First Lady leave the White House, as if they're not depressed enough, one of the very first things they're forced to do is make arrangements for their own funerals. State funerals are national events that need to be mounted in a few hours, almost always without any notice—which is why the Pentagon gives the President a checklist of all the gruesome details: whether you want to lie in state in the Capitol, if you want a public viewing, whether you want the final burial at your library or in Arlington, how many friends, family, and dignitaries should attend, who should do the eulogies, who *shouldn't* be invited, and of course, who should be the pallbearers.

Once, they even sent the military honor guard to our offices at the Manning Library to practice carrying the casket that would eventually hold him. I tried to keep Manning from coming to his office that day. But there he was, watching from his window as they carried his flag-covered weighted-down casket to the meditation garden in back. "I look heavy," he'd joked, trying his best to make light of it. Still, he was quiet as they passed by. He's more quiet now.

"Mr. President, I'm not sure that's the best idea anymore. After last night—"

"That was her own doing, Wes. You know that. Her own doing. And her undoing as well," he says as his voice again breaks. He's trying hard to be strong—to be the Lion—but I can see that he's gripping the back of his brown leather chair to stand. However it happened, it's still his wife. Looking like a shell of the man I used to know, he sighs and sits down. We both sit there in silence, staring at Lincoln's fist.

"Did the Service say anything about Nico?" I finally ask.

"His fingerprints were all over the car. The blood in the backseat was his. No question he pulled the trigger. But as far as where he disappeared to, they're still looking," he explains. "If you're worried he's coming after you, though, I've already asked the Service to—"

"He's not coming after me. Not anymore."

Manning looks me over. "So in the cemetery . . . you spoke to him?"

"Yes."

"You made peace with him?"

"Peace? No. But—" I pause to think about it. "He's not coming back."

"Good. I'm glad for you, Wes. You deserve some peace of mind."

He's generous to say it, but it's clear his mind is elsewhere. That's fine. So is mine.

"Sir, I know this may not be the best time, but I was wondering if I could—" I stop right there, reminding myself I don't need his permission. I look up from Lincoln's fist. "I'd like to talk to you about my status."

"What status?"

"My job, Mr. President."

"Of course, of course—no . . . of course," he says, clearly caught off guard.

"I thought that under the circumstances—"

"You don't have to say it, Wes. Regardless of the end result, you're still family to us. So if you're wondering if the job's still yours—"

"Actually, Mr. President, I was thinking it's time for me to move on."

Our eyes lock, but he doesn't blink. I think he's most shocked by the fact it's not a question.

Eventually, he offers a small, gentle laugh. "Good for you, Wes," he says, pointing. "Y'know, I been waiting a long time for you to say that."

"I appreciate that, sir."

"And if you need help finding a job or a recommendation or something like that . . . don't forget, it still says *President* on my stationery, and let's hope there're still a few people out there who're impressed by that."

"I'm sure there are, sir," I say with my own laugh. "Thank you, Mr. President." The way he nods at me—like a proud dad—it's a truly sweet moment. A warm moment. And the perfect moment for me to leave. But I can't. Not yet. Not until I find out.

"So what do you plan on doing next?" he asks.

I don't answer. Shifting in my seat, I tell myself to forget it.

"Wes, do you have any plans f—?"

"Did you know?" I blurt.

He cocks an eyebrow. "Pardon me?"

I stare right at him, pretending they're not the most awkward three words to ever leave my lips. Steeling myself, I again ask, "Did you know about the First Lady? About your wife?"

Across from me, his fingers lace together, resting on the desk. I know his temper. The fuse is lit. But as he sits there and watches me, the explosion never comes. His lips part, and the lacing of his fingers comes undone. He's not mad. He's wounded. "After all our—you really think that?" he asks.

I sink in my seat, feeling about three centimeters tall. But that doesn't mean I'm not getting my answer. "I saw the crosswords—your ratings—even from the earliest days, you were obviously worried. So does that—? Did you know she was The Fourth?"

At this point, he has every right to wring my throat; to argue that she was tricked and innocent. But he just sits there, pummeled by the question. "Wes, don't cast her as Lady Macbeth. She was many things—but never a mastermind."

"I saw her last night. Even in the best light—even if she didn't know who The Roman was when he first approached her—once Boyle got shot, all these years, and she never said *anything*? Doesn't sound like someone being manipulated."

"And I'm not saying she was. My point is simply that what you found in those puzzles . . . even what you saw firsthand yourself . . ." He cups a hand to his mouth and clears his throat. "I'm not a moron, Wes. Lenore is my wife. I'm well aware of her weaknesses. And when it came to staying in the grand white castle—c'mon, son, you saw it too. You were there with us—when you fly that high, when you're looking down on all the clouds, the only thing that scared her was losing altitude and plummeting back to earth."

"That didn't give her the right t—"

"I'm not defending her," Manning says, practically

pleading for me to understand what's clearly kept him up all night. He can't share this with the Service or anyone else on staff. Without his wife, he's got no one to tell but me. "You know how desperate she was. Everyone wanted that second term. Everyone. Including you, Wes."

"But what you said . . . with the clouds, and knowing her weaknesses . . . if you knew all that—"

"I didn't know anything!" he shouts as his ears flush red. "I knew she was scared. I knew she was paranoid. I knew that in the early days she used to toss details to reporters, like the early internal arguing, or the fact she wasn't consulted for redecorating the Oval—because she was convinced that if she could make them like her, they wouldn't kick us out and take it all away. So yes—*that* part I knew." He puts his head down and massages the front of his forehead. "But," he adds, "I never *ever* thought she'd let herself get dragged into something like this."

I nod like I understand. But I don't. "After you left office and it all calmed down, why'd . . . ?" I search for softer words, but there's no other way to say it. "Why'd you stay with her?"

"She's my wife, Wes. She's been by my side since we were hand-painting campaign posters in my mother's garage. Since we were—" Finally lifting his head, he closes his eyes, struggling hard to reclaim his calm. "I wish you could put that question to Jackie Kennedy, or Pat Nixon, or even the Clintons." He looks back at the photos with his fellow Presidents. "Everything's easy . . . until it gets complicated."

"So when Boyle was shot . . ."

He stares at me as I say the words. He doesn't have to tell me a thing. But he knows what I've given him all these years. And that this is the only thing I've ever asked in return.

"We knew it might happen, but had no idea when," he says without even hesitating. "Boyle approached me a few weeks earlier and told me about his offer from The Three. From there . . . well, you know how fast the Service moves. I did everything I could to protect my friend. They gave him a vest, stocked his blood in the ambulance, and did their very best to keep him safe."

"Until I put him in the limo."

"Until Nico put a bullet in his hand and chest," he says, turning back to face me. "From there, they rushed him to the Marshals Office, who patched him up, shuttled him from city to city, and put him straight into the highest levels of WITSEC. Naturally, he didn't want to go, but he knew the alternatives. Even if it wrecks families, it saves more lives than you think."

I nod as the President stands from his oversize seat. The way he leans on the armrest to slowly boost himself up, he's more tired than he's letting on. But he doesn't ask me to leave.

"If it makes you feel better, Wes, I think she regretted it. Especially what happened with you."

"I appreciate that," I tell him, trying to be enthusiastic.

He studies me closely. I'm good at reading him. He's even better at reading me. "I'm not just saying that, Wes."

"Mr. President, I never thought otherwi—"

"We prayed together before bed. Did you know that? That was our ritual—ever since we first got married," he explains. "And during that first year? She prayed for you every night."

The number one mistake most people make when they meet the President is they always try to extend the conversation. It's a once-in-a-lifetime moment, so they'll say the dumbest things to make it last forever.

I stand from my seat and motion to the door. "I should really get going, sir."

"Understood. Go do what you have to," he says as he crosses around from his desk. "I'll tell you what, though," he adds as he follows me to the door. "I'm glad she made you a pallbearer." He stops and catches his breath. "She should only be carried by family."

Halfway through the doorway, I turn around. I'll carry those words with me for the rest of my life.

But that doesn't mean I believe them.

He reaches out to shake my hand, and I get the full double-hand clasp that he usually saves for heads of state and presidential-level donors. He even lingers a moment, engulfing part of my wrist.

Maybe it was unspoken. Maybe he figured it out. For all I know, she could've even told him outright. But one thing is clear—and it's the only thing he said that can't be argued: Leland Manning is not a moron. He knew Boyle was planning to say no to The Three. So when Boyle went down, he had to've suspected they could've gotten someone bigger.

As I head out through the living room and toward the front door, I spot the huge black-and-white photo of the view from behind his desk in the Oval. Sure, those four years were great. But for him, it would've been even better to have four more.

"Let me know if you need *anything*," the President calls out from the living room.

I wave good-bye and say a final thanks.

The Cowardly Lion may not have courage. But he's certainly got a brain.

He knows I was running around with a reporter. He knows she's waiting for my call. And most important, he knows that when it comes to political touch, the best touch is when you don't feel it at all.

For eight years, I haven't felt anything. Right now I feel it all.

"Got everything you need?" the bald agent asks as he opens the front door.

"I think so."

Stepping outside, I pull my phone from my pocket, punch in the number for her hospital room, and head down the red brick path. When Herbert Hoover left the White House, he said that a former President's greatest service is to remove himself from politics and public life. Time for me to do the same.

"You speak to him?" Lisbeth asks, picking up on the first ring.

"Of course, I spoke to him."

"And?"

At first, I don't answer.

"C'mon, Wes, this isn't the gossip column anymore. What'd you think of Manning?"

Up the path, outside the garage, half a dozen brand-new agents watch me carefully as the closest one tries to usher me toward the Suburban. Outside the front gate, the wolf pack of reporters shake their heads inconsolably as they scramble together video montages to honor the fallen First Lady. With her death comes the inevitable outpouring of sadness and support from commentators who spent their entire careers ripping her to pieces. I can already hear it in their hushed, reverential tones. They loved her. Their viewers loved her. The whole world loved her. All I have to do is keep my mouth shut.

"It's okay," Lisbeth says. She knows what the press'll do to my life if I'm the one who spills it. "I'll just tell them to go with the original story."

"But what abou—?"

"You already fought your battle, Wes. No one can ask any more of you than that."

I pull the phone close to my mouth and once again remind myself that every opportunity I've had in my life came directly from the Mannings. My words are a whisper. "Have them send over your laptop. I want you to write it. People need to know what she did."

Lisbeth pauses, giving me plenty of time to take it back. "You sure about this?" she finally asks as a Secret Service agent with a flat nose opens the back door to the Suburban.

Ignoring him, I walk past the car and head straight for the tall wooden gate and the swelling crowd of mourners outside.

"And, Lisbeth?" I say as I shove the door open and the firing squad of cameras turns my way. "Don't hold back."

116

Two weeks later

A rare Italian snow sprinkled down from the dusty sky as the man crossed Via Mazzarino and lowered his chin toward the lapels of his herringbone wool coat. His hair was blond now—short and barely grown in—but he was still careful as he approached Sant' Agata dei Goti, the fifth-century church that seemed to hide on the narrow cobblestone street.

Passing the front entrance but not going inside, he glanced up at the facade. The relief above the door was an ancient carving of Saint Agatha holding her severed breast on a plate, the victim of torturers who'd attacked her when she refused to renounce her faith.

"Praise Him," the man whispered to himself as he cut right, followed the signs to the side entrance on Via Panisperna, and quietly marched up the bumpy brick driveway that was blanketed in the light snow.

At the end of the driveway, he wiped his feet on the

battered welcome mat, shoved open the brown double doors, and winced as the old hinges shrieked. Inside, the smell of damp wood and rose candles welcomed and transported him right back to the old stone church where he grew up, right back to the Wisconsin winters of his childhood, right back to when his mom passed.

The hinges shrieked again—and he winced again—as the door slammed shut behind him. Wasting no time, the man scanned the empty pews, eyed the empty altar, then glanced between the Oriental granite columns that ran down the center aisle. No one in sight. His eyes narrowed as he listened. The only thing there was a single hushed whisper. Praise Him. Just like it was supposed to be.

Feeling his heart punch inside his chest, he raced toward his destination, tracing the faded colors of the mosaic floor to the mahogany stall on the far right side of the altar.

As he got closer, he followed the faint whisper from inside. He'd never been here before, but when he saw the picture in the travel brochure—he knew to always trust fate.

Unbuttoning his coat and taking one last glance around, he kneeled in front of the mahogany stall. The whispering stopped. Through a square cutaway in the booth, a small burgundy curtain was pulled shut, and the priest inside stopped praying.

It was only then, only in the screaming silence of the empty Sant'Agata dei Goti church, that Nico lowered his hcad toward the confessional.

"Bless me, Father, for I have sinned. It's been—"

"Let's go, Nico—make it quick!" the tall orderly with the sweet onion breath shouted.

Glancing over his shoulder, Nico looked past the

industrial beige carpet, the cheap oak lectern, and the dozen or so metal folding chairs that made up the small chapel on the fourth floor of St. Elizabeths' John Howard Pavilion, and focused hard on the two orderlies who waited for him back by the only door to the room. It'd been nearly two weeks since they found him in Wisconsin. But thanks to a new lawyer, for the first time in years, he finally had chapel privileges.

Without a word, Nico turned back toward the wooden cross attached to the otherwise bare front wall of the room. Within seconds, the carpet, the lectern, and the folding chairs once again disappeared and were replaced by the mosaic floor, the ancient pews, and the mahogany confessional. Just like the ones in the pamphlet that his counselor gave him.

". . . it's been far too long since my last confession."

He took a deep breath of the rose candles—the sweet smell that was always on his mom—and shut both eyes. The rest came easy.

God provided an ending. And brought him back home for a new beginning.

EPILOGUE

The biggest wounds in life are all self-inflicted.
—President Bill Clinton

Palm Beach, Florida

Just yourself?" the waitress asks, approaching my table in the corner of the café's small outdoor patio.

"Actually, I've got one more coming," I tell her as she puts a water glass on my place mat to keep the wind from blowing it away. We're at least two blocks from the ocean, but thanks to the narrowness of the street, it always packs a nice breeze.

"Anything else to drink besides w—?" She freezes as I look up. It's the first time she sees my face. To her credit, she recovers quickly, faking a smile—but the damage is already—

"Wait . . . you're that guy," she says, suddenly excited.

"Excuse me?"

"Y'know, with the thing . . . with the President . . . that was you, wasn't it?"

I cock my head, offering the slightest nod.

Studying me for a moment, she cracks a tiny smile, tucks a strand of straight black hair behind her ear, and calmly heads back to the kitchen.

"Holy salami, what was *that*?" a familiar voice asks from the sidewalk. On my left, Rogo rushes up to the low wrought-iron railing that surrounds the outdoor patio.

"Rogo, don't hop the—"

Before I say it, he throws a leg onto the railing, boosts himself over, and plops into the seat across from me.

"Can't you use the door like the rest of the bipeds?" I ask him.

"No, no, no—no changing the channel. What was that rendezvous with the waitress?"

"Rendezvous?"

"Don't play dumb with me, Ethel—I saw it—the longing glance . . . the hair tuck . . . the little finger-phone where she held her thumb to her ear and whispered *Call me* into her pinkie."

"There was no finger-phone."

"She recognized you, didn't she?"

"Can you please stop?"

"Where'd she see you, *60 Minutes*? That's the one, isn't it? The girls love the Morley Safer."

"Rogo . . ."

"Don't fight with me, Wes—it's an unarguable fact: A waitress can make the dining experience or ruin it. Read the signal. She's trying to make it. Make it. *Maaaake iiiiiit*," he whispers, rolling his eyes upward as he reaches over and steals a sip of my water. Noticing the menu in front of him, he adds, "They got fajitas here?"

"It's a panini place."

"Panini?"

"Y'know, with the bread and the—"

"I'm sorry, do you have a cramp in your ovaries?"

When I don't laugh, he twirls the straw in the water, never taking his eyes off me. Right there, I know what he's really after. "It's okay, Rogo. You don't have to use every conversation to try and cheer me up."

"I'm not trying to cheer you up," he insists. He twirls the straw again as the waitress returns with another place mat and some silverware. He's silent as she puts it in front of him. When she leaves, I glance back at him.

"Still trying to think of a clever comeback to make me happy?" I ask him.

"I was until you just *ruined it*," he sulks, chucking his straw into his water like a mini-javelin.

When I still don't laugh, he shakes his head, finally giving up. "Y'know, you're really not a fun person."

"And that's it? That's your best retort?"

"*And!*" he adds, pointing a finger at me. "And . . . and . . . and . . . *and*—" He cuts himself off. *"C'mon,"* he whines, "just put a smile on your face—please. If you do, I'll order an orange juice and do the fake-laugh thing at the waitress where I make it come out of my nose. It burns like the sun. You'll love it."

"That's very generous of you, Rogo. I just need—just give me a little time."

"Whattya think the past two weeks have been? You're moping around like it's an Olympic event. I mean, it's not like your life sucks: interviews coming out the ying-yang, you get all the credit for saving the day, *and* semi-hot waitresses are recognizing you and bringing you water with little slices of lemon. You've had the greatest fourteen days of your life. Enough with the woe-is-me."

"It's not woe-is-me. It's just . . ."

"... you're sad to watch them go down in flames like that. I heard the speech yesterday, and the day before, and the day before: *They gave you so many opportunities. You feel like Benedict Arnold.* I understand, Wes. I really do. But like everyone in your office said—the one thing the Mannings *didn't* give you was much of a choice. That castle you were in was built on sand."

I stare out at the pedestrians walking past us on the sidewalk. "I know. But even so . . . I've been by Manning's side for the better part of a decade. I was there before he got to the office, and I didn't leave until he headed upstairs for bed. And not just weekdays. *Every* day. For nearly *ten years*! You know what that's—?" I close my eyes, refusing to say it. "I didn't go to your sister's wedding; I was in the Ukraine during my parents' thirtieth wedding anniversary; my college roommate had a baby, and I haven't even met him yet."

"It's a *she*, but don't feel guilty."

"That's the point, Rogo—to go from *every single day* to *never again* . . . I didn't just leave my job. I left—I feel like I left my life."

Rogo shakes his head like I'm missing the point. "Haven't you ever played Uno?" he asks calmly. "Sometimes you have to lose all your cards to win."

Looking down at my water, I watch the ice cubes bob and crackle inside the tall glass.

"You know I'm right," Rogo says.

A sharp fissure ricochets like lightning through an ice cube at the bottom. As it splinters, the cubes on top tumble down with it.

"Look at it this way," Rogo adds. "At least you're not Dreidel."

I stab the ice with my straw. This time, I'm the one

shaking my head. "I wouldn't cry for Dreidel just yet." Reading the confusion on Rogo's face, I explain, "Don't forget why he got the nickname. He may not be sitting in Congress next year, but mark my words, he'll be somewhere on top."

"What about Violet, or whatever her real name is? When that came out . . ."

"Dreidel laid low for the requisite week, then strategically started leaking the story of how he brilliantly helped the Marshals throughout their investigation of The Three. Believe me, the moment I saw him and his girlfriend in that hotel, he was prepping his smile for the highlight reel."

"But with Violet—he hit her—and he's—"

"—the only one of us who made an advance deal with the government. God bless America, I heard he's got a new radio show that's being lined up as we speak, while the book rights sold yesterday for seven figures, plus bonuses when it hits the best-seller lists. And when the paperback comes out, I'll bet good money he tucks in a special addendum chapter with a mea culpa to Violet, just to sell a few extra hundred thousand copies."

"Wait, so the editor who bought the book rights—is that the same guy who called you last week abou—?"

"Very same guy. Very same offer, including the best-seller bonuses."

"Oh, God—strike me with lightning!" Rogo shouts at the sky as a few fellow diners and an older woman on the sidewalk turn to stare. "You let Dreidel *take that*?"

"He didn't take anything. Besides, I promised the President from day one: I'd never cash in on him."

"His wife almost—" He turns to the man staring from the table diagonally across from us. "Sir, go back to your soup. Thank you." Looking back at me, Rogo lowers his voice and leans in. "His wife almost had you killed, jackass. And even if you can't prove it, *he* may've known about it all along. So while I'm sure your buddy Dreidel had that same, dumb code-of-honor thing going—and believe me, my momma taught me to appreciate loyalty—attempted *murder* is usually a pretty darn good sign that you can part ways guilt-free and stop sending invites to each other's birthday parties."

Slightly up the block, a meter maid driving in an enclosed golf cart marks tires with a piece of chalk on the end of a long metal pole. "Doesn't matter," I tell Rogo. "I'm not profiting off them."

"Bet Dreidel sells the film rights too (though he'll probably only get movie of the week)."

"No profit, Rogo. Ever."

"And what's Lisbeth say?"

"About the book rights or Dreidel's radio show?"

"About everything."

I stare up the block at the meter maid, who's writing a ticket for a pale yellow vintage Plymouth Belvedere. Following my glance, Rogo turns and looks over his shoulder.

"I'm only gonna get him off, Richie!" Rogo yells out.

"Only if they're dumb enough to hire you," the meter maid calmly teases back.

"I think Lisbeth understands where I'm coming from," I tell him.

"She understand anything else?" Rogo asks, still eyeing the yellow Plymouth.

"What's that mean?"

"You know what it means. You two went through the grinder together—plus you let her write the story as a final gift."

"So?"

"So I know you talk to her every night."

"How d'you know I talk to her?"

"I pick up the phone to see who you're chatting with." Finally turning back to face me, he adds, "C'mon, what's the story with our favorite redhead? You in there? You counting freckles? You trying to figure out if they make constellations?"

"Pardon me?"

"Don't play naive. You digging for clams, or you still on the beach?"

I roll my eyes. "Can you please not be so—?"

"Clamdigger!"

"No. Stop. Of course, I haven't."

"You swear?"

"I swear."

He leans back in his chair and puts his hands behind his head. "Okay. Good."

I pause and cock my head. "Why *good*?"

"Nothing," Rogo says.

"Rogo, why *good*?"

"I dunno," he says, already playing dumb. "I just figured, y'know, if you're not swimming in that pool, I might try to dive in and—and maybe just—and maybe take my own little skinny dip."

I can't help but laugh. "Wait. You? *You're* gonna ask Lisbeth out?"

"Why, you think I don't have a chance?"

"Let me be honest with you." I pick the words as carefully as possible. "You don't have a chance."

"What're you talking about? I'm short and fat; she's a little on the plus size. It's a good match."

"Yeah, that makes complete sense. Maybe you should just go ring shopping right now."

He lowers his chin, and his jaw shifts off-center. "You're not supposed to root against the rabbit getting the Trix."

"Listen, you do what you want. I'm just warning you—I think she might be seeing someone."

"Lisbeth is? Says who? Her? Or you just making it up?"

"I'm telling you . . . I could hear it in her voice."

"Did she say who it—?" His face falls. "It's not Dreidel, is it? Oh, I'll stab needles in my eyes if he—"

"It's not Dreidel—no way," I tell him.

"You think it's someone from her work?"

I glance over Rogo's shoulder, where a brand-new lime-green Mustang cruises up the block, slowing as it approaches. "Kinda from work," I say as it pulls into the fire lane that's directly across from our table on the patio. The lime-green car bucks to a stop. There's no mistaking the driver's red hair.

"Whoa, paninis!" Lisbeth calls out as she leans out the window of her car. "Do they actually serve estrogen there, or did you take your shots before you arrived?"

Rogo looks at her, then me, then back to her. "*No . . .* But you said—"

"All I said was I hadn't made any constellations," I tell him. "But that doesn't mean I'm not trying," I add as I reach across the table and pat my hand against his cheek. "At least you got to slam a car door on Dreidel's hand." Before he can even digest it, I stand from my seat, hop over the railing, and head for the lime-green car.

"Sweet mother of Harry S. Truman," Rogo mutters, already following me over the railing. "Wes, *wait*!"

For once, I don't look back.

At the opening of his Presidential Library, Manning

told a reporter that his favorite comic strip when he was little was *Prince Valiant.* The next day, an op-ed ran pointing out that in said strip, Prince Valiant once had a curse that he'd never be content. The op-ed called it the curse of every President and former President. And it is. But it's no longer the curse for me.

Crossing around to the passenger side of Lisbeth's car, I pull open the door and duck down for a quick hello. "Did I miss the part when paninis became feminine?" I ask her.

"You did the same thing with apple martinis. And Volkswagen Cabriolets," Rogo interrupts, cutting in front of me and sliding into the backseat. "You should read *Jane* magazine. That's what *I* do. *Oooh*, new-car smell."

"Nice to see you too, Rogo," Lisbeth offers.

Looking side to side in the backseat, Rogo raises an eyebrow. "Wait, how'd you afford this thing? Did you get a book deal too?"

Ignoring him, Lisbeth turns to me. From the expression on her face, I sniff trouble. "Good news, bad news," she says. "You choose."

"Bad news," Rogo and I say simultaneously. I shoot him a look over my shoulder.

"Bad news," I say again to Lisbeth.

She fidgets with the bandage on her hand, which guarantees it's serious. "Remember that *San Francisco Chronicle* job I told you about?" she asks. "Well, they made me an offer—real news too, no more gossip. But they said—not that I'm surprised—they said I need to move to San Francisco."

"So, away from here?"

"Really away," she says, staring out the front windshield.

"And the good news?" I ask.

She grips the steering wheel, then slowly turns to face me. "Wanna come?"

My cheek leaps into the air. Now I'm the one wearing the butcher's dog grin.

"Waitaminute," Rogo calls out from the back. "Before we do anything rash, do we know the full picture of their speeding ticket problems out there? Because a man with my particular practice and expertise—"

I turn back to Rogo, and the grin only gets wider. "I'm sure we can look it up."

"And let's not forget about lax traffic laws and the slip-shod judicial system that supports it. If they're not there? Those two are deal breakers."

"You're really worried? It's *California.*"

"Plus," Lisbeth adds, "in San Francisco, I bet they have crazy amounts of accidents with all those hills."

"See, now that's what I like to hear," Rogo says, beaming as the car cruises up the block. "Oooh, do me a favor," he adds. "Pull up to that old Plymouth with the ticket on the windshield? If I'm gonna pay for this move, we need us some new clients." From his wallet, he pulls out a business card and tries to squeeze forward and lean out my open passenger-side window. "Wes, scootch your seat up?"

"Here, try—*here,*" Lisbeth offers, poking a button on the dash. With a whir, the convertible roof retracts, revealing the aquamarine-blue sky and making plenty of room for Rogo to reach outside.

With his stomach pressed against the interior side of the car, he leans out from the backseat and wedges one of his business cards in the seam of the Plymouth's driver's-side window. "Downwithtickets.com!" he shouts to the few people who're staring from the sidewalk. "Now go back to your sheltered lives! Go! Flock! Conspicuously consume!"

Lisbeth pumps the gas, the tires bite the pavement, and the car takes off, sending an air pocket of wind whipping against our faces. With the top down, I watch the royal palms that line the street disappear behind us. Effortlessly, the car roars up Royal Park Bridge, where the polished waves of the Intracoastal are so bright they're almost blinding. As I tip my head back and soak in the sky, the ocean wind knots its fingers through my hair, and the sweet sun bakes against my face.

Nico was wrong. The Book of Fate isn't already written. It's written every day.

Some scars never heal.

Then again, some do.

AUTHOR'S NOTE

History has always been filled with exaggerations—and so, a few words about the Freemasons. In this book, the historical details about Freemasonry are based on three years of research. All the historical figures identified as Masons—such as Voltaire, Winston Churchill, Mozart, and certain U.S. Presidents—have been documented as Masons. Throughout history, Thomas Jefferson has been rumored to be a Mason, but the evidence today, as acknowledged in the novel, does not support that assertion. Nevertheless, Jefferson, Washington, and architect Pierre Charles L'Enfant, while designing the city of Washington, D.C., did build the most famous Masonic symbol (the compass and square) and the five-pointed pentagram into the city grid. There are disagreements over who had the most influence over the final street plan, but I believe the grid speaks for itself. For over two hundred years, those symbols have been hidden in plain sight. It is also true that on October 13, 1792, Maryland's Masonic Lodge Number 9 did lay the cornerstone of the White House in a Freemason ceremony. The same was true during the laying of the cornerstone of the U.S. Capitol Building, where George Washington himself presided over the Masonic ceremony. Washington's Masonic trowel was also used at the cornerstone laying of the Washington Monument, the U.S. Supreme Court, the Library of Congress, the National Cathedral, and the Smithsonian. To be clear, those details are what intrigued me and inspired me to pursue further investigation.

Yet these facts in no way mean that the Masons are trying to overthrow the world's governments, open the devil's door, or unleash secret satanic plots.

So why parse truth from fantasy—especially in a work of fiction? Does it even matter? Well, in this world where fact so easily dances with fiction—and where, for six novels, I have prided myself on my research—it is important to me, as both author and armchair historian, to make sure I don't add even more misinformation to whatever small section of the public consciousness I am so thankful to touch.

So I encourage you to read the historical documents yourself. Any secret fraternity that had John Wayne, Winston Churchill, Benjamin Franklin, Harry Houdini, five Supreme Court chief justices, fifteen U.S. Presidents, and my Uncle Bernie as members just has to be worth checking out. Plus, you should see what symbols they built into the street plan of Sandusky, Ohio. Really. Go to: www.bradmeltzer.com/fatesecrets.html.

Brad Meltzer
Fort Lauderdale, Florida, 2006

Brad Meltzer returns to Washington, D.C., to tell a story of lies and deception at the highest levels of government—secrets whose roots go back to our Founding Fathers and whose effects could have deadly and terrifying repercussions today.

Please turn this page for a preview of

The Inner Circle

AVAILABLE IN JANUARY 2011.

In 1989, during his final minutes in the White House, outgoing President Ronald Reagan scribbled a secret note—and, it was reported, a picture of a turkey. The note said, "Don't let the turkeys get you down." He then slipped the note into the Oval Office desk and left it for his successor, President George H.W. Bush.

In 1993, President Bush left a private note in the desk for Bill Clinton, who left a note for George W. Bush, who left one for Barack Obama.

But there were two things no one knew.

The tradition didn't start with Ronald Reagan. It started with George Washington.

And the picture Reagan drew? It most definitely was *not* a turkey.

He knew the room was designed to hold secrets.

Big secrets.

The briefcase from Watergate was opened in a room like this. Same with the first reports from 9/11.

He knew that this room—sometimes called The Box or The Tank—held presidential secrets, national secrets, and *pine-box* secrets, as in, the kinds of secrets that came with coffins.

But as he stood in the back corner of the small, plain beige room, swaying in place and flicking the tip of his tongue against the back of his front teeth, the archivist with the scratched, black reading glasses knew that the most vital thing in the room wasn't a classified file or a top-secret sheet of paper—it was the polished, rosy-cheeked man who sat alone at the single long table in the center of the room.

He knew not to talk to the rosy-cheeked man.

He knew not to bother him.

All he had to do was stand there and watch. Like a babysitter.

It was absurd, really.

But that was the job.

For nearly an hour now.

Babysitting the most powerful man in the world: the president of the United States.

Hence, the secure room.

Yet for all the secrets that had been in this room, the archivist with the scratched, black-framed reading glasses had no idea what he'd soon be asked to hide.

With a silent breath through his nose, the archivist stared at the back of the President, then glanced over at the blond Secret Service agent on his far right.

The visits here had been going on since President Orson Wallace was first elected. Clinton liked to jog. George W. Bush watched baseball games in the White House Residence. Obama played basketball. All presidents find their own way to relax. More bookish than most, President Orson Wallace travelled the few blocks from the White House and came to the National Archives to, of all things, read.

He'd been doing it for months now. Sometimes he even brought his eight-year-old son. Sure, he could have every document delivered right to the Oval Office, but as every president knew, there was something about getting out of the house. And so, the "reading visits" began. He started with letters that George Washington wrote to Benedict Arnold, moved to classified JFK memos, and on to today's current objects of fascination: Abraham Lincoln's handwritten Civil War notes. Back then, if there was a capital case during a court-martial, the vote of "life or death" would come straight to Lincoln's desk. The president would personally decide. So in the chaos of President Wallace's current life, there was apparently something reassuring about seeing the odd curves and shaky swirls in Lincoln's own handwriting.

And that, as Wallace scribbled a few personal notes on his legal pad, was a hell of a lot more calming than playing basketball.

"Four more minutes, sir," the blond Secret Service agent announced from the back corner, clearing his throat.

President Wallace nodded slightly, beginning to pack up, but never turning around. "Is Ronnie joining us or no?"

At that, the archivist with the scratched reading glasses stood up straight. His supervisor, Ronald Cobb, was one of President Wallace's oldest friends from law school. It was Cobb who usually managed the visits and selected which treasured files the President would read. But with his recent diagnosis of pancreatic cancer, Cobb wasn't going anywhere for a bit.

"Mr. Cobb's at a chemo appointment, sir," the archivist explained in a voice that seemed strained even to himself.

Again, President Wallace nodded without turning around, flipping his legal pad shut.

It was the quick motion of the legal pad that caught the archivist's eye. For a moment, as the pale yellow pages fanned forward, he could swear one of the brown, mottled Lincoln letters was tucked inside.

The archivist squinted, trying to see. But from the angle he was at, diagonally behind the left shoulder of the president, the Lincoln document was—

No.

This was the President of the United States. He'd never…

No, the archivist told himself.

No. Not a chance. No.

"Before we go, I just need to hit the little vice president's room," President Wallace said, using the joke that always got him easy laughs with donors. He stood from his seat and held his legal pad at his side.

According to research psychologists, when faced with an awkward social situation, the average person will wait seventeen seconds before breaking the silence.

"Mr. President," the archivist called out without even hesitating. "I'm sorry, but—"

President Wallace turned slowly, showing off his calming gray eyes and flashing the warm, fatherly grin that had won him the governorship of Ohio as well as the White House. "Son, I just need to run to the restroom, and then we can—"

"It'll just take a second," the archivist promised.

The room was no bigger than a classroom. Before the archivist knew it, he was standing in front of Wallace, blocking the president's path to the door. The blond agent stepped forward. Wallace motioned him back.

"Tell me the crisis, son," the president asked, his grin still keeping everything calm.

"I just... urr..." The archivist stammered, slowly starting to sway. "I'm sure it was just an honest mistake, sir, but I think you may've accidentally... huhh... In your notepad." The archivist took a deep breath. "One of the Lincoln letters."

The president laughed and went to step around the archivist.

The archivist laughed back.

And stepped directly in front of the President. Again.

President Wallace's gray eyes slowly shrank into two black slits. He was far too savvy to lose his temper with a stranger, but that didn't mean it was easy to keep that grin on his face. "Victor, I need you to excuse us a moment."

"Sir..." the blond agent protested.

"Victor..." the president said. That's all it took.

With a click and a loud metal crunk, the metal door to The Vault opened and Victor joined the other three agents stationed in the corridor outside.

Staring at the archivist, the president squeezed his fist around the legal pad. "Son, I want you to be very careful about what your next words are."

The archivist craned his neck back, taking in the full

height of the president, who was so close the archivist could see the golden eagle and the presidential seal on Wallace's cuff links. *We have a set of LBJ's cufflinks in our collection*, the archivist reminded himself for no reason whatsoever. And as he looked up at the most powerful man on the planet—as he studied the leader of the free world—it took far less than seventeen seconds to give his answer.

"I'm sorry, Mr. President. But those Lincoln documents aren't yours."

For a moment, the president didn't move. Didn't blink. Like he was frozen in time.

There was a deep *thunk* from behind the archivist. The metal door to the room clicked open.

"I toldja, right, Mr. President?" a familiar Midwestern voice called out as the door clanged into the wall. The archivist turned just in time to see his boss, Ronnie Cobb, hobble inside, faster than usual. "I told you he'd come through. No reason to bother with Beecher."

The President smiled—a real smile—at his old friend and put a hand on the archivist's shoulder. "Good for you," he announced.

"I-I don't understand," the archivist said, still focused on Cobb. "I thought your chemo..." He looked at Cobb, then the president, then back to Cobb, who was beaming like a new father. "What the heck's going on?"

"Didn't you ever see Willy Wonka?" Cobb asked as he limped a few steps closer. "The big prize goes to the one who tells the truth."

The archivist paused a moment, looking at the two men. "What're you talking about? Why'd you mention Beecher?"

"Relax—we've got something a lot better than a spooky chocolate factory," President Orson Wallace said as he closed the door to The Vault, once again keeping his Secret Service agents outside. "Welcome to The Culper Ring."

The Furies

Book One

Turn Loose Your Wolf

CHAPTER I

The Chapel

SHE AWOKE LATE IN the night. At first she thought she was resting in her room, on the second floor of the adobe building local custom dignified with the name Gura's Hotel. It was a hotel, of sorts. But the small, well-kept establishment on Soledad Street served customers other than those who wanted a meal, a glass of *aguardiente* or a bed to be used for sleeping—

For a few drowsy, delicious moments she believed she was back there. Safe. Secure—

Her mind cleared. Reality shattered the comforting illusion. Gura's Hotel might only be a few hundred yards west of where she lay in the darkness, one torn blanket affording poor protection from the chill of the moonless night. But much more than distance cut her off from all that the hotel represented.

She was cut off by the four-foot-thick walls of the roofless chapel of the mission of San Antonio de Valero. She was cut off by the trenches among the cottonwoods —*los alamos*—that lined the water ditches outside. She was cut off by the heavily guarded plank bridges over the San Antonio River. She was cut off by an enemy force estimated to number between four and five thousand men.

Yet something other than the physical presence of an army was fundamentally responsible for her separation from the hotel. No one had forced her to come to the mission some said was nicknamed for the cottonwoods, and others for a garrison of soldiers from Coahuila that had been stationed here early in the century. Her own choice had isolated her.

In those lonely seconds just after full consciousness returned, the woman whose name was Amanda Kent de la Gura almost regretted her decision. She lay on the hard-packed ground, her head against a stone—the only kind of pillow available—and admitted to herself that she was afraid.

She had been in difficult, even dangerous circumstances before. She had been afraid before. But always, there had been at least a faint hope of survival. Only the most foolishly optimistic of the hundred and eighty-odd men walled up in the mission believed there was a chance of escape.

Turned on her side, her best dress of black silk tucked between her legs for warmth, Amanda stared into the darkness. In memory she saw the flag that had been raised from the tower of San Fernando Church on Bexar's main plaza. The flag was red, with no decoration or device to signify its origin. To the men and the handful of women who took refuge in the mission when the enemy arrived, however, the meaning of the flag was clear. It meant the enemy general would give no quarter in battle.

Amanda's mood of gloom persisted. Only with a deliberate effort of will did she turn her thoughts elsewhere. Pessimism accomplished nothing. Since she couldn't sleep, she ought to get up and look in on her friend the colonel—

But she didn't move immediately. She listened. She was disturbed by the silence. What had become of the night noises to which she and the others had grown accustomed during the past twelve—no, thirteen days?

She yawned. That was it, thirteen. It must be Sunday morning by now. Sunday, the sixth of March, 1836. The first companies of enemy troops had clattered into San Antonio de Bexar on the twenty-third. Counting the extra day for a leap year, today would mark the thirteenth day of the siege—

She couldn't remember when the night had been so still.

There was no *crump-crump* of Mexican artillery pieces hammering away at the walls. No wild, intimidating yells from the troops slowly closing an armed ring around the mission. No sudden, terrifying eruptions of music as the enemy general's massed regimental bands struck up a brassy serenade in the middle of the night, to keep the defenders awake; strain their nerves. The general knew that tired men were more susceptible to fear—and less accurate with their firearms—than rested ones—

None of those tactics had worked, though. If anything, the resolve of the garrison had stiffened as the days passed; stiffened even when it became apparent that Buck Travis' appeals for help, sent by mounted messengers who dashed out through the enemy lines after dark, would not be answered.

Colonel Fannin supposedly had three hundred men at Goliad, a little over ninety miles away. Three hundred men might make the difference. But now everyone understood that Fannin wasn't coming. He hesitated to risk his troops against such a huge Mexican force. That message had been brought back by one of Travis' couriers, the courtly southerner Jim Bonham. He had risked his life to return alone when he could have stayed safely at Goliad after delivering Travis' plea to Fannin.

Oh, Buck Travis still talked of relief columns from Brazoria. Perhaps from San Felipe. But there really was no Texas army—nor any organization to this rebellion as yet. All Travis could honestly hope for—all any of them could hope for—was to hold the mission as long as possible; make it an example of the will of the Anglo-Americans to resist the Mexican tyrant. No one could get out any longer, not even under cover of darkness. The

Mexican trenches and artillery emplacements had been advanced too close to the walls.

But why was this night, of all nights, so silent—?

She pushed the soiled blanket away from her legs. The quiet unnerved her. She wished Crockett would take up his fiddle as he'd done on several evenings when Mexican grape and canister whistled and crashed against the walls. Crockett's lively fiddling, counterpointed by the wild wail of John McGregor's bagpipes, would have been welcome. It would have lifted her spirits as it had before—

But I'd settle for just a cup of coffee, she thought, standing; stretching; brushing the dust from the black silk skirt spotted with beige patches of dried mud. She was weary of corn and beef and peppered beans served up without coffee. She and the dozen other women—Mexicans, mostly—cooked for the garrison. Although the women did their best, the men complained about the lack of a hot drink to wash down the meals. Amanda didn't blame them.

She folded the blanket, laid it on the ground and turned toward the east wall of the chapel. There, on a platform reached by a long ramp of earth and timber, she glimpsed the dim shapes of the twelve-pounders—three of the mission's fourteen cannons. She thought she saw a couple of men slumped over the guns, sleeping. Worn out. If only there'd been a little coffee to help everyone stay awake—!

Suddenly she wondered whether the enemy general knew they had none. Perhaps he did, and was gambling that a night of quiet would cause the defenders to fall into exhausted slumber. Did that mean a surprise attack was imminent—?

As she pondered the worrisome possibility, her right hand strayed to her left wrist. Unconsciously, she touched the fraying bracelet of ship's rope, its once-bright lacquering of tar dulled by time. The bracelet was a link to a past that now seemed wholly unreal.

But it *had* been real, hadn't it? There *was* a great house in a splendid eastern city. And ample meals. And clean bedding. And a tawny-haired cousin with whom she'd fled when her mother was killed and the family printing house burned—

Her fingers closed on the bracelet. God, she wished she were out of this place. She felt guilty admitting that, but it was true. The probability of death had become an inescapable reality. Too much to bear—

With an annoyed shake of her head, she overcame her gloom a second time. Such feelings were not only unworthy, they were wasteful of precious energy. She could still see to her good friend's welfare, even if she could do nothing about the fact that, very soon now, she might die—

Along with every other Anglo-American walled up within the mission that those in Bexar, Anglo and Mexican alike, referred to as the Alamo.

ii

A huge mound of stones blocked the center of the chapel's dirt floor. The rubble was left from last year, when the Alamo had been occupied by soldiers under the command of General Martin Perfecto de Cos, the elegant brother-in-law of the President of the Republic of Mexico. Cos and his men had been driven out by Texans—and the President himself had mustered a new army, marching north from Saltillo to punish those who had dared to fight his troops and resist his repressive laws.

A short twelve years earlier, a newly independent Mexico had welcomed American immigrants to its Texas territory. Under special legislation of 1824 and '25, *empresarios* such as the Austins, father and son, were encouraged to purchase land at favorable prices; to recruit settlers and bring them to the new Mexican state. The Americans all promised to become Catholics, but the government seldom bothered to enforce the vow once it was made. One of the most popular men in all Texas was a genial padre named Muldoon, who frankly didn't care whether the immigrants ever set foot in his church. To be a "Muldoon Catholic" was perfectly satisfactory to the Mexican government—

Indeed, the government's generosity to foreigners had very little to do with winning souls to the Mother Church. It had a great deal to do with the general feistiness for which Americans—particularly those on the western frontiers of the nation—were famous. The Anglos were intended to serve as a buffer between the marauding Texas Indian tribes and the more heavily settled Mexican states below the Rio Grande.

The Americans who came with the *empresarios* were hardy people. They defended their land, cultivated it, and thrived under the easy benevolence of the republican government. More and more Anglos arrived every year—

Until a series of political upheavals brought Mexico's current President to power.

Fearful of Andrew Jackson's well-known hunger for territory, and aware that the number of Americans in Texas was growing daily, the new President had instituted a series of harsh laws, including one in 1830 that prohibited further immigration. Another struck at the heart of the state's agricultural system, abolishing the sale and use of black slaves.

Friction resulted; then outright hostility. When Stephen Austin visited Mexico City in 1834, intending to press Texan claims about infringement of liberties, the President jailed him. From that time on, relations between the capital and its northern province worsened—

Erupting at last into open warfare.

The preceding June, a little army of Texans had swooped down on the port of Anahuac and driven out the officer responsible for enforcing newly imposed customs duties that made exporting of crops and importing of essential commodities all but impossible for the settlers. Anahuac marked the start of the armed struggle led by the Texas War Party, of which Buck Travis was a leading member. Now most of the Americans in Texas—about thirty thousand in all—were openly talking about, or waging, a rebellion—just as their forebears had done sixty years earlier, to protest the taxes and repressive policies of the English king who had ruled the continent's eastern seaboard.

When the Texans had driven General Cos from the Alamo in December, he had retreated back across the Rio Grande. Not a Mexican soldier was left in the entire state—until the President himself, stripped of his last pretense of friendliness, had led his new army and its horde of camp followers north to Bexar.

The President's arrival split families, as their members took sides. His presence sent a good portion of Bexar's population into frantic flight, their belongings piled in carts. The President secured the half-deserted town that had formerly held about four thousand people. He raised the red flag on the church. Those Texans determined to resist had already retreated to the Alamo. So began the siege, the President steadily advancing his fortifications at night, his goal to ultimately storm the mission on the east side of the winding San Antonio River—

All of the resulting turmoil and uncertainty seemed summed up for Amanda in the rubble pile she now circled with quick, precise steps. Moving briskly required effort. She was tired. She felt unclean. She wished she had a brush for her lusterless hair.

And coffee.

But somehow, as she walked on, a hardness that had been forged within her by years of risk-filled living reasserted itself. She wanted to survive this siege. But failing that, she could at least end her life in a way she could be proud of—

I don't want to die here, she said to herself. *I've come so close to death so many times, I thought I'd earned a reprieve for a few years. But if this is the end, I ought to face it the way my own grandfather did when he fought against the British king—*

Her grandfather had survived the American rebellion and died of natural causes in 1801, two years before her own birth. Yet because her father, Gilbert, had told her so much about grandfather Philip—whose rather stern portrait she remembered from the library of the house in the east—he remained a very real presence. So real that she often thought of him as if he still lived and breathed:

I wouldn't want him to be ashamed of how I die. I would never want him to be ashamed that I belong to the Kent family.

That she was probably the family's last surviving member was perhaps the saddest part.

iii

The Alamo chapel dated from the 1750s. Franciscan friars from Spain had built it, as part of a doomed effort to win Christian converts among the predatory Indian tribes. Unfortunately, the tribe the fathers chose as their chief target was notorious for a lack of belief in higher powers. Of all the Indians Amanda was familiar with, the Comanches came the closest to uniform atheism.

The chapel was located on the southeast corner of the sprawling complex of stone and adobe buildings that had grown to cover almost three acres. Invisible beyond the chapel's stout doors was the two-story long barracks, which ran roughly northeast to southwest. The barracks formed one wall of the great open rectangle known as the Alamo main plaza.

On the plaza's ramparts and in the rooms below, the defenders were awaiting the inevitable final assault by several thousand Mexican foot and cavalry. Some said there were a hundred and eighty-two men in the mission. Others put the number at one more than that. It included thirty-two who had ridden in from Gonzales knowing there was almost no chance of escape.

On Friday, Lieutenant Colonel William Barret Travis had called them all together in the main plaza and given permission for any man who wished to leave to do so. Only one had accepted the offer.

Strangely, hardly anyone called the man a coward. Perhaps it was because gnarled little Louis Rose was a friend of Colonel Bowie's. Or perhaps it was because he had long ago proved himself in combat. Rose had fought with Napoleon in Russia before taking ship to the Americas. He was no longer young, he explained, and he'd faced death too often. Once more would be pushing his luck too far.

Clearly the little soldier had no innate loyalty to the cause that held the rest of them together. Travis told him to collect his belongings and go over the wall while there was still time. By first light, Rose had vanished.

Amanda paused to glance into the sacristy, one of the few rooms adjoining the chapel that still had a roof. The sacristy, where most of the women and children slept, was dark and still.

She moved on, her expression pensive. How would the President treat the wives and youngsters after the battle? That the rebels would lose the battle hardly seemed in doubt any longer. Almost miraculously, not a man had been seriously injured during the thirteen-day siege. But things would be entirely different when the enemy launched a direct attack on the walls. The Mexicans had rifles with bayonets and, presumably, ample ammunition. The personal armament of the Americans consisted of squirrel guns, pistols, tomahawks and knives. And powder and shot were running low inside the mission. Some of the Alamo cannons had fired rocks and hacked-up horseshoes in the past couple of days—

Given all that, the Americans remained in reasonably good spirits. They managed to act contemptuous of Santa Anna's nightly artillery bombardment, and made bawdy jests about the midnight band music. It struck her that, with Louis Rose gone, there wasn't one man who could truly be called a professional soldier.

She knew of four lawyers among the hundred and eighty. There was a physician—Dr. Pollard, who attended Bowie. Bill Garnett, only twenty-four, was an ordained Baptist minister. Micajah Autry, one of the Tennessians whom Crockett had brought in, wrote passable poetry. There were several men from England and Ireland; even another Rose—first name James—who claimed he was ex-President Madison's nephew. Most had been lured to the southwest by the promise of new land; a second chance. In the border states, it was said, many a man simply shut his cabin door, carved or chalked *G.T.T.*—Gone to Texas—on it, and walked away.

Some of the more recent arrivals, though, had come in direct response to appeals by the Texans for help in resisting the Mexican dictator. Crockett was one of those. He'd marched into Bexar in February, with a dozen sharpshooters tramping along behind him. There was not only the promise of a fight here, he said, but maybe a new start afterward—and that he needed. His anti-Jacksonian politics had caused his defeat in his most recent run for Congress. In a fury, Crockett had told his constituents, "You can go to hell—I'm going to

Texas." In the Alamo, he joked about getting the worst end of the bargain.

She saw him now as she approached the entrance to the baptistry at the chapel's southwest corner. A lean man, Crockett was seated on a stool beside the cot where Bowie lay, his pneumonia-wasted face lit by a lantern on the floor. The tail of Crockett's coon cap hung down over the back of his sweat-blackened hide shirt. His shoulders moved, but Amanda couldn't see what he was doing.

Bowie didn't hear her approach. His bleary eyes were fixed on Crockett's hands, which finally became visible to Amanda from the doorway. The Tennessean was ramming a charge into one of the relatively new percussion-cap pistols. Another, matching pistol lay in Bowie's lap, alongside the nine-inch hilted knife that had given the big, sandy-haired Colonel of Volunteers the reputation as a dangerous man, a killer. Jim Bowie hardly fitted that description now, she thought sadly.

Crockett turned. So did Bowie's black slave, Sam, who squatted in a corner, his young face showing strain. In a moment Crockett stood up. Like Bowie, he was exceptionally tall. Not bad-looking, in a raw-boned way. He pretended to be a rustic, but Amanda had talked to him often enough to know that he was widely read, and had constantly worked at educating himself during most of his fifty years. The tales about his prowess as a frontiersman—spread throughout the United States in campaign biographies—had been craftily designed, often by Crockett himself, to help him win his races for Congress.

Now Crockett touched the muzzle of the pistol to his cap. "Miz de la Gura. You're up early."

She stepped into the light, the once-elegant black silk dress rustling. "I seem to have gotten used to going to sleep to band music, Colonel," she smiled.

"Know what you mean." Crockett smiled too, but uneasily.

The lantern light revealed Amanda as a fairly tall woman, five feet seven, with a full, well-proportioned figure. She'd lost about ten pounds in the preceding two weeks, and it showed in hollows in her cheeks, and half-circles beneath her large, dark eyes. Her nose was a trifle too prominent for perfect beauty. But men still found her immensely attractive. She knew it, and in the past she'd occasionally capitalized on the fact.

Outside, in the chapel, a child began to fret, as though caught in a nightmare. Amanda identified the voice as belonging to Angelina Dickinson, eighteen months. The child's mother, Susannah, was married to Captain Almeron Dickinson, in charge of the garrison's artillery. Almeron was undoubtedly up with the chapel cannon. His eighteen-year-old wife was the only other Anglo woman in the mission. The rest were wives or sweethearts of the Mexicans such as gunner Gregorio Esparza who had sided with the Americans against Santa Anna.

Bowie's big fingers shook as he tried to pick up the pistol Crockett had laid beside its mate and the knife. He acknowledged Amanda's presence with a blink of his eyes, then a labored question:

"How are you, Mandy?"

"Well enough, Jim. You?"

"Passable."

"Has Dr. Pollard looked at him tonight?" Amanda asked Crockett.

The Tennessean shook his head. "I think he's catching a few winks like the rest of the boys."

Sam, the black, said in a tense voice, "Santy Anny—he pretty quiet this evening."

Amanda nodded. Crockett said, "Too blasted quiet."

The Dickinson girl's fretful crying faded. No doubt Angelina was sleeping wrapped in rags and her father's

Masonic apron—the warmest covering available. Bowie's sunken eyes remained fixed on Amanda as she spoke to Crockett again:

"There must be a reason for the silence, Colonel. Do you think the troops are moving closer to the walls?"

"Can't be certain with those clouds hiding the moon." Crockett dug a nail against an upper gum, then spat out a bit of meat. "I'd expect so, however." He inclined his head toward the man on the cot. "I reckon Jim feels the same way. He sent Sam to find me, so I could load his pistols."

"You—" Her voice shook now. "—you think it may be tonight—?"

Crockett shrugged. Gone was the ready grin that had buoyed the spirits of the defenders so often. He said:

"There's a good chance. If I was Santy Anny, I'd expect everybody to catch up on their rest when it was quiet—which is exactly what's happened. Even Colonel Travis is asleep."

"Tha's right," Sam nodded. "I seen Joe a while ago. He tol' me the colonel was sleepin' like the dead."

Amanda looked at Bowie again, not certain that he was recognizing her any longer. She thought about the strange partnerships that fate often arranged. No two men could be more dissimilar than James Bowie and William Barret Travis—

Amanda was a long-time friend of the massive, forty-year-old Bowie. He was a Catholic, with a checkered history of dueling, slave-running and land speculation. Grief had brought him to Gura's Hotel often these past couple of years.

Bowie had orginally shared command at the Alamo with Travis. Suffering the first symptoms of pneumonia, he'd kept on working—until his ribs were crushed in an accident that happened while he was helping to raise a cannon to the plaza wall. Since then he'd been lying here in the chapel, with command of the garrison completely in Travis' hands.

Neither man liked the other very much. They had height in common, and sandy hair, but little else. Travis was nominally a colonel of the lately formed Texas cavalry. Bowie led the volunteers. Most of the men at the garrison preferred him to the ambitious Baptist lawyer from San Felipe de Austin—

It was said that Travis had come to Texas after murdering a man in Alabama for trifling with his wife. Perhaps his wife hadn't been altogether unwilling, since Travis had left her behind and had lately been courting another young woman. He was envious of Bowie's popularity with the rank and file, and scornful of his rival's fondness for alcohol. Yet a common love of Texas, and a common plight, had finally destroyed the barriers between them. When the accident put Bowie out of action, he ordered the men under his direct command to follow the twenty-seven-year-old Travis without question.

Crockett started out. "I expect I'd better get back to the wall and see to loading Old Betsy." He touched Amanda's sleeve. The sleeve's puffy leg-of-mutton shoulder was a tatter now.

Looking at her, he added, "You know, Miz de la Gura, you're to be admired for staying here. But you should have gotten out while there was a chance. Or never come in."

She shook her head. "I've heard that from Jim too. But he needed someone to look after him—Dr. Pollard has a gun to handle. Jim and I are friends. His father-in-law helped me straighten out some deed problems when I opened the hotel with the money my husband left."

The father-in-law she referred to was Juan Martin Veramendi, who had been vice-governor of Texas and one of Bexar's leading citizens. Bowie had wed Veramendi's lovely yellow-haired daughter Ursula.

She, her father, her mother and the two children of her marriage had all perished in 1833 while Bowie was off in Mississippi, attending to some business. The family had been stricken at the Veramendi resort home down in Monclova by one of the tendrils of the cholera epidemic that had been spreading worldwide out of Asia for the past ten years. The same disease had carried off Amanda's husband a year earlier.

Bowie had never recovered from the loss of his loved ones. Even the physical charms of Henriette, one of the three girls who inhabited second-floor rooms at Gura's Hotel, failed to comfort him for long. More and more frequently during recent months, Bowie had taken to dropping by Gura's solely to drink and talk with Amanda. But he downed four glasses of *aguardiente,* the powerful cane-based liquor, for every sip she took. There weren't enough women, enough words or enough alcohol in the world to mitigate his pain—

Amanda's three girls were gone now. She'd urged them to leave Bexar when the Mexican army was reported on its way. Two of the girls, mixed-blood Mexican-Comanche wenches, had probably returned to their tribes. Henriette had headed for Nacogdoches under the protection of a middle-aged customer who sold Bibles.

The Tennessee frontiersman clucked his tongue:

"Well, I guess there's nothing any of us can do about escaping now. I do sort of wish old Santy Anny would hurry up and come on. I'm tired of being hemmed in by walls. Never liked the feeling. I'd sure like to get a look at him, too. He sounds like a pompous little piece of shit —oh, I beg your pardon—"

Amanda smiled. "No need to apologize, Colonel. I've heard every cussword in the book, and then some. And you're right about the President. They say he is pompous. But clever, too."

"Just can't believe that," Crockett returned. "A man

can't have his head on straight if he goes around calling himself the Napoleon of the West."

"Perhaps with justification. He's managed to stay on the winning side through all those changes of government, remember. People are afraid of him. For one thing, they say he's tall—several inches taller than I am, which is unusual for a Mexican. He cuts a commanding figure—"

"That may be. But I think Señor Napoleon's going to get more than he bargained for when he tries to take this place. What's so damn—so blasted infuriating is that we could hold out for months if we had supplies and a thousand men!"

Bowie's hoarse voice rasped from the cot:

"We'll give 'em a run with what we've got, we—"

He started coughing, his face convulsed with pain.

Amanda darted to the stool Crockett had vacated. Sam crawled forward on his knees, likewise alarmed by his master's coughing. From the doorway, Crockett said:

"Yes, we sure will. There's only one thing I'm really sorry about. I wish I'd got here soon eough to grab me a piece of ground and farm it a while. I'm about old enough to settle down, and I'd like to see if this land's as almighty fertile as you people say—"

Amanda laid her palm on Bowie's sweaty left hand. The coughing stopped. The lines in his face smoothed. His blue-gray eyes sought her face, as if hunting relief from his pain. Under his plain linsey shirt, he was wrapped in bandages, Dr. Pollard's only means of repairing the damage done to his ribs when the cannon fell from its tackle.

A moment later Bowie glanced at Crockett:

"You can bet it is. Mandy, tell him what your husband used to say about the soil in Texas—"

Half-turning to Crockett, she forced a smile:

"He said it was supposed to be so rich, you could

plant a crowbar at night and by morning the ground would sprout ten-penny nails."

The words were heavy, humorless. Bowie's illness had made him forget that Amanda's husband had usually repeated the remark with great cynicism. Crockett, though, knew almost nothing about her history. He laughed.

"My kind of country," he said, re-settling his cap. "Pity it doesn't belong to the United States. I heard once in Washington that President Jefferson thought he bought Texas as part of the Purchase. But Spain said no. Well, I guess that doesn't make much difference now—"

"No," Bowie breathed, "all we can do is follow your advice, Davy." He paraphrased a frequent remark of Crockett's: "Be sure we're right, then go ahead."

That widened Crockett's smile all the more. "Yep," he said. Then he touched his coon cap. "Miz de la Gura—good morning to you."

Silently, the tall frontiersman melted into the shadows of the chapel. Out there, two of the Mexican women had wakened and were talking softly. One was Señora Esparza. Ironically, her husband Gregorio, the gunner, had a brother, a sergeant, in the besieging army.

"Davy's correct about one thing," Bowie said. "I think an attack's due most any time."

"That scares me, Jim."

"And me," he admitted. His left arm lifted, fingertips brushing against the sun-browned, work-toughened flesh of her hand. "You've been a good friend, Mandy. The best anyone could want—"

It almost broke her heart to hear how weak his voice had become; to see his huge, muscular body so feeble and wasted. She clasped his hand in both of hers:

"I only wish I'd been able to bring Ursula back to you. And the children. They were good people. So was your father-in-law. He was kind and friendly even though most of the *respectable* citizens of Bexar wouldn't deign to walk on the same side of Main Plaza with me."

"Well, you weren't—" Bowie realized he was speaking in past tense; corrected with a pained smile: "—aren't in the most respectable of professions."

That roused her wrath:

"I made sure the hotel was never a public nuisance! That the girls were honest—and examined by a doctor once a month. I ran a straighter place than the owners of the cantina! Their liquor was watered, their cards were marked—"

"Yes, Mandy, I know that and you know that. But to most other people, Gura's was still a whorehouse. Period."

She looked crestfallen. "I don't claim I've lived a perfect life. Sometimes, just to survive, I've done things I'm not proud of. But at least I've never concealed them. Which is more than you can say for a man like *el presidente*. Santa Anna twists whichever way the wind blows—"

A little more animation showed on Bowie's face. "Here we are jabbering like a couple of old folks. Looking back. As if everything's over."

"It is, Jim." She fingered one of his pistols. "Isn't that why you asked Colonel Crockett to load your guns?"

Bowie didn't reply. She thought he'd fallen asleep. Then, with a little wrench of his shoulders, he stirred. He asked her to help prop him against the wall at the head of the cot. As she did, she caught a glimpse of Sam staring at his master. The black saw death in Bowie's face. Death for all of them, perhaps. But the tears in Sam's eyes were not for himself.

"Forty—" Bowie yawned. "Forty's plenty long enough for a man to live. But you're young, Mandy."

"Thanks for the compliment, but it's not true. Thirty-three is getting on. Like Colonel Crockett, I really have only one regret. I wish one of my children had survived."

"I forget how many there were—"

"Two."

"Ah, that's right. I don't know why I can never remember."

"Probably because they were both born before Jaimie and I ever met you." She stared at the lantern's flame, seeing the past. "The boy was stillborn. The girl lived six weeks. When she died, it broke Jaimie's spirit. He didn't want to work the farm any more. It was almost as if our failure to have children put a curse on everything else he was doing. Blighted it—made it unbearable—" She smiled in a melancholy way. "I knew it was partly an excuse but I never said anything. It was time we tried something else. Jaimie and I weren't good farmers—"

She realized Bowie had closed his eyes. Alarmed, Sam said:

"Is he all right?"

"He's just dozing, Sam. You rest too. I'll watch him."

In the ensuing silence, her mind began to drift. Away from the chapel. Away from the trap that had closed around them all. Even though much of the past had been sad, remembering it soothed her now; drained away some of her tension. She thought fondly of her husband, Jaimie de la Gura, and of her weary thankfulness when he had decided to abandon the thirty acres near the Brazos that the two of them had worked for several years, to provide a livelihood for the family that never became a reality—

They had worked that land to exhaustion. But Jaimie lacked the instinctive kinship with the earth that seemed to be a requirement for raising cash crops at a profit. Jaimie's neighbors could produce forty to eighty bushels of corn for every acre they owned. He was fortunate if his fields yielded twenty.

In their last two years on the farm, the life had become hateful to both of them; the two-room, dog-run cabin more and more disagreeable. Even now Amanda grew queasy when she recalled the smell of the swine Jaimie tried to raise and fatten for market. Her idea of hell was a limbo without purposeful sight or sound—with nothing to torture the lost soul but the smell of pigs.

A year before the birth and death of their daughter, they had discussed trying to plant the prime cash crop, cotton. But working cotton fields required plenty of laborers. Jaimie might have been able to negotiate a loan to buy a few slaves. But he was against the system in principle. As a boy in New Orleans, he'd sided with his mother when conscience drove her to complain about the original source of the de la Gura money—West Indian blacks brought illegally through the bayous in defiance of the law of 1807 banning the importation of slaves from Africa.

Jaimie's mother had been a devout Catholic. Slavery violated Christianity as she understood and practiced it. She had filled her son's mind with her beliefs—and he carried some of that youthful indoctrination with him until he died.

Whenever he and his Brazos neighbors discussed the slavery question, Jaimie liked to remind them that President Jefferson, though a slave-holder himself, had prophesied a "revolution of the wheel of fortune" for blacks. He could quote a couple of lines from the President's *Notes on the State of Virginia*—lines that reflected Jefferson's mortal fear of a coming apocalypse—

"Indeed I tremble for my country when I reflect that God is just: that His justice cannot sleep forever."

So cotton was out of the question for the de la Guras.

The whole miserable enterprise came to an end when they buried their daughter. With the money they got from the sale of their land, they had negotiated for a house in the growing riverside settlement of Bexar.

Soon after, Jaimie had set out for New Orleans to buy some needed furnishings, to visit the cemetery where his parents were buried and to order merchandise for a store he intended to open. But in New Orleans, cholera had struck him down—and his diseased body had been hastily dumped into a grave there, so it wouldn't infect anyone else. Amanda learned of the death by means of a letter from a public official.

What grieved her almost as much as the loss of her husband was the guilt she felt about that journey to New Orleans. Jaimie didn't want to live in Bexar, let alone operate a mercantile establishment. He had been driven to it by his need to escape from all the bad memories the farm represented. He had chosen Bexar for her—knowing full well that the confinement of a town didn't suit him and never would. He had lived outdoors—hunted and trapped in the north along the Missouri river—for much of his adult life, and he knew he'd be no better selling calico than he had been at raising corn.

After Jaimie's death, Amanda wanted nothing to do with storekeeping. But she had to find some way to earn a living. She knew she had some skill in the domestic areas that were the assigned provinces of women, and she decided that the natural place to apply that skill was in managing a decent hotel—which Bexar lacked.

So, late in 1832, she had sold her house, bought an available adobe building on Soledad Street, borrowed heavily from a wealthy Mexican friend of the Veramendis to buy some beds and chairs and washstands and have the place refurbished—and by early in 1833, the first, rather spartan version of Gura's Hotel was open. She had barely been able to meet expenses during the early months.

The young sons of the town's better Mexican families began frequenting her public bar in preference to the cantina. She poured an honest drink. But the young gentlemen complained about Bexar's lack of feminine companionship. The two overweight prostitutes who occupied a filthy crib behind the cantina weren't fit to touch, let alone kiss. The young gentlemen didn't mind stains on their reputations from visiting such women, but they didn't want pox sores in the bargain.

Listening to that sort of thing night after night, Amanda had an inspiration. She soon added the desired service—with appropriate decorum and discipline—to the back rooms of her second floor. After that, her ledger showed a substantial profit every thirty days. She paid off the loan by year's end, and began purchasing some better items of furniture.

She saw nothing overwhelmingly immoral in converting part of Gura's Hotel into a brothel. She had spent her adolescence and young womanhood among the Teton Sioux, and had come to regard sexual activity not as a great many white people did—unavoidable but somehow unclean—but as the Indians saw it: of almost inestimable importance because of its connection with the creation of life. Anything so important could only be engaged in one way—joyously.

The Sioux were not a promiscuous people. Quite the opposite. Adultery, though never formally punished, was frowned upon. The virture of young women was protected with elaborate rituals of courtship—though Amanda had never been so protected. When she had been sold to a young man of the tribe, she had already lost her virginity. Because of that—and because of her white skin—the rules didn't apply.

Gradually, she came to understand and share the happy duality of the Sioux attitude toward sex. The physical act of love was regarded with mystical reverence—and this produced an earthy appreciation of the act itself. Sex was not a sin but a celebration; a wondrous and necessary part of a fulfilled life.

What a far cry from the views of those white women who whispered about the subject with revulsion. Amanda felt sorry for such warped creatures. The Sioux, both male and female, had a much healthier attitude.

To the Indian philosophy of love she had added her own: a man and woman taking comfort from each other was not half so immoral as the casual taking of human life, a common occurrence on the frontier—and one with precious little moral stigma attached. Witness her friend Bowie's respectability.

She did recognize that charging for the services of her girls injected a certain commercial taint. But which was more reprehensible? Selling a man a jug of popskull that dulled his senses and, over the long run, could ruin his health? Or selling him an hour's pleasure and peace in the arms of a woman?

Perhaps the pious would declare than an *honest brothel* was an impossible concept. But an honest brothel was what she had tried to run.

The puritanical segments of Bexar's population couldn't approve, let alone understand, such an attitude, of course. Although she prospered, she was only tolerated, never accepted, by the best families. Until his death, Veramendi remained one of her few influential friends. Another, surprisingly enough, was the parish priest, a thoughtful, tolerant man named Don Refugio, who had considerable respect for the religious convictions of most Indians—Comanches excepted—and found them in some ways more "Christian" than many of his flock.

But the ostracism she'd suffered seemed trivial in the light of what she was facing now. Her gaze was almost unconsciously drawn to the symbols of the coming struggle: the pistols in the drowsing Bowie's lap. The pistols and the infamous knife—

Copies of Bowie's knife were in demand all across Texas. Even in the States, people said. The inch-and-a half wide blade had a wickedly honed false edge that permitted a backstroke during a duel. There was also a concave scoop where the back curved to meet the edge at the point.

The prototype had been given Jim Bowie by his brother Rezin in 1827. Bowie had often laughed about the various legends that had sprung up concerning the original knife and its successors—

That each had been forged with a piece of meteorite thrown into the cauldron of molten metal.

That he was in league with the Devil, who had provided the knife's inspired, lethal design in return for a claim against Bowie's soul. There was almost no limit to the wild stories that were circulated.

Bowie had once remarked to Amanda that it was the man more than the weapon that determined the outcome of a fight. But he also admitted he was flattered when others assigned supernatural properties to the knife—

Abruptly, Bowie's eyes fluttered open. He blinked; brushed at the stubble sprouting on his chin. When he spoke, it was evident that he had no awareness of having slept for a short time:

"Still say, Mandy—" He coughed "—what Crockett said. You should have stayed outside. Maybe the Mexican's would have left you alone."

"What do you think I am, Colonel?" she teased. "A turncoat? I may run a whorehouse, but that doesn't mean I lack principles!"

Bowie laughed. Amanda smiled too, then continued more seriously:

"I knew what I had to do when Buck Travis gave his little speech at the fandango on George Washington's birthday. He said Americans down here had to stand up for liberty. My grandfather did just that back in Boston, sixty years ago."

"Travis is wrong."

"What do you mean, wrong?"

"Wrong about the issue. It's dictatorship."

"You're not making sense. What's the difference?"

"We're fighting because Santa Anna centralized all the power of the government in Mexico City. Overturned the constitution of 1824. Dissolved the state legislatures—"

"That's tyranny, Jim—and the other side of the coin is liberty."

"Depends on what you mean by the word. I mean the rights we were guaranteed in twenty-four. I don't mean independence from Mexico."

Finally she understood. "Well, Sam Houston and the others at Washington—" She meant Washington-on-the-Brazos, the provincial capital that had been established after the outbreak of hostilities "—may have different ideas by the time they've finished their deliberations. Santa Anna will never give in to demands that the constitution of twenty-four be put back into effect. Coming here with his army is proof of that. So maybe it *is* time for another declaration of independence."

"So we can join the United States?"

"Or become an independent republic."

"Well—" Bowie sighed, closing his eyes a moment. "—however it works out, we won't know."

Behind her, Amanda heard Sam's sudden intake of breath. Occasionally during the thirteen days of the siege she had witnessed similar reactions from others at the Alamo, as the possible finality of their position struck home.

"We had to make the stand, Jim," she said. "It was that or surrender. Or run."

"I know. But sometimes it seems downright idiotic to die in a broken-down church. This place is of damn little military importance and everyone knows it."

"Yes, but as Colonel Travis says, it's how we fight, not where, that counts most. If General Santa Anna pays highly for a victory, he'll think twice before he tries to win another."

A moan from the chapel made her start. Only Angelina

Dickinson, she realized. She knotted her hands in her lap. The lantern light glinted on her dark hair as she gazed at Bowie.

"I'm sounding a lot braver than I really am, Jim."

"But you still came into the mission."

"Because of you. Your illness. And—well, there's no getting around it, and I don't mean to sound overly sentimental. But I *am* an American, just like most of the settlers in this part of the country. I've kept track of what's happened these past couple of years. I happen to think the settlers are right, asking for reinstatement of the constitution they lived under when they first came out here. If it comes to fighting, and I have to choose sides, why would I choose any side but my own?"

A moment's silence. Bowie closed his weak hand around hers:

"You're a strong woman, Mandy. Some would just give up and let it go at that."

She smiled. "The people in my family may get scared to death, but one thing they *don't* do is give up easily—"

She heard the slave Sam, mumbling fearfully to himself. She tried to offer some words for his benefit:

"But I really think that red flag must be a bluff."

"Wouldn't count on it."

"Aren't there any rules in warfare? I mean about sparing non-combatants? The nigras? The children—?"

" 'Course there are. Santa Anna knows the military customs. But he won't offer terms. There's been an open rebellion. His country stands to lose all of Texas. He means to prevent that—*and* punish us. Hard. If some innocent people are hurt, he'll shrug and look the other way. That's the kind of unprincipled son of a bitch he is—"

A series of loud sounds brought Bowie's drowsy eyes fully open. Sam yelped in alarm. Amanda jumped up, ran to the door of the baptistry—

Out in the darkened chapel, a woman was wailing.

Boots hammered on the ramp leading up to the cannon platform. She heard Almeron Dickinson shout:

"They're coming! From all quarters. The foot—the cavalry too. *They're coming*—!"

iv

At last Amanda heard it for herself: the low, tumultuous drumming of men—a great many men—running over hard ground beyond the walls. The noise flooded into the roofless chapel from all directions.

On the gun platform, Captain Dickinson was cursing someone; demanding that he wake up, pronto. Amanda realized her original guess had been correct—silence to allow the defenders to doze off must have been part of Santa Anna's strategy. Dickinson's oaths and yells proved the Texans were less than ready for the assault—

A squirrel gun banged from the other side of the closed chapel doors. Then, above the steadily increasing pound of running feet, a bugle pierced the night. It was joined by another, then by all the brass in the Mexican regimental bands.

The bugles and the fast-cadenced drums were playing an unfamiliar tune. Yet the wild, almost savage music started Amanda trembling as she stood in the baptistry door.

Abruptly, the sky over the chapel burst alight. By the reddish glow of the Mexican rockets, Amanda watched men scurrying into position along the cannon rampart. The wild, pealing music grew louder. Behind her, Bowie said:

"I know that call they're playing. It's the *deguello*."

Struck by the rawness of his voice, Amanda spun. Bowie's emaciated hands closed around the butts of his pistols.

"Comes from an old Spanish word, *degollar*—" He

licked his lips. "It means to slit the throat. There'll be no terms. No mercy—"

Grimacing, he wrenched his shoulders higher against the wall, then gestured with the pistol in his right hand:

"Go back to the other women and the children, Mandy. Maybe you'll have a chance that way."

"Jim, I won't leave—"

The cocks of his pistols rasped as he thumbed them back.

"Yes, you will. I'm one of those they want most."

He waved a gun, a furious arc in the air:

"You *get out*—you hear me?"

"Better do what he say, Miz Mandy," Sam told her. "I look after the colonel from here on—"

Amanda whispered to Bowie, "God keep you, Jim."

"And you. Now *get!*"

She whirled and rushed into the darkness of the chapel. The rockets sprayed fire across the heavens. Long matches were glowing on the gun rampart. The night resounded with the sudden blast of cannons, the howls of the Mexican foot rushing toward the walls—and the drums and bugles blaring that melody which meant no quarter.

CHAPTER II

The Massacre

AMANDA HAD SELDOM BEEN dissatisfied with the sex conferred on her by the accident of birth. Occasionally, she'd even found her femininity to be a decided advantage. But she didn't feel that way as she huddled in the sacristy, surrounded by frightened women and children. This morning, she wished she were a man.

The dimness of the room seemed to heighten her sense of helplessness. She would have preferred to be in the main plaza, where the fighting was taking place. But a few moments after she'd left Bowie, Travis had sent a man to the chapel with explicit orders. The women and children were to stay hidden.

The noise of the battle had already become an uninterrupted, unnerving din. Beyond the door of the sacristy, men ran back and forth between the cannon ramp and the powder magazine, a room in the north wall. On the gun platform, Susannah Dickinson's husband bawled, "Fire in the hole!" every minute or so, and one of the twelve-pounders roared, filling the chapel with a brief glare of ruddy light. From the main plaza, there was a continual crash of musketry, screams and curses in English and Spanish—and the boom of Mexican artillery bombarding the walls.

Surrounded by her four children—three boys and a girl—Señora Esparza prayed aloud in her own tongue. Most of the other women were quiet, too terrified to speak or move.

All at once little Angelina Dickinson began to struggle in Susannah's arms. Amanda stopped her pacing, held out her hands to the child's mother:

"Let me take her a while."

Her face pale and streaked with dirt, Susannah Dickinson lifted the little girl. Amanda bent from the waist, picking Angelina up and closing her in a soothing embrace. The roofless chapel glared red again. Seated on a stone, Susannah began to sway, twisting her hands in her lap as she fought hysteria.

The child pushed against Amanda's shoulder, whimpering. Amanda said softly:

"Be still, Angelina. Put your head down. Close your eyes."

But the words had small effect. Only the strength of Amanda's arms kept the little girl from wrenching away.

Amanda concentrated on holding Angelina, and murmuring to her. Somehow that relieved her own anxiety and frustration. The yelling and the gunfire grew steadily louder—

How long had it been going on? Half an hour? An hour? She was losing track. The sacristy had grown stifling. The odor of human sweat mingled with the reek of burned powder.

Angelina finally realized Amanda wouldn't release her. Her body went limp against Amanda's breast. Amanda squeezed the child's waist reassuringly, felt the small head droop to rest on her shoulder. The sound of firing lessened suddenly.

A lean shadow loped past the doorway. Susannah jumped up, ran forward:

"Almeron—?"

"Don't come out!" Dickinson warned. "I'm going to the barracks to see what's happening—"

A moment later, Amanda and the others heard the squeak of hinges. The great chapel doors had not yet been barred from within.

Susannah Dickinson turned back to Amanda. She ran a hand over her daughter's hair, her voice panicky:

"We've lost everything. Even if the men can hold out, we've lost our homes, our—"

"Don't talk like that!" Amanda exclaimed. "We're still alive. Nothing else matters."

She wished she believed it. She was falling prey to the same despair that made Susannah tremble. Everything *was* gone. Her reasonably settled life in Bexar was over. God alone knew what would become of them—

Renewed firing, more shouts brought Amanda's head up. One of the Mexican women cried out as someone lurched through the door. Amanda recognized the Fuqua boy, one of those who had ridden in from Gonzales. He was only sixteen. He'd been hit in the face by a musket ball.

The left side of the boy's jaw was a glistening ruin of blood and bone. Weaving on his feet, he tried to speak to Susannah. His mouth produced only grotesque gurgling noises.

The harder the boy tried to speak, the more pathetic his attempts became. His lips kept moving, blood oozing from one corner—

"Galba, what is it?" Susannah Dickinson pleaded. "What are you trying to say?"

The boy's jaws worked frantically. He grunted like an animal. Blood ran down to the point of his chin. All at once his eyes filled with tears.

"I can't understand you!" Susannah cried.

Obviously in great pain, Galba Fuqua clamped hands on his lower jaw, as if he hoped to force the ruined bones to articulate properly. The result was the same as before—gibberish. With a sob and an angry shake of his head, he fled back into the smoke that now filled the chapel.

Amanda and Dickinson's wife exchanged glances,

both stricken silent by the boy's suffering. Then Amanda looked out at the sky above the chapel walls. Light was brightening behind the smoke. Dawn—

The Mexican cannon rumbled again. Shrieks and shots and throaty Spanish yells came from every direction. How many assault columns had the Mexicans hurled against the mission? From the sound of it, many more than one.

Haggard and out of breath, Almeron Dickinson appeared. He swiped the back of his hand across his powder-blackened face as his wife ran to his side.

"Great God, Sue—" he panted. "The —the Mexicans are inside the walls!" Señora Esparza covered her face.

"Travis is dead on the north rampart," Dickinson went on. "They're coming over with ladders—climbing over their own dead—hundreds of them—my God, there's no stopping them, Sue—*get back inside and stay there!*"

He shoved her, hard. Then he spun and vanished in the smoke. Moments later, one of the twelve-pounders thundered.

Several Mexican women besides Señora Esparza had understood Dickinson's English. Two of them were on their knees, hands clasped in prayer. Susannah walked slowly back to Amanda, took her daughter from the other woman. Silent tears shone on Susannah's face. Susannah was clearly ashamed of her inability to contain her fear. Amanda glanced away, staring down at her own filthy, work-toughened hands. No matter how she struggled to fix her mind on something else, one thought asserted itself—

The Mexicans were *inside the walls.*

The shouts and gunfire in the main plaza seemed closer than ever. Bugles blared. Amanda closed her eyes, recognizing the notes of the *deguello*—

No quarter.

ii

The Alamo plaza fell first, then the individual rooms of the long barracks where some of the remaining defenders had barricaded themselves. The chapel doors, barred at last, shook and splintered under heavy cannon fire. Finally they crashed open.

The smoky chapel filled with Mexican infantry. The soldiers wore blue cotton jackets with shoulder-knots of blue and green, dirt-stained white trousers and white cross-belts. Their headgear—tall felt shakos with pompoms—showed their commander's preoccupation with things Napoleonic.

Daylight had come, though the thick smoke weakened and diffused the brilliant sun. Some of the running infantrymen were little more than blurs. But Amanda could still see the bayonets jutting from their muskets—

Hunched over, a man hurled himself into the sacristy. Weeping, Sam hunted a familiar face. He stumbled forward, clutching Amanda's arm:

"The colonel's dead, Miz Mandy—"

"Oh, God, Sam, no!"

"A whole bunch come after him soon's they busted the doors. He killed about half a dozen 'fore they grabbed his knife away. I begged 'em to kill me too but they jus' laughed—"

The crying slave grew incoherent. On the verge of tears herself, Amanda ran a hand back and forth over Sam's black hair. She felt him trembling against her arm. She spoke as calmly as she could:

"Sam? Sam, you must answer me. Do you know what's happened in the plaza and the barracks?"

"Dead, they—all dead. Colonel Crockett wen' down with ten, maybe twenty on top of him. Santy Anny's soldiers, they gone crazy. After our boys fall, the soldiers jus' stand there shootin' at the bodies. Shootin' dead men an' cuttin' them with the bayonets—I swear I never seen anything like—like—oh, Jesus, Miz Mandy, Jesus—"

He flung his arms around Amanda's neck and buried his wet face against her shoulder.

At Amanda's side, Susannah whispered. "Almeron's dead. I know he's dead."

"Stop that! We can't be sure about—"

"But there's no more cannonfire. Don't you hear? The cannons haven't fired for at least a minute. *Almeron's dead—!*"

Screaming it, she flung herself toward the door. Amanda wrenched away from the grieving slave, dashed after the younger woman, caught her and pulled her back from the entrance. As she did, she glimpsed a ghastly sight. Above the milling Mexican infantrymen, bodies were sprawled across the silent twelve-pounders on the rampart. She thought she recognized Jim Bonham. And Señora Esparza's husband. She didn't see Dickinson.

She pushed the half-hysterical Susannah back into the center of the sacristy, then glanced outside again. A man came lurching down the ramp from the platform, his clothing tattered, his skin blackened by powder. In his right fist Major Evans clutched a flaring torch.

Amanda put a hand to her throat. She knew what Evans intended to do with the torch.

Ignite the remaining powder. Blow them all up—

He never had a chance. Before he reached the bottom of the ramp, kneeling Mexican infantrymen fired a volley. Evans literally flew upward, smashed by balls that pierced his forehead, blew out one eye, opened bloody holes in his belly before he fell.

Several soldiers charged the corpse. A moment later, Evans' body was being tossed in the air, jabbed and kept aloft by dozens of bayonets. The Mexicans cried one word over and over:

"Diablo! Diablo!"

Devil was one of their favorite epithets for Texans. Now they were yelling it as a joke. But Evans wasn't the only victim of the barbarity. A quick glance toward the baptistry showed Amanda another group engaged in the same sport. She pressed her knuckles against her mouth; averted her head.

The body being lifted and stabbed was Jim Bowie's—

Wild with grief. Susannah Dickinson tried to rush by. Amanda grabbed her:

"You mustn't, Susannah! Stay here. Don't let them see you—"

What a pathetic plea, she thought then. As she manhandled the younger woman back into the sacristy for a second time, she knew discovery was inevitable.

iii

The musket-fire boomed and echoed in the dim, cramped room. A fatalistic calm had settled over the women and children. Señora Esparza stared into space. The eldest of her three sons, a handsome twelve-year-old named Enrique, gazed fiercely at the ceiling, his lips forming words no one could hear. Amanda understood the meaning, though. Very few times in her life had she seen such hatred on a human face.

Unbelievably, the soldiers were still riddling the corpses on the gun platform. Through rifts in the smoke, Amanda saw bodies jump and jerk as the balls struck. The crazed behavior of the Mexicans told her a good deal about the fury of the battle in the plaza. Only incredible losses could explain the savagery of the attackers.

Another bent figure came darting out of the smoke.

How Jake Walker, a gunner from Tennessee, had thus far escaped death Amanda couldn't imagine. Then she saw that he had been hit. He seemed to be looking for someone. Suddenly, he rushed forward:

"Miz Dickinson—if they let you live, you got to get a message to my wife. You got to tell her—"

"Jake, not so loud!" Amanda warned.

Too late, Walker whipped his head around. He realized his shout had attracted attention. Soldiers converged on the sacristy door, muskets raised.

Amanda flung herself at Susannah and Walker, hoping to thrust them out of the way. Walker took a step backward. Amanda drove Susannah to the ground, tumbling on top of her.

Walker gaped at the hostile faces in the doorway. He yelled something, raised his hands in front of his face—

The muskets exploded. Walker shrieked as a ball struck him in the throat. He fell, blood gushing down over his chest.

On hands and knees beside the gasping Susannah, Amanda watched a boy belonging to one of the Mexican women clamber to his feet. Tugging a blanket around his shoulders as if he were cold, the boy started to speak. A soldier aimed and shot the boy through the stomach.

The mother moaned and fainted as the boy struck the ground. Enraged, Amanda jumped up, running at the soldiers, shouting at them in the Spanish she knew so well:

"God damn you for a pack of animals—!"

Muskets were leveled again. She ducked as two went off. Susannah cried out—and Angelina too. The little girl clutched her right leg where the ball had hit.

A soldier slammed the butt of his musket against Amanda's forehead. She sprawled, hitting hard. As she struggled to take a breath, half a dozen soldiers crowded into the sacristy and surrounded Jake Walker. As they'd done with Evans and Bowie, they lifted the body on their bayonets and tossed it. Amanda gagged, averting her head. She felt warm blood from the corpse spatter her face—

Then, abruptly, she heard a new voice, loud and deep. Something whacked against skin. A soldier squealed.

Amanda pushed up from the ground, gained her feet. She was still short of breath; blinking from the thick smoke beginning to fill the room. Her head ached suddenly. She expected a bayonet stroke any instant—

It never came. A man she couldn't immediately identify was flailing the soldiers with the flat of his saber. They fell back, muskets raised to parry the blows.

Her vision cleared a little. The man using his sword to drive the infantrymen into the chapel was a hatless officer in a red-faced blue coat stained with blood and dirt.

"His Excellency gave no orders for slaughtering women, you whoresons!" he shouted. "Get out! Leave these people alone!"

The officer's fury sent the soldiers milling into the smoke. When they were all gone, he touched Jake Walker's corpse with the toe of one boot, getting blood on the leather. His mouth twisted in disgust.

Amanda stood panting and rubbing her watering eyes. Finally she got a clear look at the officer. He was in his thirties; stout. His skin was swarthy, his hair black and wavy. His glance shifted from Walker to the dead boy tangled in the blanket. Looking pained, he tapped the flat of his sword against his trousers and turned his attention to the surviving women and children:

"I assume that most of you speak Spanish? I am here to help you—"

Still sickened by the brutality she'd witnessed, Amanda stepped forward. The officer pivoted. His round face might have been a merry face in different circumstances. Now it showed surprise as Amanda bent her head and spat on the officer's boots.

One of the women groaned, obviously afraid that Amanda's defiance would produce more violence. The officer's jaw whitened. But he didn't raise his sword. He glanced down at the spittle glistening on his reddened boot. Then back at Amanda:

"I will overlook your disrespect, señorita—" He'd glanced at Amanda's left hand and seen no ring; she had put it away permanently after Jaimie died. "—because I understand how you were driven to it by the excesses of our men. Sequestered in here, you undoubtedly have no idea of what they have been through. Indeed—"

A bitter amusement shone in his dark eyes. He had an almost boyish countenance, Amanda decided. But the essentially benign features had been hardened by weather, and by war. The officer was clearly no coward, but neither did he seem to be cruel. She began to hope she and the others might survive.

The officer shrugged in a tired way, continuing, "—indeed I doubt whether the army can withstand another such victory." The last word was tainted with sarcasm.

"I am Major Cordoba," he went on. "I must inform you that you are the prisoners of His Excellency General Antonio Lopez de Santa Anna, President of the Republic of Mexico." He pointed his saber at Angelina Dickinson. The little girl was leaning against her kneeling mother, crying and clutching her bloodied skirt to her wounded leg. "I shall attempt to secure a litter for the child—"

Still with a bitter edge to her voice, Amanda said, "Don't trick us, Major. If we're going to be taken somewhere and shot, I for one would just as soon get it over with right here."

Cordoba's lips compressed. He was angry. "Señorita—"

"My name is de la Gura. Señora de la Gura."

Amanda's insolent tone made Cordoba color even more:

"Señora, then! You are foolish if you refuse to entrust yourself to me. I have been sent specifically—"

"How can we trust men who shoot children?" Amanda retorted, pointing at the fallen boy.

"The boy's death is regrettable, but—"

"*Regrettable?* It's inhuman!"

Wilting under her glare, Cordoba muttered, "Yes, granted—granted!" Louder then: "But it is impossible to control men who have just concluded an engagement such as this. I repeat—you have no idea of what our troops suffered at the hands of your people."

There was grudging respect in Cordoba's last statement. Amanda's anger cooled a little. The man did seem intelligent—decent, even. That couldn't be said of most of the soldiers.

"Major?" Susannah Dickinson said in English. "My husband was on the gun platform. I—I assume he's dead, but—"

"Please," Cordoba interrupted in Spanish. "It would be easier if you would speak in my language."

"I don't know it very well," Susannah replied, her voice shaky. Amanda hurried to her side and cradled an arm around her shoulder. Clinging to her mother and crying softly, little Angelina looked ready to swoon with pain.

"Ask your question," Amanda said to Susannah. "I'll translate for him."

"Will I have a chance to look for my husband's body? I'd like to see him decently buried."

Cordoba glanced at Amanda. She put the query into Spanish. When she concluded, Cordoba shook his head:

"His Excellency has instructed that only our soldiers are to be buried. Unfortunately, the señora's husband is considered a traitor to the republic. Therefore—"

"For God's sake spare us your lectures, Major!"

"I was only attempting to explain why the señora's husband would be denied burial. I am afraid it will also be denied to yours."

"My husband died four years ago."

"I see."

Cordoba eyed her speculatively while she told Susannah what he had said. Almeron Dickinson's wife closed her eyes and shook her head, looking more defeated than ever.

Cordoba tried to be conciliatory: "For your own safety, I beg you all to remain here while I see about the litter. We will escort you out of the mission and back to Bexar as soon as possible. I suggest that as we depart, you do not look too closely at the sights in the main plaza. For the sake of your own sensibilities—"

The sentence trailed off into awkward silence. All at once Amanda felt completely drained of anger. She was exhausted, and desperate to get out of this death-choked place—

Cordoba started to leave. It was Señora Esparza who stopped him this time:

"We will look our fill. Butcher."

"Please, señora!—you and I are not enemies. We are people of the same nation—"

"No. I am a Texan, like my husband Gregorio. I hate your Santa Anna just as he did. When my children and I go out, we will see what your dictator has done—and remember it until another time. Then we will repay you."

Cordoba smiled in a humorless way. "I don't doubt His Excellency worries about that very thing. That's why he is in such desperate haste to put an end to the rebellion."

The major vanished into the sunlit smoke. A few seconds later, Amanda heard him summoning men—cursing in the process.

Cordoba's command of obscenities made her wonder

about him. Was his apparent concern for the welfare of the non-combatants only a pretense? Or was the bluster, the cursing, the false part? She supposed it didn't really make much difference so long as Angelina received prompt attention, and no one else was hurt.

Another burst of musket-fire drew her attention to the chapel. The Mexicans were still mutilating the dead. Laughing, even singing, in celebration of the slaughter—

Amanda's face hardened. As Señora Esparza had said, it would be a long time before the people of Texas forgot the dreadful dawn just past.

iv

In the final assault on the Alamo, Santa Anna's army had pounded the walls with cannons, then scaled them with ladders and pushed the defenders back in hand-to-hand combat to last-ditch positions in rooms in the long barracks. But even Major Cordoba's warning hadn't adequately prepared Amanda for what she saw as armed soldiers escorted the survivors into the main plaza.

The plaza was literally a field of corpses; hundreds of them. For every American, there seemed to be ten of the enemy. There was a stench of blood and powder that the morning sun couldn't burn out of the air. The faces and limbs of the dead were black with flies.

Several of the women began crying again. One of the Esparza children vomited. Amanda dug her nails into her palms and swallowed sourness in her throat. It was apparent that the Texans had given ground a foot at a time. The soldiers who had reached the chapel had done so over small mountains of bodies.

Amanda recognized almost all of the Texan dead. She had cooked for the men, joked with them—and now she saw them lying in grotesque postures, lifeless hands clenched around pistols and knives. She fought to keep from weeping herself.

By the time the captives and their guards were a quarter of the way to the open gate, Amanda's shoes gave off a squishing sound. She glanced down, sickened. So much blood had been spilled, the hard ground couldn't absorb it all. She had stepped in a sticky red pool of it.

Mexican soldiers searched for souvenirs among the heaped bodies. But near the wall, she noted an unusually large mound of corpses that the human scavengers seemed to be avoiding. Most of the dead appeared to be Mexicans, but she recognized one American among them. He lay on his back, his face a patchwork of bayonet-cuts. At least two dozen other wounds had torn his hunting shirt and trousers.

Pacing at her side as he had since they left the chapel, Cordoba noticed her stare:

"That man in the fur cap—is he the one called Crockett?"

"Yes."

"I'm told it took a score or more to bring him down."

"That doesn't surprise me."

"You can see the soldiers fear to go near him even now—"

The sight of Crockett's stabbed body unleashed new rage within her. It found a ready target in Cordoba's continuing presence:

"I don't need your personal attention, Major. In fact I resent it."

"Understandably," Cordoba nodded. His brown eyes kept moving back and forth from one group of soldiers to another. Some of the soldiers watched the prisoners with sullen fury. "However, you must accept it until we are safely outside. I want no incidents—"

"What sort of incidents?"

"Non-combatants are to be spared—that was His Excellency's order. But it won't be obeyed voluntarily. I really think you still fail to understand the importance of this engagement, señora."

"What do you mean?"

"Just this. Your General Houston has boasted too often that, with five hundred men, the province of Texas could be liberated from Mexico. His Excellency had to win this battle—at any price. To do so, he inflamed the passions of his men—"

Cordoba inclined his head toward a pair of soldiers busily plying knives. One soldier was sawing through the bone of a Texan's ring finger in order to claim an emerald signet. His sweaty-faced companion had a different purpose. While Amanda watched, the soldier whacked off the ear of a dead man she recognized as one of Crockett's twelve from Tennessee. With a gruff shout, the soldier displayed the souvenir to other Mexicans nearby. They laughed and applauded. Grinning, the soldier tucked the ear into his pocket.

"—indeed, señora, the very spirit with which your people resisted only heightened the desire for revenge. That's why looting must be permitted. And why the faces are being cleaned—"

He pointed to other soldiers using rags to wipe the dirt from the fallen, Mexican and American alike.

Amanda shook her head, not understanding. Cordoba explained in a somber voice:

"His Excellency wishes no mistakes made about the identity of each body. As I informed you, our soldiers will be buried. Your people will be burned."

"Scum," she breathed. "Murdering scum, that's all you are—"

"Alas, señora, war is seldom an ethical business."

"There could have been terms! Honorable surrender—"

"No. An example was needed. Besides, would your people have accepted terms?"

She pushed back a stray lock of dirty hair from her forehead, unable to reply. Thank God the gate was only a sort distance away. Susannah Dickinson, accompanying the litter on which her daughter rested, had already reached the body-strewn ground between the mission and the river. Two black men were just following her out the gate. One was Sam, who had come from the sacristy. The other was Travis' slave, Joe, captured in the long barracks. Both men were crying.

"Well, señora?" Cordoba prodded. "*Would* the Texans have accepted terms of any kind?"

She turned her head, gazing at the disheveled major. He was still something of an enigma. He had the erect bearing and outward flintiness of a professional. Yet there was a certain softness in his eyes that suggested another, more elusive man behind the façade. For the first time she noticed his tunic. It bulged noticeably; his belly was growing fat. And he looked tired.

Less angry, she answered:

"I doubt it. When Anglos get pushed too far, they usually fight back. There's a saying they use when someone threatens them—"

"A saying? What is it?"

"Turn loose your wolf."

"In other words—do what you will?"

"Do what you will—but you'll regret it."

Cordoba sighed. "That was obviously the case here. However—"

Stumbling, Amanda uttered a little cry. The major caught her arm. One of the enlisted men walking with the captives noticed Cordoba's quick reaction, and smirked.

Cordoba glared. The soldier blinked and swallowed, intimidated by the fury of the major's eyes.

Amanda carefully disengaged her arm from Cordoba's hand. He refused to look at her, staring instead at her cordage bracelet. His round face was still flushed.

By all rights she ought to hate him. Yet she couldn't bring herself to it.

"Where are you taking us?" she asked finally.

"You and the Señora Dickinson are going to His Excellency. The Mexican women and children will be set free."

A ripple of dread chased along Amanda's spine. "And Susannah and I won't be?"

"I can't say. His Excellency received reports of noncombatants in the mission, and I was instructed to bring them to him for his personal disposition."

"Where is he?"

"I am not certain of that either."

"Maybe I'll be lucky. Maybe he got killed."

"General Santa Anna? Never. Do you imagine he would lead an assault in person—?" Was there faint contempt in his voice? If so, it was quickly hidden: "You may find yourself reasonably well treated, however. His Excellency has a certain fondness for attractive women."

Amanda realized he meant it as a compliment. But this hardly seemed a suitable time or place. She didn't bother to respond. Cordoba then said:

"You do know His Excellency took a wife in Bexar—?"

Startled, Amanda shook her head.

"It was the night we bridged the river. One of the general's aides discovered a most charming young woman—and her mother—living just over there."

Amanda's eyes followed his pointing hand. She recognized the house he was indicating.

"Would the young woman's name be Señorita Armendariz?"

"That's it, I believe. Quite a beauty."

"I have a different word for her." The Armendariz girl and her mother were two of those who had refused to speak to Amanda on the streets of Bexar. Señora Armendariz had even urged the *alcalde* to close Gura's

Hotel. "I'm not surprised that little bitch advanced herself with the general—"

Cordoba almost smiled: "Alas, I don't believe he had marriage in mind. But the señorita's mother insisted."

"Who married them? Don Refugio?"

"The parish priest? No, I'm afraid he would have considered such a ceremony—shall we say—irregular? The 'priest' was actually one of Colonel Miñion's aides. A lad who's quite an actor. His Excellency is already blessed with a wife in Mexico City."

"You mean Santa Anna deceived the girl?"

"*And* her mother. Evidently his desire got the better of him."

"You don't sound as if you approve."

Expressionless suddenly, Cordoba shrugged. "Whatever my personal feelings concerning His Excellency, I am a soldier. I serve him without question."

"Is that right?" Amanda studied him as they approached the gate. "Would you have served him without question if you'd been assigned another kind of duty? If you'd been required to kill Texans?"

"I would have obeyed orders."

"If they included wholesale brutality?"

"I see no purpose to such a discussion," Cordoba said quickly. "It's purely theoretical."

But Amanda realized she'd touched a sensitive spot. Her earlier suspicion was confirmed. It was Cordoba's curse to be afflicted with a conscience.

"Then answer a question that isn't. What do you honestly think Santa Anna will do with Susannah and me?"

"Señora, it is impossible for me to guess. He might be in an expansive mood as a result of the victory. He might parole you at once."

Amanda halted in the gateway, turning to gaze back at the dead in the plaza.

"Major, how many men did you lose this morning?"

"Ten for every one of yours—at minimum. By the end of the third charge against the walls, for example, the Tolucca battalion under General Morales had little more than a hundred men remaining. Its original strength was almost eight hundred and fifty."

"I doubt His Excellency will be in a mood to forgive that kind of loss."

As if to confirm her fear, Cordoba didn't answer.

▼

The stench of the dead and wounded was even worse outside the Alamo than it had been within. Bodies of Mexican soldiers lay along the base of the wall. Here and there the wreckage of scaling ladders testified to the difficulty of breaching the mission defenses.

Details of men were already moving across the shell-scarred ground, dragging corpses toward the bank of the San Antonio. Overhead, buzzards were gathering.

As she walked, Amanda was conscious of Major Cordoba dropping behind. She didn't see the frankly admiring way he continued to watch her. She was pondering what might befall her in the next few hours. Surely it couldn't be any worse than the horror just concluded. Surely—

Something about the light interrupted the thought. She studied the angle of the sun and realized it couldn't be much later than eight o'clock. The day had hardly begun. Sunday. God's day. And so many had died—

But His Excellency was wrong if he believed cruelty would destroy the Texans' will to resist. As Señora Esparza had promised, it would probably have the opposite effect. It did on her.

She turned again, gazing past Cordoba to the mission's shot-pitted walls. The tricolor and eagle of Centralist Mexico had been raised above the long barracks. Hate welled within Amanda at the sight of the flag flapping in the sun.

Tired as she was, the hate would give her strength; sustain her through whatever might come before this day ended. She wouldn't grovel in front of the self-styled Napoleon of the West, that much she promised herself.

Shoulders lifting a little, she trudged on toward the river. Her shoes left faint red traces on the hard ground.

CHAPTER III

The Bargain

AMANDA CROSSED THE San Antonio on one of the plank bridges erected by the Mexicans. It seemed to her that she was returning not to a familiar town, but to one that was alien . . . alien and not a little frightening.

Northward, the low hills were covered with tents and wagon parks. Units of cavalry and infantry were re-assembling noisily, raising huge clouds of dust.

Cordoba's men soon encountered difficulty moving ahead toward the Main Plaza. The narrow streets of Bexar, so drowsy and pleasant only a few months ago, swarmed with soldiers and poorly dressed Mexican women. Many of the women were dragging children whose clothing was equally dirty and ragged.

The women were hurrying in the opposite direction, toward the mission. Band music drifted from the river now—music celebrating the victory. The women jeered at the captives. Amanda was glad Susannah couldn't understand Spanish.

Some stones were flung. One struck Señora Esparza. Cordoba drew his sword and ordered his men to close up around the prisoners. After that, the *soldaderas*—the camp followers—had to content themselves with verbal attacks.

Despite her determination not to succumb to despair, Amanda found her spirits sinking with every step. Her mouth felt parched. Her head hurt. Her arms and legs ached. She wished for the peace and privacy of the tiny walled garden behind the hotel. There, whenever she was lonely or depressed, she had always found solace in simple physical labor. She yearned for the garden now. She imagined the sight of her tomato vines bursting with heavy red fruit in the mellow Texas sunlight. She savored the remembered aroma of strings of onions and yellow and red peppers drying in the shadow of the wall—

Gone. It was all gone. The sense of defeat swept through her like a poison. It seemed that every time she put her life back onto a stable course, something disrupted it. That had been the case for almost as long as she could remember—

She thought of her mother, dying in the street outside the Kent house in Boston. She thought of the terrible morning in Tennessee, when the man who claimed to be a preacher had beaten her cousin Jared, then raped her and carried her off to St. Louis, where he sold her to trappers traveling up the Missouri. She thought of her first night in the tepee of the young Sioux warrior who had bought her from the trappers—

She had endured all of it, calling on an inner strength bequeathed to her in some mystical chemistry of birth by her frail father, Gilbert Kent. She had endured hunger and pain and near-paralyzing fear, buoyed by her will to survive. In an hour, a month, or a year, she told herself, she would find an end to the suffering. And so she had—

But there always seemed to be more waiting.

Grief had nearly destroyed her after Jaimie's death. She had fought with it like an enemy who wanted her life. She had fought, and she'd won another reprieve. Opened the hotel. Fussed over the three girls. Taken comfort from the feel of the garden earth against her hands whenever doubt and sadness threatened her—

And now, because she'd decided she had no choice but to go into the mission, she was forced to begin still one more time—as a stranger in a town of enemies. She wondered whether she could do it.

She noticed a party of officers approaching on foot. Among them was a stout, mustachioed civilian wearing flared trousers, a tight-fitting velvet jacket and a sombrero. The *alcalde*, Don Francisco Ruiz.

Though never her close friend, Don Francisco had always been cordial. He realized that Gura's Hotel fulfilled a need in Bexar, and he had resisted pressure from the Armendariz family and others when they wanted it closed. Don Francisco glanced at Amanda as he passed. One of the officers said something to him and he looked away quickly, without so much as a nod of greeting.

There had been shame in his eyes, Amanda thought. But the shame wasn't powerful enough to make him speak to her. The *alcalde* understood very well who controlled Bexar now. Later, she learned that he had been sent to the mission by Santa Anna himself. He was to search through the bodies of the Texans and confirm to His Excellency that William Travis, David Crockett and James Bowie were indeed dead.

Don Francisco's rebuff brought tears to Amanda's eyes. She was ashamed of herself, yet she couldn't hold the tears back. A *soldadera*—a young, coarse-faced woman with immense breasts and a large mole near the point of her chin—saw her crying, snatched up a stone and lobbed it between two soldiers.

The stone struck Amanda's forehead. The pain jolted her from her self-pity. Eyes flashing, she closed her hands into fists and started after the Mexican girl.

Cordoba was quicker. He brandished his sword and cursed. The young woman laughed and hurried on as soldiers kept Amanda from pursuing her.

The major reached for Amanda's arm. "Are you all right, señora?"

She avoided his hand. "Yes. And I told you before—I don't need any help from you."

Cordoba stared at her for a moment. "Don't be too sure."

Furious, she gathered her skirt in both hands and walked on. In an instant, her eyes were dry.

She'd show him how strong she was. She'd show them all.

ii

The prisoners were taken to the spacious, airy house of Bexar's second-ranking political official, *jefe* Don Ramon Musquiz. Servants carried Angelina Dickinson to a bedroom while the others—Amanda, Susannah and the two blacks—were led to the don's comfortable office overlooking an ornamental garden.

Susannah grew distraught when she wasn't permitted to accompany her daughter. But Cordoba assured her the child was not seriously hurt. After absenting himself briefly, he returned to say that Santa Anna's personal doctor had already been summoned to dress the little girl's wound.

Susannah's dirty, bedraggled appearance showed Amanda what she herself must look like. She sank into a chair, her attention caught by the paper-littered desk. She had been in Musquiz's office before. She recognized a number of articles that didn't belong there: an ornate silver tea service; a liquor decanter with a fat silver stopper; a silver spittoon.

A sandaled servant, an elderly Mexican, entered with a tray. On the tray were cups, a wine bottle and a plate of hardtack. The servant knew Amanda. But, like Don Francisco, he thought it prudent not to acknowledge the fact. He concentrated on putting the tray on the desk without disturbing the papers.

Avoiding Amanda's eyes, the old man addressed Cordoba:

"His Excellency is inspecting the mission. He will return shortly. He ordered that the prisoners were to be given refreshments."

"How kind of him," Susannah said in a bitter voice. "Is it our last meal?"

"Very good, thank you," Cordoba said to the servant. As the old man left quietly, Amanda rose and walked to the younger woman.

"A little wine might make you feel better, Susannah."

"Nothing will make me feel better." Almeron Dickinson's widow clenched her hands. "Nothing. Nothing."

Major Cordoba acted embarrassed. The four soldiers who had accompanied him into the office appeared to be engrossed by *el jefe*'s fig tree just outside.

Amanda realized she was incredibly hungry. She saw no reason to refrain from eating the enemy's food. She picked up the plate and walked to the two blacks to serve them.

Sam took a piece of hardtack. Joe shook his head, still looking utterly miserable. Amanda returned to the desk. She poured half a cup of wine, drank it, then picked up two pieces of hardtack and sat down again.

The office was cool and still. With an annoyed expression, Cordoba began wiping the buttons of his uniform with his cuff. He polished off some of the dirt, but not enough, apparently, to satisfy himself. He kept frowning.

Amanda finished the first piece of hardtack. She was raising the second to her lips when she remembered something. Cordoba saw her wry, sad smile; gave her a quizzical look.

She held up the hardtack, explaining:

"Jim Bowie said there'd be an attack sooner than we expected. He heard that the bakeries in the border towns were working night and day, making this. He said only an army would require that much hardtack."

"If you had that kind of advance warning, señora, why were there not more men in the mission?"

"Travis thought Jim was crazy. He said your army would never march in the winter. Not until the grass grew and the horses could forage. Jim told him we were fighting Mexicans, not Comanches. Travis laughed it off. If he'd listened to Jim, he might have sent for reinforcements sooner—"

She stopped, following Cordoba's tense glance toward the corridor. Boots clicked out there. She heard men speaking. Then one of the soldiers in the office pointed toward the garden wall:

"They've started burning them."

Amanda looked. A black plume of smoke was climbing into the sky. Her hand closed, crumbling the hardtack—

A party of several officers and one civilian appeared at the far end of the hall. One of the men was noticeably taller than the others. He was perhaps forty years old, and not bad looking. His uniform overflowed with silver frogging, buttons, epaulettes.

Moving briskly, the man led the others toward the office doorway. Just as he entered, he touched his middle, belched, then winced. Amanda's last question about the man's identity vanished. Santa Anna was known to suffer perpetual dysentery.

Cordoba snapped to attention; saluted:

"These are the prisoners, Excellency."

General Antonio Lopez de Santa Anna nodded. "Very good. Take your ease, Major."

But Cordoba remained rigid. The general turned to the civilian member of the group, a willowy fellow carrying a sheet of foolscap.

"Read me the first line again, Ramon."

The secretary cleared his throat. " 'Victory belongs to the army, which at this very moment, eight o'clock A.M., achieved a complete triumph that will render its memory imperishable—' "

Santa Anna touched the paper. "Amend that. A complete and glorious triumph." The secretary's head bobbed. "Have it inscribed and return it to me for signature. I want it dispatched to the minister of war in Mexico City by noon, understand?"

"Perfectly, Excellency." The secretary bowed and hurried out.

Santa Anna turned next to a suave officer who was appraising Amanda's figure with insolent directness. "Colonel Almonte!"

The officer jerked to attention. "Excellency?"

"I believe we should arrange a victory review in the plaza before the day's over. I will give a short oration. See to it, please. Make certain all the town officials are present."

Almonte saluted, pivoted smartly and left the room.

The general returned his attention to his captives, studying them with an affable expression. The past few seconds had already confirmed what Amanda had heard about the dictator's enormous vanity. And she knew too much about his rapid shifts in allegiance on his climb to power to be lulled by his smile.

iii

Santa Anna slipped into the chair behind the desk. He opened a drawer and took out a gold snuff box. A charnel stench drifted in from the garden. The Texan dead, burning—

From the box Santa Anna removed a pinch of white powder. He placed the powder in one nostril and inhaled. Then he handed the box to another of the officers:

"Ask Doctor Reyes to refill that for me." As the

officer hurried out, Santa Anna smiled even more broadly at the two women and the blacks. "It has been an eventful twenty-four hours. A bit of opium powder is marvelous for relieving tiredness, I find."

None of the prisoners offered a comment. Frowning, Santa Anna said to Cordoba:

"You will identify these people, please."

One by one, Cordoba supplied the names of the four, beginning with the blacks and ending with Susannah:

"Señora Dickinson is not fluent in our language, Excellency. But Señora de la Gura can translate."

"De la Gura," Santa Anna repeated. "That isn't an Anglo name."

"My husband was Spanish."

"Spanish—*Excellency*," one of the officers said, taking a step forward. Santa Anna waved him back, trying to soften Amanda's frostiness with another smile:

"Spanish—do you mean Mexican?"

"I mean what I said. My husband was born in New Orleans."

"He was an American citizen, then?"

"After the Purchase, yes."

Santa Anna frowned at the obvious pride in Amanda's voice. He tented his fingers; scrutinized her in silence; finally said:

"It's unfortunate for you that I chose not to divide the survivors simply by consulting a list. With that name, you might have been lost and forgotten among the Mexican women Major Cordoba found in the mission."

His eyes were much less friendly now. But Amanda refused to turn away from the intimidating stare. The general abruptly switched back to cordiality:

"There is an excellent establishment in Bexar bearing the name Gura, I recall."

"The hotel I own," Amanda said.

"The hotel you *formerly* owned. It has been taken over as a billet for my senior staff. That should not be a great loss, however. You could have lost your life. So I presume you will be suitably thankful when I permit you —all of you—to leave Bexar unharmed."

Sam gasped loudly. Susannah looked at Amanda, who told her:

"He says we aren't to be killed."

"Angelina too?"

"I presume so." She repeated the question for Santa Anna.

"Of course, of course! I looked in on the child just before I stepped in here. A delightful creature. Lovely! Reyes, my personal physician, assured me she would be fit to travel within a day or two."

Again Amanda translated. Susannah looked blank: "Travel? Travel where?"

"She wants to know where we're supposed to go," Amanda said.

"Why, back to your own people!" Santa Anna said, speaking to Susannah in Spanish. "I thought briefly of sending you to Mexico City, as proof of our victory. But I've concluded it would be more useful for you to go to Gonzales. I'll send an escort—my own orderly, Benjamin. He was an Anglo—although a slave—before he joined my service. When you're once again among your own—"

"What do you mean, her own?" Amanda fumed. "Her husband died at the mission. Murdered by your men!"

Santa Anna sat forward suddenly, losing his relaxed manner. "Murder is a very ugly word, señora."

"But it fits."

"No. Those who died were casualties of war. By their traitorous behavior, they arranged their own executions. It was no doing of mine."

Amanda laughed then, so loudly and contemptuously that the officer who had reproved her before drew his sword.

Standing by Susannah's chair, Cordoba tried to warn Amanda with his eyes. She ignored it:

"No doing of yours? Who raised the no quarter flag from the church, may I ask? Who gave the command for the playing of the *deguello?*"

"God, what hypocrites you Anglos are!" Santa Anna snarled. "You cavil at the harshness of war while your white brethren in the United States—and here in Texas until I put a stop to it!—trade in human flesh without a qualm of conscience. Blood of Jesus, woman, don't prattle to me about inhumanity!"

Santa Anna's slashing gesture stunned Amanda to silence. Before she could accuse him of taking refuge behind an issue entirely unrelated to the battle, he barked at Cordoba:

"You will please assume the duties of translator, Major. I dislike this woman's contentious attitude. Especially since I have generously decided to permit the noncombatants to go free."

Seething, Amanda exclaimed, "You'll forgive me, Your Excellency, but I'm suspicious of this sudden outpouring of compassion—"

"Excellency—" The officer who had drawn his sword stormed around the desk. "I suggest that kindness is wasted on this American slut."

"Kindness *and* rational argument, it seems."

"Then let my dragoons have her."

Santa Anna pursed his lips. "A possibility. A distinct possibility—"

"If you're going to kill me, do it and be done!" Amanda raged. "I've had enough of Mexican mercy for one morn—"

"*Amanda!*" Susannah Dickinson cried. "For God's sake be civil to him! I don't know what you're saying, but you're going to make everything worse. Almeron's dead, Angelina's hurt—" Suddenly she began to weep.

"I want to live. I want to get out of this place. *I want to live—*"

Amanda held back an angry remark. She had no right to endanger Almeron Dickinson's widow or the blacks because of her own hostility.

Presently the color that had rushed to Santa Anna's cheeks faded. He rose, moving out from behind the desk:

"What did she say, Major? I caught a little of it, but not everything."

Cordoba repeated the sense of Susannah's plea. Santa Anna nodded; said to Susannah:

"I am glad you show some appreciation of the realities of the situation, señora—" He paused, allowing Cordoba time to translate. "Your people were foolish to oppose the Centralist regime. I trust that when you leave Bexar—supplied with food, blankets and money—you will lose no time in communicating to your fellow Texans that resistance is futile. I am more determined than ever to see the rebellion crushed now that the so-called Council at Washington has taken its ill-advised step—"

Cordoba cleared his throat. "I don't believe any of those in the mission knew about the declaration, Excellency."

"Ah, yes, you're probably right." He turned toward the blacks, his tone caustic:

"You are now citizens of the independent Republic of Texas. Not free citizens, of course. I'm sure freedom will be reserved for those with white skins."

The slaves gaped. Amanda asked, "When did it happen?"

"The declaration? Just four days ago. Señor Burnet has been named president, and Señor Houston is general of the army—if there is one."

Amanda was speechless again. The news was both sad and surprising. The sadness came from realizing that none of the men who had died at the Alamo had known they were fighting for a newly independent country.

"I find Houston's appointment particularly amusing," Santa Anna said. "The poor sot the Indians call Big Drunk commanding a few farmers and storekeepers as ill-trained as he is—"

Amanda managed to speak: "Sixty years ago, another army just like that won a war for independence—"

"True, señora. But I shall not make the same mistakes the British king did—nor be so gentlemanly to those I oppose." He stalked toward the blacks. "When you rejoin your people, tell them their so-called republic will be gone in three months. Tell them what you saw here. Tell them what they can expect if they continue to fight—" The deep voice grew louder. "That is the only price I'll extract for your freedom—that you spread my message. Resistance will be crushed without pity. The sensible course is immediate surrender."

Cordoba finished translating for Susannah. She stared at Santa Anna, then slowly bowed her head.

The general glanced to the blacks again. Their uneasy eyes showed him they understood what he wanted—and, like Susannah, agreed to it. Santa Anna smiled with genuine pleasure. The word of his military might would be spread through the little Texas settlements, to demoralize the government that had emerged at last from the wrangling and factionalism prevalent for months at Washington-on-the-Brazos.

Santa Anna approached Amanda:

"And you, señora? If you are set free, will you tell your people that surrender is the only way to avoid annihilation?"

"That's the last thing I'll do—Excellency. I will tell them how you ordered a massacre—"

"*Don't!*" Susannah cried, understanding Amanda's fierce expression all too clearly. "He's only asking us to report the truth. We can't win against them—why do you want to pretend we can?"

For a moment, Amanda wavered. Susannah might be right—

For most of her adult life, she had put survival foremost on her list of priorities. Was she foolish to change those priorities now?

No, she decided, thinking of Crockett's slashed body. Of the boy in the blanket shot down in the sacristy. Of Bowie's bayoneted corpse. *No—*

She couldn't scorn Susannah or the two slaves for their desire to live. She knew Susannah probably believed the Texans could never hold out against the Mexican army. Amanda wasn't sure they could either. But in spite of that, the price Santa Anna was asking for survival was higher than she wanted to pay.

Trying to keep her voice steady, she said, "Take the general's offer, Susannah. I can't. If I go to Gonzales—" There was a catch in her throat; her stomach churned as the smell of the burning bodies worsened "—if I go there, I'll tell everyone His Excellency deserves to be shown exactly the same mercy he showed at the Alamo. I'll tell them it's better to die for an American republic than surrender to a Mexican killer—"

Santa Anna was livid. "I do not speak English well, señora. But I understand a little of it. You will regret what you have just said." He lost control. "*By God, you will—!*"

He pounded a fist on the desk, overturning the creamer of the tea service. Thick droplets fell from the edge of the desk, striking the inlaid floor with a loud *plop-plop.*

The officer who had mentioned turning Amanda over to the dragoons started to repeat the suggestion. Before he'd spoken half a sentence, she was struck just under her left breast—viciously—by a man's fist.

She spun, raising her arms to protect herself. With shock and disbelief, she saw the contorted face of her attacker.

It was Cordoba.

iv

"You've said enough, you ignorant whore!" Cordoba yelled, drawing his hand back to hit her again.

Susannah Dickinson tried to rush to Amanda's assistance. Two of the enlisted men seized her and wrenched her back as Cordoba slammed his fist into Amanda's stomach, then flung her to the floor.

The room darkened; distorted. She pressed her hands against the wood, trying to rise—trying to comprehend the inexplicable change that had come over the major. He was flushed; breathing hard as he bent his leg backward at the knee, then kicked her in the belly.

Amanda cried out. The room began to swing back and forth. Cordoba's voice sounded faint but furious: "Let me take her and discipline her, Excellency."

"Better she be shot outright," another of the officers said.

Cordoba again: "No, no, Colonel—if you please! I'll see that she suffers for her insolence. Much more than she'd suffer if you killed her."

Santa Anna: "I find your request a bit unusual, Major. You said nothing during her outbursts—"

"My astonishment—my anger—robbed me of suitable words, Excellency."

"Nor are you known for your temper—"

"Except when my commander is insulted, Excellency."

"Well, that's the proper attitude, certainly."

"Then let me have her!"

Amanda tried to sit up. She was too weak and dizzy.

She fell back, her black silk dress tangled around her legs. She'd thought Cordoba possessed some small degree of honor. Like Santa Anna's generosity, that honor had been revealed as a sham. Over the ringing in her ears, she heard him pressing his request:

"—I promise you I'll work her till she drops, Excellency. I lost my serving-woman on the march from Saltillo. *Telele* killed her—the fever from bad water. So if you'll put her in my keeping, I'll teach her to respect Centralist authority—"

Several of the officers muttered about Cordoba's proposal—whether for or against it, Amanda couldn't be sure. Finally, she heard Santa Anna shout for silence. The voices cut off abruptly. The dictator sounded amused again:

"Very well, Major, you may have her. See that she fully enjoys the perquisites of her new station—and that she comes to regret her refusal of my clemency. But mark this—!"

He struck the desk again. The sound was loud as a shot.

"Under *no* circumstances is the offer to be repeated. By you or any other officer. She will not go free now or ever. Of course, if she finds the work of a camp woman too difficult—if she should sicken and die—that's your affair. No questions will be asked."

The room seemed cloaked in darkness. Amanda let it sweep into her mind, blotting out Santa Anna's soft, satisfied chuckle.

v

A fly buzzed. There was a sensation of intense heat. She opened her eyes.

Above her, she saw an expanse of light. After a moment she realized she was lying on hard ground, gazing up at the sloping side of an officer's marquee, one of dozens that dotted the flat land and the hillsides around Bexar. The sun was broiling down on the other side of the canvas, lighting it to brilliance.

She still ached from the punishing Cordoba had given her. Slowly, she rolled her head to the side and saw a mussed cot. A rickety table. A washstand holding a razor case, brushes, a dented copper basin—

Then, in the periphery of her vision, she noticed boots. Boots marked with dried blood and dirt. One of the boots was resting on a small wooden box. Hands were drawing a cloth back and forth across the stained leather—

She turned her head a bit more. Cordoba took his foot off the box, dropped the cloth. He stood staring down at her, his uniform blouse unbuttoned. Black hair curled above a sweat-grayed singlet.

The inside of the marquee was broiling. She drew in a breath of the unpleasant air. It was ripe with the smells of horse droppings, the burning dead, male sweat. Cordoba continued to watch, his expression a blank.

She gathered her strength, attempted to sit up. The effort pierced her side with a pain that made her wince and cry out softly.

"You stupid, intemperate woman!" Cordoba exclaimed, grabbing her wrists and pulling her to her feet. As soon as she was upright, he let go. She sat down hard on the cot, gasping.

Rage still colored the major's cheeks. But it was a different kind of rage than he'd displayed in front of the general. Puzzlingly different—

Cordoba strode forward. Outside, several mounted men clattered by, laughing and joking in Spanish. She raised her hand to strike him. Cordoba caught her wrist; pushed her arm down:

"Listen to me! I have very little time before I must attend that wretched review—"

The officer's fingers were hard, like a vise. Behind the mild countenance that had turned so hateful in the Musquiz house, there was unsuspected strength—a strength he exerted to keep her immobilized on the cot as he said:

"Do you know that you nearly got yourself sentenced to a firing squad? Or worse?"

"Let me go, God damn you!"

"No! Not until you hear me out! You made His Excellency furious. He was ready to order you shot—or to turn you over to those dragoons Colonel Fialpa mentioned. In the latter case, a hundred men would have taken you. Then you'd have been thrown to the *soldaderas*. To die—if you were lucky."

She laughed at him, a raw, raging sound:

"Don't start telling me how generous *you* are, Major!"

"I had to mistreat you, don't you understand that? I knew of no other way to get you out of there!"

"You're telling me what you did was—was a *sham?*"

"Yes! Completely!"

"Well, it was too damned realistic!"

"For that, I am truly sorry. It was the only way—" He loosened his grip. "If you promise not to run, I'll release you."

She debated; finally sighed and nodded:

"All right—though I still don't quite believe what you're saying."

He let go.

"God—" She massaged her belly. "You hurt me."

He shrugged. "A trifle."

"You call broken ribs a trifle?"

"Compared to the ministrations of the dragoons, yes. Besides, I don't believe any of your ribs are broken. While you were unconscious, I looked at—that is, ah—I examined—never mind! Take my word, you'll survive."

He stood back, rubbing his reddened cheek. It was

beginning to show a sweaty growth of beard. As the red faded, he said:

"Let's get down to the issue, Señora de la Gura. It's quite simple, really. You can stay with me and I'll treat you decently—with a few public demonstrations of cruelty to impress my fellow officers, naturally. Or I can turn you back to Santa Anna and you can take your chances. You lost your opportunity for freedom when you provoked His Excellency. So I trust you understand the choice is no longer liberty or the lack of it, but whether you want to live with me or die with someone else."

Wearily, Amanda gazed at him. She saw an emotion in his eyes that almost made her laugh out loud. He looked as earnest and hopeful as a small boy. She didn't laugh because she couldn't quite bring herself to humiliate him.

After pondering his offer a while, she said, "I realize you're trying to help me, Major. But I'd feel like a traitor staying with you."

"A traitor to whom?"

"To my own people."

"*Ah!*" He gestured sharply. "Better to be alive—with hope—than dead with none. His Excellency predicts total victory soon, but I am not so certain. Especially now that you Anglos are fighting for a country you have declared to be your own."

"I'm not fighting for anything, Major. I'm a prisoner."

"There is always the chance you could be rescued."

"Highly unlikely, I think. I just don't understand your concern for my welfare. What kind of man are you?"

"A man whose *soldadera* died, and who needs—"

"That's not what I mean and you know it."

"What else can I tell you?" he exclaimed, his skin growing pink again. "My life is commonplace—quite unextraordinary. I'm a professional soldier with a duty to perform—and with little fondness for the style of my commander."

"Now we're getting somewhere. You don't like Santa Anna?"

Still flushed, he sat down on the small box. It creaked under his weight but, staring at his hands, he seemed not to notice.

"That is understating the case, señora." After a cautious glance at the tent entrance, he went on, "His Excellency demands the best for himself. The tastiest food. The choicest wine. Snowy linen, polished silver—my God, the man has a passion for silver such as I've never seen before—!"

Fascinated, Amanda watched the major growing angry again.

"You may be sure His Excellency was comfortable on the long march from Saltillo. He slept under fur robes, with a brazier burning in his marquee, when the blizzards struck the hills of Coahuila and the men had no tents and no fires. He pretended not to see the wretched Mayans from the Yucatán battalion lying like bundles of rags at the roadside—dying because they couldn't withstand the northern cold. We were short of provisions from the beginning, so His Excellency cut rations to half—for everyone except himself. Can you imagine how I liked ordering my men to fall out and search for their suppers? *Search?* They ate mesquite nuts—have you ever tasted them?"

"Yes. Bitter."

"Compared to our usual fare, they were a banquet, I can assure you! We lost men by the hundreds—both from desertion and—you'll forgive me—diarrhea. In his haste to mete out punishment, His Excellency also overlooked the small matter of providing enough doctors, medicines and ambulance wagons—but of course he made sure his personal physician was always close by! My God, you wouldn't believe the chicanery the man condones! You can imagine how our wounded need blankets and bedding today. But every stitch in Bexar has been appropriated by His Excellency's brother-in-law, Colonel Dromundo. It's available—to any hurt or dying man who can pay Dromundo's price—"

Glumly, Cordoba shook his head. "They would slit my throat if I said any of this in public. But His Excellency General Santa Anna is fighting for his personal power, not for Mexico."

"Then why do you obey him?"

"Because, for better or worse, he *is* Mexico—at the moment. Don't make any mistake, señora. Despite my dislike of him, I'll honor my promise. You won't go free. And if you try to escape, I won't stand in the way of your punishment. Beyond that, I guarantee you good treatment. My wants are minimal. Decent meals. Clean laundry. My boots polished—I hate a dirty uniform. It's unprofessional."

Amanda thought it over. She was still undecided when Cordoba jumped up. "Believe me, señora, I'm offering you a better bargain than you'd get from most in this encampment!"

He was probably right. And becoming a camp follower was no worse than some of the other things she'd done to stay alive.

"All right, Major," she said. "I accept."

He clapped his hands, delighted as a child:

"Wonderful! Now the first thing you must learn is how to say my first name correctly—"

"Major."

"What is it?"

"There's one subject you overlooked."

"Yes?"

She patted the cot.

He turned red again. "I make no demands there, señora. Clean smallclothes and a hot meal at night will satisfy me."

"Then you're one of a kind."

He shrugged, almost scarlet. "I am what I am."

"Don't you like women?"

He looked at her steadily.

"Some women."

She honestly didn't know what to make of Cordoba. At the moment, he resembled a shy boy more than a man. At least he didn't frighten her any longer, and to be free of fear even for a little while was welcome.

He cleared his throat. "Uh—señora—my name—"

"Oh yes, I'm sorry. Tell me what it is."

"It is Luis."

"Luis," she repeated.

"Good, that's just right—"

Still flushed, he pulled out a cheap pocket watch, then began buttoning his uniform blouse hastily.

"I don't think you'll find me too unpleasant. I am not a violent man. I am a narrow one, I regret to say. All my adult life has been spent in the army. I've had no time for other pursuits—nor any interest in them. But you know something? The older I grow—the more I see of the politicians who direct any army—the more I wonder whether I should have done something else with my life. Campaigning's no pleasure under a man like His Excellency."

As he finished dressing, he added in an apologetic way, "I trust you won't attempt to escape while I'm gone."

"No, I won't." She stretched; wriggled her shoulders, thankful that the aches were lessening.

"You'll have many an opportunity in the weeks ahead. You won't be guarded, or even watched very much—"

"Major, you saved my life."

He waved. A shade too quickly, she thought. "For purely practical purposes, I assure you."

"Even so, I owe you something for that. And I made a bargain. I'll live up to it."

"I do think I should station a corporal's guard outside for a few days. For the sake of appearance—"

"Go ahead if you want. I'm going to lie down for a little. Then I'll tidy up the bed, and try to find some branches to sweep this place out."

"Please, señora—just rest. You have seen horrible sights today. There is no need to busy yourself so soon."

"Yes there is," she said softly. "If I work, maybe I'll forget what I saw."

His eyes met hers, large and melancholy.

"Do you honestly think that's possible, señora?"

"No. But God forgive me, I wish it were."

"So do I."

They stood a moment longer, staring at one another. Then Luis Cordoba snatched up his shako and batted dust off the pompom. After a last look at the bedraggled woman in the center of the sunlit marquee, he touched respectful fingers to his brow and went out.

CHAPTER IV

The Camp Follower

THE ARMY MOVED EASTWARD, and Amanda with it. Cordoba brought her word of terrified Texans fleeing ahead of the Mexican force. The major said Sam Houston himself had ordered the retreat, fearing more slaughter of the kind that had taken place at the Alamo. Susannah Dickinson and the two blacks had evidently reached Gonzales with an account of the massacre.

The weather was rainy and miserable. Trudging in mud beside the wagon carrying Major Cordoba's marquee and equipment, Amanda saw frequent signs that the spirit of resistance had been broken. Homesteads, abandoned and torched, billowed black clouds into the gray sky. Herds of cattle broke the horizon-line and trembled the earth, set free as their owners piled belongings on muleback, left their small ranches and hurried east.

The village of Gonzales was still smoldering when Santa Anna rode in at the head of his host. Amanda walked wide-eyed through the dirt streets, listening to the talk of the *soldaderas*. Houston had insisted on burning Gonzales so there would be no shelter for Santa Anna's troops, the woman said.

But a few rickety buildings survived. In the doorway of one, an old blind woman, an American, listened to the clatter of the army passing, clutched a mangy white cat to her breast and wept.

Amanda was some distance down the street when she

heard a shot. She looked back. The doorway was empty. One of the *soldaderas,* surrounded by laughing friends, was waving a pistol—

"General Urrea has taken Colonel Fannin at Goliad," Cordoba told her two days after Palm Sunday. Amanda already felt bad enough without hearing that. Her period had come. She was miserable from the stickiness and chafing of the rags tied beneath her dress.

"Fannin was the one who should have come to the aid of the mission, wasn't he?"

Amanda nodded in a dull way.

"They say he had four hundred men when he was captured. Palm Sunday morning, they all thought they were being paroled. A detachment of Urrea's troops took them to a woods near the village. Urrea had other men hidden among the trees. Fannin and his four hundred were shot to death." There was no satisfaction in Cordoba's voice when he said it.

Amanda lost track of the days. Rain fell intermittently, sometimes a shower, sometimes a torrent. The drenched plains took on a wearying sameness. The Texans were still reported in wild flight. Santa Anna was in high spirits, confident he'd catch the rebel leaders before they reached the sanctuary of American soil beyond the Sabine.

March became April, but Amanda was hardly aware of it. Constant bad news only compounded the weariness produced by the hard routine of the march.

She rose before dawn every day, stiff from sleeping on blankets laid at the foot of Cordoba's cot. Her first chore was to go outside to the communal cook fire, jostle a place among the other camp followers and begin brewing the major's coffee.

At first she had been crowded away from the fire. Taunted with obscene remarks. Even threatened. A couple of incidents in which she'd used her nails, her teeth and her fists to defend herself put an end to the harrassment. The other *soldaderas* never spoke to her directly. But they allowed her room to work.

After breakfast, she was expected to help Cordoba's orderly strike the marquee and pack it for transportation in the baggage wagon. All day she followed the wagon on foot, breaking the routine occasionally by dropping back to the wagons of the civilian sutlers.

With money Cordoba had given her, she bargained for food. She refused the tainted meat always offered first, and demanded fresh. She swore and gestured and haggled until the inflated price came down to a satisfactory level. Here, at least, her experience on a farm and at the hotel made her the equal of most of the other women—and superior to some. Quite a few of the *soldaderas* were young girls, unlettered and ignorant of the fact that the sutlers routinely tried to sell spoiled food at ten times its worth.

She did get a rest every afternoon. War or no war, the Mexicans demanded a siesta. But as soon as the army camped for the night, work began again.

She prepared the major's evening meal. And whenever there was a stream nearby, she carried his laundry there, washing it with yellow soap that left her hands raw. She slapped the clothes damp dry on stones, Indian fashion.

Illness was still rampant in the army. So once a week, she insisted on plunging the major's wash into a kettle of boiling water. She boiled his drinking water as well. Although these unusual procedures elicited more laughter from the camp women, Cordoba remained healthy while many of his fellow officers succumbed to dysentery.

She spent a considerable amount of time polishing boots and uniform buttons. Cordoba was almost fanatic about a neat appearance—a reaction, she suspected, to the sloth and disorder prevalent in the camp. Cordoba's gleaming leather and metal were an expression of his outrage—and one of the few aspects of a chaotic world that he could control absolutely.

There was one part of the *soldaderas'* routine in which Amanda refused to participate, though. Every night, the women worked together to dig open trenches. Whenever they had to relieve themselves, they squatted over the trenches like so many hens, chatting amiably with their skirts hiked above their waists and their bottoms clearly in view.

Perhaps because of her city upbringing, Amanda couldn't expose herself that way. She had to seek the privacy of a grove of trees, or at least some shrubs. Occasionally, the lack of such foliage near the campsite kept her in excruciating pain while she waited for darkness.

The other women laughed about her fastidiousness, just as they laughed about her cooking of the clothes. One *soldadera* in particular seemed not just scornful, but hostile. This was the coarse-faced young woman with the mole; the girl Amanda had encountered in the street the morning after the massacre.

Now and again Amanda would run into the girl at the sutler's or along a creek at laundry time, and the girl would be sure Amanda heard some particularly filthy reference to her parentage, or her relationship with Cordoba.

Each time, Amanda met the girl's ugly gaze squarely—almost daring her to lay hands on her. But she didn't. Amanda asked a few questions of Cordoba's men and learned that the girl lived with a captain of the artillery. For a woman belonging to a man of lesser rank to attack the *soldadera* of a senior officer was a violation of the camp's rough protocol; and it was that which kept the girl's hostility from degenerating into the physical. But Amanda was sure the ranks of their respective men fueled the girl's fury; she was probably jealous of an Anglo woman enjoying the favors of a major.

If the girl only knew! Amanda thought. During their first weeks together, Cordoba didn't so much as touch her.

She had frankly expected him to order her into his bed, despite what he'd said that first day. But he treated her with punctilious politeness. He complimented her often, praising the flour biscuits she baked, or the whiteness of his dress shirts:

"I swear to heaven, no man ever had a better *soldadera*. You take to this life as if you were born to it."

"I wasn't, and I don't like it."

"Nevertheless, you're extremely skilled."

She shrugged. "All it takes is making up your mind."

In response to his puzzled frown, she elaborated: "I didn't have a lot of schooling, Luis. And what I did have, I didn't care for very much. But when I was growing up, I managed to learn something that's as important as what they teach in classrooms."

"What is that?"

"I can do almost anything I want if I want to do it badly enough."

"Such confidence!"

"I'm not trying to brag—the same thing's true of most people. They just don't want to put forth the effort, that's all. When I was young, I lived for a while with a tribe of the Sioux—"

His mouth dropped open. "With *Indians?*"

"Yes."

"You continually astonish me, Amanda. Do go on."

"I was the property of one of the dog soldiers—the warriors who police the buffalo hunts. To satisfy the man I lived with—and keep him from hurting me—I had to learn how to make love like a grown woman—when I wasn't much more than twelve years old. I had to learn to broil the meat of a buffalo hump the way he liked it. I'd never cooked anything in my life—but I learned because it was necessary. And because I didn't want to seem weaker than the Sioux women, I learned every game they played—and practiced until I was better than they were. The man I stayed with was so proud of me, he ordered his first wife out of his tepee forever. And whenever white traders came to the village, he put guards over me and kept me hidden. He was afraid I might be stolen away—"

"I trust you were appropriately flattered."

"Yes—but maybe not for the reason you think. Not because of vanity. His attitude showed me I'd done what I set out to do. Survive. Even thrive. The man I was living with was killed, and I left the Sioux. But before I went, the old chief—the father of my man—told me he'd never seen a Sioux girl who could play the double-ball game—handle the rawhide and the sticks—as well as I did. He couldn't give a higher compliment to any woman. The point is, I don't think learning the game took special talent. Just the will to do it."

"I think you underestimate your abilities."

"Will counts for a lot in this world, Luis. I'll trade money or education for will anytime."

Cordoba was silent. There was a look akin to awe on his swarthy face.

His reticence about sex continued to bother her. At night, he seldom glanced her way as she brushed her hair and prepared for bed. She slept in the same black silk dress she wore all during the day. Could that be part of the trouble? she wondered. The dress, clean but ragged now, struck her as decidedly unfeminine.

One warm evening in the first week of April, she was awake long after Cordoba had fallen asleep on the cot. She moved her head from side to side, uttering a small sigh once in a while. There was a tightness in her body that she couldn't deny.

Jaimie de la Gura had been dead a long time. And there had only been a very few men since then; an occasional customer of Gura's Hotel to whom she took a fancy. The last one, a wandering trader bound for Taos, had slept in her arms more than half a year ago.

She alone was responsible for the unsatisfied hunger, she knew. It was ironic—the brothel madam who could no longer give herself casually. She had given herself that way early in her life, when it was necessary to use her good looks and her sex for survival. But after Jaimie, she changed. Without a basic liking for the partner, she was unwilling—even though her body made its need manifest in aches and sleeplessness.

The need this particular night grew almost unbearable. She finally rose on one elbow; whispered softly in the darkness:

"Luis?"

The major answered with an exhausted snore. She stretched out again, uncomfortable and unhappy. She had come to like Cordoba. But beyond that, his lack of interest made her feel there must be something wrong with her.

True, she was dirty and unkempt most of the time. That didn't seem to make any difference to other men in the army, though. They rutted with women who smelled like a sty.

Cordoba stirred. Said something in his sleep. She propped herself on her elbow again, listening.

The major was mumbling a name. Her heart beat a little faster in the hope that it might be hers—

A moment later, she was ashamed of the foolish conceit. She slid her hands down her belly, pressing her palms against herself. She couldn't go to the cot and waken him now. She knew it would have made him miserable afterward.

In torment, she lay still. It was an hour or more before she fell asleep and dreamed erotic dreams that left her grumpy in the morning.

ii

The army marched into San Felipe on the Brazos on the seventh of April. Once more the Texans were gone, though Cordoba said scouts had sighted Houston and three or four hundred men downriver at Thompson's Ferry.

That the tiny Texas army had recently been in San Felipe was evident when Amanda went down to the Brazos in the red twilight. Carrying Cordoba's laundry, she passed two pirogues with their bottoms staved in. The prow of a third poked up from reeds near the shore. Houston had destroyed any craft the Mexicans might use to cross the rain-swollen river.

Up and down the bank, chattering *soldaderas* kneaded and pounded their men's clothing. As Amanda walked by a group of four, she noticed the girl with the mole. Kneeling in the mud, the young woman stared at her.

Amanda hurried on. She heard the girl and her companions talking. Suddenly she yelped, stumbling as a stone struck the back of her head.

She dropped Cordoba's shirts and underdrawers in the mud; turned; saw the girl wiping her hands on her blouse.

The girl hoisted her skirt and began tucking it into the rope belt she wore, unconcerned about revealing her grimy thighs and a black tangle above. One of the older *soldaderas* caught her arm:

"Ah, let the white slut alone, Manuela. She behaves herself—"

"Which is more than can be said for your friend!" Amanda called, rubbing her scalp, then bending to retrieve the laundry.

Head lowered, Manuela started walking toward her.

Amanda wondered why the young woman looked even more haggard than usual.

"I'm sick of seeing her parade herself," Manuela said to her companions. "She thinks she's a queen, living with a major—"

Only a step away now, Manuela reached out and twisted a lock of Amanda's hair around a stubby finger. She breathed out the smell of wine as she went on:

"But she's an ice queen, this one. I have a friend who belongs to a sergeant in one of Cordoba's platoons—"

Amanda said, "Let go," then pulled back. But Manuela held the lock of hair. Amanda winced.

"—and I hear Cordoba's marquee is silent all night long. Never any sounds of pleasure. Just the ice queen farting in her sleep."

Amanda's cheeks darkened as she realized she'd been spied on. She supposed she should have expected it. Manuela kept winding the strand of hair tighter around her finger:

"Probably the major regrets taking an Anglo into his tent. Anglos are as weak between the legs as they are in their bellies—"

Amanda wrenched suddenly, tearing away. Manuela stepped back with a curse. Then she squatted, fingers digging in the mud until they closed on a pointed stone.

A barking dog and half a dozen ragged boys from San Felipe came running along the sunset-reddened bank, drawn by the promise of a fight. Amanda's stomach flipflopped. Manuela meant to do her physical harm—

"You'd better get her away," Amanda warned the other three women. "I don't want a quarrel. But if she pushes it—"

"Yes? What will you do?" Manuela demanded. She spat. "Nothing!"

"She lost her captain three days ago," one of the older women blurted. "He was knifed in an argument over cards—"

Amanda understood the reason for the girl's haggard look. But that didn't lessen her fear. Manuela held out the rock, showing Amanda the point:

"After I finish with this, the major will need another companion."

"I don't think so."

"I do. He may be surprised when I come back in your place. But I don't think he'll be disappointed. I think he'll welcome a woman who knows how to spread herself properly."

Amanda's racing mind sorted the ways she might deal with the situation. Appealing to logic wouldn't work. Manuela obviously had a gut hatred of Texans. And now the loss of her captain had removed any reason for restraint.

The boys had stopped nearby, smirking and nudging one another in anticipation. Manuela shuffled forward again, her bare feet squishing in the mud:

"The fact of it is, I need a man. I'm sure you won't mind surrendering yours since you bring him no happiness—"

Determined to try to bluff her way out, Amanda said, "Unless you want to get hurt, leave me alone."

"Perhaps if you beg me, Anglo."

"*Beg!* The hell I will, you—" Unthinkingly, she resorted to the kind of slur she would never have used when she was calm: "—you greaser bitch."

Manuela licked her lower lip. "I am going to make you hurt for that, Anglo."

"All right." Amanda nodded. "Turn your wolf loose."

"What?"

"I mean go ahead and fight. You'll wish you hadn't."

Briefly startled, Manuela laughed with false bravado:

"Eh, the ice queen shows a little fire! What are you going to use to fight me?" She ground her heel on one of Cordoba's shirts. "Dirty laundry?"

Before Amanda was quite prepared, the girl rushed

her. The point of the stone slashed toward Amanda's eye.

Amanda lunged aside, lost her footing in the mud. As she fell to her knees, the stone raked her temple. A second later she felt the trickle of warm blood above her eyebrow.

Snarling obscenities, Manuela jumped around behind her. She seized Amanda's hair with one hand, used the other to smash the stone against her scalp. Amanda pitched forward, gasping. Manuela stepped on the back of her neck, driving her face into the mud.

Sputtering and fighting for air, Amanda rolled aside frantically as the young girl started to kneel on her stomach. Mud clogged her eyes, her nostrils. But somehow she avoided the next swipe of the rock and kept rolling—straight into the shallows of the river.

Manuela stormed after her, kicking up droplets that glowed red in the sunset. The dog was barking loudly. The boys clapped and encouraged Manuela, who struck for Amanda's head again.

Amanda grabbed Manuela's forearm with both hands, jerked it to her mouth and bit. Manuela squealed. Amanda shoved her backward. The stone almost slipped from the younger woman's grasp, but she caught it.

Soaked and moving slowly because of it, Amanda still managed to get behind the girl and use her own tactic—a yank of the hair. But Manuela was strong; strong enough to slither free and spin, hacking at Amanda's face with the rock.

Amanda dodged again, laced her hands together, kicked Manuela's leg. The girl doubled over. Amanda's locked hands came down on Manuela's exposed neck with terrific force.

Crying out in real pain, Manuela sprawled face first in the shallows. The stone flew from her fingers, splashed and disappeared under the water. Amanda thought about calling a halt. But if she did, she'd never be safe in the encampment. She had to defeat the Mexican girl completely; decisively—

She gazed around for a weapon. Something Manuela had said came to mind. She darted for the bank, grabbed one of Cordoba's shirts, dipped it in the water and lashed Manuela's cheek.

Floundering in the shallows, Manuela cried out. She tried to grab Amanda's leg. Amanda whipped the girl's face again. Again. Her eyes were red with the glare of the sunset as she struck—

She laid ten, twelve, fifteen strokes on Manuela's face, neck and shoulders. When the shirt showed blood, she stopped. Whimpering, Manuela crawled away in the water—

Amanda was shaking. She stumbled up the bank. The boys and Manuela's companions stared at her in amazement.

She wiped her brow with a soaked sleeve, then stared at the blood from the cut over her eye. She dropped the shirt she'd used as a whip, retrieved the rest of Cordoba's laundry. Manuela was still on her knees in the water, shaking her head in a groggy way. Amanda hooked a toe beneath the bloody, ruined garment, and kicked it toward Manuela's three companions:

"Clean her up. And tell her the major has a lot of other shirts."

Walking as steadily as she could, she moved on down the bank in the stillness.

iii

"God above, what happened to you?" Cordoba exclaimed when she entered the marquee sometime later, the clean laundry bundled under one arm.

She put the laundry on the washstand, her hand none too steady. "Nothing," she said. "I'm all right."

Cordoba was bare-chested. The black hair below his throat showed glints of sweat in the light of the hanging lantern. At the waist of his trousers, his stomach bulged. He laid a palm over the roll of fat, as if ashamed to have her see.

She sank down on the cot. "I'm afraid I lost one of your best shirts, though."

Cordoba seemed not to hear. "How did you cut your forehead?"

"It isn't important."

"I insist that you answer." She didn't. "At least let me find some alcohol—"

"No, I only need to rest a minute."

"Damn you, woman! Tell me who hurt you and I'll see him flogged!"

If she hadn't been so spent, she would have laughed. The major looked furious.

"Not *he,*" she said. "It was one of the *soldaderas*. She won't bother me again." Her generous mouth curved in a wry smile. "She had designs on you. She lost her own man, and—well, let's just say she wasn't thinking very clearly."

She lay back. Closed her eyes. She sensed Cordoba crouching down beside her.

"I still want to know the woman's name. I intend to see her punished."

"It's not necessary, Luis—I took care of it."

"You might have been killed!"

"I wasn't."

She studied him. His deep-set eyes seemed unusually dark in the shadows beneath his brows. Teasing, she added:

"Maybe you would have preferred her. She claimed she could please a man better than I do."

Cordoba gathered both her hands in his. She felt the weight of his forearm against her left breast. She was touched by the almost child-like tenderness of his expression:

"You have pleased me more than any woman I have ever known, Amanda. You have made this filthy campaign bearable. Brought me comfort just with your presence. You know I'm poor at talking like a romantic—I am a soldier. I'm trying to say you are the dearest—"

Swallowing, he stopped. The familiar redness tinted his cheeks again.

She smiled. "But I don't seem very good at giving a man what he wants most from a *soldadera*—" She was only partly teasing now. His closeness—the warmth and hardness of his arm—stirred something in her that was part passion, part hunger for reassurance. "I've really wondered why you never touch me."

"Because—" His eyes brimmed with pain. "Because I have a wife."

He bowed his head.

She reached her right hand across her breast; ran the palm down the faint stubble on his face.

"I know that, Luis."

He jerked back. "You *know—?*"

"Well, I guessed. One night, in your sleep, you spoke a woman's name several times. I decided it was the name of a sweetheart or, more likely, your wife."

Each word cost him effort: "I have wanted you very much, Amanda. But I dared not ask—"

"Always so honorable—" Gently, she touched his forehead. "That's a terrible burden to bear in a dishonorable world."

"I told you before—I can't help what I am. I know I must go home to my wife in the capital one day—"

"That could be a long time in the future."

He said nothing.

"Do you have children?"

"Alas, no."

"Well, I wouldn't want you to do anything that would make you feel ashamed later—"

"Stop!" he exclaimed. "It's only on your account that I've held back. You're a beautiful woman—and a decent one. If you were just a camp whore, I'd have taken you and thought nothing of it. Well—almost nothing. You deserve better. I could never dishonor you with lies. False promises—"

"I don't need promises, Luis. I just need you."

Again he averted his head:

"Sometimes I wish I'd never seen you. But I did. And I have come to—to love you with all my being. More than I have ever loved any woman." He raised his head. "Any woman."

"If that's how you feel, nothing else is necessary. Blow out the lamp and lie down with me—"

She saw the dawning wonder in his eyes. Wonder mingled with suffering. He was still agonized by what he had revealed about himself. She tried to relieve his conscience with a light tone:

"It is about time you treated me as a proper camp follower! Besides, I'm too sore to sleep on the ground one more night."

Slowly, slowly, a smile forced itself across his mouth. A tentative smile that turned to joy as he reached upward for the lantern.

iv

In the darkness, he cursed, then apologized. He'd tangled his feet in his breeches as he pulled them off.

He lowered himself beside her on the narrow cot, touching her cheek almost hesitantly. She circled his neck with her arms, turning her head to the proper angle for a kiss.

When their lips touched, much of Cordoba's restraint disappeared. He pressed his mouth hard against hers. She felt his yearning in the sudden clasp of his arms beneath her back—

He murmured her name over and over as they embraced. He spoke lovely, courtly Spanish as he caressed her body. She sighed with pleasure when his hands closed on her bare breasts.

A moment later, she maneuvered beneath him, guiding him and laughing when he gasped at her boldness. He entered her gently, although his breathing roared loud as a storm in her ear. When she urged him to speed, he complied, and with each quickening movement of his body, she understood again that this was no weak man, only one who was tender and humane in a world that sometimes derided those virtues. With the straining of her own flesh, the movement of her hands, the press of her mouth, she tried to show him that she admired and prized what he was.

He was quicker than she, bursting into apologies afterward. She stilled them with a kiss, then drew him into the curve of her arm. Holding him close, she murmured that, before the night ended, there would be another time. A better one—

"Oh," he said, alarmed, "I don't know if that's possible for me—"

"It is. You'll see."

She caught the sound of a boot scraping in the dirt street outside. Another eavesdropper?

She felt sorry for him, whoever he was. Skulking in the April dark, he could only hear the sounds of lovemaking. He would never imagine the sense of completion and peace and—yes, admit it—affection that warmed her soul after long, long months of privation.

▼

After that night, Manuela never bothered her again. An even happier result was the change in her relationship with Cordoba.

Before, their conversations had been largely superficial: the events of the day's march; the suspected position of Sam Houston's little army; the latest example of incompetence or dishonesty on the senior staff. But once they had shared each other's embraces, she and the major wanted to share the whole sum of themselves as well—their hopes and histories; their dreams and disappointments.

As the army worked its way south toward Thompson's Ferry, their evening lovemaking usually ended not in langorous slumber but in quiet conversation. Nights when they were both too tired, conversation sufficed.

The only subject Cordoba wouldn't discuss was his wife. Otherwise, he held nothing back. What he had said about himself was true: his background—his world—was limited to soldiering.

He had been born in Veracruz, the fourth of his father's children, and the only son. He was a young subaltern in the army when the political upheavals began in the 1820s. His father, a prosperous importer, remained loyal to Spain. After much painful deliberation, Luis Cordoba put himself on the side of independence, helping to overthrow the Spanish government, then that of the professed revolutionary Iturbide, who had turned on his separatist followers and maneuvered himself into the role of emperor.

Iturbide had been deposed in 1823. A year later, a revised, democratic Mexican constitution began luring the Anglo-American *empresarios* to Texas. Through it all, Cordoba said, he had remained loyal to Mexico first and the army second:

"When the separatist movement developed, I had the highest of hopes. I thought that, at last, I could fight for something other than simple military victory. For principle. Over the years I've learned how easily principle can be crushed by those with ambition. Now I'm virtually back where I started—obeying orders. Hoping to win if there's an engagement. Not daring to look too deeply into why we're fighting. A man can die in many ways, you know. Death in battle is perhaps the most final, but the least grievous. It's much worse to struggle for a cause, then perceive that you've struggled for nothing. I felt that way—cheated; dead—when His Excellency jettisoned the constitution."

"There's no hope of unseating Santa Anna?"

"Next to none. He's firmly entrenched. God—what a poltroon he is! In its short history, your country has been fortunate to escape his kind, Amanda."

"Oh, we've had our share of poltroons, I think—" She shook her head. "I get such an odd feeling when you speak about the United States."

"Odd? What do you mean?"

"It *is* my country. Yet sometimes it doesn't seem so any longer. My grandfather did fight in the Revolution—"

"Did he! And survived?"

"Yes, though he was wounded. He limped for the rest of his life."

"The Americans have a positive passion for rebellion! Even more so than those of us south of the Rio Grande, I think."

"That isn't always a good thing, Luis. Do you know that when we fought Britain again, twenty-five years ago, several of the northern states wanted to secede because they hated the war? And four years ago—I remember being shocked when I read it in the papers—

South Carolina nearly left the union because of Nullification."

"I don't know the term."

"It means a state placing itself above the law of the country. South Carolina didn't like one of the government's tariffs. So the state legislature nullified it. Said it didn't apply to South Carolina. Old Hickory—"

"The president, Jackson?"

"Yes. He said it did, because no state could declare itself separate from the union. He promised to send in troops if South Carolina continued to disagree. The state gave in. I suppose that was proper. I remember hearing my father say that once the country was formed, no one could tear it apart. I didn't understand—I imagined huge ditches in the earth. Now I know what he meant —and how serious the question is."

"Your country is still divided on at least one great issue."

"You mean slavery?"

He nodded.

"That's where our passion for rebellion as you call it could prove our undoing," she said in a somber way. "There are people in the east—mainly in New York and Boston—who call themselves abolitionists. They want to do away with slavery completely. The south can't afford that. There's trouble coming—you can tell even by reading the papers out here."

Boston, Amanda revealed, was the city in which she'd grown up. She had lived in a splendid house owned by Gilbert Kent, her father, a well-to-do printer of books and newspapers.

Gilbert Kent had died at a relatively young age, leaving Amanda in the care of her pretentious and somewhat unstable mother, Harriet. Gilbert's widow had made a poor choice of a second husband—a wastrel named Piggott. He had succeeded in gambling away most of the family's assets, including the printing house, Kent and Son.

"The loss was probably no accident, I learned later. My cousin Jared—the son of my father's half-brother Abraham—served in the navy in the 1812 war. There was an officer aboard Jared's ship—Stovall, his name was—who fancied boys and men in preference to women—"

Cordoba snorted in disgust.

"Jared got in a scrape with Stovall. Injured Stovall's face—scarred it. Permanently. The man never forgot. After the war, he came to Boston in secret. He was the one to whom my stepfather lost Kent's."

"You think this Stovall planned it? Maneuvered your stepfather into a game and cheated him?"

"I'm almost certain of it. Anyway, my cousin had a terrible temper in those days. He set fire to the printing house and shot and killed Stovall's general manager, a man called Waltham—Walpole—something like that."

"In heaven's name, why take vengeance on some flunky?" Cordoba exclaimed.

"Jared didn't intend to—he was aiming for Stovall."

"And so those tragic circumstances marked the end of the family business?"

"I've no way of knowing. Books are fairly scarce out here—especially among poor people. Now and then I've asked questions. No luck. Besides, if the firm burned to the ground, it might not have been rebuilt at all. But I never heard that Stovall had any connection with publishing. His family operated an iron works of some kind."

"How about the fellow himself? Is he living?"

"There again, I've been too busy staying alive to look into it—and I'm not trying to be clever saying that. It's God's truth. I haven't had the money—or the necessary eastern contacts—for making an inquiry. I know our family employed a Boston law firm, but the name is another of those details that's completely slipped away from me. Sometimes, I think I'm much better off leaving the whole question alone. I'm afraid that if I learned Stovall was still alive, I'd spend all my energy on schemes to repay him."

"You have a deep hatred of him, obviously—"

"Without ever having set eyes on him. If he hadn't lured my stepfather into a gambling game with the firm at stake, my mother might have lived. She died the same day Jared burned Kent's and shot the general manager."

"How did she die?"

"She was run down by a dray right in front of our house on Beacon Street. Everyone called that an accident too, but my mother's second husband caused it. My mother had a fight with Piggott. He told her he'd lost the printing house. She rushed out, intending to go straight to the firm. She stumbled on the curb—the drayman couldn't stop in time—"

Amanda paused, re-living the scene in her mind. Cordoba whispered a word of sympathy. She let a shudder work itself out, then went on:

"That same night, Jared crept back to Beacon Street and told me what had happened. That he'd set fire to the firm because he couldn't stand the thought of someone like Stovall taking over what the Kents had worked so hard to build."

"This Jared sounds like a headstrong sort. Did he have no one to discipline him?"

"No. My mother tried, but she and Jared despised one another."

"What became of his parents?"

"Abraham, his father, tried to homestead in Ohio. Jared's mother was killed there. By Indians. Abraham gave up and came home. A few months later, he disappeared completely. On the very night I was born, in fact. I remember hearing very little about him except that he was a noisy, quarrelsome man. He was drunk most of the time—anyway, the night the printing house burned,

Jared convinced me that we had to leave Boston together. We had no one except each other, and he was afraid of being arrested for murder. We started for New Orleans. I can't remember much about the early part of the trip, except that it was winter. We were always half frozen and half starved. We met a few kind people. I recall one little girl named Sarah, in Kentucky—her mother and father were farmers. They treated us well and helped Jared recover from a sickness. We didn't get far after we left Knob Creek, though. Only to Tennessee—"

From the pain of the past, she summoned the rest of it: her rape and abduction by the bogus preacher, Blackthorn, who sold her in St. Louis to a trader named Maas. He in turn sold her to a warrior of the Teton Sioux, a young, not unhandsome man whose Indian name translated to Plenty Coups:

"Some of this you've already heard—"

Cordoba grinned. "How you were experienced with men at age twelve, for example? I'm certainly fortunate to have the benefit of all that training—"

She pinched him. "I didn't ask for it, Luis! I was pretty well filled out by the time I was twelve—"

He rolled his tongue in his cheek. "That is not hard to imagine."

"Oh, be serious! Do you want to hear this or don't you?"

"I do. Please continue."

"Being a woman was the only weapon I had when I was sold to the Sioux. If I hadn't used it, I would have been treated a lot worse by Plenty Coups."

"How long did you stay with the Indians?"

"Eight—no, closer to nine years. Like you, I never had any children. For some reason, Plenty Coups couldn't."

"I'd say you were lucky to survive such an experience."

"I've told you before, it wasn't all luck."

"Ah, yes. The old chief's compliment when you left—"

"Determination was only part of it. Something else helped me get through those years—and the ones since. Somehow I've always been blessed with almost perfect health. I never realized how precious that was—how rare among women especially—until I saw all the sick squaws in Plenty Coups' village. Work and childbirth and white men's diseases killed more of them than I can remember—"

She told him the rest on succeeding evenings: how Plenty Coups had been injured in a fall from his horse as he rode in to strike a huge bull buffalo with his coup stick during a hunt. Three weeks later—just about the time, they figured out, that Iturbide had been at the height of his power as Emperor Augustin I of Mexico—she was a widow.

A month after Plenty Coups' death, a party representing John Astor's American Fur Company had visited the tribe.

"Jaimie de la Gura, my husband, was one of those men. The American and French winterers and the Delawares who worked with them called him Spanish Jim. He was very handsome—"

Cordoba pulled a face. "More handsome than I?"

"Just about the same." She leaned up to kiss his lips.

"You told His Excellency your husband came from New Orleans—"

"That's right. His father was quite well off. Ran an elegant coffee house. But that was when he was older. Civilized, you might say. There was a wild streak in the de la Gura family. Jaimie's father came by most of his money running slaves with the Lafitte brothers. He wanted Jaimie to enter the clergy or perhaps study law. Jaimie wouldn't do either. He didn't like town living very much. He ran away up the Mississippi when he was eighteen, went to work for a fur trader in St. Louis, and traveled west from there—"

"To find you in the Sioux village."

"Yes. I was allowed to be seen by white men after Plenty Coups died. Jaimie took a liking to me. He asked me to go with him—and he was willing to pay the old chief in trade goods for my freedom. My life with the tribe had come to a kind of ending, so I said I'd go. Jaimie was ten years older than I was. A good man."

"And obviously one of impeccable taste."

She laughed. "We were married in St. Louis. We spent our honeymoon in a real hotel, with solid walls, and beds with the most marvelous sheets and blankets—I'd forgotten what that sort of existence was like. Jaimie still didn't care for it, though. And he was too independent to work for one employer very long. He didn't keep on as a trapper because he felt the life was too hard for a woman. We went south. He worked at odd jobs—we covered a lot of territory before he finally decided we should come to Texas and try farming."

She described the events that had led to Jaimie's death and her subsequent venture with the hotel:

"So you can see I've done a good many things in thirty-three years, Luis—some of which I'm a little ashamed to talk about."

He brushed his mouth against her cheek, as if to dismiss her concern. Then he shifted his position so she could lie more comfortably. He asked:

"This Jaimie—did you really love him?"

"I think so. He was kind to me. I never felt any great outpourings of emotion when he was alive. But I liked him—I enjoyed being with him—at least until things went sour for us. I mourned a long time when he died. If that's love, then yes, I loved him."

The major touched the rope bracelet. "Did he give you this?"

"No, my cousin Jared did. He made it from cordage on the *Constitution,* the frigate he served on during the war."

"Do you know where your cousin is now?"

She shook her head. "That day in Tennessee was the last I ever saw of him. He may be dead. He might have gone back to Boston, though I doubt it—"

"You sound sad when you speak of this Bos—" He had trouble pronouncing it. "Bos-ton. Do you miss it?"

"I miss never being hungry, or cold, or worried about tomorrow. I sometimes feel Boston's where I belong."

"Because of the comforts?"

"No, that's not it. My father came of a very independent, idealistic family. I can still see him in the front sitting room one night when I was little. He was speaking to Jared. I can't recall the exact words, but I understood his meaning, and it made a great impression. My father said anyone who belonged to the Kent family had a duty in this world. A duty to give, not just take—"

Lost in the reverie, she closed her eyes. The images in her mind—a flickering hearth; her cousin's tawny hair and blue eyes; her father's sallow face and frail body beside the mantel; a long, polished muzzle-loader; a gleaming sword; a small green bottle—were incredibly vivid:

"I can hear his voice to this day. And see the things above the mantelpiece. A little bottle of dried East India tea my grandfather collected when the colonists dumped the shipment in Boston harbor. There's a sword my grandfather got from the French general, Lafayette—and a Virginia rifle—"

She opened her eyes.

"Those things were important to my father. I remember him saying they had to be preserved, as tokens of what the Kents stood for. I have no idea what's become of them—"

"Would you like to go back and try to discover that?"

"Yes, I would. Everyone has one special dream they cherish, I suppose—a dream that doesn't stand a chance of being fulfilled. Going back to find those things is mine." Her smile was rueful. "I expect they were sold for junk years ago."

"If you have such a consuming desire, I would have expected you return to Bos-ton long before this. You've had opportunities—"

"After Jamie died?"

"Exactly."

"I thought of it. But there's a funny kind of pride involved, Luis. I think I told you the Kents were once a wealthy family. I promised myself I'd never go back unless I could be worthy of the name."

"You mean go back as a rich woman?"

"At least well off. So I could properly face anyone who might remember the family. Especially that son of a bitch Stovall or his heirs—" She paused a moment. "You probably think I'm crazy."

"To be truthful, I should prefer to say unrealistic."

She snuggled against the muscle of his naked arm. "I admit it."

"Then again, perhaps I'm the one who is unrealistic. I listen to you, and I can believe you *will* go back one day."

"I don't think I'd be a very good caretaker of those things my father prized. The Kents are supposed to be people who contribute, remember? I've done nothing much but keep myself alive—"

"Nonsense, Amanda! You're a generous, loving woman. An honorable woman! You made that clear when you faced His Excellency—"

She laughed softly. "I love you for saying things like that. But I'm afraid it's your heart talking, not your head."

"It's the truth!"

"Oh, Luis, we won't really find out what we are until it's too late to do anything about it. The Sioux believe the only honest verdict on a human life comes when it's all over."

"Are you saying that trying to live honorably is useless? I can't accept that."

"I can't either—but I do believe the Sioux are right when they claim we see ourselves imperfectly. Untruthfully. And only someone else can judge us—"

Quietly, Cordoba asked, "Do you mean God?"

"The name isn't important, is it? The Mandan Sioux, for instance, believe that when you die, a great vine sprouts from the ground near your body. A vine that's invisible to everyone else. The vine leads straight up to the sky—to paradise. Your spirit rises and begins to climb. About halfway up is the critical point. Either you go all the way unmolested—or great hands reach down from paradise and break the vine, and your spirit falls back to earth, denied heaven because you lived an unworthy life." Amused, she added, "Can you guess who those hands belong to?"

"Why, to whoever those Mandan call their God."

"No, to an agent of the high spirit. An intermediary."

"An Indian Christ?"

Merrily, Amanda said, "A very formidable woman."

"A *woman?* That's blasphemous!"

"I think it's delightful. I must say your attitude's typical of men, Luis."

They laughed again, and then he returned to the original thread of the conversation:

"Well, I can't worry about the afterlife—I have enough problems with the present."

"And no dreams?"

There was a long moment of silence. Then:

"None that will come true. You, though—you have your Bos-ton. Hold onto that, Amanda. You may still see your home before that remarkable vine appears. You have the will—" He began to stroke her hair. "Right now, though, your home is here. If only for a short time."

"I sometimes wish it could be for a long time, Luis."

He pulled her closer.

"I wish that constantly, Amanda. Constantly."

When she fell asleep against him, his cheeks were wet.

vi

On the eleventh of April, Santa Anna's troops captured a flatboat at Thompson's Ferry. They began crossing the Brazos the following day.

On the fourteenth, an apparition appeared on the river—a smoke-billowing monster that chugged and rumbled. Great revolving paddle-wheels propelled the boat through the water. There wasn't a human being anywhere on deck.

Infantrymen lining the banks grew terrified at the sight—though a few had enough presence of mind to unlimber their muskets and fire at the boxy pilot house, where dim figures crouched over a wheel. Amanda, watching with a group of terrified *soldaderas,* tried to calm them:

"That's no demon. It's a boat driven by an engine."

"Engine—?"

Round, frightened eyes signaled a total lack of comprehension.

"Well, just take my word for it—there aren't any imps in the boat's belly. Just a machine that moves a shaft and drives the wheels by means of steam."

"Steam—!"

She gave up. They didn't grasp any of it.

Amanda herself had never seen a steamboat before. But she had read about them in Texas newspapers. She knew they were changing the nation in which she'd been born; speeding the pace of its river commerce and drawing the frontiers closer to the cities. Fascinated, she watched the steamboat churn by—

As its stern came into view, she noticed bright red lettering:

YELLOW STONE

Only the night before, Cordoba had told her Houston was using a small steam vessel of that name to ferry his fleeing army across the Brazos. Now, apparently, the retreat was complete—

A handful of the more courageous officers rallied some men and rushed to a point of land where the river narrowed. Using ropes, they tried to snare the steamboat's smokestacks as she chugged by. Pistol shots from the pilot house scattered the would-be ropers. *Yellow Stone* was soon gone around a bend. Amanda stood staring after it, somehow saddened by the sight.

She turned away from the bank, still gripped by wonder and melancholy. That marvelous boat without oars or tow-ropes represented the world in which she'd been born. Unbidden, dim pictures slipped through her mind—

The cozy glow of a fire in a grate.

Ice skaters gliding in a white landscape.

While church bells pealed, she rode in a carriage, finely dressed; recognized as Gilbert Kent's daughter—

With a fierce shake of her head, she returned to reality. Nothing remained of the steamboat but traces of smoke in the sky. Her convictions about the power of her own will seemed pathetic all at once. Her dream of seeing Boston again was just as insubstantial as the vanishing smoke.

vii

Late that same day, dispatch riders sped to Santa Anna's marquee with news that the president of the Republic of Texas, Señor Burnet, could be caught at the settlement of Harrisburg, a scant thirty miles away. Before dark, His Excellency had a picked force moving forward: seven hundred infantry; fifty dragoons; a six-pound cannon, the necessary wagons and, of course, the *soldaderas*. Cordoba's men—and Amanda—were with the special detachment.

The forced march was grueling. The advance party of dragoons reached Harrisburg the following midnight.

No Burnet. The Texas government, such as it was, had fled again.

And where was Houston? Somewhere up the Brazos? No one was sure.

The Mexican citizens of Harrisburg wanted to be helpful, but they lacked information. The Texans who foolishly stayed behind—including three Anglo printers still churning out English-language newspapers—suffered arrest and maintained stoic silence under interrogation. Santa Anna torched the town and sent his cavalry eastward on a probing expedition.

Again riders brought back news that whetted the general's appetite for a final slaughter of the only "army" that stood between him and total conquest of the rebellious province. Houston and his men had been sighted. Moving east—to the sanctuary of the land beyond the Trinity River. To reach it, they would have to cross the San Jacinto, probably at Lynch's Ferry.

Once more the army moved with all speed. For Amanda the march was a nightmare blur of walking, sweating, going without meals, fording flooded creeks, struggling to help free mired wagons—

On April the eighteenth, the Mexicans made rendezvous with their cavalry in the town of New Washington on Galveston Bay. His Excellency granted his men a night's rest while dragoon scouts combed the countryside that was cut by river channels and bayous. On the morning of the twentieth, the scouts galloped back into camp at eight o'clock.

Within an hour, the drums were beating the signal to advance.

viii

As the marquee came down, Amanda noticed how pale Cordoba looked. She asked him why.

"Because—" He swore. The belt that held his saber had to be loosened another notch before it would fit around him. "—because His Excellency is feeling so splendid. Houston has been sighted less than eight miles from here. But I spoke with the dragoons myself. Houston and his men are facing us, not Lynch's Ferry."

She shook her head. "I don't understand what's wrong with that."

"Why, nothing!—except that we have been operating from one assumption all along. The assumption that Houston is in wild retreat before us. I wonder. If he's retreating, why has he stopped?"

Cordoba drew his saber; quickly sketched a crude map on the ground.

"Even His Excellency seems to have forgotten that we are now separated from the main body of the army. In our eagerness to pursue the Texans, we have left Sesma with a thousand of our best at Thompson's Ferry—"

He stabbed the sword at the ground.

"Urrea at Matagorda—"

Another stab.

"—and God knows what's become of Filisola and his two thousand!"

Stab.

Swift strokes obliterated the map and markings as the bugles and drums sounded. The first of the baggage wagons began to roll.

"I wouldn't presume to advise His Excellency, of course," Cordoba said sourly. "I only pose the question

—are we chasing frightened men? Or being lured by clever ones? Are we the pursuers or the pursued? I don't like the smell one bit!"

He moved to Amanda. Swept an arm around her and buried his mouth against the curve of her throat:

"Whatever happens, you remain with the women and the wagons. I don't want anything to harm you."

Then he was gone through the dust behind a cantering squad of dragoons.

She should have drawn comfort from Cordoba's concern. Instead, she felt afraid.

Not for herself.

For him.

CHAPTER V

The Corn of San Jacinto

A MOSQUITO TICKLED Amanda's neck. She reached up quickly and squashed it. One of the *soldaderas* sitting near her in the simmering shade of the baggage wagon opened her eyes.

The woman saw nothing of importance. She closed her eyes again. Perspiration trickled down Amanda's nose. She wiped it away.

The whole camp was taking siesta; Santa Anna had insisted. Because of the heat, the general had left his carpeted marquee of striped silk. She could see him stretched out beneath the great oak tree that crowned the hilltop, his hands folded on his belly.

The oak stood approximately in the center of the campsite chosen last evening. Around the sleeping general, officers sat talking quietly or studying maps. Few were as relaxed as their leader.

Major Luis Cordoba was standing up, staring toward the forward section of the encampment. There, infantrymen in mud-stained white fatigue suits dozed against a semi-circular barricade of packing boxes, pack saddles and other gear. The makeshift breastwork was located just where the hilltop began to slope down to a broad expanse of wild grass.

What time was it? Amanda guessed three o'clock. Dawn on this twenty-first of April had been clear and beautiful. But the temperature had risen steadily. Now the air steamed.

At nine that morning, General Cos had appeared with

an extra five hundred cavalrymen. They too were resting, at the extreme rear of the camp. The horses cropped grass while the men napped in whatever shade was available.

Restless, Amanda pushed up from where she'd been sitting. She walked to the end of the wagon. She saw Cordoba glance her way, but the distance was too great for her to read his expression. She assumed he was worried.

His Excellency didn't seem worried. His relaxed slumber was a marked contrast to his fury at sunset yesterday—

Early on the twentieth, the Mexicans had located Houston's force with very little trouble—almost confirming Cordoba's fears. The Texans—reportedly numbering only about half of Santa Anna's fifteen hundred —had gone to ground in a forest of oak trees festooned with Spanish moss. All during the afternoon, they had refused to come out and fight.

Instead, riflemen sniped at the Mexican lines from the gloom of the wood, and two six-pounders fired rounds of fragmented horseshoes. Santa Anna's sole six-pounder replied occasionally, with little effect.

Late in the day, a Texas cavalry unit had probed the Mexican position, only to be driven back—without losses. Santa Anna's curses roared through the encampment until night fell. When Amanda and the major went to bed in his marquee after dark, he told her that, tomorrow, His Excellency intended to take the initiative—

If so, when? The afternoon was already waning.

From the end of the wagon, she gazed at the barricade. Some of the infantrymen were asleep. Others were nervously checking the mechanisms of their antique muskets. Amanda fanned herself, dizzy all at once. She shut her eyes; drew deep breaths of the stale air—

The dizziness passed. She still felt uneasy. Her loyalty really belonged to those unseen men hiding in the wood along Buffalo Bayou. Yet she was deeply concerned for Cordoba, too.

The forest where the Texans hid rose at the far end of a great meadow. Santa Anna had chosen to camp on the hilltop because of its commanding view of the wood and the meadow. From the barricade, his marksmen could rake the meadow's lush grass, which in many places grew taller than full-grown wheat.

Studying the meadow now, Amanda realized something was wrong. The air around her was still. But the grass stirred as if blown by a gentle wind—

She blinked. Were men moving out there?

With one hand on the wagon, she stood on tiptoe for a better view. Along the barricade a number of soldiers had risen and were watching the unusual motion of the grass.

She glanced to the oak. Santa Anna's staff showed increased activity. Men were running back and forth between the tree and the barricade. One was Cordoba, racing toward the oak and brandishing a spyglass.

With a yawn, Santa Anna roused. Beyond him, she saw movement where the cavalrymen had been dozing only a moment ago. Dragoons hurried to their horses, hazy figures against a distant growth of trees. The trees screened a swamp that drained into the little San Jacinto River, which ran down from the north to intersect Buffalo Bayou.

Just as she turned her attention back to the meadow, the notes of a Mexican bugle split the drowsy air. All the men behind the barricade scrambled up, readying their muskets. At a place where the meadow grass wasn't so high, Amanda glimpsed other men advancing with rifles, and a rider jogging on a white horse.

The riflemen quickly left the highest grass behind. While the Mexicans took siesta, the Texans had begun their advance—perhaps counting on the inactivity in the enemy camp. They moved steadily toward the base of the hill, spreading out in a wide semicircle. The horseman in the center of the line grew more visible moment by moment. He towered in the saddle—

It was Sam Houston. The man the Cherokees of eastern Tennessee had christened Raven.

Amanda had met Houston before, in Bexar. On his last visit, he'd spent an hour in the public bar of Gura's Hotel. He was a strapping Scotch-Irishman, with good manners and obvious education. Yet Amanda found there was something primitive about him, and he seemed to defy easy classification.

He indulged his temper as readily as he did his intellect. He spoke of reading Julius Caesar for relaxation, but he was so fond of a particular cussword that some Mexicans called him—and thus any Texan—*Señor God-damn.* In the meadow, his height and the milky whiteness of his horse Saracen identified him beyond all doubt.

An officer at the barricade bawled a command. Muskets lifted, cracked and spurted smoke and orange fire. The volley sent the Texans diving for cover.

Houston wheeled his horse aside, bending low over its neck. The infantrymen reloaded, began firing again. Now the whole camp was in motion. Men raced to join those already in place behind the improvised rampart. The *soldaderas* screeched in alarm and rushed to protect their belongings—

Amanda remained at the end of the wagon, watching. Acrid smoke drifting along the barricade obscured her view for a few moments. Then she saw the meadow again. Houston's men were still moving forward, that long, sweeping arc closing on the base of the hill. Incredibly, the Texans had yet to fire a single shot.

She heard music. The *tap-tap* of a drum, then a fife. The Texans were advancing to the melody of a popular romantic ballad, *Come to the Bower.*

Noise in the Mexican camp soon overpowered the

music. Men shouted orders. Hoofs thudded and gear creaked as the cavalry milled at the rear of the hill. In the confusion, Amanda lost sight of Cordoba.

Running, the first Texans reached the base of the hill. The infantrymen fired steadily. And still no shots from the attackers—

Even as Amanda realized this, a volley thundered from the bottom of the hill. On the barricade, a white-suited soldier spun around and fell. From somewhere behind the advancing line, the Texans' two six-pounders boomed.

The fire was brutally accurate. Amanda ducked behind the corner of the wagon as geysers of earth erupted just in front of the breastwork. When she looked again, she saw that a gap had been blasted in the center of the barricade.

Behind her, *soldaderas* wailed and ran in every direction. Through the thickening smoke, she glimpsed Santa Anna berating an orderly. The man sprinted off—for what purpose, she couldn't guess.

Then she heard another sound from the unseen slope of the hill. A raw, animal sound. For a moment, the sound made no sense—

When it did, she shuddered. The Texans were screaming as they climbed the hillside. Shooting and screaming—

"Remember Goliad!"

"—the Alamo—"

"Remember the Alamo!"

The first Texans reached the gap in the barricade and stormed through, firing rifles and pistols point blank at the few defenders brave enough to remain near the opening. Bearded and dirty, the Texans spread out, clubbing men down with rifle butts and attacking them with knives and tomahawks.

A steady stream of Texans poured through the gap. Others came jumping over the barricade. Houston rode through the opening, mounted on a bay horse now. Evidently the white one had been shot from under him. He fired pistols from both hands.

Amanda spun around. All across the camp, an incredible scene of panic was unfolding. Mexicans streamed away from the barricade. Groups of terrified soldiers surged back and forth, leaderless—then began to run. Not toward the barricade. The other way.

Clouds of smoke and dust blew across the hilltop. The dragoons were moving too. Not toward the barricade. Away.

Under the oak, Santa Anna clambered onto a black horse whose rein was held by the orderly she'd seen before. Sword still sheathed, His Excellency went galloping off toward the rear of the hill.

A Texan ball blasted the corner of the wagon. Amanda leaped back, her cheek stabbed by flying splinters. The fife and drum could no longer be heard at all. The Texans were howling too loudly.

They fanned out across the hilltop, almost crazed. They shot and cut and killed—

"Remember Goliad!"

"REMEMBER THE ALAMO!"

She saw Houston's bay stumble and fall, blood spurting from its belly. Houston dragged himself from under the horse, then doubled as a ball tore into his boot. But he recovered quickly. He shot a Mexican cavalryman out of the saddle. When the Mexican hit the ground, Houston tore the man's pennoned lance from his hands and stabbed it into his throat. In seconds, Houston was mounted on the cavalryman's horse, shoulders hunched and blood welling from the top of his right boot—

The frightened screams of the Mexicans blended with the howling of the Texans. The last of the Mexican infantry broke from the barricade, flung down their weapons and ran toward the rear. Amanda saw a boy hardly out of adolescence twist and raise his hands defensively as two lanky Texans caught up with him.

The boy shrieked, "Me no Alamo! *Me no Alam—*" One of the Texans disembowled him with two slashes of a bowie.

The Mexicans ran—but not fast enough. They died by the tens and twenties, shot down, clubbed down, kicked and stepped on. Everywhere, Amanda heard the same hysterical plea—

"Me no Alamo! *Me no Alamo!*"

There were a few who didn't try to save themselves that way. One Amanda caught sight of suddenly was Luis Cordoba. With a small group of enlisted men, he was attempting a pathetic defense near the oak.

The major was surrounded by seven or eight men, most struggling to reload their muskets as a band of Texans charged them. Saber drawn, Cordoba shouted for the soldiers to load more quickly. Two pitched over, killed by pistol shots. Amanda started to run toward the tree, dodging between bearded Americans. One leveled his rifle at her, checking his fire only when he saw her white skin.

Amanda had already flung herself on the ground in anticipation of the shot. She buried her head on her arms as other Texans behind her volleyed at a troop of retreating cavalry. When she looked up again, she saw that Cordoba and three other survivors were fighting hand to hand with twice as many opponents.

A rifle butt felled one Mexican soldier. The other two threw down their pieces and dashed around the tree. With all the noise, Amanda couldn't hear what they cried. But she knew—

"Me no Alamo!"

His uniform ripped and bloody, Luis Cordoba stood his ground. He raised his saber for a defensive stroke. Amanda lurched to her feet, nearly bowled over again as Houston rode past, shouting commands.

She raced through a litter of Mexican bodies, holding up her black silk skirt and crying Cordoba's name. The Texans backed him toward the oak; crowded around; wrenched the saber from his hand. Blood smeared his forehead. His eyes were huge and fearful suddenly—

A Texan thrust a pistol to within six inches of Cordoba's face and pulled the trigger. The major slammed back against the tree, his mouth gushing blood. Amanda screamed, "*Luis!*" as he sank from sight, the back of his head leaving blood and gray matter on the bark.

Someone grabbed her, flung her aside—"Get out of the way, you Spanish slut!" Two young Texans raced by as she struck the ground, the wind knocked out of her.

Her mind burned with an image of Cordoba dying, the victim of a code of honor that hadn't permitted him to run or beg for mercy—even though he was more entitled to mercy than most of those shrilling, "Me no Alamo!"

With her cheek in the dirt, she wept for him in the brief seconds of incredible noise—hoofs, shrieks, shots—before she fainted.

ii

The battle of San Jacinto lasted no more than twenty minutes. The pursuit and capture of the demoralized Mexicans lasted well into the night. Though most of the senior officers were either caught or surrendered voluntarily, Santa Anna got away.

Amanda was carried to a large tent erected for the use of the Texas army's surgeon, a mild, kindly man named Ewing. She was put on a cot among those occupied by wounded men, some of who complained about the presence of a woman until Ewing ordered them to be quiet.

Ewing gave her brandy and a chance to tell her story. When he heard it, he promised he'd arrange for her to repeat it to Houston himself after the general awoke from the heavy sleep into which Ewing had drugged him. Houston had lost a good deal of blood as a result of the wound in his right leg.

Next morning, while most of the Texans were sleeping off their raucous celebration of the victory, Sam Houston propped himself under the oak where Santa Anna had rested and Cordoba had died. He began penciling dispatches to President Burnet hiding somewhere on Galveston Island, and to President Jackson in the east. He was still working when a detachment returned with yet another captive—a rather tall Mexican wearing a dirty blue smock, leather cap and slippers of red felt.

The man claimed to be a private who had run away. He said he'd stolen the smock and cap from a slave cabin in the neighborhood. He had been discovered hiding in the sedge grass along Vince's Bayou. He had wanted to swim across, but didn't know how.

What made the prisoner of more than passing interest was his cultivated speech, unusual among ordinary line soldiers. The man was telling his story as the detachment rode into camp. Suddenly some soldiers imprisoned in a rope corral exclaimed, "*El presidente!*"

Very shortly, the prisoner stood in front of Houston. With a preening smile, the Napoleon of the West admitted his identity and shrugged off the failure of his ruse.

The Texans shouted for a lynch rope. Houston ordered them silent. When Santa Anna requested opium to calm his nerves, Houston had it brought from the fallen marquee. By noon, the marquee was set up again. Inside, the dictator got to work writing orders that called for the total evacuation of all Mexican troops north of the Rio Grande.

Amanda heard the story from Doctor Ewing late in the day. He'd come into the tent where she was resting.

After describing Santa Anna's capture, he said Houston might have a few minutes to receive her before supper. The general was anxious to see his old acquaintance who had been at the Alamo, then been held captive by the Mexicans, Ewing told her.

Amanda nodded in acknowledgement, wishing she didn't feel so dispirited. She should have been happy. Her good friend Bowie and all the others butchered at Bexar had been avenged. The Texans had won a splendid victory against a force twice as large as theirs. And done it with incredibly small losses—six killed, two dozen wounded.

The enemy toll was more than six hundred dead and something like twelve hundred captured. Cordoba's prophecy had been right. Houston was a better strategist than Santa Anna had ever suspected—

Cordoba. She couldn't get him out of her mind. That was the problem.

She forced herself to pay attention to Ewing; agreed with his comment that it seemed a little unfair for Santa Anna to be paroled and allowed to return to Mexico City. But Houston was adamant, Ewing said. Though the new republic of Texas had won its independence with savage fighting, it would now conduct its affairs honorably.

Honor. Amanda's mouth pursed in a bitter way. Honor had earned Luis Cordoba his grave.

Puzzled by her dour mood, Ewing said, "I would think you'd show a little more pleasure, Señora de la Gura. You were rescued. Your own side carried the day—"

"Don't misunderstand, doctor. I'm glad Santa Anna was beaten. He deserves much worse than he's getting. But you see—" She gazed at his silhouette against the red sun visible outside the tent."—nothing is ever clear cut. The Mexican officer who kept me was a fine man. A brave one. He didn't run away yesterday. He didn't cower and pretend he had no part in the Alamo killings—though the truth is, he didn't. But he was still shot down. And Santa Anna's alive. I'm sorry it wasn't the other way around."

Doctor Ewing didn't know what to say. Looking uncomfortable, he tugged out a fobbed watch:

"We'd better go. The general said five sharp."

As she started out, a young man with a bandaged leg glared at her from an adjoining cot:

"You a Texican, woman?"

"Yes."

"Well, I heard what you said. I'll be blasted if I can see how you'd grieve for one of those fucking greasers. I just can't understand that at all."

"No," Amanda said, "I suppose you can't. I don't suppose anyone can."

Her face stark, she followed Ewing into the late afternoon heat.

iii

Amanda expected the interview with General Sam Houston to be difficult. As she walked with Doctor Ewing toward the oak, she saw groups of Texans at cook fires glance her way. Some pointed; scowled; made derogatory comments. She tried to ignore them. Tried to walk with her head up and her expression composed. But it took great effort.

Sam Houston saw her coming. He sat up a little straighter on the blankets spread at the base of the tree. His bootless right leg was swathed in bandages from foot to mid-calf. On either side of him, several packing boxes formed an improvised office. She saw an inkstand, pencils, books, foolscap writing paper—

And a number of Texans loitering on the tree's far side. The side on which Cordoba had fallen. Thank God she wouldn't have to stare at the bloodstained bark—

But the faces of the Texans bothered her. The men seemed just as hostile as those at the campfires.

Houston smiled and waved as she and Ewing approached. The general was more than six feet tall, with a long, blunt jaw, wavy, gray-streaked chestnut hair and bright blue eyes. His skin was pale. His fine shirt was torn and powder-blackened. So was his claw-hammer coat. A distinctly rumpled and weary-looking Raven—

Houston had been given the name in his youth, when he'd run away from his widowed mother to live with the Indians. He had served in the army, studied law, been elected to Congress as a Jacksonian Democrat, and then won the governorship of Tennessee. In 1829, he'd abruptly resigned in the middle of a campaign for a second term, fleeing the state and an eighteen-year-old bride who had left him after three months of marriage.

Amanda had heard both sides of the story. Houston's partisans insisted the girl had been cold, and Houston had every right to leave her. His enemies claimed the girl feared him; said he was insane—jealous beyond reason; and that his sexual appetites were a disgrace even in the marriage bed.

Whatever the truth, Houston had disappeared for a time along the Arkansas River, where the government had resettled his old friends, the Cherokees. He used liquor to blot out the past. So much liquor that the Cherokees gave him a second, less flattering name—Big Drunk.

In the early 1830s he had emerged from his alcoholic wanderings and re-established his old ties with the president under whom he'd soldiered in the Creek War. Some in Bexar hinted that Houston had come to Texas for a purpose other than the one publicly announced: to help American traders negotiate treaties of peace with the marauding Indian tribes. The rumormongers said Houston's real mission was to foment a movement for Texas independence, thus paving the way for the territory's eventual union with the United States.

It might have been true. Certainly since the beginning of the Mexican trouble, Houston had been in the forefront of the Texan cause—

"Amanda!" Houston exclaimed in his deep voice as she entered the dappled shade of the oak. "I can hardly believe it's you! When I heard you were a prisoner of the Mexicans, I was almost as surprised as I was when Santa Anna showed up wearing bedroom slippers."

"My compliments on the victory, General," Amanda said. The remark brought snorts and some ugly glances from the men in buckskin and homespun on the other side of the tree.

"You're mighty formal all at once. What's wrong with the names we used in Bexar?"

"A lot's happened since then, General."

"Goddamned if it hasn't. I trust you'll forgive me for not standing up. Orders of Doctor Ewing there. Push those books off that case. Sit down and tell me how you got here."

"She got here because she was yella," one of the men beyond the tree said in a false whisper. Houston glared:

"The next man who utters a remark like that will answer to me." He glanced back to Amanda. "Passions are still running pretty high. I'm not too popular myself since I refused to let the men hang our Mexican friend."

"I can understand their feelings. I was in the mission."

"So I learned from Almeron Dickinson's widow."

"I saw what the Mexicans did—on Santa Anna's direct order."

"I'd like to hear your account of it."

She told him, trying not to let the words conjure sounds and sights and smells. But they did. She was glad when she finished the story.

He reached out to grasp her hand. "Thank you.

You've confirmed everything that was reported to me. I suppose I shouldn't have asked. The memory is obviously unpleasant—"

"I try to forget how it sounded—how it looked—and how sickened it made me. I can't."

"No one can forget—even those of us who weren't there. I told His Excellency much the same thing this morning. Before he decided we'd be easy to beat, he should have remembered the Alamo." He squeezed her hand. "Are you up to telling me the rest of your experience?"

She nodded and, in a subdued voice, described how she'd been made a prisoner. She omitted the more personal details of her relationship with the major, characterizing him only as a man who had treated her in a humane way. At the end, she said:

"I hope his body can be sent back to Mexico City. He—he had a wife there."

"That may not be possible. Some of Santa Anna's staff officers are going to do what they can about notifying next of kin. There's no need for you to worry about such things—you're a free woman now."

Some of the men beyond the tree didn't like that either. Houston's lids flickered; he heard the angry whispers. But he didn't turn to acknowledge them. Instead, he went on:

"You can join in the work to be done in Texas. We've got to rebuild. Get the government functioning—"

His hand strayed beneath one of the mussed blankets. He pulled out an ear of corn. Some of the kernels had been nibbled away.

"My afternoon meal," he smiled. His thumb accidentally flicked three kernels from the ear. One of the men on the other side of the tree scrambled forward to snatch them up:

"I could take this corn home an' plant it, General."

Houston glanced at the ear in his hand, then suddenly began shucking kernels from it:

"Here—all of you take some. Plant it in your fields. It's time to cultivate the arts of peace now that you've shown yourselves masters of the art of war."

Pleased by his flattery, the men crowded forward. Amanda was momentarily forgotten as the Texans laughed and jostled one another, straining to get some of the corn Houston dropped from his outstretched hand.

"By God, we ought to call this Houston corn!" one of the men shouted.

The general shook his head. "Honor yourselves, not me. Call it San Jacinto corn."

With his forefinger he worked another kernel loose, then tossed the ear into the crowd. Noisily, the Texans swarmed around the man who caught it. Not a one of them was paying any attention to Amanda now. She wondered whether the byplay with the corn had been a ploy to divert them and blunt their hostility.

Not entirely, she realized, as Houston held out his hand:

"You take this one. It's time for all of us to start thinking about the future."

Amanda tried to speak. She couldn't. With bleak eyes, she stared at the kernel resting in her palm.

"Doctor Ewing," Houston said, "I think you'd better conduct the señora back to the surgical tent. If any man so much as touches her, report it to me and I'll have him whipped till he can't walk."

She leaned on Ewing's arm in the twilight. Along the way, the kernel of corn dropped from her other hand. She was aware of the loss. But she didn't turn back to search. She had no field to plow and plant. Nothing to give the future meaning and value. That she was safe and unhurt seemed of small importance. The fabric of her life had been ripped to ruin—again.

iv

On a gray and showery afternoon in June, Amanda walked through the rubble in the lobby of Gura's Hotel. With her was a small, finely-boned man in cleric's robes, the parish priest, Don Refugio de la Garza.

Don Refugio wrinkled his nose at the smell of human waste left in a corner. Amanda surveyed the smashed counter, then a pile of scrapwood and horsehair—all that remained of the lobby furniture.

Her dress was the only touch of color in the whole dreary scene. It was homespun, dyed yellow with root dyes. A sunbonnet kept her face in shadow as she studied the wreckage. She had been back in Bexar for several weeks, escorted by an amiable soldier in a wagon Houston commandeered for her. The journey had been difficult. She felt weak most of the time, and was troubled frequently by nausea.

Shortly after she'd arrived, she'd been informed that Gura's Hotel was no longer fit to be lived in. Don Refugio had advanced her a small sum to rent a room elsewhere in town. This was the first day she'd been able to summon the courage to visit Soledad Street and see the devastation for herself.

"It's a pity, but there's not much left," Don Refugio said as Amanda gazed at the whitewashed wall. Someone had used charcoal to scrawl a filthy remark about Texans. "There was a good deal of drinking and carousing while Santa Anna's senior officers were quartered here. Also, they were not particularly respectful of property belonging to an Anglo."

Amanda sighed. "Is it the same upstairs?"

"Worse."

"Then there's not much point in going up. I suppose the land and the building will bring me a little money."

The priest's gray eyebrows shot up. "You don't intend to re-open the hotel? I know it would require a great deal of work, but I thought—"

"I'm going to sell, padre. As is. There's bad feeling toward me in this town."

"Yes, I realize. Still—"

"It's even worse than before, when I had girls upstairs."

"You can admit the ill will is understandable, can you not?"

"No. I was the one American woman who survived the battle at the mission *and* stood up to Santa Anna—in return for which, I was made a prisoner. To the Americans around here, that somehow makes me a traitor. Susannah Dickinson, on the other hand, took Santa Anna's clemency—"

"She saw her husband die, Amanda! She was utterly demoralized—"

"I know. I'm not finding fault, just stating a fact. She *did* accept his offer—and spread the message he wanted her to spread. For that, she's a heroine. I don't imagine my name will ever appear on the list of the women who lived through the massacre. I'm confident hers will."

"Ah, but a name on a paper tells nothing! If your name is recorded, you will probably be listed as a Mexican—"

"True. Anyway, that's not the point. I wouldn't accept Santa Anna's so-called generosity—and look where it's gotten me."

"But people wonder why you didn't run away from the Mexicans."

"Because I gave my word to the officer who saved me from execution! Oh, what difference does it make? They hate me, and that's that."

"It will pass, Amanda."

"Will it? I know what people are saying. That I should have refused to go with Cordoba. Broken my word. Fled. And if that wasn't possible, I imagine they believe I should have done away with myself! Well—" Her mouth twisted. "I've always had a strong survival instinct. I gather that's no longer permitted in Texas."

"Nonsense," Don Refugio snorted. "Do you know how many, here and elsewhere, actively supported Santa Anna when it seemed the Texan cause was lost? I assure you the number is not small."

"People might even think differently if I'd lived with a different sort of man," she went on, staring at three holes drilled in the wall by pistol balls. "But Major Cordoba was decent—and I've made no secret of that. Evidently decency on the part of the enemy is also unthinkable."

"That we are all God's creatures, with an equal distribution of devils and saints among all nations, is seldom remembered in wartime."

"General Houston remembered," she said. "He, at least, was kind to me."

The priest nodded. "He has grown to be a man of immense wisdom, I think. They say there'll be an election in the next few months. Burnet will step aside. Houston is almost certain to be named president of the republic. He's your friend, and I'm sure he'd see that you were treated fairly. For that reason, you might want to reconsider your decision. I assure you the hatreds will be forgotten. We are all Texans now. We may eventually become Americans, if the rumors are true."

"The rumors about annexation?"

"Yes. Houston is in favor, is he not?"

"Very much so. He told me before I came back that he may petition Congress—or at least ask the people to vote on whether a petition requesting annexation should be sent. But the newspapers say Jackson's cooled on the idea. He doesn't want a protracted war with Mexico, so he has to maintain neutrality. It's all very muddled—especially since the Mexican legislature repudiated Santa Anna's treaty recognizing the republic's independence. Who knows how it will come out?"

Her words trailed off with an empty sound. The priest pondered, then agreed:

"Yes, in some ways Santa Anna's defeat only compounded the confusion. The matter of chattel slavery will becloud annexation, no doubt—"

Thinking of the dead in the mission, she made a derisive sound. "I trust you heard how Quincy Adams referred to the rebellion? Denounced it in Congress as nothing more than a scheme to restore slavery down here, and bring another slaveholding state into the nation? The fool!"

"There are some who would hope for that," Don Refugio told her. "Here and in the United States."

"Well, I won't be present to see how the whole thing's resolved, padre. I've made up my mind. I have to start over somewhere else. With a new name. Or an old one, rather. The name I had before I was married. I need a fresh start at everything."

The little priest tried to read her face in the shadow cast by the bonnet's brim. He couldn't. But he heard the strain in her voice:

"Whether I've done right or wrong is something someone else will have to decide. Maybe the woman who guards the vine—"

"Who?"

"Never mind."

"Amanda, I beg you to think carefully before—"

"I can't stay in Bexar any longer, padre. There are—too many memories. My husband—my friends murdered in the chapel. The major—"

Her voice broke. She shook her head as if angry with herself. Don Refugio laid his slim fingers on her arm, squeezing gently to comfort her.

"Where will you go?"

"I don't know. Further west, I suppose. I can travel with one of the pack trains. Perhaps to Santa Fe. Even on to California—I hear that's beautiful country."

"Comfortable, certainly. But you would be a subject of Mexico again."

"I'm not trying to escape a government, just the past. Besides, more and more Americans are settling there all the time. Coming up from Santa Fe, or from the east by ship—"

"And across the mountains one day, perhaps."

"The mountains? I doubt that."

"So did I, at first. But a number of the itinerant traders claim the fur companies have sent wagon shipments quite far west to equip their brigades. They believe it's possible to traverse the mountains and reach the Pacific with a wheeled vehicle." He looked amused. "America has a ravening hunger for land. Few obstacles will deter its satisfaction, least of all mountains. I expect your people won't be content until they claim the continent from coast to coast. So I'd have a care about choosing California. You might find yourself embroiled in the same political turmoil you've just endured here."

"There's always the Oregon Territory."

"One more area ripe for dispute and rebellion! Don't the British and the United States occupy it jointly, by treaty—?"

"It doesn't make any difference where I go—so long as it's away from here!"

After a moment, Don Refugio sighed in a resigned way:

"If your mind is made up, I am at your disposal to help with arrangements."

"Thank you." She smiled, but without much feeling. "I won't be going immediately, much as I'd like to. I won't be in any condition to travel for a while. You see, I—"

She experienced a bursting sense of relief at finally admitting it to someone:

"I'm fairly certain I'm going to have a child."

V

"Push," the fat old midwife said with a singular lack of compassion. She rested hard hands on Amanda's huge, heaving belly.

She tried. The pain was intense, and growing worse. The contractions seemed to torment her whole being.

She lay on a table in a room Don Refugio had provided in a wing of the San Fernando church. Her knees were bent, her feet braced against blocks of wood the priest had nailed to one end of the table. Don Refugio, dimly visible at the edge of a circle of lantern light, was in attendance because he'd acquired certain medical skills over the years. But Serafina, the midwife brought in from the country, was in charge.

There was a howling in Amanda's ears. Was it the wind outside the church, carrying sleet and rain from the northwest this gloomy day in January, 1837? Or was it only an imaginary echo of sounds from the past? The melody of the *deguello?* The shrieks of the dying in the mission? The pitiful cries of the routed soldiers at San Jacinto—?

"Push, for the Virgin's sake!" Serafina cried. "I can see the head!"

The insides of Amanda's thighs were wet. She lay naked, only her breasts covered by a scrap of rag. Her hands gripped the ends of a length of pine wood the midwife had given her to bite.

She dug her teeth into the soft, fragrant stick and closed her eyes, writhing.

"Hold her still!" Serafina exclaimed. Don Refugio's hands pinned Amanda's shoulders. The contractions were no longer distinct; they blended into a single, consuming pain. She felt the thick thrust of something being expelled from within her body—

"Push, woman. *Push.*"

She lost her sense of time and of place, catching only fleeting visual and aural impressions as her mind blanked out, then re-awoke—

The thickness between her legs was gone. She saw Don Refugio, white rags draped over one arm of his robe. She heard water splash as Serafina bathed her red-stippled hands and forearms.

She heard a muted gurgling, too; then the midwife's grumbles as she manipulated twine, tying the cord once near the opening from which the child had emerged and a second time close to the belly of the unseen baby. The child must be resting on the mound of rags between her thighs, Amanda realized—

The midwife stepped back.

"Cut the cord, padre."

The sudden glitter of a bowie knife almost made her scream aloud. Then she remembered she wasn't in the mission, nor on the hill of San Jacinto, but in an adobe room with a winter rainstorm raging outside.

Don Refugio's hands dipped out of sight. Immediately after cleaving the cord, he whipped the rags off his arm and began to bundle the infant. Amanda glimpsed a tiny, plum-colored face puckered in a struggle for breath. The baby's skin was wet and shimmering—

"A very good child," Serafina announced. "Now we must wait."

A second later, Don Refugio said, "I don't believe she hears you."

"The Pope send me packing, but it's a mystery to me how you celibates can presume to minister to women. Nothing personal, mind you—" A shrug. "You're a lot better than some I know." A pointing finger loomed before Amanda's eyes. "She hears me. She just doesn't feel like chattering."

"A thousand pardons!" Don Refugio said. "I forget this is your domain, not mine."

Amanda's grimace gentled into a smile. She stopped biting the stick so hard; released her hands from the ends. The priest melted into the darkness as the baby began to squall. In the church tower, the wind struck wild clangs from the bells.

Amanda let her heavy eyelids close. She opened them suddenly at the midwife's cry:

"Ah, Jesus have mercy! She's gotten rid of everything but she's still bleeding—"

Don Refugio's white-haired head bobbed above Amanda. He laid a dry hand on her sticky forehead. Suddenly her loins felt thick again—Serafina had thrust her right hand and forearm into her and was massaging vigorously to stop a warm flow she could feel on her legs.

The midwife grunted anxiously as she worked. At last she withdrew her red hand, disappeared, and once more Amanda heard the sound of flesh being plunged into water.

Presently Serafina returned. She stood immobile, her gaze focused between Amanda's legs.

After what seemed like hours, she nodded:

"The bleeding has stopped." For the first time, she allowed herself a smile. "You can sleep now, señora."

"I—I'd like to see the baby—"

"All right, but only a moment." She swung toward the darkness. "Step lively, padre!"

Amanda heard sandals scraping stone; Don Refugio obeyed the midwife just as any novice would have obeyed a superior.

"You've had babies before," Serafina declared, moving up beside Amanda's torso and re-arranging the cloth that had shifted away from her left nipple.

"None—that lived. I want this child to live."

"Oh, I think he will. He's a hefty one."

"He?" Amanda repeated. "A boy—?"

"From every observable sign," the older woman said with a wry smile. "What will you call him?"

Drowsily, Amanda answered, "Luis, I think. Luis Kent. Only spelled—" She labored for a breath. "American fashion—with an o in the first name."

Louis Kent. How good that sounded! Then she thought of something else:

Now there's someone to carry on the family. I can take him with me if I ever go back to Boston. I can show him where his grandfather and great-grandfather lived—and teach him to be proud he's a Kent.

"Louis, eh?" The midwife sniffed. Amanda barely heard:

Now that I have him, I will *go back. We'll go back together—*

"Louis—well, I suppose that's all right. Though everyone these days is naming their newborns after the men who fell at the mission. I'd have thought you might pick a hero's name too."

"I—did. The baby's father—was with the Mexican army—"

"Ah yes, I heard they held you captive for a while."

"He—could have killed—a great many. But he didn't—"

"Well, the decision's yours. Why the baby was named will soon be forgotten anyway. Your people and mine, we're no longer much different, it seems. We're all citizens of the republic. Living under the new republican flag with that one star. Judging by the way the voting went in October, I might even be an American presently. It's a remarkable world—"

She whirled to the shadows:

"It's about time, pad—mother of God, keep the feet covered! *Covered!*"

"My profound apologies," the priest murmured, surrendering the child to the midwife. "I'm a mere man—"

"That's quite apparent, I'm sorry to say." Serafina in turn handed the small warm bundle to Amanda. Then the midwife and the priest stood gazing downward, their shoulders touching and their banter forgotten.

Fighting sleepiness, Amanda lifted a corner of a rag aside and stared at the slitted eyes, the wrinkled pink flesh, the mouth that sucked air noisily. Suddenly she clutched the little boy tight against her breast.

"In God's name handle him gently!" Serafina said. "You'll suffocate the poor thing."

But Amanda clutched her newborn fiercely, feeling him squirm, then hearing him squall.

What a strange turn of events, she thought, remembering the tiny kernal Sam Houston had dropped into her hand beneath the oak at San Jacinto. He hadn't known—nor had she—that an entirely different kind of seed would germinate from the war's bloody ground. A seed that would yield this miracle of living flesh within her arms; give her a purpose; a new reason for going on when it seemed that all the rest of her reasons had been destroyed—

The future no longer terrified her because of its emptiness, its uncertainty. Let the wolf run; she wasn't afraid.

Louis Kent howled louder. She had never heard such a sweet, sweet sound—

Serafina slapped her hips:

"Merciful heaven, padre, I give up. Now she's crying too!"

The Journal of Jephtha Kent, 1844:

Bishop Andrew's Sin

April the 30th. Arrived in New York City after a wearying journey by coach, my annual stipend not being large enough to permit riding the rail roads. I have joined my brethren here for General Conference. Am stopping at a modest hotel where the appointments are few but clean, though of course the establishment cannot compare with other local hostelries. Adjoining one of its rooms, The New York Hotel has installed a separate, private facility for the purpose of bathing—or so I was told by my companion, the Reverend Hodding, with whom I took a brief walking tour late this afternoon.

Hodding is a pleasant, if opinionated, fellow. He itinerates in the vicinity of Chester County, Pennsylvania. We compared our situations, which are not essentially different, except in one regard. Freedom for the enslaved Negro is a goal much sought by Hodding, as well as by many of those to whom he ministers.

I in turn attempted to present Hodding with the views of those Christian men and women I have served the past two years from my location at Lexington, in Virginia's valley of the Shenandoah. But I did not press a strong personal view upon him. I have none. Whenever I think on the subject, I end in a quandry.

As evidence of the moral failure of our own Church, Hodding spoke scornfully of the treatment accorded men and women of color at Lovely Lane in Baltimore, where the "Afric" may sit nowhere but the balcony, and receives the sacrament only after it has been served to white persons. He also mentioned St. George's in Philadelphia, where Negroes must hold their own services at an hour different from that at which the whites worship. Clearly my companion is one of those enraged by the failure of the Methodist Episcopal Church to declare a position on the slave issue; twice during our stroll, he repeated Mr. Wesley's claim that the system of black bondage in this nation is "the vilest that ever saw the sun."

I continued to refrain from argumentation because, as I noted, I am not sure of my own heart—and also because I cannot d--n out of hand those whom I serve in Virginia. To do so, I would have to d--n the very woman with whom God has favored me, blessing our union with Gideon—

Gideon. A splendid little boy! I must not overlook his coming birthday. I must take a trinket home.

Before we parted, Hodding insisted the Conference would address the slavery question. I pray not. Such disputation can only lead to divisiveness of the sort which has already led the Reverend Orange Scott of Lowell to withdraw from the Methodist connection.

I fear a confrontation, and wonder why. Is it because there is epic risk of fostering ill will within the Church? Or is it because I know that, if forced to search my own conscience, I will find a lack of personal conviction?

Later. Prayed an hour for guidance, but remain as worried and uncertain as before.

*

May the 1st. One hundred and seventy-eight pastors have gathered. As the proceedings commenced, I was restored and refreshed by the preaching and the singing. How good to hear those stout voices inquiring of each other's welfare as the opening hymn, *And Are We Yet Alive?*, soared forth.

Bishop Soule, occupying the chair for the opening session, sounded a warning to those who would disturb our work among the people of color. Their souls are for saving but all else is beyond us, the bishop declared in his address. "To raise them up to equal civil rights and privileges is not within our power. Let us not labor in vain and spend our strength for naught."

His remarks produced a few dark looks up and down the benches, but no open dissent. I trust the Bishop's admonition will be heeded for the sake of the Church's tranquility and, I shamefully admit, mine.

*

May the 2nd. A quiet day. Another walking tour late in the afternoon. Even though I twice visited Boston while a student at the Biblical Institute in Vermont, the splendor and squalor of New York City far surpass anything I have beheld elsewhere.

There are a great many Irish present, and more arriving by ship each month. Simply by listening to street conversation, one is made aware of the animosity directed toward them. A Mr. Harper, a book publisher like my great-grandfather, is to run for mayor here. Harper is what is called a reform candidate, for the city"s affairs are in disorder and badly need setting straight. Whether Mr. Harper is dedicated to that task remains questionable, since I was informed that his partisans are preparing banners bearing a campaign appeal that seems to have little to do with reform, and everything to do with stirring hatred of the slum Irish. The slogan is, "No Popery!" Let us hope the campaign will not producc the sort of anti-Catholic rioting which recently struck Philadelphia.

Obtained an edition of Mr. Greeley's *Tribune,* which contains this remarkable information—the rail road trackage within the country now totals close to four thousand miles, with more being laid all the time as new lines open. The United States has several times the trackage of the entire continent of Europe, the paper says. "Thou *art* the God that doest wonders!"

*

May the 3rd. Today, Friday, the cataclysm is upon us. The sectional quarrel which has inflamed tempers in Congress and the press has reached even here. The Conference to which the Reverend Orange Scott formerly belonged put forward a petition opposing slavery, whereupon the meeting erupted into shouting of a most unseemly sort.

The chair has appointed a Committee on Slavery to accept other memorials on the same subject. Hodding told me such petitions are sure to come, then went on to confirm a suspicion I have not uttered or written before, though many of my southern brethren have expressed it to me:

The anti-slavery delegates are operating according to a plan drawn long before we assembled. The ultimate target of the strategy is the worthy and well-regarded Bishop James Andrew of Georgia, whose sin is this: he is the unhappy possessor of a mulatto girl and a Negro boy, neither of which he purchased. Both were bequeathed to him in the estate of his first wife. His second wife is also the inheritor of slaves. Under Georgia law, neither the bishop nor his spouse can manumit the slaves.

When Hodding mentioned Andrew in a most challenging way, then asked my opinion on what should be done, I once again took refuge in excuses that hide my own equivocation. I said I did not feel qualified to take part in any general debate, being among the most recently ordained of all those gathered; I became a pastor not quite two years ago. I said I felt doubly unqualified by reason of age, having just observed my twenty-fourth birthday.

Did Hodding suspect my evasion? His smirk made me believe so.

Later. I thought much of my beloved wife Fan, and of our son. I asked myself what the anti-slavery delegates would offer Fan's father, Captain Tunworth of Lexington, as well as her numerous relatives in South Carolina, in return for the black labor on which they depend. That, it seems to me, is one of the sticking-places:

Even many in the south accept the fact that the peculiar institution is, in a great number of respects, inhumane. But abolitionist agitators such as Mr. Garrison of Boston, whose *Liberator* newspaper insists upon full freedom for Negroes, never propose any plan by means of which the southern agriculturist can replace his Negro labor. And without the labor, there is no prosperity for those who cultivate the land. The snare is a cruel one, since human beings north or south are not prone to abandon that which fosters their survival.

At supper, we fell into a heated discussion of one alternative to slavery which has been proposed for nearly thirty years by the Colonization Society—namely, the freeing and re-settlement of the Negro in Liberia. Hodding bitterly chastised several of the more moderate brethren who favor this idea. He said the scheme is based on an unspoken belief that the Negro is inferior to the white—and will somehow contaminate the nation with his continued presence. Hodding then proceeded to put a theological cast on the subject.

John Wesley, the beloved Asbury, Coke—the pillars of our faith—were unequivocal about the absolutes of good and evil. Good and evil are the fixed stars in our struggle as itinerants. Our aim is, first, conversion—admission of sin—and then redemption; the eradication of human wickedness through the grace of Our Lord Jesus Christ. No one could disagree with those extremities, and the lack of a middle ground. Then Hodding closed the trap.

If there is no middle ground in our theology, so there can be none regarding the slave question. If slavery is acknowledged an evil, it must be destroyed, just as confessed sin is overcome by redemptive love for Christ. Several shouted at Hodding—one subject, they cried, is spiritual, the other temporal! Hodding sees no difference; he sees, in fact, an irrefutable connection.

I sat silent throughout. Hodding's logic troubled me sorely, but not as much as the intemperate speech of my brethren on both sides of the argument. It seems to me the affair of Bishop Andrew is exacerbating tempers to a dangerous degree.

*

May the 10th. A resolution has been put forward "affectionately" requesting Bishop Andrew to resign his office. And a curious thing has occurred—the use of the word "slavery" has become infrequent in our sessions. Andrew's alleged transgression has somehow been transmuted into a question of Church authority: whose will is paramount? That of the General Conference? Or that of the bishops?

It is a screen, nothing more. The fundamental issue is Andrew's ownership of black men and women.

Screen or no, Bishop Soule today sounded another, even more dire warning. He said that permitting the Conference to remove Andrew without a proper ecclesiastical trial would rend the organization of the Church "beyond repair."

*

May the 14th. The debate continues, heated and unsettling. I absented myself for a time this afternoon, having realized that I will be forced to take a stand unless the committees laboring in private can effect a compromise, which I think unlikely. By leaving the gathering, I hoped to free my mind of the dismaying subject—only to discover it turning to another almost as troublesome.

My thoughts returned to my conversion six years ago by the Reverend Lee of the Willamette Mission in Oregon. Jason Lee was the great man who first revealed to me that my name, Jephthah as it is spelled in the Old Testament, means "God opens." The conversion did not please my father, to whom I have not written in far too long.

Many years ago, my father Jared Kent put the eastern part of the continent behind him forever, accepting both the freedom which the western lands afford, and the struggle they require for even meager success. My father came to love the free spaces, their natural beauties and abundance. He wanted me to remain a westerner as he is. I could never convince him that my given name must have had a pre-ordained significance unknown to him when he bestowed it, for, through the Reverend Lee, God truly did open my soul to His message, and I felt a compelling call to train myself for the ministry. My answering of the call wounded my father not a little.

As I walked along the Broad Way, I was overcome with pity for my father, who saw me onto the ship for the east with the greatest reluctance. His rheumatism, developed from many years spent in icy streams trapping for plews, has made his existence as a wheat farmer trying in the extreme. His sorrow was increased when my beloved mother, Grass Singing, went to her grave three years ago. Thinking of him alone now in Oregon, my guilt was, for a time, nigh unbearable.

Desperate to relieve it, I sought refuge in an act I freely acknowledge as a pandering to human vanity. In answer to my wife's earnest request, I inquired about, and was directed to, a studio where the remarkable Daguerreotype is available.

The sitting required less time than I expected—a

minute, no more. But all of the kitchen funds which my dear Fan gave me for this express purpose were required to purchase the little copper plate which now reposes in a silk-lined box on my bureau.

Although the visit to the studio was worldly indulgence, the experience refreshed my spirit in an unexpected way. On the plate I first saw not myself but the Almighty's handiwork—for surely the Frenchman, Daguerre, was blessed by heavenly inspiration when he perfected his method of capturing the human face on a bit of metal.

On returning to my hotel, I continued to marvel at the plate, which is somehow treated with silver salts and then exposed to the light to create an image. I discovered again why my brethren chide me good-naturedly with the name "Indian Preacher." I have the light eyes of the Kents but the dark and unruly hair of the Shoshoni. All in all, mine is a curious and severe countenance. For a few moments, I fancied that, in the eyes of the image, I saw my guilt over the unhappiness I had brought to my father, and I fancied that I also saw my doubt about where I would stand on the question now being debated at the Conference in increasingly heated language.

*

May the 25th. All the city agog with news from Baltimore, where, only yesterday, there was received an actual, audible message transmitted in code from the Supreme Court room in the capital by means of the electric telegraph of Mr. Morse. He is the inventor of the device as well as the code. Four words were sent: "What hath God wrought?"

As the debate grinds on, I ask the same wracking question about the presence of the black man in America. Why was this tribulation visited upon him—and upon us? Why were we so unlucky, or so foolish, as to find this form of labor most suitable to the requirements of an economy founded on tobacco, rice, cane and cotton crops?

Is Garrison correct in his jeremiads? Is our precious Constitution "a covenant with death and an agreement with hell" because it recognizes the right of an owner to apprehend Negroes who have committed the felonious act of fleeing from their servitude? As Garrison claims, does the Constitution at the same time guarantee Negroes every right of citizenship that whites enjoy? Even many in the northern states find that concept too radical—yet the extreme abolitionists have been propounding it for more than a decade.

Decent people disagree on both questions just noted. Mr. Justice Story of Connecticut, for example, expressed a majority opinion of the Supreme Court when the Pennsylvania Act of '26 was struck down two years ago. The opinion was founded on the Court's contention that neither Pennsylvania nor any other individual state has the authority to prevent the owner of an escaped Negro from reclaiming him—even if the Negro has reached non-slave soil. Mr. Story clearly believed that the owning of slaves confers an unquestionable Constitutional right to recapture that slave—that piece of property.

In further opposition to Garrison and his followers, the opinion also implied that our American liberties are solely for the benefit of members of the white race. Story and the Court ignored the Constitutional promise of due process. Conclusion—it simply does not apply to any man or woman with dark skin.

Who is wrong and who is right? I do not know; I do not know!!

*

May the 27th. There is no way in which I can evade the issue before the Conference, so I have given up trying. I am, instead, struggling to reach my own decision.

After digesting the various arguments and praying on the whole matter, I am for the moment tending to side with the faction which would unseat Bishop Andrew, even though the bishop is clearly a man without onus; a Christian man; a Methodist man; a good man. If my present mood prevails, I will in effect turn my back on my own dear wife and her family.

Am I capable? And is it *right?*

Later. Mr. Polk and Mr. Dallas have been nominated as presidential candidates by the Democrats in Baltimore—the news "telegraphed" for the first time in the nation's history. Either Polk or Mr. Clay, the candidate of the Whigs, will be forced to resolve the stormy issue of annexation of Texas. Mr. Clay is in opposition because the Texan Republic has not been recognized by Mexico, and there is talk afloat that annexation will mean war.

Of more pertinence, if Texas should be admitted to the Union, it will come in as a slave state, further promoting sectional strife. It is already known that a treaty of annexation prepared by Secretary of State Calhoun and currently before the Senate will be rebuffed. But opposition to annexation does not end there. The politicians who espouse Garrison's radical philosophy are adamantly against the extension of slavery into any new territory whatsoever—a thorny problem since the country's mood is generally expansionist; among some sectors of the population—the restless and the poor, whose universal answer to unhappiness or failure is westward migration—wildly so.

The northern radicals will never be content merely with blocking the admission of new slave territories, however. They would prefer to completely upset the fragile balance of the "spheres of interest" established by the Missouri Compromise of 1820, by means of which slavery was prohibited in all Louisana Purchase lands north of approximately the thirty-sixth parallel—Missouri excepted—but made permissible south of that line, while Maine was admitted as a free state to balance Missouri's presence.

They say former president Jefferson, a very old man in those days and but five years from his death, spoke of the Compromise as "a fire bell in the night," warning of a sectional dispute that could rend the nation. I fear he was correct. The abolitionists want the institution of slavery destroyed wherever it exists, and forbidden forevermore.

My wife's people, of course, believe Texas should and will come in slave. So no matter how the issue of admission is decided, the outcome will only provoke more bad feelings—nationally, and in whatever is left of the Methodist Episcopal Church after the Andrew question is resolved. My southern brethren and I now recognize that if the Andrew matter is put to a vote, we will be outnumbered and defeated—

A sorrowful conceit, the inscription of "we"—I am still tormented, uncertain—but tending toward the other side.

•

May the 30th. Perused the book stalls this afternoon. The Conference is recessed while the committees labor, in hopes that some compromise may yet be worked out. Discovered the bins are a-bulge with guidebooks purporting to inform those afflicted with "the Oregon fever" as to the best way to equip themselves for the journey across the mountains.

In the past few years the "fever" has become epidemic. The trains of wagons leaving Missouri in the good weather number in the dozens, so the newspapers say. I would as soon never meet one of those eager pilgrims, for I would be forced to report the truth: that homesteading in the Oregon valleys is fraught with risk.

For one thing, the border dispute with Great Britain remains an irritant and a potential source of conflict. Everyone cries, "Fifty-four forty or fight!" But informed opinion maintains that England will never accept the fifty-fourth degree of latitude as Oregon's northern boundary. For another, homesteading is best left to those thoroughly skilled in agriculture. This I have seen for myself.

My father traveled to Oregon with my mother and me after the summer fur rendezvous of '37. At that time, the price of a plew was already down to the disastrous low of one dollar, due to beaver hats at last passing from fashion. My father and his fellow trappers saw the demise of their trade in that depressed price—but my father, unlike some too old or too disheartened to begin again, was determined to find an alternate livelihood. Although he has worked diligently at wheat farming in Oregon, my father has not fared well, lacking the proper experience—and the temperament; he was always more suited to the boisterous, unfettered life of the brigades with which he marched and rode for some twenty years.

Yet I can understand why the Oregon territory holds such allure today. The vale of the Willamette is truly beautiful, and this I know my father appreciates, despite the rigors of the labor and his scant success. If he sorrows at what many would call a life of small accomplishment, it is a gentle sorrow, rendered less stinging by what God has shown him of the lovely, though demanding land beyond the Mississippi. "I have looked on wonders," he remarked once, "and while I live I hope I never lose the hunger to behold more."

If my father regrets anything deeply, I suspect it is the stormy temper which plagued him during his early years. I can never forget his quiet confession about taking the life of a man named Walpole; a man involved in a scheme to seize control of the Boston printing firm my great-grandfather Kent founded. My father set fire to the firm to leave the schemers nothing but ashes, then fled the city of Boston with his young female cousin.

The confession took place one night when I was thirteen or fourteen, my father saying I was at last old enough to hear the story. I can still see him reclining in our tipi that evening while my mother sewed him a new hide shirt.

I see his sun-lightened yellow hair streaking to gray, and his thick-knuckled fingers, stiff from the cold beaver streams, turning and turning his one tangible reminder of his younger days—a fob medallion struck for him by his father's half-brother, Gilbert Kent, who operated the firm for a time. The medal bore the family symbol, and a Latin motto—*Cape locum et fac vestigium.* Take a stand and make a mark.

The former my father felt he had done. He had put the past behind him forever, and ventured into the far west, both to make a new life and to search—fruitlessly as it turned out—for his cousin, Gilbert's orphaned daughter, whom he lost to an abductor in Tennessee in 1814. As to the latter—making a mark—my father openly doubted his success.

Because my father speaks of the past as closed—an indication, perhaps, that its memory still holds a power to hurt him—I have felt it kinder never to write him about my two visits to Boston while I was studying at the Institute. I not only saw the house on fashionable Beacon Street where my father lived—a house now occupied by an unknown family—but I also saw, rebuilt, a publishing company called Kent and Son.

What called all this to mind is a volume I discovered

among the guidebooks in the stalls—an expensive and obviously new edition of a currently popular historical romance by the Frenchman, Dumas. The book is entitled *The Three Musketeers.* The spine was damaged, no doubt accounting for the volume's presence in the bin.

I opened the book, smitten by a most ungodly urge to read something other than Holy Scripture. There on the title page was the family device which my father carried on the obverse of his medal—the partially filled bottle of tea. Accompanying the symbol were the words *Kent and Son.* I located the date of publication. 1844. The firm still survives.

Before I replaced the novel, I briefly entertained the idea of sending it to my father with my next, long overdue letter. I decided against it for the same reason I said nothing about my discoveries in Boston. To hide the truth from a man who prized his family heritage and saw it lost, remains, I believe, the most Christian and compassionate course.

Later. Did I do right about the book? I am so unsure of everything, though I try to let no one see. Only these private pages, an outlet for my turmoil now and for my hopes and apprehensions during the past two years, know of my misgivings—only these pages, and Him Who Sees All.

May He have mercy on my weakness and my doubt.

*

June the 1st. All compromise has failed. The will of the Conference majority has proved paramount. A substitute resolution, requesting Bishop Andrew to cease his ecclesiastical function, was adopted one hundred ten to sixty-eight. Having spent a sleepless night in which I prayed almost continuously, and recognizing that I may have committed a grave sin, I abandoned my earlier flirtation with the majority and cast my vote nay.

I did so with the image of my dear Fan's face in my thoughts. When I was assigned the itinerancy in Virginia, I took the people as my own. I discovered my wife among them, and even though God may one day judge them sinners despite their professions of conversion, I cannot condemn them. I chose to stand with them.

In this perhaps I erred. But I am somewhat comforted because I do not believe my beloved mother would see it so.

The Shoshoni are a remarkable people. During the years my mother and I wandered with my father, first with his partner, Weatherby, and then with my father alone after Weatherby perished of the small pox, many of my mother's spiritual beliefs were implanted in my mind, forever coloring my imperfect understanding of Christian tenets.

The Shoshoni do not deny the existence of evil. They only hold a unique view of its source. To my mother and her race, the evil man was not merely sinful, but deranged—a subtle yet important distinction. The man who carried out some heinous act was obviously not in full possession of his God-given reason. Had he been, he would have recognized that his behavior was harmful to himself and, by extension, harmful to the tribal community. Patience and moral instruction, not punishment, were the remedies for such behavior. Perhaps it is from a secret, all but unadmitted faith in my mother's principles that I turned from the shrill posturings of Hodding and the others of the anti-Andrew faction and sided with the slave-holding bishop and, therefore, with those to whom I minister. Perhaps I acted from an unvoiced belief that, if we have sinned collectively, we can one day come to understand our derangement and correct it.

It may be a vain hope. I pray it is not an excuse for cowardice.

Many at the Conference yearned for compromise, but that longing was frustrated by the vote. Lovick Pierce of

Georgia has declared the southern Conferences will lodge a "manly, ministerial and proper protest" concerning the Andrew affair. I have this very night heard talk of the form the protest will take:

Separation. The sundering of the Church into two bodies, north and south.

*

June the 2nd. The Conference winds to its grievous end; I will begin my homeward journey tomorrow. Even the name of my lovely little town in Virginia has become as ashes in my mouth—for I have not been able to escape the memory that, near another Lexington, my great-grandfather first stood with those country marksmen who dared to pledge their lives to the promise of liberty which this nation represents.

But liberty for whom? Whispers the worm of conscience now that the vote is done. I could not rest all night, seeing faces of color scorning me for rejecting their cause. My mind is a maelstrom. Is the agitation I suddenly feel on behalf of black men and women a temptation of the Devil, to divert me from my chief task of redeeming souls? What of the souls of my own kind in Lexington—?

In the gloomy hours before dawn, I wrestled afresh with these questions—and Heaven saw fit to deny me an answer. This morning I encountered Hodding. He did not speak. His glance d---d me for lack of courage. Yet even that bothers me less than what his loathing suddenly portended.

After he hurried on, I saw with utter clarity that we must discover a solution to repair this terrible schism. A solution both sides can accept—and one which will deal properly and fairly with the person of color as well. That the black man has a soul the Church does not deny. That he is entitled to be a communicant of American liberty is what tears us asunder. Whether that idea is right, or only an aberration, the side ultimately found to be in error must be persuaded to admit and amend its error.

Who will lead us in a search for truth and accord? Who will speak reason and effect the means of escape from our dilemma? Unless such means are found, I fear passions will rise even as they rose during the dreadful business in St. Louis in '36, when white hysteria inspired by the columns of the Congregationalist Lovejoy's antislavery paper, *The Observer*, led to all manner of mistreatment of Negroes, and to the death of a poor black riverman the mob caught, chained to a tree and burned alive. Hodding has self-righteously recalled the incident to me on more than one occasion—as well as the fate of Lovejoy himself, who fled to free soil in Alton, Illinois, only to be killed by five bullets while another hysterical mob wrecked his fourth printing press.

Such damaging passions are present north and south. How often have I heard Captain Tunworth speak fearfully of the deranged Turner? The slave led perhaps as many as one hundred of his fellows on a rampage throughout Virginia's Southampton County in '31, slaughtering fifty-seven white persons, including women and children. Captain Tunworth swears the black man is a beast, to be chained for the protection of society. He says he would die defending that view.

So where is the answer? Passion is rampant on both sides. I have seen that here, in a meeting of men purportedly pledged not to animosity but to its antithesis—compassionate love. Will God show us the path soon, after we have endured His testing and renewed our vow to follow His Son's teachings? Or has He already abandoned us in rage and sorrow because we are so blind; so incapable of governing our passions, and bringing Christian order from them?

Should God turn aside from us, will not the Federal Union find itself in the same wretched state as the Church does today? Irretrievably sundered? Should that transpire, the prospect is holocaust—for we preachers, contentious as we may be, still waged our little war this month with debate and document and resolution. Even with a gulf now opened between northern and southern Conferences, a modicum of Christian love remains for the brethren on the other side—

Will men outside the Church feel that restraining affection?

I fear not.

Later. I have re-read what I wrote earlier. I am humiliated and ashamed and increasingly filled with dread.

How can there be hope of a solution if even men of Christ have come this far, failing to find it? I go back to Virginia not only wondering whether I have done the right thing, but whether these thirty troubled days are but a harbinger of much worse to come.

A man such as my father-in-law, Captain Tunworth, will not yield. The abolitionists still thunder with the ancient Roman jurist, "Let justice be done, though the heavens fall!" Above the whole tumult rings the black man's anguished cry.

Those who seek a middle ground may be cursed and shouldered aside. I feel it—Almighty God, *I feel it terribly*—

Still later—en route. Very hard to write; coach bouncing; and my hand unsteady. So distressed was I during my last hours in the City, I forgot to buy a bright trinket for my little boy Gideon. I fear I am bringing him instead a legacy of much darker hue.

Book Two

Gold

CHAPTER I

Cry in the Wilderness

ON A BRILLIANT MORNING in the second week of April 1848, the clipper *Manifest Destiny* sailed into the bay, having been en route from the hongs of Canton an intolerable sixty-two days. The clipper dropped anchor opposite the settlement of Yerba Buena, a straggling collection of frame and adobe buildings set near the water against the background of the southern peninsula's grassy hills.

The ship was owned by the Ball Brothers Line, New York. She had slid off the ways only two years before, christened by her builders in a burst of patriotic zeal. In the pages of *The Democratic Review*, Mr. O'Sullivan had referred to the nation's steady expansion toward the Pacific as a "manifest destiny." The words had caught the fancy of Congressmen and China traders alike.

At thirteen hundred and sixty tons, *Manifest Destiny* was a lean and beautiful vessel. But as her canvas came down, and a lighter operated by the local hide merchant put out from the beach, her captain was still cursing her roundly. He had hoped for a straight, swift passage from China, around the Horn and up to New York. Like most captains of clipper ships—so called because their construction helped them clip time from existing speed records—he was always trying to beat some other skipper's performance. His current target was the seventy-eight-day mark of Captain Waterman's extreme clipper *Rainbow*, set in '45. He didn't like Waterman. Few in the

China trade did, including Waterman's crewmen, who had nicknamed him Killer.

A typhoon in the South China Sea—a freak storm, blowing months after the fall season—had nearly dismantled *Manifest Destiny*'s masts as she started her homeward run. The damage forced her back to Macao for a refitting. With the chance for a record—and the resulting prestige and increased business for Ball Brothers—gone, the clipper's captain had decided to concentrate on profit.

Manifest Destiny had called at the Hawaiian Islands, adding another two tons of Alaskan sealskins to the sixteen thousand tons of tea already in the holds. The clipper then set sail for Yerba Buena, the sunny little port on the California coast. Here the captain would squeeze aboard whatever hides and tallow were available. The captain's primage was calculated at a generous seven and one half per cent of the delivered sale price of the cargo. Since he was already far behind schedule, the more he brought home without making the clipper plow under, the greater his earnings.

Yerba Buena had one other attraction besides the possibility of extra cargo. As the lighter headed for shore, the captain began to think of that, and with considerable pleasure. It took his mind off his anger at the ship, the weather and himself.

The captain sat in the lighter's bow, the oilskin-wrapped parcel from New York tucked under one sleeve of his trim blue sea jacket. He wore a peaked cap and his best black silk neckerchief. He was a tall, slim man with a sharp chin and gray eyes that tended to intimidate those who served under him. Though he was just forty, white hair already showed around his ears. His name was Barton McGill. His home—birthplace, rather—was Charleston, South Carolina.

While the lighter plowed through the chop, he scanned the small crowd gathering on shore. Such a crowd always formed when a ship of size entered the roads. The permanent population of Yerba Buena was right around five hundred, perhaps half of those being Americans. Even at some distance from the beach, Bart McGill could easily spot the Yankees. The darker ones were Coloma Indians, Mexicans, Chileans and Peruvians. There were even a few Hawaiians in the village. He saw white and colored waving with equal enthusiasm; heard halloos across the water—

Then, approximately in the center of the crowd, he spied an extremely tall, yellow-skinned Negro. Bart McGill's eyes were momentarily cool. He and Israel didn't get along too well. But the Negro's height helped the captain spot the person he really wanted to see—

Sure enough, there was Amanda. Standing a little to one side of Israel, and waving. A few steps behind her was her son Louis, recognizable because of his size—he was eleven—and his jet black hair.

Goddamnedest thing in the world, finding someone like her in this penny-ante port, Bart thought, smiling. He'd been married twelve years to a proper Charleston bitch who had borne him three daughters, none of whom had survived infancy. At last the bitch had done the decent thing and left him a widower while he was somewhere in the Indian Ocean in '43. But he'd had to visit California two years ago to discover a woman he really cared for; a woman older than he was; most miraculous of all, a woman who didn't want to knot him up in matrimony.

He didn't call often at Yerba Buena. But everyone knew Amanda was Captain McGill's woman, as well as the proprietor of Kent's, a tavern and eating house on Portsmouth Square—where, he noticed as he squinted into the sunlight, the stars and stripes still appeared to be flying.

Commander Montgomery had sent that banner up the staff for the first time in '46, when the Americans in

California heard the news of their country's war with Mexico. That same year, a treaty with Britain had settled the disputed northern boundary of Oregon not at the fifty-fourth parallel but the forty-ninth. With a potential enemy out of the way, the United States had turned its attention to a real one. Provoked by the annexation of Texas, Mexican soldiers had attacked a U.S. dragoon company near Matamoros, and the war was on—

Realizing how out of touch he was, Bart McGill turned to one of the oarsmen:

"Did General Scott capture Mexico City last fall? I sailed right after he took Chapultepec—"

"Yessir, captain, he did. The greasers done signed a treaty, too. I heard Washington got all o' Texas, New Mexico and Upper Californy. Guess it's true—"

"Which was practically American anyway after the Bear Flag revolt and General Kearny's capture of Los Angeles," Bart said in his mellow southerner's voice. "Will California come into the Union, then?"

"Too soon to tell," the oarsman answered. "The treaty ain't more'n a couple of months old. Can't see much reason why the Union'd want us, either," he added. He bent forward and drew back on his oar.

Bart McGill turned his gaze inland, to the green and tan hills receding to the distant bluish haze that might have been only a haze—or the great Sierras. The land was indeed desolate; a wilderness—though he'd heard there was good hunting in the Sierra foothills. He wondered about the territory's status if, at some remote time in the far future, it acquired enough people to entitle it to statehood. The request would touch off another debate about slavery, no doubt. Being a southerner, he had views on the subject of slavery. But he much preferred the sea to the settled east because he got sick of hearing nigra, nigra, nigra. In New York, nobody could talk for half an hour without launching an argument over the south's peculiar institution.

"Bart? Here we are!"

The faint cry borne on the breeze took him away from the tedious and disagreeable subject. A couple of Mexicans with cornets began tootling a welcome. There was some desultory cheering. But the crowd seemed skimpy, even for Yerba Buena.

His eye fixed on Amanda—forty-five years old and looking ten years less. God, what a handsome woman. If only she'd been able to conceive a child. But her time for that had ended relatively early—before he met her.

She strained on tiptoe, her dyed cotton dress a sparkle of red amid the drab rags of most of the other inhabitants. Her son Louis wore a flannel shirt and homespun trousers. Bart didn't even notice what Israel, the tall mulatto, was wearing. He was concentrating on the vibrant, dark-haired woman who kicked off her shoes and dashed to the water's edge, awaiting the lighter.

Bart felt unusually sentimental just then. During all the years of his marriage, his wife had never once generated emotion of the kind that gripped him as he watched Amanda barefoot in the white foam. She was a prize; a genuine prize—

She'd been married once; lived in Texas a while, then in the pueblo of Los Angeles. She'd been in Yerba Buena for the last four years, and on the surface seemed content to earn a meager living selling food and drink. But he knew how deceiving that air of contentment was. He knew because of things she asked of him, and because of the parcel he bore under his arm.

She was waving hard now, her hand flying. On her wrist he saw that peculiar rope bracelet given her by the vanished cousin she spoke of occasionally. She claimed she could have been a Boston heiress if the right cards had fallen. But here she was on the California coast, scraping out an existence in a single-story building she'd put up with the last of her savings after paying sixteen-fifty American for her fifty-vara lot—

And damned if he wasn't glad about the whole business.

Better watch yourself, McGill, he thought, or you'll do some fool thing like deciding you love this woman enough to marry her—and there goes independence and a handsome living with the Messrs. Ball.

The lighter grounded. The cornets blared as Bart prepared to jump down into the surf. Amanda spun toward the crowd:

"Louis? Come here and see Captain Bart—"

"Oh, they's one more thing I forgot to tell you," the oarsman said suddenly.

Bart turned, an inquiring look on his face.

"Folks around here got tired of the old name for the town. Some of 'em are starting to call it after another settlement that used to be near here."

"What settlement?"

"San Francisco."

ii

"Bart!" Amanda cried, throwing her arms around his neck. "I nearly fainted when Louis ran in to say they'd sighted your clipper from the hill. I thought you were going straight back to New York this trip—"

"Planned on it. Ran into an out-of-season blow." He bussed her cheek, relishing the clean, soaped smell of her skin. Even in such a public place, the touch of her body produced a decided physical reaction. "Tell you about it later," he added as he hugged her. She felt him, all right:

"I can tell you've been away a while. Lord, how I've missed you—!"

He grinned. "That's why I don't come around too often. I reckon we'd get pretty tired of each other if we slept in the same bed year in and year out—" He planted another kiss on her cheek. "I swear you just keep growing prettier, Amanda."

"No. I'm getting gray, Bart."

She was; strands of white showed in the dark glossiness of her hair.

"It's becoming. You take it from one who's seen all kinds."

"Nice of you to flatter an old lady, Captain McGill—" She caught his arm as they walked from the surf to the damp sand. She picked up her shoes, still teasing him: "You know some of the local women think I'm scandalous, keeping company with a youngster like you—"

"The hell with 'em. Five years' difference is no difference at all." He peeked around her at the sturdy, black-eyed boy with swarthy skin and broad shoulders. He held out his hand.

"How are you, Louis?"

"Very good, Captain Bart, thank you," Louis Kent said with a cheery smile. Bart gave the obligatory nod to the hulking yellow scarecrow lingering a respectful distance away:

"Israel. Things well with you?"

"About the same, cap'n."

In the opaque brown eyes, Bart detected the hostility he'd encountered before. Amanda said Israel bore southern-made scars on his back—Bart had never cared to ask to see them—and so all southerners were anathemas to the mulatto. Israel made no secret of having run away from a Mississippi cotton plantation. How Amanda could treat the ex-slave as an equal, Bart McGill's experience and education did not permit him to fathom.

Amanda had met Israel in Los Angeles, where he'd gone as a member of one of the trading brigades coming up from the southwest. That was early in '44. She'd hired him to accompany her north to Yerba Buena, where she'd hoped to find a more prosperous economy than the one she'd left in the pueblo. In that, she had been disappointed.

Together, Amanda and Israel, who was about thirty now, had built Kent's. It tickled Bart that Amanda approached physical work with an almost masculine directness. He'd watched her split a log for firewood once, and laughed aloud when she raised her palms to her mouth, spit on them, and clamped a grip on the axe—treating him to an arch look because he laughed. He'd assured her he was only laughing because her behavior was such a delightful contrast to the vaporish ways of eastern ladies—including his unlamented wife—who probably would have gone to their graves rather than let anyone see them spit *or* chop wood.

The mulatto had helped supply the knowledge of carpentry required to put up the tavern. He and Amanda had shared the labor equally. He'd remained her devoted—and free—employee ever since. For no rational reason, Bart distrusted him—an inheritance from his own upbringing, he occasionally admitted to himself.

The crowd was dispersing. Amanda and the clipper captain started up the beach toward the crude buildings that comprised the setttlement. Israel and Louis followed.

"Feels good to be on shore again," Bart said.

"Feels good to have you here."

"Reckon we should celebrate with a little music after you're finished for the day."

"Not just with music," she laughed, squeezing his arm.

"Miz Kent already hung up the sign saying we're closed," Israel remarked from a pace behind.

Bart was annoyed at the Negro eavesdropping on private conversation. But Amanda's bubbling voice took the edge off his irritation:

"I'm going to cook you the biggest meal you've had in months. And Louis and I want to hear some songs—"

"Got a new one I think you'll like," he said, taking her arm. He noticed her dark eyes straying to the parcel in his other hand. "But you're more interested in these, aren't you?" He bent to whisper. "There's a price on 'em."

Her eyes brimmed with warmth, and she was only partly teasing when she replied:

"You don't have to bargain for that, Bart. You know how much I long for you while you're gone—"

"Still say you couldn't stand me if I was around all the time."

She kept eyeing the parcel. In answer to the unspoken question, he said:

"Yes, Kent editions, every one. Three Coopers. A collection of stories by Hawthorne—*Mosses from an Old Manse*, I think the title is—and a bunch of peculiar—oh, supernatural tales, I guess you'd call them. Written by some fellow named Poe. I didn't care for 'em much. That particular book was second-hand. I was told the public doesn't care for 'em much either."

Amanda's ebullient mood seemed spoiled by the mention of the books. Soon after they had met for the first time, she had spoken candidly about her childhood, who she was and who her father had been. She said she had never imagined her father's firm was still in existence until, by pure chance, she had come across a tattered copy of Headley's *Napoleon and his Marshals* in Los Angeles.

The book was being sold among other odds and ends by a wagon-trader who had passed through the pueblo. It was the twelfth edition of the popular work, published at Boston in 1839 and carrying the words *Kent and Son* and a design representing a bottle of tea on its title page.

After that very first visit, Bart had brought her Kent books on every trip. Whenever possible, he also brought her answers to questions.

Listening to the story of her early years, he had learned in the bargain how she'd traveled this far west. He had been thunderstruck by the account of what she'd endured, and not a little disturbed by her unpleasant expression when she spoke of the man who had won the family firm from her stepfather in a dice game—

Her face had the same grim look now. In New York the past autumn, he had found the answers to some new questions. He wondered whether he should tell her. He disliked seeing the angry streak in her nature assert itself—

She didn't leave the choice to him. She quickened her step so they drew ahead of Israel and the boy. They swung past a smith's and walked on toward the oddly quiet Portsmouth Square. Even Brannan's mercantile emporium looked deserted. Abruptly, Amanda said:

"What about Stovall?"

"What about him?"

"Bart, don't string me along. Did you find out everything I wanted to know?"

He sighed. "Most of it."

"Well, then—is Stovall still running Kent and Son?"

"Yes."

She swore as vehemently and violently as any of his able seamen. He finally interrupted:

"I don't know where you learned all those words, sweet, but I'm suitably impressed. Now you want to let me finish?"

"I'm sorry, go on."

"Stovall's running the company, but through underlings, not personally—"

"The way you say that, you make it sound like I put you to some terrible chore—"

"I'm out of my depth investigating a muckety-muck

like Mr. Hamilton Stovall. Steel's a far cry from shipping, and I got plenty of peculiar stares at the saloons where the newspaper writers hang out—"

"You also got answers, didn't you?"

"Eventually. But those reporter fellows sure as hell wonder why a sea captain's buying them rounds and asking about the third biggest steelmaker in the whole United States."

Amanda seemed not to hear:

"Where is he living?"

"A fancy mansion in New York—he and his wife."

"He's *marrried?*"

"He is. The woman's a good deal younger. They have no children."

"I'm not surprised. From what Jared told me, I can't imagine Stovall being interested in a woman—unless she could confer some kind of respectability on him."

"Perhaps that is why he married. He's certainly not the same man you described to me—at least not in public. He's eminently respectable."

"But treating the book company like a stepchild—"

"Not exactly. A couple of clerks told me Kent's is still a popular and successful imprint."

"Which he keeps going solely because it makes money?"

"Why else would he keep it going?"

"My father and my grandfather believed printing books served a useful purpose."

"So it does. It lines Mr. Stovall's pockets."

"I'm talking about educating people. Having a point of view and not being afraid to express it."

"It's my impression Stovall cares very little about the state of the public mind. The clerks said the Kent and Son list is growing less substantial every year. And the house publishes nothing controversial—though come to think of it, I did see a Kent edition of *Awful Disclosures.*"

"I've never heard of it."

"Caused a real stir when it was issued in '36—and discredited soon after. It was written by a girl named Maria Monk. That is, her name's on it—hacks probably prepared the manuscript. Maria claimed to have been a nun. Later it was proved that the closest she got to the Roman faith was a religious home for wayward girls. The whole book's fiction, but it's lip-smacking stuff. Nuns submissive to the carnal will of priests—midnight revels in a Montreal convent—illegitimate babies baptized, then strangled, nine months after the aforesaid revels—"

"That's disgusting."

"But you can't call it controversial. Too many people believe such tales about Catholics."

"Does Stovall?"

"Can't say. But I imagine that if he published the Monk book, he hates the papists—especially all the Irish filling up the eastern cities."

"Did you ask about his politics?"

"Forgot. You know I don't give much of a damn who votes for what. Again, *Awful Disclosures* would lead me to guess he's a Know-Nothing."

"God!" Amanda seethed. "If my grandfather knew a bigot like that was publishing books under his name—" She was too angry to continue.

"I did discover a couple of things about Stovall's main business," Bart went on. "He's opening up a new mill in Pittsburgh. The railroads are using more steel than he can produce. And he's changed the company name from the Chesapeake Iron Finery to the Stovall Works."

"Did you find out who's actually running Kent and Son?"

He shook his head. "But I know who's general manager of the Stovall Works. One of the boys from the *Sun* stood me to a schooner of beer after I bought him three. He got to talking pretty freely. He said—"

Bart's hands grew chilly. How he despised the sight of Amanda's lovely face when it was this white; this intense. She got that way whenever she discussed Stovall—

They had reached the edge of Portsmouth Square. The stars and stripes snapped in the breeze above the rows of turned earth; the square was Yerba Buena's potato patch.

Bart still hadn't finished his last sentence. In front of the Old Adobe, the town hall, Amanda stopped, blocking his path:

"Go on with it, Bart."

"Jesus! You could let me get to your place, at least—"

"*Tell me right now!*"

"All right. The reporter happened to mention the name of the fellow in charge of the steel operation. It's one of the names you remembered. But you didn't have it quite right—" He hesitated again. "It's not Waltham, it's Walpole."

"*Walpole!*"

Louis, who had been dawdling behind with Israel, ran to her:

"Ma, what's the matter?"

"Nothing—nothing."

"You sounded so mad—"

"You and Israel go on to the tavern—*go on!*"

The gangling yellow-skinned man drifted up:

"Do like your mama says, Louis." He took the boy's hand and started off. The sight of black skin pressing white made Bart McGill feel slightly unclean. He'd been brought up to loathe that kind of familiarity between the races.

Amanda showed no sign of moving. One hand shielding her eyes from the sun, she was waiting for the rest. He figured he might as well get it over:

"Walpole," he repeated. "The same name as the fellow your cousin shot."

"He's a relative—one of Walpole's sons?"

"He's the same man."

"That—that can't be!"

"Who asked the questions, you or me?"

"But Jared killed Walpole!"

"I know that's what you said. But I'm the one who spent three gold pieces on more beer and two telegraph messages. The *Sun* reporter contacted a man he knows on a Baltimore paper. The man wired information back the next day. Walpole's old—almost ready to retire. There are employees at the company who've heard him speak of being shot by one of the Kents way back in fourteen or fifteen—whenever it was that Stovall took over your father's firm."

"Then—Stovall let Jared think—"

"Think what? Your cousin never waited to discover what really happened. You said both of you ran away the very same night—" He grimaced. "I'm getting weary of this blasted detective work, Amanda. What I've found out hasn't done any good at all. It only makes you more miserable. When are you going to realize it's downright unhealthy to harbor a grudge for so many years—?"

She paid no attention:

"He let Jared think he'd done *murder*—"

"Jared never gave himself a chance to find out otherwise!"

"Stovall could have tried to locate—"

"Oh, come on, sweet!" Bart broke in, angered that the past had cropped up so soon. It always did eventually. But it seldom produced the degree of rage seething in her right now. Well, he'd guessed this might happen. But he tried to make her see reason:

"Stovall didn't care a damn for your family. Hated them, in fact—you said so yourself."

"And all this time, he let Jared believe that he killed—"

"*All this time!*" he echoed in a sarcastic way. "Your cousin's probably dead."

"That makes no difference. By God, I'm going back there—!"

He sounded tired: "You've told me. Over and over."

"Ten years ago, I had the same idea—but for a different reason. I just wanted to see where the family lived—search for some mementos my father owned. When I came across the Headley book, everything changed. I want Kent and Son out of Stovall's hands!"

"Maybe the first reason was better. This jeremiad against Mr. Stovall eats on you worse every year—"

"Because I'm getting older. I may not have many years left. I swear, if I can ever put together more than twenty dollars at one time, I'm going back and take the company away from him. I'll do more than that to him if I can—"

Inexplicably chilly in the sun, Bart said, "Sometimes, Amanda, you scare the bejesus out of a man. I know this much. You get involved in trying to destroy someone and you'll wind up suffering as much as he does. Hate works that way. It hurts the one who gets it *and* the one who gives it—"

I have first-hand experience.

"—Christ amighty, that's exactly what's happening back east right now. One section against the other—the tempers hotter, the words more vile and unreasonable with every day that passes—before it's over, people on both sides are liable to be killing each other!"

She didn't want to hear. She snatched the book parcel from his hand, her fingers almost colorless as they clenched the oilskin:

"*If I only had some money—*"

"Dammit, woman, don't you *ever* listen to what I say? I've told you a dozen times you don't need money to pay your way east. Say the word and I'll take you and Louis aboard—"

"I'm not talking about money for passage. I'm talking about a lot of money."

Exhausted and unsettled by the discussion, he was snappish:

"What if Mr. Hamilton Stovall doesn't care to sell Kent and Son the minute you say so? Did you ever think of that?"

Outwardly, she remained the same Amanda Kent: full-figured, with a deliciously wide mouth, lovely dark eyes—and yet the fury in those eyes produced a subtle distortion; the total effect was spoiled.

"I'll make him sell. No matter what I have to do."

"Then you're just as crazy as you claim he is!"

"Thank you."

"Amanda—"

"Thank you very much, Captain McGill!"

Jamming the parcel of books under her arm, she whirled and hurried away.

"Amanda, come back here! I didn't mean to make you fly off—"

She didn't stop or look around. He swore a few blistering words, then followed her slowly across the sunlit square.

iii

She dashed straight in the front door of Kent's and slammed it after her. He noticed the *Closed* sign Israel had mentioned. Puzzlingly, similar signs hung on the door of Sam Brannan's store, and on the door of the small, jerry-built office of the *Star* immediately adjoining. Brannan owned the paper as well as the mercantile establishment.

But Captain Bart McGill had things to worry about

besides the curious absence of the town's most industrious citizen. The visit to Yerba Buena had gotten off to a catastrophic start. All he'd wanted to do today was spend a while enjoying Amanda's company—talking with her of inconsequential things; laughing with her; touching her. And then, at an appropriate hour when Louis was bedded down and Israel had retired to his shanty behind the tavern, he would have climbed into her bed and loved her—

Instead, he'd wrecked her customary composure with the one thing capable of doing that—the past; the past she constantly picked over so the wound could never heal.

Goddamn, why had he ever spent so much time and energy on those inquiries? Why hadn't he refused to discuss the contents of the parcel, or what he'd learned last autumn, until later? Until it was dark and calm and they'd taken their sweet fill of one another—?

He knew why. He'd questioned the reporters in New York, and answered her promptly this morning, because she asked—because he liked to please her.

But she *was* getting too old for silly notions about bringing the Kents back to the position of eminence she claimed they'd once enjoyed. Forty was an average lifetime; five years beyond that, she was lucky to be in such astonishingly good health. She should be enjoying what was left of her life, not dedicating it to some fool scheme that soured her disposition and didn't stand a chance of succeeding. Wealthy or not, she'd be no match for a powerful man like Hamilton Stovall—who logically couldn't be expected to hand over Kent and Son to a member of the family he despised.

Yet Amanda was a determined woman; that he knew very well. Maybe she *could* succeed if she tried hard enough, and had a touch of luck. What upset him was the fact that her ambition was so closely tied to an almost fanatic hatred of Stovall. And as he'd tried to tell her, hate was a costly, destructive emotion—

Except when some shipboard crisis sparked him to a fury and drove him to action, Captain Barton McGill was a calm, detached sort of man. He'd been raised in a Charleston home where two aristocratic people of high temper had clashed often. Among his most vivid memories of childhood were the sounds of argument—

Cursing.

Crying.

Crockery smashing—

He'd been fortunate to discover the haven offered by a career at sea. His parents—both dead now—hadn't objected to his leaving home when he was quite young. He felt they had little interest in him, and suspected they were glad to be rid of him. But he'd married unwisely; married a woman who had much the same disposition as his mother and father. Her anger, easily roused, had driven him deeper within himself. He developed a kind of spiritual kinship with the spotted turtle he'd kept as a pet when he was eight or nine—

Kept, that is, until one of the stormiest of the arguments between his parents. His father snatched the turtle from its box on the porch and hurled it at his mother. She dodged and the spotted turtle hit the house, its carapace cracked even though it had frantically withdrawn its legs and head—

The turtle died that same night. Bart never forgot. Over the years he concluded that those who indulged their tempers for any but the most practical and pressing reasons were fools doomed to destroy others, and be destroyed. Even turtles weren't perfectly protected from the wrath of such fools, but at least they had some armor. His was intellectual.

He abhorred, and took no part in, the venomous debate the slave question produced in the north and south. He jeered at the hysterical abolitionists and their bombastic, foully slanted pamphlets and newspapers. But his contempt was nearly as strong for those cotton-kingdom demagogues who puffed out clouds of gas about states' rights and offered sly threats of separation—secession—to *scare* those northern bastards—

No matter what the motive, hate bred hate and, in the end, chaos. He had long ago weaned himself away from such damaging passions. He preferred the steady, soothing beat of the ocean against a clipper's hull; the spirited but essentially civilized bargaining in the Chinese hongs. In the Far East trade, a man could do his task, take pride in it, and make a little money without staking his life on worthless angers and wooly ideas—such as Amanda's notion that Kent and Son was supposed to do more than bring in a profit; that it had some higher responsibility to inform and inspire the people who bought the books bearing its imprint. Ideas like that—turned into crusades—only brought people to grief—

Damnation! He should have lied about the questions she'd put to him on his last visit. Lied outright:

"Kent's isn't owned by Stovall any longer. No one's heard of Walpole in years—"

As he stared glumly at the closed front door where she'd vanished, he realized that if he'd thought things through a little more—or if he cared for her a little less—he *would* have lied.

Now it was too late.

iv

Whittling, Louis Kent looked up as Bart McGill approached the shadowed rear stoop of the sun-bleached frame building. Out back, Israel was pottering in the garden next to his shanty.

Bart wanted to go on inside; into the building's rear room, a large, square chamber partitioned into sleeping space for Louis, and a second, somewhat bigger alcove for Amanda. He could see the room's furnishings—the piano he'd brought on one voyage; the walnut dining table and chairs that had come on another. Amanda and her son entertained visitors at the table, and took meals there. Food came from the tavern's small kitchen, located between the rear living room and the more spacious public room in front. Kent's didn't waste money on fancy fixtures. A plank bar and several cheap tables and chairs satisfied the diners and drinkers of Yerba Buena—

He saw it all, fondly, but he didn't go in because he suspected Amanda was probably still upset. She'd let him know when she was composed enough to see him again.

He sat down beside the boy on the splintery step. "Louis, I've been wondering something."

"What is it, sir?"

"Have I got my days mixed up? I swear last night, my log read Tuesday. But places around here are closed tight, just like it's Sunday."

"You mean Mr. Brannan's store?"

"And his paper," Bart nodded. "Where is the old money-grubber, off palavering with brother Brigham?"

"Oh, no, Captain Bart, Mr. Brannan's given up the Mormon faith."

"He has! Why?"

"He and Young fell out over the place those Latter-day Saints were going to settle after they got run out of Missouri. Mr. Brannan brought some families to Yerba Buena by ship, you know—"

"Yes."

"—and he tried to persuade Young this was the promised land. I guess old Mr. Young saw it differently, back at that salty lake they say lies east of the Sierras. Young threw Brannan out of their church—"

"Good God! I beg your pardon, Louis. Continue."

"—and he said he wanted all the money Brannan had collected in tithes, too. Ma said Mr. Young claimed it was the Lord's money, so Mr. Brannan said he'd return it as soon as Young sent him a receipt in the Lord's handwriting. That Mr. Brannan's pretty good at turning a dollar—"

"Almost as good as your mother," Bart observed with a wry smile. "But you haven't told me where he is."

"I think he must have gone up to Captain Sutter's mill."

Bart blinked. "You mean the fort on the Sacramento? New Helvetia?"

"No, I mean Captain Sutter's sawmill. I guess it's been built since you were here last. About forty or fifty miles beyond the fort, on the American River. Mr. Brannan probably went up to see about the gold—along with Mr. Kemble, the editor of the *Star*."

"What gold are you talking about, Louis?"

The boy shrugged. "Probably isn't real. Probably just pyrites."

"Found in the river?"

"Yes, sir. Mr. Marshall, who was putting up the mill, spied it first." Louis fished in his pocket, produced a crumpled clipping. "This was in the other paper last month. I tore it out—I got pretty excited. But ma calmed me down quick enough. She said a lot of the yellow stuff had showed up around here before—and all of it busted apart the minute someone laid it on an anvil and hammered it. That's one way you tell fool's gold, they say."

Bart scanned the story from Yerba Buena's other occasional newspaper, *The Californian*. The item was dated the fifteenth of March:

> GOLD MINE FOUND.—In the newly made raceway of the Saw Mill recently erected by Captain Sutter on the American Fork, gold has been found

> in considerable quantities. One person brought thirty dollars worth to New Helvetia, gathered there in a short time. California, no doubt, is rich in mineral wealth; great chances here for scientific capitalists.

He didn't read the final sentence, because Louis interrupted:

"Nobody believes that now."

"But a few still went to look for themselves—?"

"Yes. Mr. Brannan even fetched along some *aqua fortis*. I don't know what that is, but he said if you poured it on gold, nothing would happen, and that's another way you tell real gold from pyrites."

"Explains why the town's so quiet, anyway. Strikes me that if there were gold up along those rivers, someone would have made certain by now. It's April already—"

"Does seem funny, doesn't it?"

Bart changed the subject: "How are you coming along with your studies?"

"Pretty well. Ma helps me three nights a week. I'm good with sums—I can make change fast in the tavern. My handwriting's only fair. And I don't like all that poetry and those stories she makes me read—"

"Well—" He tousled the boy's dark, curly hair. In the blue shadow of the stoop, Louis might have passed for a Mexican, so coppery were his cheeks. "—you'll have to suffer. Reading's the mark of a cultured man. I brought a new batch of books. Maybe you'll like that Poe fellow's eerie concoctions—"

The door opened behind them. Bart rose. But even before he swung and saw Amanda's smiling face, he was gratified by her calm voice:

"Come in, Bart. And forgive me for carrying on a while ago—?"

Her smile was so warm, he promptly forgot the worry

and turmoil caused by her reaction to the Kent books:
"Nothing to forgive, sweet—'less you refuse to pour me a good strong drink."

V

The remainder of the day was merry and satisfying. Amanda cooked up some beef brought in a few days earlier from the fort of the somewhat bizarre European, Captain John Sutter. The fort lay beyond the central valley, where the Sacramento and American Rivers flowed together.

While Amanda worked, Bart told her all the news he could remember from the previous fall—old news, to be sure, but she welcomed it. There were some newer tidbits as well, the most recent concerning the failing health of the famous Mr. Astor.

He was dying at eighty-four, so enfeebled he could take no nourishment except milk from the breast of a woman hired for that purpose. To provide him with exercise, his household servants laid him on a blanket and lifted and lowered him. But sick as he was, the legendary millionaire still kept track of payments made by individual renters of his various real estate properties—and demanded his agents collect a small amount of money owed him by a widow who had fallen on hard times. The gossips said Astor's son had taken the sum from his own pocket, and sent it to his father by special messenger. The dying man was well pleased, Bart said.

He and Amanda exchanged eastern and western perspectives on the war just concluded under the leadership of two Whig generals, the military commander of the southwest, Zachary Taylor, and the commander of all United States forces, Winfield Scott—both avowed political opponents of President Polk.

Though both men were Virginians, a greater personal

contrast could hardly have been found. Scott's preoccupation with protocol and proper dress had earned him a national nickname—Old Fuss and Feathers. Taylor, unassuming and unspectacular, seldom wore a uniform, preferring farmer's clothing, with only a cap carrying a general's emblem identifying his rank. While cogitating, scanning dispatches or issuing orders, he usually sat with both legs hanging down one side of the old white nag he rode. His style won him a nickname too—Old Rough and Ready—and Bart said some in the east were already calling him presidential material.

Like previous American wars, the one against Mexico had been unpopular in certain quarters. Many northerners saw it as a means of guaranteeing the presence of a huge slave state, Texas, in the Union. Bart spoke with some derision about a rustic philosopher of Massachusetts, a chap named Thoreau, who had actually refused to pay a poll tax to protest the "immoral" war. He had gone to Concord jail instead.

Amanda had a somewhat more personal, less political interest in the outcome of the war. She'd had first-hand experience with the Mexican president, Santa Anna, back in Texas in the thirties. Bart knew the story; he knew who had sired young Louis, and under what circumstances.

With relish, Amanda described Santa Anna's abdication after the capture of Mexico City in September of '47:

"I only hope they've gotten the treacherous son of a bitch out of office for good this time!"

She said conditions in California were settling down now that Mexico had renounced claim to the land. The territory was currently being governed by a garrison at Monterey under the command of one Colonel Mason. Exactly as Louis had said, she dismissed the rumor of gold at Sutter's mill as just that.

She served supper in the late afternoon, while the

sunlight began to diffuse behind the fog gathering out on the Pacific. At Amanda's request, Louis pronounced the grace. Then the boy asked:

"Isn't Israel going to eat with us, ma?"

"No, he has a touch of the stomach complaint."

She and Bart both knew it was an excuse. Israel didn't enjoy the captain's company. Bart was glad the former slave wasn't around.

He ate and ate, complimenting the cook frequently. After the meal he lit a Cuban cigar and moved to the room's most cherished object, the small, compact piano he had freighted from New York.

Before going to sea as a cabin boy in the Far East trade, he had been forced to study music. Despite his youthful dislike of practice, he was accomplished. Music had become a companion for his adult years; a companion who never argued over damnfool *ideas,* or got het up, except as the composition and the performer dictated—

He ran through the popular song he'd mentioned in the morning, a lively novelty called *Oh, Susannah!* that everyone in the east was whistling. Louis and Amanda quickly learned the words. The trio sang the song four times through, with foot-stomping and hand-clapping to hide the flaws in their voices.

Next Bart played some Chopin for Amanda, finishing with a fiery yet somehow melancholy fantasy—Opus 66 in C sharp minor—whose central passage seemed to speak of unfulfilled hopes and dreams. Amanda rocked in the rocker, her eyes closed, her sun-burnished face golden in the light of the lamp.

Bart finished the piece and looked around. Louis had slipped out, not caring for "fancy" music. He watched Amanda rocking for a moment.

"Amanda."

"Mm."

"What are you thinking about?"

She opened her eyes. "Gold."

"You said there wasn't any."

"I know. If there were, Captain Sutter would certainly have made more of the fact by now."

"Unless he's afraid the gold might bring a lot of people tromping over his ground."

"You know, I never thought of it that way. You're right. He's a farmer at heart—"

"A farmer who pretends he was once a soldier."

She smiled. "Everybody calls him captain out of respect. No one really believes he served in the Swiss Guards in France—any more than they believe in the gold. Still, it's a lovely dream—"

"What is?"

"Owning a piece of ground with a lot of gold in it."

He didn't like the brief, predatory expression in her eyes. He puffed on his cigar, rose and stretched:

"Who does own this country? One of the men on the lighter sounded like nobody's sure."

"That's true. Anyone who wants land around here can claim it, except in town."

"Let's hope they don't want it. Changing the name of this place is too much change already. I prefer Yerba Buena just like it is. Quiet—"

He walked to her side, bent and kissed her forehead. "With you always here."

She reached up to touch his face, her fingertips warm against his skin. How soft and beautiful she looked in the lamplight. The predatory quality was gone. He stroked her hair:

"You're an amazing woman, Amanda."

"Why do you say that?"

"I want another free meal tomorrow."

They laughed together. Then he went on, "I say it because most females would have tried to lash me up legally long before this."

She shrugged, the movement tightening the fabric over her breasts and reminding him of his long-unsatisfied need.

"You said one marriage was enough. Besides, even though I'm regarded as something of a loose creature around here, I continue to believe it's the loving, not the document, that counts most. If you wish to consider that an invitation, Captain McGill, please d—what on earth's wrong? Why did you pull such a terrible face?"

"Just thinking of the poor devils still on board the clipper. They don't get leave till morning. While I wallow in debauchery—" He grinned.

"No debauchery permitted until children are in bed. Do you want to help me find Louis?"

"With speed, sweet. With the utmost speed."

As she stood up, he leaned forward to kiss her mouth. She caressed his face again.

"Make sure of that," she whispered.

He wheeled and sped out into the clammy fog, shouting her son's name.

vi

She was full of eagerness and heat too long contained. With Louis bedded down in the smaller cubicle, and the curtain carefully pulled across the entrance to hers, they made love with almost desperate haste, Amanda not even allowing Bart to slip out of his trousers before her hands were on him, pulling him to her.

The alcove grew warm. They lay together drowsily afterward, Amanda laughing about how shameless it was for a woman midway through her forties to enjoy a man's body. She teased him about the difference in their ages, calling herself a seducer of innocents—whereupon he rolled over and kissed one of her breasts while his other hand slid down the smoothness of her belly:

"I'll show you how innocent I am. Would you care to learn a certain way Chinese girls make love?"

She laughed and poked him:

"What Chinese girls, you deceitful bastard?"

"Unimportant. Just pay attention—"

"And I thought southerners were honorable men."

"In public. Shut the bedroom tight and we rut just as hard as the next. Harder, maybe. Better, for sure—"

Laughing, hugging, kissing with their lips parted, they went more slowly this time. The play of hands and limbs drove Bart into a frenzy, until he was floundering on her, parting her legs with insistent fingers, opening the way for himself, thrusting forward with a haste that matched her own—

She cried out happily at the impact—only to jerk her head from the mussed pillow an instant later. Her sudden movement jolted him:

"What the hell's wrong?"

"Someone's shouting—"

"Let them shout."

"I hear people in the square—"

He listened. Caught the unintelligible bellow of a bass voice.

"We've had trouble before, Bart. Drifters liquored and starting a scrape. Setting fires—hand me my robe."

"Oh, goddamn it, all right," he said, severely peeved.

She lit a lamp on the walnut table. Louis popped out of his cubicle, asking what was wrong.

"You go back to sleep," Amanda said, reaching past the pile of new books to a board hanging on the wall. Pegs jutted from the board. Two of them supported one of the revolvers manufactured by Colt's of Hartford. The gun was an 1840 holster model, .36 caliber, with a barrel a full foot long. Amanda handled it expertly, flipping out the fold-in trigger and checking the five chambers to be sure they were loaded. Through one curtained window Bart glimpsed a running figure with a torch—the mulatto, Israel, heading for the square—

Amanda rushed through the kitchen and into the public room, Bart a few paces behind. She unlatched the front door, dashed out on the stoop. Struggling to pull on his shirt, Bart saw her stiffen, silhouetted against the weak glow of several torches being carried through the fog toward the source of the shouting. He heard the bass voice again. This time he understood some of the words:

"By God, I tested it myself! Come and look if you don't believe me—"

He ran toward the door as Amanda disappeared in the thick fog. Moments later, shivering, he joined a growing crowd of people who surrounded a spent, bedraggled man. The man held up something that glowed yellow in the blaze of the torches.

Sam Brannan's thick black hair literally bounced on his forehead as he emphasized his words with shakes of his head:

"It's gold, I tell you—" He brandished the half-full quinine bottle. "Right out of the American river!"

Someone on the far side of the crowd went racing away to summon others:

"Brannan's back! He's got gold from the American—"

Within seconds, it seemed that a half dozen voices began to bawl the word through the fog:

"Gold!"

"Gold!"

Lights bobbed as people came running with more lanterns and torches. Bart McGill stared at the faces ringing the stocky Mormon displaying the quinine bottle. The faces were sleepy or stunned or stupidly amused—all except one.

Amanda didn't see Bart watching—nor see him shiver a second time. Her dark hair was lit by the fuming torch in Israel's hand. She was staring at the sparkling yellow dust in the bottle. Staring thoughtfully—speculatively—

She had the look of a predator again.

CHAPTER II

The Fever

THE ARRIVAL OF THE *Manifest Destiny* was a welcome interruption of young Louis Kent's undemanding, if monotonous, routine.

Louis customarily rose before daylight. He laid and lit the fire in the cast iron stove in the kitchen. While his mother cooked for the men who took breakfast at Kent's, he waited tables, collected money and ran dirty dishes back to Israel, who washed them in two large wooden tubs. When the breakfast business slacked off about eight-thirty, everyone began preparing for the noon trade, which actually started closer to ten.

At that hour, Israel moved out front to take charge of the liquor kegs. A phlegmatic Mexican girl named Concepcion took over the serving chores while Louis was demoted to dishwasher for the afternoon and evening. He wasn't especially fond of any of the work, but dishwashing was particularly boring. He knew the work helped his ma keep the place going, though, so he accepted his responsibilities with no complaint.

But the nocturnal shouting in the square, followed by Amanda's departure with her revolver, altered his life more drastically than the return of Captain Bart ever had.

The following morning, he learned the cause of the commotion. Merchant Brannan had rushed back from the American River with a bottle of genuine gold dust.

Almost immediately, Louis noticed a change in his mother. Her mind seemed to be on something other than the operation of the tavern. He hoped she wasn't finally planning the return to Boston that she discussed from time to time. Even though life in Yerba Buena was far from ideal—he had no playmates, for instance—he wasn't sure he wanted to go.

Oh, she painted an elegant picture for him. She said the printing business her family had once owned would be his one day. She promised him fine clothes, and marvelous sights, and an existence that no longer included a broom, scalding water and garbage scraps. He supposed it might be nice to have some friends his own age. And it would be interesting to see the huge cities at the other end of the continent, though truthfully, he couldn't imagine any place as large and crowded as New York. He hardly believed half of Captain Bart's descriptions.

And could faraway Boston give him the fine, free feeling that swept over him when he and Israel roamed the hills of the peninsula, sniping at jackrabbits with the mulatto's antique squirrel gun? He doubted it.

His reservations sprang from something other than simple fear of the unknown, however. When his ma spoke of Boston, a peculiar, almost ugly look came into her eyes. She seemed like a stranger, somehow.

He finally figured out that his mother's absent air was directly connected to the furor over the gold, though Boston might be mixed up in it. He knew a lack of money was all that prevented their return to the east. And now there was a kind of money available right in the inland rivers.

He didn't like the whole business one bit. Practically overnight, his ma stopped smiling—and she always smiled a lot whenever Captain Bart visited. She grew a little curt with him, and with everyone—Israel commented on it. Louis wished Mr. Brannan hadn't raised such a fuss and set the whole village buzzing. He wanted his mother gay and easygoing again—

But things were never to be what they had been before.

Two days after Brannan's return, Captain Bart stormed into the public room about ten A.M. Louis, pushing the straw broom, glanced up and saw the captain wham his peaked cap onto one of the tables.

"Where's your mother?"

"In—in the kitchen, I think," Louis said, next to speechless.

The captain sank into a chair. "Tell her to fetch me a cup of coffee. Then you can uncork that rum keg and pour me—" He jumped up. "No, I'll get the damned rum myself. You get your mother."

Louis put down his broom and raced for the curtain separating the front from the kitchen. He discovered Amanda in the center of a cloud of steam. Perspiring, she was stirring a kettle of beans with a horn spoon.

"Captain Bart wants coffee, ma."

She laid the spoon aside. "I thought I heard someone come in—" She lifted the lid of the battered pot. "The coffee's gone. We had so many customers this morning, we ran through four gallons."

"Where are all those people coming from?"

"Up from the south—out of the hills—from the sky! There must be fifty more men in town than there were this time yesterday."

"Maybe that's why the captain's in a bad temper. I've never seen him so stormy—"

"Louis, for Christ's sake, the rum keg's empty!" McGill shouted.

"Ma, you better hurry—"

Amanda wiped her hands on her apron. "Find Israel. Have him bring another keg from the storage shed. We drained the one out in front last night."

She disappeared beyond the curtain. As the boy headed out the back way, he heard McGill thunder:

"I sent Louis for you *and* some coffee, goddamn it!"

"Don't you talk to me that way, Bart McGill! What in the world's become of that reserve you're so proud of—?"

Her voice faded as the boy darted into the sunlight. He hailed Israel, who was emptying a tub of dishwater behind the privy. A few minutes later, the two re-entered Kent's, the lanky mulatto balancing a small keg on his shoulder.

Israel removed the empty from its cradle behind the plank counter and set the new one in place. Captain Bart was tapping his cap against his knee while Amanda studied a piece of paper. In a moment, she shook her head:

"It's almost ludicrous, Bart."

"A man does ludicrous things when he smells easy money. Jesus, I need *something* to drink—" He jumped up again and stalked toward the counter.

"I'm sorry about the coffee—" Amanda began. McGill paid no attention. Israel reached for a tin cup. The captain snatched it from him:

"I'll pour my own, if you don't mind."

He put the cup back on the shelf and picked up another. He maneuvered the cup under the bung and got the keg open. But his hand was shaking. Rum splashed, soaking the cuff of his blue jacket. He swore under his breath, oblivious to Israel's venomous stare.

The boy realized Israel was mad because the captain refused to let him handle his drinking cup. Louis saw that his ma noticed, too. She tried to blunt Israel's anger with an explanation:

"Two of Captain McGill's crew jumped ship last night."

"My cook and my third mate," McGill said. "Took off up the Sacramento—" He downed a swallow of rum, then gestured with the cup. "The mate left a note for his father. If he thinks I'm going to see it delivered to New Hampshire, he's got shit between his ears."

Amanda glanced at her son. "Bart—"

"Sorry," the captain muttered in a perfunctory way. He drank again.

In a toneless voice, Israel asked, "What's the note say, Miz Kent?"

"Go on, you can read it to him," Bart said to Amanda.

"I can read it for myself," Israel said. "My momma taught me in the pine woods, even though it was against the law. Bark for a tablet. A white oak stick for a pen. An oak ball soaked in water to make ink—and fifty apiece across the back when the driver finally caught momma and me sneaking off together for a lesson. There isn't any nigger more dangerous than an educated nigger, is there, captain?"

"I don't need any goddamn sass from you!" McGill exclaimed.

"Maybe you gonna get some anyway. And something else besides," Israel said, stepping forward.

Bart McGill slammed his cup on the plank counter. Louis saw with alarm that the ex-slave's fingers were fisted. Amanda rushed between the two, a hand on each of them:

"I forbid that kind of behavior around here, and both of you know it! Israel, you go back outside—Bart, you settle down." She tugged his arm. "Come on—" She glanced over her shoulder. "Israel, I'm asking you to leave—"

"Asking or telling?"

"Asking. Please!"

His dark eyes resentful, the lanky man finally shrugged, turned and walked out. McGill was still seething. After the door banged, he exploded:

"That snotty son of a bitch acts like I'm one of those

Mississippi cotton barons! The McGills never owned a slave. Not one!"

"But Israel sees all white men alike because a few of them treated him badly. Unfortunately you have the same kind of irrational feelings about colored people—"

Louis heard Amanda with only half an ear, having inched his way toward the table where the paper had fallen. He managed to glimpse a few of the scrawled lines:

> *—frenzy has seized my soul. Piles of gold rise up before me at every step. Thousands of slaves bow to my beck and call. Myraids of fair damsels contend for my love. In short it is a violent attack of what I can only term gold fever—*

"Now settle down and think about your men," Amanda urged. "Are you going after them?"

McGill started refilling his cup. "By every law on the book, I should. But I decided against it. I plan to load the hold as fast as possible and weigh anchor. I can't afford to lose anyone else—I've already got the first and second mates standing guard. They rounded up the whole crew this morning and sent 'em back to the ship. They have orders to shoot if anybody takes a header over the rail. I hope the cook and the mate dig to hell and find nothing but a ton of those pyrites!" He slumped at the table, staring moodily into the cup.

Amanda's face had acquired that intense look Louis disliked:

"How does a man collect gold, Bart? You've called in Peru and Chile, surely you've heard—"

His head jerked up. "Why the hell are you so interested? You planning to sail off to the American too?"

Louis knew his ma was hiding something when she answered:

"No, I'm just curious. Gold-hunting must take some equipment—"

"Not much more than a pick, a shovel and a pan for placer mining. You wash the dirt out of a pan of water and because the gold's heavier, it stays put. It's hard labor. Even harder if you're working solid rock instead of a river. The South Americans have mechanical contraptions—*arrastras*—for separating gold from quartz."

He finished his drink, jammed the paper in his pocket and his cap on his head:

"I'll see you for supper—provided I get enough hides loaded. I want to get out of this lunatic place—"

When he was gone, Amanda moved quickly to her son:

"Louis, I'd like you to do an errand."

Uneasily, he said, "What is it?"

"I need a new iron pan for the kitchen. Fetch twenty cents and run to the hardware. While you're there, see how many shovels are in stock."

"Ma!" he cried. "You haven't got the gold fever too?"

Amanda laughed in a harsh way. "No, I'm not that addled. But I've been noticing how many people have come to town just in the past twenty-four hours—"

She gave him a pat on the bottom:

"You hurry along and get that pan."

ii

"I need an iron pan, Mrs. Holster," Louis said to the stout woman tending the hardware counter. She pointed to an empty shelf:

"Sold the lot not two hours ago."

"Who bought 'em?"

"Sam Brannan. He bought every pick and shovel, too.

Paid twice the going price for everything. He's loading them out in back right this minute."

Disappointed, Louis headed for the front door. Courtesy jogged him into acknowledging the owner's absence: "Is Mr. Holster feeling poorly this morning?"

"You mean because he's not here?" The woman sniffed. "He hired Andy Bellamy to pole him up the river to Sutter's fort. Mr. Kemble the editor went with him. You won't be reading the *Star* around here for a while—or seeing Mr. Holster selling nails! I swear, I don't know what's got into people, traipsing off to nowhere thinking they can wash a fortune out of a stream—"

But Louis knew. He'd read the third mate's note. The fever explained everything from the influx of strangers and his ma's odd behavior to the sudden turnover in hardware.

To verify that last, Louis walked around to the rear of the building. Bare-chested and sweating, Sam Brannan was lashing a canvas over the bed of a small wagon. Louis said hello, then shinnied up one wheel for a look into the bed:

"What are you shipping, Mr. Brannan? A whole lot of pick-axes, huh?"

And pans and shovels, he noted before Brannan shooed him off and covered the cargo completely:

"That's right, Louis. Going to peddle them in the store I lease up at New Helvetia. I figure just one pan will bring me anywhere from half an ounce to one ounce of dust, flake or lump gold."

"How much is that in money?"

"Oh, about eight to sixteen dollars American."

Louis whistled. "How can you ask so much for a twenty-cent pan?"

"Because men need 'em, my boy. And what men need, they'll pay for—handsomely. Like I told Mrs. Holster—" He grinned. "Spades are trumps now.

If there's as much gold in the American as there seems to be, it's going to be that way for a long time."

Louis ran back to the other side of Portsmouth Square and reported to his mother. She thanked him, but her eyes didn't seem to be focusing on the immediate surroundings. She acted much the same as she did whenever she discussed returning to Boston.

"You go help Israel," she said. "I want to look over my account book—"

She left him. He scuffed the toe of his boot against the kitchen floor. Maybe living by herself—without a man—had something to do with these peculiar spells. Maybe it wasn't entirely the fault of the gold—

Amanda always refused to answer Louis' questions about his father. She put him off with a promise that she'd clear up the mystery when she thought the time was appropriate. Did that mean he was still too young? He assumed so.

Every once in a while he keenly missed having a father. Now was one such time. A man might help his ma keep a level head. A man who was around more regularly than Captain Bart might help cure his ma of the fever—to which Louis was convinced Amanda had succumbed, whether she'd admit it or not.

iii

That night Amanda completely forgot her son's lessons. Captain Bart arrived for supper about seven, but the tavern was so busy, she had no chance to serve him until half past nine—which put him in another foul mood. Louis could tell from the sort of music the captain hammered on the piano before and after he ate—wild, noisy music, full of heavy chords in the bass.

Louis couldn't sleep because of the racket. He pushed the curtain aside and asked whether he could go out to the privy. Amanda didn't answer. She was seated at the walnut table, her pencil moving rapidly over a sheet of paper. She was doing sums, he noticed. Puffing on a cigar, Captain Bart stared out a window.

"Ma? Did you hear me?"

Without so much as glancing up, Amanda said, "What? Oh, yes, go ahead."

Frowning, the boy walked toward the back door.

He sat awhile on the rough, splintery board. But the request had been a pretense. Presently he pulled his flannel nightshirt down and stepped out of the reeking little building. The night air was chilly, damp-smelling. Fog drifted. Out in the bay, blurs of light showed the location of Captain Bart's clipper and a small steam packet that made coasting voyages as far north as Oregon.

A lantern was burning in Israel's shanty. Captain Bart started pounding the piano again. Louis didn't especially want to return to the noise. He walked across the damp ground and knocked on the shanty door.

He heard Israel draw in a sharp breath:

"Who's there?"

"Just me, Israel."

"Oh—Louis. Come on in."

The place was cramped but scrupulously neat. A table, a chair, a cot and a box for Israel's few clothes comprised the furnishings. The tall man lay on the cot, one of the new books—Mr. Poe's—propped on his bare stomach.

As Israel sat up, Louis caught a glimpse of the Negro's shoulderblade. Like most of Israel's back, the yellow skin there was a crosswork of hard brown scar tissue. Israel often said—with a certain air of pride—that he'd been whipped more than any other slave on the Mississippi plantation from which he'd run away when he was twenty.

"The captain's music keeping you awake?" the ex-slave asked.

"Yes, that and—" Louis stopped, feeling vaguely foolish.

"And what?" Israel prompted.

"And all the craziness in town."

Israel nodded. "Know what you mean. I heard almost a hundred more folks showed up today."

"I just don't understand the reason, Israel. Why is everybody so excited about gold? What can you do with it?"

The tall man reflected a moment. "The truth is, nothing much—except use it to replace a bad tooth. Gold's not like iron or copper. You can't turn it into needles or kettles or plows."

"Seems to me it's worthless, then."

"No, you can buy things with it. They say it lasts a mighty long time. And it's not found in very many places in the world. Guess that's why it's so valuable—there isn't much of it."

"I still don't see why people would bother to hunt for it."

"That's because you don't think like a grown-up, Louis. Some grown-ups put a lot of stock in being rich."

"Is owning gold like owning people of color? The more you own, the richer you are?"

Israel's gentle smile disappeared. "Yes and no."

"What do you mean? What's the difference?"

"For one thing, a human being can produce something—provided he's scared bad enough. A lump of gold doesn't think, either. Or shed a tear. Or have any feelings to speak of—"

He said it quietly enough. But his eyes were so somber, Louis shuddered.

"I wish they'd never found any gold at Sutter's!" he declared finally.

"Could make California mighty prosperous, Louis. Could be even more important than that—it just might start this part of the country filling up with people like nothing else could."

"But ma's thinking about it too much!"

"How do you know?"

"Well, she's either thinking about gold or Boston. She's hardly spoken to me since supper."

Israel tried to smile. "I expect she's caught a light case of the fever. It'll pass."

Louis shook his head. "I think she has a bad case. She wants money mighty strongly, Israel. You know how she's always talking about going east—"

"Yes, I do, and I have a peculiar feeling that going there wouldn't be good for any of us. I know I couldn't abide the crowds. Guess it's none of my affair, though. You better hurry back inside. You've been out here a while—"

"Bet they'll never notice how long I was gone. Goodnight, Israel."

"Goodnight, Louis."

He left the shanty and crossed the foggy yard. Amanda glanced up from her sums as he entered. She said nothing. McGill sat at the piano, staring into space.

Louis walked to the cubicle, drew the curtain and threw himself in bed, feeling miserable. He could have stayed out half the night—he could have jumped in the bay or run off to the American—and she probably wouldn't have said a word!

iv

The sandy-haired man walked into the public room about nine the following evening. Nine was the normal closing time. But it was already apparent to Louis that, with all the new arrivals, Kent's could have extended its hours till eleven or twelve and done a brisk business in liquor.

He presumed the tavern would soon be open that long every night. But right now his ma was occupied with those scraps of paper on which she'd been ciphering last evening and most of the day. She was at it again, in the back, leaving Israel and Louis to hang out the *Closed* sign, sweep and clean the place, blow out the lanterns and lock up. The Mexican girl, Concepcion, had already gone.

The public room was empty of customers but the front door was still open when the sandy-haired young man entered. Israel pointed to the sign lying on the table nearest the entrance:

"We're closed. I was just about to hang that up—"

"I'm powerful hungry," the young man said. "Couldn't I see a bill of fare?"

"Isn't any," Israel informed him. "For supper we serve salt pork, beans, biscuits and coffee—and what's left is cold."

The sandy-haired fellow glanced at the open front door. Nervously, Louis thought. Busy with the broom, he still didn't miss the wood-handled bowie sheathed over the young man's left hip. The stranger was in his twenties, with a homely face. His flannel shirt and trousers looked brand new. Hardly a trace of dust anywhere. The shirt bagged, much too large.

"Couldn't you rustle up a couple of biscuits?" the young man asked. "I don't care if they're cold—I'm plumb near starved."

Israel shrugged and headed for the kitchen. Presently he returned, and set a plate in front of the stranger. "You collect his money when he's finished, Louis," he said as he left again.

The sandy-haired man wolfed two biscuits and was starting on a third when he noticed the boy watching him:

"What are you staring at?"

"Nothing, sir."

"Tend to your work!"

The abruptness of it—and the flash of color in the young man's cheeks—alarmed Louis somehow. Ill at ease, he glanced down at the pile of sweepings. A horse clopped along the street. The sound stopped suddenly. The young man whipped his head around, staring through the door into the darkness. Perspiring all at once, he swabbed his forehead with the back of one hand—

He started when another man appeared in the doorway. A lean, severe-looking Army officer in his late twenties. The officer's dark blue fatigue jacket and light blue trousers were powdered with dust. So was his face, which hadn't been touched by a razor in several days. His reddish beard, wrinkled clothing and fatigued eyes were in marked contrast to the mint-bright barrel of the Army revolver in his right hand.

"Evening, Private Pepper," the officer said. His glance shifted to Louis, then back to the young man, who looked as scared as anyone Louis had ever seen.

"How—how'd you track me so fast?" the young man asked.

"Do you imagine it was hard with you on foot and me on horseback? You had a good head start, but I don't suppose I was more than half an hour behind you by the time you got here."

"I—I know I didn't leave any trail—"

"Where else would you be likely to come but the mouth of the Sacramento? I'd have shown up sooner but I had to stop and ask questions. I just came from the store where you bought those new clothes. You should have bought a hat to cover up your hair, too. I knew people would remember your hair if they didn't remember your face—" A humorless smile curled the officer's mouth. "I'm becoming very experienced at chasing deserters, Pepper. You're the third in as many days—though the other two didn't get as far." He gestured with the revolver. "Come on, we'd better start back to Monterey—"

The young man sighed and stood up. The officer turned his head toward Louis:

"Sorry to trouble you, young man—"

Suddenly the deserter leaped to the side and flung an arm around Louis' throat. The next thing Louis knew, the long blade of the bowie was pressed against his throat:

"I don't want to hurt this tadpole, Sherman. But I will if you don't let me go."

"My God, Pepper, what's become of your brains? You pull something like this, Colonel Mason'll order a whole troop after you!"

"Talking won't change my mind," Pepper said. Louis' heart hammered in his chest. He gulped air through his mouth, feeling the deserter tremble. Any sudden move might get him the bowie through the throat—

"Stand clear of the doorway," the deserter ordered. "And put your revolver on the counter."

The officer remained motionless. Louis winced as the point of the knife dug his throat:

"Sherman, you do what I say or I'll cut him!"

A board creaked. Someone was creeping from the kitchen. The officer's eyes jumped past the deserter, startled—

The younger man jerked his knife hand away from Louis' throat and whirled, cursing, just as Israel swung an iron skillet.

Louis felt something warm and wet trickling down his neck. The bowie had pierced the skin. Israel tried to slam Pepper's head with the skillet—and missed as the deserter sidestepped.

A look of panic crossed Pepper's face. Off balance, Israel staggered toward him. Pepper shot his knife hand straight toward the tall man's belly—

Louis jumped, both hands closing on Pepper's forearm. The deserter snarled, lifted a knee and rammed Louis hard between the legs. The boy crashed against the barrels supporting the counter, clutching his groin and fighting back tears. Somewhere in the back of the building, Amanda cried her son's name—

Israel regained his balance and darted forward again, both hands locked on the skillet's handle. Pepper jabbed with the knife. It raked the iron bottom, struck sparks, skittered off. While the officer shouted for everyone to clear away so he could fire, Israel clenched his teeth, dodged another bowie-jab and swung the skillet at Pepper's skull—

Still dazed, Louis heard the frightful crunch—then Pepper's moan. He saw the bowie tumble from the deserter's hand and impale itself, humming, in the floor. Pepper fell beside it, a stain darkening his trousers. Covering his face with his forearms, Pepper rolled his head from side to side, whimpering—

"What in damnation is going on—? *Louis!*" Her Colt's revolver clutched in one hand, Amanda rushed toward her son.

"My deepest apologies, ma'am," the officer said, leaning down to free the bowie and pitch it onto the counter. "Things got just a trifle out of hand. But the young man was very resourceful—"

"He's not hurt badly, Miz Kent," Israel said as Amanda knelt, laid the revolver aside and took Louis' head in her hands. Despite the horrible pain between his thighs, the boy seconded the lie:

"No, ma, not bad."

"Someone better explain why there are knives and pistols and *fighting* in this restaurant—and damn fast!" Amanda said.

The officer looked flustered. "I'm Lieutenant Sherman, ma'am. Lieutenant William T. Sherman, from the Monterey garrison. That fellow's a runaway—"

"A deserter?"

"That's right. We're beginning to lose them at the rate of one or two a day. I imagine it'll get worse. The struggle between right, and six dollars a month, and wrong, and a possible seventy-five or hundred per day, is a pretty severe one—"

Sheathing his revolver, Sherman dragged the cowed young man to his feet.

"You'll wish you'd never touched that boy, Pepper, because the attack will go on the bill of charges." He glanced at Israel. "Do you have any rope to tie him?"

Louis lost track of what happened next, busy fending his mother's hands and answering her anxious questions. Yes, the man had seized him and pricked his skin and kicked him but, no, he wasn't seriously injured; Israel had seen to that.

"Well, you're coming straight back to bed," Amanda declared. "I want you to take those clothes off so I can look at you. Israel, you lock up. Lieutenant—thank you for your courtesy, but I must see to my son—"

Louis limped a little; the pain in his genitals was still pretty fierce. The last he saw, Israel and Lieutenant William T. Sherman were lashing the prisoner's hands behind his back. The youthful offender looked abject, his moment of crazed courage long past. Nothing remained except a doleful contemplation of the trouble into which his yearning for gold had gotten him.

It drives people out of their heads, Louis thought as Amanda helped him through the dark kitchen. *It really does—*

He was stricken anew with fear for his mother.

V

The next evening, Louis lay rigid in his curtained alcove, wakened from sleep by the harsh sounds of an argument:

"If you stay here one day longer, you're a damned fool."

"Bart—"

"Those are the only words for it—damned fool. It doesn't take a biblical prophet to see what's going to happen to this place. More and more drifters—riffraff—piling into town—and you're willing to expose your son to that kind of existence?"

"Believe me, I've thought it over pretty hard—"

"And what have you decided?"

"I've decided to stay."

"*Jesus!* Louis might have been *killed* last night!"

"He wasn't, he came through just fine. He showed a good deal of pluck, Israel said."

"Pluck isn't worth shit if it lands you six feet under!"

"Bart, keep your voice down. Why are you so angry with me?"

"Because I want to see you *safe!* We're sailing in the morning—come with me. I'll take you and Louis—even that uppity nigger if you insist—straight to New York."

"I thought you didn't approve of my going east."

"I don't. But I like the idea of your staying here even less."

"Well, I won't go back without money—and there's money to be made in San Francisco. A lot of money. Now what about the loan from the primage you'll collect at the end of the voyage? You can easily spare a thousand dollars—"

"Am I supposed to do your damn shopping, too?"

"I told you I'd pay you fifteen percent on your money if you would. That's twice as much as you get from the cargo—"

"How the hell can I inform the Ball brothers I'm loading a thousand dollars' worth of pick axes and iron pans for a female acquaintance? It's against company policy. Besides, they'd think I was out of my head."

"They won't think anything because you won't tell

them. And you'll figure out a way to hide the extra cargo, I know you will. Why are you so averse to profit all of a sudden? You heard what Sam Brannan's doing. You know you'll make your fifteen percent half an hour after you bring in the shipment—"

Louis lay utterly still, disheartened by the severity of his mother's tone:

"I've never had a chance like this. Never in almost forty-five years. I'm in the right place at the right time. I can make something of myself! For Louis—"

"Pardon me if I say bullshit to that."

"Please, Bart—"

"You're not thinking of Louis, you're thinking of that damn printing company—and how good it'll feel to take it away from Stovall."

"I'm losing patience with—"

"Fuck your patience! It's true, isn't it?"

"May I remind you this is not a New York dock? Your language—"

"Is no worse than what you indulge in when you're mad. Isn't what I said the gospel truth? *Isn't it?"*

Silence. Louis dug his nails into his palms and shut his eyes, wishing they'd stop.

"I'm not going to argue my motives, Bart," Amanda said, very quietly. "I've never made any demands on you before—"

"No demands? What about all that damn investigation—?"

"You could have refused. I was very clear on that."

"You're saying I can't refuse this time?"

"Not if what we've been to each other means anything—"

Louis wanted to cover his ears when McGill shouted:

"So the account's finally due, is that it? The whorehouse madam finally presents her bill for services rendered?"

Silence again. Dreadful silence. What did McGill

mean, calling his ma a whorehouse madam? Louis knew what a whorehouse was—Yerba Buena had one—but the connection with Amanda was a mystery as impenetrable as the riddle of his unknown father.

Finally, he heard his mother speak in a whisper:

"That's absolutely vile. You promised you'd never bring up what I told—"

"Christ, I know," he interrupted, sounding miserable all at once. "I'm sorry. I truly am. But I can't stand what's happening to you, Amanda! All of a sudden you're acting like the rest of the moon-heads in this town—thinking you can have El Dorado in your pocket before snow flies in the mountains!"

"You're wrong," she said in a hushed voice. "I'm not like the rest of them. I'm not going to the mines. I've talked to Sam Brannan. I know the odds. Men are staking out claims no bigger than twenty feet on a side. Only one in a thousand will strike anything big. There'll be many more losers than winners. I can make a killing off both."

"*A killing*—you see? It's even affected the way you talk!"

"Bart, I am almost forty-five years old! Sometimes I can't sleep at night, thinking of what that means. I'm going to die. I'm really going to die. But I swear, before it happens—"

"Now who's yelling?"

"I don't care! I won't throw this chance away! Will you buy the merchandise for me or won't you?"

Louis was perspiring. He drew a slow, careful breath, fearful of making the slightest sound.

"I shouldn't," McGill said. "I should cart you away from here bodily—"

She laughed then. "Impossible, and you know it."

Through the curtain, Louis heard him sigh:

"Yes, I do. So I guess I'll help you. But Jesus!—you sure do take advantage of a relationship."

"Bart, I'm handing you an opportunity to earn fifteen percent on your money! If you're smart, you'll risk two thousand, not just one."

"I already reached the same conclusion."

He didn't sound overjoyed about it. Amanda was, though:

"Oh, Bart, thank you, thank—*now* what are you angry about?"

"Losing my temper, goddamn it!" But at last his voice had a smile in it. So did hers:

"Not typical of you, Captain."

"Only two things ever get me wrought up. Trouble with the ship, and women."

"Any women?"

"No, sweet, just those I care about."

"How many does that include?"

"One. But she's damn near more than I can handle—"

Louis heard muffled sounds; the sort of sounds which usually accompanied that funny custom of men kissing women—the prelude, he surmised, to what animals indulged in without benefit of hugs or kisses.

In some ways, Louis Kent wasn't overly fond of Captain Bart McGill. The captain treated Israel shabbily. But lying in the dark and listening to the murmurous voices beyond the curtain, this was one time he believed Captain Bart was right.

Because of the gold, Yerba Buena was changing. It was no longer a pleasant place. Maybe not a safe place, either. He'd seen some of the rough characters drifting into town. He'd felt the young deserter's knife against his own throat. He feared there'd be more of the same in the months to come—

Right then, he altered his thinking about the east. It might be better if they left California—

But they weren't going to leave. His ma had won the argument—as usual.

The gold was changing her too, though. Changing her into a new person. Someone even more forbidding than the stranger who spoke of Boston. That he feared most of all.

CHAPTER III

Christmas Among the Argonauts

"CONFOUND IT, AMANDA! Forty-eight thousand, then."

"Not for sale, Sam," Amanda said, handing cups of Thirty Rod to the miners elbowing Brannan at the plank bar. "Lord knows why you need another piece of property—"

"Not need, my dear. Want."

"Your wants should be well enough satisfied by the dozen plots you've already bought. Not to mention that shipload of carpet tacks which I hear you're selling to carpenters at four times cost."

"Don't act so damn virtuous. Wouldn't you do the same thing?"

"Of course. That's why pouring you a Christmas drink is the limit of my generosity for the evening."

"One side, one side!" Israel yelled, pushing past the crowd at the bar. He held two platters of grizzly meat with side helpings of oysters. Two more were precariously balanced on his forearms. He was jostled and shoved, but he managed to deposit the food on one of the tables. Out in the kitchen, Felix, the recently hired Frenchman, was screeching about the inhuman pace of his work.

Israel's expression made it evident he didn't enjoy the duties of a waiter. But the Mexican girl, Concepcion, had quit to work in a bordello for much higher wages. He scribbled a chit and flung it down. "Pay the boy when you leave." He pointed an elbow at the podium by one of the front windows.

Behind the podium, Louis Kent sat on a stool. On the podium stood a quill and inkstand, a balance and a set of weights. Immediately to Louis' left, six-foot Billy Beadle lounged at the front door, a big slung-shot conspicuously displayed at his belt.

Billy kept watch on the men packing away food and drink in Kent's public room. He was one of the lately arrived Sydney Ducks—Australians transported to San Francisco by a government desperate to rid itself of the criminals in its overcrowded jails. Bruises on Billy's face testified to his fondness for brawling. His size and obvious strength helped keep the customers from sneaking out without paying—or from wrecking the place. Virtually all the customers were miners down from the diggings on a holiday, or would-be miners heading for the camps. Hardly a one of them was sober.

The air in Kent's was heavy with tobacco smoke and the aromas of its eclectic menu. The miners demanded everything from the hottest Mexican chili to duck, plover, trout and antelope. The stink of sweat mingled with the more exotic odors; most of the miners were none too concerned about their grooming.

As he struggled back toward the bar, Israel reflected that white folks had always looked pretty similar to him. That certainly was true of the men who came down from the American and the Yuba and the Feather and all the other obscure forks and branches and intersecting creeks on which strikes were being made. The men the newspapers called the modern Argonauts tended to dress alike after a few weeks in the diggings: flop-brimmed hats which they never bothered to remove indoors; flannel shirts; dark pants; heavy boots. Their individuality was further blurred by an almost universal adoption of chest-length beards. In the whole noisy, smoky, smelly place, Amanda Kent was the only person who looked distinctive and halfway appealing this Christmas Eve in the year 1849. Of course she was also the only woman.

At the bar, Brannan was saying, "You should realize forty-eight thousand dollars is a damn generous offer!"

Israel stopped, leaned over the exasperated man's shoulder and said, "Don't you settle for less than a hundred thousand, Miz Kent."

"A hundred thousand!" Brannan exploded. "Your nigger's a bigger swindler than I am!"

Unexpectedly, that hurt more than Brannan's use of the word nigger. Israel had made his remark without thought. Now he realized he was unconsciously being caught up in the mood of avarice that pervaded Kent's these days.

He showed no anger at Brannan's term for a colored man. With the exception of Amanda and her son, every white person used it. He didn't like it, but shrugging off a word was a lot easier than avoiding outright trouble in San Francisco any more. He thought he'd escaped that sort of trouble when he fled Mississippi—

He walked warily wherever he went. Fear was his companion again, just as it had been on the plantation. There a man toted his cotton basket to the gin house fearing he'd be whipped if he brought in even a few ounces less than his quota. At the same time he feared that if he brought in too much, he'd be expected to deliver the same quantity the next night—and would be whipped if he failed. Israel had been free of that kind of constant fear for quite a few years—and now it was back.

"Sam," Amanda said, "do you want some Christmas whiskey or don't you? You're not going to buy Kent's this evening or anytime. I told you last month and again last week—the property isn't for sale."

She said it with a charming smile. Yet the smile somehow seemed less genuine than the ones Israel recalled from their first days together down south.

Amanda Kent was very alert, brisk and energetic for a woman of her age. In fact she drove her employees—and herself—twice as hard as a man might have. And she always looked handsome in the bargain—

That was true tonight. Her hair was neatly done—though turning grayer, Israel had observed of late. Her dress of yellow taffeta was the sole spot of bright color in the restaurant. She had chosen the dress from the pages of a *Godey's Lady's Book* McGill had brought her. The dress itself had come with the captain's most recent cargo. He was on the lucrative New York-California freight run now; three round trips since that regrettable night over a year ago when Brannan had returned with his quinine bottle full of gold.

At the moment McGill was eastbound around the Horn. Israel was glad. He and the captain would never be friends. And while McGill made an excellent business partner for Israel's employer—and was also her lover, he knew—he wasn't sure the arrangement was doing Amanda any good.

Oh, she'd prospered—mightily. She'd realized four hundred percent from her first investment in a quantity of pick axes and pans. Then she'd switched to lumber, which couldn't be milled fast enough up in the hills to feed San Francisco's construction boom. Kent's itself had used part of the lumber, adding a second floor—a thirty-man dormitory. For bed and breakfast, Amanda charged twelve-fifty.

Like everything in town, the price was inflated. But the hopeful, pathetically over-equipped arrivals from the packets and clippers paid it without protest, staying a night or two before they bought passage on a river skiff, or set out on foot for the diggings. Right this minute, through the ceiling, Israel could hear one of the gold-hunters bellowing an exuberant celebration of his future:

"Then blow, ye breezes, blow!
"We're off to Californi-o—"

Brannan refused the drink Amanda had offered. "All right, Sam," she said. "I don't want to be rude, but you're taking up space for a paying customer." Shaking his head, Israel started on for the kitchen.

"There's plenty of gold,
"So I've been told,
"On the banks of the Sacramento!"

The singer slurred the last notes into a whoop and a couple of stomps that vibrated the flimsy planks overhead. The mulatto's frown deepened. A lunatic with no future except an imaginary one that fumed out of a liquor bottle was of no consequence to him. But Amanda was. And her behavior worried him. She no longer had time for anything but business. No time for the boy, for instance; Israel had taken over Louis' lessons.

"Israel? Hey, chum!"

The yellow-skinned Negro turned in response to the shout from Billy Beadle.

"There's a chap outside who'd like to talk to someone from the establishment."

Israel pointed to Amanda. But she was busy filling cups with Sixty Rod, the godawful whiskey that was twice as strong as its counterpart, Thirty Rod. A whiff of either was supposed to flatten the unwary at the indicated distance; even around corners.

"See what the man wants, Israel," Amanda called as Brannan jammed his silk hat on his head and left.

With a sigh, Israel started for the front. He overheard snatches of conversation. One miner bragged he'd soon see color on his claim now that he'd teamed up with some partners and installed a long tom. Another complained that it was a crime the way greasers could walk the streets as freely as whites. Greaser was a catchall term for the Mexicans, Peruvians and Chileans pouring into the town along with Americans, Frenchmen, Englishmen, Australians and even a few Germans.

The remark put another scowl on Israel's face. Then he reminded himself that he was a free man. If he didn't like the situation in San Francisco, he could always leave—

Yet he stayed, and would stay, because he was loyal to his employer, as well as fond of her. Amanda Kent was one of the few human beings who had ever treated him as a person. To most of the others he'd known during his thirty-two years, he'd been either sub-human, or property, or both.

His wife Cissie, whom he'd married at age sixteen in Mississippi, had been property. He'd been forced to stand by and see her whipped when she was pregnant with their baby. She'd brought in too little cotton to the gin house, so the big boss ordered a pit dug in the ground; a pit in which her bulging belly fitted as she lay face down. He was whipped unconscious when he tried to interfere. When he woke much later, he learned that Cissie had lost the child. She was sold off within two months. No white person on the plantation had expressed one word of regret to Israel, and he'd never seen his wife again—

Amanda Kent wasn't that sort of white woman. She was kind; thoughtful of others. At least she had been until the damn craziness struck the whole town—

One more example of it was waiting outside. In the spillage of lamplight through the smoke-grayed plate glass windows, Israel spied a young, yellow-haired miner on muleback. Reeling drunk. Armed with a pistol and a knife, too. A bad combination.

At the door, Billy Beadle said:

"Don't know what the bucko wants, but he's got fat saddle bags."

"So I see." As Israel stepped out to the plank walk, Louis gave him a wan smile. *Isn't exactly the kind of Christmas Eve a boy should have,* Israel thought.

He stopped at the edge of the walk Amanda had installed at her own expense. "Something we can do for you, mister?"

The stranger kept himself from falling by hanging onto the mule's neck. He squinted at Israel:

"You a white man?"

Israel gnawed his lower lip. Christmas, he thought sourly.

"That make a difference to you?"

"Well, if you ain't white, you sure as hell ain't the owner of this place."

"The owner sent me out to ask what you want."

"Simple. I want a good swallow of Sixty Rod—"

Puzzled, Israel shook his head. "Then bring in the bags. You've got dust in them, haven't you?"

"Damn right I have. I been up at Sullivan's Creek, pulling out a hundred, two hundred dollars in every pan."

Israel rolled his tongue in his cheek. If the young miner was telling the truth, he was one of the lucky ones; the few lucky ones. There were supposedly fifty thousand men in the diggings; men who had come by ship around Cape Horn, or over the Panama isthmus with a change of vessels, or the whole way across the continent in wagon trains from Westport and Saint Jo back in Missouri. Israel had heard that more than seven thousand wagons had rolled toward California during the good weather this year.

"You want a drink, come on in," Israel said, still not understanding the delay.

The miner leaned forward. He would have tumbled

into the mud—it was San Francisco's rainy season now—if Billy Beadle hadn't dashed from the doorway and propped him up.

"For—" The miner belched. "—for a coon, you're a mighty dumb one. I don't want to walk in and drink. I want to *ride* in and drink."

Billy said with a grin, "I don't think your mule would fit through the door with those bags hanging on him."

"I don't want to ride through the door," the young man replied. "I want to ride through *that.*"

He jabbed a finger at one of the two glass windows.

Billy looked dumbfounded. Israel started back inside; the windows were recent additions, and costly:

"You better find someplace to sleep, mister. You're already dreaming."

"No goddamn coon's gonna tell me—" the miner began, reaching for his pistol.

"None of that, chum," Billy exclaimed, seizing the miner's wrist just as another voice interrupted:

"What on earth's taking you so long out here?"

Amanda stood in the doorway. The miner saw Billy's other hand lift the slung-shot from his belt, and all at once lost his urge to fight.

Grinning again, Billy took the heat out of the situation: "Why, nothing much, Mrs. Kent. This laddy just asked to ride through the window and have a drink."

"Ride through—?"

Amanda stopped, studying the miner. Thunderstruck, Israel watched her smile:

"That's a pretty peculiar request. Why do you want to ride through a window, young man?"

"Ain't ever done it before. Ain't ever seen a window that big, either."

"Don't you have glass windows where you come from?"

"I come from a farm in Illinois and, no, we don't, 'cause my poppa's poor."

"But that doesn't really explain—"

"Listen, are you the owner?"

"That's right."

"Well, we're making progress, anyway. I wasn't gettin' anywhere with the coon." He swept off his filthy hat. "They call me Flaxtop up in the diggings, ma'am—"

"I don't give a damn what they call you—you *get!*" Israel said, reaching for the mule's bit.

"Calm down, Israel!" Amanda snapped. "If you can't keep your temper, go inside."

Astonishment sapped Israel's anger almost instantly. He rubbed his eyes. Lord, he was tired of this upside-down existence, where you never knew what to expect next. He was tired of working seven days a week. He was tired of the noise in town—even on Christmas Eve, shouting and laughter and piano music poured from the plank and canvas and brick hotels and gambling dens and brothels that spread out from Portsmouth Square, lighting the peninsula with hundreds of glowing lanterns. The night was so bright, he could even see the masts of the abandoned ships in the bay—seventy or eighty of them, left to rot at the end of one-way trips from Panama or New York. Their crews had rushed to the diggings right along with their passengers—

It was mass insanity! And Amanda had fallen victim to it. Why, she'd even considered hiring four Chilean whores for the second floor until he talked her out of it, convincing her it wouldn't be suitable with young Louis on the premises.

As further proof of the way her wits had deserted her, Amanda was actually treating the miner's request seriously:

"You really want to ride through one of my windows?"

"I sure do. I struck paydirt and I want to celebrate. I got the dust to pay for the privilege—" He reached back to slap a saddle-bag. "Plenty of it."

Israel headed inside. No doubt she was just being courteous to the young fool—

He pulled up short at the sight of her face. Lord God in heaven. She was *considering* it!

With a cool smile, she said, "Your fun won't come cheap, Flaxtop."

"I guessed not, ma'am. How much?"

She pondered. "Seven hundred and fifty dollars for the window—there's no plate glass manufactured in the United States, you know. It's imported from Europe. Add another two hundred and fifty for general damage. The Sixty Rod will be on the house."

Even Billy Beadle gaped. Israel performed some quick calculations. Allowing for freight charges, Amanda could order a new window from the east coast for maybe five hundred; repair some broken furniture for a hundred or a hundred and fifty. Her terms were outrageous; but she'd presented them with an absolutely straight face. His stomach started to hurt.

"You're sayin' a thousand—?"

"One thousand," she repeated. "If that's too steep for you—why, Merry Christmas."

She pivoted away from the miner. Israel marveled at the way she bluffed. It worked:

"Hang on! I—I guess I can afford it. You got yourself an arrangement, ma'am."

Amanda acted unruffled, as if what was happening was an everyday occurrence:

"Fine. We'll give our guests a little holiday entertainment with their suppers. Billy, you carry those bags inside. Weigh out the equivalent of a thousand dollars. Flaxtop, you wait right here until I move a few tables."

The miner slapped his mule's neck and uttered a long, piercing yell. Louis appeared, drawn by the noise. Amanda spoke to Israel:

"We're out of Thirty Rod. Walk over to Dennison's

Exchange and see whether they'll let me have twenty gallons."

"Sure they will," Israel said. "Your credit's good all over town."

Amanda swept back inside. Billy Beadle chuckled, started to unstrap the saddle bags. The mulatto glanced at Louis:

"You walk along with me to the Exchange."

The boy's face fell. "I want to see him bust the window."

"I said you come along! It isn't fit for a youngster to watch grown men act like fools—" Muttering gleefully to himself, the miner paid no attention. "You watch enough of 'em, you'll start behaving the same way. Come on, now—I'll need help rolling the cask through the mud."

He said it harshly, still upset by the way Amanda had taken advantage of the tipsy miner. He yearned for the old days: Yerba Buena quiet and mellow in the sun; a relaxed pace at the tavern; a few slow-moving residents hoeing potatoes in the square—

What the devil had come over her? *What was driving her?* He was afraid he knew the answer.

"Clear away, boys, clear away!" he heard her shouting inside. "Move your legs, mister, we've got a customer coming in by a different route. Billy? Hurry up with those bags!"

"Come *on*," Israel said, with such a savage gesture that Louis shied back. After a moment's hesitation, the boy stepped down from the plank sidewalk. Instantly, the mud hid the soles of his boots.

"You're gonna miss a real fine show, mister coon," the miner said. Israel grabbed Louis' hand and didn't look back.

I mustn't let it twist me up, he thought. *I've listened to every dirty slur ever invented for a black man. I've watched the Hounds beat up Frenchmen and rip down the tents of the Chileanos on Alta Loma, and I haven't let any of it bother me too much because I'm a free man, I can walk away any time I want.*

Maybe I will. She's not the same woman any more.

ii

Israel tugged the boy's hand, pulling him to the left: "Watch your step!"

Louis had nearly stumbled into the top of a cast iron stove. The rest of the stove had sunk into the mud produced by the December rains.

Neither man nor boy was much surprised by the sight of the stove top. Discovering that charges for shipping heavy freight to the diggings were astronomical, the gold-hunters who came by ship discarded all sorts of personal goods in the public thoroughfares. Speculators who attended the beach auctions and bid on the cargos of the incoming vessels sometimes had to take every item in a shipment when they wanted only part of the shipment. The unwanted merchandise was abandoned in the same places the would-be miners left their heavier belongings. Rotting sacks of flour, expensive commodes, unopened cartons of dress shirts—you could find damn near the whole residue of civilization buried in the winter slime of San Francisco's streets.

One of the stove lids lay in the mud just beyond the sunken obstacle. Angrily, Israel flipped the lid over with his toe:

"I bet when Jason and his Argonauts went hunting the golden fleece, they never left a trail of garbage!"

As the boy and the Negro crossed the square, the noise remained constant. Men and women laughed in the bars. A brass band blared *Deck the Halls* from the lobby of the Parker House. Barkers shouted from the entrances of the gambling tents—*"Come on in, gentle-*

men, come on in and try to find the little joker! Here's the place to get your money back!"

They circled around a bearded, wild-eyed fellow in parson's weeds. Clutching a Bible under one arm and exuding a smell of gin, the man bellowed at them:

"Divine services tomorrow morning! Eight sharp in the tabernacle just a few steps up Kearny. Divine services unless there's news of a strike tonight!"

"Thimbleriggers—cheap women—rum-sots—*trash!*" Israel declared, his yellow face changing as he and Louis passed from shadow into the blaze of lanterns. Everywhere, men walked or ran or staggered—going to perdition!

He guided Louis around a signboard on a pole at the edge of a particularly sinister-looking mudhole. The sign bore the words:

THIS WAY IMPASSABLE!

Below, in a rougher hand, someone had written:

not even jackassable

"You surely don't like San Francisco any more, do you, Israel?" the boy said at last.

"No, sir, I don't. They say we have twenty-five thousand people, and that's twenty-four thousand five hundred too many. You no sooner blink an eye than somebody reports one more camp opened up, with fool names that are an insult to the English tongue. Gouge Eye—Whiskeytown—Mad Mule Gulch—Murderers' Bar—people've lost their minds even when it comes to christening towns! Old Polk should have kept his mouth shut."

"What's the president got to do with it?"

"Why, Louis, if President Polk hadn't stood up when Congress opened its session a year ago—"

As he spoke, his eyes were never still. He saw half a dozen rats prowling over a heap of garbage. Heard a passing miner make reference to his color. A Peruvian in rags loitered in the shadows, watching him and stroking the edge of a knife across his thumb. Every time he ventured out these days, it felt like Mississippi again. He needed to arm himself.

"—if he hadn't blabbed about the gold Colonel Mason sent to the Philadelphia Mint in a tea caddy, it might have been a lot longer—years, maybe—before the country got excited about California. Polk should have just gone out of office quietly and let Taylor take over—but no, he had to pop the cat from the bag. They say he always wanted land. The whole continent under one flag. I don't object to that, but I do object to him giving the fever to every rascal, fool and failure on three continents—"

Without a smile, Louis said, "I told you 'most a year ago that ma had a bad case. You didn't believe me."

"I know. Proves how wrong a man can be."

"Know something?"

"What?"

"I don't like it either. I mean, here it is Christmas and we don't even have a holiday pine with some candles on it. And nobody's got time to make presents—we're too busy fixing to serve dinner all day tomorrow—" The boy sighed. "I try not to think about it too much. Most of the time that's easy. I'm so frizzled out from working, there's nothing on my mind but sleep."

"We keep on this way," Israel said, "we're liable to wind up the richest folks in the graveyard."

"Not ma. She's tough."

"Tougher all the time."

"She wants to go to Boston something awful, I guess."

Israel didn't answer. The boy only knew the surface reason Amanda worked so hard. The mulatto, on the other hand, had heard her speak at length about Hamilton Stovall—not only about how he'd gained control of Kent and Son, but how he'd ruined her cousin's life. He believed Amanda had kept that latter part of the family's history from her son.

The man and the boy reached the large canvas tent whose signboard read *Dennison's Exchange*. Like the other establishments around Portsmouth Square, it poured noise into the Christmas Eve darkness—and, from outside, it shone like one immense lantern. Suddenly men yelled in the distance; glass shattered.

Louis spun. "Oh my Lord, she really let him do it!"

Israel refused to look. His face was as bleak as his thoughts:

It's that Stovall driving her. Stovall and those books McGill brings in. She doesn't see what it's doing to her, either—and what it could do to her boy.

To speak to Amanda on that subject would have been overstepping. Israel could argue with her about the advisability of women on the second floor; even though that too concerned Louis, that was business. But he didn't dare intrude in more personal areas. After all, she was his employer—

A white woman.

Once, he'd practically been able to forget about that. But gold had drawn men to California. Men who bore hatreds. The source—the way they'd been taught, or the lack of any teaching at all—didn't matter. Either way, they were dangerous. He'd begun to feel the fear again—

He heard the tipsy young miner, Flaxtop, saying *coon*. The memories tumbled one upon another. The crack of the whip at the gin house. The feel of it flaying his back while he clenched his teeth and struggled to keep from crying out. Cissie's screams as she lay with her belly in the hole, taking her punishment—

Confused and angrier than ever, he jerked Louis through the entrance to the Exchange. His yellow face looked thunderous in the hazy lantern-light.

He knew he was in a bad temper. Told himself so—and that he ought to simmer down. He made an effort—

Then he saw who was on duty behind the bar.

iii

The preceding year, San Francisco has been plagued by ruffianism unusual even for a boisterous frontier town. The source of the trouble was a group of men once called the First New York Volunteers—the last word hardly being appropriate since most of them had been forced to join up or languish in eastern jails.

The Volunteers had been shipped to California to reinforce Kearny during the Mexican trouble. When they arrived, the fighting was over. The unit had disbanded, and some of its members had drifted north a few months after the discovery of gold.

In San Francisco, the men boastfully called themselves the Hounds—because they roamed the streets in packs, harassing women and foreigners with obscene remarks and their favorite weapons: slung-shots and metal knuckles.

The men professed an affiliation with a splinter political party in the east, the American party, which had sprung from an earlier group calling itself the Native American Association. The title capsuled the group's purpose, and that of the party which emerged from it—to keep America the exclusive preserve of those white Protestants who had been born there. Members of the party had secret rituals, passwords and handshakes—never revealed when they were questioned: "I know nothing." An eastern editor—Mr. Greeley, Israel believed it was—had contemptuously christened the party Know-Nothing.

For months, the local counterparts of the Know-Nothings had occupied a tent headquarters at Commercial and Kearny. The tent, its nickname *Tammany Hall* also borrowed from the east, was gone now; torn down as the result of a public outcry when the Hounds invaded Little Chile up on the hill called Alta Loma the preceding July. The Chilean immigrants had been beaten, their women raped, their hovels demolished—and San Francisco had finally risen in outrage. Amanda had contributed fifty dollars to help organize a company of volunteer peace officers who razed Tammany Hall and drove the Hounds out of town.

Officially, they were gone. But some had come back. One, a bald, blue-chinned man named Felker, had found employment as a bartender at the Exchange.

Israel approached Felker warily. He was sure the man would recognize him. Amanda had once used her Colt revolver to back down three Hounds who tried to come into Kent's for a meal; she wouldn't allow the hooligans on the premises. But an offense to one Hound was an offense to all.

Felker was busy telling a story to a trio of miners leaning on the bar:

"—and so the nun says to the priest, let's fuck now, father, and you can hear my confession later."

Scurrilous jokes against Catholics were a staple of the Know-Nothings. Two of the bearded miners laughed. The third, dressed much like the others but standing a little apart, fiddled with his whiskey cup. The man's blue eyes registered his dislike of the story.

Israel stepped between Felker's cronies and the loner. Behind him, Louis watched the conclusion of a three-card monte game. The pale-skinned dealer raked in a two-thousand-dollar bet from his glum victim, whose loss the watchers cheered and applauded.

Felker kept talking with the two miners. The lantern hanging from the canvas directly above him cast an oily light on his bald head. The thin, weathered loner scratched his almost pure white beard and studied Israel, then Felker, who continued to ignore the Negro. Israel in turn scrutinized the miner from the corner of his eye. The man's long hair showed a few streaks of yellow among the gray. He was a decent-looking sort. And Israel guessed he might need help handling Felker.

He was correct. The bald man wouldn't even look at him for the better part of two minutes. Finally, struggling to contain the anger that had been building within him during the evening, Israel slapped a palm on the bar.

"Felker."

A slow, almost smug smile tugged up the corners of the bartender's mouth. Behind Felker, Israel saw a knotted rope hanging from a nail in one of the tent poles. When patrons grew too rowdy, men who tended bar used such a rope as a substitute for a ship's cat.

"Merry Christmas," Felker said in a sarcastic way. Israel started to dig in his pocket, then remembered he was supposed to put the order on credit. Felker mis-interpreted the move, reaching across the bar to fasten a hand on the mulatto's forearm:

"I know the rules around town say a nigger is entitled to one drink in any public place. But the rules are suspended when I'm tending the store."

Israel's hand clenched. He jerked free of Felker's grip.

"I came to buy twenty gallons of Thirty Rod for Kent's. We're out."

"So am I."

His stomach starting to hurt again, Israel pointed to a keg on a cradle "Doesn't appear that way."

"Empty," the balding man shrugged. "You try somewhere else. Niggers give this place a bad odor. 'Course, I have a pretty keen nose. I can smell coon twice as sharp as any hunting dog."

That brought a snicker from one of the two miners on Israel's right. He knew he should leave. Perhaps on a different evening, he would have. But everything that had happened tonight had made him testy.

"All right," he said. "But first I'll have a whiskey."

"No," Felker said. "No, you won't."

"Israel, I think we'd better go along," Louis said.

His brow hot, Israel drew a coin from his pocket. Felker seemed to be bouncing up and down, almost expectantly.

"Pour me one, Felker."

"I said no."

"Pour me one or I'll pour it myself."

Dennison's Exchange grew still. The racket from the street only heightened the silence as the mulatto and the white man stared at one another.

iv

For a moment, Israel didn't believe what he was seeing. Felker shrugged again, as if giving up.

The two miners had stepped back just a little in case of a confrontation. The lone miner, hunched over his drink as he had been ever since Israel and the boy walked in, watched the bartender. Felker wiped his hands on his apron, started to turn and reach for a cup—

Israel's astonishment slowed his reflexes. He wasn't prepared when Felker grabbed the rope from the tent pole, whirled and lashed at Israel's face.

The rope's knotted end nicked Israel's left eye, made him yell in surprise. Blinded and enraged, he shot his hands out to fasten on Felker's neck.

Israel gripped hard, his height helping him lean halfway across the bar. Felker squealed, hit at him with the rope. Israel heard Louis pleading with him to let go, then caught the sound of men rushing forward. But the flick of the rope on his eyeball had shattered his control. He choked Felker harder—

The two miners reached for him. The loner stepped away from the bar. Israel heard the cock of a pistol, then the miner's voice:

"You two stay out. And that goes for everyone else. Let them settle it."

Slobbering curses, Felker tried one more slash with the rope, bringing it up and over his shoulder. The end snapped against the hanging lantern, knocked it off its hook, sailed it behind the kegs where it broke and spilled oil that ignited a second later.

"Jesus Christ, a fire!" one of the monte dealers shouted as flame spurted up the canvas wall.

The canvas caught almost instantaneously, the whole rear wall of the Exchange turning to flame. Israel held Felker's throat, taking satisfaction from the way the man's eyes were starting to water. He applied more pressure, the heat from the canvas popping sweat onto his yellow face—

He wasn't choking Felker alone. He was choking the drivers who had beaten his mother so that she died before her time. He was choking the owner who had sold Cissie. He was even choking old President Polk, who had turned a sleepy little village into a stink-hole—

Felker's eyes bulged. Time held still for Israel, the hate in him almost intoxicating. The fire reached the tent's side walls and ceiling. A pole behind the bar became a column of flame, gave way—

Louis shouted, *"Israel—!"* as the ceiling started to buckle.

Israel let go, shoved Felker backward against the kegs. The bald man fell, flailing. The lone miner seized Israel by the shoulders, pulling him away:

"The ceiling's coming down—!"

The patrons had started a wild trample for the street. Somewhere a bell began to clang. "Go on, Louis!" he yelled, shoving the boy out of danger as the miner leaped away too. Israel stumbled against a rickety table that collapsed beneath him, tumbling him to the dirt floor—

A third of the canvas ceiling ripped and fell, enveloping Felker. He shrieked and disappeared in roaring flames. Lying on his belly, Israel screamed too when scorching canvas struck the backs of his outstretched legs—

"Burned that white man to death!"

"—own damn fault—"

"Get moving, get moving!"

The distant bell grew louder. Sobbing, Israel dug in his elbows, dragged himself out from under the canvas. His trousers smoldered, caught fire. He rolled over, thrashing the backs of his legs in the dirt. Overhead, another section of canvas tore loose—

"Boy, help me!"

That was the lone miner. Israel felt hands at his collar; vainly tried to focus his eyes. All he saw were leaping tatters of flame and, deep in the center, a charred, crawling thing that bleated like an animal as it died, Felker—

Hands hauled him along. His head banged against the ground. The ceiling glowed red-orange. He wondered whether he was going to hell for murder—

The flames disappeared in total darkness.

v

When Israel regained consciousness, he was lying in the mud of Portsmouth Square. He was dimly aware of people milling against a backdrop of glaring light. He heard loud crashes as the fire swallowed frame and canvas structures near the Exchange.

Bit by bit, his awareness returned—bringing pain that consumed him from his thighs downward. He writhed, groaning.

"Lift his legs, lift his legs! Where's that damn lard they sent for—?"

He thought that voice belonged to the miner who had pulled him out of the blazing tent. He felt hands on his brow, then a cheek pressed to his forehead:

"You'll be all right, Israel. We'll get you fixed up—"

The words grew incoherent as Louis broke down and cried.

"Stand back! Here come the pumpers!"

If he hadn't been in such agony, Israel might have laughed. San Francisco's fire equipment was worthy of nothing but laughter, and no one had taken steps to remedy the situation, even though people were extremely conscious of the hazard posed by the town's shoddy buildings. He thought he saw spokes blurring as men dragged one of the hand-driven pumpers toward the conflagration. Was it the antique from Hawaii, or the old wreck from the east that President Van Buren had once used to water his garden? *Odd,* Israel thought, *odd how your mind works when you're hurt bad—*

"I think we got him out soon enough," the lone miner said, sounding far away. "I hope so. Let's turn him—"

Israel screamed when men rolled him over, tore away the remains of his trousers and began to smear lard on his calves.

"Ma, ma—this way!"

That was Louis. With a great effort, Israel lifted his chin from the dirt. Sure enough, elbowing and pushing, there was Amanda—

Oh God, he thought, *she's getting mud all over that pretty yellow dress.*

Unconcerned, she hiked up her skirt and dropped to her knees beside him. Through his pain, he felt an almost overpowering happiness. She didn't care about her fancy dress. She cared about him. Maybe he'd been too hard on her—

He started to cry, just like Louis. Even the agony of

hands patting lard on his legs didn't bother him now—

Somewhere out of his field of vision, the lone miner asked, "Ma'am, does this man belong to you?"

"No—that is—he works for me—dear God, Israel, what happened?" She stroked the side of his face. He felt the roughness of that old, worn bracelet of rope. "Louis—someone—*tell me what happened!*"

A half dozen voices babbled at once. To Israel, the men around him were no more than fire-etched silhouettes. But Amanda's face was visible. He saw her flame-lit eyes widen when the miner grabbed her arm.

"What's the matter with you, are you crazy? Let go of—"

"Where'd you get this piece of rope, woman?"

"Damn you, let go!" She started to punch the miner.

"Where did you get it? What's your name?"

Curious, Israel thought, his pain so intense that it actually numbed and soothed him and sent him drifting back toward sleep. Most curious, the way Amanda was staring into the dark where the miner must have been standing. Her face had the strangest expression—

"My name's Amanda Kent. I don't see why you—"

"Amanda—"

Very strange, how that miner sounded as if he were about to weep too:

"I'm Jared. *Jared Kent—*"

Israel heard no more.

CHAPTER IV

To See the Elephant

JARED ADAM KENT couldn't remember when he'd celebrated a more remarkable and joyous Christmas day.

He didn't feel the least bit tired. His occasionally crippling rheumatism—a legacy from the years of trapping with Weatherby in the cold streams of the beaver country—hardly bothered him at all.

He should have been exhausted. He was already weary when he reached San Francisco after the long ride from the mining camp called Hopeful located all the way up on the east branch of the north fork of the Feather River. He hadn't slept a single minute since glancing up outside the burning saloon and seeing a woman whose face stirred a memory; a woman whose wrist, circled by a worn bit of rope, brought a miracle he'd never dreamed he'd witness.

In the first hour after Amanda's mulatto had been dragged from the flames, Jared barely said half a dozen coherent words to his cousin. They'd wept and hugged each other for a couple of minutes, but things were too frantic for much more than that.

Amanda saw to Israel's removal to his shanty behind the restaurant she owned. Then she summoned a doctor. The sleepy physician dressed and bandaged the Negro's burned legs. He dosed the groaning man with brandy, assuring Amanda that although Israel would suffer pain for a few weeks, as well as the unpleasantness of skin sloughing away, in his professional opinion Israel would eventually be good as new.

With that problem attended to, Jared and his cousin spent three quarters of an hour surveying the damage done by the fire. It had leveled several blocks surrounding the Exchange before being brought under control. Booming gambling houses such as the Verandah and McCabe's El Dorado had disappeared into smoldering ashes. Had the wind been blowing in a different direction, Kent's would very likely have burned too.

Amanda introduced Jared to a man named Sam Brannan who apparently owned a good deal of real estate in the town. Brannan predicted San Francisco could expect many more fires in view of the building boom and the flimsy nature of most of the construction. He suggested that volunteer fire companies be organized, and better pumping equipment secured. Amanda pledged financial support of such a program. But Jared somehow had the feeling her heart wasn't in the promise.

Finally, toward midnight, they returned to her place, to begin building a bridge of words across the years since 1814. They talked all through the night.

Now it was Christmas morning. Jared was relaxing in a chair by a back room window, with Amanda's handsome, swarthy young son curled up at his feet.

Jared wiggled his nose. "Smells mighty good, Amanda. My, you've come a far piece in the world. I've never met anybody else who had a French cook."

Because of all the excitement, Amanda hadn't bothered to change her mud-spotted yellow gown. She was seated on the piano bench, hands in her lap, and he had to admit she'd amply fulfilled the promise of beauty she'd shown as a child. She was slender but full-bosomed. Her dark eyes were as lively as ever. And the gray in her hair seemed to enhance her beauty, not detract from it.

Jared's mind could hardly hold all that she'd told him in the breathless bursts of conversation before dawn:

Her life with the Teton Sioux. Her marriage to a Spanish trapper. Her difficult experience in Texas. The Mexican officer, Cordoba—and Louis' birth. Then her migration to California, and now sudden prosperity brought on by the discovery of gold—

Still, all night long, he'd sensed she was holding something back. At those times, her eyes had a hard glint difficult to reconcile with the sight of the happy, self-assured woman seated opposite him, or the memory of the young girl he'd last seen at Stone's River in Tennessee—

"Felix is a jewel," she said. "He came from Paris. He keeps talking about going to the gold fields, but I make it worth his while to stay here. He's cooking something special for dinner. Eggs and oysters. It's quite delicious, the way he spices it. Oh, Jared—" Laughing, she hugged her knees. "This still seems like a dream."

"If it is, I hope we don't wake up before we eat. I'm damn near starved to death."

"We'll sit down the minute Billy finishes nailing boards across the broken window."

From Jared's feet, Louis asked, "Could we sing a Christmas carol first, ma?"

"Why, yes. Though with Bart gone, we've no one to play."

"Who's this Bart fellow?" Jared asked.

Louis glanced questioningly at his mother. From the front of the building, the steady beat of Billy Beadle's hammer thudded. At six in the morning, Amanda had taken what Louis said was a most unusual step. She'd ordered the burly Australian to hang out a sign announcing that Kent's would be closed the entire day.

Still smiling, Amanda told her cousin, "His full name's Barton McGill. He works for a New York ship line. Captains one of their clippers. I guess you could call him my gentleman friend—"

"He's from Charleston," Louis put in. "We don't get to see him often."

"Well—" Jared stretched luxuriously, then leaned back in the chair. The mellow December sun highlighted the few strands of yellow still visible in his white hair. "—I'd be happy to have him here to share this wonderful day. I wish my son were here too."

"A Methodist minister." Amanda shook her head. "I can hardly believe it."

Jared's expression was tinged with sadness for a moment. "I couldn't either when he first broached the idea after his conversations with Reverend Lee. Then I got to thinking. There's a peculiar streak on my side of the family. Rebellious. The Fletcher blood, your mother used to call it. I expect Jephtha inherited it from me. So it was probably natural for him to strike off in some unexpected direction."

"Where is your son, sir?" Louis had missed all of the night's conversation.

"In Lexington, a little place in the Shenandoah valley in Virginia. He and his wife Fan have had four children so far. Three have survived. All boys." He ticked them on his fingers. "Gideon was born in forty-three, Matthew a year later. Annabelle lived only two weeks in forty-five. Jeremiah came along fourteen months after that—"

"Is Jephtha happy in Virginia?" Amanda asked.

Jared frowned. "If I read his letters correctly, no. His last one came on a packet just before I left Oregon. Gloomier than ever. It's the chattel slavery question that upsets him. He's loyal to his wife and her people—they're southerners. And when the Methodist Episcopal Church split over slavery five years ago, he stayed with the southern faction. But what he sees of the system torments his conscience. Of late, unbearably."

"Well, we're a long way from those problems out here," Amanda said. "Though one of these days, I expect I'll be right in the middle of them." She gazed at her cousin. "Eventually I'm going back east."

Jared noticed the way young Louis began to fool with the loose sole of one of his boots. The boy was frowning. Amanda went on:

"I want to see our old home. That's one of the reasons I'm working so hard to make money."

Jared flexed his fingers; examined his swollen knuckle-joints. The hard glint had returned to her eyes. It bothered him.

"You didn't mention that last night—" he began.

She shrugged, gazing past him to the sunlit window. "It's something I decided a couple of years ago—" Her stern look softened. "We can discuss it after dinner."

Louis tried to re-direct the conversation to a more agreeable topic:

"Was your wife really an Indian, cousin Jared?"

"A Shoshoni," he nodded. "A fine woman. She was called Grass Singing."

"That's a pretty name."

"I wish I'd been able to make a pretty life for her—"

He cut off the thought, much as he'd cut off an earlier frustration by leaving the failing farm in the Willamette Valley in the late summer of '48.

"—but all in all—" He spoke for his cousin's benefit now. "—I have very few regrets. I sired a son to keep the Kent name alive—without ever imagining you'd be doing the same, Amanda. For a long time, I made enough money to live just the way I wanted. I loved the fur trade until my partner, Elijah Weatherby, died. His passing took some of the joy out of it—maybe because it made me realize I was getting old. Then business dropped off. I thought raising wheat in Oregon might be a good thing to try. I was wrong there. Like my father, I wasn't cut out to be a farmer—"

A sadness touched him. His imagination showed him dim pictures of the house on Beacon Street from which he'd fled after setting fire to the printing house and shooting the man who had helped Hamilton Stovall steal Kent's. He could look back on all of that without anger. Once, he'd harbored hopes of revenge. But they had been burned out of him by distance, and time, and his gradual acceptance of the life he'd made for himself in a land he found beautiful—

Aware of Louis and Amanda watching him, he resumed, "I sold the farm when Oregon got the news of the gold. I always did like seeing new sights, and Captain Sutter handed me a perfect opportunity. I tramped down the coast on foot and went straight to his fort. There, I heard about a strike in a new camp called Hopeful, so that's where I headed. I've done pretty well, too. That is, the Ophir Mineralogical Combine's done well—"

Louis said, "Ophir what?"

"Mineralogical Combine." Jared grinned. "Fancy name for a pretty grimy operation. There are three of us in it. We each had adjoining claims along the stream. The first men on the site agreed no claim would be larger than a hundred square feet. By putting three together and building ourselves a cradle to speed up the processing of the dirt, we see more color than we would if we worked alone. Color means the yellow color of the dust or flakes," he added in an aside to Louis.

Amanda inquired about Jared's partners.

"One's an Englishman. He was a draper over in Liverpool. The other man's a little Baptist storekeeper from Georgia. He came across the mountains with a wagon train. He's the one who slapped on the splendiferous name. He said that in the Bible, in King Solomon's time, Ophir was a land famous for apes, ivory, peacocks—and gold. We're getting a fair amount of it, but we could get a lot more if we could hire decent help."

Louis raised his eyebrows. "You mean some of the men in the diggings don't have claims?"

"The ones that are too lazy. They'll pick up a few dollars for day wages, then go on a week-long tear. We've tried hiring a few Pikes. Every one of them's proved to be worthless."

"What's a Pike, sir?"

"Originally it meant a fellow from Pike County, Missouri. Now the name sticks to anybody with small education and a big temper. If a man says he's a Pike, you can be halfway certain he's running from the law, too. There are a lot of men of that sort in the diggings. They even make up tunes about 'em—"

Leaning back, he began to wave his hand to and fro, smiling at Louis as he croaked in an off-key way:

"Oh, what was your name in the States?
"Was it Thompson, or Johnson, or Bates?"

Louis clapped in delight. Amanda looked impatient.

"Did you murder your wife,
"And then run for your life?
"Say, what was your name in the States?"

"I'll have to teach that one to Captain Bart—"

Amanda interrupted: "How much gold are you mining, Jared?"

"Lately it's averaged out to near twenty-four, twenty-five hundred dollars a week—"

He was startled by her look of intense concentration: "You could wind up a millionaire."

"Sure—in about thirty years."

"Thirty! I calculate nine or ten."

"You forgot my partners. It's share and share alike."

"Yes, I did forget that."

"The claim may peter out, too. A great many do."

She looked disappointed. What in the world was going on inside her head?

Louis diverted him with another question: "Do you work every day?"

"Every day except Sunday. It's not a matter of miners being godly—just worn out. Sunday's actually the wildest day of the week in Hopeful. Sometimes we have dances—"

"Are there women in the camps?"

"Once in a while a female of—call it low character—shows up and spends a couple of nights. If you don't believe grown men can go crazy, you should be there when a woman arrives. Women of that sort aren't interested in dancing, though. For dances, the men take turns tying ribbons on their arms and acting the woman's part. But no matter what you do to liven up the routine, camp life still gets boring as the devil. My partners and I drew lots to see who took the first holiday. I was lucky, I picked the short straw. So I got to come down to see the elephant. I've always wanted to see one elephant or another," he sighed. "I guess that's why I never really lived up to this—"

From his pocket he drew a tarnished medal, handing it to Louis for inspection. On the obverse was a design of a tea bottle and an inscription in Latin. The reverse bore the words *Kent and Son* and a date—1810.

"Your grandfather gave me that," Jared explained. "It was part of a fob, but the green ribbon's long gone. The Latin means take a stand and make a mark."

But Louis was more interested in something else the bearded man had said:

"There aren't any elephants in San Francisco, cousin Jared."

"Oh, that's only an expression. From an old story of the farmer who had read about elephants but never set eyes on one. The circus came to a town near his home, so he loaded his wagon with eggs he meant to sell and drove in to watch the circus parade. The elephant frightened his horse, the wagon overturned, and all the eggs broke. But the old farmer shrugged it off—'I don't give a hang, I've seen the elephant.' It means living through a bad experience. Or, the way some miners use it, just satisfying your curiosity."

He retrieved the medal and slipped it back in the pocket of his worn trousers.

"That's practically all I've done since Weatherby and I went up the Missouri in 1814, chase elephants. I suppose a man could do worse, though—"

"But now you're a rich gold miner!" Louis exclaimed.

"Not rich by a long shot, son. Not yet."

Amanda leaned forward. "What are you going to do with your share?"

"Just enjoy it while I can. I've never had much money. I'd like to take a trip back east myself. See Jephtha and my grandsons—"

A stranger looked at him from her eyes:

"And Boston?"

"No, Amanda, that's past history."

"Maybe not." But she didn't amplify the remark.

The back door opened. Billy Beadle ducked as he entered, slapping his hammer against his thigh:

"When's that bloody frog going to serve dinner? I've worked up a proper appetite—"

Amanda rose. "I'll go ask him." As she started out, she noticed the Australian frowning.

"Something wrong, Billy?"

"Nothing much," Billy replied with a too-quick shrug. "Thought you should know that a couple of Felker's chums wandered by while I was nailing—"

"Hounds?"

"Yes, ma'am. I've seen them before, though I'm not familiar with their names. They passed a few remarks about what happened to the little bast—excuse me, Louis. To Felker. Seems they don't think too kindly of any of us. I expect they're all bluff and brag, though."

Jared pointed to the corner where he'd put down his bag and his old Hawken rifle; he'd fetched them from a cheap hotel where he'd taken a room before going to the Exchange.

"I expect that'll handle them if they cause a fuss."

"I doubt they'd do it on Christmas," Billy said. "We can just relax and enjoy the grub."

Jared chuckled, amused at the way California slang had found its way into the Australian's vocabulary. Billy Beadle was a convicted thief, Amanda said. But he seemed a sunny, even-tempered sort.

"I'll stow my hammer," he said.

"And I'll prod Felix—"

Amanda and the Australian left. Jared stretched again, feeling drowsy in the sunlight. His knees had begun to ache a little. But he was supremely content; totally unworried about the dead man's friends.

ii

They began the Christmas celebration with a discordant but boisterous rendition of *Hark! The Herald Angels Sing,* which Billy Beadle directed with considerable flourish. Then Amanda said:

"Louis usually offers the grace, Jared. But if you don't object, I wish you'd do it—being the oldest of the family."

"Don't know whether that's a compliment or not," he smiled, then bowed his head along with the others.

It took a while for him to collect his thoughts. Even when he did, the words were hesitant:

"Lord God, this is Jared Kent speaking to you. I, uh, mention the name because I haven't been one of your most faithful followers. But I—we thank you for the blessings of this holy day, most particularly because—"

He cleared his throat and knuckled his misting eyes.

"—because you saw fit to re-unite the Kents, and for that we are in your everlasting debt. We thank you for the food of which we are about to partake, and for the kinship of loved ones after so many years of—"

He couldn't go on for a moment.

"After so many years," he repeated in a whisper. "Thank you, Amen."

Amanda slipped her hand over his and squeezed, not letting go for a good long time. Jared got himself under control and, smiling again, finally raised his head.

Amanda nodded briskly to the cook who had crossed himself at the completion of the grace:

"Felix, we're ready. Do your utmost."

He bowed low. "Madame Kent—that I have already done. You shall see!"

He bustled out, returning with platter after platter. The meal included his egg and oyster specialty, salmon, wild duck with rice, loaves of bread he'd baked before daylight, and plenty of rum and French champagne to lubricate Jared's tongue and deaden his rheumatic pains.

Amanda left once during the meal, to go out to the shanty and see to Israel. While she was gone, Jared carved himself a second slice of duck. The slightly greasy handle of the knife slipped in his hand. He nicked a finger. Louis ran for a bit of clean rag while Jared sat pale as milk, his stomach churning with the old, inexplicable nausea that had plagued him since childhood.

He had never been able to look at a wound—his or anyone else's—without being overcome by a few seconds of paralyzing sickness. He'd long ago given up trying to fathom why he was so afflicted. By force of will he usually managed to keep his reaction hidden while he waited for the infuriating nausea to pass, as it did now.

By the time Louis returned with the rag scrap and knotted it around Jared's finger, he was his old self again. Amanda came in to report Israel was sleeping comfortably.

Louis insisted on hearing Jared describe his life as a trapper. He obliged, sprinkling the story with anecdotes about the friends he'd made—his partner Weatherby; Old Gabe Bridger; the bandy-legged and pugnacious brigade captain, Kit Carson—and examples of the humor peculiar to the tough, often illiterate mountain men. He repeated their jokes about the Platte River—"The only water in America you have to chew."—and the spaciousness of the country they roamed:

"Since an echo takes eight hours to come back, you just shout 'Time to get up!' when you go to bed. Then of course there's the glass mountain—"

Louis was smiling but dubious.

"I've seen it!" Jared said. "A whole mountain exactly like the lens of a spy-glass. You can look through it and watch elk grazing twenty-five miles away. But it's so clear, there are thousands of dead birds around the base. They try to fly through it and knock their brains out."

"Glass mountain or not," Louis said, "it sounds like you've done some mighty exciting things."

"I've done what I had to do," Jared answered, with considerable truth. He drained the rum in his cup, gazed across the table at Amanda. "I never did find your mother, though. Weatherby and I searched two whole seasons, asking for her among the Teton Sioux—"

"They kept me out of sight whenever white traders arrived. I never got so much as a peek at visitors."

"I do recall a village where there was a brave named Plenty Coups," Jared reflected. "Weatherby and I visited it a year after I threw in with him. No one said a word about a white girl in the tepees. My God—" He shook his head. "If we'd only had sense enough to search a little on the sly—"

"We were probably closer than we knew," Amanda agreed.

"At least we didn't spend all our lives without seeing each other. I was plain lucky to draw the first holiday—"

"And we're delighted your mine's a success, sir," Billy Beadle said, toasting their visitor with a cup of champagne.

"Delighted and envious!" Felix growled from his place beside the Australian. "I should leave the kitchen! Go to the diggings—"

"You'd have a hard time," Jared advised him. "It's sad to say, but the Americans are pretty intolerant of foreigners."

"The same is true here, sir," Billy remarked. "I often wonder if it's a national disease—"

"Sometimes the behavior of Americans does make you think so," Amanda said. "I do get astonished at how easily people forget that everyone in this country is a foreigner—except the Indian."

"I would be happy to take my chances if I could find gold," Felix declared.

"Not many do," Jared said. "I'd guess ninety percent of the men in Hopeful will end up poorer than when they chased out here. I suppose I should count myself fortunate. At the rate the Ophir's producing now, it won't make me wealthy by the time I die. But at least I'll be comfortable."

"Comfortable enough to go east to see Jephtha—" Amanda began.

Unaccountably annoyed, he hedged:

"At this stage, it's no more than a thought—"

"A good thought. Louis and I could go with you. We could visit your son, and then Boston."

Louis' cheerful expression vanished. He snatched a slice of bread, tore it in two and stuffed a half in his mouth. Jared shook his head:

"Talking about Boston is pointless, Amanda. I have no desire to go there."

"I think you'll change your mind."

She didn't say why, though; just gave him an odd, challenging stare. Her face looked chalky in the pale orange light suffusing the room. Jared again had the feeling she wanted to tell him something. He almost urged her to it. But she stood up suddenly, murmuring that the coffee pot was empty.

Felix jumped to his feet. "I will go, madame—"

"No, you sit still." Before she turned away, Jared saw that hard glint in her eyes.

He frowned and plucked a crumb from his beard, wondering sadly whether they could ever be genuinely close again. As he well knew, time and hardship changed a person. It seemed to have changed her.

Yet he felt there was more to it. She was inexplicably tense; expectant—

I'm getting old, he thought. *I'm seeing phantoms where I should be seeing only a capable, grown-up woman who can't help being a stranger in many ways—*

But he wasn't convinced. She was hiding something. What was it?

Gazing at the curtain falling into place across the kitchen door, he asked himself whether he truly wanted to discover the answer.

iii

It was well after dark. A whale oil lamp glowed on the small table next to Jared's chair by the window.

Louis was already tucked into bed in his alcove. Billy Beadle had gone off to sit with Israel. The doctor had called at five, saying Israel would begin to experience a good deal of pain soon, and would need liberal doses of alcohol throughout the night. Felix had departed to circulate among the celebrants in the saloons. Even on Christmas, San Francisco had resumed its revelry.

Jared yawned, sleepy from the huge meal and the rounds of rum and coffee afterward. Amanda entered; she'd gone to settle an argument between two of the paying guests upstairs. He marveled at the expert way she handled the long-muzzled Colt's revolver—

She replaced the revolver on its pegs, then moved to a shelf of books he had noticed earlier. She drew one down and handed it to him.

Puzzled, Jared examined the stamped spine. *"Napoleon and his Marshals,"* he read aloud. "If you're recommending this to put me to sleep, I don't need it."

She ignored his wry smile: "Look at the title page."

He turned the first couple of leaves.

"My God! Kent and Son."

Amanda leaned over him, pointing:

"The date, Jared. Ten years ago."

His hand shook as he closed the cover. Now he understood what had caused her tension. He felt as if he'd walked to the rim of a chasm; a chasm from which he'd retreated years ago. The whale oil lamp made her eyes glare with a fierceness he found frightening.

"Where—where did you get this, Amanda?"

"From a trader down in the pueblo of Los Angeles." She pointed to the shelf. "Captain McGill has brought me others since then." She took hold of his shoulder. *"Stovall rebuilt the company!"*

Jared's head lifted, his eyes revealing his confusion. "I wonder if Jephtha knows. He attended divinity school in New England. He might have seen some books with the Kent imprint—"

"Entirely possible."

"If he did, why didn't he write me?"

"To spare your feelings, perhaps. He might think it was wiser to let the past stay buried. He might assume nothing could be done about it. That's where a minister and I would disagree. I believe something can and should be done."

Fingers still trembling, Jared laid the book aside. He covered his eyes with a palm; whispered:

"I knew there was something you were waiting to tell me. I could feel it all day—"

He dropped the hand to his lap, massaging the enlarged knuckles. The peace of Christmas had left him, replaced by a chaotic churn of emotion. He saw images—

The deck of the frigate *Constitution* on which he'd sailed when he was still a boy.

The hateful, foppishly handsome sixth lieutenant, Hamilton Stovall, who had tried to make him a party to shameful male degeneracy.

He saw Stovall aim a pistol in the smoke that hung over the frigate after its battle with *Guerriere*; saw the defensive slash of his own cutlass sever a cannon's breeching ropes.

He saw the cannon rolling free, and Stovall falling against it; he heard Stovall's shriek as his hands, then his right cheek struck the searing metal of the still-hot gun—

And he saw the morning when Hamilton Stovall, swinging a cane, had strolled into Kent's with his general manager to announce that he'd won the firm by cheating Aunt Harriet's husband at cards and dice—

He didn't want to ask the question that fairly screamed in his mind. But he did:

"Who's operating the printing house now? Stovall?"

"His employees."

"You're sure?"

"Positive."

A long silence. He covered his eyes again.

"I must say, Jared, I expected a stronger reaction."

"What kind of reaction?"

"Interest. Anger."

He shook his head. "Indulging my anger made a shambles of everything. I knew I had to begin a new life or I'd always be a prisoner of the old one." He drew a breath. "Forget Stovall. I have."

"How could you? *He took what belonged to us!*"

"In another life—another world. I'll never see Boston again."

She whispered, "I will."

"Is—is that the real reason you're working so hard out here?"

"Yes. Ever since I found the Headley book, I've worked for nothing else. Jared—"

She turned and walked slowly toward the piano bench. As she sat, her hand brushed the treble keys. A wild, jangling burst of notes filled the lamplit room, then slowly died away.

"—Hamilton Stovall is still alive. Living in New York City—controlling the company from there—I've had Captain McGill make inquiries. He's ruined the firm. It publishes outdated reprints and scurrilous books that run counter to everything our family stood for. I've got to bring Kent and Son back into the hands of its rightful owners!"

"Not for my sake. I don't care any more."

Her mouth thinned. "You don't care that Stovall's let you believe you were a murderer all these years?"

"Let me believe—? What do you mean?"

"Do you remember the man you shot at the printing house?"

"The man I killed? Walpole? Yes—"

"You didn't kill him."

"What?"

She rushed to him, kneeling and gripping his arms: "He didn't die. He's alive today—just as Stovall is! Stovall probably laughs about it. Jared, believe me. Captain McGill confirmed it—Walpole is *alive*. Isn't that reason enough to fight for the company? *And* hurt Stovall if he gets in the way?"

His emotional defenses broke. Hate seethed through him—fully the match of the hate he saw in his cousin's eyes.

iv

At last, terrified of where the discussion could lead, he fought back his rage:

"No, Amanda—no. I'm done with Stovall. I buried the past—"

"You can't bury the fact that you're a member of the Kent family!"

His mouth wrenched. "Hardly an outstanding one—"

"If that's how you feel, now's your chance to change things!"

"I don't think you and I are talking about the same kind of accomplishment—"

"What the hell does that mean?"

Jared drew the medal from his pocket; held the obverse toward the light:

"I remember your father speaking to me before I went out on the *Constitution* the second time. He talked about the Kents always taking the high road. The road of cause. Contribution. Commitment—I think those were the words he used. If so, I haven't lived up to them. But at least I've lived so I'm not ashamed of myself—"

"By God, I don't see any shame in taking what's ours!"

"But you talk about hurting Stovall at the same time—"

"He deserves it! If he tries to block us, let him suffer!"

Jared shook his head. "I don't want anything like that on my conscience. I'm satisfied with what I finally made of my life. I married a good woman. I earned a living honestly. I fathered a boy who angered and disappointed me when he went his own way—then I finally realized it was a worthy way. In Boston I was—I was headstrong—vindictive—"

The medal disappeared as he clenched his hand.

"I've tried to live differently as a grown man. I don't want to go back to the past! As if we ever could—"

"We can. And it's our duty."

"Not mine. I'm an old man. Fifty-one—"

"An old man? Or a weak one?"

Stunned, he stared at her as she knelt beside him:

"I don't think I know you any more, Amanda."

She pounded a fist on his knee, not realizing the pain it caused:

"I only want what's rightfully ours! We've both lived too long with too little—"

"What is it you're really after? Stovall's money? Stovall's life—?"

"I want *justice,* goddamn it! I want Kent and Son! For myself—and my boy."

"And you don't care what you do to get it?"

A brief silence. Then:

"No, I don't."

In the crucible of memory, Jared saw the face of Hamilton Stovall on the day the printing house burned. He saw the white silk bandana hiding Stovall's scarred flesh, and remembered his own intense rage—

But trying to undo a wrong more than thirty years old was futile. Futile and destructive. He saw the latter very clearly—on Amanda's own face.

His anger left him again. Gently, he touched his cousin's forehead:

"Don't do it. Trying to hurt Stovall, you'll only hurt yourself. And your son. Do you notice how he looks at you when you talk about Boston? He's afraid of you—just as I was afraid of my father before he disappeared—"

He pressed her cheeks with both hands:

"Amanda, I beg you—don't go back."

She jumped up, whirling away:

"God, you've turned spineless!"

Grieved, he shook his head. He stood up; took a step toward her. Darkness seemed to close in from the corners of the room. He thought he heard a foot fall outside; probably Billy Beadle walking in the yard—

"Not spineless: Sensible. The more you hate, the more it poisons y—"

"Oh, yes," she broke in, "I've heard that pious little sentiment before. From Captain McGill, among others. Spare me!"

"Amanda—"

His shoulders lifted. Some of the age seemed to drop from him; his blue eyes grew nearly as fierce as hers.

"—I'm afraid this is going to be a short reunion."

That finally gave her pause:

"Short? Why?"

"Because I don't want any part of rebuilding the Kent family in the way you propose to do it."

"Jared, *Jared—!*" She came to him, speaking more calmly. "I only want to see the family live again!"

"There's nothing wrong with that—except the price you intend to pay."

"I had hoped you'd pay your share."

His eyes narrowed. "With what I'm taking from the claim?"

"Yes. In a year or two we could rent a decent house in the east. Find that law firm whose name I can nev—"

She stopped, her eyes flicking to the glass beyond the lamp.

"There's someone out th—*Jared, move away from the window—*"

Her rush to push him came too late. Two pistols exploded in the back yard. He heard glass shatter an instant before he was slammed forward against the piano, struck in the back.

v

Amanda screamed. Louis burst from the alcove—*"You stay in there, Louis!"*—and Jared dropped to his knees, trying to grip the leg of the piano. He was short of breath. His spine hurt. The skin beneath his flannel shirt was warm and sticky—

"Sneaky, murdering *bastards*—!"

He heard Amanda's voice from afar; she'd run outside. Her revolver boomed once, then again. In the dormitory upstairs, men shouted questions at one another. Billy Beadle yelled in the yard, but the words made no sense.

He lost his grip on the piano leg, struck the carpet, his beard twisted under one cheek. His eyes filled with tears of pain. Peculiar, disconnected thoughts tumbled in his mind:

Too much cold water gets every trapper one day—

I'm old—

Oh, God, I hurt—

"Cousin Jared?"

That was Louis. He tried to answer. The pain was too consuming. He fainted.

vi

Voices. Faces. Indistinct. Hard to identify.

"—some of Felker's cronies, I don't doubt. Bloody scum! They got clean away in the dark—"

Who was that? He struggled to focus his eyes. He was lying in the shadow of the walnut table. Above him, a blurred figure in the lamplight, he finally recognized Billy Beadle.

Amanda spoke:

"Billy, you run for the doctor. Run like hell!"

The Australian vanished. In his place Jared saw his cousin. But he was only marginally aware of her. His mind distracted him:

So this is how it ends. Unexpectedly—at the wrong time—with too many words unsaid—too many things undone—

He cried his son's name; fought to sit up—

Amanda knelt. Her cool palm pressed him down. He thought he detected tears in her eyes. An inner voice spoke with bitterness:

At least she has enough heart left to weep.

Then he thought of the claim—the Ophir Mineralogical Com—

Com—

The last word eluded him.

What would become of his share?

He knew. The knowledge only sharpened his fear:

I've given her exactly what she shouldn't have—

"Don't," he said in a barely audible voice.

Amanda shook her head; shook it so hard, tears flew from her eyes. He wasn't speaking loud enough.

She rested her cheek against his. How warm her lips felt through the tangle of his beard—

"What did you say to me, Jared?"

"Said—don't take—the Ophir gold—"

"No, that belongs to your son."

"But he's—not worldly, he probably—won't want—"

He had no strength to say more.

"I'd never take it, you know that, Jared," she said, grief jumbling the words together. "But if Jephtha will permit me, I—I'll be the—the steward—of it—"

I know why. DON'T!

Pain shot upward through his neck into his head. A heavy haze obscured his sight of Amanda. He realized she was still on her knees, asking another question.

Through the roaring in his ears, he finally deciphered part of it:

"—attorneys."

"What?" The sound emerged as a guttural. His lips moved again, slowly: "What?"

"The name of the family attorneys—Boston—can't remember—"

Merciful God, how terribly he hurt! If only he'd drawn the long lot—never come to San Francisco—he might have seen his grandsons—

But not Amanda. Why were things never clear-cut? Why was there darkness and this unbearable pain? Why hadn't he been given time to persuade her to abandon her scheme for—

"Jared, please—tell me the name!"

Don't, Amanda. That's not the way your father wanted you to live—

"Jared, you're my blood kin. *You've got to tell me!*"

His lips jerked; a whisper:

"Ben—"

"What? Jared, try. *Try!*"

"Ben—" He spoke it as separate words. "Bow."

"Benbow. Benbow—yes, oh God, that's it!"

Was he wrong to tell her? The question savaged him as he arched his back and cried aloud, afraid because the lamplight had grown so dim.

Was he wrong? Was she only planning to do what needed to be done—?

No. It would harm her. He didn't want her harmed. He loved her. He tried to tell her as she leaned her cheek against his again, their tears mingling:

"Jared, oh Jared, don't die, we're all that's left to bring the Kents into the world again—"

Againagainagain wailed the echoes in his mind. The pain was lessening; the dark deepening. One last, clear thought eradicated his fear, now that he realized even fear wouldn't help him:

I have to go, Amanda. All of us have to go to see the elephant.

CHAPTER V

The Man Who Got in the Way

THE TWO MOUNTED FIGURES were dwarfed by the immensity of the dripping spruces and pines. A gray haze, not so thick as fog and not quite rain, hid the slopes of the Sierras they'd last seen at sunset the preceding evening. The mules struggled over the rocky terrain. Israel, leading the way, frequently had to resort to quirting the animals.

Most of their gear was packed in bags that bulged from the flanks of his mule. His trousers bulged as well. His legs were still wrapped in bandages.

Although the mulatto's burns could have been far worse, they'd nevertheless caused him considerable suffering. He'd never complained once—but the pain had shown on his face from the first day he'd hobbled out of his shanty and taken half a dozen steps before halting in the center of the back yard, sweating and drawing deep breaths.

Amanda had been watching from inside. Israel resumed walking in a moment or so, wincing each time he put weight on his feet but clearly determined to reach his goal. He'd finally come up the steps into the back room. Even though he'd made rapid progress since that first passage across the yard, walking was still difficult for him. Riding muleback was much less of a strain.

"Israel? How much further, do you think?"

"I calculate a mile or so. Unless we took the wrong fork a while back."

"I surely hope not. I'm worn out."

"So'm I. And the Sabbath's supposed to be a day of rest!"

The shod hoofs of the mules rang against rocks on the barely discernible trail. From their right drifted the purling of water, a stream hidden by the murk. Only by copying down the most explicit directions at Sutter's had they been able to wind their way up to this branch of the Feather.

Amanda's statement to Israel was no exaggeration. They'd been on the way from San Francisco six days now, making slow progress because of their unfamiliarity with the country. It was a trip she'd decided they must take, hardship or not.

But she'd be thankful when they reached their destination. Winter dampness seeped up the sleeves of her fleece-lined coat and penetrated the fabric of the jeans trousers tucked into her stout boots. Her thighs hurt from the bouncing and scraping of the saddle. With her hair pinned up beneath a flop-brimmed wool hat, and the holster of her revolver showing beneath the bottom of her coat, Amanda hardly resembled a woman. Nor did she feel much like one.

Since the dark of Christmas night, a kind of daze had enveloped her. Even now, more than three weeks into January of the new year, 1850, she hadn't entirely freed herself of despondency. To find Jared with such abruptness, then lose him just as abruptly, and all within a space of twenty-four hours, had been the profoundest sort of shock.

She had wept over his body for nearly an hour after the breath went out of it. It was Billy Beadle, she learned later, who finally pulled her away. She'd been hysterical. She didn't remember.

She was ashamed she'd behaved that way. She'd always prided herself on her strength. But flesh could only bear so much, and that one Christmas day had strained her physical and mental resources almost to the breaking point.

In the days that followed, she'd alternated between periods of depression whose only antidote was a stiff drink and the security of her bed, and other periods of almost frantic activity. During the latter, she tramped San Francisco with Billy, asking in the saloons and gambling halls for information about the identity of the men who had shot her cousin.

That the murderers were cronies of Felker's she didn't doubt. But the disbanded Hounds proved to be more than close-mouthed. They were elusive. Every known member of the group had vanished suddenly, perhaps fearing civic wrath of the kind that had caused the destruction of the Hounds' headquarters.

Amanda offered five hundred dollars for information, but got nothing more than a few useless scraps: this man had been seen playing cards with Felker; that one had accompanied him on a tour of the brothels. One man mentioned was at last identified as one of the pair who'd spoken to Billy on Christmas morning. He too was gone. The guilty had fled along with the innocent. Amanda soon realized she'd probably never locate the two who fired the fatal shots.

That wasn't the only cause of her troubled state. Jared's burial in San Francisco's crude hillside cemetery had been an ordeal.

The mourners were few. Amanda; Israel; solemn-faced Billy; Felix; and Louis. Only their nearness, and her own vow not to surrender totally to despair had made it possible for her to endure the brief service. She'd hugged Louis to her side, her other hand clutching Jared's fob medallion. As the earth rattled on the plank coffin, she closed her hand tighter and tighter on the medal's edge, using the physical pain to deaden the pain of her heart and her mind—

Afterward, she found herself constantly wishing Jared had been given a few more days at her side. She remembered his eyes during their argument just before the pistol balls shattered the window. He had looked at her with surprise—sorrow—and finally with loathing—

Or did she only imagine that?

Accompanying her depressed feeling was an almost abnormal awareness of the hampering effects of age. She'd been conscious of gradual changes for several years. Her energy seemed to drain away before a day was half done. She was frequently wakeful at night. Routine tasks sometimes looked too formidable until she rested a bit. For a week or two, she dwelled on this deterioration in a morbid way, unable to stop thinking of the ultimate end of the process.

The heightened sense of her own mortality brought on intense self-questioning. However briefly, perhaps Jared *had* seen her more clearly than she saw herself. Perhaps her determination—the determination that had burst inside her like a long-smoldering fire when she first saw the Headley book—had become a ruinous influence.

She'd long believed it was right to plan and work and save in order to go back to Boston. She thought the Kents' past and her son's future demanded it.

Yet recalling Jared's eyes and his dying plea for her to leave the gold alone, she doubted.

Was she letting the fury of wounded family pride warp her?

Or was she on the right course?

She didn't know.

But when it struck her that she should at least look after Jared's interests up in the diggings, she didn't put the idea aside. Instead, she immediately informed Israel that they were going.

Louis had received word of the forthcoming trip in

somber silence. To add to the gloom of the departure, she was worried about Bart McGill. The morning she and Israel set out, his ship was seven days overdue. He'd often spoken of hundred-knot winds that created an extreme hazard on the Cape Horn passage—

Now here she was, winding up a muddy track beneath sodden trees. She felt more than a little out of her element. How ridiculous for a woman almost forty-seven years old to go traipsing into the gold country like the very fools she'd once condemned.

Someone had to settle Jared's affairs, though—

To whose benefit? was the immediate response of her questioning conscience.

Confused again, she took comfort in remembering what she'd once told Luis Cordoba about the Mandan's vine to paradise. A human being did what seemed necessary and right, and left it to someone else to judge whether the sum of thousands of such decisions equaled a life lived with honor, or the lack of it. If her plan to recapture Kent's, tainted as it was by her hatred of Stovall, was impure—why, so was life itself. Despite Jared's warnings—and Bart's—she would go ahead. She had in effect made that choice the moment she informed Israel about the journey.

A sudden change in the irregular clopping of the mules' hoofs drew her from introspection. Ahead, between two great shoulders of granite, Israel had brought his mount to a halt.

"Guess we've arrived safe and sound," he called. He pointed. "There's civilization."

Amanda grimaced. Just beyond the mulatto, a hanged man dangled from the branch of a tree.

The corpse twisted as the rope unwound slowly. The tree limb creaked. A young man, Amanda saw as she rode up beside Israel. A young man with a black beard and distended eyeballs and flesh discolored by death.

She wondered what his crime had been—and what heaven's verdict on his life would be. The earthly decision was unmistakable.

The two mules clopped by the hanging tree to a place where the trail again descended. Listening, she heard a fiddle scraping *Old Dan Tucker*. The camp itself was still invisible in the mist.

They rode on till they came to a crudely lettered sign on a post driven into the ground:

welcom to Hopeful

Another sign—rather, the sheared-off top section—lay discarded nearby. Amanda leaned forward to read what had been painted on the board:

War! War! ! War! ! !
The celebrated Bull-killing Bear
KIT CARSON
will fight a Bull to the Death on Sunday
the 15th inst. at 3 p.m.

The rest was gone. Somewhere ahead, a gun went off. Men shouted. Her shoulders felt heavy. Foolish old woman, she thought.

Then she recalled the fob medallion in her pocket, and sat up straight. Two more shots exploded. She said:

"We may be sound, but who knows how safe?"

She unbuttoned her heavy coat; laid her right hand on the holstered revolver. Israel fell back to let her take the lead as the mules negotiated the muddy track that led toward lanterns now visible as smears of yellow in the murk.

ii

Even in San Francisco, Amanda had seldom seen such a confusion of humanity as she did that Sunday morning.

Hopeful straggled for more than half a mile along the bank of the Feather's branch, hemmed in on the landward side by nearly perpendicular hills covered with dark firs. The camp consisted exclusively of improvised housing—tents, scrap-lumber hovels and even a number of large packing cases from which the sides had been removed. Inside one of these, a man lay reading. In another, a couple of bearded miners played cards.

Amanda kept her hat brim pulled down as she and Israel rode along the main street. She saw no women anywhere. Men milled aimlessly on either side. Most were white, but here and there she spied a darker face; a Mexican; a Chilean. Two stocky youngsters appeared to be Kanakas from Hawaii. Most of the miners were dressed as Jared had been—heavy coats and trousers. There was an almost universal display of mustaches and chin whiskers.

Being hatless, Israel immediately attracted attention. A group lounging outside a tent identified as Sacramento Tom's started pointing. One man lobbed a stone. Another shouted:

"Ain't no claims for niggers here!"

Israel went rigid. Amanda laid a hand on his arm. He swallowed and gazed straight ahead.

Inside Sacramento Tom's, the fiddle-scraper swung into *The Old Oaken Bucket*. A man approached Amanda's mule, weaving. He doffed a filthy felt hat:

"Welcome, pilgrim! You don right, comin' to Hopeful. We're takin' it out of the ground with jackknives—"

Head down, she didn't respond. The man shrugged,

executed a half-turn, unbuttoned his pants and began to urinate in the mud.

On Amanda's left, three bearded fellows were carrying a wounded man out of another gambling tent, to the amusement of a small crowd. Had this been the source of the shots? She heard one of the watchers yell to someone in the tent:

"Frenchie, you be in miner's court at five sharp. The court'll decide whether Dick provoked you. That is—" A glance at the wounded man being borne away. "—if Dick's still alive to state his case."

A somewhat larger tent on the right announced itself as *The Bear Flag Palace.* From all the lanterns burning inside, some positioned above others, Amanda realized an enterprising soul had somehow rigged an upstairs section for the hotel. Immediately beyond the Palace, a general store—another tent—was doing a brisk business. Out in front, a shirt-sleeved clerk waved a pair of boots to half a dozen customers:

"Cowhide, double-soled, triple-pegged and guaranteed waterproof. Fit your road-smashers exactly! Who's going to start with a bid of two and a half ounces? Do I hear two and a half ounces of dust—?"

"You hear three!"

"Three and a half!"

"Four!"

Before Amanda passed by, the boots sold for nine ounces of dust. She admired the auctioneer's audacity.

She was so intent on watching the auction's conclusion, she failed to see another man, more tipsy than the first, who came lurching toward her mule from the left. He stumbled against the animal. The mule brayed, bucked—and Amanda went toppling off.

She struck on her right side, sinking three or four inches into the ooze and gasping for air. Her cheeks and forehead were splattered with mud. Israel tried to control his nervous mule as Amanda gained her knees. She grabbed for the top of her head. Her hat had fallen off—!

The tipsy gentleman, pink-faced, middle-aged and bearded, gaped:

"God bless us all, a woman! Madam—" He extended a pudgy hand. "Otto Plankveld, late of Albany, New York. Allow me to assist you—"

"No thanks, I'm all right," Amanda said, jumping up and jamming her hat on her head—too late:

"A woman! The Dutchman's got a woman—!"

"Ah, he's just blind drunk again—"

"No, you are. She's standin' right out there!"

Instantly, men rushed toward Amanda from both sides. The commotion spread, attracting others from up and down the street. The damp air grew so full of alcohol fumes, she might have been inside a distillery.

Poor Otto Plankveld was promptly elbowed to the rear of the crowd. Hands reached out. Teeth shone in sudden grins:

"Hey, dearie, you a workin' girl?"

"How much for a toss in bed?"

"How about in the mud? Is that cheaper?"

"Hell, she ain't no whore, she's too damn old—"

"Yeh, but she's got her nigger bully with her—"

"Gentlemen," Amanda began, not a little alarmed by the ring of jostling, inebriated men, "I'm looking for the Ophir—"

Before she could finish, a particularly foul-smelling fellow with a long white streak down the center of his sandy beard grabbed her left arm:

"The Ophir boys can wait a while to take their turn. There ain't another creature in Hopeful that's got what you got—"

With his other hand, he reached for her crotch.

She jerked out of his grip and took a hasty step backward.

"Hey, Pike, leave her alone, we seen her first!"

The man paid no attention, his smile fixed and ugly.

The portly Dutchman had squeezed his way up front again. He stepped between Amanda and the man identified as Pike. Not his name, probably, Amanda thought, recollecting Jared's remarks about the type.

The Pike shoved Plankveld:

"Back off, you fuckin' little sausage-eater."

"No. Can't you see she is a lady?"

"Shit, why would a lady come up here—'less it's to do business?"

"You've swilled too much liquor, Pike. She's a lady. You got to treat a lady decent. Especially on the Sabbath—"

"I'll Sabbath you, you two-legged jackass!" the Pike said in a slurred voice. He shoved Plankveld hard.

The crowd surged back as Plankveld staggered, then righted himself. Amanda intervened:

"Stop it! You've both drunk too much. I'll thank you to get out of my way."

Plankveld almost retreated. The bearded Pike refused, grinning as he faced the German. He wriggled his fingers, an invitation for the other man to attack.

Amanda's mule had wandered to a spot just beyond the two antagonists. The crowd closed in again. Israel, still mounted, was behind her. The only way to reach her mule was to remove the two drunks from her path:

"*Did you hear me?* Stand aside."

The Pike called her a filthy name.

Muddy and exhausted from the long journey, her temper was short. She saw the quarrelsome Pike as an infuriating obstacle. She started to yell at him. Before she could, he reached for Plankveld's neck.

The German tried to fend him off. The Pike's arms were longer. He locked hands on Plankveld's throat, yanked him forward and drove a knee into his genitals.

Plankveld cried out. The Pike flung him into the mud, laughed. A few watchers applauded. The crowd, completely ringing Amanda, Israel and the mules, grew larger every second. The Pike raised his right boot and brought it down on the German's temple.

This time Plankveld screamed, the right side of his head driven deep into the mud. Amanda shot her hand toward Israel, snatched the quirt from the mulatto's hand. Just as the Pike started to boot the German a second time, she laid the quirt across the back of his neck:

"Now will you stop and get out of the way?"

The Pike stood up to his full height. A hand darted to the back of his neck where the quirt had drawn blood. Amanda's palms started to sweat. Whimpering, Plankveld tried to crawl away.

The Pike faced Amanda. "Well, ain't the little bee got a sting—"

Israel kneed his mule forward to block the Pike's lunge at her. The bearded man pounded both fists into Israel's ribs. With a yell, the mulatto slid off the side of his mule just as Amanda had done, landing on his rump in the mud. Someone flung a handful at him, smearing his face. Almost at the same moment, the Pike stabbed a hand under his tattered coat and pulled a pocket pistol, a cheap copy of the popular large-caliber weapons built by the Philadelphia gunsmith Henry Deringer.

"I got me a sting too, woman—"

Behind Amanda, men yelled and scattered.

Perhaps if she hadn't been so tired and so furious at having been stupidly balked in the middle of the main street, she might have reacted in a different way; tried to reason with the Pike. But he was mad and so was she. His right hand lifted for a shot at close range. She saw the man not just as a witless bully but as a symbol of everything that stood between her and what she wanted—

The Pike pointed the stubby muzzle at her eyes. She darted to one side, freed the revolver from her holster while the Pike tried to correct his aim. Because he'd been drinking, his forearm shook. He closed his other hand over the one clutching the pistol, squinting as the muzzle steadied—

Amanda extended the revolver to the full length of her arm and fired.

The reverberations of the shot died slowly. The pocket pistol slipped from the Pike's hand. He dropped to his knees, astonished at the reddening hole drilled in his flannel shirt between the lapels of his old coat.

He lifted his head and stared at Amanda for one gruesome moment. Then his eyes shut. He fell face down in the mud.

Someone exclaimed, "By Christ, she killed him outright!"

Amanda whirled. "He was going to kill me!"

"He was too drunk to shoot straight. He'd have missed you sure—"

"And I was supposed to take a chance on that? No thank you!"

Men surged around her, shouting. Israel shoved them back:

"Get away! You get away from her—!" He bent to whisper, "Keep the gun handy, Miz Kent. We may need it before we're out of here—"

A violent argument erupted between factions in the crowd. Some claimed Amanda had committed cold-blooded murder, others that she had only defended herself against a man who would have done murder himself. Her right hand was shaking so badly, she could barely hold the Colt's.

Israel slipped an arm around her shoulder. A man demanded she attend miner's court at five. In the midst of the yelling, Plankveld picked himself up and tried to out-shout the others:

"*Nein*, no court! He attacked her! A worthless Pike—everybody knows he had a terrible temper—"

"I'll be in court!" Amanda said.

"Walk with me," Israel whispered, cradling her

against him and easing the revolver from her hand. "You bring the animals, will you please, sir?" he said to Plankveld.

The red-cheeked German nodded, grabbing the reins of the two mules. Amanda felt the unsteadiness of Israel's gait; he was favoring his left leg, the one burned worst.

Faces swam around her; glaring eyes; mouths bawling this or that point in connection with the argument. She and the lanky yellow-skinned man took two steps; then two more. They could go no further.

Israel raised the revolver. *Oh God, he's forgotten to revolve the cylinder. What if they notice—?*

Israel spoke politely to the men in front of him:

"We're looking for a claim called the Ophir and we'll be obliged if you permit us to go on our way."

Ugly grumbles. Israel swallowed again, glancing around the ring of miners. He adjusted his grip on the revolver he was holding at waist level. Several men eyed the barrel apprehensively.

"I'm asking you all to stand aside," Israel said.

"Shit," a man grumbled, "the Pike ain't worth gettin' killed over. Let the nigger through, you boys."

"Thank you," Israel said quietly. The men fell back.

Dizzy for a moment, Amanda closed her eyes. "Come on," Israel whispered.

"Hurry—I got the mules," Plankveld said from behind them.

"I can walk," Amanda said. "You ride, Israel. I know your legs are hurting—"

"Be that as it may, just lean on me till we're clear—thank you, gentlemen, thank you—"

He led her past the miners and out into the open. After they'd gone a short distance up the street, he relaxed a little:

"Well, we got out of that. For the moment. Sure wish you hadn't killed that fellow—"

Infuriated, she wrenched away:

"He was aiming that hide-out gun straight at me!"

The mulatto's sad gaze accused her. "Yes, but it holds only one ball. Those men called it right—the Pike was full of whiskey, and wobbly. I think you could have dodged him."

"That's not your place to say!"

Israel glared suddenly:

"Miz Kent, don't you forget—I don't have any *place* except the one I pick."

"All right, all right—I'm sorry."

"Never seen you so riled as when you pulled the trigger—" He sighed. "Guess it's too late to do anything now."

She held back a retort because she knew he was right. She'd lost control; aimed for the Pike's chest when a leg would have served. But her pent-up anger and her desire to reach the claim had pushed her beyond reason. She was terrified to discover that she was capable of such irrational rage when she was opposed.

iii

The Ophir Mineralogical Combine was a plot of ground thirty feet long and ten deep along the excavated bank of the stream. Plankveld led them to the claim's boundary, stopping near a large tent. A piece of mining equipment stood on a sandbar three yards out from the bank. Constructed of wood, it resembled an oversized child's cradle. A long chute jutted from one end.

The bedraggled German handed the reins of the mules to Israel, who kept shifting his weight from foot to foot. Amanda's revolver was back in the holster, but she still felt the after-effects of the shooting—which apparently had already been forgotten by most of the camp.

Fiddle music and laughter drifted down to the claim.

"Madam," Plankveld said, "take my advice. Do not go alone anywhere in Hopeful today."

"Why not?"

"Scurrilous as he was, the Pike had one or two friends."

"All right, I'll do as you say. Israel will come to court with me. Where is it?"

"The Bear Flag Palace."

"At five. Thank you for helping us, Mr. Plankveld. I'm sorry you got dragged into a scrape because of me."

"The Pike—Armbruster, I think that was his real name—he was known for his bad ways—" The German picked at a gob of mud in his beard, then aimed a thumb at the lamplit tent. "Those boys won't be too unhappy over what happened. The Pike worked for them four days, got drunk and smashed up their cradle. Cost Mr. Nichols plenty to buy lumber for another—"

"Mr. Nichols is one of the partners?"

"*Ja*, one of the three. Just two left now. Another, Mr. Kent, he went down to San Francisco and never came back. Too bad, you know? The Ophir, she's one of the best. Starting to produce close to a thousand dollars a day—"

Amanda caught her breath. The tent flap lifted:

"I say—someone there?"

She turned to confront a spare, rather handsome man of about thirty. He was bearded and dressed like the other miners. But one touch distinguished him—a bright sash of scarlet silk.

She answered the query in a voice still a bit unsteady:

"Yes, my name is Amanda Kent—"

The man's debonair smile faded. "Kent, did you say?"

She thought of Jared living with guilt all his days. She thought of the man who had caused that guilt. And suddenly, her own guilt over shooting the Pike vanished. She spoke with authority:

"That's right. A third of this claim is mine."

iv

Francis Pelham, the former draper from the British Isles, and Joseph Nichols, the rotund little Baptist from Georgia, welcomed Amanda into the tent. Nichols brought a basin of water and a few rags. After she'd cleaned her face and hands, they listened to her story. At the end, Nichols shook his head:

"I'm sorry indeed to hear of Jared's demise, Mrs. Kent. You have my most sincere sympathy. Your cousin was a straight sort."

"Can't say the same for that rascal Armbruster," Pelham remarked. "We took him on and later regretted it."

"So Mr. Plankveld told me," Amanda said.

The interior of the tent was crowded with shovels, pick axes, three cots, crates, a small stove and a table with a crooked leg. A set of balances rested on the table. Amanda saw no evidence of gold. She asked about that.

"We have a sort of community bank in Hopeful," Pelham explained. "Each miner pays a share to cover the wages of the clerk and three guards who work eight-hour shifts. Three other chaps watch the guards so they're not tempted. As you discovered, the atmosphere in this camp borders on the unbalanced—"

"Damnation!" Nichols jumped up from the crate on which he'd been sitting. He squashed his palm against his left leg just above the knee. Then he blushed:

"I beg your pardon for the profanity. We're all afflicted with the quicks and slows."

"Joseph means fleas and lice," Pelham said. "Are you sure I can't warm a biscuit for you, Mrs. Kent? You look a trifle pale."

"I'm fine," she lied.

"And nervy," Nichols said. "I 'spect you realize by now that you risked your life coming here."

She shrugged. "I had no choice. I heard from miners in San Francisco that any man who gets killed or disappears forfeits his claim."

"Entirely correct," Pelham returned with a precise nod. "We had all but given Jared up for lost. I share Joseph's grief at his unhappy end."

"Well, that's past," Amanda said.

"Would you perchance like some coffee?"

"I'd like some whiskey if you have it."

"We do—for medicinal purposes," Nichols told her.

Pelham grinned. "And the Sabbath."

Nichols poured. No mention was made of refreshments for Israel, who'd been standing silently ever since the four entered the tent. Nichols gaped as Amanda downed the half cup of liquor in four swift swallows.

The alcohol was cheap and raw. It hurt her throat and stomach at first, but quickly began to exert a soothing effect. Feeling a little stronger, she said:

"Israel might like something—"

She didn't miss Nichols' frown. The mulatto noticed too. Amanda realized he was thinking of her welfare when he refused to turn the remark into an issue:

"Thank you anyway, Miz Kent, I'm not hungry or thirsty."

Amanda nodded, addressed the partners:

"To business, gentlemen. I came here principally because my cousin has a son in Virginia. I'll probably be going to visit him soon—"

"You wish for Joseph and me to buy out your cousin's interest?" Pelham broke in.

"No, I don't. I intend to take over Jared's third."

Pelham frowned. "Absentee ownership is not too practical. Every partner must share in the work—"

She turned her head toward Israel, who was standing

near the table. Despite the condition of his legs, his posture was erect. Amanda suspected that was probably for Nichols' benefit. She knew what the effort must be costing the mulatto.

"Israel has agreed to act as my representative," she said.

Joseph Nichols scratched his nose. "Well now, ma'am, I ought to caution you about one thing. Nigras don't receive a very cordial reception in the diggings—"

"Do they anywhere?" Israel asked. Nichols looked flustered.

"Mr. Nichols," Amanda said, "My cousin told me you're from Georgia—"

"That's true."

"Do you object to working with a man of color? As an equal?"

After a moment Nichols replied, "I can't pretend I've ever done it before. On the other hand, the Nichols family doesn't support the idea that slavery is an immutable institution, or even a good thing. Not all southerners do, you know. Too much fuss about cotton at the expense of everything else has caused the south to lag badly in manufacturing—"

"I should clear up one point," Amanda interrupted. "Israel is a free man. He'll return in a few weeks and work as hard as either of you. For that, he'll be paid a percentage of my cousin's share."

"Joseph—" Pelham confronted his partner. "Can you accept a colored man?"

Amanda shook her head. "There's no question of *acceptance*. I'm asking how Israel will be treated by—"

"Please, Miz Kent," the mulatto broke in. "Let him answer. If this is to be a going operation—"

Piqued, Nichols said, "It *is* a going operation."

"All right." Israel replied calmly. "Then if it's to continue as one, we have to be honest about how we feel toward each other. I'll do my portion of the hard labor, that I promise. But I won't sleep outside, or take my meals anywhere but right here."

Nichols reddened again. "I must say you're mighty assertive for a nigra—"

"You'll get used to it."

"Freedom *is* the law in California," Amanda said. "I assume you know the new government down in Monterey adopted an anti-slavery clause in the state constitution—?"

"Yes," Pelham said, "though we were frankly too busy to vote on the constitution. Not that I could, of course—I'm still a citizen of Her Majesty's country. But I do think it's remarkable that California declared itself a state before your federal union did so—"

"The question remains," Amanda said, "will Israel be welcome, or are you going to cause problems for him? If you are, you'll have problems with me."

Unsmiling, Francis Pelham answered, "Based on Armbruster's fate, Mrs. Kent, I would take that for granted. The decision is really Joseph's."

Nichols scratched his armpit. Shook his head, rose and walked to the coffee pot. Painfully conscious of everyone watching, he poured a cup. Then, slowly, he walked back to Israel.

"It'll take some effort, but I guess I can get used to it." Abruptly, he thrust the cup forward. "You sure you're not thirsty?"

With a grave smile, Israel said, "I believe I am now."

"Then here—help yourself."

Israel took the cup. "Thank you, Mr. Nichols."

"You all have any name besides Israel?"

"I don't," the mulatto admitted. "Some slaves adopted the last names of their masters but I refused."

Nichols looked startled: "You a runaway?"

"Many years ago. I was born on a plantation. My

papa was a white man. My momma never told me his name. She hated him, I guess. I ran away first chance I got. Is any of that important?"

"No, I 'spose it isn't—"

"Definitely not," Pelham said. "We've no time to dwell on past history, we're too bloody busy. It requires four men to work a claim efficiently, you know. Two must dig, a third must alternately shovel the dirt into the hopper of the cradle you saw outside, and pour in water. The fourth man rocks the cradle to filter the dust and flakes down the chute. The gold is caught behind the chute's transverse riffles, while the water and mud wash on—"

Israel nodded: "I'm familiar with placer mining, Mr. Pelham."

"Ah, but Joseph and I don't want to limit ourselves to placer mining." He began to speak with more animation, waving his cup as he paced back and forth. Amanda decided she liked the cut of Jared's partners. Israel too was interested in what the Britisher had to say:

"We're drawing a fine profit out of the claim now. We can do better if we can ever hire a dependable helper."

"Better than a thousand a day?" Amanda asked.

"In my opinion, yes."

Nichols said, "I heard Chinee boys are showing up in some of the camps, Francis. Hard workers. Maybe we'd have better luck with one of them—"

"And I wouldn't feel so outnumbered," Israel said. Nichols actually chuckled.

"A possibility," Pelham agreed. "My point is this, Mrs. Kent. If there is abundant gold in and along the rivers of California, it follows that it must wash down from somewhere. The Mexicans are undoubtedly correct when they speak about a *veta madre.*"

"A mother vein?"

"The boys around here call it mother lode," Nichols told her.

"Go on, Mr. Pelham."

"Men are already striking off for the slopes of the Sierras. The land's for the taking—no one's quite thrashed out the laws of ownership as yet. Separating gold from the quartz rock will require heavier equipment, however—"

"You've studied the subject, haven't you, Mr. Pelham?"

"I have. I did not leave my relatives—the city where I was born—and the pittance I earned in the drapery shop in order to enjoy a holiday in America. I came here for a purpose."

"Excellent."

"As soon as Joseph and I—"

"And Israel," she said.

"Quite so. As soon as we can lay up sufficient funds and hire trustworthy chaps to work *this* claim under the supervision of one of us, the other two will go to the mountains. As you undoubtedly know, the size of claims is settled by the common consent of those who arrive first. It's my plan to locate a promising site no one's discovered, and set the limits to suit ourselves." Pelham smiled. "Naturally we'll require your approval of such a venture, Mrs. Kent. But I gather from your remark of a few moments ago, you would not be averse to a speculative expedition—?"

"I wouldn't. If there's more money to be made, I insist you go."

"Capital!"

"The one thing we aren't going to do," Nichols declared, "is squander gold from here *or* the mountains on alcohol, games of chance and traveling prosti—fast women," he amended, beet-colored. "Like Francis, my home's a long way off—and not worth going back to, either. A big combine from Atlanta put up a general store four times the size of the mine and just half a mile away. Drove me out of business. I suffered the miseries of the damned on the Overland Trail. I dosed myself with gunpowder and Dr. Zoril's cure-all medicine and wore one of those blasted asafetida bags to prevent the cholera. Until I got used to the stinking alkali water, I thought a chamber pot would be my life's companion. We never saw an Indian—not one—but I was always scared of being murdered by some fool handling a gun without knowing how. One man in our train thought he heard an Indian whoop, jerked his rifle out of the wagon barrel first and shot himself to death. Why, there were guns popping day and night—!"

"I've heard the overland route is trying," Amanda said.

"Disillusioning would be more like it. I had to throw out most of the heavy goods I freighted from Georgia to Missouri with the last of my savings. I dumped a Franklin stove, a pile of furniture—anyone can find California just by following the trail of abandoned bedroom suites! But I got here, by heaven. I carved my name on Independence Rock, crossed the mountain ranges and even survived the stench of the rotting carcasses of horses and mules that collapsed in the Humboldt Sink. After all I went through, I'm not going to behave like that stupid Armbruster, throwing his dust away as fast as we paid him. I don't mind telling you we had some fierce conbobberations concerning his errant ways—"

"Conbobberations?" Amanda repeated.

Amused, Pelham said, "Arguments. If it's English they speak in this part of America, they're jolly well inventing it more quickly than I can learn it. However, Joseph addresses a valid point. I've observed that those who strike it rich, as the saying goes, need more than a spot of luck. Success requires ample perspiration and a diligent, scientific approach. We can control those two factors. If we also have luck when we move to the higher elevations, we could all be exceedingly wealthy. At very least, this claim alone should keep us comfortable for a long time."

"Comfortable isn't good enough, Mr. Pelham. I prefer rich."

He saluted her with his cup. "We shall do our best to shower you with gold, dear lady."

"My cousin's son is a preacher. I don't think he'll have much use for it. But I do, believe me."

At that, Israel stared down into his cup, visibly unhappy.

V

Amanda stood up. "Do they serve dinners at that so-called hotel on the main street?"

"The Bear Flag?" Nichols said. "You bet—pretty good ones."

"Outrageously over-priced, though," Pelham added.

"I'll pay the bill, so let's not worry about price. Since I have to be there for court at five, we might as well go up to the hotel now. We can eat and discuss more of the details of this—"

She noticed Nichols studying his muddied boots.

"You're not hungry, Mr. Nichols?"

"Ma'am—" A quick glance at Israel. "—please, now, don't anyone be insulted, but the Bear Flag has a policy—that is—"

Scarlet again, he stopped.

"Joseph means they don't serve persons of color," Pelham said quietly.

Weary as she was, Amanda still spoke firmly:

"I think they'll suspend their policy—" She moved her right hand to the butt of her holstered revolver. "—just about as quickly as that jury of miners will clear me when I tell my story."

"God save me," Pelham grinned, "you *are* a determined woman."

"Miz Kent usually gets whatever she goes after," Israel said. A second later he added, "Sometimes that can be downright harmful to a person."

He didn't mean the remark as a joke. Amanda knew she should call him down for it. With Nichols present, she concealed her anger and didn't.

That Israel spoke the truth was a risk she'd already accepted.

CHAPTER VI

The Parting

CAPTAIN BARTON McGILL hauled back his right foot and kicked the rock he'd stumbled over:

"Son of a *bitch!*"

The rock went skittering down the path that led to the top of the semaphore hill. A few steps above him, Amanda waited, her face hidden by her bonnet.

"My," she said as he joined her, "you're in a fierce temper."

"Are you surprised? I go away for three and a half months—" He linked her arm in his. They resumed their climb toward the ramshackle house and the wooden signal tower perched on the hilltop. "—and when I come back, nothing's the same. I waited two hours for the lighter from shore!"

"You just made the mistake of anchoring on the day the mail boat arrived, Bart."

"Ship," he grumped. "Mail ship."

A fragrant cigar clenched between his fingers streamed smoke into the clear air of early evening. For February, the weather was unusually warm and beautiful. He took a puff of the cigar, asked:

"How often are they sending that steam monstrosity out here?"

"Twice a month."

"Never seen such crowds! Kicking, punching each other—must have been a couple of thousand people in those lines at the Post Office."

"You can turn a nice profit if you get a place at the front of a line. You can sell it to someone else for twenty-five, sometimes fifty dollars."

They circled the side of the hill about fifty feet from the summit. On the front porch of the house, the elderly man raised the arms on the semaphore tower to signal when a ship was sighted sat rocking slowly. A paper in his lap snapped in the wind.

Bart's gray eyes searched the soft gold sky, then the shadowed hills across the channel to the north. He didn't want to look behind him. He didn't care to be reminded of what he'd seen when he stepped on shore: masses of people; pack animals and every sort of wheeled conveyance; new buildings of raw pine or red brick—the only word for it was chaos.

What pained him most were all the abandoned ships in the harbor. It was unconscionable that worthy vessels should be left to rot. Their crews had succumbed to the lure of the diggings. Bart's own officers were standing armed guard on the *Manifest Destiny*. He'd threatened to whip and chain any man who attempted to jump ship.

The changes in San Francisco were only part of what troubled him, though. Certain changes in Amanda's situation—and in his own state of mind—were equally responsible. Feeling dour, he was sharp with her:

"That all you can think about these days? Profit?"

She wheeled to face him, her dark eyes catching the western light. He marveled at how lovely she was. She possessed a beauty no girl of sixteen or seventeen could hope to match. She was assured, not gawky; calm-spoken but purposeful. Secretly, he admired her strength, though he wouldn't have admitted it. Her strength was one reason he feared he'd lose her—

He realized he was extremely nervous. He had been worrying about this moment ever since the harrowing passage through the Strait of Magellan. For a time, he'd thought *Manifest Destiny* was going to founder and break apart in the violent winds and towering seas.

They'd run against the gale six days and six nights. Even now he could hear the roar of the waves smashing over the bows; feel the bite of the ropes that held him lashed to the helm.

He'd fought the storm as if it were a human enemy, dogged by a conviction that his luck had played out, and he'd never reach San Francisco. But he refused to give up. Finally, the clipper escaped the worst of the weather.

Although he'd already been awake seventy-two hours straight, he'd sprawled in his bunk for another two or three, thinking. Sorting out what he wanted of life and what he didn't. He reflected that perhaps only the prospect of imminent death could force a man to arrange his affairs. Lying there with the cabin lamps unlit, he'd reached a decision.

The freight-laden clipper arrived in San Francisco harbor nine days behind schedule. He'd been on shore since noon. He'd yet to speak to Amanda concerning the decision. He was fearful she wouldn't care about it. Besides, she had much to tell him about the past weeks—

And now the walk had taken a bad turn. Alone with her, away from the rowdy town, he'd hoped to tell her what was on his mind. Instead, just a moment ago, his nervousness and uncertainty had prodded him to make a remark better left unspoken.

She tugged off her sunbonnet as she faced him. Evening sunlight set her dark hair ablaze.

"Bart, that was unkind."

He studied the cherry-colored tip of his cigar: "Mentioning profit?"

"No, what you implied about me."

"Maybe so, sweet. But you have a look you didn't have last time I was here."

"I told you—a great deal has happened."

She leaned against him, letting him feel the curve of her body. The contact somehow heightened his uneasiness. He felt exactly like a callow boy, angry with the world because he expected it to reject him—

He tried to smile:

"I found that out the minute I walked into Kent's and Felix informed me Sam Brannan was the new owner. How much did you squeeze out of him?"

"I asked ninety thousand. Firm. He complained but he paid. It's prime real estate."

"That uppity nigra of yours told me he got himself a last name, too."

"Why shouldn't Israel adopt a last name? He's a free man. And he'll have a responsible position, helping to manage the claim—"

"Israel Hope." Bart shook his head. "The whole world's haywire. Niggers naming themselves after mining camps—Billy paid off and gone chasing up the Yuba—your cousin showing up from Oregon one day and getting shot the next—" He fixed her with an uncompromising stare. "And you weren't there when the lighter tied up at the pier."

"I've already apologized for that. I had to sign papers with Brannan."

"Well, it makes no difference."

"You sound as if it does."

"What the devil's my opinion worth? I'm just a common sea captain—" His bitterness grew uncontrollable. "I've never owned a speck of gold. And believe it or not, I've never killed a man."

Amanda stiffened. "How did you learn—?"

"Israel."

"He had no right—"

"Oh, don't score him for it. He was only recounting what happened in the camp. Besides, it'll be all over San Francisco soon. Someone from Hopeful is bound to come down here and talk about it."

"There's no reason why they'd—"

"There certainly is. Most women don't know which end of a gun to pick up, let alone how to shoot one. Have you decided what you're going to say to Louis when he finds out?"

"That I'm not guilty of any crime! The miner's court brought no charges against me. I can explain the shooting to him—"

"For his sake, I hope so."

Bart turned away, glowering down at the sprawling town. Lanterns beginning to wink in the dusk softened its jumbled look. Westward, darkness was thickening above the channel. A fog bank hid the horizon. The air was growing chilly.

He was ashamed of the things he'd said. Yet he'd said them, hadn't he? Hell! He ought to head back for the clipper this instant. The confusions of shore life were too much for him to handle any longer. Ferocious as the tides and winds could be, they were antagonists a man could understand, and master. Here, he understood nothing—not how to deal with the demons that drove Amanda, nor how to control himself so he didn't hurt her.

And he *had* hurt her—to the point where she couldn't even summon anger:

"Would you care to listen to my side of the shooting scrape, Bart?"

"No. The Pike got in your way. And nothing—no one—is allowed to do that, correct?"

She shook her head. "It sounds like you don't think much of me any longer."

Bitterly: "I think more of you than you'll ever realize. That's why I wish I'd never helped you find those books, or asked those damn questions. Now you won't stop until you own Kent's again. I suppose that means you won't be coming back here—?"

She avoided his eyes. "I haven't decided."

"You don't fib very well, sweet."

Her cheeks darkened.

"You going straight to Boston?"

"No, Virginia first—to visit Jared's son. He deserves to know what happened to his father."

"You could write him."

"I considered it. That sort of news isn't easy to deliver in any fashion. But I think I can soften it better in person."

He had no comment. After a moment, he said, "Suppose you get all your humanitarianism out of the way and approach Stovall and he refuses to sell—what will you do then? Aim a gun at his head?"

"You're unreasonable. And very unpleasant, I might add!"

She spun to gaze at the thicket of bare masts in the bay. He all but abandoned his plan to discuss what he'd decided after surviving the storm.

"I plead guilty to unpleasant," he said. "But not to unreasonable. Putting your personal crusade aside, you still don't know what you're getting into by deciding to settle in the east."

"I know very well."

"Permit me to disagree. There's real trouble brewing. Has been ever since that damn Democrat from Pennsylvania tried to tack his anti-slavery proviso onto the Congressional bill for money Polk could use to negotiate with Mexico."

"I've heard some people actually approve of Mr. Wilmot's proviso."

"Nobody down south approves of it! Wilmot tried to violate the 1820 compromise line. Tried to make sure slavery would be banned in any new land acquisitions, north *or* south. The proviso passed in the House, but the Senate voted it down, thank God. Still, ten state legislatures in the north endorsed it. Not that it makes much difference to me personally, but I'll be flogged if I can see how the federal government has any business interfering with the rights of states, new or old. There's no such thing as a state surrendering a little bit of her sovereignty. Just as old John Randolph of Roanoke said thirty years ago, that's like asking a lady to surrender a little bit of her chastity."

"It was my impression you avoided thinking about politics, Captain McGill."

"Who the hell can avoid it when everybody on the east coast talks of nothing else? The hotheads on both sides of the Congress are screaming because of Wilmot. Someone's got to settle the question of slavery in the new territories. And figure out a better system of enforcement for the fugitive slave laws. It better happen soon, too."

"The newspapers on the last mail packet said Mr. Clay proposes to work out a compromise of some sort."

"Yes, he's supposed to introduce a flock of bills to calm the abolitionists *and* the secessionists—"

The last word brought a sharp glance from Amanda.

"That's right, the southerners are raising that threat again. The damn fanatics in the north are driving them to it! You'll be drawn into it if you go back. Nobody can stay neutral—"

Now it was her turn to sink a barb:

"Except at sea?"

"I'm not ashamed to say I've retreated. I don't want any part of such quarreling. It never decides anything, it only hurts people. I hope the situation doesn't get worse, but I'm afraid it may. Zach Taylor was a capable soldier, but as a president, he's a failure. So it's up to the Congress to resolve the differences peaceably."

"Peaceably?" she repeated. "What other way is there?"

"There's war."

"Oh, Bart, the states would never fight over—"

"Slavery? Don't you be too sure. There's a terrible violent streak in this country, Amanda—your own experiences should prove that. In New York, just last spring, the mob nearly tore down the Astor Place Opera House—the one you can't walk into unless you wear kid gloves—"

"I think I read a short item about that. I don't recall any mention of the cause."

"A ridiculous feud between Forrest, the American actor, and Macready from England. The feeling against the high-toned Mr. Macready boiled over when the Opera House booked him in *Macbeth.* The city called out more than three hundred police—the militia—even artillery and cavalry. There were thugs packing the theatre—and thousands milling in the streets. Why, Christ, before it was over, water hydrants were knocked open, the pavement was torn up and chucked through the Opera House windows—more than twenty got killed, and about a hundred and fifty wounded. The police arrested that Judson fellow—the one who writes those pieces against foreigners under the name Ned Buntline—for trying to set fire to the building—while it was still occupied! They dragged him away screaming, 'Working men! Shall Americans or English rule?' If people will behave like maniacs because an English actor spouts his lines on a U.S. stage, just imagine what they might do over the nigra question. I sometimes think we were immortal fools to start this country with a revolution. It's helped put a stamp of respectability on violence ever since."

Amanda had no answer for his assertion. Maybe he'd broken through her unspoken confidence that she could deal with any problem, no matter how large; deal with it and overcome it—without being harmed by it. He pressed his momentary advantage:

"If those Congressional compromises are put to a vote, I've heard Calhoun may go to Washington, sick as he is. He knows the situation's desperate—he and

Webster and Clay and the other big thinkers. A big thinker I surely am not. But I'm content with my life because it lets me stay sane—no, you hear me out. You're a good woman, Amanda. A strong woman. But there's another part of you that's dangerous. In some ways you act like the windbag abolitionists—you've somehow got it in your head that you're one of those avenging goddesses of the Greeks or the Romans, I forget which—I read about them at the academy when I was no more than Louis' age. But the difference between you and one of the furies, sweet, is just this. They lived forever. You can't. You can be injured. Back east, you'll have to take sides politically. On either side, you'll be putting yourself in jeopardy. And you've already done it by declaring war on Stovall. So you're doubly vulnerable. I read some Bible when I was a boy, too. I remember St. Matthew. Jesus in the garden of Gethsemane—"

He gazed at her, hoping the meaning wouldn't be lost:

" 'All they that take the sword shall perish with the sword—' "

The wind murmured in the silence. The darkness was lowering rapidly. It muted the ugliness of the town below—but not the determination in her eyes:

"I'll take my chances."

"Yes—unfortunately—" He tried to smile. Failed. "That's the kind of woman you are."

"Why won't you understand, Bart—?" Unconsciously, she touched the rope bracelet. "Jared's death made it impossible for me to turn back. I would never have wished him murdered. But once it happened, I accepted it—and decided to make the most of it. I'll never have the same kind of opportunity."

With considerable cynicism, he said, "You're certainly counting on your cousin once removed wanting no share of what belonged to his father."

"He's a preacher. I don't think he'll be interested. Besides, all I intend to ask of him is the use of the money for a while. He'll be rewarded. Eventually I'll give Jephtha Kent ten times what he'd earn otherwise. I've discovered how to use money to make money—"

She brightened then, her head lifting as she whirled to face the dark eastern sky:

"Try to look at it from my side, Bart. Even apart from wanting to own the company again, it's exciting to think of going home. There's so much I've never seen. The cities. Fine houses and those huge factories they say are springing up everywhere. I want to ride a horse-car and a railroad—I'll have to educate myself, too. Learn good manners, and how to dress properly. And teach everything to Louis—"

"Staying out of the way of the political trouble all the while? It can't be done. I especially don't think you can do it."

"Why not?"

"Just the way you are."

"Would you mind explaining that remark?"

"For one thing, you have a peculiar liking for nigras—"

Amanda bristled: "And which side were you on during the Astor Place riot, Captain McGill?"

"What?"

"You sound like you might have joined the thugs trying to keep the American stage for Americans only!"

"Nonsense. I never take sides. I was still in the Atlantic, thank God. Besides, I was just using that as an example of the way people in this country knock each other in the head over any trivial—"

"I wouldn't call the slavery question trivial."

"No, I expect you wouldn't. You treat that damn Israel like an equal."

"I treat anyone I respect as an equal! I always have. It didn't matter whether it was a Sioux dog soldier, or a Mexican officer, or a black man—"

"God," he muttered, "you do have an inordinate fondness for inferior sorts."

"Such as my grandfather? You're absolutely right. My grandfather Philip was one of those *inferior sorts*—he was nothing when he came to this country. A penniless bastard boy. But he thought America might offer him something Europe couldn't then. A chance to succeed because of what he could do, not what he was. I'm of the opinion this country stands for that. And if my attitude means I'll get involved in this political furor you're so afraid of, then I guess I will. But first of all, I'm going to bring the printing house back into the family."

Bart shook his head. "You won't listen to reason on any subject, will you? Do you really imagine Stovall's going to sell out to someone named Kent?"

"I thought of that. For a while, I'll use my married name."

Bart's cigar had burned out long ago. With a grimace of disgust, he flung the stub into weeds beside the path. He noticed the old man on the porch of the house watching them, roused from his doze by their loud voices.

A sense of desperation filled him then. He was convinced Amanda was charting a course much more dangerous than she was able to recognize. He had to stop her if he could. There was one possible way. He'd glimpsed death in the seas of the Strait of Magellan, and reached a decision. He *had* to tell her—

"Look, sweet," he began, "I think I've said a lot more than I should have about your personal affairs—some of it in a pretty nasty way. I apologize."

Her expression gentled. "Accepted—if you'll accept mine."

He waved that aside. "We've wandered pretty far from what I wanted to say this evening. I told you about the storm we struck rounding the Horn—"

"Yes—Lord, I was frantic with worry when the clipper didn't arrive on schedule—"

"You aren't the only one whose life has changed. I thought we were all going to die before we outran that blow. When we got through it, I realized it was time to make some changes of my own—"

He reached for her shoulders and pulled her against him, inhaling the fresh-scrubbed scent of her skin. His fingertips moved lightly down her back.

"I thought a good deal about what I wanted. I decided what I wanted more than anything was you. I don't mean just occasionally. I mean all the time—"

He hugged her impulsively, and for a moment, silent in the wind, they savored the closeness. The dark had engulfed the semaphore hill and hidden them from the old man watching.

Finally Bart resumed:

"I'm about to say something I never imagined I'd say to another female after I got rid of the one who played hob with my life for twelve years—"

A hesitation.

"I love you."

She clasped him tightly. "Oh, Bart—you probably won't believe it because of the way I scold you for some of your notions—"

"Scold me!" He managed a chuckle. "Lop my fool head off with a verbal ax, you mean—"

"You hush and let me speak."

"All right."

"I love you too."

Stunning, unexpected joy welled inside him. Emotion made his words halting:

"I—I hardly see how it could be possible. God knows I'm not perfect. Tonight I've demonstrated that amply—"

"A woman doesn't ask for perfection and love in the same package, Bart. To love you, I don't have to agree with every word you utter—"

"Some men expect that of their women."

"Well, you know better than to expect it from me."

He chuckled again. "I surely do. I reckon that's one of the reasons you stick in a fellow's mind—"

Holding her close, his fears of rejection began to seem groundless. He went on with rising enthusiasm:

"If what you say about loving me's the gospel truth, Amanda—"

"It is."

"Then don't go back. Stay here with me. Away from the stump speakers and the wild-eyed philosophers and —all the things that can hurt you. Even though California's filling up, we'll be safer than we would be in Charleston, or New York. I'll make a good life for you. For your boy, too—"

He wiped his eyes. When she spoke again, her words and her tone told him she didn't yet understand all he was attempting to say:

"You work out of New York, Bart—"

"In the desk in my cabin, there's a paper I drew up three days ago. My resignation. I'll hand it to the Ball brothers at the end of this voyage. The next time I sail to California, it'll be for good. I can find a captain's berth on one of the coastal packets, I know I can—"

Again that affectionate merriment in her voice:

"My, it must be love if you're willing to learn to pilot one of those hateful steam ships—"

"To be with you I'd do damn near anything. Marry me, Amanda—"

He held her waist and poured out all the longing that had grown within him after the perilous passage:

"Marry me."

She drew in a breath; she was astonished:

"I had no idea you meant to propose—"

"What's so strange about it? People marry all the time!"

She kissed his cheek. "And I love you all the more for asking me. But—"

He pulled back, cold and fearful all at once:

"The answer's no?"

"I have an obligation, Bart."

"An obligation to what? To some Latin on a cheap piece of metal?"

"Please don't say that. I wouldn't have shown you Jared's medallion if I thought you'd make sport—"

"I'm *not* making sport! I'm trying to save you from what you're going to do to yourself!"

"It's my duty to go to Boston. I came from a family that—"

"A family that's nothing any more. Nothing! Your splendid *family* consists of one Methodist gospel-shouter and one former owner of a Texas whorehouse—"

He could almost feel her wrath like a physical blow:

"You certainly have a very peculiar way of demonstrating your affection, Captain McGill."

"Amanda—"

"Do you enjoy being cruel?"

"I'm trying to show you the truth! I care about what happens to you!"

He spun and stalked off into the high grass, hands clenched at his sides.

He'd suspected from the first that she'd refuse him. That was why he'd been so nervous. And now her refusal had unleashed rage again. He hated her strength almost as much as he hated his own lack of self-control—

He stood with his head down until his trembling worked itself out. Then, over his shoulder but loud enough for her to hear, he said:

"I've botched everything tonight. I'm sorry. I truly am, Amanda—"

He heard her footsteps in the grass. Felt her body against the back of his blue sea jacket. But something in him was dying. Not responding to the clasp of her arms around his waist from behind, nor to the press of her cheek against his shoulder:

"I understand why you're upset. You risk a lot—including pride—when you propose to a woman. I only wish I could say yes—"

His last hope died then; died and disappeared as completely as the house and tower had disappeared, only a short distance above on the hill's black summit. He blinked a couple of times, then pried her hands from his waist. He didn't want to let her know how much he was hurting. He tried to banter:

"All right. If there's anything a man should avoid, I reckon it's a committed woman—"

"If what you say about the east is true, I don't think you can stay uncommitted either."

"You just watch! Five thousand miles from New York, I won't be worrying about anything except course and cargo."

"No, you're talking differently than you did a couple of years ago. You're much more conversant with both sides of the political argument."

"The hell I am!"

"Then, you thought men who championed states' rights were fools. A while ago, you said the federal government shouldn't tamper with those rights. Maybe you've taken sides yourself. Unconsciously—"

That fueled his wrath all over again:

"Never. *Never!*"

"You *are* a southerner—"

"I'm a seaman—period. The only territory with a claim on me is the deck of a clipper!"

He stepped away from her, unwilling to discuss the subject further. She'd pointed out something of which he was totally unaware, and it had shaken him profoundly. He practically barked the next sentence:

"It's time we went back." Then—with a faint undertone of threat: "I've got a business offer to think over."

"An offer? You didn't say anything about—"

"No point in mentioning it earlier. I thought I'd be berthing out here from now on. Since I won't be, this other proposition has a lot to recommend it. Gentleman approached me just before I weighed anchor this trip. The manager of the New York office of the Royal Sceptre Line."

"Sounds like a British firm."

"It is. Headquarters in London. Most of their trade's with Africa and India. Guess I've built a pretty fair reputation with Ball Brothers—Royal Sceptre offered me a mighty handsome command on a brand new clipper, the *Prince Consort*. Might be just what I need to get me away from the mess in this country. 'Specially since there are no personal reasons for staying—"

"Would you be based in London?"

"Yes."

Unhappy, she fell in step beside him, letting him speak again when he was finally moved to it:

"Concerning your own trip, Amanda—I trust you don't have any thought of traveling on *Manifest Destiny*—"

"Why, yes, I do."

"You know there isn't passenger space."

"What about your cabin? You've offered it before."

"Not this time. It—it wouldn't be good for either of us. You find passage on another ship."

A silence, interrupted only by the crunch of their steps on the path.

"Will I see you in the east, Bart?"

"Can't say for sure."

"Does that mean you're going to England?"

He didn't answer.

Negotiating a steep place, she hung onto his arm for support. He almost pushed her hand away.

He smelled the night breeze. It was cold, and carried a salt tang. Already most of the lamps of the town were haloed by fog. But the hateful noise—the music, the braying laughter—grew steadily louder as they descended.

"Bart—"

"What?"

"Will you at least stay with me while you're in San Francisco?"

"Maybe it would be better if I didn't—"

"I want you to stay. I want us to have that much."

"We could have a lot more."

"I know. I'd say yes in a minute if it weren't for—"

"The family," he finished. "I guess I'll never appreciate what that family means to you. But I'll say this and be done. A family feeling as strong as yours is a curse, not a blessing."

"You're wrong," she said. "It's both."

ii

Amanda, Louis and Israel saw him off four days later.

The visit had been strained and anticlimactic, because the parting had really taken place on the semaphore hill. Their two subsequent attempts at lovemaking had been perfunctory. One hadn't even come to completion because something not merely physical shrank his flesh before they were half done.

And yet he stayed, unwilling to surrender his last hours with her even though she was occupied with other matters—packing, purchasing tickets on another vessel, buying Louis a proper traveling outfit. He'd actually seen more of the boy than he had of Amanda.

To fill the time, he taught Louis the fundamentals of playing the musical instrument he'd brought him as a birthday present. Louis was quick, and seemed to welcome the diversion. He obviously didn't relish the idea of leaving San Francisco, though he never said so directly. But he attacked the music lessons with such ferocity that Bart knew the boy was troubled. He suspected Louis was just as conscious of the new hardness in his mother as were any of the adults around her.

In a couple of days, Louis could blow *Oh Susannah!* with only a couple of sour notes, though he absolutely couldn't remember the proper name of the instrument—aeolina—and settled for the easier one, mouth organ.

One afternoon Bart sent out to the clipper for a similar instrument he'd bought for himself. They perfected a pretty fair duet on *Sweet Betsy from Pike*. But the session was strangely cheerless. Neither of them ever laughed aloud.

The morning of Bart's departure was gray and gloomy. He was going home with the holds of *Manifest Destiny* only scantily filled with hides. All the profit these days came from the westbound run. The quicker the clipper returned to New York for another load of freight, the better.

Trim and tall in his best blue jacket, black neckerchief and peaked cap, he said his farewells one by one:

"Israel—"

He forced himself to grasp the other man's hand and shake it. The mulatto looked startled, then pleased.

"—I count on that new last name to bring you good luck in the diggings."

"Thank you, Captain Bart. I'm mighty glad to be getting out of this wicked, overcrowded town. Hopeful isn't a capital of virtue, but at least they christened it sensibly."

Bart glanced past Israel to Amanda. She was wearing the yellow taffeta he liked. At the moment she was fussing with the sleeve of Louis' new coat. The boy was sprouting. He was almost thirteen; slimming down as he grew taller. His dark eyes were a mirror of his mother's but his swarthy skin and jet hair echoed the man who had fathered him in Texas.

So Amanda wouldn't hear, Bart said to Israel:

"I don't think much of her going east, you know."

"Gathered that. I don't either."

"We finally agree on something."

"Indeed we do."

Smiling without feeling it, he moved on. He extended his hand to Louis:

"Take care of your mother."

"I'll try, sir. Are you going to come visit us?"

"Don't see how I can. I don't know where you're planning to settle."

Uneasily, the boy glanced at Amanda. "I'm not sure myself—"

"Besides that," Bart said, "I'll probably be out of the country."

He took the last two steps with great effort. Amanda started to reach for his hand. He noticed the old, worn rope bracelet—little more than a few frayed strings now—and quickly brought his hand up to the brim of his cap in a small salute.

She looked at him, surprised and saddened. But he couldn't touch her. He couldn't or he'd break.

"That was a very decent thing you did for Israel," she said.

He shrugged. "I try to make a conscientious effort not to be a son of a bitch all the time. God keep you safe, sweet."

"Bart—please. Don't cut it off this way. Come find me in the east."

"I'm sure that wouldn't be difficult. Given your money and your ambition, I'm sure that after a couple of years go by, you'll be well known. Eminent, in fact. Unless—"

Unless that man Stovall is more than a match. Fights you—and wins—

"Unless what?"

"Nothing."

It could go either way, he decided. She was smart, sturdy and strong-willed—more of the goddamned Kent family inheritance!

Unexpectedly, he saw tears shining on her cheeks:

"Bart, I beg you—come find me. Just—to say hello—"

He was unintentionally curt:

"Doubt that'll be possible. Right now I feel pretty favorable toward that offer from Royal Sceptre—"

And I don't think I'd want to see how you've been hurt.

Or how you may have hurt others—

"Goodbye, sweet."

"Bart—!"

He spun away as she cried his name, stalking toward the end of the creaking pier where the lighter waited.

As he climbed down the ladder to the bobbing boat, he kept thinking of the ominous passage of scripture that had come to mind on their hilltop walk. It fit her perfectly. She was too determined; too unwilling to moderate her stand or limit the means she'd use to achieve her goal. In a way, she was like the zealots—the fanatics—in the north and south who were surely going to bring destruction down on the whole nation one day—

An oarsman spoke to him. He didn't hear. He was listening to an inner voice.

Put up again thy sword into his place: for all they that take the sword shall perish with the sword.

iii

Aboard *Manifest Destiny*, Barton McGill immediately turned command over to his first mate and sailing master, with orders that the clipper depart as soon as possible. He went below.

In his cabin he opened the drawer of his desk and

drew out the resignation he'd labored to phrase properly. He was satisfied with the language. He intended to submit the letter the moment he docked—but not for the same reason he'd written it.

With a shake of his head, he returned the resignation to the desk and opened the locker where he stored his whiskey.

To make room for the bottle on the desk, he cleared away his log and the one Kent and Son title he'd purchased in New York—some sort of trashy romantic novel. *A Frenchman's Passion*. The unknown author had adopted an obvious, and ridiculous, pseudonym—Mrs. A. Penn. Yet a clerk had informed him, disdainfully, that this latest offering of the once dignified and prestigious Kent house was attracting thousands of readers, principally feminine. Bart had somehow balked at taking the book ashore, and now he flung it on the deck.

He poured a drink, downed it, poured another and shucked off his jacket. He took his boxed aeolina from one pocket. With his sleeves rolled up and the bottle for company, he started playing the central melody of the Chopin fantasy in C sharp minor. Because of the sunless day, the cabin was dark. He sat with his back to the windows that overlooked the abandoned ships in the bay, letting the music speak his grief and his fear for the woman he loved.

The Journal of Jephtha Kent, 1850:

A Higher Law

January the 17th. A most disagreeable dinner-time. Captain Tunworth and my mother-in-law present, but neither ate more than a few morsels, preferring to fulminate against President Taylor. They condemn Taylor as a traitor to his class, and his state, because of his easy compliance with the will of certain northern Congressmen under whose influence he has fallen. Chief among these hated advisors is Seward of New York, who takes an inflexible stand on the slave issue.

Prodded by the northerners, Taylor leans toward admitting California to the Union under the constitution which the state has already adopted, viz., the constitution prohibiting slavery. If this happens, the "South's Sentinel," ailing Calhoun of South Carolina, predicts the cotton states will leave the Union. Captain Tunworth is all in favor—not surprising, since he is the master of twenty-nine ill-treated bucks and wenches.

So deep has the ideological chasm become, I find even my own modest table in Lexington divided. I listened in dismay as my dear Fan hotly seconded her father's views. I think she and Tunworth noticed my silence.

If there is to be peace in our household, I dare not speak what is in my soul. As the preceding pages of this private book will attest, I am coming all too close to complete rejection of Mr. Calhoun's claim that the idea of freedom for the blacks originates in "that blind, fanatical zeal which made one man believe he was responsible for the sins of others; and which, two centuries ago, tied the victim that it could not convert to the stake."

Christ teaches that I *am* the keeper of my brothers and sisters, whatever their color. But am I "blind and fanatical?" I pray not.

The Methodist Episcopal Church, South, will not permit me to voice my convictions, or even my doubts, from the various pulpits to which I itinerate up and down the valley. But even more saddening is my growing fear that should I present even a single counter-argument to the Captain at my own table, my dear wife would look upon me with vexation and, yes, even anger.

*

January the 29th. God has let the merciful light of His compassion shine! A way out of the nation's awful dilemma may exist after all—

In surprisingly temperate conversation with Fan before she retired this evening, I won a concession from her. She agreed that the omnibus legislation which Mr. Clay is bringing to the Congress may offer the last, best chance of averting strife and disunion.

Though she has grown increasingly partisan, Fan yet recognizes the urgency of a program of compromise. If we are to continue to enjoy tranquility throughout the nation, the dispute over fugitive slaves must be resolved. So must the status of the new western lands, which have been thrust into great prominence as a result of the discovery of California gold—an event, I should judge, which has forever altered the course of the country by generating a gigantic migration—thus inevitably filling all the territory between the Mississippi and the Pacific.

Under old Clay's various legislative proposals, California would be admitted to the Union as a free state. The New Mexico and Utah lands would be organized as territories, but without reference to slavery. The boundaries of Texas would be settled, and her debts assumed. Slave auctions in the District of Columbia—an odious sight to diplomats from foreign nations—would be prohibited, though slaves already present would not be tampered with—this as a sop to Maryland, which ceded the land for the District.

Finally, Clay offers one great bone for the south—a fugitive slave law which will at last be supported by vigorous federal enforcement. Any person found guilty of aiding a runaway black would be fined and imprisoned. An escaped slave apprehended in the north would not be granted a jury trial to decide his fate, nor be permitted to testify in his own behalf. A federal official would have power to settle questions of ownership, his fee being five dollars if he decides for the slave, but ten if he decides for the master.

It is the continual escape of slaves—and a lack of effective redress—which most rankles men such as the Captain. Perhaps Clay's bill will pacify them. But I do not believe any law will hamper the activities of certain other persons in our district—of white color—who, in secret and at the risk of their lives, assist blacks in reaching the north. No law will damp the fervor of these "conductors of the under-ground railroad."

But at least Clay's compromise may exert some soothing effect upon those who talk publicly and thoughtlessly of secession.

*

March the 9th. The momentous debate in Congress occupies the minds and fills the conversations of most people throughout the valley and, it is my impression, in the north as well. Two days ago, with the galleries packed and the chamber overheated to nearly one hundred degrees, the eloquent Webster of Massachusetts rose and spoke for three hours in reply to Mr. Calhoun. The substance of Webster's impassioned plea for accord was reprinted today in a newspaper which reached our house from Richmond.

The hour is late, Webster said. Men of good will must reach an accommodation or there will be disunion and war. The senator stated—rightly, I think—that "peaceable secession" by the southern states is a contradiction in terms—

Impossible.

*

March the 15th. How vile and bitter are the attacks upon Webster already! Having boldly stood for the principles of compromise, peace and Union, he is scorned by radical elements of the northern press as "the lion turned spaniel." He is accused of "fawning on the masters whose hands he licks for the sake of the dirty puddings they might choose to toss him."

To a congregation with whom I was visiting, I lauded the senator's courage in risking his reputation and, indeed, his treatment by posterity. I found about half of those gathered agreeing that Webster had taken a noble stand. But there are also those who resist all compromise. They will neither forget nor forgive the bayings of the abolitionists who accuse the south of being "one great brothel where half a milion women are flogged to prostitution."

Alas, the president himself, who should be the foremost spokesman of the cause of Union, favors a more limited program than Clay's. He is jealous, they say, of Mr. Clay's renewed notoriety! How mean and petty are the ambitions and angers of some men in high places!

*

March the 31st. A giant has perished. The news was flashed to Richmond and brought on from there—yesterday, Calhoun succumbed to a lung sickness.

Against the advice of friends and physicians alike, he went to Washington earlier this month to address the Senate on Clay's proposals. He was so enfeebled, he could not speak aloud. He sat huddled in a blanket in the chamber's dreadful heat while Senator Mason read his remarks.

Calhoun could not embrace the Clay legislation wholeheartedly. He believed the north has made the south its hapless victim, abusing its people and abridging their rights—and it was in response to this stern view that Senator Webster pleaded for three hours.

When I first read of Calhoun's reaction, I reflected again on the unfathomable purpose of God in creating a race of colored men. Without the existence of such a race, the old "Sentinel" might never have veered from the position he took in Congress nearly forty years ago, when he championed an improved system of national highways and waterways with the cry, "We are under the most imperious obligation to counteract every tendency to disunion!"

But the presence of the black man upon this continent—and Calhoun's conscience, which not even the most rabid northern agitator dared call into question—slowly worked its change. Just before he fell out with Old Hickory over the Nullification issue, he had already replied to Jackson's toast on Jefferson Day—"Our Federal Union! It must and shall be preserved!"—with one that expressed his own conviction—"The Federal Union—next to our liberty most dear." After that, he swung ever closer to his final position—that slavery had somehow been vindicated as "a good—a positive good" and that any other view was "moral and political evil."

To the end, he was a Unionist—but not at any price.

Captain Tunworth is fond of quoting Calhoun's remark during the debate on Wilmot's Proviso—"I desire above all things to save the whole; but if that cannot be, to save the portion where Providence has cast my lot." In his last appearance in the hall he loved, a sickly figure listening to another man read the outpouring of his heart, he remained true to his principles.

Shamefully, I cannot claim to have emulated him, except in these pages. I grow more and more circumspect in my remarks to Fan. She will grant that Clay's compromise offers the one chance of averting a separation of the sort which sundered my Church. But like Calhoun, she will not admit there is any wrong in holding men and women in bondage. I fear to dispute with her because Gideon, Matthew and Jeremiah are in her constant care, I am gone a good deal, and she has stated without qualification that she will not permit the boys to hear any of my "softness toward the nigra."

*

April the 10th. Seldom have I heard invective to rival that which Captain Tunworth directs toward Seward of New York. During the March debate in Washington, the Whig senator referred to "a higher law than the Constitution, which regulates our authority over the domain." Nothing worse could have been said to inflame southerners, who insist the Constitution protects the rights of slave owners because of these words:

"No Person held to Service or Labour in one State, under the Laws thereof, escaping into another, shall, in Consequence of any Law or Regulation therein, be discharged from such Service or Labour, but shall be delivered up on Claim of the Party to whom such Service or Labour may be due."

How I weary of hearing the Captain parrot that passage! It is the foundation of his belief that the federal government must assist in returning escaped slaves.

True, the word "slave" is not mentioned. But the Captain says the meaning is unmistakable.

The failure of the abolitionist politicians to heed the clause—plus the passage, in some northern states, of those disputed "liberty laws" forbidding recapture of runaways—has led to the controversy which Clay's new fugitive slave proposal would hopefully abate. Clay's bill would in effect enforce the Constitution to the letter—

But while men are struggling for peace, Seward rants of a law "higher" than the Constitution!

Seward, many say, has presidential ambitions. If so, he has destroyed himself with his statement. He has placed himself permanently among those the Captain villifies as "no better than mad dogs."

In truth, Seward was already very nearly classified that way because of his membership in the Whig party. When Calhoun fell out with Jackson, he promptly joined the new Whigs, a faction opposing Old Hickory's autocratic behavior. The faction took its name from the English party which traditionally fought against the unlimited power of the king.

For a time, the Whigs served the interests of an uneasy alliance of southern gentry and northern businessmen. They sought to curb the mounting power of the Jacksonian Democracy, which draws its strength from, and has become increasingly dominated by, persons of lower social standing. The factory class, as Captain Tunworth calls it.

But the Whigs have also come to be dominated and controlled by a certain segment of society—namely the abolitionist element. This drove Calhoun to abandon them and rejoin the Democracy. Thus by his party affiliation, and most assuredly by his statement about "a higher law," Senator Seward has conjured a ghost which will hover close to him for years—and thwart whatever ambitions he might harbor.

*

April the 14th. Returned from the circuit to find—again—no letter from my father.

Two of mine, sent to him in care of the postal office in Sacramento, have gone unanswered. His last to me from California, written in September, stated that he was journeying to a remote area in the hope of locating a profitable claim. I have heard nothing since.

I thought my father's decision to leave Oregon would refresh his spirits and provide him with a new opportunity much needed since his farming efforts came to nothing. Now I think my enthusiasm may have been ill advised. Spent the better part of an hour praying he is safe and well.

*

April the 27th. Damp weather has brought on a fever and confined me to my bed. The household is disturbed again because of the escape of a prime buck, Amos, belonging to a neighbor of Captain Tunworth.

The Captain raged in our parlor for an hour this afternoon, his voice carrying up to the bedroom. He believes the operatives of the "freedom rail road" aided Amos in his flight. The Captain will join the effort to recapture him.

*

April the 29th. Some thirty miles above Lexington, the runaway was caught by a party of armed men which included Captain Tunworth. They came upon Amos wandering south instead of north. The illiterate slave had grown confused because the inclement weather hid the heavens and made it impossible for him to locate the North Star. Being incapable of reading written directions of any sort, he was following the star. When it was lost from view, he blundered straight into the arms of his pursuers.

All this I learned when Captain Tunworth returned tonight. He could not refrain from coming to my room to inform me of the details. He first described the crude pass, with the signature of Amos' owner forged, which the slave had been carrying. Every black out after nightfall must have such documentation of his right to be abroad, or he becomes immediately suspect.

The Captain and his associates interrogated Amos for nearly four hours, using all manner of inhuman persuasion, since it was obvious a literate person had provided the fugitive with the forged paper. My father-in-law said he and his friends suspect Syme, who operates a small granary on the outskirts of Lexington. Syme is a Connecticut Yankee by birth. He inherited the granary from a relative. He has been heard to remark in public that he loathes the "peculiar institution." In an effort to make Amos confess the name of his abettor—Syme or someone else—the slave's owner ultimately resorted to—

It sickens me to attempt to put the actual words on this page. They are an abomination to my sight, and to the eyes of Him who sees all. I will state the despicable truth as decently as I can:

Captain Tunworth's neighbor employed a long knife. It was applied to the private parts of Amos, destroying his manhood and, soon after, his life. He bled to death without revealing the identity of his benefactor. May God have mercy on him, and on his master—

On Captain Tunworth, too. He sees nothing wrong in such base cruelty. He swore that if one of his blacks ever escaped, he would pursue him to the ends of the earth and punish him. Unable to contain my wrath, I ordered him from my room.

Approximately an hour later, when I called to Fan and asked her to bring the boys up to say goodnight, she refused.

*

May the 5th. Itinerating again. I have been unable to banish the death of Amos from my thoughts. It has had a profound effect upon me, beyond all description. Last night, when I rose to offer a meditation at prayer service, I felt as if a mighty hand had seized me, shaking from my lips a condemnation of the cruelty perpetrated against the runaway.

A dozen in my congregation promptly left. Those who remained were obviously stunned and unsettled by the interjection of a secular subject, though afterward, three were bold enough to approach me and whisper their belief that I was right.

I fear repercussions but cannot shrink from them. Some Voice other than mine spoke from within me. I think the Almighty has finally decreed that I shall keep silent no longer.

•

May the 9th. Household atmosphere most unpleasant following my return today. Fan has removed herself to a separate sleeping room. My sons barely speak at all; I fear she has harangued them in my absence—

Too grieved to write more.

•

May the 11th. While doing an errand this afternoon, I was accosted by Syme. He is a small, unpleasant-looking man with a pocked face and nervous eyes.

He greeted me cordially enough. But then he began to speak in a curiously guarded way about my recent remarks at the prayer service, which are fully known in Lexington. I can tell from the hostile stares of those I previously called my friends. Twice I have been stoned by small boys—no harm done, though both incidents deepened my sadness.

A transcript of Syme's words could never be used against him, so carefully and obliquely did he speak. Yet his meaning was unmistakable:

Should my conscience dictate a more active participation on behalf of the enslaved blacks of the district, he would assist in finding "a means for expression of my will."

I rebuffed him. My affairs are troubled enough without embroiling myself in conducting runaways to freedom. He tipped his hat and departed, his manner as contemptuous as that of my father-in-law—though for an entirely different reason.

It becomes increasingly clear that a man of moderate views can find no peace in Virginia. Perhaps he cannot anywhere in the nation.

*

June the 3rd. Unable to write a line for three days. Immense and stunning surprise fell on our house, coupled with immense grief.

My father is dead. Foully murdered in California. The news was conveyed by a visitor who has since departed just as she came—swiftly and forcefully as a summer storm. It was my cousin once removed, a handsome, splendidly-dressed woman of middle years—the very woman for whom my father searched for so long. Her unexpected arrival, all the way from California in company with a thirteen-year-old boy of dark complexion and almost Latin appearance, plunged the household into confusion.

She arrived in a carriage secured at Norfolk. She brought much luggage, but there was no hired driver; she handled the reins herself. She goes by the name Mrs. Amanda Kent de la Gura, having been married to a Spanish fur trapper; the father of her son Louis, I presume. She did not specify.

She began her visit in a mood of cordiality and sympathy, relating how she had discovered my father by chance in the city called San Francisco. She described the manner in which he lost his life at the hands of some local toughs. She then stated she was on her way to Boston, but her exact plans were presented in only the sketchiest detail. I gathered she has some desire to buy back the family printing house, of whose existence I told her I knew.

During those first remarkable hours, Fan had the good sense to conceal all hints of the tensions which have divided our family. She treated my cousin once removed and her somewhat willful boy in a friendly and gracious fashion. Regrettably, Captain Tunworth was not so courteous when he called unannounced.

In ten minutes, he and my cousin developed an unconcealed dislike of one another. Mrs. de la Gura chanced to mention that she had employed a runaway slave in California, which caused the Captain to launch a diatribe against those who harbor fugitives. My cousin's retorts were caustic. If not an outright abolitionist, Mrs. de la Gura obviously approaches that persuasion. The Captain departed in foul temper—and Fan's restraint was visibly tried.

She abandoned politeness entirely next morning, when our guest put forth another revelation. Before his death, my father apparently became a partner in a modestly successful gold-mining enterprise. I am heir to his share.

Mrs. de la Gura, who prior to leaving California appointed a representative to act in her stead, urged me to permit her to continue managing my father's interest. I told her I had no experience in business affairs, and so would be willing, provided any monies due my family were scrupulously accounted for. She assured me of it, promising that if she were given leave to administer my father's share of the claim, my sons would benefit to a greater extent than if I were to take an active role.

So strong and lucid a case did she present—remarkable on two counts; she is a female, and no longer young—that I of course consented. This produced an awful argument from Fan. In my cousin's bold and forthright manner, she saw some fancied scheme to deprive our sons of what is rightfully theirs.

At last, after much stormy language, I was forced to demand Fan's silence. I then signed a paper giving Mrs. de la Gura authority to act on my behalf. For the remainder of the visit, she and Fan were decidedly hostile to one another.

Mrs. de la Gura is a person not easily opposed, that much was clear soon after she arrived. She repeated more explicitly her determination to see the printing house restored to the hands of the founding family. In this pursuit, she said she would require the use of the California gold. Fan construed her words as glib fraud. Nothing I said would change her mind.

Before my cousin departed—having assured me she would be in touch when she was permanently located—my wife and I had yet another reason for disagreement. It was caused by an ugly scene which marred the farewell.

My second son, Matthew, six, owns a pet toad of repulsive mien and phlegmatic disposition. The boy Louis wished to examine the creature. Matthew, in one of those contrary moods which seize children from time to time, did not desire to have his treasure handled by anyone else. He refused—politely at first, then more vehemently as Mrs. de la Gura's son continued to insist. Finally the latter snatched the toad from Matthew's hand—whereupon my son burst into tears and the toad hopped into the shrubs, never to be seen again. When my cousin struck her boy's cheek to admonish him, his eyes glowed with fury, and I thought for a moment that he might strike her back.

He did not, fearing her, I suppose. But she was visibly upset by the young man's behavior. I cannot help but observe that he only imitates the behavior of his mother, who descends upon a person like that storm of which I wrote, and sweeps all away before—

When the carriage had departed, Fan berated me. I was so exercised that I could barely keep from speaking un-Christian words in reply.

I wanted to console Matthew over the loss of his pet but he would not admit me to his room. As a result of my cousin's visit, I am more than ever an outcast in my own home.

*

June the 29th. Today I received a communication from my bishop. I have paid dearly for my discourse at the prayer service.

The bishop chastised me for speaking against the cruelty of the death of Amos. My remarks were in violation of the ordinances of the Methodist Episcopal Church, South. The bishop reminded me that the Church is apolitical, concerned only with the saving of souls, not the freeing of physical bodies from bondage.

In his closing paragraph, he removed me from my itinerancy.

*

July the 5th. President Taylor died yesterday, from ingesting too much iced water and a large quantity of cherries. The stomach ailment struck him after he participated in a celebration of our nation's Independence in the capital. Mr. Fillmore has already been sworn in.

On hearing the news of the president's death, I almost

wished a similar fate might befall me. I am a pariah in my Church, my own house, and throughout Lexington. Only Christ's ever-present and strengthening hand enables me to endure the tribulation.

*

July the 21st. I can find no employment—no means of supporting my family. Fan and I fell into another terrible argument because of it. I refused her demands that I make a public retraction of my statements concerning Amos, and seek the bishop's forgiveness.

My wife, became as a stranger to me, spoke words about my character whose bitterness I cannot begin to capture on paper. She accused me of robbing my own sons by giving control of the gold claim to Mrs. de la Gura. I confess without shame that I left the house with tears in my eyes.

My son Gideon was scything weeds in the yard. I spoke to him and he turned away. I suspected that Fan had been speaking against me, but this day I saw the proof.

As I stumbled from the yard, I cried silently, "Father, if thou be willing, remove this cup from me!"

When I realized it was not to be, I was shaken by a mighty wrath—and only with the greatest effort did I pray the remainder of Our Lord's appeal—

"Nevertheless not my will, but Thine be done."

I tramped the countryside until dark, pausing once to fall on my knees and clasp my hands. Humiliated by my anger against the Lord, I admitted my sin in prayer. Despite the day's anguish, my convictions remained firm. I vowed I would neither flee Lexington nor the proximity of my family, in the hope that love and the bonds of Christian marriage would restore me to Fan and the boys. I love her, I thought. I love them. Yea, I love those who scorn me, for that is Christ's way.

A short while later, at dusk, I returned to my home in the hope of effecting a reconciliation. Fan ran out to meet me in the yard. She told me there was no place within her house for a traitor. She then brought out a few of my belongings and, when I requested it, my Bible and this book.

And so I crept away again, to the residence of a man in Lexington who I hoped would display Christian charity—the good Doctor William White, pastor of the First Presbyterian congregation. He has permitted me to sleep in a hut on his property.

By moonlight, seated in the hut's doorway, I scribble out these lines—feeling for all the world exactly like a felon, and praying that the cup indeed may pass; that time may heal the injuries of the dispute with Fan, for whom I still find love within my heart.

But I will not effect reconciliation at the price of recantation. I have pondered long on what I was moved to say at the prayer service. I believe the Lord revealed His truth when he spoke with my tongue. Amos was a child of God just as much as any white man. If that be heresy, let me suffer for it; yea, let me burn!

Later. I feel the Lord's presence. A voice whispers what I would have called unthinkable a year ago—

There is, as Seward said, a higher law. God's law of love and justice for all His creatures; a law which men have perverted.

Believing that helps ease my pain somewhat. I have been tardy in taking my stand. I will follow the heedings of that inner voice even to the gates of Hell.

•

September the 10th. I am reduced to penury—living in a hovel and tending the stables for the smartly dressed young cadets at the Military Institute. I am an outcast among those I sought to serve. Only Dr. White's merciful intercession enabled me to remain in Lexington at all, gaining for me as he did this lowly position. Captain Tunworth has assumed responsibility for the worldly needs of Fan and the boys—and is providing for them more handsomely, I am sure, than ever I could on my slim stipend as an itinerant preacher.

It is an irony that my cousin once removed, would I but make the effort to locate her, could rescue me from this wretched state by virtue of my father's gold. Yet I am not willing to take steps to contact her. To throw myself upon her mercies would be to deny the dictates of my conscience—

So I wear rags. Subsist on the coarsest of fare. Perform menial work while enduring the jibes of some of the cadets. I know I am considered the worst sort of fool—a self-condemned martyr.

I also suspect that many in Lexington wish I would leave. I am conscience made visible. A pricking thorn. That is why I will not go. My resolve has become as a stone. I answer to God and His Son Jesus Christ and Their higher law, and to no others.

*

September the 11th. Only my faith gave me the courage to endure an incident which transpired this afternoon. I saw Fan and the boys on the grounds of the Institute, bound upon some social errand or other.

Little Matthew would have spoken, but Fan pulled him sharply away and struck his hand when he resisted. Gideon showed no expression whatever; I believe he knows it would not please his mother if he recognized me.

Jeremiah, four, is too small to do so—especially as I am an unkempt, threadbare figure—no longer the same man physically or spiritually that I was a mere six months ago.

I watched them until they passed from view. Not even Matthew would look back.

•

September the 12th. A professor at the Institute informed me this morning that California has been admitted as a free state. After much struggle and many portents of failure, Clay's program is at last being maneuvered through the Congress—largely with the help of a senator who belongs to the Democracy, Douglas of Illinois, whose support had not previously been counted on.

Old Webster is now in Fillmore's cabinet, Secretary of State. Clay, exhausted, has gone to Rhode Island to rest. Neither can directly engage in the legislative battle. But Douglas has seen the danger, and responded to it—

If the rest of the compromise bills can be passed, perhaps the Union can be saved. That now appears more likely than it did at the start of this tumultuous season.

Autumn is coming to the valley. The coloring of the countryside, the hue of change, reminds me that men too must undergo change. So I have done, by speaking my beliefs and enduring the consequences.

I do not hate those in Lexington who abuse me openly or in private—the cadets; Captain Tunworth. I pray for reconciliation. I pray the Union may be preserved, though I am frequently pessimistic. I fear the issues are too deep and divisive for Clay's compromise to bring more than a temporary tranquility.

Later. The voice of the higher law spoke to me again. I cannot remain passive in my protest—though I will be circumspect, so that I may be useful to the Lord for many months to come.

Tomorrow, I will seek out Syme and reveal my willingness to help him perform the secret work I am convinced must be done.

Book Three

Perish With the Sword

CHAPTER I

The Legacy

OUTWARD BOUND FROM Boston harbor, the gigantic six-masted steamship belched smoke from her stack. Louis Kent, watching from the port rail of *Yankee Arrow,* a much smaller coastal steamer, nearly lost his broad-brimmed wide-awake to a sudden gust of wind. He caught the hat as it tumbled off his head, then exclaimed:

"I can't make out her name. But I see the British flag—"

A few steps further along the rail, clutching her parasol with one hand and her spoon bonnet with the other, Amanda turned to her companion, a broad-shouldered, six-foot Negro in his early thirties. He had a prominent nose, deep eye sockets that accentuated the darkness of his eyes, and skin of a lustrous bronze hue. His long hair, neatly trimmed at the line of his collar, tossed in the wind. He was faultlessly dressed in a frock coat and strapped trousers whose elastic bands fitted under the soles of polished-boots.

"Is that one of the Cunard steamers, Mr. Douglass?" Amanda asked. She and Louis had made the gentleman's acquaintance on the voyage up from Norfolk—he had boarded at Philadelphia—and had dined at his table, despite the purser's whispered suggestion that they needn't segregate themselves in that fashion. Amanda had remarked tartly that the other white passengers were the ones segregating themselves—foolishly

—since the gentleman was delightful and provocative company.

"No," Douglass answered in a mellow voice. "I believe that's a sister ship of the *Great Britain*. A competitive line. At the end of my lecture tour in '47, I came home on the *Great Britain*. She's screw-driven—just like that one. Those masts are an innovation too. All but one's hinged. They can be lowered to the horizontal for less wind resistance and greater speed. *Great Britain* brought me to America in just under thirteen days."

Amanda marveled: "Thirteen days from Europe. Imagine! It seems machines are changing the whole world—"

Mr. Douglass smiled in a rueful way. "Every part of it except the most important. The human mind. Two years ago, I was the only male delegate at the conference on women's rights in Seneca Falls. Afterward, I said publicly that I agreed with the ladies attending the conference—society does discriminate against women. The good folk in Rochester treated me as if I were twice a leper. Leprous once for being black, leprous again for daring to suggest women are entitled to equal treatment under the law. Those Rochestarians thought I was crazy! There's not much a steam engine can do to change attitudes of that sort, I'm afraid."

"I still don't see why she carries sails," Louis said, absorbed by the sight of the huge ship putting out to sea. He'd hooked his elbows over the rail and was hanging onto his wide-awake with both hands. He looked smart in his trim black jacket, vertically striped railroad trousers, button boots and dark green cravat.

"For the same reason we do," Douglass said, gesturing to the masts of the *Arrow*. He spoke loudly because of the thump of the *Arrow*'s engines and the steady roar of water spilling down from her enclosed paddlewheels amidships. "To conserve coal—and the engines—when there's a fair wind," he explained to the boy. "To provide motive power if the engines fail."

He settled his white summer top hat on his head. "We'll be at the pier shortly. I'd better go below and sign that book for you, Mrs. de la Gura."

"I thank you for that, Mr. Douglass—and for the pleasure of talking with you during the voyage."

Amanda smiled as she said it. But she was decidedly uncomfortable in the four-foot-wide skirt of crinoline and the flounced, stiffened muslin petticoat beneath. Summer-weight the materials might be. But all the clothing was a burden to someone accustomed to the more casual dress of California.

Still, she was determined to get used to wearing what was proper. She looked quite attractive in the expensive outfit. Her hair was done in the style that had been popular for more than a decade: parted in the center, with the sides drawn down and beneath the ears and pinned up in a bun in back. Mercifully, daytime fashion permitted her to go without the annoying ready-made side ringlets held in place by cumbersome combs. The ringlets were mandatory in the evening.

As Douglass started away, she added, "I do hope I may be able to make a donation to your paper soon."

The black man turned back, pleased. "A shortage of money is the constant plague of *The North Star*. Without the help of friends, my paper would never survive, and my message could never be spread so broadly. As it is, I spend too much time running from city to city presenting lectures and soliciting donations. Your contribution would be very welcome. An address reading Fred Douglass, Rochester, New York will bring it to me—"

"I'll remember."

As Douglass disappeared down a companionway, Amanda turned toward the panorama of Boston, a murky jumble of piers, hills, residences, and commercial buildings that poured smoke from tall chimneys into the already gray air of the late June morning.

"I'm not sure all those factories are as great a boon as everyone claims," she remarked to Louis. "Look at the dirt they spew into the sky."

The boy was more interested in their departed companion:

"Is Mr. Douglass really famous, ma?"

"Louis, I've reminded you before—it's time you began saying mother."

The dark-eyed boy scowled. "What's the difference?"

"One sounds more genteel than the other. And to answer your question—yes, Mr. Douglass is just about the most famous runaway slave in America. People pack his lectures."

"Then why wouldn't anyone else sit with him in the dining room?"

"Because he's a black man."

"But he's very nice." His scowl deepening, Louis surveyed the passengers along the rail. "People should be whipped for treating him that way."

Amanda said nothing. The remark about whipping disturbed her. Louis was beginning to display some less than admirable traits. She recalled the dreadful row with Jephtha's son over a toad during their visit in the Shenandoah Valley.

She tried to recall when she'd first become aware of the boy's aggressive attitude. In California, she decided. Soon after she told him of the shooting in Hopeful. She'd taken pains to explain that the man had threatened her, but it was the fact that she'd killed him that seemed to make the greatest impression on Louis. Quite a few times since, she'd noticed him watching her with a speculative expression.

Now, while his attention was diverted, it was her turn to study him. He was handsomer than Cordoba. Yet he seemed to lack the Mexican officer's softening humanity.

On the long voyage from San Francisco, she'd finally told Louis about his father. The experience had been harder on her than it seemed to be on him. He'd asked a few questions about Cordoba's appearance and character, and accepted Amanda's statement that the officer was an honorable man whom she'd loved.

She deliberately refrained from cautioning the boy about mentioning his illegitimacy to others; he had no friends with whom to discuss it, and she was afraid that undue emphasis would lend it an unhealthy importance it shouldn't have.

Louis hadn't brought up the subject since that one and only discussion. In many ways, the boy was an extremely private person. Not surprising, since she'd been occupied with so many other things these past few years. And would be in the weeks and months to come. She wondered whether their new life in the east would be good for him—

A bit too late to think of that, she reflected. Still, his words about whipping put her on guard. If she were required to perform any unpleasant actions in connection with Hamilton Stovall, the boy must never become aware of them.

The pilot maneuvered *Yankee Arrow* through the crowded harbor. Amanda felt just a bit intimidated by the great city rising before her. She was angered by the reaction. Here she was, about to step ashore to begin a new life just the way her grandfather had done eighty years ago, and her gloved hands were trembling!

Despite her anxiety, she was fascinated by the sprawl of the city, the gush of smoke from the manufacturies, the crowded confusion of the docks becoming visible off the bow. Boston, like the other cities she'd glimpsed on the trip, seemed to symbolize the wealth, the power, the human energy and inventiveness of the industrialized east. In all her years, she'd never seen anything that even resembled this part of America.

There were nearly twenty-five million people in the nation now. Population, according to Mr. Douglass, had grown at an unprecedented rate of thirty-six percent in ten years. And there appeared to be no limit to the mechanical genuis of the country's citizens.

For two decades, McCormick's reaper had been improving the productivity of the farms. Three rival inventors—Howe, Wilson and Singer—were vying to produce a device for mechanized sewing. She'd overheard a man on the steamer discussing a fellow named Otis, who proposed to build some sort of oversized box to lift and lower passengers within a shaft inside a building. The man had made an extravagant prediction: structures as tall as eight, ten or twelve floors would be commonplace if Otis succeeded.

The marvels were by no means limited to the large and spectacular. In her cabin, Amanda had a half-dozen samples of a remarkable little invention called a "safety" pin, perfected only a year ago. The sharp end was springy, and hid away within a small metal cap when the pin was fastened.

She was both fearful and excited at the idea of creating a place for herself in this restless, fast-changing society. It would be an important place, too. She had the means. In her portmanteau, she carried the document Jephtha had signed, granting her the right to administer the California claim—

For a few moments she pondered the sad enigma of the Reverend Jephtha Kent, a pious, haunted-looking young man who scarcely resembled his father. Something was seriously wrong in Jephtha's family; she'd sensed that all during her visit.

Perhaps it was friction over the slave problem. Jephtha's petite and attractive wife had made it clear she was a partisan of the system. His father-in-law, a detestable rogue named Tunworth, had been even more outspoken; positively vitriolic. But Jephtha himself had given few hints of his own convictions. To Amanda that suggested he didn't feel free to voice them. Having secured what she came for, she'd been glad to leave the tense household.

Thoughts of her cousin once removed reminded her of Bart's warning about the stormy political situation here in the east. She had seen another tangible example aboard the *Yankee Arrow*: the public shunning of a noted man who happened to be black.

Perhaps the socially generated turmoil was one more reason she felt uneasy. She didn't want to be drawn into it. And yet, quite without realizing she *was* being drawn in, she'd taken Louis to sit with Douglass in the dining room. No great damage done by that—snickers and glares could do her no harm. But she'd have to be careful of any deeper involvement. It could divert her from her purpose.

ii

With her autographed copy of the *Narrative of the Life of Frederick Douglass* tucked under one arm, Amanda waited impatiently near the open door of a private office at Benbow and Benbow.

Yankee Arrow had let down its gangplank less than an hour ago. Clerk's pens had stopped scratching the moment she and Louis walked into the dusty-smelling outer room of the law firm.

She was still conscious of eyes turned her way.

Louis raised his head at the sound of faraway thunder. At the open door, a clerk was speaking to the invisible occupant of the private office:

"—a Mrs. de la Gura, sir."

A somewhat high-pitched male voice snapped back, "The Benbows have no clients by that name. If she insists on seeing someone, refer her to one of the junior partners—"

Amanda stepped forward. "If you'll excuse me—" The clerk had to move or be bowled aside. "—I insist on speaking to one of the senior partners." She stopped in the doorway. "Is your name Benbow?"

At an ornate desk in front of a wall bookcase jammed with reference volumes, an elderly man with thin white hair and pale skin swung his spectacles back and forth from one hand. He studied his visitor disapprovingly:

"Yes, madam, I'm William Benbow, Junior."

"Well, I'm not precisely a client as yet. But before we finish our interview, I will be. Now if you'll dismiss this young man, I'd like to discuss my business—"

Benbow flung down the spectacles. "See here! I am preparing an important brief. If you insist on seeing me, make an appointment for sometime next week."

Amanda shook her head and walked into the gloomy office:

"You don't understand, Mr. Benbow. I've come all the way from California, and I don't propose to wait. I'm Gilbert Kent's daughter."

William Benbow, Junior, was seized with a fit of coughing. He groped for a crystal water jug and overturned one of the tumblers before he poured and gulped a drink. It was a full minute before Amanda was sure the old man wasn't going to faint away.

Turning to the clerk, she said, "You may go." She took hold of the door and pushed to make certain he would. Louis grinned and darted into the office before the door shut.

iii

"Incredible," William Benbow, Junior, said at the end of Amanda's rapid summary of her history—the portions of it she cared to reveal, that is. "Absolutely incredible. You do resemble your father. At the time he died, my father—" A gesture toward a dour portrait on one wall. "—was his attorney. I was still clerking in the outer chambers." The lawyer wiped his eyes with a kerchief, replaced his spectacles. "You mentioned business—if it has anything to do with your gold claim, I should advise you that the Benbow firm has no expertise in that area."

Amanda replied, "No, it has nothing to do with the California property. I may need your help with a simple real estate transaction."

Benbow looked a trifle crestfallen: "Real estate?"

"I assure you, Mr. Benbow, if you serve me capably in this small enterprise, I'll probably have a good deal of work for you later on."

"You plan to stay in the east permanently?"

"That depends on a number of factors we needn't go into right now. Are you familiar with the house my father owned on Beacon Street?"

"Quite familiar," Benbow nodded, his manner growing more cordial. "My father took me there to visit on several occasions. A handsome residence—"

Louis was seated in a chair beside his mother's. He scraped the toe of his boot on the carpet. Benbow frowned, as though the noise had interrupted his train of thought. Amanda noticed that Louis stared right back at him, without so much as a blink.

"Who lives in the house now?" she asked.

"Why, let me see—" Benbow thought. "A family named Wheeler. Mr. and Mrs. Charles Wheeler. He's a furniture merchant. He and his wife have owned the home for nearly twenty years, I think."

"I'm asking because my father once kept certain family mementoes in the house. I'm anxious to see whether they might have survived. The items would be of no intrinsic value to another owner—but there's always a slim chance they weren't discarded. Would you imagine the Wheelers would let me inspect the property? Search the attic, and the cellar?"

"Doubtful. Wheeler's an arrogant sort. His wife is quite conscious of her fancied social position."

Amanda smiled without humor. "You're saying they might not permit some strange woman from the west to prowl through their house?"

"Yes, you've put it accurately. I doubt very much that they would."

"Would you guess that items that might have been stored in the house would still be there?"

"I've no way of knowing, Mrs. de la Gura. Wheeler and his wife are antiquaries. I'm told they've packed the place with art objects purchased on tours of Europe. That may indicate a penchant for saving things—but it's still thin evidence on which to base a positive answer to your question."

"Then the only way to answer it is to buy the house."

Benbow's spectacles, swinging in his hand again, fell to the carpet. "You want to live in it?"

"No, I just want to go inside."

"You—you've certainly chosen an extravagant means of entry!"

"I don't think so. The location of the property still makes it valuable, I assume—"

"Very definitely."

"Then it's a good investment. I'll be happy to have the house back in the family. After I inspect it, you can lease it to someone else."

Benbow was speechless. Annoyed, Amanda said: "I'll be glad to pay whatever fee you require, Mr. Benbow. But I want you to approach the Wheelers and tell them you have a purchaser for the property. How much is it worth?"

"Why—why, I suppose—in that area of town—forty to fifty thousand—"

From her reticule Amanda drew an envelope, and handed it across the desk. "Inside, you'll find a bank draft representing the sale of some real estate in California. The sum of ninety thousand dollars. I'm prepared to pay up to seventy thousand for the Beacon Street house, though if you can get it for less, so much the better. You must stipulate that nothing stored in the house when the Wheelers purchased it is to be removed. Nothing—no matter how worthless the object seems."

Benbow retrieved his spectacles, pulled the draft from the envelope and examined it, shaking his head and blinking. Amanda frowned:

"What's the matter? The draft is perfectly good—"

"Of course, of course. I am only—only—"

"Shocked at my way of doing business?"

"To put it mildly."

"Time is precious to me. I'll call on you tomorrow to learn whether you've been successful."

"Tomorrow?" Benbow gasped.

"Certainly." Amanda drew one of his old-fashioned quills from the inkstand; wrote on a slip of paper. "You'll send a representative to the Wheelers this afternoon, I assume—" She tapped the quill feather on the slip. "You can reach me here—the American House—should you get a favorable response at once."

"Very well," the lawyer gulped. He nearly dropped the envelope containing the draft. "But please take this. I'll feel more comfortable if you deposit it with a bank. I suggest the Rothman Bank on State Street—where your father had his accounts. Ask for the president, Mr. Joshua Rothman. He's the grandson of the founder. I —I think you'll find he has some important information for you—"

Thunder rumbled again, louder this time. "What sort of information?"

"I would prefer you learn that from him," the lawyer said, still acting stunned.

iv

Mr. Joshua Rothman was a slim, dark-haired young man with graceful hands and thoughtful dark eyes. Behind his high-backed chair, rain spattered the windows of his private office.

The office was conservative, as befitted an important Boston bank, yet opulent. Thick carpeting deadened sound. The marble top of Rothman's desk showed not a speck of dust. Wood paneling reflected the bluish light of the gas jets hissing within wall-mounted glass bowls. Until today, Amanda had never been in any building with gas illumination, though her hotel, the American House, boasted that it had installed gas fixtures in its rooms and upper halls in 1835.

From beyond a heavily carved door came a sudden, rapid clicking. Curious, Amanda swung toward noise.

"My apologies for the racket, Mrs. Ken—Mrs. de la Gura," Rothman corrected. "That's a private telegraph wire. The bank maintains constant contact with Wall Street. Where large sums are involved, fast and confidential communication is important."

The young banker rose, walked to the door and opened it. He said to Louis, "You're welcome to go in and watch the operator."

Louis shook his head, clearly unhappy at being trundled from office to office. Joshua Rothman shrugged, closed the door and strolled back to the desk where Amanda was seated.

"I only wish my grandfather Royal were here to greet you in person. He often spoke of the Kents—and with great fondness. The publishing house your grandfather founded has added luster to Boston for a long time."

"I have the impression absentee management has dimmed that luster quite a bit."

"Hamilton Stovall, you mean? Yes, his orientation is —how shall I say it? More blatantly commercial than that of the Kents. You know, I've always been curious about the loss of the firm to Mr. Stovall. There's still a fanciful tale that the transfer came as a result of a wager—"

"The story's correct," Amanda said. "My mother's second husband was cheated by Mr. Stovall. In a gambling game."

"Is that a fact. I never believed it. I do know the printing house burned. I heard the fire was started by— ah, but forgive me for bringing up an unpleasant subject."

"It may be unpleasant, but it's the truth. My cousin set the fire. He died in California. That part of the past is closed."

The banker nodded without replying.

"I'd like your opinion on something, Mr. Rothman. Suppose that in a few years, I were to accumulate a substantial amount of money from the mining claim I described. What are the chances of my purchasing Kent and Son?"

"I would say excellent."

Relief swept over Amanda as the young man went on:

"The firm earns a decent return, I'm told. But Mr. Stovall has a reputation for being more interested in the current balance sheet than in long-term stability and growth."

"He milks the company, in other words."

"Exactly. He does the same with his steel factories. He's in his mid-fifties, but he's still quite preoccupied with—ah—call them worldly pursuits. He's not a favorite of the lending community because he gives too little attention to sound management. He prospers only because the domestic market for steel is voracious. Since he devotes even less time to the publishing operation, I should imagine he'd be happy to dispose of it if he could realize a profit."

With never a flicker of change in her expression, Amanda stored away the bits of information about Hamilton Stovall—including the hint of licentiousness in Joshua Rothman's choice of the words *worldly pursuits.* She stored the information away just as she'd already taken note of the use of a private telegraph line.

"Very good," she said. "The draft I handed you for deposit should convince you I'm serious about purchasing my family's former home—well, I'm every bit as serious about buying Kent and Son."

"I don't doubt you for a moment, Mrs. de la Gura. But you needn't delay making an offer to Mr. Stovall."

For the first time since entering the busy bank, Amanda was genuinely surprised:

"What do you mean?"

"Rothman's has enjoyed a peculiar relationship with the Kents over the years. The bank has been the steward of certain assets of your late father of which you are probably unaware."

"What assets?"

"Have you ever heard of a cotton spinning firm in Pawtucket, Rhode Island, called the Blackstone Company?"

"Never."

"My grandfather Royal, your father, Gilbert Kent, and a number of other local men founded the Blackstone Company in 1803. It's still operating. Very successfully, I might add. For certain reasons of his own, your father preferred that your mother not be aware of his investment of one hundred thousand dollars in the firm—forgive me if this is offensive in any way—"

"No, go on," Amanda said softly, a strange expectancy gripping her.

"Your father, in short, took steps to protect a portion of his estate by placing his Blackstone voting stock in the bank's keeping. Your mother drew income from, and controlled, only the printing house."

Immediately Amanda understood why. The way in which Harriet Kent's poorly chosen second husband had gambled away Kent's made her father's decision wholly comprehensible.

"Rothman's has long since assumed there were no Kent heirs," the young man went on. "Nevertheless, we have administered the Blackstone shares as if there were. Contrary to much popular opinion, bankers are not thieves. You are the recipient of your father's legacy—which has grown to be worth a great deal of money."

"How much money, Mr. Rothman?"

"At current market value—conservatively—six million dollars."

V

"Oh my Lord, ma! Six *million?"* Louis burst out. She was so overcome, she quite forgot to correct his use of the word ma.

The initial shock passed in a few moments. But not her awareness of the stunning possibilities opened by the young banker's announcement. While the rain ticked at the windows and a glare of lightning paled the gaslight, she collected her thoughts. She said finally:

"For the time being, Mr. Rothman, I want the bank to continue administering the shares."

"Certainly. The dividend income will be credited to your new account."

"I'll also want to inspect the Blackstone Company."

At that, he looked dubious:

"If you wish, I can arrange it. But not even the male stockholders go there very often. It's a noisy, unwholesome place—a typical factory, I'm afraid."

"But I own part of it—"

"Yes, a substantial part."

"You said it's voting stock—?"

"It is."

"How can I cast intelligent votes if I've never seen the business? What it does, or how?"

"Why—" He smiled in an admiring way. "You can't, obviously. I'll be happy to schedule a visit at your convenience."

"Excellent. I'd appreciate your doing two other things for me. First, approach the owner of Kent and Son regarding a purchase. Operate through Benbow if you wish, but above all be discreet. I don't want it known that I'm a member of the family. Mr. Stovall might not be willing to sell to a Kent. He harbored quite a grudge against my cousin. That's why he took the firm away in the first place."

"So I remember hearing," Rothman murmured. "We can make the proposition this way—you are a woman of means who seeks to diversify her business holdings. At all times, we'll refer to you by your married name."

Amanda smiled. "You're very quick, Mr. Rothman. We'll get along splendidly, I think."

"I think so too. But I wish you'd call me Joshua."

"Very well—Joshua."

"You mentioned a second request—"

"Mr. Frederick Douglass is in Boston to present a lecture at the Park Street church—"

"My wife and I plan to attend." His glance said he was testing her political sentiments.

"I met him on shipboard, and I promised him a donation. Send him a draft for one hundred dollars, drawn in my name so he knows I kept my promise."

"With pleasure." He started to make a note, then noticed her upraised hand. "Yes?"

"A week from now, send a second draft to him in Rochester. Don't identify the donor."

"Is the sum also a hundred dollars?"

"Five thousand."

"Your generosity's commendable. But why give so much anonymously?"

Amanda's face looked oddly pale in the gaslight. She framed her reply with care:

"Two reasons. One, I don't think the purpose of charity is to earn public approval for the donor."

"Nor do I—though many people wouldn't give a penny to any cause unless they were honored for doing so. Still, Mr. Douglass is hardly in the same category as churches and orphan's homes. Boston *is* the center of abolitionism, but there are also quite a few local citizens who detest Garrison, Douglass and everything they stand for—"

"That's my second reason. I prefer not to be too closely identified with the movement. A small sum attracts small notice. A large one attracts a great deal. I'm sure you understand."

He did, but he said nothing. Amanda knew she'd diminished herself in his eyes. But she was determined not to become actively involved in the slavery dispute. Whether Joshua Rothman thought she was cowardly or not, she had no time for extraneous struggles. Kent and Son came first.

"I have one final question," she said. "Negotiations with Stovall will take some time, will they not?"

"Yes, though we'll make our initial approach immediately."

"I'd like to see the firm."

Rothman tented his fingers. "I'd refrain until we have at least sounded out the owner on his amenability to a sale. Actually, it would be better if you didn't visit Kent's at all—"

"That's out of the question."

"Very well—" He was obviously not happy. "I'll inform you when I think it's all right. I'd only caution you that when you do inspect the property, do so in a businesslike way. Keep your remarks very general—you'd be astonished at how a seemingly trivial word or action can sometimes upset a negotiation."

"I'll follow the advice, thank you."

The banker smiled.

"You're amused?"

"Forgive me—I am. I have an odd feeling you'll accept advice from Rothman's when it agrees with your wishes—and disregard it when it doesn't."

"You're an astute young man, Joshua," Amanda said, smiling back. "Good afternoon. Come, Louis."

vi

July rain streamed down the marble headstones in the little burying ground in Watertown. Amanda's parasol was soaked through.

The thunderstorm had blackened the sky. Behind her, at the edge of the narrow drive, the carriage horse whinnied. She didn't look around. Her eyes were moving across the rain-blurred inscriptions on the monuments.

Philip Kent

Anne Ware Kent

That was her grandfather's first wife. She was the daughter of a Boston patriot, a member of the small band of men who had led Massachusetts into open rebellion against George III. Amanda knew Anne Kent had been lost at sea during the Revolution; no mortal remains lay beneath the headstone, which stood to the right of Philip's. An equal distance to the left rose the marker belonging to her grandmother.

Peggy Ashford McLean Kent

To its left—she walked that way in the driving rain—the final monument.

Gilbert Kent

A bird had left a spatter of white on the top of the stone. It made her angry. Heedless of dirtying her glove, she smeared the white until the rain dissolved it and washed it away. Then she put the parasol on the ground and laid both hands on the wet marble and let the tears pour down her cheeks.

Presently the sadness passed. She had discharged a small debt by coming to the graveyard. Now she must discharge a larger one—and give new life to the name a stonecutter had chisled four times. Lightning glared on it—

Kent

She was home. Home and ready to return that name to its rightful eminence.

The parasol offered no protection as she groped her way back toward the closed carriage, her eyes still damp and her emotions as turbulent as the thundery skies.

"All ready," she called to the soaked driver huddled on the seat.

In the carriage's small oval window, a lightning-burst showed her the handsome face of Louis Kent. The lightning flickered out. The face vanished.

She had asked, but not ordered him to leave the carriage and walk to the graves with her. He wasn't interested.

What sort of emotional legacy was she passing on to him? she wondered. Was there *anything* he cared about?

vii

Below, the cavernous rooms of the house on Beacon Street steamed in the heat of the late September evening. With a whale oil lamp in one hand, Amanda slowly climbed the front staircase toward the second floor landing. The lamp's flame cast shifting patterns on the wall beside her.

She was vaguely aware of Louis making noise as he wandered back in the kitchen. She heard occasional shouts and catcalls from the Common. A torchlight procession had ended there at seven. Bald, bespectacled Garrison was addressing a crowd about the injustice of the recapture of a slave named James Hamlet.

The escaped black had been seized in New York City, only a few days after the Congress had passed the new fugitive slave law. Clay's compromises had finally won through, even though important legislators on both sides—including Senator Seward of New York and Senator Jefferson Davis of Mississippi—had withheld their support.

The Kentucky statesman had endured the worst sort of personal abuse during the debates on the bills. At one point, an opponent had gone so far afield as to jeer at Clay's thwarted presidential ambitions. Clay had replied that the work of averting national catastrophe was far more important than personal considerations. He would rather be right, he'd declared, than be president.

Once the various bills had finally been passed, the ringing of bells and an orgy of public drunkenness throughout the north celebrated the Union's salvation. But the members of the noisy throng listening to Garrison undoubtedly hadn't taken part in the revelry. The Massachusetts Anti-Slavery Society had been denouncing the compromise as a betrayal of American liberty.

Slowly, Amanda started toward the third floor. The darkness depressed her. She thought of Bart McGill; longed for him—for the simple physical presence of someone she cared about. A son could never satisfy that need in quite the same way—

Her knees ached as she climbed the stairs. Age. Time was running out for her. Thinking of that, she almost regretted refusing Bart's proposal—

Why was she troubled by regrets so keenly now? The matters she had set in motion early in the summer were moving toward completion. Through the Benbow law firm, Joshua Rothman had made his first tentative offer on Kent's. The sum had been rejected by Stovall's New York attorneys, but the door was left open for further negotiations at a higher price.

And the Wheelers had succumbed when Benbow increased his offer on the house to sixty-seven thousand dollars. The Wheelers had removed the last of their belongings only this morning, transferring them to a new residence in Cambridge.

In California too the future looked promising. Amanda had received a letter from Israel Hope the last of August. The letter said the Ophir Mineralogical Combine was generating ten thousand dollars in gold per week, and on the basis of this, Francis Pelham was purchasing equipment for a prospecting trip into the Sierras.

Despite all the favorable developments, she was still depressed. Louis' behavior was one reason. He was surly with the tutor she'd engaged to instruct the boy in their hotel suite. Louis did his lessons in a perfunctory way, or not at all—it depended on how he felt that particular day. He bowed to Amanda's discipline, but with the greatest reluctance. She hoped the waywardness was merely the effect of adolescence, and that it would pass. Soon.

But you can't blame the boy for the way you're feeling, she thought as she climbed on toward the narrow landing outside the attic door. *The blame's yours. You rejected Bart. You decreed that you had to go your own way. Alone—*

Sometimes she questioned the worth of the effort. And even wished she didn't feel such a strong family obligation.

With a sigh, she approached the attic door. She pulled back the latch, then walked into the musty, cluttered interior. True to their bargain, the Wheelers had left any number of old crates scattered about the attic.

Amanda set the whale oil lamp on the floor. She tried loosening the slats on the side of one crate. The wood was thin, and so old she could break it bare-handed.

She opened the crate, coughing as dust clouded from feminine garments that smelled of mold. Old clothing of her mother's? Or the possessions of the people who had owned the house before the Wheelers? Impossible to tell.

She walked around the lamp and started to insert her fingers between two slats of another crate. Something standing against the back of the crate caught her attention. She swept off the tattered muslin cover—

A framed painting. A large oil. She pulled it into the light—

A dark-haired, almost truculent man gazed at her from the canvas. In her mind's eye, she saw the stern face in its proper setting—the wall of the library downstairs.

Philip Kent's painted eyes stared at the cobwebbed attic and the woman who wept with happiness as she attacked the slats of the second crate.

viii

"Louis? Louis, come see—!"

At the open front door, the boy turned. Amanda came rushing down the darkened stairs, grime on her cheeks and fingers, her gray hair festooned with cobwebs. On the Common, the mob yelled and waved torches.

As Amanda hurried to her son's side, she noticed a figure above the crowd on the far side. A man storming back and forth across an improvised platform, waving a piece of paper—

"Louis, I found them!" She gripped her son's shoulder. "Your great-grandfather Kent's portrait—the sword, the rifle, the bottle of tea—all packed away in the attic. Come see them!"

The boy shook his head, pointed at the scene on the Common:

"I want to watch this. A man who went by told me the fellow speaking is Mr. Garrison. He's going to set fire to a copy of the Constitution."

Disappointed, Amanda said, "I really feel you should show an interest—"

"I want to watch!" Louis declared, turning and dashing out on the stoop.

Someone passed a torch to the platform.

"Look, mother—he's going to do it!"

Just as the boy uttered the last word, the mob howled and the paper in the hand of the distant figure burst alight. The roar died gradually as the man with the burning paper gestured for silence. Amanda heard him shout:

"—so perish all compromises with tyranny! Let all the people say amen!"

The mob roared, *"Amen!"* Garrison flung down the charring document and stamped on it.

"We must go to hear him speak sometime," Louis said. "It takes a lot of nerve to burn the country's constitution—"

The boy turned, a smile on his handsome face.

"Mr. Garrison's a lot like you. He does exactly as he pleases and no one dares to stop him."

One bright eye caught the torch-glare as Louis waited for her to respond to what he fancied was a compliment. Cold clear through, Amanda started to speak.

She couldn't. She turned and walked slowly back into the darkness, leaving her son staring after her, first with confusion, then outright anger.

CHAPTER II

Of Books and Bloomers

THE STREET TO WHICH the carriage brought Amanda several weeks later testified to the parsimony of the firm's owner. Kent and Son had been relocated in a dingy district of warehouses and chandler's shops near the North End piers. Despite the October sunlight and the brisk, salty smell of the air, Amanda was in a cheerless mood when she alighted from the carriage, paid the driver and told him to return in an hour.

As the hired rig clattered off, a scrofulous man in a blue jacket limped from a nearby doorway. A grubby blue bandana was wrapped around the man's forehead, hiding his eyes. Amanda noticed him sidestep a rotting fish carcass.

The man extended a dirty hand. "Penny for a Mexican veteran, ma'am?"

Furious over the appearance of the frame building that housed Kent's, she whipped up her closed parasol and whacked the beggar in the side of the head.

"Jesus Christ! Have you no charity, woman?"

"I'm as charitable as you are blind, my friend. Go cheat someone else. But first I suggest you pull that bandana down more snugly. I can see your eyes move."

Muttering, the man hobbled away. The limp vanished after he'd taken a few steps. And he did adjust the bandana before he slipped down an alley, cursing her.

Well, his anger wasn't any stronger than hers. The building was a disgrace. Its warped, split clapboards were layered with grime. So was the signboard swaying from an iron fixture over the door. The board's gilt lettering was blurred by accumulated dirt. The lower half of the e in Kent had flaked away, and the o in Son was totally gone. The tea-bottle design was barely discernible. She swung up the parasol and gave the sign a smack to set it swinging. Then she headed for the door.

While Joshua Rothman continued to negotiate with Stovall's attorneys, she had deliberately avoided driving by the firm. Now she decided that had been a mistake. She should have prepared herself gradually for the sorry state of the company.

Finally Rothman had given grudging consent to the visit. She had set out from the American House this morning with great enthusiasm. That enthusiasm was already destroyed.

At the door, she stopped, recalling the banker's caution about behaving with restraint. Rothman believed the seller's lawyers might well approve the current offer. She didn't want any actions of hers to upset that—nor did he.

She got her anger under control. But it took her almost two full minutes to do it.

ii

Sunlight from the open door spilled over the stained floor. The light seemed to stir the resentment of the five decrepit men bent at desks covered with untidy piles of paper. They blinked like animals roused in a cave.

The front office area was badly lighted. Only two oil lamps hung from ceiling fixtures. The management evidently relied on daylight through a pair of plate glass windows flanking the door. The smallness of the windows—each was less than a yard on a side—was another indication of Stovall's niggardly ways. On a gloomy day, Amanda imagined the office would be stygian. It wasn't much better now.

The five men watched her from their desks. Not a one of them looked younger than fifty. All had a dispirited air. Three went back to work as she slammed the door, cutting off the sunlight.

The floor vibrated. The presses—located in the basement, she guessed—had a slow, ponderous sound, as of someone laboring for breath.

"Who is in charge here?" she asked, advancing toward a rail that separated the desks from the small waiting area. Her voice made one of the employees start. The gutta-percha cane leaning against the back of his chair toppled over and clanged on a spittoon. The floor around the spittoon showed that the spitter missed frequently.

One of the human wrecks shuffled to the rail.

"Mr. Payne is chief editor and general manager, madam. He's busy."

"Where's his office?"

"There—" A veined hand fluttered toward two partitions walling off the back part of the room on either side of a corridor. "But I tell you he's occupied. Conferring with one of our authors."

"Who are you?"

"Mr. Drew. Office manager. May I ask your business? Are you a bookseller interested in the Kent line?"

"If I were, one look at this place would convince me the Kent line is probably as outdated as—never mind."

Watch your tongue, she thought as she pushed through the gate in the railing. But she was still angry.

"See here!" Drew snorted as she headed down the aisle toward the partitioned offices. "You have no right to thrust yourself—"

She wheeled around. "I certainly do, sir. I'm trying to buy this company. I've come to look it over."

He gaped. "You're the one—?"

"Yes, and if I'm successful, I guarantee there'll be some immediate changes!"

Sullen, Drew watched as she continued on, her cheeks scarlet.

iii

The narrow corridor dividing the walled office space ran straight to the back of the building. At the extreme rear, Amanda glimpsed a dark stair leading to the upper floors. The first door on her left bore a small, tarnished metal plate reading *T. Payne*. The door was ajar.

She reached out to knock, only to be stopped by the weary sound of a man's voice:

"Of course I don't like the manuscript. But I don't have to like your vaporish fantasies to publish them. I have instructions from Mr. Stovall! Drew will write your check before you leave the city."

"Theo—"

Amanda blinked. The voice, deep and almost masculine, belonged to a woman.

"—I frankly get goddamned sick of your Harvard snobbery. You know how many copies *A Frenchman's Passion* sold. *Bartered Virtue* did twice as well. This manuscript will outstrip both of them put together."

"The title makes me ill."

"What's wrong with *Convicted by Love?*"

"If you don't understand, I can't possibly explain. Will you stop puffing that disgusting weed in my face?"

Amanda's mouth rounded. She'd assumed the unseen man was the source of the cigar fumes. In response to the complaint, the woman laughed—a rich, cynical laugh that somehow tickled Amanda.

"Indulge me, Theo. You have your habit, I have mine. And I can't plunk myself down at Commodore Vanderbilt's dinner table and smoke a cigar. I have a position to maintain in New York! That's why I like coming to Boston to bring you a manuscript—and discuss the words dropped from *Bartered Virtue*. Here's the list. Sixty-two adjectives, eighty-nine adverbs—"

"Good writing doesn't need those crutches, Rose."

"Who said my writing's good, dear boy?"

"Not I, certainly."

"Theo, were you drunk when you edited the manuscript?"

"That's insulting."

"Well, goddamn it, I corrected the proofs till my eyes watered! I put back every word you took out. And you ignored them!"

"Rose, please," the man pleaded, sounding tired. "You know Mr. Stovall has given orders—expenses are to be kept to an absolute minimum. We can't bear the burden of re-setting once I've edited the copy."

"You'd better *start* re-setting, or I'll take my next manuscript to Mr. Harper in New York. He'll appreciate the value of my work! If it weren't for the sales of my novels, you couldn't afford to publish that dull literary drivel everyone praises and no one buys. I understand the book trade better than you do!"

"Then why don't you take over my job? I happen to be thoroughly sick of it. God, I wish I'd never quit the newspaper!"

At that point, Amanda finally knocked and thrust the door open:

"Excuse me—"

The man behind the cluttered desk was about thirty-five. He was small-boned, with pale skin, bloodshot hazel eyes and a thick pink nose. His neck-cloth and silk shirt had seen better days. He smelled of whiskey.

"This is a private conference, madam! Deal with one of the gentlemen up front."

She was amused rather than annoyed. The little man in the large chair resembled a small boy physically; his face, by contrast, suggested a hundred years of debauchery crammed into a third of that time.

The woman with him, exceptionally robust, was about Amanda's age. She had a blunt chin, forthright blue eyes and white hair. Her crinoline skirt was wider than Amanda's—and far more expensive. In one gloved hand she held a green-wrappered cigar, half smoked.

"I prefer to deal with you," Amanda said, turning sideways and tilting the bell of her skirt to maneuver it through the door. "My name is Mrs. de la Gura. I hope to purchase Kent and Son."

His reaction was similar to Drew's: *"You—?"* He jumped up. The top of his head barely reached her shoulder. "—I had no idea—that is, Mr. Stovall's attorneys wrote that someone was interested, but no names were mentioned—"

"I've come to look over the premises."

"You mean Stovall's going to sell?"

"It's a distinct possibility."

"Jubilee!" the editor cried, doing a little jig. "I think I'll go out and get a drink to celebrate."

"Not right now, please," Amanda said. "What's your first name?"

"Theophilus."

"I prefer Theo. I heard your guest using it—"

She acknowledged the stout woman gazing at her through a curl of smoke from the cigar now clenched in her teeth. Realizing he'd neglected introductions, Payne blurted:

"Oh, excuse me—Mrs.—de la Gura, you said? This is Kent's romantic novelist, Mrs. Rose—that is—"

His cheeks turned as pink as his nose. His eyes appealed to the elegantly groomed woman. She rescued him:

"It's all right if she's going to own the place, Theo." She extended her hand. "Rose Ludwig. Mrs. Adolph Ludwig of New York City."

"I'm pleased to make your acquaintance, Mrs. Ludwig."

"Down in New York, nobody knows I'm Mrs. A. Penn," the woman confided. "Being an authoress isn't an occupation my late husband—or his friends—would consider proper."

"I'll keep your secrets," Amanda told her.

Rose Ludwig drew the smoldering cigar from her mouth. "Including my vice?"

Laughing, Amanda nodded. "Now, Theo, although the sale hasn't been consummated, it's far enough along so that you and I should get to know one another. I'm buying Kent and Son to diversify my holdings—" The lie came glibly. "—and if Mr. Stovall comes to terms, I'll probably want you to continue acting as editor and manager. Provided you and I find we can deal with one another."

Payne took the candid remark as a threat. He started perspiring. Amanda decided that Hamilton Stovall had reduced the man to a state of fear.

Rose Ludwig settled herself in a chair beside Payne's cluttered desk. "Where are you from, Mrs. de la Gura?"

"California."

"One of those new gold millionaires?"

"Not quite yet."

The woman intimidated Amanda a little. She'd caught the reference to Commodore Vanderbilt, the steamship magnate. Mrs. Ludwig obviously had important social connections.

But she didn't act as if she did. She disarmed Amanda by tossing her cigar butt in Payne's spittoon and nodding emphatically:

"Well, by God. I'm glad you're here. I like your cut. How about you, Theo? Isn't she a big improvement over Mr. Stovall?"

"Careful!" Payne warned, a finger at his lips. He mouthed a name silently. *"Drew."*

Amanda realized the doddering office manager must be a spy for the owner. She kept her voice low as she asked:

"Do you know Stovall personally, Mrs. Ludwig?"

"Unfortunately I do. My late husband forced me to entertain him several times. Adolph once owned a fairly substantial block of shares in the Stovall Works. The last time Mr. Stovall graced our house, he drank too much—nothing personal, Theo—ignored his wife—she's dead now and I'm not surprised—and fawned over another guest. A gentleman," she added pointedly. "And he pretends to be so respectable! He's really a dreadful man—a grotesque. He wears a white silk scarf that covers half his face, and never takes his gloves off indoors because his hands are scarred, they say."

Theo Payne shut the office door and added to Rose Ludwig's comments in a whisper:

"He's also a political primitive. He boasts about membership in the Order of the Star Spangled Banner."

"I'm not familiar with that," Amanda told him.

"The inner circle of the Know-Nothing party."

Amanda merely nodded. It was evident Payne detested Stovall's politics, and perhaps hoped to draw her out about hers. She changed the subject:

"It's obvious you're not happy here, Theo. Why haven't you resigned?"

Scratching his pink nose, he walked back to the desk. "I have four youngsters in my family, Mrs. de la Gura—and positions aren't easy to locate these days."

Amanda wondered whether he meant he personally had a hard time finding jobs because of a fondness for alcohol. She tried to reassure him:

"Well, I hope you'll stick with it a while longer. If the sale can be completed, perhaps you'll be happier with your situation."

"As you said, that depends on whether we can work

together. Also on what changes of policy you might institute—"

Again Amanda stayed on safe ground:

"I can assure you I'd do anything to keep Mrs. A. Penn content." She turned to Rose. "I saw two women at the American House carrying copies of your last novel."

"Did you, now. I know Theo's right—the books are trash. But I have to do something to keep from suffocating in that mausoleum Adolph left me!"

Amanda turned back to Payne, who had slumped into his chair:

"I do think new management could find the money to re-set corrected copy for Mrs. Ludwig—provided you and she settle your differences on style, of course."

"Jesus Christ, that's an improvement already!" Rose declared. "Just for that, Mrs. de la Gura, I'll treat you to dinner this evening. If you're free—"

"I am," Amanda said, delighted. "Could we take a short tour now, Theo?"

"Yes, of course."

"Mrs. Ludwig, would you excuse us for a while?"

"No, I'm going to tag along. I hope you realize Theo and I don't really hate each other," she continued as they left the office. "Those goddamned Harvard literature courses softened his mind a little, but he's still a smart boy. And he works under very trying restrictions. Instead of Mrs. A. Penn—with or without adjectives—he'd rather publish tracts on abolitionism—"

"Not so loud!" Payne said, glancing down the corridor. Amanda turned and saw the emaciated Mr. Drew dart back out of sight.

iv

Amanda found herself growing angry again as they walked through the cramped, disorderly warehouse area on the top floor. She saw bins full of cheap reprints of popular works—novels by Scott and Cooper—issued first by other publishers. When they passed a bin containing Maria Monk's *Awful Disclosures*, she exploded:

"You're still selling this?"

Payne grimaced. "Mr. Stovall's orders."

"You can be sure the moment the company changes hands, we'll destroy all copies."

"I'd be happy to see it gone from Kent's list."

Another appalling sight waited for Amanda in the basement. It was noisy, damp and badly lighted. It smelled of ink and the sweat of eight slovenly men in leather aprons who operated the antiquated flatbed presses. Amanda raised her voice to be heard above the rhythmic thumping:

"Doesn't the ink take a long time to dry in this dampness, Theo?"

"Of course it does," he shouted back. "And I can't tell you how many sheets we smear and ruin. But Mr. Stovall's accountants reckon that loss to be smaller than the cost of installing proper ventilation."

"I don't know much about the printing business, but it's obvious this equipment doesn't belong in a cellar."

"No, it belongs on the second or third floor."

"Why isn't it located there?"

"Too expensive to brace the flooring properly."

"How old are these presses?"

"Oh, thirty or forty years."

"Isn't there anything newer on the market?"

"Certainly. Mr. Hoe of New York has perfected steam-driven rotaries that print much faster. Some of the newspapers have installed them—"

"We really will have quite a few changes to make," Amanda said as they left the basement.

Payne burst out suddenly, "I hope you'll permit changes in our list as well—I mean beyond dropping the Monk book. We've been severely limited by Mr. Stovall's tightness with money on one hand, and his political bias on the other. For instance, two years ago, I wanted to buy the American rights to *Jane Eyre*. Too costly, I was told. One of the country's foremost poets, Professor Longfellow, lives just over in Cambridge and we can't afford him either—"

"With all this emphasis on culture, we can kiss Mrs. Penn's future goodbye," Rose sighed.

"Definitely not," Amanda laughed. "I told you before—I wouldn't lose Kent's most popular writer."

"But I *am* controversial to certain clergymen, Mrs. de la Gura—"

"Call me Amanda, please."

"My pleasure. You *do* know some churchmen find my books offensive?"

"Does the public?"

"Not generally. I practice moderation. When Mr. van Dugdale, the horse-car tycoon, raped Mercy Twickington in *Bartered Virtue*, I closed the bedroom door well before the actual moment—and only alluded to the deed afterward. Still, I know why women read my books. The subjects of sex and money are irresistible—sometimes an author doesn't even need money! Look how handsomely Mr. Hawthorne's doing with *A Scarlet Letter*. Theo's right, though. Kent's could stand the addition of some substantial authors writing on important subjects."

"I had a chance to bid on the right to reprint Fred Douglass' autobiography," Payne said. "I didn't even raise the question internally because I knew the owner would veto the idea."

Amanda shook her head, outraged:

"And that book's done well!"

"Exceedingly well. As a category, narratives of the lives of escaped slaves are highly popular. They also serve a worthwhile purpose," he added as they reached the entrance to his office and went in.

Amanda realized she was approaching controversial ground again. But she asked one more question:

"I assume most of the authors of such books have professional help in preparing their texts—?"

"Generally, yes. Douglass did his own—he's a rarity."

"It's premature to say this, Theo, but I know a man in California who might be persuaded to assemble notes on his experiences as a slave in Mississippi. The man's a mulatto. He manages my share of a mining claim—"

The mention of California caught Rose Ludwig's attention:

"You really do come from the far west?"

"Yes, I spent some years in Texas, and then California."

"Then you're just the person I'm looking for! You can help me with background for my next book. Theo, I haven't mentioned this to you, but I'm fed up with sighing heroines. That's one of my quirks, Amanda—I'm easily bored. After Adolph was buried, I started writing because I was bored, and after three novels with a New York setting, I'm bored again. The growing, important part of this country is the far west. I want to do a tale about a genuine western hero."

Payne looked dubious. "I doubt the public would accept that kind of novel from Mrs. Penn."

"Of course they will if it's interesting and the detail's authentic. And here's my source!"

"If you'll settle for an imperfect recollection of my husband's career—he was a fur trapper—I'll provide you with whatever detail I can," Amanda said.

"I knew you were a proper sort the second you walked in!" the other woman declared. "Theo, I believe we're all going to be much happier as a result of this meeting."

"So do I," Payne agreed. "I hope the sale goes through promptly."

Amanda asked, "You will keep everything we've discussed in absolute confidence?"

"Naturally, naturally!"

"When the lawyers finish haggling and we have Mr. Stovall's signature, I'll be in touch with you by telegraph."

"Telegraph?" Payne repeated. "You don't plan to remain in Boston?"

"I intend to buy or build a home in New York City. That's the financial center of the country, and that's where I must be if I'm to make my business ventures a success. I may install a private telegraph wire between my home and my local bank, though."

"My God, Mrs. de la Gura, do you have any notion of how expensive that will be?"

"I don't," Amanda replied. "If I have to worry about the cost, I'd have no business doing it."

Rose Ludwig laughed. "Theo, I think you've met your equal. Maybe your better—even though she didn't go to Harvard."

V

That evening, under the gaslights of the dining room at the American House, Amanda and her son shared a table with the authoress. Amanda had already confirmed her first reaction to the deep-voiced woman. Rose Ludwig was outgoing, opinionated, occasionally profane—and the two of them got along famously.

On the carriage ride from Kent and Son, Rose was candid about her beginnings. Her father had been a lock-tender on the Erie Canal near Buffalo. Her first meeting with her deceased husband, the owner of a fleet of brightly painted canal passenger boats, had been accidental. Ludwig had been touring the Erie system—

which was still in operation, but gradually declining in importance because of the spread of the railroads.

Rose frankly admitted she was drawn to Ludwig's wealth and his status as a widower more than she was to his physical assets:

"He was four inches shorter than I am. A wispy little fellow. His head had this unfortunate point—which his baldness didn't help. On the other hand, he was no fool. And he was kind to me the first time my father introduced us. So when he came back on another inspection trip a year later, I was ready for him. My God, I was thirty already—a spinster!—because I refused to marry the first canal-boat captain who came along! I'd learned my lesson from my older sister Lily. She rushes to the altar the moment some man makes her pulses flutter—and she never worries about the wisdom of the choice until afterward. She's had seven—no, eight husbands—the poor creature's been wed so many times, her cheeks are pitted from the rice. The last one who carried her off pretended to be a Bavarian duke. I think Lily's in Europe with him right now—no doubt having discovered he's only a pastry cook with an accent. That's not my style. I wanted to be sure I had a good catch. The second summer that Adolph happened by, I'd looked through enough old newspapers to be certain he was the one. I hooked him in record time. Six days, two hours and twenty-three minutes. I think that's why I took to you, Amanda—you're as direct as I am. That is—as direct as I am when I'm hobnobbing with Theo. In New York. it's a different story."

"I'd like to hear about your life in New York when we have dinner," Amanda said.

"I'm afraid most of my comments will be negative. I despise so-called society. Unfortunately, by virtue of marriage, I'm considered part of it. By and large, the people are pretentious mummies—except for one or two, like Vanderbilt, who can cuss the paint off a wall, and does. God, I hate these hoop skirts—!"

She writhed on the carriage seat, cursing so floridly that the driver opened the sliding partition behind his feet to see what was wrong.

At her own hotel, Rose Ludwig brought Amanda up to her suite while she rid herself of the hated muslin petticoat with its four steel hoops sewn into the fabric. Amanda, who had thus far relied on stiff petticoat material to give her skirt the fashionable bell shape, inspected the hoops with interest. The style was coming into fashion.

End to end, the hoop at the top of the skirt measured about a yard and a quarter, she guessed. It was a complete circle of steel. The three lower hoops, increasingly longer, didn't meet in front; there was an opening of about ten inches in each.

"No matter how carefully you walk," Rose called from the bedroom, "they jab the hell out of your thighs. I'd be in a fix if I was young enough so a man would want to look at my thighs—"

She appeared in the doorway in a costume that brought a gasp to Amanda's lips: a jacket and knee-length skirt in cerulean blue and, underneath, men's trousers of the same material, gathered at the ankle. "But I'm not supposed to say a word like thighs, am I? Women don't have *thighs*, *breasts*, *stomachs*—or some other anatomical features I'd be ostracized for mentioning—Amanda my dear, why are you staring?"

"I'm sorry, I've never seen real bloomers before. Those *are* bloomers?"

"Copied after the very ones worn by Amelia Bloomer herself. I don't dare put them on in New York as yet, though I predict they'll be popular in less than a year, no matter how the churches howl about immodesty. I hope I won't be barred from the dining room at the American House—"

She almost was. The head waiter frantically clenched his teeth and darted his eyes from the bloomers to the turned heads of scandalized guests. Amanda tipped the man heavily to overcome his moral scruples and, with Louis in tow, she and Rose sailed toward their table. They did grant the head waiter a little amnesty by permitting him to seat them in a corner. The position of the table hid the lower part of Rose's costume from most of the room.

Rose Ludwig's presence had one additional benefit. Louis was overwhelmed by his mother's new friend. He was more polite and biddable than he'd been for several weeks.

As the three sat finishing their dessert ices, Amanda concluded her considerably censored account of the circumstances that had brought her to Boston. She had told Rose of her family connection with the printing firm, and won her promise of secrecy. But she implied the firm had first changed hands in a normal manner. Rose looked surprised:

"Theo's always said there was some scandalous story about it being lost in a gambling game."

"I don't know how fictions like that get started," Amanda replied, concentrating on her ice. She felt the other woman studying her. Did Rose believe her? If not, she didn't make an issue:

"We certainly have a lot in common, Amanda. We both had rough beginnings. Fortunately, once I snared Adolph, my way was smoothed. Though it wasn't all pie and roses! I immediately had entree to the best homes. You'll be spared that tribulation."

"What do you mean?"

"You won't have to mingle with all those dreadfully self-important people. You *don't* have any notions about cracking society, do you?"

"No. You heard what I told Theo Payne—I'm moving to New York because it's the business center."

"Good. Then you won't be disappointed. Really, you'd be amazed at the number of Ohio widows who remove themselves to New York with a little capital, thinking they'll soon be dining with the Rensselaers and the Belmonts and the Vanderbilts. Society has closed up like a clam in the last twenty or thirty years. Today you're either born into it, you marry into it—or you wait a generation before you get your first invitation to tea with Mrs. Belmont. Some poor creatures foolishly try to shorten the wait—"

And she launched into an anecdote about one such parvenu, a young woman who learned that New York gentry frequently rode on a certain bridle path above Forty-second Street early in the morning. Though terrified of horses, the young woman contrived a system of straps to keep herself lashed to her saddle. She made herself visible on the bridle path, where she attempted to strike up conversations with affluent bachelors:

"Now God as my witness—this is true, Amanda. One morning a thundershower struck. The horse reared and the young lady was dumped on her ass—excuse me, Louis; derriere—with all her hidden straps, and her pretensions, exposed. She left the city a week later."

Amanda laughed. "I don't want to meet any bachelors, Rose. Or any society people, for that matter."

Except one.

"Good for you." She leaned her elbows on the snowy tablecloth and pointed a finger at Amanda's nose. "You did promise to tell me what you know about frontiersmen. I'm sure Theo loathes the idea, but I'm convinced the public's ready for a rousing western tale."

"I'll tell you everything I can."

"Wonderful! Why don't we travel to New York together?"

"I'd love that. As soon as we arrive, I want you to show me where to buy a pair of bloomers."

"Delighted. You'll forgive an old lady for being sentimental, but I think we're going to be the best of friends. Friendship's a rare commodity—I have hundreds of acquaintances, but I'll bet I've had no more than two real friends all my life. No, three—I considered Adolph a friend. It's much more comfortable being married to a friend than to a lover, you know. I like you, Amanda—"

She reached across and touched Louis' dark hair. "And I like your son. My God, with those eyes, he'll be breaking hearts in a few years. If I weren't such a tottering wreck—oh, well." A sigh. "Are you two finished? I'm about to perish for want of a cigar. Bad vice I picked up from Adolph. He smoked them even in the bath. Have you ever looked at a tub full of floating ash? Ugh!"

As they left the dining room, still drawing shocked stares and comments, Amanda was immensely pleased. At long last, it seemed that events were moving in response to her will, instead of at the random whim of chance. Before the year was out, she'd be well established in New York—

With Kent and Son in her possession.

vi

Two mornings later, a grim Joshua Rothman called at Amanda's suite in the American House. She was in the midst of packing, with trunks open everywhere.

"Mrs. de la Gura, what did you say when you visited the publishing company?"

She looked chagrined. "A little more than I should have, perhaps—"

"That became evident first thing this morning."

Amanda set aside the skirt she'd been about to fold into one of the trunks. "What do you mean?"

Upset, Rothman stamped to the windows:

"A banker can be of no use to you if you refuse to

follow his suggestions!" He spun around. "You made some remarks about getting rid of a certain anti-Catholic title on the Kent list? Some other comments about wanting to publish an autobiography by a runaway slave—?"

"What if I did? I got angry at what I saw at Kent's—the decay—the indifference—besides, I only spoke to the general manager, Mr. Payne. In private. He promised not to repeat a word."

Rothman leaned across the top of a trunk:

"Theo Payne is a notorious drunk! An excellent brain—but a loose tongue when he imbibes. And he imbibes constantly."

A little knot of dread tightened in Amanda's stomach. "I—I did catch some hint of that," she admitted.

"Did you also meet a gentleman named Drew?"

"Briefly."

"Mr. Stovall's informant within the firm. After you left, Payne was so delighted, he spent all afternoon in an alehouse, celebrating. As I get the story, he returned late in the day, barely able to walk, and boasted to the entire staff about all the changes you intended to make. The *entire* staff—including Mr. Drew. You should have stayed away—I warned you. More important, you should have avoided political subjects at all costs—that, I didn't warn you of specifically. So we're both paying for it."

"Get to the point, Joshua."

"This morning, Stovall's attorneys wired from New York. The negotiations have been broken off. Permanently."

"Oh my God."

"It's my error for not telling you Stovall's an active member of the Know-Nothings—"

"No, don't blame yourself. I was aware of it."

"Then how could you imagine he'd sell out to someone who plans to turn Kent and Son a hundred and eighty degrees politicially?" Rothman sighed. "I'm sorry—it's not my position to speak so frankly—it's just that I know how much you want the company—"

"I didn't stop to think about the danger in Payne's drinking. The blame's mine, Joshua. I accept it."

"That won't make Stovall relent, I'm afraid."

"If we can't buy the firm straightforwardly, we'll have to get control some other way."

Thunderstruck, he stared at her.

"Are you serious?"

"I am. This is a setback, nothing more—"

But she felt it much more deeply than the words suggested. She hadn't been all that outspoken at the firm—yet she *had* realized she shouldn't be speaking. Her anger had overcome caution.

Stovall's immediate reaction to her comments spoke volumes about the sort of man he was; the sort her grandfather would have detested—

In a calm voice, she resumed:

"I'm sorry you've labored so hard, only to have my carelessness undo your efforts." She touched his arm. "I'll see you're well compensated when we finally get control."

"Mrs. de la Gura, I really think you'd be wiser to abandon any hope of—"

"No," she said, "I won't."

"I can see no open, legal means of—"

"Then we'll do it secretly if we have to! Illegally! One way or another, Joshua, *I am going to own Kent's.*"

CHAPTER III

The Man Who Thundered

SOME SIXTEEN MONTHS LATER—a Friday evening in February, 1852—Amanda and Rose Ludwig were seated in a box at The Bowery Theatre, a structure already twenty-five years old but distinguished among New York's playhouses because it had been the first to install gas.

The jets throughout most of the auditorium had been turned off for the meeting, which was being held in lieu of a performance of the Bowery's current attraction. Together with the footlight candles, the gas fixtures flanking the proscenium opening illuminated the half dozen speakers seated behind the podium. The six were paying dutiful attention to the preacher addressing the three thousand people who had packed the main floor, the boxes and the galleries.

A few feet upstage from the half-dozen chairs, a drop painted to represent a European drawing-room added an incongruous note; the theatre management had declined to remove all the scenery for the comedy now playing six nights a week. But since the comedy was not particularly successful, the management had been happy to rent the theatre for an abolitionist rally.

The preacher, a Congregationalist, had been talking for twenty minutes. His function was the same as that of four of the men behind him—to lengthen the program and build anticipation for the featured address by Frederick Douglass. The guest of honor sat directly behind the podium, motionless and attentive.

Mr. Bryant, who was to introduce him, began consulting his notes, conscious from the flow of adjectives that the cleric was reaching his conclusion. And so he did, with much arm-waving and a shrill burst of oratory devoid of logic but long on heat. He called down divine damnation on the entire south—but drew only perfunctory applause from the restless crowd. They'd heard essentially the same message four times already.

An audible sigh ran through the dark theatre as the preacher sat down, mopping his forehead. William Cullen Bryant, the Massachusetts lawyer turned poet and journalist, straightened his two pages of notes and stood up. A hush settled on the hall. Amanda heard Rose murmur:

"Finally! Old Horace has fallen asleep over there. So has my rear end."

Gazing across the main floor to the front box on the far side, Amanda saw the publisher Greeley straighten up in his chair, roused by the applause that greeted Bryant's arrival at the podium. She glanced to the box directly behind Greeley's; it was still a puzzle. No one seemed to be occupying it, though every ticket for the meeting had been sold for weeks. If there were people in the box, they'd seated themselves quite far back, to avoid being seen.

"Ladies and gentlemen," Bryant began, "I shall be brief in my introduction—"

A raucous cry of approval rang down from the gallery. The audience laughed. Bryant smiled. He was in his late fifties, held the editor's chair at the *New York Post,* and appeared tonight as one of the city's most outspoken foes of slavery. In the national election of '48, Bryant had been a member of the Barnburner faction that had split off from the Democratic party, enraged because the party adopted a platform containing only one plank of substance: a vague endorsement of the conduct of the Mexican war. Out of the Barnburners—

who had offered former president Van Buren to the electorate in '48—had come the even more militant Free Soil party, ardent reformers unalterably opposed to the extension of slavery into any new United States territories.

But Bryant refrained from comments on the meeting's theme, confining his remarks to a quick summary of the career of the man everyone had come to hear.

He touched on Douglass' birth as a slave in Maryland; mentioned his early years in Baltimore, when, through the kindness of an enlightened master, Hugh Auld, he had been able to learn to read and write while serving as a houseboy and a laborer in Auld's shipyard.

It was Auld's death, Bryant reminded the audience, that had brought Douglass to St. Michaels, below Baltimore, and confrontation with another Auld, Thomas, who proved less liberal.

Douglass had already begun to feel resentment of his bondage. He was quarrelsome. Auld took steps to correct that. He hired out the young black to a noted slave-breaker named Edward Covey.

Covey attempted to apply the whip once too often. Douglass turned on him, and fought. After the struggle, Covey, all but defeated, never again touched the Negro whose spirit he had been paid to destroy—

"And thus," Bryant said, "in our distinguished guest's own words, a slave was made a man!"

Applause. Amanda and Rose joined in. Then, as the clapping died away, they heard a startling sound from the darkened box behind Greeley's.

The rest of the audience heard too. Heads turned. There were scowls. Greeley rose all the way out of his chair and tried to see who had hissed.

It wasn't uncommon for foes of the abolitionists to attend their programs. Sometimes the unwelcome guests tried to disrupt a meeting. That was evidently the case tonight. Amanda's vantage point still prevented her from seeing the occupants of the box in question.

Bryant was plainly angered. He lost his place in his notes and took a few moments to resume. Douglass looked unperturbed.

Rapidly, Bryant went through the rest of his introduction, describing the speaker's first, aborted effort to escape to the north, and his second, successful one in 1838. With seventeen dollars and an identification paper borrowed from a free Negro seaman, Douglass had boarded a train in Baltimore and waited nervously for the conductor to collect his fare and examine the paper. The conductor gave the paper only a casual glance. After a boat trip from Washington to Philadelphia, then a train ride, Douglass arrived in New York, a free man.

Bryant paid tribute to Douglass' family; to his long and earnest dedication to freedom for America's enslaved blacks; to his career as editor and publisher of *The North Star* at Rochester. Then, folding away his notes, he said:

"It is my great pleasure and high honor to present Mr. Frederick Douglass."

The audience surged to its feet, applauding wildly. Douglass smiled for the first time, tilted his head to one side to acknowledge the ovation and approached the podium.

ii

The speaker began quietly, using no notes:

"Mr. Bryant—ladies and gentlemen—I too shall be brief. My message to you is essentially a simple one. But just let me state that I never stand before an audience like that which I see before me without feeling my incompetence to do justice to the cause which I am here to advocate—"

He allowed himself another faint smile.

"Or to the expectation which is generally created for me by the friends who precede me. Certainly, if the eulogiums bestowed on me this evening were correct, I should be able to entertain this audience for hours by my eloquence. But I claim none of this. While I feel grateful for your generosity, I can certainly claim very little right to your applause—for I was once a slave. I never had a day's schooling in my life. All that I know, I have stolen—"

The oblique reference to his escape produced a scattering of cheers, which he acknowledged with another of those carefully controlled smiles. As the cheering faded, there was another loud hiss.

This time, a man in the orchestra leaped up and shook his fist:

"Shame, shame!"

Others took up the cry. Douglass didn't dignify the dark box with so much as a glance. He held up his hand, settling the crowd into silence.

"I wish at once to relieve you from all expectation of a great speech. That I am deeply and earnestly engaged in advocating the cause of my brethren is most true, and so, this evening, I hail your kind expressions toward me with the profoundest gratitude. I will make use of those expressions. I will take them home in my memory. They shall be written on my heart, and they will give me courage as I travel throughout this land of boasted liberty and light—"

His voice had grown stronger.

"—yet this land of abject slavery, for the purpose of overthrowing that system and restoring the Negro to his long-lost rights!"

Applause louder than before greeted this first emotional peak in the speech. Amanda watched the dark box. Sure enough, just as the outpouring of sound began to diminish, the hiss was heard again, prolonged and ugly.

More yells of anger burst from the audience. One burly fellow started out of his seat, intending to go up the aisle and on to the box. His two companions restrained him.

Douglass moved quickly to the subject of his address —Section Two of Article IV of the Constitution. He first quoted the Section's third paragraph verbatim. Then he reminded his audience that the authors of the Constitution had included the paragraph in order to acknowledge the right of slave owners to reclaim runaways in non-slave territory, even though the paragraph carefully avoided the use of the word *slave* in favor of the more general *person*.

"Upon the face of this," Douglass said, "there is nothing of injustice, nothing of inhumanity—it is perfectly in accordance with justice, perfectly humane. But what does it *really* mean in the United States?

"It means that if any slave shall in the darkness of midnight, thinking himself a man and entitled to the rights of a man, steal away from his hovel or quarter—

"Shall snap the chain that binds his leg—

"Shall break the fetter that links him to slavery—

"It means that if he shall do these things, then by night and by day, on his way from a state where slavery is practiced to one where it is not, he shall also be liable to be hunted down like a felon and dragged back to the bondage from which he has escaped!"

Amanda leaned forward, stirred by the man's eloquence. Douglass' forehead showed a light sheen of perspiration. He still had no scrap of text before him. But he obviously needed none. Much more than thought had gone into what he was saying; his life's fears and angers and hopes had gone into it.

He let go of the podium, his hands clenched.

"This clause of the Constitution," he thundered, "is one of the greatest safeguards to that slave system which we have met here this evening to express our detestation of!

"This clause of the Constitution—upheld and endorsed by an abominable fugitive slave bill promulgated by misguided men in the Congress—gives to the slaveholder the right at any moment to set his blood-hound upon the track of the fugitive, hunt him down and drag him back to the jaws of slavery!

"This clause of the Constitution consecreates every rood of earth in this land over which the star-spangled banner waves as SLAVE-HUNTING GROUND!"

The booming voice was drowned under a roar of, *"Shame! Shame!"* If the unseen antagonist in the box bothered to hiss, no one heard.

Douglass then launched into a ringing demand that all men of conscience disobey the Fugitive Slave Act. While Amanda had applauded during the earlier portions of the speech, here she held back. She wasn't certain the speaker was right. Congress had passed the law in the hope of mitigating sectional strife and preserving the Union. Douglass rejected such compromise. He said the law was immoral—and perhaps it was. He said it should be overturned—that might be true as well. But when he said that until the law was repealed, it should be ignored, Amanda found herself disagreeing.

"This being the state of things in America—" Douglass' quieter tone immediately hushed the hall again. "—you cannot expect me to stand before you with eloquent outbursts of praise for my country. No, my friends, I must be honest with America—

"Unmask her pretensions to republicanism!

"Unmask her hypocritical pretensions to Christianity!

"Denounce her pretensions to civilization!

"Proclaim in her ear the wrongs of those who cry day and night to heaven—'HOW LONG, HOW LONG, OH LORD GOD!' "

The Bowery Theatre literally shook from the handclapping and foot-stomping. Douglass bowed his head, breathing hard and clinging to the podium for support.

The ovation continued for one minute; two; three. Rose was clapping furiously. Even Amanda cast aside her reservations and joined in, caught up in the spell of the man's oratory.

Finally, when the tumult died, Douglass resumed: "Let me say this to you in conclusion. Despite the dark picture I have presented—despite the iniquity of the present law which can only be an abomination in the eyes of all men who consider themselves believers in the principles upon which this nation was founded—no, despite all this, I do not despair of America.

"There are forces in operation which must inevitably work the downfall of the unjust law and the entire system of slavery. 'The arm of the Lord is not shortened.' The doom of slavery is *certain!*"

Once more, little by little, he had begun to build volume. Amanda's spine tingled. The stately figure held every eye in the theatre.

"While drawing encouragement from the Declaration of Independence—from the great principles it contains—and from the genius of American institutions, my spirit is also cheered by the obvious tendencies of the age in which we live.

"No nation can now shut itself up from the surrounding world and trot around in the same old path of its fathers. A change has come over the affairs of mankind!

"Walled cities and empires have become unfashionable. The arm of commerce has borne away the gates of the strong city. Intelligence is penetrating the darkest corners of the globe. It makes its pathway over and under the sea, as well as on the earth. Wind, steam, and lightning are its chartered agents. The fiat of the Almighty—'Let there be light!'—has not yet spent its force. No abuse, no outrage can now hide itself from the all-pervading and cleansing light of decency, democracy, and honor.

"Unjust laws shall perish. Unjust men shall die unmourned and dishonored. There will be universal freedom if we dedicate our hearts, our minds and our mortal souls to its accomplishment—if we resist the tyranny of the law where it must be resisted—and if our prayer of fervent aspiration forever remains that of William Lloyd Garrison—"

Douglass flung his hands high over his head, roaring:

"'God speed the year of jubilee—the wide world o'er!' "

iii

It took Amanda and Rose nearly twenty minutes to work their way through the long line of people filing onto the stage to congratulate Douglass. He was particularly gracious with Amanda, recalling their meeting on the steamer to Boston, and thanking her warmly for the donation she'd sent. She promised to send another, then said:

"But I must tell you honestly, Mr. Douglass, I can't agree with you on one point in your address."

"Which point is that, Mrs. de la Gura?"

"That the Fugitive Slave Act must be disobeyed. Overturned—perhaps. But as long as it *is* the law—"

"I can understand your attitude—even though I consider it wrong. The working of that particular law remains an abstraction for you. Something you read about, and consider intellectually. I think you'd change your mind if you were face to face with one of the law's victims. Or were a victim yourself."

"I'm not certain of that, Mr. Douglass."

He smiled. "But I am."

The press of the line behind them forced Amanda to break off the conversation. As she followed Rose up one of the aisles, she glanced at the box from which the hissing had come. If the box was still occupied, it was impossible to see by whom.

Presently the two women reached the packed lobby. Through the open outer doors, Amanda saw that snow had started falling in the February darkness. Forward movement was almost impossible.

The crowd filled the lobby and spilled outside. Lines of hacks and carriages waited three deep. As each vehicle maneuvered for a place at the curb and loaded its passengers, she and Rose were able to take another step or two. But progress was infernally slow.

As she slipped her hands deeper into her muff, Amanda felt Rose tap her shoulder. She turned and saw Mr. Greeley of the *Tribune*.

Amanda had met the Whig publisher at a Christmas fete at Rose's mansion in Gramercy Park. She'd been struck by his aura of age. Though Greeley couldn't have been much more than forty, his mutton-chop whiskers were already whitening. His piercing eyes seemed those of an old man who viewed the world with simmering discontent.

Greeley had been intrigued when Rose mentioned that her friend had survived the Alamo massacre. He had also been openly skeptical, reminding the women that there were no American survivors save a lady named Dickinson.

Amanda pointed out that the list of Mexican survivors was much less precise. She expected she'd be shown on the record not under her maiden name but under her husband's, which was Spanish, if the record carried any mention of her at all.

A few details of the massacre soon convinced Greeley that Amanda was telling the truth. He suggested an interview with one of his reporters. She declined, saying that the idea of personal publicity struck her as ostentatious, and she didn't care to be painted as any sort of heroine; she'd merely survived as best she could. Actually, her real reason for turning him down was a wish to avoid any chance of the Kent name appearing in print. Mr. Greeley had been testy with her the rest of the evening.

Now, though, the incident was forgotten. He tipped his hat in a cordial way:

"Mrs. de la Gura—Rose—good evening."

"Happy to see you awake again, Horace," Rose said.

Greeley ignored the jibe. "Douglass gave a splendid talk, didn't he?"

"Splendid," Amanda agreed.

"Marred only by those disgusting interruptions from the box behind me."

"Did you see who was doing it?" Amanda asked.

"Of course. A certain gentleman who enjoys making his obnoxious opinions known in public. A member of the exalted Order of the Star Spangled Banner. I prefer not to discuss the subject any further. His performance made me sick."

"But Horace, who was it?"

Greeley paid no attention to Rose's query. He was staring at two men in the crowd. With a sour expression, he said:

"And I'm experiencing the same feeling right now."

Amanda recognized handsome, blue-eyed Fernando Wood, a wealthy politician with ambitions for the mayor's office. With him was his brother Ben. Both were Democrats, and hence Greeley's foes.

Fernando Wood and his brother were arm in arm with a pair of gaudily dressed young ladies who might have come straight from a Paradise Square brothel—but then, the Woods made no secret of having the poor, and even most of the city's criminal element, in their political camp.

The Woods had grown rich in real estate, and also by operating as licensed gamblers, under a dubious "charter" granted them in Louisiana. They were close friends of the Tammany politician Isaiah Rynders, who bossed the Sixth Ward, owned several slum saloons—and could always rally a street gang to harry an opposition candidate. Rynders was notorious for his hatred of blacks and foreigners—his Irish constituents excepted. He had been in the crowd that had started the Astor Place riot. The ringleader, some said.

But none of this seemed to rub off on the Wood brothers tonight. They waved and chatted with friends as they worked their way out of the lobby. They saw Greeley; Fernando Wood said something that was obviously contemptuous. His brother and the young girls laughed. Greeley's jaw showed a tinge of scarlet as he turned back to the women.

"By the way—have either of you read Mrs. Stowe's novel?"

"It's not due out until next month, is it?" Rose asked.

"No. But Jewett's of Boston is distributing advance copies."

The conversation touched off Amanda's anger. If only the secret campaign she and Joshua Rothman were waging had proceeded a little further—if only she'd been in control of Kent and Son—the firm might have had a chance to publish what everyone predicted would be the literary sensation of the year. Perhaps of the decade. She forced herself to speak calmly:

"I'm afraid Rose and I aren't important enough to be on Jewett's list. How did you like the novel, Mr. Greeley?"

"Oh, not very well. I read several episodes when it was serialized in the *National Era*. The complete version's more of the same—too sentimental for my taste. The book's purpose is worthwhile, though."

"Rose introduced me to Mrs. Stowe's brother last

week," Amanda told him. "We drove over to Plymouth Church in Brooklyn to hear Reverend Beecher preach."

Greeley whipped a small pad from his coat and jotted on it with a pencil:

"Must remind Dana to send a reporter over there to see whether Henry's still planning that mock slave auction. Last time I saw him, he was trying to find a good-looking young Negress who wouldn't object to being paraded before a crowd, and sold from his pulpit—"

As Greeley put the pad away, Amanda said, "The Reverend told us they're working up a dramatization of *Uncle Tom's Cabin* for Purdy's Theatre in the fall."

"Meanwhile," Rose said, "I'll have Kent's send you another review copy of *The White Indian*. It's obvious you misplaced the first one."

"I doubt that," Greeley retorted.

"Really, Horace! You should pay attention to the book. We've gone to a fourth printing already."

"Rose," Greeley said, "I'm very fond of your hospitality. But not of your characters."

"Not so loud!" she cautioned. "You're one of the few people in New York who knows Mrs. Penn's identity."

"Well, I wish Mrs. Penn would change her style. Characters who make four-page declarations about virtue of courage put me in a torpor."

"I can certainly say the same for those incomprehensible foreign features you're publishing!"

"Mr. Marx and Mr. Engels are astute observers of the European social and political scene."

"I fall asleep after the second paragraph. Many more essays of that sort and I'll start reading Gordon Bennett's paper. Or the *Times*."

"The *Times!*" Greeley sputtered. "Upstart rag! I'm astonished it's survived this long. It certainly won't last till the end of the year. As to your fable of the fur business—"

"The story may be fictional, but Amanda here provided me with the background. It's absolutely authentic."

Greeley still looked put upon. "All right, send another copy to my editor, Mr. Dana. At your own risk!"

The stout woman pulled a face. "Horace, you can be positively vicious."

"The function of the free press is to provoke, not pacify, dear lady."

"But I thought you fancied the west."

"The real west," he nodded, with a clear implication that he still believed Rose had written about something else. "It's astonishing how the public prefers fancy to fact. I'm already enthroned for having urged some anonymous young-man to go west, when it was Mr. Soule, who edits the *Express* out in Terre Haute, Indiana, who actually turned the phrase last year. I merely repeated it in a letter to a friend—which he promptly made public."

Rose teased him: "The price of fame, Horace."

With another sarcastic expression, Greeley tipped his hat. "There's my carriage." He began to elbow his way outside.

Rose stood on tiptoe, trying to find her own driver in the confusion of vehicles and stamping horses in front of the theatre. A few gusts of snow began to blow into the lobby. Suddenly the heavy woman exclaimed:

"I've had enough of being pushed and shoved—let's do a little of our own. Follow me, Amanda—"

She turned sideways.

"I wonder if you'd excuse us—we're trying to get through—*damn it, get off my skirt!*"

The man turned abruptly. Inside her muff, Amanda dug her fingers into the palms of her hands.

She'd been in New York City for over a year. And although she'd driven by the immense house just off Washington Square a number of times, she'd never set eyes on its owner—though she'd kept track of his activities through items in the press.

And now, unexpectedly, he was directly in front of her, slender and erect despite his age—fifty-eight or thereabouts. If Rose's outburst had angered him, he didn't show it. His shoulder cape displayed its crimson lining as he raised a glove to the brim of his black top hat. In his other hand he held a gold-headed cane.

A white silk scarf was tied around his head. It cut obliquely from the left side of his forehead, across the bridge of his nose to the right side of his chin. The scarf fluttered in the wind. Amanda glimpsed a bit of ugly, discolored scar tissue. The man's left eye, brown and amused, seemed to glow like a dark gem.

Amanda held herself rigid, somehow afraid to speak or even be noticed.

"My sincere apologies, Mrs. Ludwig," Hamilton Stovall said.

CHAPTER IV

Suspicion

"MR. STOVALL! I DIDN'T see you in the audience—"

"I don't sit with the *audience,*" he said. "I always take a private box."

Rose's eyebrows shot up. "Behind Mr. Greeley?"

"Quite right."

"So it was you interrupting Douglass!"

Stovall chuckled. "Really, the man's incredible. If he didn't have such a grip on so many minds, baiting him would be amusing. Under the circumstances, I view it more as a public duty—"

Thus far he'd hardly taken notice of Amanda. She was trying to breathe evenly; maintain a polite but none-too-interested expression.

"I wonder if there's a city ordinance prohibiting a baboon from dressing in a man's clothing," Stovall went on. "If not, there should be—and it ought to be enforced against Mr. Douglass. However, I do apologize for making my presence known to you so clumsily, Mrs. Ludwig."

Stovall's words carried a faint sarcasm that robbed them of any sincerity. He turned to a man twenty years his junior hovering at his elbow.

"May I present my secretary, Mr. Jonas? Jonas, this is Mrs. Rose Ludwig—"

"Ah yes, one of the bloomer ladies," Jonas replied, his eyelids drooping briefly. He had an effeminate face, and pink, pouting lips.

Stovall turned to Amanda. "I'm afraid I'm not acquainted with your companion, Mrs. Ludwig."

Amanda felt her cheeks must be red. To be so close to the man who had made Jared suffer was almost unbearable. She wanted to strike at his face—

She fought the irrational impulse. She tried to appraise Hamilton Stovall without emotion, as she would a business adversary. It was obvious he had once been exceedingly handsome. But his exposed cheek had a purplish, blotchy look. What little she could see of his hair was pure white. His teeth were so perfect—and so yellow—she was certain they were false. Their artificial uniformity gave him a sort of a skull's grin. His glittering brown eye seemed to spike into her mind, drawing out all her secrets—

Foolish! Get yourself under control! He doesn't know who you are—

Rose remedied that in an instant:

"Amanda, let me introduce Mr. Hamilton Stovall. This is Mrs. Amanda de la Gura."

Stovall's good eye blinked. But it was young Jonas, standing unusually close to his employer, who spoke first:

"Indeed! So you're the free-thinking lady who tried to buy Kent and Son!"

Amanda's stomach hurt. "Yes, I tried to buy it. The rest is your judgment, Mr. Jonas."

Stovall's eye held hers. "I'm fascinated to make your acquaintance at last. Of course I regret it was impossible for me to accept your offer—I could have put the money to excellent use. But I simply couldn't turn the firm over to someone whose views are so far removed from mine. Misguided, if you don't mind my saying so—" He obviously didn't care if she did. "I might even go so far as to call them dangerously radical."

Hoping she sounded sufficiently calm, she replied,

"Making you aware of those views was my error, Mr. Stovall."

"You're quite correct." The yellow-tinged teeth glared in a fixed smile. But his eye held no humor.

"Of course I wasn't aware you had informants at the firm."

Stovall dismissed it: "Oh, one must—to protect one's own interests."

Abruptly, Jonas asked, "You're from California, are you not?" Amanda's stomach quivered again. Stovall had checked into her background.

"I am." She gave them no more to work on. But Stovall refused to quit:

"Why in the world would someone with substantial mining and textile holdings—"

He knows that too.

"—abruptly decide to venture into book publishing?"

"I was searching for a way to diversify. A publishing house seemed a sound investment."

"Yes, I do recall hearing some such explanation from the gentlemen who acted on your behalf. I find one thing odd, though."

"What's that?"

"I'm not aware that you've attempted to buy another book firm. Was Kent's the only one in which you were interested?"

Amanda hedged:

"At the time we negotiated—yes."

"The fact is, you've bought no other properties at all—at least under your own name. Forgive me, but it's almost as if you had some reason other than a business one for wanting Kent's."

"That's purely your speculation, Mr. Stovall."

"I admit it. There could be no personal basis for your interest, could there?"

"None."

"We've never met before—"

"Never."

"Well—" He shrugged. "I must be wrong."

"A rare occurrence with Mr. Stovall," Jonas informed them with a smug smile.

The outrageous flattery pleased the older man, though. He touched Jonas' gloved hand in an almost affectionate way. Then he said to Amanda:

"Financially speaking, I really wish we had been able to reach an agreement. Publishing is a risky enterprise—another circumstance which makes me wonder why you chose it for diversification. I have very little interest in the firm, actually—only in what it earns. I never wanted the company except as the means to an end. But perhaps you don't know the story. I assumed ownership many years ago as a result of a sporting wager—"

Amanda heard Rose's sudden intake of breath. Stovall's brown eye watched her for a reaction—

Or did she just imagine that?

"—and a desire to see the founders, a clan of wild-eyed Boston mobocrats, put out of business." He licked a snowflake from his lower lip. "The heirs of a Mr. Gilbert Kent. Despicable people."

Amanda's lips pressed together. She was trembling. Hands clenched tight inside the muff, she was conscious of both Stovall and Rose watching her closely. She hoped she hadn't given herself away—

"I know nothing about them other than the name, Mr. Stovall. I've spent most of my years out west."

"Of course," he murmured. "Well, there's no need for civilized folk to quarrel over an aborted transaction—" He patted the secretary's arm. "Jonas, be a dear chap and see what you can do to hurry the carriage."

The secretary started for the curb. He whistled and motioned. Again Stovall touched his top hat.

"Mrs. de la Gura—Mrs. Ludwig—my distinct pleasure."

His good eye raked Amanda as he turned away. Did he know more about her than he was revealing?

No, that was impossible. Outside of her immediate household, only Rose, William Benbow and Joshua Rothman knew she was Gilbert Kent's daughter—

A man blocked Stovall's route to the carriage door which Jonas was holding open. Stovall lifted his cane and prodded the man with the ferrule:

"One side!"

The man, much less elegantly dressed, whirled around:

"Who the hell are you poking with—?"

"You, my shabby friend. It's quite obvious you couldn't afford a private carriage—while mine's waiting just there." Stovall pulled the gold-headed cane close to his chest, as if ready to lash outward with it. His voice had a savage note in it: "If you want to be impudent, I'll give you impudence that'll lay you up for a week!"

The man glared, then shifted his glance to the cane head. Amanda couldn't see Stovall's face, but the other man obviously had a good view of it—and it intimidated him. Stovall's voice was equally intimidating with its unmistakable suggestion of violent temper held in check.

The man stepped back.

Hamilton Stovall climbed into the carriage. Jonas touched him, apparently to assist him on the step. Then the carriage door slammed. The driver whipped up the matched grays and the vehicle lurched off.

Amanda watched it until it was completely hidden by the wind-driven snow. *I blundered,* she thought. *After the Kent negotiations fell through, I blundered by not covering myself with another purchase—immediately.*

And had she reacted too visibly to Stovall's remarks about the family? That worried her most of all; she might well have given herself away—or at least aroused his suspicion to the point where he'd think about making further inquiries. Perhaps even in California—

That's too far-fetched, she decided.

But was it?

Abruptly, she realized Rose had spoken to her. The stout woman repeated what she'd said:

"The carriage is at the curb. Do you want to go home? Or just stand here all night?"

She glanced around. The lobby had finally emptied. "I'm sorry—certainly, let's go."

She was conscious of Rose scrutinizing her as they hurried outside.

ii

The city of New York looked almost beautiful this February night, covered as it was by fresh snow.

New York's population had climbed to almost three-quarters of a million people. A construction boom was steadily pushing the northern boundary toward the Croton Reservoir at Forty-second Street. Tonight, the ugliness of an expanding city of rich and poor—its unfinished buildings, its piles of uncollected refuse, its free-roaming herds of pigs and cows—was hidden by the wind-blown whiteness.

The streets were empty for a change. It always seemed to Amanda that half the city's inhabitants must be Irish—and indigent. They were forever loitering on the main thoroughfares. In some areas ruled by the immigrants, a lone woman—or a lone man who wasn't Irish, for that matter—dared not walk after dark. Michael Boyle, who would be waiting for her at home with the late afternoon's business matters yet to discuss, was a product of one such festering district, the Five Points.

The inside of Rose's carriage was ice cold. Or was the coldness within her? She couldn't escape an uneasy feeling about her reaction to Stovall's mention of the Kents.

Lamps and gaslights in passing buildings lit the carriage interior from time to time. The wheels jolted into a rut in the unpaved street. The driver whipped the team. The carriage lurched. Rose swore, singeing her glove on the locofoco she'd been trying to apply to the end of a cigar.

When the cigar was lit, she slid a window down and tossed the charred match into the storm.

Amanda felt questions were imminent; perhaps some of her own would forestall them:

"Rose, you spoke about Stovall's wife once. When did she die?"

"Oh, let's see. Early in fifty, I believe. She came of a good family. Baltimore—precious Hamilton's own city."

"When did he marry her?"

"Years ago—and only so he could use her family's capital to shore up his steel business. Or so I've been told."

"He has no heirs, isn't that right?"

"None."

"And I assume his wife died of natural causes—"

"That was the story—publicly."

"What do you mean?"

"I heard a whisper or two that it was suicide."

Amanda smiled without humor. "Perhaps she found out Stovall's not quite so respectable as he pretends to be."

Thoughtfully, Rose puffed out smoke. The thick blue cloud made breathing difficult.

"Well, he does admit to a few vices. He drinks a good deal. He's been known to gamble heavily. But if you removed everybody who does either one, New York would have a population of approximately forty-six. I had a peculiar feeling about that Mr. Jonas, though. I wonder if he's something more than a secretary—"

"He might be Stovall's lover."

"That was exactly my suspicion."

"There's evidence to support it."

"What evidence?"

"Michael goes back to the Five Points now and again," Amanda explained. "To visit some of the friends he knew when he worked on the docks. There's a story circulating about Stovall to the effect that he occasionally takes a little holiday with some people on Mulberry Street. Under another name."

"Who does he visit?"

"A young whore—and her brother. I gather they're all part of a—call it a triangular relationship."

Rose shivered. "My God. I fancy I'm liberal about a lot of things, but I don't care to know any more details of a sordid situation like that!"

"Maybe Stovall's wife caught a hint of it—"

"Perhaps," Rose nodded. "Stovall's tony friends didn't, I'm sure. I've heard nothing like that about him. If he prefers male companions instead of female—"

"I've been told there are some who like both."

"Well, you can be sure he'll be careful no one can prove it. Any more than people can prove your relationship with Michael Boyle's something other than business."

Aghast, Amanda said, "Do they accuse me of having Michael for a lover?"

"Naturally! I've told you—the ruining of reputations is a popular sport of some of our finer citizens."

"I didn't realize I was sufficiently well known to merit that kind of attention."

"In a little over a year, my dear, you've made the city very much aware of your presence. You'll still never crack that so-called social barrier we've discussed before—but a rich, good-looking woman who owns gold in California and part of one of the most successful textile companies in the northeast is grist for the conversational mills of society."

"I had no idea there'd been filthy talk about Michael—"

"Well, my God, he *is* good-looking. He *is* your private clerk—and you *did* give him a room as well as a position."

"He's a bright young man. Why shouldn't he have a better place to live than the slums? I'm disgusted about the stories—"

"Oh, stop," Rose chuckled. "At least Michael's the right sex—which can't be said for Mr. Stovall's employee. Stovall will have to give that up if he's serious about marrying again."

"*Marrying—!* That, I hadn't heard."

"It's true."

"Who's the woman?"

"Miss Coralie Van Bibb. Her father's a pushy clod, but he's done handsomely building carriages—this is one of his vehicles, I think. The irony's delicious. The best people ride in the products of Van Bibb's Westchester factory, and he can't get past their front doors."

"What's his daughter like?"

"Unattractive. She's thirty-four and never had a husband—doesn't that tell you? Pious as a Plymouth puritan, too—if what you say is correct, dear Hamilton will have to mend his ways. Or make a mighty pretense of it. No more Mulberry Street excursions. No more Mr. Jonas—unless he sticks strictly to business. Any sensible girl wouldn't let Stovall court her, you know. But he does have a certain dubious social standing—which old Van Bibb's desperate to share. For his part, Stovall won't be acquiring a wife so much as another source of financing. Papa Van Bibb's money—"

Amanda's eyes narrowed. "Yes, that would jibe with something Joshua Rothman told me. Stovall's trying to float a big loan for modernization of his Pittsburgh plant. He's having a difficult time of it—the eastern banks don't consider him the best of risks."

"No wonder! He refuses to devote the time needed to

run the company properly—and his board is hand picked so he encounters no opposition."

Quietly, Amanda said, "That's right. He has two cousins on the board—his only relatives. And he owns by far the largest single block of stock. Forty percent. No other shareholder owns anything close to that."

Rose took another puff of the cigar. "You seem damn conversant with Mr. Stovall's affairs."

"No more than you. I've found out some things about him since he refused to sell Kent's, that's all. The information from Michael came quite by accident."

"You don't have any hope of trying to buy the printing company again, do you?"

"No," Amanda said, truthfully. *I'm going to get hold of it another way.*

"Do you think he suspects who you really are?"

"I hardly see how he could, Rose—unless I gave myself away completely tonight."

"Not completely, though your reaction *was* noticeable. Amanda—" She hesitated. "We're friends, aren't we?"

"The closest of friends, Rose—you know that."

"Then I wish you'd be honest with me."

"About what?"

Rose leaned toward her, the cigar in her hand casting just enough light to put pinpoints of orange in her eyes. "Stovall alluded to having won the firm in a wager. When we first met in Boston, you gave me the impression he'd bought it. Which is it?"

Amanda sighed. "Stovall was telling the truth. I misled you. At the time I thought it was prudent."

"That's why you kept your family connection out of the negotiations—the Kents have a grudge against him?"

"And vice versa. He cheated my family years ago—"

"Is that the real reason you're in New York, not Boston? Because he's here, and you can make inquiries about him?"

"Partly."

"Two can play the game, you know."

"That I realize."

"Do you honestly mean to say you've given up doing anything further about taking over the company? That's not in character, my dear."

"Rose, I think we should drop the subject—"

"Sorry, but I can't. I don't want anything to happen to you. And Mr. Hamilton Stovall isn't the sort one crosses swords with in a casual fashion. You saw what he almost did to that poor chap in front of the theatre —a man he didn't even know. He's vicious. And based on what Michael told you, maybe even a little deranged. Leave him alone, Amanda. Whatever reasons you have for hating him, leave him alone—he could hurt you."

The warning echoed ones she'd heard before. But too much past history remained to be set aright for her to be frightened off by one failure—or an unfounded fear that she might have given her feelings away when Stovall insulted the Kents.

"I've faced worse than Mr. Stovall, Rose. I'll be careful."

"Then you haven't abandoned the idea of taking the firm away from him—"

"No," she admitted. "But there's no point in dragging you into it."

"He refused to sell! What other legal options do you have?"

Amanda didn't answer. Rose glowered at her cigar.

The carriage was slowing. Amanda glanced out the window. They'd arrived in Madison Square, one of the more fashionable residential areas developed in the last decade. Light from large homes dappled the snow with patches of yellow. The carriage swung up the east side of the square and under the portico of a three-story brownstone house Amanda had purchased, gutted and rebuilt after consultation with an architect Rose had recommended.

The driver climbed down and opened the door. A snow-dusted figure, he stood shivering in the night wind. The lights of Amanda's home lit Rose Ludwig's dismayed face.

"Rose, don't be angry with me—"

"I am not in the least bit angry! I'm worried. I'd as soon go strolling in Five Points naked and carrying gold ingots as keep up a feud with Stovall. You'll be the loser. He already suspects you wanted his company and no other. And after tonight, he knows the name Kent produces a reaction. He may figure out a good deal from that—"

"Yes, I'm afraid it's possible."

"Then for God's sake leave him alone, Amanda. Please!"

"Good night, Rose. I enjoyed the dinner and the lecture. Let's have lunch early next week—"

"Amanda—"

She shut the carriage door.

She stood in the blowing snow at the foot of the balustraded marble stairs. The carriage careened out of the drive, its lanterns rapidly diminishing to blurs. A sleigh crowded with young ladies and gentlemen went skimming by on the opposite side of the square. Laughter and the sound of bells lingered long after it had passed from sight.

She was tired; drained by the confrontation with Stovall, and by jousting with Rose. But she couldn't call it a day just yet. She had to deal with the problem of Stovall's suspicion.

Perhaps nothing would come of it. But if he did look further into her background, she couldn't afford to wait and discover it after the fact. She had to accomplish what she wanted to accomplish *now,* before he found out any more—

She hurried up the steps into thc house.

CHAPTER V

The Girl Who Refused

LOUIS KENT CAME DOWN the staircase, walking past the entrance to the dining room on his right and the music room—containing the piano no one played—on his left. The clock in the library chimed nine.

Despite the chill permeating the house, his cheeks felt hot. *Not much more than an hour left—*

All evening he'd thought about her; wild, confused thoughts that set his heartbeat racing. All evening he'd struggled to convince himself that what he wanted to do was perfectly proper for a wealthy boy going on fifteen. Some of his classmates at Professor Pemberton's Day School—the sons of merchants and professional men—boasted of their affairs with household girls. One boy repeatedly bragged that he'd begun when he was twelve!

That, Louis could hardly believe. But the boasting left him feeling inferior all the same. Finally, when his mother had hired the new Irish girl a few weeks ago, he'd decided to go ahead.

The other two maids and the cook were older; unattractive. Kathleen was neither. She was seventeen; on the plump side, but pretty. Clean-smelling, too—though he recalled she hadn't been the first day she presented herself for an interview. She came from a tenement somewhere in the Five Points.

His mother had left at three to have dinner and attend an abolitionist lecture with Mrs. Ludwig. The opportunity was perfect. But he was afraid. Inexperience heightened his certainty that he'd blunder; that Kathleen would refuse him. Or laugh. So instead of waiting for her upstairs—she began her rounds of the three occupied bedrooms shortly after nine every night—he'd fled down here to the first floor. Now he was telling himself his scheme was entirely too dangerous.

He walked softly across the Oriental carpeting of the long front hall. On his left, forward of the music room, the doors to the drawing room were shut. The library, on the right between the dining room and the front sitting room, showed light, its two doors ajar. In the hall, a single gas jet flung Louis' shadow on the huge front doors. He opened one and let out a gasp of surprise. Snow was falling in Madison Square.

He remained at the open door for a few moments, unable to keep his mind off Kathleen. *You don't ask them, Lou,* the boys at Pemberton's said, *you tell them. You threaten 'em with discharge if they hesitate. Anyway, most are eager for it. They'll say no a few times. But then they'll relent.*

Why had he listened? Why had he rashly promised that he'd bring it off before classes resumed next week? He'd actually gotten in another fist-fight when two of the boys scoffed—

Of course he could lie on Monday. But they'd question him. Demand intimate details. He feared that if he tried to pretend, they'd trip him up.

And it *would* be a relief to end the nightly wakefulness in which he imagined bare breasts, and legs, and lips caressing his face—more and more these past months, he thought of such things frequently. Dreamed of them, too, in dreams that caused an embarrassing aftermath.

He pressed his belly against the edge of the open door. No matter how he tried, he couldn't prevent his flesh from betraying his feelings at the most unexpected moments—

I must do it, he said silently. *Tonight, while it's quiet and ma's away.* He still thought of her as ma, though Amanda had long since trained him to use the word mother when he spoke.

Sweating a little, he watched the falling snow. He knew he'd never be heard upstairs. Except for Kathleen, the servants didn't venture beyond the first floor. Right now, before going home for the night, they'd all be taking supper down in the mansion's raised basement—

The insistent pressure between his legs refused to go away.

But it's too risky!

An inner voice mocked him:

It isn't too risky. You're frightened, that's all.

What would his ma do in a comparable situation? He thought he knew. She did whatever she wanted; went where she pleased, and brooked no interference. That had been apparent to him ever since the time in California when he heard she'd shot a man who interfered with her up in the mining camp—

His swarthy face troubled and his dark eyes focused at some remote point beyond the snow-whitened square, Louis slowly backed up and shut the door. He was afraid of his mother. Her toughness and her preoccupation with business affairs made her forbidding, somehow. Yet he admired her—

He decided he was being foolish to worry about repercussions. *She* never seemed to—

All right. What he wanted, he'd take. That was the privilege of wealthy people, wasn't it?

Turning, he stepped on the tail of the white tomcat before he realized it. The cat, whose name was Mr. Mayor, had evidently crept out of the library and approached him silently.

Mr. Mayor miaowed loudly and went bounding back toward the library doors—which opened all the way a moment later.

From the doorway, Michael Boyle looked at Louis. The boy was sure Michael could see guilt on his face.

Mr. Mayor sought protection behind Michael's legs, peering at Louis with green eyes that caught the gaslight and shone. Suddenly Louis realized what he needed in order to proceed with his plan. He should be able to get it, too. In the darkened dining room—

If only Michael didn't suspect, and try to stop him.

"What are you doing skulking out here, Louis?" the young man asked, cheerily enough. "I thought I'd caught myself a burglar."

"I was only looking at the snow."

Louis walked back toward the entrance of the library. He wanted to glance down, to see whether there was a telltale bulge to give him away. He didn't dare.

ii

Michael Boyle was a head taller than Louis. Almost six feet. He was twenty-two, with a handsome, fair face, rust-colored hair and golden-brown eyes. He had wide shoulders, a narrow waist, and looked elegant in whatever he wore—tonight a loose-fitting white silk shirt, snug gray trousers and expensive Wellington boots. Only a long white scar across his forehead marred his appearance.

The scar was the result of trouble on the piers. Michael Boyle had worked as a longshoreman since he was eleven years old. At twenty, he had joined a worker's movement to increase wages five cents per hour during the twelve-hour day.

The bosses who controlled the dock crews worked more on behalf of the ship owners than on behalf of their own men. Someone had informed on the leaders of the wage movement. One by one, those longshoremen had suffered mysterious accidents. On his way home one evening, Michael Boyle had been waylaid by unknown assailants and beaten until he could barely crawl. During the beating, a man had slashed at his throat with a knife. Michael had dodged. The blade cut his forehead open.

After that, he'd never been able to get employment as a longshoreman. All the dock bosses knew him as an agitator. He had worked at odd jobs until a year ago, when Amanda had hired him over eleven other applicants who had presented themselves in response to a newspaper advertisement for a confidential clerk. The advertisement was one of the few in the paper that didn't carry the line *No Irish need apply.*

From all Louis could tell, Amanda was well pleased with her choice. Michael was self-educated; a voracious reader—something uncommon in the Five Points. His parents had come from a village in County Antrim, where his father had belonged to the Hearts of Steel—one of the gangs that harassed the English landlords. "A brawling boy," Michael had once said of his father, without implying praise or admiration. "The village matched his temperament exactly. My father often repeated a joke—true or not, I can't say—about one of the local ladies who walked out of her cottage one morning and said with a smile, 'A lovely day—ten o'clock and not a blow struck yet.' "

When the first of the famines devastated Ireland in '22, the Boyles had removed to America—going no further than New York because they had no funds, and because they were soured on the idea of working land; the land in Ireland had already rejected them. Five years after Michael was born, his father had died in a bloody confrontation between two of the Five Points gangs. His mother had lasted only two years more. Michael had survived by determination and his wits.

Louis admired the young Irishman's obvious strength. He liked his quiet cheerfulness. At the same time, he occasionally resented Michael's growing closeness to his mother.

Now Michael leaned down and scooped up his white cat. Mr. Mayor was a huge, rather sinister-looking tom. He regarded Louis from the crook of his master's elbow. The young man said:

"You're looking odd, Louis. Got a bellyache?"

"No," Louis replied, too quickly. "I'm fine."

Michael grinned. "Whatever you say. I've a plate of mutton in the library. Care for some?"

"No thanks."

"Come in and keep me company for a bit, at least."

Louis hesitated. To lull Michael's suspicions, he'd better do it:

"All right."

He followed Michael through the double doors into the overheated room.

About half of the library's wall space was filled with ceiling-high bookcases. Near the outer windows stood a desk littered with papers and ledgers. Along the wall on Louis' right, another table held the telegraphic equipment that connected the house with the Rothman Bank in Boston.

Michael's booted feet scraped on the carpet, a sound slightly louder than the hissing of the two gas jets over the mantel. Four logs burned in the grate. Beside Michael's chair, a small taboret bore a platter heaped with slices of meat.

Mr. Mayor jumped from Michael's arms. The cat had come with the young man from Five Points, his only possession. Michael had christened him Mr. Mayor "because he's ten times as intelligent as most incumbents, and could do a better job even without the power of speech—which in the case of a politician is usually a hindrance, since it permits his idiotic ideas to be heard."

The cat put his forepaws on the edge of the taboret, shot out his head as if to sample a bit of the mutton. Michael batted him away.

Then, stepping carefully between two piles of manuscript paper at the foot of the chair, Michael sat down. He helped himself to a slice of mutton which he tore into smaller pieces, stuffing them into his mouth one at a time.

"I've never seen one person eat so much, so often," Louis said. "And how can you stand this heat?"

"Because I spent the winters in the streets when I was growing up. Never felt the warmth of a fire—nor tasted decent food, either. I expect in forty years, I might get my fill of both."

Louis wandered to the mantel, gazing at the French infantry sword hung horizontally above the Kentucky rifle. The small green glass bottle half filled with powdery tea shimmered in the gaslight.

He heard Michael riffling some of the manuscript sheets; then caught the distant creak of a floorboard overhead.

Kathleen.

Turning down the beds—

He couldn't stay here long. Not if he meant to do what he'd promised his classmates.

"How is Professor Pemberton treating you?" Michael wanted to know.

Louis turned, wondering why Michael had raised that subject. He avoided the young man's eyes, gazing instead at the oil painting of his great-grandfather hanging on the outer wall. On a smaller table underneath the painting and behind the desk, a glass display case with wooden ends held cousin Jared's medallion. The medallion stood vertically, wedged into a slot in a small velvet pedestal. Lying on the velvet in front of the pedestal was a frayed circlet of tarred rope.

Louis answered the question carefully:

"The school's boring."

"Ah, but you must suffer through if you're to go on to Harvard as your mother intends."

"I wonder if she'll let me use my right name in college. I feel funny being called Louis de la Gura. Everyone thinks I'm a foreigner."

Bitterness crept in when Michael replied, "And *foreigners* aren't the most popular souls in New York, are they?"

"Michael, do you know why I'm not allowed to call myself Louis Kent?"

"Why, how should I know that? I'm only hired help. What does your mother say when you ask her?"

"Nothing that makes much sense. She just says it's necessary to keep the Kent name hidden a while longer—"

He shook his head, gesturing at the sword and rifle: "If she's so proud of our family, you'd think she'd tell everyone who we are."

"I can't give you an explanation. It's not in my province," Michael answered, his voice so flat, Louis suspected the clerk knew more than he was saying. He'd brought up the subject with Michael once before, receiving the same sort of evasive answer.

"I wish you'd stop your fidgeting, Louis. You're making me nervous."

Louis forced his hands to his sides. "Was I fidgeting?"

"You were. Are you sure nothing's bothering you?"

"No," Louis lied. His eyes slid to the wall clock above the telegraph equipment. The hands had reached ten past the hour.

I must go upstairs. She'll be finished soon—

"What is Professor Pemberton having you read these days?"

"Plutarch."

"In Latin or English?"

The boy grimaced. "Latin. I just can't get the hang of it—the other boys have studied it for much longer—"

"Don't feel discouraged. I've listened to Latin mass for years, and I can't get the hang of it either."

Mr. Mayor jumped up on Michael, purring audibly. After digging his claws in Michael's trousers a couple of times—earning a gentle knock between the ears—the cat settled down in the young man's lap. Michael slid the polished toe of a boot toward the stacks of manuscript:

"If you need something to read, perhaps you'd find this a little more interesting. It came late this afternoon, delivered from one of the California Steamers."

Louis craned around to study the closely written sheets. "What is it?"

"The autobiography of your mother's nigger manager."

"I don't understand why she had him write it—Kent's will never publish it, will they?"

"Not under present management," Michael agreed. "Your mother had the nigger go ahead because she's confident she'll own the company soon."

"How?"

Michael's eyes moved away. "Oh, she's working on it in various ways—" Another evasion.

"Is the manuscript any good?"

"Not half bad, actually."

"Mr. Hope's a bright man."

"Also an enterprising one. The parcel contained a letter saying the Ophir Combine's about to begin work at the claim in the mountains. They've completed the flume that brings in water, and Hope and Mr. Pelham look for handsome profits." He grinned. "You're going to be richer than ever."

Louis didn't answer.

"I am a bit surprised a colored fellow could do so well in business," Michael added. "And turn out an acceptable manuscript."

"You don't care for the colored, do you, Michael?"

Michael Boyle's bright hair glittered as he raised his head.

"I don't hate them, if that's what you're asking. Neither do I think all this effort on their behalf is warranted. You see, Louis, the famines in the old country have grown worse and worse. You know how many boatloads of Irish dock in New York every year—"

"Dozens."

Michael nodded. "I've read we may have two hundred thousand arrivals this year alone. Hoping for a fresh beginning—which includes work. To every such family, a black face means competition for the job that can spell the difference between survival and starvation. It's not surprising abolitionism is hated in the slums. If the abolitionists had their way, there'd be just that many more free nigger laborers pouring into the northern cities. Poor white people are starving to death not twenty blocks from here, Louis! Yet some of the great thinkers can talk of nothing but the unfortunate colored man. They should look closer to home! To the babies who die out in the heat of Mulberry Street in the summer, put there because some girl can't afford to feed her own mouth, let alone her infant's when it grows. I've seen other babies who were gnawed to death by rats that got into their cradles. The babies were left alone while their mothers strolled Paradise Square to earn twenty-five cents with a man. Walsh knows the way it is, right enough—"

He was referring to a colorful, audacious city politician. With the aid of a group of raucous roughnecks

Walsh called his Spartan Band, he had finally forced recognition of New York's Irish constituency by the Tammany Democrats, and gone on to represent the constituency in the State Assembly and, in 1850, the Congress.

"—Walsh told those dogooders in Washington that the only difference between the nigger slave in the south and the white wage slave up here is that one has a master without asking for him, while the other has to beg for the privilege—!"

He was interrupted by the rhythmic clanging of a gong attached to the wall above the telegraph equipment and just to one side of the clock. He jumped up—ruffling Mr. Mayor, who stalked off to a corner.

Michael crossed to the table as the Morse sounder clicked off a rapid series of dots and dashes. He scowled at the sounder until it was silent.

"That's the third time the bank's telegraphed since five o'clock. I keep telling them she hasn't returned—"

Louis knew Rothman's kept a telegraph operator on duty in Boston until midnight five days a week, and until noon on Saturday. His mother paid the operator's wages.

Michael pulled a chair up to the table, noted the time of the query on a pad between the sounder and the transmitting key. He wiped his fingertips on his trousers, then began to operate the key, a horizontal knife switch that opened and closed the circuit to form the dots and dashes. Louis walked quickly to the door—the interruption provided a good excuse—but Micahel had trained himself so thoroughly in Mr. Morse's code, he was able to keep sending his message and swing around to look at Louis at the same time—

But Louis was already out the door. As he shut it, Michael's golden-brown eyes fixed on his, puzzled—

—*He suspects something,* Louis thought, flushed again.

All at once he resented Michael's curiosity. The

young Irishman *was* just an employee, not a member of the family. It wasn't his business if Louis had decided to—

To—

He couldn't even complete the thought.

Did he have enough nerve to go ahead? If only he hadn't made those rash promises to his classmates—!

But he had. So there wasn't much choice, was there?

All right, he'd take the first step and see what happened.

He stole into the darkened dining room. At the sideboard, he pulled out a decanter of whiskey. He'd tried whiskey before, surreptitiously, and destested it. But he'd heard whiskey made a person bolder. He unstoppered the decanter, tilted it and let a little of the liquor trickle down his throat.

He winced, wiped his eyes, shivered in the darkness as the telegraph key went silent on the other side of the dining room wall. He listened. Heard Michael's footsteps. Then silence. He'd evidently returned to his chair. Somewhere below. rattling crockery told Louis the servants had concluded their meal—

Except for Kathleen. She would be finishing the bedrooms. Lighting the gas; plumping the pillows; arranging the coverlets—

One more swallow of whiskey set his head to aching faintly. He drew a deep breath, returned the decanter to the sideboard and, after a soft belch that burned his throat, started for the rear hall.

As he climbed the steps, the brief headache passed. He felt warmer. Almost bold. What did he care if Michael Boyle wondered about his behavior? What did he care what anyone thought? His mother was a wealthy woman whose money permitted her to do anything she wished. He was no different—

He felt the stiffness again, without shame. He'd have a juicy tale to report on Monday.

iii

Louis stole along the second floor corridor toward the spill of light at the open door of his room. As he approached, he could hear small sounds. The rustle of bedding; Kathleen humming—

He squared his shoulders and pressed his palm to his mouth to hold back another belch. The whiskey had produced a feeling of confidence that enabled him to smile as he turned in at the bedroom door.

He was on the point of speaking when he noticed the curve of Kathleen's hip. She was leaning over the large bed, adjusting the covers. Her shiny black skirt shimmered in the glare of the gas. Snow ticked against the far windows.

The sight of Kathleen bent that way, the curve of her buttocks accentuated by her posture, brought him to full and painful rigidity. He knocked on the open door.

Kathleen screeched and spun around. One hand flew to the bosom of her dress. She had coppery hair all but concealed by her cap, a blunt chin and heavily freckled cheeks. Her mouth was full, her eyes pale blue. Her black dress and over-the-shoulder apron fit her ample breasts snugly.

"Good evening, Kathleen," he said, taking a step inside but blocking the door.

"Good evening, master Louis," she said, still red in the cheeks. "You came in so softly—startled me half to death."

"Thinking of something else, were you? A gentleman friend—?"

The girl was obviously stunned by his directness: "No, sir, I—I don't have any—"

She swallowed.

"I'll be finished in a moment."

"Good," he said, pivoting away. Kathleen's eyes had a peculiar, almost alarmed look. She hadn't missed the telltale bulge of his trousers.

Louis strolled to the window. His palms itched as he stared out at the snow-dusted roof of the mansion next door. But he didn't really see it. He saw only Kathleen's body—

"All done, sir. I'll be going now—"

He turned around. "Close the door."

For a moment she appeared not to understand. She took a hesitant step backward.

"Master Louis, did you say—?"

"You heard very clearly what I said. Walk to the door and close it."

Fright shone in her eyes. She shook her head:

"Sir, that isn't proper—"

"I don't care what's proper, I want you to close the door!"

He moved toward her. His hand shook as he raised it to her left breast. She closed her eyes and shuddered. With his other hand fisted and quivering at his side, he touched her breast with the back of his hand, then pressed upward. Kathleen appeared on the point of tears:

"Please, master Louis, may I leave?"

"You may not. I've been taken by your looks ever since my mother hired you, Kathleen. I've wanted to talk to you—get acquainted—"

Her eyes opened, tearful and angry:

"And what else, sir?"

"Oh, don't act so innocent. Don't tell me you've never had a man before—"

"Jesus and Mary be my witnesses, I have not! I'm a decent person—"

He guffawed, his dark eyes like black stones. "Come on! No Irish wench from the Five Points stays decent for long."

"That's a nasty thing to say! I've taken no man, and I won't till I'm properly wed by a priest."

"I think you're going to change your mind very shortly, Kathleen."

"You've been at the whiskey!" she exclaimed, pulling away from the press of his hand. "I can smell it. The whiskey's the reason you're saying all this—"

"I'm saving it because I like you."

She lunged for the door:

"I won't stay here another—*ah!*"

She cried out when he caught her forearm and dragged her back, stretching out his leg to catch the door with his toe and set it moving. Softly, the door clicked shut.

He maneuvered against her, his hands slipping around her waist. He drew her close. She shook her head and muttered incoherent syllables. She tried to pull away from the stiffness thrusting against her skirt but he held her fast, working his fingers in the fabric of her skirt—

"I ask you for the sake of decency, master Louis, stop this—"

"I won't—"

He put his mouth near her left ear, aroused all the more by the tickling touch of her hair and the lace of her cap.

"—because I know you're like all Irish girls. I know what you really want—"

"You don't! It's filthy of you to accuse me of—"

Angry at her protests, he slid his mouth across her cheek and found her lips.

At first they were cold and unyielding. She continued to struggle. But after a moment he felt a little heat.

He laughed, a soft, harsh sound. He held her tight as he pushed his tongue between her teeth.

Her tongue touched his for a fraction of a second. Then, as if realizing her own feelings were getting out of control, she wrenched her head away:

"You mustn't do this! If your mother should find out—"

"She won't. We'll be done before she's home."

"I swear to you, I'm virgin—"

"We'll remedy that."

He slid his hand down the front of her apron and pressed, feeling the curve of her belly. He moved his hand lower, his head all at once throbbing from the whiskey. The gaslit room seemed isolated; cut off from the real world. And the pressure between his legs had grown unbearable—

When he tried to thrust her back onto the bed, she broke away again, slipping around him toward the door. She'd nearly reached it when he called out:

"*Kathleen!*"

Slowly, she looked back. Her blue eyes widened at the harshness of his face.

"What—what is it?"

"Do you want to be arrested for thievery?"

Her mouth shaped into a horrified *O* She could barely repeat the word:

"*Thievery?*"

He gestured to a bureau where he kept loose change. "I'll say I found you rummaging through my belongings —searching for money—unless you do exactly as I say."

"Oh, God, master Louis, you wouldn't—"

"I would unless you undress and lie down on the bed, Kathleen."

Her eyes grew hateful then; so hateful that he was terrified; tempted to let her go and be done with it.

But she hid the hatred, begging:

"I need this position. I'm the only one of the McCreerys old enough to work—"

"Very well. If you value your six dollars a week, do what I say."

"You—you imagine you have a right to demand—"

"I *do* have the right." He wiped his perspiring upper lip. "What's it to be Kathleen? The six dollars—or a charge of thievery? It'll follow you wherever else you try to work—"

She started crying, the tears dampening her freckled cheeks as she glanced helplessly from one side of the room to the other. Seeing how she weakened so easily, he laughed aloud.

"You—" Her voice was ragged. "—you're only a child. Not even fifteen—"

Flushing, he said, "I have a man's cock, if that's your worry."

"But not a man's heart. Not a speck of Christian kindness—"

"I want to love you, Kathleen."

"—anything you want, you think you can take!"

"I can."

He took a step toward her.

"*Don't touch me!*"

Then, less stridently:

"Not—not till I'm ready."

He stepped to the door and slid the bolt.

"Just pull your skirt up and bare yourself, that'll be satisfactory—"

He heard the bed creak as she lowered herself onto it. He heard garments rustling; then her voice again:

"Will—will you be good enough to turn the gas down?"

"I don't think so. I want to see you—"

Unfastening his trousers, he faced her, his heart hammering in his chest as he moved his gaze slowly, slowly upward along her freckled white legs.

iv

She lay still beneath him, her eyes open and fixed on the ceiling. Louis slid between her thighs and probed, hurt at first by the roughness of her flesh.

Finally, her body changed in reaction to his presence. He jerked back and forth. Within a few seconds, his loins quivered and exploded. He felt a deep sense of disappointment—

Kathleen maneuvered her hips so their bodies were no longer joined. He rolled onto his side, stretching a hand toward her wrist as she stood up and started to lower her skirt.

The moment his fingers closed, she glared at him, miserable and angry at the same time:

"I've given you what you wanted, haven't I?"

"Once," he nodded, feeling distinctly sober and angry himself. The experience had been much less fulfilling than he'd imagined; a quick abrasion of flesh on flesh, then an abrupt end—nothing worth boasting about—

"Lie down again."

Disbelieving, she shook her head:

"You can't again so soon—"

"But in a little while—Kathleen, damn you, *lie down!*"

"I must go—"

"No, we—" He yawned. "—we've plenty of time." It seemed that way; it seemed as if only a minute or so had elapsed since he'd entered the room. "Besides, no one ever disturbs me after I've shut my door for the night."

She bowed her head, knelt on the bed and stretched out, weeping softly again. He was caught in a storm of conflicting feelings:

Satisfaction because he'd had his way.

Fear that he shouldn't have done it; he tried not to dwell on the hate he'd glimpsed in her eyes.

And a peculiar sadness that came over him because the act so long anticipated had been so curiously coarse and unrewarding.

The second time would be different. He'd enjoy it and so would she—

She lay with her back toward him. He pulled her over and forced her fingers to curl around him. She didn't want to touch him that way—her palm was cold; she cried harder—but he held his hand over hers and forced her, staring at the ceiling as she had done earlier, awaiting the first tingle of a response from his own flesh.

CHAPTER VI

Of Stocks and Sin

AMANDA LET HERSELF INTO the dim front hall. She drew off her hat and cast the snow-dampened muff aside, then paused to study her face in a peer glass.

She'd be forty-nine before the year was out. She felt every one of those years this evening. The glass showed wrinkles around her eyes, and more gray in her hair. How much of that gray had been put there by her preoccupation with Stovall—?

Feeling incredibly weary, she drew a deep breath and walked to the library doors. She opened them and gasped at the heat.

Busy cleaning himself on the telegraph table, Mr. Mayor paused with a paw athwart his nose. He recognized her and went back to bathing. Michael rose from the chair beside the hearth.

"Hallo, Mrs. A," he said with his mouth full.

She was always amused by Michael's passion for food and warmth. He never seemed to sweat, or put on an ounce of fat. She understood the reason for both cravings and seldom said anything about either—although withstanding Michael's temperature preferences required a good deal of forbearance.

"Bad weather out there," he went on as she came toward him. "I was growing a mite concerned. How was the lecture?"

"Douglass is an eloquent speaker. It's hard not to be

moved by what he says. His chief target was the fugitive slave law."

Michael's pleasant expression vanished. Amanda knew his feelings about those who championed the cause of slaves. The young Irishman would have preferred to see the same amount of time and energy spent improving the lot of his own people, who had come to the United States to escape the privation and the legal tyranny they'd endured for generations. Instead, the Irish had found tyranny of a different sort—the kind produced by hatred of foreigners. As a result, they'd found privation too.

"I told Douglass I'd send him another draft soon. Will you take care of it? A hundred in my name, and two thousand anonymously."

At the desk, Michael jotted a note without saying anything.

"Stovall was at the theatre."

He spun around. "What the devil was he doing at an abolitionist meeting?"

"He wanted to disrupt Douglass' speech. He didn't succeed."

"Did he have a crowd of cronies with him?"

"No, just one companion."

"My Lord, Mrs. A, that takes brass."

"Stovall's been accused of a good many things, but I don't believe cowardice is one of them."

"Did you speak to him?"

She sank down in the chair opposite Michael's. Her eyes moved to the piles of manuscript. But her mind was elsewhere:

"It was unavoidable. Rose introduced us afterward My tactics have gotten me in trouble, I'm afraid. Stovall knows my story about diversifying was a sham. He knows I've bought no other properties—"

Rapidly, she described the encounter at the Bowery Theatre. Some six months earlier, when she'd decided she could trust Michael Boyle, she'd revealed her plans concerning her adversary—and her reasons for them. He had to know if he was to function as her confidential assistant. She suspected he didn't wholly approve of her effort to regain control of Kent and Son. But he kept his personal views to himself, and always executed her orders without question.

She concluded, "It's possible Stovall will look more closely into my background—"

"Why should he?"

"Apparently I reacted very visibly when he made a derogatory remark about the Kents. I didn't mean to—it simply happened."

"Um."

"I think I'd better instruct Rothman's to move faster."

Michael gestured to the telegraph equipment:

"You can take care of that yet tonight. Mr. Rothman's operator has queried you three times since five P.M. I told him to try again at ten-thirty."

"Is there a problem?"

"I gather so. Something to do with an emergency meeting of the Blackstone board. If you were in Boston, communication would be less of a problem. Of course I realize Stovall is *here*—"

She looked up at the broad-shouldered young man. "You think I should drop the campaign to take back the firm, don't you? You—and Rose."

"It uses up a hell of a lot of your time. And your strength, I should imagine. Still, it's not for me to say whether you should or shouldn't. I am after all just your employee."

"Nonsense, Michael. You know you're closer to me in some ways than my own son. Where is he, by the way?"

"Popped off to sleep, I think."

"Rather early."

"He seemed—oh, nervous. Quite nervous, as a matter of fact."

"Did he say there was anything wrong?"

"No, *he* didn't say—"

Thinking about Louis, she didn't catch the significance of the emphasized word. She mused aloud:

"I'll have to talk with him in the morning—"

She smiled then, reminded of something her friend had said:

"Would you like to hear a bit of gossip Rose passed along? It seems some of the finer folk of New York have come to the conclusion you and I are lovers."

Michael burst out laughing. Amanda loved the sight of his smile. That such a handsome young man should be marred for life by the ugly scar on his forehead was a kind of blasphemy.

Still shaking with mirth, he turned to warm his hands at the hearth:

"Didn't mean to bray like that. It just tickles me that the filthy sods would come up with such notions. They've missed the truth entirely—" He faced her. "I am fond of you. But not for the reasons they imagine. No one's ever treated me more decently than you. I'd never dare say this to anyone else for fear of being hooted at—but you're as kind as I imagine my own mother would have been, had she lived."

His words heartened her; helped soothe away some of the tension she'd felt ever since the encounter with Stovall.

"That's sweet of you, Michael." She teased him: "I hope it's not pure blarney."

"An Irishman only dissembles with those he depises, not those he loves—" He pivoted back to the fire. "Faith, I'm carrying on like some convent girl—"

"I don't mind one bit."

They looked at one another for a moment.

"What's that manuscript on the floor?"

"Ah!" He scooped up a few of the pages. "Your nigger—beg pardon, I forgot you don't like me saying that —Mr. Hope's narrative. Delivered from the docks late this afternoon. There's also a letter describing the promising nature of the new mining claim in the Sierras. Plus one from your cousin in Virginia, and two others—"

Amanda scanned the few sheets Michael handed to her. Mr. Mayor put his forepaws on her skirt, studied her to see whether she'd resist. When she didn't, he hopped into her lap and curled up, his green eyes closing.

She went on reading while Michael took a clay pipe from the mantel, filled it with tobacco and lit it with a splinter of wood ignited in the fireplace. The odor of the Virginia leaf sweetened the stale, overheated air. But Amanda was hardly conscious of the warmth any longer, absorbed by the flow of Israel's prose:

"He writes extremely well."

"Yes, he does. As much as the subject of—ah—nigras leaves me cold, I confess the first few chapters caught my interest. I think his title's a bit dull, though. *The Life of Israel Hope* would mean nothing to the general public—he's not famous. I suggest something slightly more dramatic if Kent and Son ever publishes the book—"

"Kent and Son *will* publish it."

Her determination brought another smile to his face. "Then why not call it something like *West to Freedom?* It avoids the cliche of a reference to the north—it suggests the escape theme—and people are intrigued about the west."

"Yes, that's very good. I'll be anxious to read all of it—"

She laid the manuscript aside, causing Mr. Mayor to open his eyes and regard her with annoyance. She was almost embarrassed to bring up the next subject:

"Did you drive down to the Royal Sceptre office?"

"I did," he nodded. "The situation's just as it was last month when your letter was returned from London. The owners of the line still don't know anything more about Captain McGill."

Saddened, Amanda ran her hand aimlessly over the tomcat's neck. He arched and purred.

What in heaven's name had become of Bart? He'd sailed back from India the preceding November and abruptly resigned his command, that much she'd learned. But he hadn't told anyone in London where he was going—he'd just walked out and disappeared.

"I suppose it's time to give up on him," she said presently.

"We've no other options that I see."

"God, I hope he's all right—"

"You loved him a great deal, didn't you?"

"More than I realized when I said no to him. However—" She shrugged to hide the hurt. "—we should be worrying about other things. How much Stovall stock do we own at the moment?"

"I can't be positive without consulting the records. Mr. Rothman and Mr. Benbow have so many friends and clients buying small amounts on your behalf, then re-selling them to the dummy company, the total changes daily."

"Where's the ledger?"

"In my room. I was trying to bring it up to date before dinner, but I confess I fell asleep. I believe Boston Holdings owns somewhere above twelve thousand shares now."

Amanda nodded. For months, she'd been engaged in a covert campaign to accumulate stock of the Stovall Works. Her strategy was simple. When she'd acquired a controlling interest, she intended to present Stovall's attorneys with a demand that Kent and Son be sold to her—in exchange for the number of shares that would return Stovall to the position of majority stockholder.

She'd planned to take as long as necessary to acquire the shares; Rothman and Benbow moved with great circumspection, approaching one investor at a time, through intermediaries. So far, she didn't believe Stovall realized the true reason for the activity in shares in his company—nor did she think he knew of the existence of Boston Holdings.

"Find the book and get me the exact figure, would you?" she asked. "Meantime, I'll read Jephtha's letter."

Michael brought it to her from the littered table, then left the room.

Amanda stared at the soiled envelope that had come from Lexington for three cents' postage. But she didn't really see her name and address written in an irregular hand. She was thinking of Bart McGill.

Yes, she had loved him. Not in the same way she'd loved Jaimie de la Gura, and then Cordoba. More deeply—that was the hurtful truth she admitted to herself.

He hadn't sent her a single letter from London, or, so far as she knew, tried to ascertain her whereabouts. And now he'd left England, and no one knew where he was. Jaimie and Luis Cordoba had been taken from her by events over which she had no control. But Bart's departure had been her own doing, and she faced that bitter truth often—especially in the dark hours of early morning when she couldn't sleep; when age made her bones ache, and the shadows around her bed seemed to whisper of her life running out all too rapidly—

She rubbed her eyes to clear them of tears, then turned her attention to the letter.

It proved almost as disheartening as her memories.

ii

The letter, scrawled with a blunted pencil, was dated three and a half weeks earlier. Either it hadn't been mailed promptly, or had been delayed in transit.

The lines slanted across the page. Jephtha's hand was uneven; far less readable than it had been two months ago, when he'd reported his continuing alienation from his family and refused her offer of the income due him from the Ophir claim. The handwriting said the Reverend Jephtha Kent—a Reverend no longer—was a tormented man. The opening paragraphs told her he was still living and working on the grounds of the Virginia Military Institute:

> *My only friend is Thos. Jackson, the professor of whom I believe I have spoken before. He is a strange, deeply religious person—a Presbyterian—who has risked unpopularity by taking an active role in support of the local Negro Sunday School. My father-in-law, by contrast, would deny the colored people even the solace of God.*
>
> *Jackson—whom many of the cadets deride with the name 'Tom Fool' despite his outstanding record in the late Mexican conflict—is opposed to all the secessionist talk. He is humane. He once taught one of his own slaves to read in exchange for the slave's help—holding a torch—while he studied. It is Jackson who renews my hope that all in the south are not prey to the philosophy of a vile human being such as Captain Tunworth.*
>
> *Jackson is married. He and his wife are the only persons in Lexington willing to welcome me into their home occasionally. It is true that his habits are peculiar. To prevent distraction when he is pondering problems in military tactics, he will turn his chair to the wall and sit motionless for long periods of time. But I am comfortable with him, and can share my thoughts freely—my sadness over Fan's continuing refusal to allow any contact between myself and the boys—and my grow-*

> *ing certainty that the south's system of servitude will bring its own dire harvest.*
> *Compromise will never avail—it is too late. We have sinned as a nation—I firmly share this belief with the noted abolitionist and Free-Soil advocate, John Brown of Ohio. Sin is always punished. So the nation will be punished. And not lightly. In the words of Paul the Apostle to the Hebrews—'And almost all things are by the law purged with blood. And without shedding of blood is no remission.'*

The gloomy prediction disturbed Amanda, because there were already signs that Clay's compromise bills had bought nothing but a temporary peace.

The Fugitive Slave Act, designed to mollify the south, had generated an even greater militancy on the part of the northern abolitionists. And influential Congressmen were toying with a doctrine which could renew sectional antagonism.

The doctrine's chief ideologue was Stephen Douglas of Illinois, a senator whose combative temperament and slight stature had earned him the title Little Giant. Sometimes the doctrine was called popular sovereignty, sometimes squatter sovereignty. Basically it stated that people in a newly organized territory had the unqualified right to determine what form their government would take; specifically, whether the government would allow or forbid slavery.

To Douglas, this was nothing more than the working of the principle of democracy. To the abolitionists, it was betrayal. If the doctrine were followed to its logical conclusion, a territory could adopt or reject slavery whether the territory lay above or below the Missouri Compromise line. Not only did the doctrine run counter to the 1820 compromise, but by its very nature it denied Congressional right to limit the spread of slavery.

Whig opponents abused Douglas as the south's toady, claiming he was advancing the scurrilous philosophy to enhance his own chances as a future presidential candidate on the Democratic ticket. Others, less partisan, said Douglas acted only out of a solid belief in the rights of the majority. But whatever the Little Giant's motives, the papers had been filled with the debate over his doctrine.

There was bound to be a test of it in the Congress in the next year or so. Legislators were already talking of the need to organize one or two large territories between Missouri and California. There had even been discussion of a transcontinental railroad, and for this to become a reality, the western lands had to be under some form of government.

If the intellectual debate led to a practical attempt to put the doctrine into effect in the organization of new territories, the Missouri Compromise would be severely threatened—and all of the efforts of Clay and Webster to secure peace might come to nothing. Some pundits predicted that if popular sovereignty ever passed into law, abolitionist groups would launch open warfare—

Open warfare. *Remission of sin through the shedding of blood—*

Sometimes it seemed to Amanda that the nation was heading inevitably toward it—and toward the even more grave Constitutional crisis that might be precipitated. The crisis was implicit in the south's traditional response to harrying by its enemies: secession.

Did one section have the right to separate itself from the rest to protect and preserve what it believed? Though she was no great expert on government, she thought not. If it did, the words *United* States would become a mockery.

Yet how to stop the quarrel before it brought disunion? Jephtha's church had broken apart over the slave issue. Even his own household was divided. How could the nation hope to fare any better?

Clearly, Jephtha didn't think it could.

The issues underlying the letter in her hand—and the letter itself—had upset her. She concentrated with great difficulty on the closing paragraphs:

> *Unhappiness is my lot. But I consider it God's will that I remain in that state; and I do what He has commanded. I continue to be engaged in certain activities at which I have hinted before, though the fugitive slave bill has made the labor increasingly difficult. Previously used points of refuge in the north are now under the closest scrutiny by southern sympathizers. We grow desperate for safe destinations for certain freight, and may be forced to call upon some we would otherwise not burden or endanger.*

Amanda gazed over the lines she'd just read, noting that the word *freight* had been heavily underscored. In previous letters, Jephtha had indeed alluded to mysterious activities, leading her to believe he'd involved himself in the work of what was popularly called the Underground Railroad.

The letter concluded with a few phrases containing her cousin's wish for her continued health and prosperity. Her eye was drawn back to the quotation from St. Paul.

And without shedding of blood is no remission.

She believed the slave system had to be done away with eventually. But was bloodshed the only course left open to accomplish it? She couldn't imagine that people of good will in any part of the country would want that kind of a solution—

Yet every paper she read told her the positions were

hardening dangerously. The furies were loose on both sides. What if the compromise of 1850 ultimately proved unworkable? What if the threat of popular sovereignty proved real, and its advocates widened the chasm again, until it could never be bridged—?

She shuddered. The white cat yowled when she jumped up, startled by the loud, interruptive ring of the telegraph gong.

iii

Amanda had taught herself Morse's code so that she could send and receive messages when Michael wasn't present. She seated herself at the table, a steel-nibbed pen poised over a pad on which the young man had noted the times of the evening's previous transmissions. A moment after she acknowledged the query from Boston with a tapped-out A. K. D. G. READY, the operator at the Rothman Bank began to send:

> APOLOGIZE LATE HOUR. SERIES OF MILL ACCIDENTS REQUIRED SPECIAL MEETING. BLACKSTONE BOARD DIRECTORS DEADLOCKED THREE FOR THREE AGAINST EMPLOYMENT TWO PHYSICIANS TO TREAT INJURED WORKERS ONE A CHILD. OPPONENTS ARGUE STEP UNNECESSARY AND EXPENSIVE. SAFETY AND WELFARE OF WORKERS NOT MANAGEMENT'S CONCERN. MR. ROTHMAN VOTES AYE HOWEVER. URGENTLY SOLICITS YOUR VOTE ON MATTER. END.

Amanda's pen flew across the pad, copying down the final words of the message. She chewed the end of the pen for perhaps ten seconds, then began to work the key:

> EXPENSE NOT FACTOR. BELIEVE WE HAVE CLEAR RESPONSIBILITY. MR. ROTHMAN AUTHORIZED TO CAST AYE VOTE FOR A. K. D. G.

The library doors opened. Michael came in carrying several papers and a ledger. While the sounder chattered out ACKNOWLEDGED WITH THANKS, he took Amanda's pen from her fingers and scribbled on her pad:

12,875 shares as of last Wednesday afternoon—representing 38% of outstanding shares.

She nodded, aware of Michael lingering just behind her as she rapped out the signal for a further transmission, then began to send the dots and dashes:

> SPEED UP ACQUISITION STOVALL WORKS STOCK BY BOSTON HOLDINGS. URGENT REPEAT URGENT WE REACH FIFTY ONE PER CENT OWNERSHIP SOON AS POSSIBLE. END.

In a moment, the sounder replied with words Amanda didn't bother to copy:

> ACKNOWLEDGED ROTHMAN'S BANK.

Satisfied, she stood up.

"You think Stovall will attempt to block your purchase of shares?" Michael wanted to know.

"Of course he will—if he finds out who I am before we have a controlling interest. I'm sure he's aware of movement in the issue. He may not realize the individual blocks have been re-sold to Boston Holdings, but he could certainly track down that fact if his suspicions were sufficiently aroused."

"You're quite right. The bank that acts as the registrar of the stock has the information. There's no legal way to prevent them having it. You're gambling they'll neglect to inform Stovall—"

"I'm gambling they haven't yet. Joshua Rothman and I have already agreed to the final step. When Joshua's intermediaries have acquired the shares representing the last thirteen percent, those shares won't be transferred to Boston Holdings in small batches, as we've done in the past. They'll all be held and transferred in a single day. It'll be too late for Stovall to do anything about the takeover then. Still, you're right—the risk has always been high—" She paused only a moment. "I think it's time we developed an alternate plan. Just in case the stock scheme's uncovered."

Michael looked wary: "What sort of plan, Mrs. A?"

"You told me some nasty gossip about Stovall—that he's spent time with a brother and sister on Mulberry Street—both of whom are prostitutes?"

Glumly, Michael nodded. "Yes."

"What are their names?"

"I fail to see how their names could be of any—"

"Tell me anyway."

His face had lost its cheerful look. "The Phelan twins. Joseph and Aggie."

"Are they still—what's the term for that sort of thing? Practicing?"

In a clipped voice: "I don't know."

"I think you do."

"I really don't inquire too deeply into such matters—"

"Well, I want you to inquire. I want you to see whether you can get a deposition from them. Concerning what goes on during any one of Stovall's visits. In detail, Michael. Such complete detail that there can be no doubt of the—the customer's identity. Or his intention."

She tried not to see his stunned look.

"Christ!" he whispered. "You don't mean that—"

"I do."

"Manipulating stock is one thing. But mucking around in slime is quite another—"

"Are you telling me you won't do it?"

A long silence. Amanda said:

"If you won't go to the Five Points, I will."

He studied her face for a sign that she was bluffing him; saw none. With a shake of his head, he said softly:

"All right. I suppose I'm obligated to do whatever you ask as long as I'm in your employ."

"And you *are* still in my employ—"

"For the moment."

The dull-voiced threat didn't even make her blink:

"Can these Phelans be persuaded to give you the information I want?"

"Mrs. A, listen! You mustn't soil yourself in this sort of—"

"Answer me, Michael!"

He sighed. "Yes, I think the information could be gotten—if the Phelans were given enough money, and frightened a little in the bargain."

"Would they speak to you in front of a notary?"

"I tell you it's all a matter of how much you pay them—and how much they imagine they're threatened. I could take not only a notary, but a couple of pretty tough lads I knew on the docks. If I were to go," he added.

"You'll go. Because I'm willing to pay the Phelans five thousand dollars—and whatever it takes above that to relocate them in another city. Someplace quite distant—out of Stovall's reach. New Orleans, St. Louis—"

Dourly, he said, "For five thousand, I imagine the Phelans would climb in your bed and put on a performance that would stop your heart with shock—and if you were still alive afterward, they'd hand you their souls in a white hanky."

"Go see them. Get me the statement. Prepare two identical copies."

"What are you going to do with the copies?"

"For the moment, nothing."

"But if you were to use them, how—?"

"Why, I expect one copy would go to Mr. Stovall—with a suggestion that the other might soon be delivered to his prospective bride. I just heard about her this evening. A very proper young woman, I'm told. He's in desperate need of her father's money."

He stared at her, disbelieving.

"I find your reactions damned annoying, Michael!"

"Be as annoyed as you please! I can't reconcile that —" He pointed to the display case holding the medal. "—with what you're proposing. You told me once the Kents always took the high road—"

"There are times," she said angrily, "when the *high road* won't get you where you must go. *I want Kent's!* The statements are only insurance. I really think we'll be successful with the stock, so let's not quarrel—" She fanned herself. "My God, I can't stand this heat a moment longer. Is there anything else we need to discuss?"

"Well—"

"Speak up before I suffocate."

"It—it concerns Louis. I think I know why he's behaving oddly. I tried to suggest as much a while ago, but you were all caught up in Mrs. Ludwig's gossip."

"Go on."

"Professor Pemberton wishes an appointment. He sent round a note. Your son isn't performing satisfactorily in school."

"You mean he's failing?"

"It's not that he lacks interest or aptitude—he simply

doesn't wish to do the work. So he doesn't. He's also indulged in a bit of scrapping—"

"A bit or a lot?"

"Well—the latter. You can read the professor's note. He says that when Louis doesn't get his way in some trivial dispute with his classmates, he swings a punch. Rather a mean one, too, I gather. You can be thankful you're not raising a coward, anyway—"

He tried to smile. The effort failed. The dispute about the Phelans had soured his mood.

She wondered sadly whether her own pattern of living was responsible for the way Louis was developing. The change in him dated from the time she'd tried to explain why she'd shot the man in the mining camp. Ever since, she'd had the uncanny feeling that her son was imitating her behavior; doing exactly as he pleased—just as she appeared to do. He didn't realize that every action she took had one motive: to see Kent and Son restored to its rightful owners. She'd have to try again to make him understand she was working toward a goal—a goal that mattered almost as much as life itself— '

She glanced up, aware of Michael studying her. He said nothing. But she felt accused. In concocting the scheme with the Phelan twins, wasn't she acting just as irresponsibly as her son? Taking what she wanted, regardless of the means—and regardless of who might be injured?

No! There *is* a difference! she thought.

But she was uneasy with the conclusion.

She didn't want Michael to see that. She spoke briskly:

"Does Louis know about Pemberton's note?"

"No. When the boy dropped in here a while ago, I asked him one or two questions about school, that's all."

"How did he answer?"

"He said he was bored."

"Let me have the note."

He rummaged on the desk. "Oh—here's one more that arrived with the late mail. A solicitation of funds from Mr. Thurlow Weed in Albany. He's the newspaper publisher, isn't he?"

"And the power behind the Whig party in the state—he and Seward. Should I read that?"

"It depends on whether you want to contribute funds to support the party's convention in Baltimore in June."

"I suppose I'm closer to a Whig than to anything else," she said. "I can't quite bring myself to be as rabid against slavery as the Free-Soilers. But I'll be damned if I'll give a penny to a party when I can't vote for it. Put that in a letter to Mr. Weed. Tell him the moment the Whigs support votes for women, he'll have my contribution."

"Do you really mean that?"

"Of course I do!" She looked rueful. "I also know it's impractical as the devil."

"You are a somewhat contradictory creature, Mrs. A."

"Did you ever know a person who wasn't?"

He inclined his head again, almost smiling as he agreed. Then:

"Shall I or shall I not write Mr. Weed?"

"Yes, write him a polite note," she sighed. "Enclose a draft for a hundred dollars."

"Very well."

"And don't forget your trip to the Five Points."

"That would be impossible," he said. "May I plead with you once more not to—?"

"No."

"You can be a hard woman, Mrs. A."

"When it's necessary."

"You've never been hard with me before. Demanding, but not hard." He rubbed his knuckles across his upper lip. "You know how much I hated the tenements—and the crookedness on the docks. You know very well I'd sooner die than be forced back to either. You're taking advantage of that. Still, that isn't what bothers me the most. So far, everything you've done to get the firm is legal. Surreptitious, but legal. The Phelans, though—that's something else."

His steady gaze frightened her; blunted her anger. Her mind echoed with Bart's biblical warning; and Jephtha's—

For remission of sin, the price was blood.

"That's my worry, not yours."

She started for the door, then swung back:

"Oh, yes—I'd better take Pemberton's letter. I want to read it before I talk to Louis in the morning."

"Here. Mrs. A—?"

"Yes, Michael?"

"I really am glad you got home safely. That storm's growing nasty outside—"

With a dispirited smile, she held up the note from the headmaster:

"It appears we've one of our own brewing inside, too."

iv

Amanda climbed the stairs slowly. She stopped on the landing to catch her breath beside the stained glass window. The window contained a small portrait of Lord Byron set above a pattern of figures representing the muses.

Under the gas fixture, she read what Pemberton had written. It was every bit as grim as Michael had hinted. Louis was willfully refusing to settle down to his studies—

Damned if she'd wait till morning to have it out with him!

Instead of proceeding to her room, she turned the opposite way on the second floor, toward his. She frowned when she tried to open the door.

Locked.

She thought she heard a voice—not her son's—whispering inside. Curious and a little alarmed, she knocked:

"Louis?"

No answer.

"Louis, this is your mother. Why do you have the door bolted? Please open it at once."

CHAPTER VII

The Box

AN IRRATIONAL DREAD settled over Amanda while she waited for a reply. The wind whined across the roof. A door closed below; Michael leaving the library. In her son's room, she heard furtive footsteps and, if her ears weren't tricking her, that unfamiliar voice.

"Louis, unless you answer me—" she began, only to be interrupted:

"I'm here, mother." The sound of a yawn—too exaggerated to be genuine. "What do you want?"

"I want you to open the door immediately."

"You woke me up."

He's lying, she thought, the knowledge a sickening shock. She'd never known her son to lie before. The other voice whispered again. This time she identified it as a woman's; the shock was instantly compounded.

Amanda had long ago realized Louis would probably have his first experience with a girl without her knowledge. She'd decided she would have little control over the time and place, and that about all she could do was exert her influence to see he didn't become involved with some diseased tart from the slums. But she hadn't expected the encounter to happen so soon. Nor in her own house—

Who was with him?

Of all the females who worked for her, she suspected Kathleen McCreery. Kathleen was young; not unattractive. Who had taken the initiative, the boy or the maid? Kathleen didn't strike her as a scheming sort. But obviously the girl knew she was working in a wealthy household—

Her mind a chaos of questions, Amanda finally realized the door was still closed.

"Louis, I'm not going to continue to speak to you this way. Let me in!"

The door opened. But not far.

That Louis had been lying to her was immediately apparent. He was still dressed. But he was barefoot. The tail of his shirt hung over his left hip. Far from sleepy, he was sweating.

"Mother, you woke me out of a sound—"

"The devil I did!" She shoved the door and rushed past him before he could stop her.

Beside the bed, looking utterly terrified, was the McCreery girl. She was clumsily trying to smooth her black skirt. And sure enough, there was the evidence: the rumpled bed with covers tossed back; a damp stain tinged pink at one edge—

Louis started to speak. Kathleen was quicker:

"Ma'am—please—believe me—he forced me—"

"What do you mean, *forced*?"

"Just—just that. I was fixing the room for the night. He came in—he said—*ohhh*—"

"For God's sake, Kathleen, don't start crying! I can hardly make sense of what you're saying as it is—"

Louis stormed between them:

"Who cares what she's saying? Every bit of it's a lie! She practically begged me—"

Kathleen's face convulsed with shame and rage:

"You filthy boy. You filthy, *filthy* boy—"

To Amanda:

"I've never been with a man before—God as my witness! He locked the door—"

"*Shut your mouth!*" Louis cried, running at her with his hand raised.

Amanda lunged, caught her son's wrist, flung his fist

down to his side. He glared at her; tried to strike her—

Amanda slapped him across his left cheek, then across his right.

The boy stumbled back, upsetting a chair. He almost blundered against one of the windows before he righted himself, staring at his mother with astonishment and fear. His normally swarthy face had drained of color. The sight of him sickened her.

She pointed to the overturned chair.

"You sit down while I listen to Kathleen's side of this. Then I'll give you a chance—"

He hesitated. But he finally obeyed, righting the chair in front of the window and sinking down. Outside, the rooftops of the square showed thickening crusts of white—so clean in contrast to the ugliness she'd discovered—

The boy watched his mother apprehensively as she shut the door. Walking back to Kathleen McCreery, Amanda felt her belly aching again, worse than ever—

She put her arm around Kathleen. With their backs to the boy, she gave the girl's trembling shoulders a gentle squeeze:

"Don't be afraid to speak. If Louis abused you, he'll be punished—"

"Oh yes?" the girl retorted. "He's never punished for anything."

"He will be this time. Now tell me precisely what happened."

Kathleen tried, her speech breathy and punctuated by loud sniffles that might have made Amanda laugh in other circumstances:

"He said that—he said he wanted me—in his bed and—if I wouldn't, he'd—he'd say he caught me—trying to steal something—"

Amanda studied the maid's red, puffy eyes. Unless the girl was a superb actress, she wasn't pretending.

"So you consented?"

"I consented because I'd have been accused if I didn't! He demanded that I undress—"

"Demanded?"

"Just the way he demands everything. Don't you know how your own son behaves with the people who wait on him?"

"No, I—I guess I don't. Evidently I've been too busy to give Louis the right sort of attention—"

But I've given him the pattern to follow, haven't I? She remembered California; the boy's odd, almost admiring smile when she talked about the man she'd shot—

Struggling against rage that was directed more toward herself than her son, she faced him. Walked to him. Stood before him, her stare fixed on his guilty, evasive eyes—

"Louis, do you deny what Kathleen says?"

"Yes—yes, I do," he answered, though without firmness. "She flaunted herself—"

"May the saints summon me this minute, *I didn't!*" the girl burst out. "I'd never do such a thing, Mrs. de la Gura. I'd never risk losing this job—I spent months searching for a house where they'd take Irish. Do you think I'd throw that away even—even if I wanted the likes of him?"

"No," Amanda said wearily. "No, that wouldn't be at all likely."

"Ma, I tell you she's making it all up—!" Louis began.

"Louis—" Her voice was pitched low, her eyes stark. "I am not going to tolerate a single lie from you. Did you or did you not demand that Kathleen obey you?"

He still evaded her gaze. She dug her nails into his shoulder:

"Louis, *answer me.*"

"I—"

He wiped his mouth with the back of his hand. Then, as if realizing he was trapped, he turned defiant:

"What if I did? Why shouldn't I have her if I want? This is my house, not hers—and she's nothing but slum trash."

Kathleen began to weep again. As Amanda let go of his shoulder, her lips were almost colorless:

"Of all the insufferable arrogance—"

"Are you taking *her* part?"

"Yes! I am! What gave you the right to think you could order her about any way you wished? No one—nothing gives you that right!"

"No?" A kind of cowering nastiness wrenched his face. "*You* seem to do exactly what you please. Anywhere—and any time."

She struck him with her fist, savagely. He toppled off the chair, fell on one knee, still glaring. She shook with fury—realizing belatedly that she'd really been striking out not at him, but at his accusation—

Because she knew it was true.

ii

She ordered Louis to remain in his room. With as much control as she could muster, she put her arm around Kathleen again, shepherded her out to the hall and led her toward her own quarters.

Amanda pitied the young girl. But she also knew what had to be done. Louis must be dealt with firmly, decisively—and at once. Kathleen's presence would only compound the difficulty of taking him in hand.

She turned up the gas in her private sitting room and eased the girl gently into a chair. Then she sat down opposite her, trying to speak calmly:

"Kathleen, I can't tell you how ashamed I am of what Louis did—"

The girl made a faltering effort to straighten her disarrayed hair. "If only—if only he hadn't used me like—like some piece of goods—"

"I'm afraid I must bear the blame for that. I've inadvertently let Louis believe he can do whatever he wishes. I intend to correct that—"

Provided it isn't already too late.

"However—" Here was the thorny place. "—I think you can realize it would only make things more difficult if you were to remain in the house."

Kathleen's head lifted. Her coppery hair glinted in the flickering glow of the gas—and so did her reddened eyes:

"You're going to turn me out?"

"I don't want to, but you wouldn't be happy here in the light of what's happened. Nor would it be good for Louis to—"

"It *is* his part you're taking. It *is!*"

"Kathleen, I assure you it isn't. I'm thinking of your welfare too."

"Then for God's sake think of how much I need this position!"

"I've considered that."

"You're not going to punish him, that's it," she declared.

"I assure you I'm going to punish him. Severely."

"No, you're getting rid of me so you can smooth it over. Pretend it never happened—"

"You're being unreasonable, Kathleen. Don't you appreciate the problems it would cause for you to see Louis every day, feeling as you do about him? I'm asking you to leave for your own sake. In fact I want you to go tonight."

"Tonight—!"

"Yes, go downstairs and speak with Michael. Tell him to write you a draft for eight weeks' wages. Give him your address, and I'll do my utmost to locate another position for you—"

"So I'm to be thrown out as though I'm the criminal?"

"You don't seem to understand I'm doing it for your peace of mind as well as—"

"I *want* him to look at me! I want him to remember how cruel he was!"

Amanda shook her head. "That won't serve any useful purpose. In a few days you'll see the wisdom of—"

"I won't be treated this way, Mrs. de la Gura. I did nothing wrong. The wrong's all on the boy's side."

"And mine," Amanda said wearily. "I've admitted that." Her voice hardened just a little. "But I still insist you go."

All at once Kathleen's eyes brimmed with resentment. Her face showed a wrath Amanda had never seen her display before:

"You'd better not do this to me—"

Amanda bristled. "Young lady, I'm trying to act in your own best interests. I won't be threatened."

"If you force me to leave, I have friends who'll take my part."

Somehow the plain words made Amanda's spine crawl.

"Friends?"

"My uncle's a pal of Mr. Rynders. You know who Mr. Rynders is, don't you?"

"Isaiah Rynders? Of course."

"I'll make sure he learns what you've done."

"Have you heard nothing I've said? I know you're the one who's been wronged. I'm trying to make what amends I can—"

To salve my conscience?

"I need this position," the girl repeated, more firmly. "It's the best I've ever had, and no one else in my family is old enough to bring home steady wages. If you put me out, Mr. Rynders will hear about it."

"And do what, may I ask? Send some of his hooligans to throw stones at the house?"

"I—I don't know what he'll do, but he'll do something. And it won't be just stones, either."

Her reddened eyes seethed with anger—the same kind of anger Amanda had occasionally seen on Michael's face when he spoke of blacks, or the crowded, filth-ridden stews of his childhood. But understanding the girl's rage didn't mean she could condone it:

"I'm afraid I'm losing patience with you, Kathleen—"

"You'll lose a lot more before this is over!"

"Don't you dare utter one more threat, young lady! You go see Michael this instant!"

The girl started to retort, recognized how deeply she'd stirred Amanda's wrath, and kept silent. With a last, hateful glance at her former employer, she rushed from the room, slamming the door behind her.

Amanda sat motionless for the better part of five minutes. Then, overwhelmed by misery and exhaustion, she buried her face in her hands and cried.

iii

When the crippling despair passed, she went to her bedroom. She found the whiskey she kept at hand for those nights when sleep refused to come easily. She poured a generous measure and drank it in swift swallows.

The effect of the whiskey was almost instantaneous. A semblance of control restored, she walked down the hall to Louis' room and knocked.

He replied with a sullen monosyllable.

"I'll be back to speak with you as soon as I've talked with Michael," she said.

Silence.

Amanda shook her head, wheeled and strode toward the staircase.

She found Michael at the desk in the library, his demeanor as melancholy as it had been following their discussion of the Phelans. She closed the doors and leaned against them.

"Has Kathleen been here?"

"Yes, Mrs. A, she just left. I wrote the draft as you instructed. She's downstairs, packing her belongings. Considering the snow and the late hour, I doubt we can whistle up a hack. I'll have to hitch the carriage and drive her home myself."

"How much did Kathleen tell you?"

"Enough to make it clear master Louis all but raped her." He hesitated. "What do you plan to do about the boy?"

"We'll discuss that in a moment. Do you agree Kathleen should go?"

Michael rose and walked toward his chair. He'd refilled his plate with mutton. He picked up a slice and bit into it without much relish. Eventually he answered: "Under the circumstances, I do."

"The girl made some wild threats about setting Isaiah Rynders on us."

Michael's brow hooked up. "The ward boss?"

"Yes. She claims he's a friend of her uncle. Could she make good on a threat like that?"

"I expect so. There isn't a major gang with which Isaiah Rynders doesn't have connections—the Patsy Conroys, the Daybreak Boys, the Shirt Tails, the Plug Uglies. If Rynders could do her uncle a favor—rather, have some of his thugs do it—he would. Such little acts of kindness insure loyalty to the Society of Saint Tammany come election time."

"Do you have any idea what they'd do?"

"None whatever. It could be a friendly little street assault when you least suspect it. Or Louis might be the target. Some of the roughest gangs specialize in such charming touches as stomping a victim with shoes in which they've embedded a couple of knife-blades—"

"Dear God!"

"They're also fond of quick raids to wreck and loot a house. Or arson—that's relatively safe. The possibilities are almost without limit—" He shrugged. "On the other hand, Kathleen's threat may be more heat than substance."

"You're not entirely convinced of it."

Michael's eyes slid away. "Not entirely."

"Well, I suppose it's time for me to resurrect my old revolver and keep it handy."

"Not a bad notion," he agreed.

"As for Louis—I know what I'm going to do. First I intend to punish him personally. Then I'm going to withdraw him from Professor Pemberton's Day School for a while. Put him to work around the house. Any sort of project that needs doing—or can be invented. I want you to take charge of that phase. Work him to exhaustion."

"What are you trying to do, Mrs. A, break him like a horse?"

That irritated her: "Do you have a better suggestion?"

"I think so—though it'll make you even more angry."

"I'm listening."

Michael drew in a deep breath. "Set him a different kind of example."

She turned red. "Just exactly what do you mean?"

"Simply this. You're a determined woman. You go after what you want, no interference allowed—and you make no secret of it. I suspect Louis is only showing his admiration of that."

"In a very warped way!" She said it sharply. But she knew Michael had touched the essential truth of the problem.

"Agreed," he said. "Still, you might find things changing favorably if you displayed—shall we say—a less aggressive attitude?"

"I can't be what I'm not."

"Certainly. But you *can* be less outspoken about your intention to own Kent and Son at any cost. Louis may not understand the reason for it, or know how you're going about it. But he can't help being aware of your hostility. You're quite a different woman when Mr. Stovall occupies your thoughts than you are, for example, when you're entertaining Mrs. Ludwig or arguing the pros and cons of abolitionism. You may not even realize the disparity—"

"I'm sorry, I don't."

"Then perhaps I've made you angry in a good cause."

Amanda gazed restlessly around the library.

At the painting of her grandfather highlighted by the flicker of flames from the hearth—

At the polished scabbard of the French sword and the lustrous wood of the Kentucky rifle—

At the shimmering green glass of the tea bottle—

She sounded almost despondent when she spoke:

"Everyone wants to convince me I'm a fool for trying to get control of the firm."

"Everyone? There have been others before me?"

"Quite a few," she said, sourly. "Rose Ludwig just this evening. My cousin Jared before he died. Captain McGill—but that's immaterial. I consider it my duty to deal with Stovall."

"I'd say your sense of duty has become a fixation."

"Call it anything you like. I won't stop now. He blocked me once, because I was careless, but he won't a second time. You must understand how I see it, Michael—Louis behaved inexcusably. But every step I've taken against Stovall, I've taken for a good and sufficient reason—"

"You could lecture Louis for days, Mrs. A, and I don't believe you'd get through to him. He's not old enough to comprehend the subtle difference between an appetite for a woman and an appetite for revenge. If there *is* a difference—"

"There is!"

His shrug said the question was debatable.

"Michael, what Louis did to Kathleen was pointless and—"

"Forgive me again," he interrupted. "I may be expressing a narrow male attitude, but a boy with a physical craving hardly considers the craving pointless. It's the most important thing in the world to him. It took me months to work up nerve the first time I—well, never mind the details."

"I am talking about the despicable way Louis went about it!" she insisted.

Michael's gaze rested on Mr. Mayor sleeping in a ball on the marble in front of the fire. "You wouldn't call my planned expedition to the Five Points despicable?"

"I was very explicit on that subject. The material from the Phelans would only be used in an extreme situation, so let's not permit that to confuse the discussion."

He flushed. "I think it's very pertinent to the discussion. You *did* ask for my suggestions—"

"Well, I don't agree with them. Hamilton Stovall and my son's behavior have nothing to do with one another."

"Who are you trying to convince? Me? Or yourself?"

"Michael, you're overstepping—!"

"The hell I am! You've enrolled me as your son's disciplinarian!"

"I told you I intend to punish—"

"For God's sake, Mrs. A, why won't you recognize that it's your obsession with Kent and Son that's damaging the boy? Until you reach that conclusion, no punishment will make a whit of difference in Louis' character. If you change, he may. Otherwise—"

"Enough, Michael."

"No, goddamn it, I want to have my say about—"

"The subject is *closed.*"

There was a heavy silence.

"And you'll take charge of Louis as I instructed."

"Ordered!" he growled, turning toward the fireplace. He saw the white cat lying in front of him. He kicked it.

Mr. Mayor woke with a start, nearly as astonished at the young man's cruelty as Amanda herself. Michael slammed a fist down on the mantel, then bent to stroke the cat, murmuring apologies almost as if he'd struck a human being.

She *couldn't* admit Michael was right. Or Jared. Or Bart McGill. She couldn't admit she was being destroyed by her own dedication to owning the printing house. She was strong. She'd survived challenges before. Survived and overcome them. She would survive this one; bring Louis into line *and* gain her objective—

Michael's back was still turned as she said, "Be sure Louis is wakened at six. I'll inform him before I go to bed that you'll be—"

A commotion at the rear of the house whirled them both toward the doors.

Michael started into the hall, only to step back as the butler, Mr. Hampton, rushed into sight, still struggling to slip his arms into his black coat. He smelled of gin; he'd evidently been relaxing downstairs before trudging home—

"Mrs. de la Gura, there is an Adams Express wagon in the alley."

"At this hour?"

"I hardly believed it myself when I saw the accumulation of snow. Nevertheless, two deliverymen are bringing in a large crate."

"We've ordered nothing big enough to be delivered in a crate—" Michael began.

"I can't help that, Mr. Boyle," Hampton said with a dogged shake of his head. "The crate has come from the railroad station, addressed to this house."

"Oh my God," Amanda exclaimed, an incredible suspicion forming in her mind. "Jephtha's letter—"

"What's that to do with a crate from Adams Express?" Michael wanted to know.

But Amanda had already dashed past him toward the butler's pantry. With astonished looks, he and Hampton hurried after her.

iv

The crate, dripping melted snow and exuding a faint acrid smell, had been brought down the rear service stairs into the room at the rear of the raised basement. The room was a cheerless place without gas fixtures, used principally for storage.

The servants clustered around the crate. One of them, Brigid, the downstairs maid, held a flickering oil lamp that cast slow-moving shadows. Two sodden and distinctly unhappy draymen stood eyeing the box as Amanda entered, Michael and the butler right behind.

The outer door blew open, whirling snow and freezing air into the room. The flame of the lamp jumped in the sudden gust. Grotesque shadows leaped across the walls and ceiling. One drayman kicked the door shut while Amanda surveyed the crate. It had been crudely addressed in black paint:

Mrs. A. de la Gura
Madison Square
New York City

It also bore a return address—*J. Jared, Clifton Forge, Virginia*—and, across the ends, an additional legend:

Books & household merchandise

The contrived name of the sender—meaningful to Amanda but to no one else—strengthened her growing conviction about the crate's contents. With a sinking feeling, she recalled a passage in Jephtha's letter about regular destinations for *freight* being unsafe—

"Come off the train from Baltimore," one of the draymen informed her. "We ain't to blame for the stink. One of the handlers down at the terminal must have pissed on—"

His companion nudged him, then held out a scrap of paper and pencil to Amanda:

"You'll have to sign."

"Why did you deliver it on such a bad night?" she asked, scribbling her name.

" 'Cos the goddamn sender paid extra," the first man grumbled. "Special delivery within an hour after it arrived—"

The draymen left. Outside, wheels crunched snow. Hoofs clopped softly. The sounds faded.

Amanda circled the box, spotting three small holes neatly drilled through the wood. She didn't know whether to laugh or weep over the additional burden thrust so unexpectedly on the already disturbed household.

Michael voiced the confusion of the whispering servants:

"Who in God's name would be shipping you books and such, Mrs. A?"

"That *J. Jared* is the Reverend Kent in Virginia. Jared was his father's name. I'm sure he painted that on the box so we'd identify the sender."

"Well, we can leave it sitting till morning, anyway—"

Amanda shook her head. "We have to open it. Fetch a crowbar."

"Why?"

She pointed. "Do you notice those holes?"

"What of them?"

"Do you remember reading in the paper last year about a black man in Virginia who had himself shipped to the Philadelphia Anti-Slavery Society? The underground railroad's used the trick several times before."

"Oh my Lord!" the cook exclaimed. "Is your cousin mixed up in that, ma'am?"

"I've had hints of it in his letters—Michael, bring the crowbar!"

In half a minute, the young man returned and fell to prying one side off the case. Amanda was outraged that the Reverend Jephtha Kent would make her a party to his illegal work without so much as a word of warning—

But there *had* been warning, she realized belatedly. In Jephtha's delayed letter, hadn't he made a reference to *calling on some we wouldn't otherwise burden or endanger?* If those weren't the exact words, the sense was the same. He'd been telling her in a cryptic way that he might need her help. Perhaps he'd avoided saying it straight out in case mail from suspected underground railroad operators was tampered with. At the time she'd read the lines, she'd simply been too dull-witted to grasp his meaning.

A nail squealed as Michael worked the crowbar. He was starting to pry loose another when the bar slipped from his fingers and clanged on the floor.

"Can't hold onto the blasted thing. There's a bit of grease on it—"

"Spit on your hands," Amanda said.

Bent over and reaching for the length of iron, Michael stared. The reaction was more pronounced from the servants. The butler uttered an audible gasp.

Amanda snapped at him:

"Haven't you ever used a little spit so you could get a better hold on something, Mr. Hampton?"

"No, madam, I have not," the butler said, plainly horrified by the idea.

"Well, you're not taking advantage of the saliva God

gave you. For heaven's sake, Michael, get that damn thing open!"

"Right away, Mrs. A—I was about to do the very thing you suggested."

He moistened his palms while Mr. Hampton raised his eyes to the ceiling.

Presently the last nail came free. Michael scrambled back as the side of the box crashed to the floor. One of the maids shrieked softly. Amanda almost felt like crying again:

Not this on top of everything else—!

Huddled inside the crate in a tangle of cheap blankets was a light-skinned colored girl. Her frayed cotton dress barely covered her emaciated thighs. Amanda judged her to be sixteen or seventeen. She looked undernourished and nearly frozen. With the crate open, the smell of urine was much stronger.

The black girl started to crawl out, tears in her eyes:

"I thought I die in there. I thought I die from the cold and the shakin' on the train—"

Amanda forced herself to stay calm. She knelt and slipped an arm around the trembling girl:

"You're safe, child. Safe. What's your name?"

"Mary, ma'am."

"Mary what?"

"Mary's the only name I got."

"I'm Mrs. de la Gura—"

"Praise God! The Reveren' Kent, he took me over to Clifton Forge hid in Mr. Syme's wagon. He stopped in some woods outside of town, an' before he nailed me in the box, he say you help me get to Canada—"

"Christ, that's all we need—black contraband!" Michael groaned.

"Hush, Michael."

"But you can be arrested for concealing a runaway sl—"

"I said hush! Mary—how long have you been shut up in that box?"

"Mos' part of two nights an' all day, I guess—what day's this?"

"Friday night—Saturday morning by now."

"The Reverend, he drove me to the Virginia Central depot Wednesday—trip's almos' thirty miles—"

"Why couldn't they simply have shipped the creature to Canada?" Mr. Hampton asked, disdainful.

"Watch your tongue, Mr. Hampton," Amanda warned. "She's not a creature—she's a human being. And a hungry one at that, I imagine. Have you had anything to eat, child?"

"Biscuits. No drinkin' water. Breathin' was the hardest. Breathin' and bracin' my hands an' feet so I wouldn't roll around and make noise when men lifted the box—"

"Does that answer you, Mr. Hampton?" Amanda asked in a waspish voice. "If they shipped her all the way to Canada, she'd probably suffocate before she got there—or make such a stink in the box someone would surely open it."

The girl grew agitated. "I couldn't help wettin' myself. I tried and tried not to—I tried hard, but I couldn't—"

"That's all right, that's all right," Amanda whispered, patting her. "You did just fine, Mary. Who do you belong to?"

The girl blinked. "To me. I get to Canada, I won't belong to nobody ever again."

"But who did you belong to in Virginia?"

"Cap'n Tunworth."

"The Reverend's father-in-law?"

"Yes'm. He a proper gentleman with other white folks, but he can be mean as hell to his niggers when the spell's on him."

Amanda nodded, her anger at Jephtha all but erased

by the courage and fragility of the young girl who had entrusted her life to two white men, and ridden rattling trains in a lightless wooden cage with mortal fear for her companion.

"I've met the captain," she said. "You've confirmed my impression of him—"

"I knew Mr. Syme could get me started to Canada. Mos' every nigger 'round Lexington knows that. I never wanted to go till the cap'n sold my mamma and papa to a man in Carolina. But the cap'n wouldn't sell me. I figure I never see my folks again, so I might as well take a chance on bein' a free person—"

"But why did the Reverend send you here?" Michael asked. "Why not to an organization like the local anti-slavery society?"

"Jephtha's letter indicated that was getting too dangerous," Amanda said.

Mary nodded. "He an' Mr. Syme say they got slave-catchers watching those places now. Watching for colored—even for boxes like the one I come in—"

Suddenly she hugged Amanda, burying her head on the older woman's shoulder.

"I hate that old box! It was all dark an' I made it smell bad—I couldn't help it—I'm so glad I'm here—I'm so glad—"

"Someone bring a couple of clean blankets," Amanda said while the girl sobbed. "We'll put her in the third floor bedroom next to Michael's until I decide what we can do with—"

She froze. At the storeroom door beyond the cluster of servants, she saw Kathleen McCreery.

Kathleen was bundled in a shabby coat. Her pale eyes rounded at the sight of the crate and the black girl in the circle of lamplight.

"Michael—!"

Amanda's warning spun him toward the door.

"Get her out of here! When you take her home, warn her that she'd better not say a word."

"I'm afraid we're not in much of a position to issue warnings," Michael whispered. He stalked to the door and thrust the dumbfounded Kathleen out of sight.

The black girl began to cry in earnest, long wailing sobs. Whether of pleasure or pain, Amanda couldn't tell. She was still fighting the impulse to cry again herself.

That Jephtha Kent had relied on her willingness to harbor a runaway—a clear violation of the Fugitive Slave Act—was upsetting enough. That the McCreery girl had seen the runaway was an absolute disaster.

▼

Michael returned to the house about half past one in the morning, reporting to Amanda in the library:

"I did the best I could but she's still in a rage. I promised her an additional two weeks' wages one month from now—*if* she keeps silent about what she saw."

"Do you think she will?"

Amanda wasn't encouraged when he answered, "It depends on how angry she's feeling in a day or two. There's one commodity that's not for sale in the Five Points, Mrs. A—an end to an Irishman's wrath once he's down on you."

"Well, let's hope for the best."

"What are we going to do with the nig—the girl?"

"Put her on the first steamer heading to Canada. You inquire at the piers in the morning."

"What about the disciplining of your son?"

"That can wait a few hours. I still must go up and speak to him—"

"You haven't yet?"

"No, I haven't yet!" she lashed out. "I've been attending to the girl! We tried to feed her and she threw up everything. I finally got some brandy down her. That put her to sleep."

"You'd better sleep a little yourself. You look exhausted."

"I'll see Louis first."

But even that went wrong.

When she climbed the staircase and reached the door of her son's room, she found it unlocked. She opened it quietly. The night sky had cleared. The winter moon shone. Its reflection on snowy rooftops cast a luminous whiteness into the room.

Louis lay on his side in the soiled bed, fully dressed. His head was all but hidden in the pillows, as if he'd tried to burrow deep into them to escape the world.

Her face drawn, Amanda stared at him for a long time, thinking.

vi

She found Michael still in the library. His legs were stretched out toward the dying fire. The white cat was dozing on his knees. He looked startled when she slipped inside.

Her glance went briefly to the display case. Jared's medallion reflected the last red gleams from the hearth.

"Michael—"

"Yes, Mrs. A?"

"I want you to forget about going to the Five Points."

He blinked. "You don't want me to contact the Phelans?"

"No."

She expected him to smile. Instead, quite soberly, he nodded:

"That's good. Because I had decided I'd resign rather than do that particular chore. I'm thankful you changed your mind. May I ask why—?"

"I looked at Louis upstairs. And I thought of what you said about the high road. I—I don't want the ruining of my son to be the price I pay for Kent's."

"Why don't you wipe the slate all the way clean? Forget the stock too. Dissolve Boston Holdings. You've more than enough money to start a new firm."

"It wouldn't be the same. The stock acquisition is legal. I'll go ahead with that and hope it succeeds." She was very much aware of how much she was staking on a single strategy.

Michael smiled then. "At least what you've decided should make you feel a mite better."

"In a way it does. At the same time, I think I've walked away from a fight. I've never done that in my life."

"I'd say your decision took more courage than any fighting ever could."

"I wish I believed you," she said softly. As she turned to go, the admiration in his eyes was of little comfort.

CHAPTER VIII

The Slave-Hunter

SATURDAY MORNING BROUGHT brilliant sunshine and the drip of melting snow from the eaves. Amanda slept until nine—three hours past her usual time for rising. When she saw the clock on the mantel of her bedroom fireplace, she got up in a rush, drew on a fur-trimmed robe and went straight to the third floor.

She found Mary just finishing an immense breakfast brought up from the kitchen. The girl seemed in good spirits:

"I never had so much food at one time in all my life! Never slept in a bed so soft, either."

"Are you feeling well?"

"Reckon I am. I couldn't eat that food fast enough."

"Good. Today we're going to look into the schedules of steamers to Canada."

"It scares me some to think about goin'," Mary admitted. "I don't know anybody there. An' the Reverend, he didn't have no names to give me—"

"I've been told there are anti-slave societies in almost every large Canadian city. I'm sure you'll have no trouble locating one. They'll help you get settled."

The girl clutched Amanda's arm:

"You don't think they send anybody after me from Virginia, do you, ma'am?"

"I think it's very unlikely," Amanda reassured her, hoping she was right. She left Mary sitting on the bed, bouncing up and down and enjoying the resilience. Mary's expression was almost rapturous.

Amanda went to her son's room next. It was empty. In Kathleen's absence, no one had yet made up the bed. She returned to her own room, dressed and hurried down the staircase.

As she descended the steps, she heard the bell of a horse-car clang on the far side of the square, then the prolonged rasp of a large chunk of snow sliding off the roof. In the front hall, the sun shone through the narrow windows on either side of the door, casting rectangles of light on the carpet. Somehow that glow restored her spirits a little. She felt more competent to deal with the problems that had arisen during the night.

Hamilton Stovall was far from her mind as she entered the dining room and saw Louis, still in his velvet-collared robe, dawdling over a cup of coffee.

He glanced at her, then back to the cup, his manner subdued. A moment later, the maid Brigid appeared. She was a plain, buxom girl in her late twenties.

"Only tea, I think, Brigid," Amanda said. "But no cream. I'm putting on too much weight."

Brigid smiled, murmured, "Yes, ma'am," and left.

Amanda unfolded the stiff linen napkin set at her place at the head of the long mahogany table. Louis was seated on the side, to her left, near a weighty breakfront displaying some two dozen pieces of fine silver. Amanda laid the napkin in her lap; she could feel the tension her presence created. Rather than confront Louis immediately, she began with another subject:

"Where is Michael?"

The boy's quick exhalation signaled his relief. "Off in the carriage already. To the steamer offices, he said. He told me about the crate Adams Express delivered last night."

"You're to say nothing about it outside this house. The girl will be gone within a few days."

Louis nodded. "I don't know who I'd tell, anyway—"

"I was thinking of your associates at the Day School," Amanda said in a quiet voice. "The ones with whom you've been quarreling."

The boy's head jerked up, his dark eyes wary.

"We had a note from Professor Pemberton yesterday. About your fighting. And your refusal to study. I've decided to withdraw you from school for a few weeks."

He almost smiled. He'd hardly consider that a severe penalty, she knew.

"As to what happened with Kathleen, I'm going to punish you for that when we finish breakfast."

"Punish me? How?"

"You'll discover in due time. First I'd like to ask you a question. Have I somehow given you the idea that you can take anything you want in this world with no thought of how you might be hurting other people?"

The boy frowned. "I don't know, ma—mother. Sometimes, I—I do have the feeling you do whatever you please—"

"Then I am to blame—even though there are good reasons why I behave as I do. You had no good reason for what you did to Kathleen. And nothing like that will ever happen again, Louis. Nothing," she repeated. "I'm afraid I've spoiled you. That too is going to change. While you're out of school, I expect you to work around the house. Under Michael's supervision."

He accepted the announcement in stoic silence.

"Now I'd like to know something else. After mistreating Kathleen last night, did you feel nothing? No shame? No sorrow—?"

He pressed his lips together, toying with the handle of his cup. When he looked at her again, she felt almost dizzy with relief. There *was* a spark of contrition in those blazing black eyes:

"Yes, I—I felt wretched." He lowered his head. "But not until it was over."

He stood up suddenly, hurrying around the corner of the table to stand beside her. "I went to sleep thinking of how I tried to lie to you—and how much you despised me. I can't stand to have you hate me, ma—"

She closed her eyes a moment, immensely relieved. Perhaps he wasn't beyond hope after all.

"I don't hate you, Louis. I love you. But I can't forgive or excuse what you did. You hurt Kathleen. You shamed her, you abused her as if she were an animal. You caused her to lose her job because I couldn't keep her in this house after what happened. No matter how rich a person may be—or how self-important money makes you feel—and it does, sometimes—that still gives you no right whatsoever to hurt another human being who's done nothing to hurt you. I'm going to impress that on you in a way I trust you'll never forget. At the same time, I acknowledge my part in your guilt—I expect I've set you a bad example because you don't understand why I do certain things."

"Would those things have anything to do with that man who still owns Kent's?"

"What do you know about him, Louis?" she countered softly.

"Why—I know he won't sell the company back to you, and that makes you mad. You bring up his name with Michael a lot, and you're mad then too. I've read in the papers that Stovall runs a huge steel factory. And I remember once in California, you and Captain Bart had a terrible argument while I was trying to sleep. I heard his name even way back then—"

Amanda sighed. "Well, you're correct. A good deal of my activity since we've come east is connected with Stovall. I expect I owe you a full explanation. You'll have it—in a week or two—when you've shown me you mean to change your ways."

She couldn't keep affection out of her voice as she clasped both of his hands in hers:

"I can't permit you to go the wrong way now, Louis. There's too much at stake—principally your future. You'll be in charge of Kent and Son one day. I want you to work with Theo Payne if he'll stay on. Learn from him—"

"But we don't even own the company!"

"We will," she assured him. "And you'll re-build it into the kind of firm your great-grandfather would be proud of. There's no limit to the possibilities open to you, Louis. A useful life—a good marriage—*entree* to the best homes—by the time you're grown," she added with a wry smile, "the sour old society ladies who consider me new rich will be in their graves. Their children will welcome you as an equal. That's what I want for you—because you're a Kent. And because I love you."

He pulled his hands loose and flung his arms around her neck, hugging her:

"I know I did wrong last night, ma. I'll make it up to you—I want you to be proud of me—"

She wrapped her arms around his waist and pressed her cheek against his chest, the relief almost unbearable—

She heard Brigid enter with her tea and broke away. The tea smelled delicious. She drank it eagerly. An image of the portrait of Philip Kent drifted into her mind. She thought, *It isn't too late. I'll turn him into a Kent worthy of the name—*

The sound of boots stamping in the front hall caught her attention. She heard Michael speaking to Hampton, set her teacup down and hurried from the room.

Michael stood in an oblong of sunlight, unwrapping a long scarf of red wool from around his collar. His hair shone almost as brightly as his smile:

"We're in luck, Mrs. A. We've only to wait until Tuesday night. There's a White Star steamer sailing from North River at ten o'clock. Straight up the coast, overnight at Boston, then along the St. Lawrence to Montreal—"

He pulled a manila envelope from his coat.

"I bought the girl's ticket."

"Wonderful!"

Michael flung the scarf onto a bench and raked droplets of melted snow from his hair. "Have you spoken with Louis?"

"Just now. He seems contrite."

"Is he ready to work?"

"He will be in an hour."

"Why the delay?"

"I've one thing yet to take care of—" Her eyes were hard.

"Very well. While I'm waiting, I'll chop up that crate and burn the pieces. As soon as Louis is free, I'll set him to clearing the slush out of the front drive. My, won't that raise eyebrows next door! Mrs. de la Gura's son doing servant's work—"

Amused, he walked toward the dining room. Amanda followed.

"Come with me, Louis," she said.

"Where?"

Michael gaped when she answered:

"The carriage house."

ii

The dapple-gray mare whickered as Amanda and her son entered the frame building at the rear of the property. The light was poor and the interior smelled of straw and manure. The mare's breath streamed from her nostrils in the cold air. She bumped the side of her stall.

Water dripped from the wheels and springs of the carriage Michael had only recently returned to its place.

Amanda reached up and drew the stiff-handled whip from its socket.

"Louis, take off your robe."

"My robe? What are you going to—?"

"You heard what I said. Take the robe off and stand against that post, facing it. Put your hands on the post, over your head."

The boy swallowed. The ferocity she'd seen on his face last night might never have existed. He looked terrified; young and vulnerable—

She ached at the thought of what she was about to do. Yet it had to be done.

Louis dropped the robe; lifted his hands to grasp the post. She watched his back prickle into gooseflesh as he waited, his head turned slightly, one eye visible.

"Now," she said, "you remember this moment, because I'll never do such a thing to you again—just as you'll never treat another person the way you treated Kathleen. I remind you once more—she did nothing to deserve the hurt you gave her. Not just the physical hurt—she'll carry the memory all her life. I want you to carry the memory of this. How it feels to be hurt by wanton cruelty. You remember, Louis—and let it keep you from hurting any other blameless person—ever again."

"Ma—" he began. The whip flicked up past her shoulder, and forward. The tip struck between his shoulderblades with a sharp, smacking sound.

Louis' hands tightened on the post. He clenched his teeth.

She whipped him again. This time he cried aloud. The cry disturbed the mare. She kicked the side of the stall. Louis' whole body was trembling. Sweat covered his cheeks. The second blow had left a thin scarlet stripe on his skin.

Amanda struck a third time. He cried louder, digging his fingers into the post. The mare whinnied, kicked again. One of the stall boards cracked.

She forced herself to fall into a rhythm: the long, flexible tip of the whip came back, then flew forward to mark him. The whip butt grew slippery in her hand—

Six strokes.

Seven—

Blood began to run down the boy's back. The mare was wild with terror, bucking and slamming her hoofs into the stall's side, smashing the boards—

Eight.

Nine—

Louis groaned, started to slide down the post. White-faced, Amanda whispered:

"Stand up. Stand up and *feel it*."

The savagery of her voice made him pull himself erect. He braced for the next blow; listened for the whisper of the whip cutting the air; closed his eyes—

Screamed when the whip flayed him.

The mare kicked, the sound thunderous. Two more boards in the side of the stall splintered apart.

"All right," Amanda said, ashen.

Louis turned. His hands jerked at his sides. He stared at her, tears in the corners of his eyes. There was no hate in that glance; only dull suffering—

She walked to the carriage, picked up a handful of straw, wiped the blood from the whip and replaced it in the socket. Then she faced her son.

"Come here."

He walked to her, stumbling the last couple of steps. She caught him in both arms, cushioning him against her, arms around his waist.

"Cry if you want. Cry—no one will hear you—"

He did, letting the long sobs free him of some of his pain. Amanda cried too, in silence, holding him close until the worst of his shuddering passed—

Finally he got control of himself. She stepped back, barely aware that the sleeves of her dress were stained red.

"If you're ever tempted to hurt someone again, remember today."

"I will, ma."

"Swear it, Louis."

"I swear. Before God, I swear it."

A knot seemed to break within her. She could barely speak:

"Now—" She wiped her cheeks with the back of one hand. "Put your robe on—"

He did, groaning when the fabric came in contact with the lash-marks.

"We'll go upstairs. I'll dress and bandage the cuts. You can rest for an hour. Then you're going to work. You'll hurt quite a few days, I expect. It's proper you should."

The dapple gray blubbered her lips, still stirring restlessly in the broken stall as the two of them walked into the winter sunlight, the boy leaning on his mother for support.

iii

At twilight on Sunday evening, Amanda was at work at the desk in the library, comfortably dressed in one of the three bloomer outfits she owned—a matching top and trousers in lavender. She was going over the list of investments she'd made using Jephtha Kent's earnings from the Ophir Mineralogical Combine. If the Sierra claim looked as promising as Israel Hope's letter suggested, those earnings should soon increase sharply.

She figured the different percentages of growth for each of the issues in which she'd invested the mining profits. None of that money had gone to purchase Stovall Works shares, as she'd originally intended. Boston Holdings operated solely on income from the Blackstone mill.

She worked slowly. Her eyes itched from scanning the columns of figures. After jotting a final note on two stocks whose poor performance merited immediate sale, she turned to the weekly edition of Mr. Greeley's *Tribune*.

She read an account of a lecture given in New York the preceding week by the philosopher, Emerson, then a review of a concert by the Swedish opera star, Jenny Lind, who was touring America under personal contract to the showman Phineas Barnum. She found both articles informative but dull. On the livelier side was a scathing feature about the poor performance of New York's police.

The writer accused the chief of taking criminal bribes —including one from the city's foremost female abortionist—and argued that city police protection would never be satisfactory until the force was given some semblance of professionalism, the first step being uniforms. But those, the police had steadfastly refused to wear ever since Mayor Harper had suggested the idea in the mid-40s. The police contended they were "free Americans," and thus should not be required to appear in public in "livery befitting servants."

A dispatch from Illinois caught her attention next. It dealt with the Whigs in that western state, and quoted a lawyer named Lincoln who had served one term in Congress during the Mexican war and was apparently becoming a power in the party.

The lawyer's first name was Abraham. Amanda wondered whether he could be the same person she'd seen briefly when she and Jared had been traveling to Tennessee years ago. Because Jared had contracted an illness, they'd stopped for a couple of weeks at a cabin in Kentucky. She remembered farmer Lincoln's boy Abraham quite clearly. Though he had only been five years old, he'd displayed an unusual curiosity about letters and words.

Expressing himself on the strength of the Whigs in Illinois, Lincoln was then quoted on his personal views about the Know-Nothings. The nature of his opinions made it instantly clear why Horace Greeley had given them space:

"How can anyone who abhors the oppression of negroes, be in favor of degrading classes of white people? Our progress in degeneracy appears to me to be pretty rapid. As a nation, we began by declaring that *'all men are created equal.'* Now we practically read it 'all men are created equal, *except negroes.'* When the Know-Nothings get control, it will read 'all men are created equal, except negroes, *foreigners and Catholics.'*

"When it comes to this I should prefer emigration to some country where they make no pretense of loving liberty—to Russia, for example, where despotism can be taken pure, without the base alloy of hypocrisy."

The statement summed up Amanda's own beliefs about as well as she'd ever been able to do herself. She decided to show the piece to Michael. It might help abate his deep-seated antagonism toward colored people, pointing out as it did that there was little difference between those who would deny the black man liberty, and those who wanted to keep the immigrant Irish in much the same kind of inferior position.

She had just started to tear the article from the page when the door opened and Mr. Mayor miaowed. She glanced up, rubbing her eyes—the older she grew, the longer they took to re-focus from close work to something more distant.

Hampton presented a silver tray bearing a rectangle of white pasteboard.

"A gentleman in the sitting room, Mrs. de la Gura. He's most insistent about seeing you."

"I wasn't expecting any callers—"

"The gentleman isn't from New York. From his

speech, I would judge he comes from one of the southern states."

The peace that had begun to settle over her since Saturday morning shattered as she snatched the engraved card and read the name.

Virgil Tunworth, Capt., U.S.A. (ret.)

iv

The card fell to the floor. Hampton peered at her: "Is everything all right, madam?"

"Yes—yes—" She retrieved the card, her pulse racing. "Where's Michael?"

"In the carriage house, I believe. He and master Louis are repairing the broken stall."

"Give him the card, bring him in here and tell him to wait—"

She started out, whirled back:

"No, go upstairs first. Lock Mary in her room. Tell her to keep absolutely quiet, no matter what happens." When Hampton seemed slow to comprehend, she exclaimed, "The man is her owner!"

Hampton frowned. "The name did seem slightly familiar—"

"Mary mentioned him the other night. How in God's name he got here, I don't know."

In the sitting room, Captain Virgil Tunworth paced back and forth before the windows overlooking the bare trees of Madison Square. The captain was a small, spare man in his early fifties. Wisps of gray hair lay across a bald skull. He spun around when Amanda entered.

Feigning cordiality, she smiled:

"Captain Tunworth—!"

She noted the sooty shoulders of his cream-colored tailcoat; a black smudge on his stand-up collar. The gaslight emphasized the white stubble on his chin; he apparently hadn't shaved for a day or more.

The captain had served in the army for several years before taking up a more profitable career—the supervision of his family's lands near Lexington. He still carried himself in an erect, military fashion, and affected a severe manner.

"Good evening, Mrs. de la Gura." His glance said he hadn't forgotten their unpleasant meeting in Virginia—and his expression quickly registered disapproval of her lavender trousers.

Still smiling, she said, "This is indeed a surprise—"

"You needn't pretend it's a pleasant one. You know why I've come."

"I'm afraid I haven't the faintest idea," she said, drying her palm on the handkerchief she kept tucked in her sleeve. She approached the bell pull. "May I ring for a drink for you?"

"Thank you, no." Politeness was clearly an effort. "I'm filthy and worn out from the train, so let's conclude our business promptly."

Amanda walked past him to the window. Saw a hack waiting under the portico, its side-lamps aglow in the lowering dark.

"What business, sir?"

In a clipped tone, he replied, "You're harboring a nigger girl who belongs to me."

"Captain Tunworth, that—that is the most astonishing—and preposterous—accusation I've ever heard!"

"Astonishing, I grant you. I'm sure you weren't expecting me. But preposterous? Hardly. You see, Mrs. de la Gura—"

He stalked toward her, openly belligerent.

"Some whose niggers run away are content to let them go. I am not. My wench Mary was conducted to Clifton Forge last Wednesday and shipped in a packing case to this house—"

He raised a hand on which a diamond ring glittered. "Before you trap yourself with denials, allow me to finish. I know how Mary got away because I whipped one of my bucks half to death—until he told me he'd seen her conferring with Mr. Syme when my wife sent Mary and the buck to town on an errand. You certainly know who Mr. Syme is—your cousin's fellow-conspirator? After the buck confessed, we caught him."

Suddenly Amanda felt terror:

"Who caught him?"

"Why, some gentlemen who feel exactly as I do about fugitives and those who assist them. Congress has passed a law denying niggers sanctuary in the northern states—and so we're entitled to their return. I regret to say that after Mr. Syme admitted his perfidy—following a little moral suasion with a board applied to his bare feet—he tried to escape. He couldn't walk, let alone run. Took a pistol ball in the back. He's dead. I'm of the opinion Syme's wife warned your cousin, the Reverend. He's disappeared—"

"Jephtha's gone?" Amanda gasped. "Where?"

"To hell, I sincerely hope," the captain replied with a tart smile. "He was interfering with the law of these United States. He conspired to rob me of my property. As I say, Mary was spirited away on Wednesday. By sundown Friday Mr. Syme had departed this earth—but not before he told us your cousin had driven Mary all the way to the Clifton Forge depot of the Virginia Central line. Some cash and some threats loosened the tongue of the express agent there. That's how I learned the destination of the box the Reverend shipped. This morning, an hour after I got off that infernal train, I fetched the local manager of Adams Express straight out of church. I only had to remind him that abetting the escape of a slave now carries serious penalties—"

Captain Tunworth's hand dipped into his coat and came up with a paper.

"He gave me this copy of the delivery order, and that's all there is to it. I don't suppose the crate is still in this house. But I imagine Mary is. Return her and there's no need for us to quarrel—or to make the incident public."

Amanda sank down on a sofa in front of the Virginian. Jephtha a fugitive! That upset her as much as the arrival of Mary's master. She fought to keep tension from her voice as she said:

"I imagine you're congratulating yourself on being rid of your son-in-law—"

"Woman, don't change the subject on me. I demand—"

"The hell with your demands!" Amanda said in a scathing voice. "I want to know what's become of my cousin!"

Tunworth shrugged. "I expect he's hiding out somewhere in the Blue Ridge. The truth is, no one in Lexington will be grieved at his going. For almost a year he's been suspected of being a conductor on the nigger railroad. His wife and boys want no part of him. Except for that crazy Professor Jackson at the Institute, he hasn't a single friend in the county. And now that we've split up his nefarious little partnership with Mr. Syme, we'll be happy to be quits with him. Let's get back to the matter of my property—"

"You're quite glib about referring to a human being as property!"

"And you're misguided to term niggers human beings."

"Then what are they, captain?"

"Well—human, I suppose I'd have to grant you that. But not to the same full degree as white persons. The nigra is basically inferior in all respects."

Amanda felt desolate. He spoke so calmly—with such an air of conviction—that she knew he'd expressed the bedrock of his belief.

"And nothing will change your mind about that?"

"Nothing. If the abolitionists have their way, the next

step after freedom for the niggers will be equality with whites. I can't accept that, I never will accept it—I'd take up arms before I would obey any law that tried to coerce me into accepting it—but you're trying to sidetrack me again, Mrs. de la Gura."

"Because discussing your so-called property is a waste of time, sir—mine and yours."

"You're getting me exercised, woman—" He wiped his forehead with his sleeve. "You can't deny she's here."

"I refuse to discuss it."

He shook the express receipt at her. "Goddamn it, I have the evidence!"

Amanda tore the paper from his hand, ripped it in half. "That's what I think of your trumped-up evidence! I'd be obliged if you'd leave, Captain Tunworth."

"Not without Mary. Not without my propert—"

A peremptory knock broke the tension and whirled them both toward the door. Michael stuck his head in:

"A word with you, Mrs. A?"

She scowled. "This is not the time—"

"Very urgent. Please!"

To Tunworth she said: "You wait here, sir."

The moment the door clicked behind her, she whispered, "What in the hell is so important that—?"

"Hampton gave me the card. How did Tunworth wind up here so quickly?"

In terse sentences, Amanda repeated the essence of what Jephtha's father-in-law had told her—including the dismal news that her cousin had fled Lexington, evidently in fear of his life. Michael shook his head:

"Then you'd better give her up without a fuss."

Amanda looked stunned. "Let him take the girl?"

"Yes. Unless you surrender his wench without a row, you may be in for serious trouble. Do you know whether he has an order from the court—?"

"He didn't mention one. He only arrived in New York this morning."

"Then he'll probably have to wait for court to sit tomorrow. That's even worse."

"Why?"

"You know fugitive slaves are juicy newspaper copy. If Tunworth stays in the city very long, one of the antiabolitionist sheets like the *Journal of Commerce* may get wind of the whole affair. If it's true your cousin's role in the escape is known—"

"It is. But what's the point?"

"The name Kent could very well be smeared all over the press, along with yours. If Mr. Stovall saw it, I suspect he'd be astute enough to make a connection—"

Amanda's face was bleak as she stared at the young Irishman. He was right. Damnably right—especially in the light of Stovall's already-aroused suspicion.

"Furthermore, Mrs. A, I should remind you that obstructing the recapture of a fugitive slave is illegal. It's one thing to send donations to radical lecturers, quite another to violate a federal law."

She paced to the front door, then all the way back, her knuckles pressed against her teeth. Quite apart from the threat to her personal plans, the question of legality was inescapable. This was the very thing Bart McGill had warned her about. The moment when she would be confronted with a line, and only two choices: step back —or cross.

Wearily, she realized Bart had been right when he said it would be impossible for her not to be drawn into the slave controversy. But she'd never imagined it would happen so precipitously—or pose such disastrous consequences—

She thought of Douglass at the Bowery Theatre. In the abstract, he'd said, the Fugitive Slave Act was tolerable to some people. But the frightened face of the girl

Mary made it intolerable—exactly as Douglass had predicted.

She faced Michael.

"I'll have to take the risk. With Stovall *and* the law."

"Captain Tunworth is entirely in the right."

"I know he's in the right—according to what's written in the statutes. But I can't be a party to sending that child back to bondage. If Tunworth was a decent master—if he treated his slaves in a half way humane fashion—it might be different. But when I was in Virginia, Jephtha made it abundantly clear the captain's a cruel man. Mary said the same thing. I won't turn her over to the likes of him."

Michael's smile was tinged with a curious sadness: "I had a feeling that might be your decision. Do you want me to come in with you?"

She shook her head. "I want to convey my answer to the captain myself."

v

When she did, and asked him to leave, Virgil Tunworth exploded:

"Damned if I will! You bring me Mary this instant!"

She smiled. "I told you she isn't here, Captain."

"And I say you're a villainous liar!" He snatched up his broad-brimmed wool hat and stormed for the door. "I'll root her out myself—"

Amanda caught his arm and jerked him around. Tunworth's eyes popped; he hadn't realized how strong she was.

"You're not going to set foot in another room in this house without an order from the appropriate authorities."

"Then by Christ I'll see the Fugitive Slave Bill Commissioner in the morning! I'll be back and I *will* look in every room!"

"Captain Tunworth," she said in a low voice, "I do pray to God that when you die, someone forbids your burial in Virginia. That a state that gave freedom—and great leaders—to America should spew up the likes of you—"

"Sermonize all you wish, Mrs. de la Gura. The fact remains, the Constitution and the law of the land give me the right to reclaim my property. I will. I know the wench is on these premises—or if not, that you know her whereabouts. Mr. Syme revealed everything, you see. *Everything—*"

He jammed his wool hat on his balding head. His smile matched Amanda's for coldness:

"A man doesn't lie when his bare feet are bleeding from fifty blows of a pine board. I'll call on you again. In company with a federal marshal."

He jerked the door open and stalked past Michael who was lounging under the gas fixture. The front door crashed behind him. In half a minute, Amanda was surrounded by Louis and the servants, all clamoring to know what had happened.

As the hack clattered away, Amanda raised her hands to stop the questions. Quickly and calmly, she explained the visitor's identity, and the reason for his call. Hampton, clearly alarmed, said:

"We should get the girl out of here at once!"

"The steamer doesn't sail till Tuesday evening," Michael said.

"Remove her to another location, then. Mrs. de la Gura, the newspapers have been most explicit. The law in effect since 1850 puts all the right on that gentleman's side—"

"The law be damned! I'm thinking about Mary. But perhaps moving her isn't a bad idea. Michael—?"

"Won't work, Mrs. A."

"Why not?"

He crooked a finger and led her to one of the narrow windows flanking the front door.

"Take a look at what I spied when you were inside with the captain the second time."

She peered out; saw a man huddled against a tree in the small park in the center of the square.

"Hell of a chilly evening to be taking the air, don't you think?" Michael asked. "There's another chap similarly occupied opposite the entrance to the alley. I saw both climb out of Tunworth's hackney. That captain may be a countryman, but he's no fool. I'll wager he was prepared for a refusal and hired those lads from some saloon or other."

"To keep watch."

"Aye. You know the law says bystanders may be summoned to help recapture a slave. Or a *posse comitatus* can be formed—"

"So if we remove her, they'll follow us."

"Undoubtedly."

"Then we'll have to keep her here for the moment. But I won't let them take her, I don't give a damn how many orders they produce. That bald bastard helped drive Jephtha out of his own home—and now he's turned him into a fugitive too—Michael, you examine all the locks and latches downstairs. Make sure they're fastened. Hampton, I want someone awake and watching the front and back entrances at all times. I'll take my turn—you will too, Louis. I've also got to speak with Mary. It isn't fair to conceal what's happened—especially since we may have unexpected visitors crashing in on us in the next day or two—"

She started for the library.

"But first I think I'd better do what I forgot to do Friday night. Locate my old revolver."

The library door closed with the sharpness of a gun firing.

Louis and the servants stared, still too stunned to react. Only Michael Boyle showed animation—lifting a hand to his mouth and rocking back on his heels as he laughed, half in admiration, half in dismay.

CHAPTER IX

Besieged

IN THE EARLY HOURS of Monday morning, the temperature climbed a few degrees above the freezing mark. Rain began to turn the last of the snow to slush. Amanda woke around five, having tossed restlessly most of the night. Her knees and elbows ached; she felt ancient.

She put on a robe and lit the gas. While the rain pelted the windows, she sat worrying about Jephtha, and pondering the dilemma created by Captain Tunworth's arrival. When it grew light, she walked to the bedroom window that overlooked Madison Square.

Among the dripping, leafless trees of the little park stood a small kiosk with latticework sides. Inside the kiosk she glimpsed a man pacing to and fro beneath the conical roof. Whether it was the same watcher Michael had spied the preceding evening, she couldn't say. But *someone* was there—

By the time she went downstairs, the servants had already lit the gas to dispel the gloom. She quickly became aware of the strained atmosphere in the house. The two remaining maids, the cook and Mr. Hampton all knew the mansion was under surveillance. They went about their work with drawn looks and few words.

She had no appetite for breakfast. She went directly to the kitchen, poured herself a cup of tea and carried it into the dining room, where Michael sat in front of an untasted platter of ham and fried potatoes. As she sank into her chair and unfolded her napkin, she asked:

"Did you sleep badly, Michael?"

"I didn't sleep at all, Mrs. A. I looked in on our guest, though. She was snoring. You *did* tell her about Tunworth—?"

"Yes."

"Well, she evidently feels reasonably secure in this house." He grimaced as Mr. Mayor prowled from under the table and leaped into his lap. "I think she's the only one," he added, stroking the cat in an absent way.

"Is Louis up?"

Michael nodded. "Polishing the woodwork on the third floor."

"I wonder how soon the captain will be back."

"Not before the end of the day, I should imagine. The court procedure will take time."

"We've got to get Mary out of here."

"I agree. But the two men are still on watch."

"Then we'll take her out right in front of them."

He blinked. "How?"

"I've been thinking about a way. I want you to take the horse-car to Rose's house. Ask her to come here in her carriage. And to wear something bright—with a shawl and a parasol or an umbrella. Also gloves—gloves are particularly important."

He smiled. "I think I see what you're driving at. It's risky—but audacious enough that it just might work."

"When you leave, use the front door. So you'll be clearly seen."

He nodded. "Do I have your permission for a slight detour on the way to Mrs. Ludwig's? I think it might be prudent if I spent a short time browsing around Paradise Square. Just to see whether there's any sign of Kathleen stirring up trouble."

"If you don't take too long at it," Amanda agreed. "Try to be back by noon."

Michael Boyle said, "I will," dumped the white cat off his lap and strode out.

ii

The young Irishman returned about eleven thirty, rain-soaked, with a paper tucked under his arm. He found Amanda in the library.

The old Colt revolver lay on the mantel next to the tea bottle. He flung his cap and scarf on the chair by the hearth and walked to the desk, where Amanda had been vainly trying to examine some figures on the preceding year's profits of the Blackstone Company. Somehow the figures blurred and refused to make sense—

She set the ledger aside with great relief. "Is Rose on the way?"

"She promised to be here inside of an hour—" He managed a grin. "She made a hell of a fuss when I showed up. I forgot she never rises until twelve."

"Oh heavens, so did I. Well, I expect she'll forgive me when I explain the urgency of the situation. What did you learn in the Five Points?"

"Nothing. All quiet. A little too early in the day, I think. I may pop back later this afternoon. Provided I'm not needed here—"

He unfolded the paper in front of her.

"Stop-press edition. Out two hours early. Most of the news is a re-hash of last week's. But there's one fresh item—"

He pointed out a feature story on the front page of the *Journal of Commerce,* a paper founded in 1825 by the Tappan brothers, who had followed a stern abolitionist policy. But the Tappans had later sold the *Journal;* its current management was pro-southern.

"Didn't imagine we could keep the affair quiet for long," Michael murmured. Pale, Amanda scanned the story:

FUGITIVE SLAVE IN MADISON SQUARE?
Virginian lodges accusation against textile heiress; seeks warrant.

A warrant permitting search of the residense of Mrs. Amanda de la Gura, wealthy resident of No. 12 Madison Square, will be sought by Captain Virgil Tunworth of Lexington, Virginia, it was learned at eight this morning by the *Journal* reporter assigned to the court of Judge Develbess, Fugitive Slave Bill Commissioner for the city.

Captain Tunworth, who arrived in New York yesterday, alleges that operatives of the so-called underground railroad did cause to be stolen from him and delivered to the Madison Square address late last week one female slave who goes by the name Mary. The Captain, who is stopping at the Astor House, informed this reporter that he anticipates Judge Develbess will issue a search warrant, together with another for the arrest of said escaped slave, late today or early tomorrow.

Tunworth charges that the fugitive was aided in her escape by a former Methodist pastor, one Jephtha Kent of Lexington. Kent is a relative of the lady who occupies the Madison Square manse, and has since fled the district from which Captain Tunworth traveled—

Despondent, Amanda laid the paper aside with the rest of the piece unread. Michael said softly:

"We can't say it was unexpected."

"I know. I only wish they hadn't dragged in Jephtha's name—"

She sat staring at the column of type, wondering whether it was being read in a certain residence in Washington Square.

iii

"Take off my *clothes?*" Rose Ludwig exclaimed when Amanda met her in the front sitting room shortly after one. "I've received some odd propositions in my life, but that has to be the most—"

"Rose, don't say anything—not till you've read this." She held out the copy of the *Journal of Commerce.*

With a puzzled expression, Rose took the paper, the unlit Cuban cheroot in her hand momentarily forgotten.

While Rose studied the front page, Amanda went to the window. She could see both the man in the kiosk and her friend's carriage under the portico. The carriage driver looked miserable in the wind-blown rain.

Once more Amanda judged the angles and the distance. From the kiosk the watcher not only had a clear view of the carriage, but of the front door as well. Yet he was far enough away so that facial features would be indistinct. Provided Mary kept the parasol down; kept her dark skin hidden—

A rustle of the paper turned her attention back to Rose. The other woman laid the *Journal* aside, her eyes grim:

"Is it true, Amanda?"

"Yes. The girl's up on the third floor." Quickly, she described most of what had taken place since Mary's arrival.

"Then you're in serious trouble with the law," her friend said when she concluded.

"I know. But that's of less concern to me than getting Mary out of the house. When Tunworth produces his warrant, there's no way I can prevent him from seizing her. And I want her on that steamer for Canada tomorrow night! Rose—"

She walked to her friend; laid a hand on her arm.

"—if you'll stay here until then, you can help Mary escape."

"How, for God's sake?"

"You were seen coming in—"

"By whom?"

Amanda led her to the window, pointed out the dim figure pacing in the kiosk. Rose peered through the rain-streaked glass:

"Who is that?"

"Some fellow Tunworth hired to stand watch. There's another keeping an eye on the alley and the carriage house. The captain was shrewd enough to realize he couldn't get the warrant issued immediately—and that we might try to spirit Mary away. I'm sure you were observed when you arrived. If that man in the park sees the same dress and umbrella going out again, I don't think he'll realize he's been tricked—"

Rose's eyebrow hooked up. "Is that why Michael insisted I wear something like this—?" She touched the sleeve of her yellow velvet dress. "Which I must say is entirely inappropriate for the season and the time of day!"

"That's exactly it. I want Mary to stay at your house until about nine tomorrow evening. Then your driver can deliver her to the White Star pier on North River. Please, Rose!" Amanda pleaded. "I wouldn't ask if I could think of another way—"

"What am I supposed to do, loll in my pantalets until Wednesday morning? I was planning to do some shopping at the Lord and Taylor store this afternoon. And I have engagements tomorrow—" She sighed. "But of course I'll do it."

"Bless you! I should tell you one more thing. We might be in for some difficulty from another quarter. Louis—well, let's just say he got into a bit of trouble with one of the maids. I discharged her. Before she left, she threatened reprisals. I wouldn't take them seriously, except that she has an uncle who's cozy with Mr. Rynders, the Sixth Ward politician. It's possible he could send some of his gang friends to vandalize the house—"

Rose sighed a second time, louder:

"When you stir up a stew, you do a thorough job of it."

"I'm not positive there'll be any trouble from Rynders. I only thought it was fair to warn you."

"Well," Rose said with an emphatic nod, "that's fair enough. Take me up to the girl and let's get her on her way."

Amanda hugged her friend, then hurried her out of the sitting room to the third floor.

iv

"I never wore a skirt like this," Mary said. "I liable to fall—"

"You won't fall," Amanda assured her, slipping a folded paper into the reticule the girl carried. Rose stood just behind Amanda, wearing an embroidered robe several sizes too small.

The gas in the front hall had been turned down so the interior would be dim when the door was opened. The yellow velvet dress with its immense hoops fitted Mary poorly. But with the shawl drawn around Mary's head, gloves on her hands, and the umbrella for additional concealment, Amanda thought the ruse could work.

"Just watch your step going out to the carriage," she said. "And give that paper to Mrs. Ludwig's butler. He'll see you're driven to the White Star pier tomorrow night."

Mary's eyes misted with tears. "Oh, Miz de la Gura, you been so good—"

She patted the girl's arm. "I want you to be safe in Canada, Mary. Safe and free—"

Peering through one of the narrow panes beside the door, Michael pointed:

"That chap in the park's paying close attention. He hasn't moved since the carriage pulled up." To Rose: "I'm worried about your driver. He's sure to notice the difference, and react—"

Rose moved up beside him. "Let me handle Carney."

Amanda knew the next few seconds would be critical. She tried not to show her anxiety as she opened the door wide. After embracing Mary briefly, she took the girl's elbow and guided her outside.

The carriage driver gaped. "What the hell's going on? Who is—?"

"Carney, don't say a goddamned word!" Rose hissed from the shadows just inside the door. "I'm staying here. The girl's going to my house—in my place. Help her into the carriage! *Look at her, not me—!*"

The dumbfounded driver climbed down. Mary's hoop skirt swayed in a gust of rain that swept under the portico. Biting her lip, she put her foot on the first step below the top one.

Amanda watched the man in the park. He had come to the near side of the kiosk, so he could observe the activity at the front of the house. There was no doubt he had a clear view of the yellow-clad figure moving unsteadily down the steps—

Mary had one hand clutched to her bosom, holding the ends of the shawl covering her head. But her other hand was rising too high; unconsciously lifting the umbrella so that it didn't conceal her face—

"The umbrella!" Amanda whispered from the doorway. *"Lower it—!"*

She did. Just as Amanda let out a relieved breath, Mary's foot slipped on one of the steps. She uttered a low cry, staggering—

"Oh, Christ, that's the game," Michael groaned.

Amanda gripped the edge of the door, her hand white. The watcher in the park ran out of the kiosk—

"Help her, Carney!" Rose Ludwig whispered.

The driver darted up three steps and caught Mary's forearm just as she started to fall.

He steadied her, his eyes wide with astonishment as he got a close look at the black face beneath the umbrella.

But he held onto Mary's arm; assisted her down the final steps and into the carriage. When the door slammed, Amanda gulped and closed her eyes a moment.

She waved and called goodbye. The driver clambered up the wheel, still mightily confused. He popped his whip and guided the team out from under the portico—

Chilled by the wind-driven rain, Amanda turned her back on the square, walked inside, shut the door and leaned against it. The faces of the watching servants were white blurs in the gloom.

Rose re-tied the sash of the robe Amanda had loaned her, then clucked her tongue:

"I imagine that added a few years to my face. I thought for certain she'd fall—"

"Do you feel like a whiskey, Rose?"

"I may drink a quart."

"I don't want that much—but I'll join you."

Michael swung from the window, grinning:

"I think we pulled it off. At least the lad across the way hasn't moved since the carriage turned the corner."

He followed the two women back to the library. Rose immediately noticed the old Colt revolver resting on the mantel. She pointed to it:

"Is that for moral encouragement—or is it loaded?"

"Look in the cylinder," Amanda said.

Rose squinted. "My God! Ready to fire."

"So long as it's handy, I suppose there's no need to

keep it on display." Amanda took the revolver down and carried it to the desk, shutting it away in a drawer.

Rose shook her head. "It's unbelievable, the things I permit myself to get into for the sake of friendship—"

"And I can't possibly repay you for what you've done," Amanda said.

The stout woman accepted the brimming whiskey glass Michael handed her. "I'll think of a way, my dear. For instance—when you finally get hold of Kent's, you can increase my royalty rate—"

Amanda smiled, but without feeling.

"Better still, I'll settle for peace and quiet until tomorrow night." She toasted the thought with an upraised glass, then consumed the liquor in several rapid gulps.

Looping his scarf around his coat collar, Michael said to Rose, "Peace and quiet are now in the hands of a certain Miss Kathleen McCreery. I'll be back in a couple of hours, Mrs. A—I'm going to make a second trip to see whether all's calm in the Five Points."

The white cat padded after him out the door.

▼

The afternoon dragged on. The February sky darkened. By three o'clock, every gas jet downstairs was turned up full.

Repeatedly, Hampton answered knocks at the front door. He turned away reporters from other papers who had seen the story in the *Journal*. Twice he got into a shouting match before he managed to slam the door in a newsman's face.

Despite the inclement weather, occasional curiosity-seekers came by, on foot or in closed carriages. One group of small boys flung stones at the house before Hampton shouted at them and chased them away.

Sequestered in the library with her friend, Amanda was still aware of the attention the house was receiving; it made her nervous; it seemed a harbinger of worse to come—

Rose had pressed for some of the details of what Amanda had referred to as the incident with the maid. Amanda finally obliged, though she concealed the fact that Louis had actually taken the girl sexually, hinting instead that it had been an attempted seduction.

"But I've permitted him to be far too headstrong. In fact I think I've encouraged him without realizing it. That will change."

Rose nodded, then yawned loudly. "Excuse me—it's that damned business of being hauled awake before noon—"

"Why don't you go upstairs and nap for a while?"

"Excellent idea. I'll be down for dinner—unless a riot wakes me sooner."

In the silence of the library, Amanda found herself again unable to concentrate on any of the business details to which she should be attending. She kept staring at the portrait of her grandfather, wondering whether he'd have approved of her aiding Tunworth's runaway. She hoped he would have—

Even now, she didn't know precisely why she'd done it; she wasn't sure whether she'd acted out of a sense of moral conviction, or from a guilty conscience—belatedly trying to live up to the Latin inscription on Jared's medallion in the display case.

A little of both motivations had played a part, she suspected.

She began to focus on other concerns. On Jephtha, for one. She knew there was little she could do to help him until he got in touch with her—if he ever did. She prayed he was safe.

She was bound to have another encounter with Captain Tunworth. She looked forward to it. When the clock showed four-thirty, she was actually a little disappointed the Virginian hadn't returned with his warrants.

Well, he'd surely arrive tomorrow. And she'd have the satisfaction of telling him that—

The telegraph gong shattered her reverie. She jumped up and hurried to the table. She tapped out an acknowledgement of the query signal, then readied her pen to copy the message:

CONFIDENTIAL WALL STREET SOURCE ADVISED FOUR P M TODAY STOVALL WORKS BOARD HAS AUTHORIZED NEW STOCK ISSUE. WILL DOUBLE NUMBER OF SHARES OUTSTANDING. ISSUE ENTIRELY REPEAT ENTIRELY SUBSCRIBED PRIOR TO ANNOUNCEMENT.

A knot formed in the pit of her stomach.

SUSPECT SINGLE BUYER OR CONSORTIUM BUT HAVE NO INFORMATION. WILL ADVISE IF SITUATION CLARIFIES. AWAIT YOUR INSTRUCTIONS. ROTHMAN'S BANK

Amanda flung down the pen; pressed her palms against her eyes. The sounder began to click again:

AWAIT YOUR INSTRUCTIONS.

Wearily, Amanda clicked out NO INSTRUCTIONS, then added her initials. In a moment, the sounder replied:

ACKNOWLEDGED. END.

The stillness of the library was broken only by the steady beat of the rain on the windows and the sound of

Mr. Mayor scampering through the main hall in pursuit of some phantom adversary. Amanda stared at the message the bank had transmitted.

"God*damn* it!" she cried, slamming her fist down on the pad while tears welled in her eyes. The last few words smeared from the impact of her hand—

She knew who had moved so swiftly to convene the Stovall board and make it impossible for her to acquire the needed fifty-one percent. It was no consolation that she'd increased the risk of discovery by her decision about Mary—and that she'd made the decision of her own free will.

When Michael returned at ten past five, looking dour, she showed him the information from the Boston bank:

"Stovall doubled the number of shares—and then bought them. He or someone acting on his behalf."

"I expect so, Mrs. A."

"Because of the *Journal* story."

"Yes," Michael said. "We've always suspected he'd be aware of steady movement in the shares over the past year or so. The story undoubtedly prompted him to look into it—very closely."

She covered her eyes again. "Then I've thrown away my last chance to own Kent's—"

Michael strode to the hearth, knelt and began laying logs on top of kindling. "I'm afraid we have more immediate concerns than that."

She wiped her eyes and looked at him. He said:

"Something's brewing in the Five Points."

"What?"

"I saw copies of the *Journal* being passed around in three saloons. Heard your name mentioned—"

He applied a locofoco to the kindling. As it began to snap and blaze, he stood up.

"—plus a lot of nasty talk about a runaway nigger. I managed to draw one of the lads into conversation. Ever since the paper came out, Mr. Rynders has been buying a powerful number of whiskeys for certain selected acquaintances—"

"You think the money I paid Kathleen—and the extra you promised—wasn't enough to pacify her?"

"That's exactly what I think. Also, Mr. Isaiah Rynders has made no secret of the fact that before the day's out, he's going to look up someone at the Astor House."

"The Astor—! That's where Tunworth's staying—"

"I'm sure Mr. Rynders read it in the paper. He's a clever bastard—Tunworth will fit into his plans beautifully. Here's how it works. Kathleen appeals to Rynders for succor. He spots the *Journal* piece. It's a fine pretext for his friends to do devilment on Kathleen's behalf. They can screen their real motive behind false moral outrage—you've concealed a fugitive slave! You've broken the law! Hell, I wouldn't be surprised if some of those gang boys showed up as part of Tunworth's search party—"

"In other words," Amanda said quietly, "you definitely believe we'll be visited."

"Tonight," Michael nodded. "Or tomorrow."

"But there's nothing they can do! The girl's gone!"

"Why, that gives Rynders' chums an excuse to act even angrier. I suggest we follow a sensible course of action. Leave. Now."

"Be frightened out of my own house? I'll be damned if I will!"

"You're also involving other people, Mrs. A. It's not fair to the servants—"

"Can't we contact the police?"

"Not until something happens—unless you're willing to admit the entire story—Mary included. That might lend credence to—"

"No! Mary won't be out of New York until tomorrow evening."

"Well, the police won't act on suspicion alone. Especially not when Mr. Rynders is a pal of quite a few of them—"

Amanda drew a long breath.

"All right. Gather the servants in the kitchen. Wake Rose. And bring Louis downstairs."

vi

What Amanda had to discuss with the assembled group seemed incongruous in the cheery atmosphere of the large kitchen. Smells of baking bread drifted from the huge iron stove. Three capons browned on the hearth spit, giving off a savory aroma.

Rose puffed one of her vile-smelling cigars—causing Hampton to cough in an exaggerated way—as Amanda spoke:

"I've asked you here because I'm afraid the dismissal of Kathleen McCreery may have put this household in a dangerous position. Michael went to the Five Points twice today. It seems clear Kathleen won't be satisfied until she takes revenge for the injustice she feels was done to her—"

Louis stared at his feet, scarlet.

"You're aware we've been under observation by men hired by Captain Tunworth. The girl's gone. But you can be sure the captain will be back. Further, Michael said Isaiah Rynders was going to the Astor House late today. It's possible he went to see Tunworth—to offer the help of some of his thugs. Hunting for a fugitive slave would be a perfect pretext for an invasion of this house—and perhaps worse—"

She left the thought there. But she saw from the faces of the servants that their own imaginations were painting vivid pictures.

"It's my responsibility to defend my own property.

But it's not yours. You normally leave late in the evening to go to your homes. I'd suggest you start leaving now, one by one. Go through the alley. I don't think you'll be stopped by the man on watch—especially when he sees you're white," she added with a touch of cynicism. "We might have trouble tonight, it might come tomorrow—or it might not come at all." She tried not to let them know she didn't believe that last.

"I don't want any of you endangered," she said. "So decide who's to go first, and leave. Rose, that includes you."

"Hell," the heavy woman shrugged behind a cloud of smoke, "I don't have any clothes to wear."

"I'll loan you something."

"Won't fit. I'm staying."

"I'll stay too, madam," Brigid said. "My old man once got his head broken by some of Rynders' bullies, 'cos he wouldn't vote the way Rynders ordered."

"Very well, it's your choice. Louis—I want you out of the house along with everyone else—"

"Leave you here with just Michael and Brigid and Mrs. Ludwig?" He shook his head.

"Louis, I really insist—"

"No, ma. I'm not scared of a fight."

As she stared at the boy, she fancied she saw Cordoba's face glimmering in a kind of lapped image. She smiled in a tired way.

"All right. But the rest of you hurry."

vii

By eleven that night, the house lay silent. Rose had gone to bed after three stiff whiskeys. Louis was keeping watch at the back entrance. The rain slashed the sitting room windows. Michael glanced out, then resumed his nervous pacing:

"Still just one chap in the park. Perhaps the rain's spared us tonight."

"The rain and Captain Tunworth failing to get his warrants," Amanda replied. "I almost wish they'd come and get it over with—the waiting's worse than the battle. It's always worse—"

A moment later, noticing her odd, bemused smile, the young Irishman said:

"Doesn't seem to me our predicament's a subject for humor, Mrs. A—"

"No." She brushed a tired hand across her forehead; her smile faded. "I was only thinking of how the past comes around and around again—like a wheel. I was remembering Texas. When I was in the Alamo mission. By my own choice. When I got out alive, I thought I'd surely never go through anything similar. But here I am, besieged again—and again with no one but myself to blame."

"Blame, Mrs. A? Why do you talk of blame? In your position, most women—men, for that matter—would have gone scurrying out of town hours ago. But you never run. That's rare—and certainly not worthy of blame."

"I ran from Stovall."

"Bosh! You canceled your plans concerning the Phelans because your family's always stood for honor. Decency—"

"Neither of which will buy Kent's now that I've lost my lever for forcing the sale."

"We're not positive Stovall's behind the big stock acquisition—"

"Don't try to be consoling, Michael. Of course he is. He saw the paper."

"Well, at least you can balance the other side of the ledger with several favorable entries. You didn't mire yourself in blackmail. You just may have saved your son from ruin. You certainly saved Mary from recapture—"

"And I lost the one thing I wanted most!"

She exhaled loudly; slumped in her chair. "I must be crazy to stay here like this—"

"Why no," Michael said, "you're a Kent. You've always said they were a brave lot—"

Amanda studied the painting of Philip. How she longed, this moment, for a fraction of the courage those eyes conveyed—

She shivered as wind spattered rain against the windowpanes.

"A member of the Kent family's no different than anyone else in one respect, Michael. Being a Kent doesn't make me any less frightened of what's going to happen."

CHAPTER X

Destruction

DURING THE NIGHT THE rain stopped. The clouds cleared. By morning, Madison Square glowed in winter sunlight.

Amanda hadn't slept well again. But she was up and dressed when Michael ran into the library a few minutes after nine:

"There's a hack at the door, Mrs. A. And some witnesses over in the park—"

"Witnesses?" She jumped up, following him to the hall.

"Eight or ten chaps who don't have the look of belonging in this neighborhood. They've been gathering for the last half hour. Expecting the hack's arrival, I imagine—"

From the window beside the front door, Amanda saw the men loitering near the kiosk. They were shabbily dressed, in patched trousers and jackets too thin for the weather. They huddled close together, their breath making white plumes in the morning air.

Under the portico, the door of the hackney opened. Captain Virgil Tunworth stepped down, followed by a portly, mustached man in a black alpaca suit and broad-brimmed hat. A bulge on the man's hip hinted at a holstered side-arm.

Brigid came up behind Amanda; started to open the door—

"No," Amanda said, patting her hair to make sure it was arranged. "I'll answer."

Puzzled by Amanda's cheerful expression, Brigid bobbed her head and stood back. Michael took up a position against the wall, his coppery hair catching the sunlight. A smile of rascally delight curved his mouth.

Before Captain Tunworth could lift the knocker, Amanda pulled the door open.

"Captain! Good morning."

The greeting confused the Virginian. He glanced at his companion, who was reaching into his jacket. The portly man produced two folded legal documents.

Recovering from Amanda's unexpected cordiality, Tunworth snapped:

"This gentleman is Mr. Bowden—"

"United States Marshal, ma'am," the other man said, rather apologetically. "I have to serve you with this warrant. It permits me—"

"To search my house for the runaway girl the captain fancies I'm hiding?"

"Yes, ma'am."

"Put the warrant back in your pocket, Mr. Bowden. It's totally unnecessary."

"What's that?"

"I informed Captain Tunworth Sunday evening that I wasn't harboring a runaway slave. He wouldn't believe me. You come in and see for yourself."

The marshal stared at Tunworth. "I thought you said she'd refuse—"

"This is some kind of damned flummery!" the captain exploded. "She's gotten rid of the nigger—"

"Why, Captain, how ungentlemanly of you," Amanda said, relishing his discomfort. "You continue to accuse me of breaking the law. Even if I had been hiding this imagined runaway, how could she have escaped?" She pointed past the stamping hack horse to the men near the kiosk. "You've had me watched day and night."

Captain Tunworth flushed; clamped his lips together. Amanda retreated a step:

"Marshal, the house is yours. I have a guest staying on the second floor. My friend Mrs. Ludwig. She came to visit yesterday and became indisposed. Brigid will show you her room—if you must search it—"

"I'm afraid we must search the entire premises, ma'am," Bowden advised her.

"Then would you be kind enough to knock before you disturb Mrs. Ludwig?"

She said it so sweetly, Bowden couldn't help smiling. "Of course."

Tunworth glared as he followed the marshal inside. Michael could barely stifle a guffaw. As the law officer stumped into the sitting room, Tunworth wheeled back to Amanda:

"You had a guest yesterday, right enough. But I know she left an hour after she arrived."

"Really, Captain! You should hire reliable men, not the dregs of the saloons. Her carriage left, that's all."

"Goddamn it, I was told explicitly! Your visitor got into—"

"Please don't swear at me, sir," Amanda broke in, that charming smile still in place. "I don't care what you were told. I'd suggest you inquire whether the man who passed on that doubtful information drank a little something to warm himself while he kept watch. Something that dulled his powers of observation—"

Her dark eyes mocked him. He in turn understood exactly what she was telling him without words: the black girl had departed and he had no way of proving it; the Federal marshal's search was pointless.

But the heavy-set official caught none of that. He came bustling out of the sitting room. "All clear in there. Shall we proceed, Captain?"

Virgil Tunworth slapped his hat against his leg and followed the marshal toward the library.

ii

Bowden took forty-five minutes to comb the house from garret to basement. Now and then he ostentatiously rapped a wall, as if searching for one of those secret rooms so popular in ladies' novels but seldom found in private homes. Amanda and Michael retired to the dining room for coffee, saying little but smiling at one another at the occasional loud sound of Tunworth's hectoring voice.

When he and the marshal reappeared in the downstairs hall, Amanda went out to them:

"Are you finished?"

Bowden nodded. "We are."

"And satisfied?"

"Yes, ma'am. I'm sorry we had to trouble you. It seems the captain was in error when he requested the warrant—"

"The nigger was in this house over the weekend!" Turnworth said. He waved his hat at Amanda. "She got the the girl out. Wearing the clothes of that harpy upstairs!"

The marshal reddened. "Afraid we did disturb your guest, Mrs. de la Gura. Can't say I've ever heard a female use such a collection of cuss-words before—"

"Marshal, you come across to the park with me!" Tunworth demanded. "You talk to the man who kept watch yesterday. This woman smuggled my slave away in disguise!"

"Unless someone can swear positively to having seen a nigra person leave the house—not just a person, Captain; a *nigra* person—you've no grounds for pressing your complaint." The marshal displayed his search warrant. "Mrs. de la Gura's allowed a complete examination of her home. I can't use the other warrant to arrest someone I can't find."

"Take her into custody! Question her! *Force* her to tell you where—"

"That exceeds my authority, Captain," the marshal interrupted, sounding annoyed for the first time. He settled his hat on his head and executed a stiff bow. "Ma'am, we thank you for your cooperation."

"I'm sorry I couldn't be of more help," Amanda smiled, ushering him to the door.

Bowden went out. Captain Tunworth stormed down the steps after him. Amanda closed the door and moved to the window to watch, Michael at her shoulder.

Louis came running from the kitchen with half a sweet bun in one hand and sugar showing at the corners of his mouth.

"Oh, ma, you sure fooled 'em! I never saw anyone as mad as that captain when he paraded through the kitchen—"

"He's still fuming," Michael said, pointing outside.

The marshal and Tunworth stood by the hack's open door. Amanda couldn't make out the words, but it was obvious Tunworth was insisting on further action, and the marshal was refusing. Finally, red-faced, the marshal thrust both warrants into Tunworth's hand, climbed into the hack and jerked the door shut.

The hack clattered off. Tunworth glared at the house, then stalked across the street. He went straight to the crowd of rough-clad watchers near the kiosk and disappeared in their midst. Amanda drew a tense breath when a couple of the men spun away and started walking toward the house.

Tunworth immediately caught them and pulled them back. Presently, the men began to drift away. Captain Tunworth headed for the opposite side of the square, alone, and was eventually lost from sight in dray and carriage traffic.

"Well," Michael said, "that's it—for the moment."

"I should think we've seen the last of the captain," Amanda said. "There's nothing more he can do."

"There's nothing more he can do *legally*. But I'll bet a gold piece those boyos who came to watch the girl's capture are friends of Rynders—"

After a moment he added, "And they operate best after dark. We've not gotten out of the woods yet."

iii

Despite Michael's pessimism, Amanda couldn't help being elated about frustrating Tunworth. She went up to see Rose, and described the search in detail. Rose complained profanely about having two men poking around her room while she was still in her bed-clothes—

Amused, Amanda asked, "Did they see something they shouldn't?"

"Hell no. They wouldn't even give me a second glance!"

"*That's* why you're angry—!"

"Not funny," Rose barked, lighting a cigar.

Presently she dressed and joined Amanda downstairs. The two ate lunch. At the end, Amanda suggested her friend go home, to insure that the black girl was taken to the White Star pier on time:

"There's really no more danger here, Rose." She sounded more confident than she felt.

Rose finally agreed. Michael walked her across the square to catch the horse-car, returning to report the park free of Captain Tunworth's spies. Amanda was more convinced than ever that Jephtha's father-in-law wouldn't bother them again. She told Michael that in the morning, he was to take the carriage and collect the servants. Meantime, he and Louis could resume their work repairing the broken stall in the carriage house.

In the library, she laid a fire, lit it and settled down in a chair to read through Israel Hope's manuscript. She couldn't concentrate on it. The morning's elation was quite gone.

She thought about using the telegraph to query the Rothman Bank concerning the stock situation. But she decided against it, sadly certain she'd hear nothing to cheer her up. The item in the *Journal of Commerce* had totally wrecked her scheme to force Stovall to sell Kent's. The more she thought of that, the more depressed she became.

One simple choice—one moment of commitment to the welfare of a girl she'd undoubtedly never see again—had undercut the effort of the past two years—and the hopes, the hard work, the struggle of many more years than that.

Amanda had never been one to dwell much on past mistakes. But with the problem of Captain Tunworth resolved, she couldn't escape a deepening despondency. If she used the telegraph, the bank would only confirm that Boston Holdings had failed in its mission—

Was the freedom of one uneducated and frightened black girl worth the sacrifice of what she wanted most in the world?

Foolish question. She knew she couldn't have refused to help the runaway. In that kind of situation, a Kent could never refuse—

But the price of Mary's safety was so high; so unbearably high—

Again she tried to read what Israel had written. It seemed pointless; by its very existence, the manuscript mocked her. It would never be published with the Kent imprint—

The words blurred. The sentences lost all meaning. The strain and exhaustion of the past few days finally caught up with her. Sometime after three, she dozed off—

She awoke with a start to find Brigid hovering beside her. Except for the glow from the hearth, the library was dark.

"Visitor, ma'am. In the hall—"

Her palms turned cold. Not Tunworth again—

"Who is it, Brigid?"

"He didn't present a card, ma'am. But he says his name's Stovall."

"Stovall—!"

Amanda seized the arm of the chair. The pages of manuscript spilled off her lap.

"Where's Michael?"

"In the kitchen, ma'am. He and Louis are eating a bite of supper I fixed. 'T'isn't as good as cook's fare, but I did my best. I looked in at seven to see if you'd want some, but you were asleep—"

"Seven? What time is it—?"

The clock showed half after eight.

Tense, Amanda picked up the manuscript pages and piled them at the foot of the chair. Brigid noticed her extreme nervousness.

"Would you like me to tell the gentleman you're indisposed?"

"No, Brigid, I—" Fear crawled in her like some venomous invader. "—I'll receive him."

"In the sitting room?"

Amanda dabbed at her perspiring upper lip; glanced from the objects on the mantel to the painting of her grandfather. Her voice grew a little firmer:

"In here. Light the gas, please. Did you bolt the front door again?"

"Of course, ma'am."

"All right. I'll see to the visitor—"

Still plagued by an ominous feeling, she left the library and walked toward the front door where Stovall waited, his gold-knobbed cane under one arm and his silk hat held in his gloved hand.

Outside, Amanda heard a carriage horse stamp. The immaculate white scarf bisecting Stovall's face had a silken sheen in the gaslight. His visible eye sparkled bright as a bird's.

Staring at him, her sense of dread worsened. Her gaze went past his shoulder to one of the narrow windows flanking the door. Except for the flare of the lantern on his carriage and the dimmer lights on the far side of the square, she saw nothing but darkness. Somehow that terrified her too—

"Kind of you to receive me, Mrs. de la Gura," Hamilton Stovall said with a slight bow. "Or would it be more proper if I addressed you by your correct name? Kent?"

iv

From a shadowed place in the hall, Mr. Mayor miaowed. The sound of Brigid's footsteps faded at the rear of the house. She kept her voice as steady as she could:

"Whatever you prefer, Mr. Stovall. Please come this way—"

"Thank you."

Amanda's arm trembled as she held the library door open. Inside, the gaslight glowed.

Stovall went in. She wanted to strike him. But she held back, struggling for control; for mastery of the inexplicable mixture of loathing and terror his presence generated.

Yet he behaved politely enough, taking the chair she'd vacated beside the hearth. She walked around the desk and sat beneath the painting of Philip, almost as if she needed some sort of physical barrier to prevent her from attacking him.

Stovall acted quite relaxed. Smiled—though there was no cordiality in his eye. His artificial teeth glimmered like old bone as he laid his cane across his knees and set his silk hat on the floor.

"It seems my suspicions weren't entirely unfounded," he said.

She didn't answer.

"You *do* recall our little encounter at the Douglass lecture—?"

"Quite—quite well."

Never had ordinary speech required such effort; never had she churned with such overpowering hate. At the same time, her fear of him grew; she was terrified of his assured manner; that skull's grin—

Almost as if he were chiding an infant, he continued:

"You lied to me. Your motive for wanting to buy Kent and Son was not entirely a matter of business—"

"That conclusion hardly seems a sufficient reason for you to call in person, Mr. Stovall."

He wouldn't be prodded:

"You can imagine my stupefaction after I browsed through Monday's *Journal* and saw the mention of your relative—"

"Get to the point!"

Her outburst amused him; he clearly enjoyed unsettling her. Breathing loudly, she brushed a stray lock of white hair from her forehead.

"Certainly," he murmured. "I drove here to satisfy my curiosity—and to pass on two items of information. Shall we take those in order—?"

He leaned forward slightly:

"Who are you?"

"The cousin of a young man named Jared Kent."

He sat bolt upright; a point scored.

"That's right," she said. "The boy who served with you aboard *Constitution*."

He touched the white silk with a gloved finger. "The boy who attacked me—"

"Oh, that's very funny—you speaking of an attack.

Wasn't it the other way around? Once in your cabin? And once on the deck?"

Now, finally, she'd cracked his defenses; he spoke with soft, seething fury:

"Jared Kent forced me to live my life as a grotesque —" *Flick* went the gloved finger against the silk. "He gave me this." He held out his gloves, palms up. "And these. Hands so scarred, I can't display them in public—"

"I think you extracted payment ten times over. You stole the printing firm from my stepfather—"

"That foolish Piggott? My dear woman, I won a wager from him!"

"Not honestly, I suspect."

Stovall's lips pressed together in prim pleasure. "Impossible to prove, of course."

"Of course. When my cousin shot your companion—"

"Poor old Walpole. Retired now. Hopelessly senile."

"—you never took steps to correct Jared's belief that he'd done murder."

"Great God, woman, what do you expect from a man who's been the target of a pistol? Charity? Compassion? Besides, your cousin fled Boston—"

"Thinking he was a murderer. He carried the guilt all his life."

"May I ask where he is now?"

"He died in California over two years ago."

"While you amassed your wealth partly in—"

A supple gesture of his right glove.

"California! Now I begin to perceive the pattern. A reunion. A pledge of retribution—in the form of regaining the family business. Really rather cheap theatrics, don't you think? Well, you have at least satisfied my curiosity. And as regards your effort to buy—or in the case of the stock manipulation, I might say steal—Kent and Son, you have failed."

He leaned forward again.

"How utterly you've failed is one of the points I wish to impress on you this evening."

She watched the play of firelight on his flesh and the concealing silk. She felt unclean. He was more than a physical grotesque; the shine of his eye said his very soul —if he had one—was malignant.

"Happily," he continued, "I checked your little stock scheme in time, thanks to the fortuitous appearance of the Kent name in Monday's press. I am not entirely the thoughtless and unqualified steward of my own affairs that I sometimes appear to be, Mrs. de la—forgive me. I simply can't use that name any longer. Mrs. Kent. For some months, I've been aware of a good deal of movement in Stovall Works shares. Much more than the firm's reputation merits, I might add. But if investors had confidence in my company, excellent! That I failed to scrutinize the movement more closely is a tactical error I readily admit. My head's been busy with other things. Attempting to float a loan. Courting a young woman—at any rate, I was not aware the acquisitions of Stovall shares were in any way organized until the *Journal* item prompted me to make certain inquiries—and very rapidly, I don't mind telling you. Naturally the information was there—in the hands of the bankers who act as registrars of the stock. Those fools had neglected to see any significance in the pattern and hence had never called it to my personal attention. All the individual purchasers, it seems, re-sold their shares to a company known as Boston Holdings. Whose principals, I learned, are the very same Jew financier and the very same attorney who attempted to arrange your purchase of Kent's—"

He kept smiling that hateful, insincere smile; his teeth glared red in the firelight.

"What was your ultimate goal? A majority position in the stock?"

She could barely nod:

"Yes."

"Which you would then exchange for control of the company you wanted?"

"Yes."

He clicked his tongue against his teeth. "I don't accept that lightly, my dear woman. Not lightly at all. You maneuvered against me—"

"Get out," she breathed. "Get out of here before—"

"Before what, Mrs. Kent? You've no trump cards to play—they're all mine. As you'll soon see—"

She shivered. His voice had dropped low. He lightened it, almost teasing her:

"Naturally when I unearthed your little manipulation on Monday, I acted. At one thirty in the afternoon, I convened the available members of the board—which now includes my prospective father-in-law, by the way. By two, we had agreed to issue the new stock. Thankfully, Mr. Van Bibb had already agreed in principle to invest in the Stovall Works. Instead of making a loan to the company, he and two associates subscribed the entire new issue. Between us, Van Bibb, his friends and I now hold a commanding majority—"

He pressed the tips of his gloved fingers together. "You want Kent's very much, don't you? I never cared for that idea once I learned of your—ah—democratic philosophies. Now I have an even more compelling reason for keeping the firm out of your hands. I assure you, my dear—it's never going to be yours."

"Mr. Stovall, you're exhausting my patience. You've made it clear that you've defeated m—"

"But I haven't! Not completely! You overlooked one additional possibility—"

Her hands pressed against the desk, she whispered: "What possibility?"

"Why—the mortality of human flesh. I am older than you by several years. Suppose I were to be struck by a sudden illness. Suppose I were to die. My estate—to be handled by my future wife and my two cousins who sit on the board—might very well accept any reasonable offer for Kent and Son. But it will never happen now. I intend to issue explicit instructions to Miss Van Bibb—to my cousins—and to my attorneys—that you never be permitted to purchase the company. Never as long as you live. Nor any of your heirs, for that matter. Ah, that hurts, doesn't it? Well, suffer with it. Till the moment you die, suffer with the knowledge that even tens of millions of dollars will never give your family what you've striven so desperately to acquire—"

Amanda absorbed the words almost as if they were physical blows. She knew he meant every one. He'd outpointed her again; she'd never thought of the contingency he'd described—

"That's what you came to tell me, Mr. Stovall?"

"That and one thing more. I want to learn a little more about you—"

The teasing smile twisted his lips. She was frightened again, trying to decipher his intent.

"That's correct—I want to know more about your background. Your life in California—and wherever else you've been. I plan to dispatch a pair of trusted investigators to the gold fields. I'm sure a woman as—determined as you can't have survived merely by the exercise of piety and the performance of good works. I'd like to know how checkered your past really is—"

Amanda shook her head, still unable to fathom his purpose. What could he possibly learn that would hurt her? That she'd shot a man? That she'd run a brothel in Bexar? Neither fact would be to her credit if it were made public. But scandal couldn't prevent her from continuing her business affairs, any more than it had prevented him. And she had no hope of being accepted in the higher echelons of society. Unearthing the past seemed a wholly futile exercise—

Or so she believed until she asked, "Why?"

She turned icy when he said, "You have a son, do you not?"

Oh God, no, she thought. Of course that was the reason.

"An heir to the name of your pretentious family?"

"I—"

"Come, I know you do! And I'm sure you have high ambitions for him. Commendable. Let's hope *his* reputation isn't blackened too terribly by whatever I might discover. Because I'll make it public, I assure you. Any shame which attaches to you will attach to him. In short, I'll do everything in my power to make his life difficult —to prevent him from rising in the world—I will smear and stain your name—and his—until any aspirations you may have had for your son achieving respectability will be quite gone. No one attacks me with impunity, my dear woman—"

The skull smile widened.

"No one."

"Stovall—" She could barely speak.

"Ah! I've touched a genuinely sensitive spot at last!"

"Don't do anything to harm my boy. This is only between us."

"Indeed it is not. And I'm encouraged by your reaction. There must be something you don't care to have aired about—" Abruptly, he seemed nonplussed for the first time. "I fail to understand why you're smiling."

It was a smile bordering on tears:

"Do you? I'll tell you. I once had a plan to use much the same strategy on you."

"What do you mean?"

"Your affairs in the Five Points—with a young man and woman named Joseph and Aggie Phelan—"

Stovall's gloved hands clenched. His cane slid off his knees to the floor.

"I know about them. At one time I thought of informing Van Bibb's daughter."

Warily: "But you didn't—"

"No, I didn't."

He breathed loudly, relieved. "Scruples. That, of course, is the difference between us."

"I didn't do it, Stovall—and I ask you to be decent enough to act with similar restraint. I don't care what kind of filth you spread about me. Just don't hurt my son—"

Almost weeping, she bent across the desk:

"Let's call a truce. You have the company. Isn't that enough?"

She was desperate now. If his inquiry agents followed the trail of her past from San Francisco to Los Angeles, then back to Texas, every chance Louis had for a respectable life could be wiped out—

His mother murdered a man.

His mother kept a whorehouse.

His mother was scum—

Humiliated and hating the man smiling at her beside the hearth, she did the hardest thing she'd ever done. She begged:

"*Please,* Stovall! A truce!"

He laughed in a merry way. "A truce?" He raised a glove to the white silk. "With a family who did this—?"

The glove lifted the silk. She pressed her knuckles to her mouth as sour vomit climbed into her throat. She averted her head; squeezed her eyes shut—

When she looked again, he had let the silk fall back into place.

"No, my dear Mrs. Kent, a truce is out of the question." His voice grew steadily louder. "If it's humanly possible—and one or two of your inadvertent reactions make me think it is—I'm going to see that your boy is never welcomed in the kind of home where I'm sure you'd wish him welcomed. Let him live with your money. Let him derive what satisfaction he can from that, because he'll never have the satisfaction of being called a gentleman—nor the satisfaction of owning Kent and So—"

The rest of the sentence was blurred by the explosive sound of shattering glass.

V

Hamilton Stovall grabbed up his hat and cane, leaped to his feet, spun toward the library doors. Another window broke. The front sitting room—

She heard the scream of a frightened horse; Michael shouting from the kitchen—

Stovall loped toward the doors. He was two steps from them when Louis burst in.

The boy stopped in the doorway, glanced briefly at Stovall, then at his mother. Amanda saw the panic on his face:

"Ma, there are men out front! Twenty or thirty—come from nowhere—"

She heard shouting; cursing; the heavy thud of fists pounding the front door.

Rynders' thugs. Waiting until dark to strike—

Stovall realized the danger, even though he didn't understand its source or cause. With a shrill yell—"Get out of the way!"—he bolted for the hall.

Louis didn't react quickly enough; didn't step aside. Stovall's cane slashed wildly. The gold knob struck the boy's temple.

Louis fell sideways, his head slamming the heavy woodwork of the door frame. He cried out; tumbled to the carpet as fists beat harder on the front door—

He's killed him, Amanda thought, all the hatred bursting loose within her. *HE'S KILLED LOUIS*—

Screaming for his carriage driver, Stovall stepped over the still form sprawled in the library entrance. Amanda wasn't even conscious of tearing open the drawer of her desk, pulling out the old Colt and firing.

A red splotch appeared on the dark fabric of Hamilton Stovall's coat, between his shoulders. He pitched forward, his hat rolling in one direction, his cane in the other. He fell at the feet of Michael Boyle, who had appeared suddenly from the rear of the hall.

Unable to speak, Michael stared at the woman behind the desk. Her right arm was extended to its full length. The gun in her hand showed no sign of motion. A tiny wisp of smoke curled out of the foot-long barrel.

vi

Abruptly, Amanda came back to life. She ran to the fallen boy, flinging the Colt on the carpet as she knelt between Louis in the doorway and Stovall's body in the hall. She touched the boy's lips—

"He's breathing!"

"What in God's name did Stovall—?"

"Hit him," she said. "With his cane—"

"There she is!" someone outside yelled. "That's the one who hid the nigger!"

She twisted around; saw white, distorted faces pressed against the narrow windows on either side of the front door.

Another voice: "Where's Mickey? Mickey has the pistol—"

A third: "Don't wait for Mickey! Break the goddamn door!"

Mr. Mayor miaowed at the noise of shoulders battering the wood. The door gave off an ominous crack. The cat arched his back and crept away from the shouting; the thudding; the fist that suddenly smashed window-glass and reached around for the bolt—

Amanda jumped up. "Take Brigid out the back. Brigid and Louis."

Michael scowled, pointing at the darkening skin just below the boy's hairline:

"It could be dangerous to move him—"

"It'll be a lot more dangerous if he stays here! Get him to a doctor! *Now!*"

"I can't leave you to face—"

"Michael, I'm not going! You can carry Louis better and faster than I. There are things here I have to protect—"

The front door splintered. Scraps of wood fell inward. The disembodied hand, bloodied by the broken glass, was still groping for the bolt. Michael's face showed his agony as he tried to decide what to do.

"I'll be all right!" She held up the revolver, turned the cylinder. "I've four more shots—and I'm sure the neighbors have already summoned the police—"

From the portico came another strident yell:

"Shoot the fuckin' horse, Mickey!"

An explosion. A wild scream of animal pain.

"There goes the driver! *Catch him—!*"

With a grind and crash, the carriage was overturned. Michel and Amanda heard the driver's shrieks—

"Damn you, Michael, *go!*"

The young Irishman rushed to Louis, lifted him in both arms. With one last look at his employer, he hurried toward the dining room. He moved swiftly; yet Amanda was conscious of the extreme care with which he held the still figure of the boy—

Let him get away, she prayed. *Let my son live—*

The red hand found the bolt at last. As she retreated toward the library, the already-ruined front door swung inward, wrenched off its top hinge by the force of the men crowding against it. In the drive, the coachman was still screaming.

Just as she started to close the library doors, she glimpsed a lick of flame. The carriage set afire—

Burly, oafish, the men spilled into the long front hall.

One who was faster than the rest leaped at Mr. Mayor. The frightened tom started to run. The thug caught him by the tail.

The white cat yowled, claws slashing. The thug swung him hard. The cat's head broke open, spattering the wall—

Amanda saw that an instant before she locked the doors. She closed her eyes and leaned her forehead against the wood, listening to the sounds of the carnage: shouts; filthy language; furniture breaking; windows smashing; draperies being ripped down—

She stumbled around behind the desk. She put the Colt on a pile of papers; picked up the display case containing Jared's medallion. She carried it to the mantel and set it up beside the tea bottle. She retrieved the Colt, returned to the mantel and stood there, waiting—

Bart said it would come to this. Take up the sword—perish with the sword.

Perhaps if I hadn't hated Stovall so much—or wanted Kent's so badly—Louis wouldn't have attacked Kathleen—

Nor this mob come—

And Stovall wouldn't have hit my son—

If, IF!—the complexities of cause and effect tormented her as she waited for the first onslaught against the library doors—

Shoulders slammed the outside of the panels. Her heart beat frantically as she positioned herself two steps out from the mantel.

The bolt housing tore loose.

The doors swayed.

Buckled—

"There's the bitch!"

"Give her what-for—"

"For Kathleen McCreery!"

She had a wild glimpse of half a dozen men milling in

the hall. One had his penis in his hand, urinating on the carpet—

The men charged her across the wreckage of the doors. She shot the first one in the chest.

He screamed and slapped his frayed jacket, slammed backwards into the arms of his companions. While she revolved the cylinder, the thugs retreated into the hall again, yelling and cursing as they tried to free themselves from the weight of the dead man. One thug stepped on Stovall's head.

"Mickey, damn ye, where are ye, boy?"

"Mickey, bring your gun—!"

The whole house thundered: heavy boots slammed the ceiling; glass crashed and tinkled; great thumps and thuds and splintering sounds built to a deafening din.

The thugs advanced cautiously outside the library doorway, using the walls to hide themselves from Amanda. One bearded face suddenly peered around the splintered frame. She aimed the Colt. The face disappeared. In the distance, bells clanged. Police wagons. Blocks away, but coming fast. Distracted by the sound, she failed to see the hand that snaked around the doorframe clasping a small, shiny-plated pistol. The moment she did see it, the pistol gave off a loud pop.

She started to duck behind Michael's favorite chair. Something struck her below her left breast. She glanced down, faint all at once. Her dress was stained dark red.

She dropped to her knees, one hand on the chair so she wouldn't fall. The wound began to hurt.

"You got 'er, Mickey!" a man howled, charging into the room. "Let's tear the fuckin' place apar—"

She shot him between the legs. The bullet lifted him off his feet and hurled him on top of the man she'd shot in the chest.

The library was smoky now. She gasped for breath;

stood up despite the pain; stretched out her left hand, groping for the mantel—

The pain was constant; hard to bear. But she wouldn't let them reach her. She wouldn't let them pull down the sword or the rifle. Wouldn't let them smash the green bottle or the case with Jared's medallion—

Another man tried. He almost had his hands on her before she blew away half his face.

That sent the attackers fleeing back into the hall, out of the line of fire.

The bells clanged louder. Hoofs rattled on concrete. Iron-tired wheels screeched. Under the portico, someone yelled:

"Police—!"

There were panicked cries; the sound of pounding feet; a last crash of glass from somewhere at the rear of the house—

Amanda held onto the mantel with all her strength. The left side of her dress was soaked red from breast to hip—

I killed Stovall, she thought, gazing down at the blood. *And what did Jephtha say—?*

Without blood there is no remission of sin—

Her blurring eyes moved to the wall clock.

Fifteen until ten.

Fifteen minutes more and the steamer would put out from North River bound for Canada—

She almost smiled.

She let go of the mantel and the Colt revolver at the same time, unconscious before she struck the carpet.

CHAPTER XI

Judgment

AMANDA KENT DE LA GURA lived seventeen days after the attack on her home. She lay in her bedroom on the second floor, conscious for short periods, and in relatively little pain at first. During one of the brief periods of wakefulness, Michael Boyle told her eight men had been caught and arrested by the police; the rest had escaped. No connection between any of the eight prisoners and Isaiah Rynders could be established, he informed her somewhat cynically.

Occasionally Amanda heard unfamiliar voices; the faint rasp of saws on the first floor; the rap of hammers. Workmen had already begun repairing the damage, estimated at eighty thousand dollars.

In Amanda's room, there was no evidence of the attack. The draperies had been replaced. The damaged furniture had been removed. The thugs had destroyed furnishings throughout the house; smashed great holes in the plaster; ripped up carpeting and defecated on the floors. But while Amanda slept, Michael supervised the quiet work of making it seem as though her bedchamber hadn't been touched.

Sometime on the second or third day, a doctor bent over her. She didn't recognize him. Since moving to New York City, neither she nor her son had ever required a doctor's care. In fact she couldn't remember the last time she'd been seriously ill.

Now, however, it was a different matter. The doctor told her the pistol ball had lodged in or near her left lung, and couldn't be removed. She knew from his expression she was going to die.

"I've also been attending your son," he said.

"Where—" At times, speaking even a few words was difficult. "Where is—?"

"Mrs. Ludwig's home. We'll move him here as quickly as we can. Young Mr. Boyle got him to me in time. He suffered a wicked concussion but I believe he'll pull through."

She fell asleep weeping.

ii

On the fourth day, Michael brought her a *Tribune* with the account of Hamilton Stovall's funeral, and a letter postmarked in the nation's capital. She could barely find strength to hold the envelope:

"I can't read it, Michael. The hand seems familiar—"

"I opened it, Mrs. A. It's from your cousin's son."

"Jephtha? He's alive—?"

"In Washington. He doesn't think he can go back to his family."

"Is—is there an address?"

Michael pointed it out. "A Methodist parsonage."

"Write him. Tell him—to come here. Shelter—"

"What, Mrs. A?" He bent close to her.

"Shelter him," she whispered as her eyes closed. "Help him—start again—"

iii

On the sixth day, Theo Payne arrived from Boston in response to a telegraph message Michael had sent. Amanda smelled the whiskey on Payne's breath the moment he entered the bedroom, turning his hat brim nervously in his hands.

He sat on a chair at the bedside, listening attentively:

"Downstairs—there's a manuscript. I want—Kent's to publish it. I want—you to stay on as—the editor."

"Stay on?"

"Mr. Benbow—has approached the Stovall estate. They are—willing to sell. The executors have no—have no—" She struggled to get the words out. "—objections to my politics, and—and my money is as good as—anyone's. I want you to teach my son all you know, Theo. I want the firm to—to stand for something again."

"You know my position. I am strongly in favor of abolitionism. I would even propose starting a newspaper similar to the one Kent and Son once published." Eagerness livened his voice. "I've had experience in that line, you know—"

"If you do start a paper," she whispered, "it must do more than—than support freedom for the slaves. It must —it must stand for that and—preserving the Union too—"

Payne looked downcast. "I'm not sure both can be done together—"

A moment later he leaned forward. "What did you say?"

Silently, her lips formed two words:

"Must be."

After several minutes had passed, he assumed she wasn't going to waken again soon. He began to tiptoe out.

"Theo—"

He started, unnerved by the unexpected loudness of her voice. He turned back. Her eyes were open; clear and alert.

"Theo," she said, "clean the sign."

"The sign? Oh—the one in front of the firm—"

"Better still, have—a new one painted. It's a goddamn disgrace."

He watched her eyes close again, then continued to the door, vaguely ashamed because he wanted to whoop with joy.

iv

Rose visited on the seventh day. It was a tiring experience for Amanda, because Rose seemed all bluster and profanity:

"Damn it, Amanda, you've got to—to get out of that bed—I don't have—another friend who'll tolerate my cigars or—or go out with me in public wearing—trousers—Jesus Christ, how horridly I'm behaving! I can't help it. *I can't help it—*"

She hid her face with both hands.

v

On the ninth day, summoned at Amanda's request, William Benbow, Junior arrived from Boston. With the door of the bedroom closed, the attorney showed her the papers transferring legal guardianship of Louis Kent de la Gura to Michael Boyle.

"Only one—mistake," she said. "Scratch out—de la Gura. His name is Louis—Kent."

Old Benbow helped guide her hand so she could write her signature. It was all but illegible.

vi

On the eleventh day, Amanda felt sufficiently alert to hold another short conversation with Michael. She wore a lavender bed gown that Brigid had helped her put on.

Her hair, unpinned, lay fanned on the pillow, so nearly white that it was almost indistinguishable from the linen. From time to time, her wrinkled face constricted with pain.

"Michael—?"

"I'm here."

She clutched his extended hand, treasuring its warmth.

"Louis is—?"

"Perfectly fine, though still sleeping a good deal."

"I wish I could see him."

"Why, you will, Mrs. A. You'll be up and ab—"

"No, I—" She coughed. "—won't and you know it. I think I—forgot to ask before. Did anyone—find Tunworth—?"

"The night of the attack? No. I expect he was safely in the Astor House when it took place. He's gone home minus one nigger."

"About Jephtha—"

"I wrote him. I invited him here to live."

"Good. Remember, all the Ophir money—is his—along with the profits of the issues I bought with part of that money—"

"I'll see he gets every penny."

"You—mustn't—say that word again, either."

"What word?"

"Nigger. I—don't like it. You're not a slum boy any longer, Michael, you're—part of my family now. You are all I have to depend on—the only one who—can take Louis in hand—see that he grows up to be—straight and decent—and learns the business under Theo Payne—"

"I won't say the word again, Mrs. A," Michael whispered. "I don't think I'm fit for the responsibility you've laid on me. But I'll try to be worthy of it."

She sighed, a faint, reedy sound. "I did so much that was wrong—"

"And so much that was right."

"But—" She seemed not to hear. "At least Kent's will be back in the family."

"Yes. Benbow says all's proceeding smoothly."

"Michael—" Frantic pressure from her feeble fingers. "You must promise me—"

"What?"

"Never tell—Louis how—Stovall died."

"I had already decided I wouldn't. One of the mobsters was found dead with a pistol on his body. A copper whacked the fellow too hard with his stick. So the story is, the dead chap's the one who shot Mr. Stovall. The press has already printed it that way. The ball from your Colt was of much larger caliber. But the police overlooked that. I—I'm afraid I bribed them to do so. There's little point in them prosecuting a woman who—"

He stopped abruptly.

"Who is going to die?"

A long silence.

"Michael—?"

"Yes?"

"When you put up a headstone—in Watertown—"

"Oh, Mrs. A, what's this morbid talk of headstones?"

"Listen to me. Along with my husband's name, I want the name Kent on it. Amanda Kent de la Gura—"

She began to drift off, murmuring it over and over: "Kent. Kent—"

Crying silently, Michael Boyle held her hand long after she was unconscious.

vii

One the fifteenth day, she thought she had begun to hallucinate. She saw a familiar face; gray eyes; hair whiter than she remembered it—

"Bart?"

"Yes, sweet, it's me."

"How—how is it possible?"

"Why, the story of the mob's attack has been telegraphed to papers all over the country. Along with the account of how you probably helped a nigra girl escape to Canada. You should hear them cuss you in Charleston! That's where I read about it—"

"Charleston! I—tried to write you in London—"

He shook his head. "I went home. Damned if I can altogether explain why—unless it was the feeling of starting to grow old among people I didn't know very well. The folk in Britain are marvelous. Polite. Hospitable—and the Royal Sceptre captaincy paid far better than I'd expected, once I added in the primage. But after I lost you, somehow I came to feel I—I didn't have anything. Not even a home. If a man doesn't have a woman—and I swore I'd never fuss with another until I met you—I suppose he should at least have a home. I never figured I'd do it, but one day I gave notice to Royal Sceptre and walked out. I confess I damn near bawled when the steamer sailed in past Fort Sumter and Fort Moultrie and I saw the Battery in Charleston again. I'm running a little cotton packet up and down the coast—"

She tried to laugh; it came out as a faint rasp:

"You—took sides after all."

"Guess I did, in a way."

"So did I—" An image of Jared's medallion drifted into her mind. "You were right, no—no one can stay out of it."

"Listen, you'll never get me to a political meeting, sweet! I'm content to savor the southern climate as is —I stay far away from platforms where Yancey and Rhett and some of the other secessionist fire-eaters puff out their sulphurous rhetoric—"

"There's—so much hate on both sides now—"

"Yes, there is." He looked at her with forlorn eyes. "It'll tear this country apart."

"The Union has to survive. The *country* has to survive—"

"Not certain it can, sweet."

"There's too much that's good at stake. Too much that was hard-won—"

"But it's a matter of principle on both sides. And the voices keep getting louder—"

"There are other voices. Kent's will be one soon. Against slavery—"

"Well, there you go!"

"But against bloodshed too—"

"Amanda," he said, "it's an impossible problem. The north will never countenance slavery, and the south will never give it up. Each wants its own way. That always leads to but one conclusion. 'Perish with—' "

Abruptly, he cut off the sentence, realizing it had a closer and more painful meaning.

She recognized his discomfort:

"You were right about that too. Stovall's dead. I shot him. He attacked Louis—might have killed him—"

"Yes, the Irish lad informed me."

After a moment, she said:

"Bart—I wish you'd bend down and kiss me. That—that's a frightful thing for an old lady to ask, isn't it?"

He put his face near hers.

"No."

"I expect I should have married you—"

"I know you should have, sweet."

"I did what I had to do. But I love you."

"Yes, I love you too. More than I can begin to tell y—"

Silence.

"Amanda? Did you hear—?"

In panic, he felt for her pulse—

Thin. But it was there. She was only sleeping.

viii

On the morning of the seventeenth day, with the draperies open to admit the sun of another bright winter morning, she felt unusually lethargic. Breathing was difficult. She was struck by the certainty that she wouldn't live much longer.

One hand rested on a blue-covered legal document. The agreement of the Stovall estate to sell Kent and Son. It had arrived by messenger from Boston late the preceding night. Michael had brought it up and laid it at her bedside so she saw it the first thing when she awoke.

She wished she could have spoken to Louis. But he was still recuperating; still sleeping a good deal, Michael said.

All at once she heard a faraway melody.

The piano. The piano in the music room; the piano no one had ever played—

And now familiar, melancholy notes rose upward through the house—

Bart. The Chopin piece.

Somehow the music soothed her. Seemed not melancholy but full of sweet promise and healing. She let her mind range peacefully back across all the years, from the tepee of the young Sioux, Plenty Coups, to her marriage to Jaimie de la Gura—the turmoil in Texas—Cordoba and the birth of her son—Bart in California—

And the end of her life here in New York.

It was time for an accounting.

On the credit side, she'd preserved the family. Put it in trustworthy hands. With Joshua Rothman and old Benbow and Theo Payne to assist him, Michael Boyle—a Kent in spirit now, if not in name—would serve well until Louis achieved his majority. She only prayed she hadn't warped her son's character too severely;

prayed Michael would be able to mold him into an honorable man. At least there was a hope of it—

Perhaps Jephtha would help when he came to the city. On Jephtha's side too, the family had heirs; his sons. Whatever their position on the divisive issues tormenting the country, they were Kents. With the proceeds of the Ophir claim in Hopeful, and with the promising reports from the Sierras, they would be wealthy men—

If there were no war to destroy them; to destroy the nation—

On the debit side, she knew she had at times been ruthless in order to survive; ruthless in obtaining her ends. So ruthless, Louis had very nearly been sacrificed. Yet from her ruthlessness had come the restoration of the Kent fortune. Perhaps that entry had a place on both sides of the ledger.

And the company. The company belonged to its rightful owners again. Her hand moved over the blue-covered document; a kind of caress—

All at once she felt quite sleepy. The sunlight burned her eyes. Details of the room melted away in the glare—

The appearance of that intense light told her the end was very near. She was terrified of dying alone. Bart and Michael had gone downstairs for breakfast with Rose, who had sat with her through the night. She tried to grasp the bell pull—

She was too feeble to reach it.

Weary and frightened, she gave up trying to assess her own life. She remembered the Mandan legend of the vine; the great womanly hands left the vine alone, or tore it, denying paradise. The meaning of the legend brought a certain comfort. Only a Divine intelligence could fully and accurately judge a human life, and find it worthy or wanting—

She'd taken lives. The man in Hopeful—and Hamilton Stovall—lingered most acutely in her mind. Those acts would weigh heavily in the judgment, she knew.

But the judgment itself was beyond her.

I am a Kent.

I did what I had to.

Let the verdict come down.

An almost child-like expression of pleasure came onto her face. Settling her head more comfortably on the pillow, she turned toward the intense light. She'd quite forgotten the light shone through a window in a specific house in a specific city in America—

Or did it?

She felt her strength waning. She was suddenly ashamed of her own fear.

Guilty she might be. But what human being was not? There were things in her past she needn't be ashamed of; things to be proud of; she wouldn't surrender so meekly to a condemning judgment—

That's not what grandfather would have done.

Slowly, her eyes closed.

It was puzzling. The light remained.

Growing steadily brighter—

Suddenly, clear and sharp, she saw the vine to paradise.

She spit on her hands and began to climb.

The long shadows of Lincoln and Davis
loom across the land,
locked in an epic struggle that tests the loyalties of the Kents,
north and south,
and threatens a love that knows no boundaries in

The Titans

Volume V

of

The Kent Family Chronicles

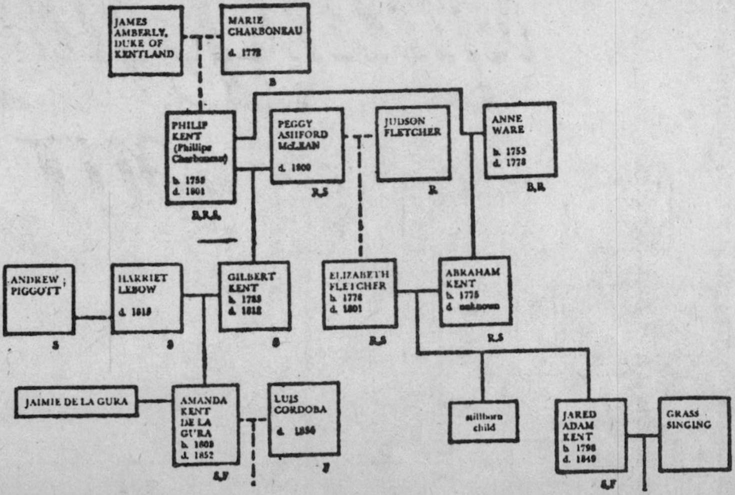
JAMES AMBERLY, DUKE OF KENTLAND
MARIE CHARBONEAU d. 1778
B
PHILIP KENT (Phillipe Charboneau) b. 1758 d. 1801
B,R,S,
PEGGY ASHFORD McLEAN d. 1800
R,S
JUDSON FLETCHER
R
ANNE WARE b. 1753 d. 1778
B,R
ANDREW PIGGOTT
S
HARRIET LEBOW d. 1818
S
GILBERT KENT b. 1785 d. 1812
S
ELIZABETH FLETCHER b. 1778 d. 1801
R,S
ABRAHAM KENT b. 1775 d. unknown
R,S
JAIMIE DE LA GURA
AMANDA KENT DE LA GURA b. 1809 d. 1852
S,F
LUIS CORDOBA d. 1836
F
stillborn child
JARED ADAM KENT b. 1798 d. 1849
S,F
GRASS SINGING

The Kent Family

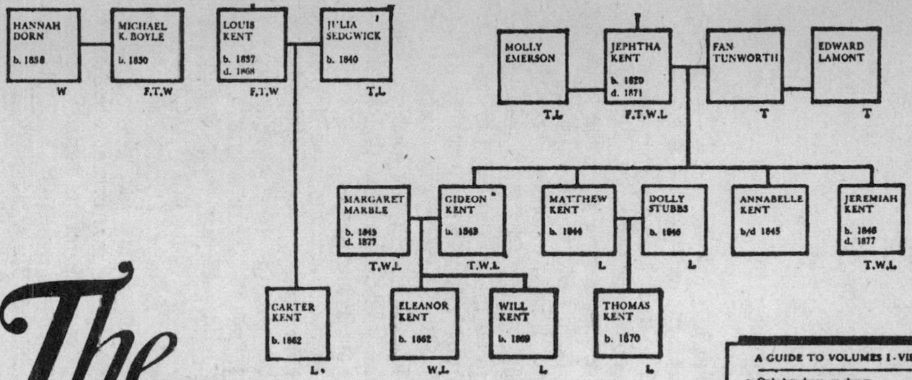

A GUIDE TO VOLUMES I - VII

- Only key dates are shown.
- Broken line indicates an illegitimate birth.
- On the chart, letters appear with the names of characters. The letters indicate in which novel or novels the character appears.

B	THE BASTARD	(1770-1775)
R	THE REBELS	(1775-1781)
S	THE SEEKERS	(1794-1814)
F	THE FURIES	(1836-1852)
T	THE TITANS	(1860-1862)
W	THE WARRIORS	(1864-1868)
L	THE LAWLESS	(1869-1877)

Afterword

The American Bicentennial Series has produced an immense and positive response from readers. One question is frequently asked: "What's true and what isn't?" A short comment may be in order.

The Kent family, of course, is fictitious—but at all times, an effort has been made to make each of the Kents *representative* of a certain type of person living in a particular era in American history. For instance:

The grim circumstances faced by several of the family members in Volume III, THE SEEKERS, reflect the reality of the period: life on the cutting edge of western expansion was stark; brutal. Many were defeated by it; many others persevered. (But to romanticize or prettify the historical realities of such a period, it seems to me, would diminish the courage and determination of those who endured and overcame its hardships.)

Factual details have helped shape the lives of the fictional characters. A good example from this volume is the escaped slave in the packing box. (What author would have the nerve to invent such a device?) In the period described, a man named Henry "Box" Brown actually made his escape to the north in this fashion.

As to actual events and people, I made a mental pledge at the beginning of the Series that I would never deliberately or knowingly distort the record, whether of a battle, or the character of an historical figure as I saw him or her through the lens of research. One or two small liberties with chronology have been taken in the first four novels, but that is the only sort of deviation I feel is defensible in books which attempt to relate the story of our common past.

I must admit to one compromise. Before I undertook the writing, I acknowledged it would probably be impossible to cover so much history without committing errors; hopefully, careful research would keep them minor —as in Volume I, THE BASTARD, which originally included a sequence in which a match was struck—long before matches of that sort were available. That one, mercifully, was caught in the galley proofs.

Accepting the probability of unintentional error was the price of seeing the work reach readers in a reasonable time; I either had to run the risk or face taking a lifetime to do the writing.

Happily, the approach, with all its hazards, seems to have been the right one. A great uumber of men and women have written to say the Series has re-kindled a desire to delve deeper into American history. No writer or publisher could ask for a greater reward.

JOHN JAKES

About the Author

JOHN JAKES was born in Chicago. He is a graduate of DePauw University, and took his M.A. in literature at Ohio State. He sold his first short story during his second year of college, and his first book twelve months later. Since then he has published more than 200 short stories and over 50 books—chiefly suspense, nonfiction for young people and, most recently, science fiction. With the publication of *The Furies,* volume four of the Kent Family Chronicles, he became the first author in history to land three novels on the best-seller lists within a single year. The author is married, the father of four children, and lists among his organizations the Authors Guild, the Dramatists Guild, and Science Fiction Writers of America. In both 1976 and 1977 he was awarded honorary doctorates for his contribution to the Bicentennial observance. He says the most satisfying aspect of the phenomenal success of the Kent family novels is "the mail which reports that a reader has been motivated to seek out some good nonfiction in order to read about American history in greater detail. That kind of direct response is what writing is all about—and it makes all the hard work worthwhile."